BORDERS®

CLASSICS

BORDERS LEATHERBOUND CLASSICS

JANE AUSTEN, *Works*
L. FRANK BAUM, *The Oz Chronicles* (2 VOLUMES)
L. FRANK BAUM, *Wonder Tales*
CHARLOTTE & EMILY BRONTË, *Works*
DANTE ALIGHIERI, *The Divine Comedy* (ILLUSTRATED BY GUSTAVE DORÉ)
CHARLES DICKENS, *Works*
CHARLES DICKENS, *The Christmas Books*
ARTHUR CONAN DOYLE, *The Classic Mysteries of Sherlock Holmes*
NATHANIEL HAWTHORNE, *Works*
HOMER, *The Iliad & the Odyssey*
VICTOR HUGO, *Works*
JAMES JOYCE, *Ulysses*
JACK LONDON, *Yukon Writings*
EDGAR ALLAN POE, *Works*
WILLIAM SHAKESPEARE, *Complete Works*
ROBERT LOUIS STEVENSON, *Selected Works*
HENRY DAVID THOREAU, *Works*
MARK TWAIN, *The Complete Adventures of Tom Sawyer & Huckleberry Finn*
JULES VERNE, *Works*
H. G. WELLS, *Works*
VIRGINIA WOOLF, *The Early Novels*

Classics of Horror (Frankenstein/Dr. Jekyll and Mr. Hyde/Dracula)
Ghosts
Grimm's Fairy Tales
Three Great American Poets (WHITMAN/DICKINSON/FROST)

VIRGINIA WOOLF

The Voyage Out

Night and Day

Jacob's Room

BORDERS.
CLASSICS

Please direct sales or editorial inquiries to:
BordersTradeBookInventoryQuestions@bordersgroupinc.com

This edition is published by
Borders Classics, an imprint of Borders Group, Inc.
by special arrangement with
Ann Arbor Media Group, LLC
2500 South State Street, Ann Arbor, MI 48104

Production team: Mae Barnard, Tina Budzinski,
Lori Holland, Denise Kennedy, Steven Moore,
Kathie Radenbaugh, and Rhonda Welton

Printed and bound in the United States of America
by Edwards Brothers, Inc.

ISBN 1-58726-109-X

07 06 05 04 10 9 8 7 6 5 4 3 2 1

CONTENTS

THE VOYAGE OUT

1

As the streets that lead from the Strand to the Embankment are very narrow, it is better not to walk down them arm-in-arm. If you persist, lawyers' clerks will have to make flying leaps into the mud; young lady typists will have to fidget behind you. In the streets of London where beauty goes unregarded, eccentricity must pay the penalty, and it is better not to be very tall, to wear a long blue cloak, or to beat the air with your left hand.

One afternoon in the beginning of October when the traffic was becoming brisk a tall man strode along the edge of the pavement with a lady on his arm. Angry glances struck upon their backs. The small, agitated figures—for in comparison with this couple most people looked small—decorated with fountain pens, and burdened with despatch-boxes, had appointments to keep, and drew a weekly salary, so that there was some reason for the unfriendly stare which was bestowed upon Mr. Ambrose's height and upon Mrs. Ambrose's cloak. But some enchantment had put both man and woman beyond the reach of malice and unpopularity. In his guess one might guess from the moving lips that it was thought; and in hers from the eyes fixed stonily straight in front of her at a level above the eyes of most that it was sorrow. It was only by scorning all she met that she kept herself from tears, and the friction of people brushing past her was evidently painful. After watching the traffic on the Embankment for a minute or two with a stoical gaze she twitched her husband's sleeve, and they crossed between the swift discharge of motor cars. When they were safe on the further side, she gently withdrew her arm from his, allowing her mouth at the same time to relax, to tremble; then tears rolled down, and leaning her elbows on the balustrade, she shielded her face from the curious. Mr. Ambrose attempted consolation; he patted her shoulder; but she showed no signs of admitting him, and feeling it awkward to stand beside a grief that was greater than his, he crossed his arms behind him, and took a turn along the pavement.

The embankment juts out in angles here and there, like pulpits; instead of preachers, however, small boys occupy them, dangling string, dropping pebbles, or launching wads of paper for a cruise. With their sharp eye for eccentricity, they were inclined to think Mr. Ambrose awful; but the quickest witted cried "Bluebeard!" as he passed. In case they should proceed to tease his wife, Mr. Ambrose flourished his stick at them, upon which they decided that he was grotesque merely, and four instead of one cried "Bluebeard!" in chorus.

Although Mrs. Ambrose stood quite still, much longer than is natural, the little boys let her be. Some one is always looking into the river near Waterloo Bridge; a couple will stand there talking for half an hour on a fine afternoon; most people, walking for pleasure, contemplate for three minutes; when, having compared the occasion with other occasions, or made some sentence, they pass on. Sometimes the flats and churches and hotels of Westminster are like the outlines of Constantinople in a mist; sometimes the river is an opulent purple, sometimes mud-coloured, sometimes sparkling blue like the sea. It is always worth while to look down and see what is happening. But this lady looked neither up nor down; the only thing she had seen, since she stood there, was a circular iridescent patch slowly floating past with a straw in the middle of it. The straw and the patch swam again and again behind the tremulous medium of a great welling tear, and the tear rose and fell and dropped into the river. Then there struck close upon her ears—

Lars Porsena of Clusium
By the nine Gods he swore—

and then more faintly, as if the speaker had passed her on his walk—

That the Great House of Tarquin
Should suffer wrong no more.

Yes, she knew she must go back to all that, but at present she must weep. Screening her face she sobbed more steadily than she had yet done, her shoulders rising and falling with great regularity. It was this figure that her husband saw when, having reached the polished Sphinx, having entangled himself with a man selling picture postcards, he turned; the stanza instantly stopped. He came up to her, laid his hand on her shoulder, and said, "Dearest." His voice was supplicating. But she shut her face away from him, as much as to say, "You can't possibly understand."

As he did not leave her, however, she had to wipe her eyes, and to raise them to the level of the factory chimneys on the other bank. She saw also the arches of Waterloo Bridge and the carts moving across them, like the line of animals in a shooting gallery. They were seen blankly, but to see anything was of course to end her weeping and begin to walk.

"I would rather walk," she said, her husband having hailed a cab already occupied by two city men.

The fixity of her mood was broken by the action of walking. The shooting motor cars, more like spiders in the moon than terrestrial objects, the thundering drays, the jingling hansoms, and little black broughams, made her think of the world she lived in. Somewhere up there above the pinnacles where the smoke rose in a pointed hill, her children were now asking for her, and getting a soothing reply. As for the mass of streets, squares, and public buildings which parted them, she only felt at this moment how little London had done to make her love it, although thirty of her forty years had been spent in a street. She knew how to read the people who were passing her; there were the rich who were running to and from each others' houses at this hour; there were the bigoted workers driving in a straight line to their offices; there were the poor who were unhappy and rightly malignant. Already, though there was sunlight in the haze, tattered old men and women were nodding off to sleep upon the seats. When one gave up seeing the beauty that clothed things, this was the skeleton beneath.

A fine rain now made her still more dismal; vans with the odd names of those engaged in odd industries—Sprules, Manufacturer of Saw-dust; Grabb, to whom no piece of waste paper comes amiss—fell flat as a bad joke; bold lovers, sheltered behind one cloak, seemed to her sordid, past their passion; the flower women, a contented company, whose talk is always worth hearing, were sodden hags; the red, yellow, and blue flowers, whose heads were pressed together, would not blaze. Moreover, her husband walking with a quick rhythmic stride, jerking his free hand occasionally, was either a Viking or a stricken Nelson; the sea-gulls had changed his note.

"Ridley, shall we drive? Shall we drive, Ridley?"

Mrs. Ambrose had to speak sharply; by this time he was far away.

The cab, by trotting steadily along the same road, soon withdrew them from the West End, and plunged them into London. It appeared that this was a great manufacturing place, where the people were engaged in making things, as though the West End, with its electric lamps, its vast plate-glass windows all shining yellow, its carefully-finished houses, and tiny live figures trotting on the pavement, or bowled along on wheels in the road, was the finished work. It appeared to her a very small bit of work for such an enormous factory to have made. For some reason it appeared to her as a small golden tassel on the edge of a vast black cloak.

Observing that they passed no other hansom cab, but only vans and waggons, and that not one of the thousand men and women she saw was either a gentleman or a lady, Mrs. Ambrose understood that after all it is the ordinary thing to be poor, and that London is the city of innumerable poor people. Startled by this discovery and seeing herself pacing a circle all the days of her life round Picadilly Circus she was greatly relieved to pass a building put up by the London County Council for Night Schools.

"Lord, how gloomy it is!" her husband groaned. "Poor creatures!"

What with the misery for her children, the poor, and the rain, her mind was like a wound exposed to dry in the air.

At this point the cab stopped, for it was in danger of being crushed like an egg-shell. The wide Embankment which had had room for cannon-balls and squadrons, had now shrunk to a cobbled lane steaming with smells of malt and oil and blocked by waggons. While her husband read the placards pasted on the brick announcing the hours at which certain ships would sail for Scotland, Mrs. Ambrose did her best to find information. From a world exclusively occupied in feeding waggons with sacks, half obliterated too in a fine yellow fog, they got neither help nor attention. It seemed a miracle when an old man approached, guessed their condition, and proposed to row them out to their ship in the little boat which he kept moored at the bottom of a flight of steps. With some hesitation they trusted themselves to him, took their places, and were soon waving up and down upon the water, London having shrunk to two lines of buildings on either side of them, square buildings and oblong buildings placed in rows like a child's avenue of bricks.

The river, which had a certain amount of troubled yellow light in it, ran with great force; bulky barges floated down swiftly escorted by tugs; police boats shot past everything; the wind went with the current. The open rowing-boat in which they sat bobbed and curtseyed across the line of traffic. In mid-stream the old man stayed his hands upon the oars, and as the water rushed past them, remarked that once he had taken many passengers across, where now he took scarcely any. He seemed to recall an age when his boat, moored among rushes, carried delicate feet across to lawns at Rotherhithe.

"They want bridges now," he said, indicating the monstrous outline of the Tower Bridge. Mournfully Helen regarded him, who was putting water between her and her children. Mournfully she gazed at the ship they were approaching; anchored in the middle of the stream they could dimly read her name—*Euphrosyne*.

Very dimly in the falling dusk they could see the lines of the rigging, the masts and the dark flag which the breeze blew out squarely behind.

As the little boat sidled up to the steamer, and the old man shipped his oars, he remarked once more pointing above, that ships all the world over flew that flag the day they sailed. In the minds of both the passengers the blue flag appeared a sinister token, and this the moment for presentiments, but nevertheless they rose, gathered their things together, and climbed on deck.

Down in the saloon of her father's ship, Miss Rachel Vinrace, aged twenty-four, stood waiting her uncle and aunt nervously. To begin with, though nearly related, she scarcely remembered them; to go on with, they were elderly people, and finally, as her father's daughter she must be in some sort prepared to entertain them. She looked forward to seeing them as civilised people generally look forward to the first sight of civilised people, as though they were of the nature of an approaching physical discomfort—a tight shoe or a draughty window. She was already unnaturally braced to receive them. As she occupied herself in laying forks severely straight by the side of knives, she heard a man's voice saying gloomily:

"On a dark night one would fall down these stairs head foremost," to which a woman's voice added, "And be killed."

As she spoke the last words the woman stood in the doorway. Tall, large-eyed, draped in purple shawls, Mrs. Ambrose was romantic and beautiful; not perhaps sympathetic, for her eyes looked straight and considered what they saw. Her face was much warmer than a Greek face; on the other hand it was much bolder than the face of the usual pretty Englishwoman.

"Oh, Rachel, how d'you do," she said, shaking hands.

"How are you, dear," said Mr. Ambrose, inclining his forehead to be kissed. His niece instinctively liked his thin angular body, and the big head with its sweeping features, and the acute, innocent eyes.

"Tell Mr. Pepper," Rachel bade the servant. Husband and wife then sat down on one side of the table, with their niece opposite to them.

"My father told me to begin," she explained. "He is very busy with the men. . . . You know Mr. Pepper?"

A little man who was bent as some trees are by a gale on one side of them had slipped in. Nodding to Mr. Ambrose, he shook hands with Helen.

"Draughts," he said, erecting the collar of his coat.

"You are still rheumatic?" asked Helen. Her voice was low and seductive, though she spoke absently enough, the sight of town and river being still present to her mind.

"Once rheumatic, always rheumatic, I fear," he replied. "To some extent it depends on the weather, though not so much as people are apt to think."

"One does not die of it, at any rate," said Helen.

"As a general rule—no," said Mr. Pepper.

"Soup, Uncle Ridley?" asked Rachel.

"Thank you, dear," he said, and, as he held his plate out, sighed audibly, "Ah! she's not like her mother." Helen was just too late in thumping her tumbler on the table to prevent Rachel from hearing, and from blushing scarlet with embarrassment.

"The way servants treat flowers!" she said hastily. She drew a green vase with a crinkled lip towards her, and began pulling out the tight little chrysanthemums, which she laid on the table-cloth, arranging them fastidiously side by side.

There was a pause.

"You knew Jenkinson, didn't you, Ambrose?" asked Mr. Pepper across the table.

"Jenkinson of Peterhouse?"

"He's dead," said Mr. Pepper.

"Ah, dear!—I knew him—ages ago," said Ridley. "He was the hero of the punt accident, you remember? A queer card. Married a young woman out of a tobacconist's, and lived in the Fens—never heard what became of him."

"Drink—drugs," said Mr. Pepper with sinister conciseness. "He left a commentary. Hopeless muddle, I'm told."

"The man had really great abilities," said Ridley.

"His introduction to Jellaby holds its own still," went on Mr. Pepper, "which is surprising, seeing how text-books change."

"There was a theory about the planets, wasn't there?" asked Ridley.

"A screw loose somewhere, no doubt of it," said Mr. Pepper, shaking his head.

Now a tremor ran through the table, and a light outside swerved. At the same time an electric bell rang sharply again and again.

"We're off," said Ridley.

A slight but perceptible wave seemed to roll beneath the floor; then it sank; then another came, more perceptible. Lights slid right across the uncurtained window. The ship gave a loud melancholy moan.

"We're off!" said Mr. Pepper. Other ships, as sad as she, answered her outside on the river. The chuckling and hissing of water could be plainly heard, and the ship heaved so that the steward bringing plates had to balance himself as he drew the curtain. There was a pause.

"Jenkinson of Cats—d'you still keep up with him?" asked Ambrose.

"As much as one ever does," said Mr. Pepper. "We meet annually. This year he has had the misfortune to lose his wife, which made it painful, of course."

"Very painful," Ridley agreed.

"There's an unmarried daughter who keeps house for him, I believe, but it's never the same, not at his age."

Both gentlemen nodded sagely as they carved their apples.

"There was a book, wasn't there?" Ridley enquired.

"There *was* a book, but there never *will* be a book," said Mr. Pepper with such fierceness that both ladies looked up at him.

"There never will be a book, because some one else has written it for him," said Mr. Pepper with considerable acidity. "That's what comes of putting things off, and collecting fossils, and sticking Norman arches on one's pigsties."

"I confess I sympathise," said Ridley with a melancholy sigh. "I have a weakness for people who can't begin."

". . . The accumulations of a lifetime wasted," continued Mr. Pepper. "He had accumulations enough to fill a barn."

"It's a vice that some of us escape," said Ridley. "Our friend Miles has another work out today."

Mr. Pepper gave an acid little laugh. "According to my calculations," he said, "he has produced two volumes and a half annually, which, allowing for time spent in the cradle and so forth, shows a commendable industry."

"Yes, the old Master's saying of him has been pretty well realised," said Ridley.

"A way they had," said Mr. Pepper. "You know the Bruce collection?—not for publication, of course."

"I should suppose not," said Ridley significantly. "For a Divine he was—remarkably free."

"The Pump in Neville's Row, for example?" enquired Mr. Pepper.

"Precisely," said Ambrose.

Each of the ladies, being after the fashion of their sex, highly trained in promoting men's talk without listening to it, could think—about the education of children, about the use of fog sirens in an opera—without betraying herself. Only it struck Helen that Rachel was perhaps too still for a hostess, and that she might have done something with her hands.

"Perhaps——?" she said at length, upon which they rose and left, vaguely to the surprise of the gentlemen, who had either thought them attentive or had forgotten their presence.

"Ah, one could tell strange stories of the old days," they heard Ridley say, as he sank into his chair again. Glancing back, at the doorway, they saw Mr. Pepper as though he had suddenly loosened his clothes, and had become a vivacious and malicious old ape.

Winding veils round their heads, the women walked on deck. They were now moving steadily down the river, passing the dark shapes of ships at anchor, and London was a swarm of lights with a pale yellow canopy drooping above it. There were the lights of the great theatres, the lights of the long streets, lights that indicated huge squares of domestic comfort, lights that hung high in air. No darkness would ever settle upon those lamps, as no darkness had settled upon them for hundreds of years. It seemed dreadful that the town should blaze for ever in the same spot; dreadful at least to people going away to adventure upon the sea, and beholding it as a circumscribed mound, eternally burnt, eternally scarred. From the deck of the ship the great city appeared a crouched and cowardly figure, a sedentary miser.

Leaning over the rail, side by side, Helen said, "Won't you be cold?" Rachel replied, "No. . . . How beautiful!" she added a moment later. Very little was visible—a few masts, a shadow of land here, a line of brilliant windows there. They tried to make head against the wind.

"It blows—it blows!" gasped Rachel, the words rammed down her throat. Struggling by her side, Helen was suddenly overcome by the spirit of movement, and pushed along with her skirts wrapping themselves round her knees, and both arms to her hair. But slowly the intoxication of movement died down, and the wind became rough and chilly. They looked through a chink in the blind and saw that long cigars were being smoked in the dining-room; they saw Mr. Ambrose throw himself violently against the back of his chair, while Mr. Pepper crinkled his cheeks as though they had been cut in wood. The ghost of a roar of laughter came out to them, and was drowned at once in the wind. In the dry yellow-lighted room Mr. Pepper and Mr. Ambrose were oblivious of all tumult; they were in Cambridge, and it was probably about the year 1875.

"They're old friends," said Helen, smiling at the sight. "Now, is there a room for us to sit in?"

Rachel opened a door.

"It's more like a landing than a room," she said. Indeed it had nothing of the shut stationary character of a room on shore. A table was rooted in the middle, and seats were stuck to the sides. Happily the tropical suns had bleached the tapestries to a faded blue-green colour, and the mirror with its frame of shells, the work of the steward's love, when the time hung heavy in the southern seas, was quaint rather than ugly. Twisted shells with red lips like unicorn's horns ornamented the mantelpiece, which was draped by a pall of purple plush from which depended a certain number of balls. Two windows opened on to the deck, and the light beating through them when the ship was roasted on the Amazons had turned the prints on the opposite wall to a faint yellow colour, so that "The Coliseum" was scarcely to be distinguished from Queen Alexandra playing with her Spaniels. A pair of wicker arm-chairs by the fireside invited one to warm one's hands at a grate full of gilt shavings; a great lamp swung above the table—the kind of lamp which makes the light of civilisation across dark fields to one walking in the country.

"It's odd that every one should be an old friend of Mr. Pepper's," Rachel started nervously, for the situation was difficult, the room cold, and Helen curiously silent.

"I suppose you take him for granted?" said her aunt.

"He's like this," said Rachel, lighting on a fossilised fish in a basin, and displaying it.

"I expect you're too severe," Helen remarked.

Rachel immediately tried to qualify what she had said against her belief.

"I don't really know him," she said, and took refuge in facts, believing that elderly people really like them better than feelings. She produced what she knew of William Pepper. She told Helen that he always called on Sundays when they were at home; he knew about a great many things—about mathematics, history, Greek, zoology, economics, and the Icelandic Sagas. He had turned Persian poetry into English prose, and English prose into Greek iambics; he was an authority upon coins; and—one other thing—oh yes, she thought it was vehicular traffic.

He was here either to get things out of the sea, or to write upon the probable course of Odysseus, for Greek after all was his hobby.

"I've got all his pamphlets," she said. "Little pamphlets. Little yellow books." It did not appear that she had read them.

"Has he ever been in love?" asked Helen, who had chosen a seat.

This was unexpectedly to the point.

"His heart's a piece of old shoe leather," Rachel declared, dropping the fish. But when questioned she had to own that she had never asked him.

"I shall ask him," said Helen.

"The last time I saw you, you were buying a piano," she continued. "Do you remember—the piano, the room in the attic, and the great plants with the prickles?"

"Yes, and my aunts said the piano would come through the floor, but at their age one wouldn't mind being killed in the night?" she enquired.

"I heard from Aunt Bessie not long ago," Helen stated. "She is afraid that you will spoil your arms if you insist upon so much practising."

"The muscles of the forearm—and then one won't marry?"

"She didn't put it quite like that," replied Mrs. Ambrose.

"Oh, no—of course she wouldn't," said Rachel with a sigh.

Helen looked at her. Her face was weak rather than decided, saved from insipidity by the large enquiring eyes; denied beauty, now that she was sheltered indoors, by the lack of colour and definite outline. Moreover, a hesitation in speaking, or rather a tendency to use the wrong words, made her seem more than normally incompetent for her years. Mrs. Ambrose, who had been speaking much at random, now reflected that she certainly did not look forward to the intimacy of three or four weeks on board ship which was threatened. Women of her own age usually boring her, she supposed that girls would be worse. She glanced at Rachel again. Yes! how clear it was that she would be vacillating, emotional, and when you said something to her it would make no more lasting impression than the stroke of a stick upon water. There was nothing to take hold of in girls—nothing hard, permanent, satisfactory. Did Willoughby say three weeks, or did he say four? She tried to remember.

At this point, however, the door opened and a tall burly man entered the room, came forward and shook Helen's hand with an emotional kind of heartiness, Willoughby himself, Rachel's father, Helen's brother-in-law.

As a great deal of flesh would have been needed to make a fat man of him, his frame being so large, he was not fat; his face was a large framework too, looking, by the smallness of the features and the glow in the hollow of the cheek, more fitted to withstand assaults of the weather than to express sentiments and emotions, or to respond to them in others.

"It is a great pleasure that you have come," he said, "for both of us."

Rachel murmured in obedience to her father's glance.

"We'll do our best to make you comfortable. And Ridley. We think it an honour to have charge of him. Pepper'll have some one to contradict him—which I daren't do. You find this child grown, don't you? A young woman, eh?"

Still holding Helen's hand he drew his arm round Rachel's shoulder, thus making them come uncomfortably close, but Helen forbore to look.

"You think she does us credit?" he asked.

"Oh yes," said Helen.

"Because we expect great things of her," he continued, squeezing his daughter's arm and releasing her. "But about you now." They sat down side by side on the little sofa. "Did you leave the children well? They'll be ready for school, I suppose. Do they take after you or Ambrose? They've got good heads on their shoulders, I'll be bound?"

At this Helen immediately brightened more than she had yet done, and explained that her son was six and her daughter ten. Everybody said that her boy was like her and her girl like Ridley. As for brains, they were quick brats, she thought, and modestly she ventured on a little story about her son—how left alone for a minute he had taken the pat of butter in his fingers, run across the room with it, and put it on the fire—merely for the fun of the thing, a feeling which she could understand.

"And you had to show the young rascal that these tricks wouldn't do, eh?"

"A child of six? I don't think they matter."

"I'm an old-fashioned father."

"Nonsense, Willoughby; Rachel knows better."

Much as Willoughby would doubtless have liked his daughter to praise him she did not; her eyes were unreflecting as water, her fingers still toying with the fossilised fish, her mind absent. The elder people went on to speak of arrangements that could be made for Ridley's comfort—a table placed where he couldn't help looking at the sea, far from boilers, at the same time sheltered from the view of people passing. Unless he made this a holiday, when his books were all packed, he would have no holiday whatever; for out at Santa Marina Helen knew, by experience, that he would work all day; his boxes, she said, were packed with books.

"Leave it to me—leave it to me!" said Willoughby, obviously intending to do much more than she asked of him. But Ridley and Mr. Pepper were heard fumbling at the door.

"How are you, Vinrace?" said Ridley, extending a limp hand as he came in, as though the meeting were melancholy to both, but on the whole more so to him.

Willoughby preserved his heartiness, tempered by respect. For the moment nothing was said.

"We looked in and saw you laughing," Helen remarked. "Mr. Pepper had just told a very good story."

"Pish. None of the stories were good," said her husband peevishly.

"Still a severe judge, Ridley?" enquired Mr. Vinrace.

"We bored you so that you left," said Ridley, speaking directly to his wife.

As this was quite true Helen did not attempt to deny it, and her next remark, "But didn't they improve after we'd gone?" was unfortunate, for her husband answered with a droop of his shoulders, "If possible they got worse."

The situation was now one of considerable discomfort for every one concerned, as was proved by a long interval of constraint and silence. Mr. Pepper, indeed, created a diversion of a kind by leaping on to his seat, both feet tucked under him, with the action of a spinster who detects a mouse, as the draught struck at his ankles. Drawn up there, sucking at his cigar, with his arms encircling his knees, he looked like the image of Buddha, and from this elevation began a discourse, addressed to nobody, for nobody had called for it, upon the unplumbed depths of ocean. He professed himself surprised to learn that although Mr. Vinrace possessed ten ships, regularly plying between London and Buenos Aires, not one of them was bidden to investigate the great white monsters of the lower waters.

"No, no," laughed Willoughby, "the monsters of the earth are too many for me!"

Rachel was heard to sigh, "Poor little goats!"

"If it weren't for the goats there'd be no music, my dear; music depends upon goats," said her father rather sharply, and Mr. Pepper went on to describe the white, hairless, blind monsters lying curled on the ridges of sand at the bottom of the sea, which would explode if you brought them to the surface, their sides bursting asunder and scattering entrails to the winds when released from pressure, with considerable detail and with such show of knowledge, that Ridley was disgusted, and begged him to stop.

From all this Helen drew her own conclusions, which were gloomy enough. Pepper was a bore; Rachel was an unlicked girl, no doubt prolific of confidences, the very first of which would be: "You see, I don't get on with my father." Willoughby, as usual, loved his business and built his Empire, and between them all she would be considerably bored. Being a woman of action, however, she rose, and said that for her part she was going to bed. At the door she glanced back instinctively at Rachel, expecting that as two of the same sex they would leave the room together. Rachel rose, looked vaguely into Helen's face, and remarked with her slight stammer, "I'm going out to t-t-triumph in the wind."

Mrs. Ambrose's worst suspicions were confirmed; she went down the passage lurching from side to side, and fending off the wall now with her right arm, now with her left; at each lurch she exclaimed emphatically, "Damn!"

2

Uncomfortable as the night, with its rocking movement, and salt smells, may have been, and in one case undoubtedly was, for Mr. Pepper had insufficient clothes upon his bed, the breakfast next morning wore a kind of beauty. The voyage had begun, and had begun happily with a soft blue sky, and a calm sea. The sense of untapped resources, things to say as yet unsaid, made the hour significant, so that in future years the entire journey perhaps would be represented by this one scene, with the sound of sirens hooting in the river the night before, somehow mixing in.

The table was cheerful with apples and bread and eggs. Helen handed Willoughby the butter, and as she did so cast her eye on him and reflected, "And she married you, and she was happy, I suppose."

She went off on a familiar train of thought, leading on to all kinds of well-known reflections, from the old wonder, why Theresa had married Willoughby?

"Of course, one sees all that," she thought, meaning that one sees that he is big and burly, and has a great booming voice, and a fist and a will of his own; "but—" here she slipped into a fine analysis of him which is best represented by one word, "sentimental," by which she meant that he was never simple and honest about his feelings. For example, he seldom spoke of the dead, but kept anniversaries with singular pomp. She suspected him of nameless atrocities with regard to his daughter, as indeed she had always suspected him of bullying his wife. Naturally she fell to comparing her own fortunes with the fortunes of her friend, for Willoughby's wife had been perhaps the one woman Helen called friend, and this comparison often made the staple of their talk. Ridley was a scholar, and Willoughby was a man of business. Ridley was bringing out the third volume of Pindar when Willoughby was launching his first ship. They built a new factory the very year the commentary on Aristotle—was it?—appeared at the University Press. "And Rachel," she looked at her, meaning, no doubt, to decide the argument, which was otherwise too evenly balanced, by declaring that Rachel was not comparable to her own children. "She really might be six years old," was all she said, however, this judgment referring to the smooth unmarked outline of the girl's face, and not condemning her otherwise, for if Rachel were ever to think, feel, laugh, or express herself, instead of dropping milk from a height as though to see what kind of drops it made, she might be interesting though never exactly pretty. She was like her mother, as the image in a pool on a still summer's day is like the vivid flushed face that hangs over it.

Meanwhile Helen herself was under examination, though not from either of her victims. Mr. Pepper considered her; and his meditations, carried on while he cut his toast into bars and neatly buttered them, took him through a considerable stretch of autobiography. One of his penetrating glances assured him that he was right last night in judging that Helen was beautiful. Blandly he passed her the jam. She was talking nonsense, but not worse nonsense than people usually do talk at breakfast, the cerebral circulation, as he knew to his cost, being apt to give trouble at that hour. He went on saying "No" to her, on principle, for he never yielded to a woman on account of her sex. And here, dropping his eyes to his plate, he became autobiographical. He had not married himself for the sufficient reason that he had never met a woman who commanded his respect. Condemned to pass the susceptible years of youth in a railway station in Bombay, he had seen only coloured women, military women, official women; and his ideal was a woman who could read Greek, if not Persian, was irreproachably fair in the face, and able to understand the small things he let fall while undressing. As it was he had contracted habits of which he was not in the least ashamed. Certain odd minutes every day went to learning things by heart; he never took a ticket without noting the number; he devoted January to Petronius, February to Catullus, March to the Etruscan vases perhaps; anyhow he had done good work in India, and there was nothing to regret in his life except the fundamental defects which no wise man regrets, when the present is still his. So concluding he looked up suddenly and smiled. Rachel caught his eye.

"And now you've chewed something thirty-seven times, I suppose?" she thought, but said politely aloud, "Are your legs troubling you today, Mr. Pepper?"

"My shoulder blades?" he asked, shifting them painfully. "Beauty has no effect upon uric acid that I'm aware of," he sighed, contemplating the round pane opposite, through which the sky and sea showed blue. At the same time he took a little parchment volume from his pocket and laid it on the table. As it was clear that he invited comment, Helen asked him the name of it. She got the name; but she got also a disquisition upon the proper method of making roads. Beginning with the Greeks, who had, he said, many difficulties to contend with, he continued with the Romans, passed to England and the right method, which speedily became the wrong method, and wound up with such a fury of denunciation directed against the road-makers of the present day in general, and the road-makers of Richmond Park in particular, where Mr. Pepper had the habit of cycling every morning before breakfast, that the spoons fairly jingled against the coffee cups, and the insides of at least four rolls mounted in a heap beside Mr. Pepper's plate.

"Pebbles!" he concluded, viciously dropping another bread pellet upon the heap. "The roads of England are mended with pebbles! 'With the first heavy rainfall,' I've told 'em, 'your road will be a swamp.' Again and again my words have proved true. But d'you suppose they listen to me when I tell 'em so, when I point out the consequences, the consequences to the public purse, when I recommend 'em to read Coryphæus? Not a bit of it; they've other interests to attend to. No, Mrs. Ambrose, you will form no just opinion of the stupidity of mankind until you have sat upon a Borough Council!" The little man fixed her with a glance of ferocious energy.

"I have had servants," said Mrs. Ambrose, concentrating her gaze. "At this moment I have a nurse. She's a good woman as they go, but she's determined to make my children pray. So far, owing to great care on my part, they think of God as a kind of walrus; but now that my back's turned—Ridley," she demanded, swinging round upon her husband, "what shall we do if we find them saying the Lord's Prayer when we get home again?"

Ridley made the sound which is represented by "Tush."

But Willoughby, whose discomfort as he listened was manifested by a slight movement rocking of his body, said awkwardly, "Oh, surely, Helen, a little religion hurts nobody."

"I would rather my children told lies," she replied, and while Willoughby was reflecting that his sister-in-law was even more eccentric than he remembered, pushed her chair back and swept upstairs. In a second they heard her calling back, "Oh, look! We're out at sea!"

They followed her on to the deck. All the smoke and the houses had disappeared, and the ship was out in a wide space of sea very fresh and clear though pale in the early light. They had left London sitting on its mud. A very thin line of shadow tapered on the horizon, scarcely thick enough to stand the burden of Paris, which nevertheless rested upon it. They were free of roads, free of mankind, and the same exhilaration at their freedom ran through them all. The ship was making her way steadily through small waves which slapped her and then fizzled like effervescing water, leaving a little border of bubbles and foam on either side. The colourless October sky above was thinly clouded as if by the trail of wood-fire smoke, and the air was wonderfully salt and brisk. Indeed it was too cold to stand still. Mrs. Ambrose drew her arm within her husband's, and as they moved off it could be seen from the way in which her sloping cheek turned up to his that she had something private to communicate. They went a few paces and Rachel saw them kiss.

Down she looked into the depth of the sea. While it was slightly disturbed on the surface by the passage of the *Euphrosyne*, beneath it was green and dim, and it grew dimmer and dimmer until the sand at the bottom was only a pale blur. One could scarcely see the black ribs of wrecked ships, or the spiral towers made by the burrowings of great eels, or the smooth green-sided monsters who came by flickering this way and that.

—"And, Rachel, if any one wants me, I'm busy till one," said her father, enforcing his words as he often did, when he spoke to his daughter, by a smart blow upon the shoulder.

"Until one," he repeated. "And you'll find yourself some employment, eh? Scales, French, a little German, eh? There's Mr. Pepper who knows more about separable verbs than any man in Europe, eh?" and he went off laughing. Rachel laughed, too, as indeed she had laughed ever since she could remember, without thinking it funny, but because she admired her father.

But just as she was turning with a view perhaps to finding some employment, she was intercepted by a woman who was so broad and so thick that to be intercepted by her was inevitable. The discreet tentative way in which she moved, together with her sober black dress, showed that she belonged to the lower orders; nevertheless she took up a rock-like position, looking about her to see that no gentry were near before she delivered her message, which had reference to the state of the sheets, and was of the utmost gravity.

"How ever we're to get through this voyage, Miss Rachel, I really can't tell," she began with a shake of her head. "There's only just sheets enough to go round, and the master's has a rotten place you could put your fingers through. And the counterpanes. Did you notice the counterpanes? I thought to myself a poor person would have been ashamed of them. The one I gave Mr. Pepper was hardly fit to cover a dog. . . . No, Miss Rachel, they could *not* be mended; they're only fit for dust sheets. Why, if one sewed one's finger to the bone, one would have one's work undone the next time they went to the laundry."

Her voice in its indignation wavered as if tears were near.

There was nothing for it but to descend and inspect a large pile of linen heaped upon a table. Mrs. Chailey handled the sheets as if she knew each by name, character, and constitution. Some had yellow stains, others had places where the threads made long ladders; but to the ordinary eye they looked much as sheets usually do look, very chill, white, cold, and irreproachably clean.

Suddenly Mrs. Chailey, turning from the subject of sheets, dismissing them entirely, clenched her fists on the top of them, and proclaimed, "And you couldn't ask a living creature to sit where I sit!"

Mrs. Chailey was expected to sit in a cabin which was large enough, but too near the boilers, so that after five minutes she could hear her heart "go," she complained, putting her hand above it, which was a state of things that Mrs. Vinrace, Rachel's mother, would never have dreamt of inflicting—Mrs. Vinrace, who knew every sheet in her house, and expected of every one the best they could do, but no more.

It was the easiest thing in the world to grant another room, and the problem of sheets simultaneously and miraculously solved itself, the spots and ladders not being past cure after all, but—

"Lies! Lies! Lies!" exclaimed the mistress indignantly, as she ran up on to the deck. "What's the use of telling me lies?"

In her anger that a woman of fifty should behave like a child and come cringing to a girl because she wanted to sit where she had not leave to sit, she did not think of the particular case, and, unpacking her music, soon forgot all about the old woman and her sheets.

Mrs. Chailey folded her sheets, but her expression testified to flatness within. The world no longer cared about her, and a ship was not a home. When the lamps were lit yesterday, and the sailors went tumbling above her head, she had cried; she would cry this evening; she would cry tomorrow. It was not home. Meanwhile she arranged her ornaments in the room which she had won too easily. They were strange ornaments to bring on a sea voyage—china pugs, tea-sets in miniature, cups stamped floridly with the arms of the city of Bristol, hair-pin boxes crusted with shamrock, antelopes' heads in coloured plaster, together with a multitude of tiny photographs, representing downright workmen in their Sunday best, and women holding white babies. But there was one portrait in a gilt frame, for which a nail was needed, and before she sought it Mrs. Chailey put on her spectacles and read what was written on a slip of paper at the back:

"This picture of her mistress is given to Emma Chailey by Willoughby Vinrace in gratitude for thirty years of devoted service."

Tears obliterated the words and the head of the nail.

"So long as I can do something for your family," she was saying, as she hammered at it, when a voice called melodiously in the passage.

"Mrs. Chailey! Mrs. Chailey!"

Chailey instantly tidied her dress, composed her face, and opened the door.

"I'm in a fix," said Mrs. Ambrose, who was flushed and out of breath. "You know what gentlemen are. The chairs too high—the tables too low—there's six inches between the floor and the door. What I want's a hammer, an old quilt, and have you such a thing as a kitchen table? Anyhow, between us"—she now flung open the door of her husband's sitting room, and revealed Ridley pacing up and down, his forehead all wrinkled, and the collar of his coat turned up.

"It's as though they'd taken pains to torment me!" he cried, stopping dead. "Did I come on this voyage in order to catch rheumatism and pneumonia? Really one might have credited Vinrace with more sense. My dear," Helen was on her knees under a table, "you are only making yourself untidy, and we had much better recognise the fact that we are condemned to six weeks of unspeakable misery. To come at all was the height of folly, but now that we are here I suppose that I can face it like a man. My diseases of course will be increased—I feel already worse than I did yesterday, but we've only ourselves to thank, and the children happily—"

"Move! Move! Move!" cried Helen, chasing him from corner to corner with a chair as though he were an errant hen. "Out of the way, Ridley, and in half an hour you'll find it ready."

She turned him out of the room, and they could hear him groaning and swearing as he went along the passage.

"I daresay he isn't very strong," said Mrs. Chailey, looking at Mrs. Ambrose compassionately, as she helped to shift and carry.

"It's books," sighed Helen, lifting an armful of sad volumes from the floor to the shelf. "Greek from morning to night. If ever Miss Rachel marries, Chailey, pray that she may marry a man who doesn't know his ABC."

The preliminary discomforts and harshnesses, which generally make the first days of a sea voyage so cheerless and trying to the temper, being somehow lived through, the succeeding days passed pleasantly enough. October was well advanced, but steadily burning with a warmth that made the early months of the summer appear very young and capricious. Great tracts of the earth lay now beneath the autumn sun, and the whole of England, from the bald moors to the Cornish rocks, was lit up from dawn to sunset, and showed in stretches of yellow, green, and purple. Under that illumination even the roofs of the great towns glittered. In thousands of small gardens, millions of dark-red flowers were blooming, until the old ladies who had tended them so carefully came down the paths with their scissors, snipped through their juicy stalks, and laid them upon cold stone ledges in the village church. Innumerable parties of picnickers coming home at sunset cried, "Was there ever such a day as this?"

"It's you," the young men whispered; "Oh, it's you," the young women replied. All old people and many sick people were drawn, were it only for a foot or two, into the open air, and prognosticated pleasant things about the course of the world. As for the confidences and expressions of love that were heard not only in cornfields but in lamplit rooms, where the windows opened on the garden, and men with cigars kissed women with grey hairs, they were not to be counted. Some said that the sky was an emblem of the life to come. Long-tailed birds clattered and screamed, and crossed from wood to wood, with golden eyes in their plumage.

But while all this went on by land, very few people thought about the sea. They took it for granted that the sea was calm; and there was no need, as there is in many houses when the creeper taps on the bedroom windows, for the couples to murmur before they kiss, "Think of the ships tonight," or "Thank Heaven, I'm not the man in the lighthouse!" For all they imagined, the ships when they vanished on the sky-line dissolved, like snow in water. The grown-up view, indeed, was not much clearer than the view of the little creatures in bathing drawers who were trotting in to the foam all along the coasts of England, and scooping up buckets full of water. They saw white sails or tufts of smoke pass across the horizon, and if you had said that these were waterspouts, or the petals of white sea flowers, they would have agreed.

The people in ships, however, took an equally singular view of England. Not only did it appear to them to be an island, and a very small island, but it was a shrinking island in which people were imprisoned. One figured them first swarming about like aimless ants, and almost pressing each other over the edge; and then, as the ship withdrew, one figured them making a vain clamour, which, being unheard, either ceased, or rose into a brawl. Finally, when the ship was out of sight of land, it became plain that the people of England were completely mute. The disease attacked other parts of the earth; Europe shrank, Asia shrank, Africa and America shrank, until it seemed doubtful whether the ship would ever run against any of those wrinkled little rocks again. But, on the other hand, an immense dignity had descended upon her; she was an inhabitant of the great world, which has so few inhabitants, travelling all day across an empty universe, with veils drawn before her and behind. She was more lonely than the caravan crossing the desert; she was infinitely more mysterious, moving by her own power and sustained by her own resources. The sea might give her death or some unexampled joy, and none would know of it. She was a bride going forth to her husband, a virgin unknown of men; in her vigor and purity she might be likened to all beautiful things, for as a ship she had a life of her own.

Indeed if they had not been blessed in their weather, one blue day being bowled up after another, smooth, round, and flawless. Mrs. Ambrose would have found it very dull. As it was, she had her embroidery frame set up on deck, with a little table by her side on which lay open a black volume of philosophy. She chose a thread from the vari-coloured tangle that lay in her lap, and sewed red into the bark of a tree, or yellow into the river torrent. She was working at a great design of a tropical river running through a tropical forest, where spotted deer would eventually browse upon masses of fruit, bananas, oranges, and giant pomegranates, while a troop of naked natives whirled darts into the air. Between the stitches she looked to one side and read a sentence about the Reality of Matter, or the Nature of Good. Round her men in blue jerseys knelt and scrubbed the boards, or leant over the rails and whistled, and not far off Mr. Pepper sat cutting up roots with a penknife. The rest were occupied in other parts of the ship: Ridley at his Greek—he had never found quarters more to his liking; Willoughby at his documents, for he used a voyage to work of arrears of business; and Rachel—Helen, between her sentences of philosophy, wondered sometimes what Rachel *did* do with herself? She meant vaguely to go and see. They had scarcely spoken two words to each other since that first evening; they were polite when they met, but there had been no confidence of any kind. Rachel seemed to get on very well with her father—much better, Helen thought, than she ought to—and was as ready to let Helen alone as Helen was to let her alone.

At that moment Rachel was sitting in her room doing absolutely nothing. When the ship was full this apartment bore some magnificent title and was the resort of elderly sea-sick ladies who left the deck to their youngsters. By virtue of the piano, and a mess of books on the floor, Rachel considered it her room, and there she would sit for hours playing very difficult music, reading a little German, or a little English when the mood took her, and doing—as at this moment—absolutely nothing.

The way she had been educated, joined to a fine natural indolence, was of course partly the reason of it, for she had been educated as the majority of well-to-do girls in the last part of the nineteenth century were educated. Kindly doctors and gentle old professors had taught her the rudiments of about ten different branches of knowledge, but they would as soon have forced her to go through one piece of drudgery thoroughly as they would have told her that her hands were dirty. The one hour or the two hours weekly passed very pleasantly, partly owing to the other pupils, partly to the fact that the window looked upon the back of a shop, where figures appeared against the red windows in winter, partly to the accidents that are bound to happen when more than two people are in the same room together. But there was no subject in the world which she knew accurately. Her mind was in the state of an intelligent man's in the beginning of the reign of Queen Elizabeth; she would believe practically anything she was told, invent reasons for anything she said. The shape of the earth, the history of the world, how trains worked, or money was invested, what laws were in force, which people wanted what, and why they wanted it, the most elementary idea of a system in modern life—none of this had been imparted to her by any of her professors or mistresses. But this system of education had one great advantage. It did not teach anything, but it put no obstacle in the way of any real talent that the pupil might chance to have. Rachel, being musical, was allowed to learn nothing but music; she became a fanatic about music. All the energies that might have gone into languages, science, or literature, that might have made her friends, or shown her the world, poured straight into music. Finding her teachers inadequate, she had practically taught herself. At the age of twenty-four she knew as much about music as most people do when they are thirty; and could play as well as nature allowed her to, which, as became daily more obvious, was a really generous allowance. If this one definite gift was surrounded by dreams and ideas of the most extravagant and foolish description, no one was any the wiser.

Her education being thus ordinary, her circumstances were no more out of the common. She was an only child and had never been bullied and laughed at by brothers and sisters. Her mother having died when she was eleven, two aunts, the sisters of her father, brought her up, and they lived for the sake of the air in a comfortable house in Richmond. She was of course brought up with excessive care, which as a child was for her health; as a girl and a young woman was for what it seems almost crude to call her morals. Until quite lately she had been completely ignorant that for women such things existed. She groped for knowledge in old books, and found it in repulsive chunks, but she did not naturally care for books and thus never troubled her head about the censorship which was exercised first by her aunts, later by her father. Friends might have told her things, but she had few of her own age—Richmond being an awkward place to reach—and, as it happened, the only girl she knew well was a religious zealot, who in the fervour of intimacy talked about God, and the best ways of taking up one's cross, a topic only fitfully interesting to one whose mind reached other stages at other times.

But lying in her chair, with one hand behind her head, the other grasping the knob on the arm, she was clearly following her thoughts intently. Her education left her abundant time for thinking. Her eyes were fixed so steadily upon a ball on the rail of the ship that she would have been startled and annoyed if anything had chanced to obscure it for a second. She had begun her meditations with a shout of laughter, caused by the following translation from *Tristan*:

In shrinking trepidation
His shame he seems to hide

While to the king his relation
He brings the corpse-like Bride.
Seems it so senseless what I say?

She cried that it did, and threw down the book. Next she had picked up *Cowper's Letters*, the classic prescribed by her father which had bored her, so that one sentence chancing to say something about the smell of broom in his garden, she had thereupon seen the little hall at Richmond laden with flowers on the day of her mother's funeral, smelling so strong that now any flower-scent brought back the sickly horrible sensation; and so from one scene she passed, half-hearing, half-seeing, to another. She saw her Aunt Lucy arranging flowers in the drawing-room.

"Aunt Lucy," she volunteered, "I don't like the smell of broom; it reminds me of funerals."

"Nonsense, Rachel," Aunt Lucy replied; "don't say such foolish things, dear. I always think it a particularly cheerful plant."

Lying in the hot sun her mind was fixed upon the characters of her aunts, their views, and the way they lived. Indeed this was a subject that lasted her hundreds of morning walks round Richmond Park, and blotted out the trees and the people and the deer. Why did they do the things they did, and what did they feel, and what was it all about? Again she heard Aunt Lucy talking to Aunt Eleanor. She had been that morning to take up the character of a servant, "And, of course, at half-past ten in the morning one expects to find the housemaid brushing the stairs." How odd! How unspeakably odd! But she could not explain to herself why suddenly as her aunt spoke the whole system in which they lived had appeared before her eyes as something quite unfamiliar and inexplicable, and themselves as chairs or umbrellas dropped about here and there without any reason. She could only say with her slight stammer, "Are you f-f-fond of Aunt Eleanor, Aunt Lucy?" to which her aunt replied, with her nervous hen-like twitter of a laugh, "My dear child, what questions you do ask!"

"How fond? Very fond!" Rachel pursued.

"I can't say I've ever thought 'how,'" said Miss Vinrace. "If one cares one doesn't think 'how,' Rachel," which was aimed at the niece who had never yet "come" to her aunts as cordially as they wished.

"But you know I care for you, don't you, dear, because you're your mother's daughter, if for no other reason, and there *are* plenty of other reasons"—and she leant over and kissed her with some emotion, and the argument was spilt irretrievably about the place like a bucket of milk.

By these means Rachel reached that stage in thinking, if thinking it can be called, when the eyes are intent upon a ball or a knob and the lips cease to move. Her efforts to come to an understanding had only hurt her aunt's feelings, and the conclusion must be that it is better not to try. To feel anything strongly was to create an abyss between oneself and others who feel strongly perhaps but differently. It was far better to play the piano and forget all the rest. The conclusion was very welcome. Let these odd men and women—her aunts, the Hunts, Ridley, Helen, Mr. Pepper, and the rest—be symbols, featureless but dignified, symbols of age, of youth, of motherhood, of learning, and beautiful often as people upon the stage are beautiful. It appeared that nobody ever said a thing they meant, or ever talked of a feeling they felt, but that was what music was for. Reality dwelling in what one saw and felt, but did not talk about, one could accept a system in which things went round and round quite satisfactorily to other people, without often troubling to think about it, except as something superficially strange. Absorbed by her music she accepted her lot very complacently, blazing into indignation perhaps once a fortnight, and subsiding as she subsided now. Inextricably mixed in dreamy confusion, her mind seemed to enter into communion, to be delightfully expanded and combined with the spirit of the whitish boards on deck, with the spirit of the sea, with the spirit of Beethoven Op. 111, even with the spirit of poor William Cowper there at Olney. Like a ball of thistledown it kissed the sea, rose, kissed it again, and thus rising and kissing passed finally out of sight. The rising and falling of the ball of thistledown was represented by the sudden droop forward of her own head, and when it passed out of sight she was asleep.

Ten minutes later Mrs. Ambrose opened the door and looked at her. It did not surprise her to find that this was the way in which Rachel passed her mornings. She glanced round the room at the piano, at the books, at the general mess. In the first place she considered Rachel aesthetically; lying unprotected she looked somehow like a victim dropped from the claws of a bird of prey, but considered as a woman, a young woman of twenty-four, the sight gave rise to reflections. Mrs. Ambrose stood thinking for at least two minutes. She then smiled, turned noiselessly away and went, lest the sleeper should waken, and there should be the awkwardness of speech between them.

3

Early next morning there was a sound as of chains being drawn roughly overhead; the steady heart of the *Euphrosyne* slowly ceased to beat; and Helen, poking her nose above deck, saw a stationary castle upon a stationary hill. They had dropped anchor in the mouth of the Tagus, and instead of cleaving new waves perpetually, the same waves kept returning and washing against the sides of the ship.

As soon as breakfast was done, Willoughby disappeared over the vessel's side, carrying a brown leather case, shouting over his shoulder that every one was to mind and behave themselves, for he would be kept in Lisbon doing business until five o'clock that afternoon.

At about that hour he reappeared, carrying his case, professing himself tired, bothered, hungry, thirsty, cold, and in immediate need of his tea. Rubbing his hands, he told them the adventures of the day: how he had come upon poor old Jackson combing his moustache before the glass in the office, little expecting his descent, had put him through such a morning's work as seldom came his way; then treated him to a lunch of champagne and ortolans; paid a call upon Mrs. Jackson, who was fatter than ever, poor woman, but asked kindly after Rachel—and O Lord, little Jackson had confessed to a confounded piece of weakness—well, well, no harm was done, he supposed, but what was the use of his giving orders if they were promptly disobeyed? He had said distinctly that he would take no passengers on this trip. Here he began searching in his pockets and eventually discovered a card, which he planked down on the table before Rachel. On it she read, "Mr. and Mrs. Richard Dalloway, 23 Browne Street, Mayfair."

"Mr. Richard Dalloway," continued Vinrace, "seems to be a gentleman who thinks that because he was once a member of Parliament, and his wife's the daughter of a peer, they can have what they like for the asking. They got round poor little Jackson anyhow. Said they must have passages—produced a letter from Lord Glenaway, asking me as a personal favour—overruled any objections Jackson made (I don't believe they came to much), and so there's nothing for it but to submit, I suppose."

But it was evident that for some reason or other Willoughby was quite pleased to submit, although he made a show of growling.

The truth was that Mr. and Mrs. Dalloway had found themselves stranded in Lisbon. They had been travelling on the Continent for some weeks, chiefly with a view to broadening Mr. Dalloway's mind. Unable for a season, by one of the accidents of political life, to serve his country in Parliament, Mr. Dalloway was doing the best he could to serve it out of Parliament. For that purpose the Latin countries did very well, although the East, of course, would have done better.

"Expect to hear of me next in Petersburg or Teheran," he had said, turning to wave farewell from the steps of the Travellers'. But a disease had broken out in the East, there was cholera in Russia, and he was heard of, not so romantically, in Lisbon. They had been through France; he had stopped at manufacturing centres where, producing letters of introduction, he had been shown over works, and noted facts in a pocket-book. In Spain he and Mrs. Dalloway had mounted mules, for they wished to understand how the peasants live. Are they ripe for rebellion, for example? Mrs. Dalloway had then insisted upon a day or two at Madrid with the pictures. Finally they arrived in Lisbon and spent six days which, in a journal privately issued afterwards, they described as of "unique interest." Richard had audiences with ministers, and foretold a crisis at no distant date, "the foundations of government being incurably corrupt. Yet how blame, etc."; while Clarissa inspected the royal stables, and took several snapshots showing men now exiled and windows now broken. Among other things she photographed Fielding's grave, and let loose a small bird which some ruffian had trapped, "because one hates to think of anything in a cage where English people lie buried," the diary stated. Their tour was thoroughly unconventional, and followed no meditated plan. The foreign correspondents of the *Times* decided their route as much as anything else. Mr. Dalloway wished to look at certain guns, and was of opinion that the African coast is far more unsettled than people at home were inclined to believe. For these reasons they wanted a slow inquisitive kind of ship, comfortable, for they were bad sailors, but not extravagant, which would stop for a day or two at this port and at that, taking in coal while the Dalloways saw things for themselves. Meanwhile they found themselves stranded in Lisbon, unable for the moment to lay hands upon the precise vessel they wanted. They heard of the *Euphrosyne*, but heard also that she was primarily a cargo boat, and only took passengers by special arrangement, her business being to carry dry goods to the Amazons, and rubber home again. "By special arrangement," however, were words of high encouragement to them, for they came of a class where almost everything was specially arranged, or could be if necessary. On this occasion all that Richard did was to write a note to Lord Glenaway, the head of the line which bears his title; to call on poor old Jackson; to represent to him how Mrs. Dalloway was so-and-so, and he had been something or other else, and what they wanted was such and such a thing. It was done. They parted with compliments and pleasure on both sides, and here, a week later, came the boat rowing up to the ship in the dusk with the Dalloways on board of it; in three minutes they were standing together on the deck of the *Euphrosyne*. Their arrival, of course, created some stir, and it was seen by several pairs of eyes that Mrs. Dalloway was a tall slight woman, her body wrapped in furs, her head in veils, while Mr. Dalloway appeared to be a middle-sized man of sturdy build, dressed like a sportsman on an autumnal moor. Many solid leather bags of a rich brown hue soon surrounded them, in addition to which Mr. Dalloway carried a despatch box, and his wife a dressing-case suggestive of a diamond necklace and bottles with silver tops.

"It's so like Whistler!" she exclaimed, with a wave towards the shore, as she shook Rachel by the hand, and Rachel had only time to look at the grey hills on one side of her before Willoughby introduced Mrs. Chailey, who took the lady to her cabin.

Momentary though it seemed, nevertheless the interruption was upsetting; every one was more or less put out by it, from Mr. Grice, the steward, to Ridley himself. A few minutes later Rachel passed the smoking-room, and found Helen moving arm-chairs. She was absorbed in her arrangements, and on seeing Rachel remarked confidentially:

"If one can give men a room to themselves where they will sit, it's all to the good. Arm-chairs are *the* important things——" She began wheeling them about. "Now, does it still look like a bar at a railway station?"

She whipped a plush cover off a table. The appearance of the place was marvellously improved.

Again, the arrival of the strangers made it obvious to Rachel, as the hour of dinner approached, that she must change her dress; and the ringing of the great bell found her sitting on the edge of her berth in such a position that the little glass above the washstand reflected her head and shoulders. In the glass she wore an expression of tense melancholy, for she had come to the depressing conclusion, since the arrival of the Dalloways, that her face was not the face she wanted, and in all probability never would be.

However, punctuality had been impressed on her, and whatever face she had, she must go in to dinner.

These few minutes had been used by Willoughby in sketching to the Dalloways the people they were to meet, and checking them upon his fingers.

"There's my brother-in-law, Ambrose, the scholar (I daresay you've heard his name), his wife, my old friend Pepper, a very quiet fellow, but knows everything, I'm told. And that's all. We're a very small party. I'm dropping them on the coast."

Mrs. Dalloway, with her head a little on one side, did her best to recollect Ambrose—was it a surname?—but failed. She was made slightly uneasy by what she had heard. She knew that scholars married any one—

girls they met in farms on reading parties; or little suburban women who said disagreeably, "Of course I know it's my husband you want; not *me*."

But Helen came in at that point, and Mrs. Dalloway saw with relief that though slightly eccentric in appearance, she was not untidy, held herself well, and her voice had restraint in it, which she held to be the sign of a lady. Mr. Pepper had not troubled to change his neat ugly suit.

"But after all," Clarissa thought to herself as she followed Vinrace in to dinner, "*every one's* interesting really."

When seated at the table she had some need of that assurance, chiefly because of Ridley, who came in late, looked decidedly unkempt, and took to his soup in profound gloom.

An imperceptible signal passed between husband and wife, meaning that they grasped the situation and would stand by each other loyally. With scarcely a pause Mrs. Dalloway turned to Willoughby and began:

"What I find so tiresome about the sea is that there are no flowers in it. Imagine fields of hollyhocks and violets in mid-ocean! How divine!"

"But somewhat dangerous to navigation," boomed Richard, in the bass, like the bassoon to the flourish of his wife's violin. "Why, weeds can be bad enough, can't they, Vinrace? I remember crossing in the *Mauretania* once, and saying to the Captain—Richards—did you know him?—'Now tell me what perils you really dread most for your ship, Captain Richards?' expecting him to say icebergs, or derelicts, or fog, or something of that sort. Not a bit of it. I've always remembered his answer. '*Sedgius aquatici,*' he said, which I take to be a kind of duck-weed."

Mr. Pepper looked up sharply, and was about to put a question when Willoughby continued:

"They've an awful time of it—those captains! Three thousand souls on board!"

"Yes, indeed," said Clarissa. She turned to Helen with an air of profundity. "I'm convinced people are wrong when they say it's work that wears one; it's responsibility. That's why one pays one's cook more than one's housemaid, I suppose."

"According to that, one ought to pay one's nurse double; but one doesn't," said Helen.

"No; but think what a joy to have to do with babies, instead of saucepans!" said Mrs. Dalloway, looking with more interest at Helen, a probable mother.

"I'd much rather be a cook than a nurse," said Helen. "Nothing would induce me to take charge of children."

"Mothers always exaggerate," said Ridley. "A well-bred child is no responsibility. I've travelled all over Europe with mine. You just wrap 'em up warm and put 'em in the rack."

Helen laughed at that. Mrs. Dalloway exclaimed, looking at Ridley:

"How like a father! My husband's just the same. And then one talks of the equality of the sexes!"

"Does one?" said Mr. Pepper.

"Oh, some do!" cried Clarissa. "My husband had to pass an irate lady every afternoon last session who said nothing else, I imagine."

"She sat outside the house; it was very awkward," said Dalloway. "At last I plucked up courage and said to her, 'My good creature, you're only in the way where you are. You're hindering me, and you're doing no good to yourself.'"

"And then she caught him by the coat, and would have scratched his eyes out—" Mrs. Dalloway put in.

"Pooh—that's been exaggerated," said Richard. "No, I pity them, I confess. The discomfort of sitting on those steps must be awful."

"Serve them right," said Willoughby curtly.

"Oh, I'm entirely with you there," said Dalloway. "Nobody can condemn the utter folly and futility of such behaviour more than I do; and as for the whole agitation, well! may I be in my grave before a woman has the right to vote in England! That's all I say."

The solemnity of her husband's assertion made Clarissa grave.

"It's unthinkable," she said. "Don't tell me you're a suffragist?" she turned to Ridley.

"I don't care a fig one way or t'other," said Ambrose. "If any creature is so deluded as to think that a vote does him or her any good, let him have it. He'll soon learn better."

"You're not a politician, I see," she smiled.

"Goodness, no," said Ridley.

"I'm afraid your husband won't approve of me," said Dalloway aside, to Mrs. Ambrose. She suddenly recollected that he had been in Parliament.

"Don't you ever find it rather dull?" she asked, not knowing exactly what to say.

Richard spread his hands before him, as if inscriptions were to be read in the palms of them.

"If you ask me whether I ever find it rather dull," he said, "I am bound to say yes; on the other hand, if you ask me what career do you consider on the whole, taking the good with the bad, the most enjoyable and enviable, not to speak of its more serious side, of all careers, for a man, I am bound to say, 'The Politician's.'"

"The Bar or politics, I agree," said Willoughby. "You get more run for your money."

"All one's faculties have their play," said Richard. "I may be treading on dangerous ground; but what I feel about poets and artists in general is this: on your own lines, you can't be beaten—granted; but off your own lines—puff—one has to make allowances. Now, I shouldn't like to think that any one had to make allowances for me."

"I don't quite agree, Richard," said Mrs. Dalloway. "Think of Shelley. I feel that there's almost everything one wants in 'Adonais.'"

"Read 'Adonais' by all means," Richard conceded. "But whenever I hear of Shelley I repeat to myself the words of Matthew Arnold, 'What a set! What a set!'"

This roused Ridley's attention. "Matthew Arnold? A detestable prig!" he snapped.

"A prig—granted," said Richard; "but, I think a man of the world. That's where my point comes in. We politicians doubtless seem to you" (he grasped somehow that Helen was the representative of the arts) "a gross commonplace set of people; but we see both sides; we may be clumsy, but we do our best to get a grasp of things. Now your artists *find* things in a mess, shrug their shoulders, turn aside to their visions—which I grant may be very beautiful—and *leave* things in a mess. Now that seems to me evading one's responsibilities. Besides, we aren't all born with the artistic faculty."

"It's dreadful," said Mrs. Dalloway, who, while her husband spoke, had been thinking. "When I'm with artists I feel so intensely the delights of shutting oneself up in a little world of one's own, with pictures and music and everything beautiful, and then I go out into the streets and the first child I meet with its poor, hungry, dirty little face makes me turn round and say, 'No, I *can't* shut myself up—I *won't* live in a world of my own. I should like to stop all the painting and writing and music until this kind of thing exists no longer.' Don't you feel," she wound up, addressing Helen, "that life's a perpetual conflict?" Helen considered for a moment. "No," she said. "I don't think I do."

There was a pause, which was decidedly uncomfortable. Mrs. Dalloway then gave a little shiver, and asked whether she might have her fur cloak brought to her. As she adjusted the soft brown fur about her neck a fresh topic struck her.

"I own," she said, "that I shall never forget the *Antigone*. I saw it at Cambridge years ago, and it's haunted me ever since. Don't you think it's quite the most modern thing you ever saw?" she asked Ridley. "It seemed to me I'd known twenty Clytemnestras. Old Lady Ditchling for one. I don't know a word of Greek, but I could listen to it for ever—"

Here Mr. Pepper struck up:

πολλὰ τὰ δεινά, κοὐδὲν ἀν-
θρώπου δεινότερον πέλει.
τοῦτο καὶ πολιοῦ πέραν
πόντου χειμερίῳ νότῳ
χωρεῖ, περιβρυχίοισι
περῶν ὑπ᾽ οἴδμασι.

Mrs. Dalloway looked at him with compressed lips.

"I'd give ten years of my life to know Greek," she said, when he had done.

"I could teach you the alphabet in half an hour," said Ridley, "and you'd read Homer in a month. I should think it an honour to instruct you."

Helen, engaged with Mr. Dalloway and the habit, now fallen into decline, of quoting Greek in the House of Commons, noted, in the great commonplace book that lies open beside us as we talk, the fact that all men, even men like Ridley, really prefer women to be fashionable.

Clarissa exclaimed that she could think of nothing more delightful. For an instant she saw herself in her drawing-room in Browne Street with a Plato open on her knees—Plato in the original Greek. She could not help believing that a real scholar, if specially interested, could slip Greek into her head with scarcely any trouble.

Ridley engaged her to come tomorrow.

"If only your ship is going to treat us kindly!" she exclaimed, drawing Willoughby into play. For the sake of guests, and these were distinguished, Willoughby was ready with a bow of his head to vouch for the good behaviour even of the waves.

"I'm dreadfully bad; and my husband's not very good," sighed Clarissa.

"I am never sick," Richard explained. "At least, I have only been actually sick once," he corrected himself. "That was crossing the Channel. But a choppy sea, I confess, or still worse, a swell, makes me distinctly uncomfortable. The great thing is never to miss a meal. You look at the food, and you say, 'I can't'; you take a mouthful, and Lord knows how you're going to swallow it; but persevere, and you often settle the attack for good. My wife's a coward."

They were pushing back their chairs. The ladies were hesitating at the doorway.

"I'd better show the way," said Helen, advancing.

Rachel followed. She had taken no part in the talk; no one had spoken to her; but she had listened to every word that was said. She had looked from Mrs. Dalloway to Mr. Dalloway, and from Mr. Dalloway back again. Clarissa, indeed, was a fascinating spectacle. She wore a white dress and a long glittering necklace. What with her clothes, and her arch delicate face, which showed exquisitely pink beneath hair turning grey, she was astonishingly like an eighteenth-century masterpiece—a Reynolds or a Romney. She made Helen and the others look coarse and slovenly beside her. Sitting lightly upright she seemed to be dealing with the world as she chose; the enormous solid globe spun round this way and that beneath her fingers. And her husband! Mr. Dalloway rolling that rich deliberate voice was even more impressive. He seemed to come from the humming oily centre of the machine where the polished rods are sliding, and the pistons thumping; he grasped things so firmly but so loosely; he made the others appear like old maids cheapening remnants. Rachel followed in the wake of the matrons, as if in a trance; a curious scent of violets came back from Mrs. Dalloway, mingling with the soft rustling of her skirts, and the tinkling of her chains. As she followed, Rachel thought with supreme self-abasement, taking in the whole course of her life and the lives of all her friends, "She said we lived in a world of our own. It's true. We're perfectly absurd."

"We sit in here," said Helen, opening the door of the saloon.

"You play?" said Mrs. Dalloway to Mrs. Ambrose, taking up the score of *Tristan* which lay on the table.

"My niece does," said Helen, laying her hand on Rachel's shoulder.

"Oh, how I envy you!" Clarissa addressed Rachel for the first time. "D'you remember this? Isn't it divine?" She played a bar or two with ringed fingers upon the page.

"And then Tristan goes like this, and Isolde–oh!–it's all too thrilling! Have you been to Bayreuth?"

"No, I haven't," said Rachel.

"Then that's still to come. I shall never forget my first *Parsifal*–a grilling August day, and those fat old German women, come in their stuffy high frocks, and then the dark theatre, and the music beginning, and one couldn't help sobbing. A kind man went and fetched me water, I remember; and I could only cry on his shoulder! It caught me here" (she touched her throat). "It's like nothing else in the world! But where's your piano?"

"It's in another room," Rachel explained.

"But you will play to us?" Clarissa entreated. "I can't imagine anything nicer than to sit out in the moonlight and listen to music–only that sounds too like a schoolgirl! You know," she said, turning to Helen, "I don't think music's altogether good for people–I'm afraid not."

"Too great a strain?" asked Helen.

"Too emotional, somehow," said Clarissa. "One notices it at once when a boy or girl takes up music as a profession. Sir William Broadley told me just the same thing. Don't you hate the kind of attitudes people go into over Wagner–like this–" She cast her eyes to the ceiling, clasped her hands, and assumed a look of intensity. "It really doesn't mean that they appreciate him; in fact, I always think it's the other way round. The people who really care about an art are always the least affected. D'you know Henry Philips, the painter?" she asked.

"I have seen him," said Helen.

"To look at, one might think he was a successful stockbroker, and not one of the greatest painters of the age. That's what I like."

"There are a great many successful stockbrokers, if you like looking at them," said Helen.

Rachel wished vehemently that her aunt would not be so perverse.

"When you see a musician with long hair, don't you know instinctively that he's bad?" Clarissa asked, turning to Rachel. "Watts and Joachim—they looked just like you and me."

"And how much nicer they'd have looked with curls!" said Helen. "The question is, are you going to aim at beauty or are you not?"

"Cleanliness!" said Clarissa, "I do want a man to look clean!"

"By cleanliness you really mean well-cut clothes," said Helen.

"There's something one knows a gentleman by," said Clarissa, "but one can't say what it is."

"Take my husband now, does he look like a gentleman?"

The question seemed to Clarissa in extraordinarily bad taste. "One of the things that can't be said," she would have put it. She could find no answer, but a laugh.

"Well, anyhow," she said, turning to Rachel, "I shall insist upon your playing to me tomorrow."

There was that in her manner that made Rachel love her.

Mrs. Dalloway hid a tiny yawn, a mere dilation of the nostrils.

"D'you know," she said, "I'm extraordinarily sleepy. It's the sea air. I think I shall escape."

A man's voice, which she took to be that of Mr. Pepper, strident in discussion, and advancing upon the saloon, gave her the alarm.

"Good-night—good-night!" she said. "Oh, I know my way—do pray for calm! Good-night!"

Her yawn must have been the image of a yawn. Instead of letting her mouth droop, dropping all her clothes in a bunch as though they depended on one string, and stretching her limbs to the utmost end of her berth, she merely changed her dress for a dressing-gown, with innumerable frills, and wrapping her feet in a rug, sat down with a writing-pad on her knee. Already this cramped little cabin was the dressing room of a lady of quality. There were bottles containing liquids; there were trays, boxes, brushes, pins. Evidently not an inch of her person lacked its proper instrument. The scent which had intoxicated Rachel pervaded the air. Thus established, Mrs. Dalloway began to write. A pen in her hands became a thing one caressed paper with, and she might have been stroking and tickling a kitten as she wrote:

> Picture us, my dear, afloat in the very oddest ship you can imagine. It's not the ship, so much as the people. One does come across queer sorts as one travels. I must say I find it hugely amusing. There's the manager of the line—called Vinrace—a nice big Englishman, doesn't say much—you know the sort. As

for the rest—they might have come trailing out of an old number of *Punch*. They're like people playing croquet in the 'sixties. How long they've all been shut up in this ship I don't know—years and years I should say—but one feels as though one had boarded a little separate world, and they'd never been on shore, or done ordinary things in their lives. It's what I've always said about literary people—they're far the hardest of any to get on with. The worst of it is, these people—a man and his wife and a niece—might have been, one feels, just like everybody else, if they hadn't got swallowed up by Oxford or Cambridge or some such place, and been made cranks of. The man's really delightful (if he'd cut his nails), and the woman has quite a fine face, only she dresses, of course, in a potato sack, and wears her hair like a Liberty shopgirl's. They talk about art, and think us such poops for dressing in the evening. However, I can't help that; I'd rather die than come in to dinner without changing—wouldn't you? It matters ever so much more than the soup. (It's odd how things like that *do* matter so much more than what's generally supposed to matter. I'd rather have my head cut off than wear flannel next the skin.) Then there's a nice shy girl—poor thing—I wish one could rake her out before it's too late. She has quite nice eyes and hair, only, of course, she'll get funny too. We ought to start a society for broadening the minds of the young—much more useful than missionaries, Hester! Oh, I'd forgotten there's a dreadful little thing called Pepper. He's just like his name. He's indescribably insignificant, and rather queer in his temper, poor dear. It's like sitting down to dinner with an ill-conditioned fox-terrier, only one can't comb him out, and sprinkle him with powder, as one would one's dog. It's a pity, sometimes, one can't treat people like dogs! The great comfort is that we're away from newspapers, so that Richard will have a real holiday this time. Spain wasn't a holiday. . . .

"You coward!" said Richard, almost filling the room with his sturdy figure.

"I did my duty at dinner!" cried Clarissa.

"You've let yourself in for the Greek alphabet, anyhow."

"Oh, my dear! Who *is* Ambrose?"

"I gather that he was a Cambridge don; lives in London now, and edits classics."

"Did you ever see such a set of cranks? The woman asked me if I thought her husband looked like a gentleman!"

"It was hard to keep the ball rolling at dinner, certainly," said Richard. "Why is it that the women, in that class, are so much queerer than the men?"

"They're not half bad-looking, really—only—they're so odd!"

They both laughed, thinking of the same things, so that there was no need to compare their impressions.

"I see I shall have quite a lot to say to Vinrace," said Richard. "He knows Sutton and all that set. He can tell me a good deal about the conditions of ship-building in the North."

"Oh, I'm glad. The men always *are* so much better than the women."

"One always has something to say to a man certainly," said Richard. "But I've no doubt you'll chatter away fast enough about the babies, Clarice."

"Has she got children? She doesn't look like it somehow."

"Two. A boy and girl."

A pang of envy shot through Mrs. Dalloway's heart.

"We *must* have a son, Dick," she said.

"Good Lord, what opportunities there are now for young men!" said Dalloway, for his talk had set him thinking. "I don't suppose there's been so good an opening since the days of Pitt."

"And it's yours!" said Clarissa.

"To be a leader of men," Richard soliloquised. "It's a fine career. My God–what a career!"

The chest slowly curved beneath his waistcoat.

"D'you know, Dick, I can't help thinking of England," said his wife meditatively, leaning her head against his chest. "Being on this ship seems to make it so much more vivid–what it really means to be English. One thinks of all we've done, and our navies, and the people in India and Africa, and how we've gone on century after century, sending out boys from little country villages–and of men like you, Dick, and it makes one feel as if one couldn't bear *not* to be English! Think of the light burning over the House, Dick! When I stood on deck just now I seemed to see it. It's what one means by London."

"It's the continuity," said Richard sententiously. A vision of English history, King following King, Prime Minister Prime Minister, and Law Law had come over him while his wife spoke. He ran his mind along the line of conservative policy, which went steadily from Lord Salisbury to Alfred, and gradually enclosed, as though it were a lasso that opened and caught things, enormous chunks of the habitable globe.

"It's taken a long time, but we've pretty nearly done it," he said; "it remains to consolidate."

"And these people don't see it!" Clarissa exclaimed.

"It takes all sorts to make a world," said her husband. "There would never be a government if there weren't an opposition."

"Dick, you're better than I am," said Clarissa. "You see round, where I only see *there*." She pressed a point on the back of his hand.

"That's my business, as I tried to explain at dinner."

"What I like about you, Dick," she continued, "is that you're always the same, and I'm a creature of moods."

"You're a pretty creature, anyhow," he said, gazing at her with deeper eyes.

"You think so, do you? Then kiss me."

He kissed her passionately, so that her half-written letter slid to the ground. Picking it up, he read it without asking leave.

"Where's your pen?" he said; and added in his little masculine hand:

> R.D. *loquitur*: Clarice has omitted to tell you that she looked exceedingly pretty at dinner, and made a conquest by which she has bound herself to learn the Greek alphabet. I will take this occasion of adding that we are both enjoying ourselves in these outlandish parts, and only wish for the presence of our friends (yourself and John, to wit) to make the trip perfectly enjoyable as it promises to be instructive. . . .

Voices were heard at the end of the corridor. Mrs. Ambrose was speaking low; William Pepper was remarking in his definite and rather acid voice, "That is the type of lady with whom I find myself distinctly out of sympathy. She—"

But neither Richard nor Clarissa profited by the verdict, for directly it seemed likely that they would overhear, Richard crackled a sheet of paper.

"I often wonder," Clarissa mused in bed, over the little white volume of Pascal which went with her everywhere, "whether it is really good for a woman to live with a man who is morally her superior, as Richard is mine. It makes one so dependent. I suppose I feel for him what my mother and women of her generation felt for Christ. It just shows that one can't do without *something*." She then fell into a sleep, which was as usual extremely sound and refreshing, but visited by fantastic dreams of great Greek letters stalking round the room, when she woke up and laughed to herself, remembering where she was and that the Greek letters were real people, lying asleep not many yards away. Then, thinking of the black sea outside tossing beneath the moon, she shuddered, and thought of her husband and the others as companions on the voyage. The dreams were not confined to her indeed, but went from one brain to another. They all dreamt of each other that night, as was natural, considering how thin the partitions were between them, and how strangely they had been lifted off the earth to sit next each other in mid-ocean, and see every detail of each other's faces, and hear whatever they chanced to say.

4

Next morning Clarissa was up before anyone else. She dressed, and was out on deck, breathing the fresh air of a calm morning, and, making the circuit of the ship for the second time, she ran straight into the lean person of Mr. Grice, the steward. She apologised, and at the same time asked him to enlighten her: what were those shiny brass stands for, half glass on the top? She had been wondering, and could not guess. When he had done explaining, she cried enthusiastically:

"I do think that to be a sailor must be the finest thing in the world!"

"And what d'you know about it?" said Mr. Grice, kindling in a strange manner. "Pardon me. What does any man or woman brought up in England know about the sea? They profess to know; but they don't."

The bitterness with which he spoke was ominous of what was to come. He led her off to his own quarters, and, sitting on the edge of a brass-bound table, looking uncommonly like a sea-gull, with her white tapering body and thin alert face, Mrs. Dalloway had to listen to the tirade of a fanatical man. Did she realise, to begin with, what a very small part of the world the land was? How peaceful, how beautiful, how benignant in comparison the sea? The deep waters could sustain Europe unaided if every earthly animal died of the plague tomorrow. Mr. Grice recalled dreadful sights which he had seen in the richest city of the world—men and women standing in line hour after hour to receive a mug of greasy soup. "And I thought of the good flesh down here waiting and asking to be caught. I'm not exactly a Protestant, and I'm not a Catholic, but I could almost pray for the days of popery to come again—because of the fasts."

As he talked he kept opening drawers and moving little glass jars. Here were the treasures which the great ocean had bestowed upon him—pale fish in greenish liquids, blobs of jelly with streaming tresses, fish with lights in their heads, they lived so deep.

"They have swum about among bones," Clarissa sighed.

"You're thinking of Shakespeare," said Mr. Grice, and taking down a copy from a shelf well lined with books, recited in an emphatic nasal voice:

Full fathom five thy father lies,

"A grand fellow, Shakespeare," he said, replacing the volume.

Clarissa was so glad to hear him say so.

"Which is your favourite play? I wonder if it's the same as mine?"

"*Henry the Fifth,*" said Mr. Grice.

"Joy!" cried Clarissa. "It is!"

Hamlet was what you might call too introspective for Mr. Grice, the sonnets too passionate; Henry the Fifth was to him the model of an English gentleman. But his favourite reading was Huxley, Herbert Spencer, and Henry George; while Emerson and Thomas Hardy he read for relaxation. He was giving Mrs. Dalloway his views upon the present state of England when the breakfast bell rung so imperiously that she had to tear herself away, promising to come back and be shown his sea-weeds.

The party, which had seemed so odd to her the night before, was already gathered round the table, still under the influence of sleep, and therefore uncommunicative, but her entrance sent a little flutter like a breath of air through them all.

"I've had the most interesting talk of my life!" she exclaimed, taking her seat beside Willoughby. "D'you realise that one of your men is a philosopher and a poet?"

"A very interesting fellow—that's what I always say," said Willoughby, distinguishing Mr. Grice. "Though Rachel finds him a bore."

"He's a bore when he talks about currents," said Rachel. Her eyes were full of sleep, but Mrs. Dalloway still seemed to her wonderful.

"I've never met a bore yet!" said Clarissa.

"And I should say the world was full of them!" exclaimed Helen. But her beauty, which was radiant in the morning light, took the contrariness from her words.

"I agree that it's the worst one can possibly say of any one," said Clarissa. "How much rather one would be a murderer than a bore!" she added, with her usual air of saying something profound. "One can fancy liking a murderer. It's the same with dogs. Some dogs are awful bores, poor dears."

It happened that Richard was sitting next to Rachel. She was curiously conscious of his presence and appearance—his well-cut clothes, his crackling shirt-front, his cuffs with blue rings round them, and the square-tipped, very clean fingers with the red stone on the little finger of the left hand.

"We had a dog who was a bore and knew it," he said, addressing her in cool, easy tones. "He was a Skye terrier, one of those long chaps, with little feet poking out from their hair like—like caterpillars—no, like sofas I should say. Well, we had another dog at the same time, a black brisk animal—a Schipperke, I think, you call them. You can't imagine a greater contrast. The Skye so slow and deliberate, looking up at you like some old gentleman in the club, as much as to say, "You don't really mean it, do you?" and the Schipperke as quick as a knife. I liked the Skye best, I must confess. There was something pathetic about him."

The story seemed to have no climax.

"What happened to him?" Rachel asked.

"That's a very sad story," said Richard, lowering his voice and peeling an apple. "He followed my wife in the car one day and got run over by a brute of a cyclist."

"Was he killed?" asked Rachel.

But Clarissa at her end of the table had overheard.

"Don't talk of it!" she cried. "It's a thing I can't bear to think of to this day."

Surely the tears stood in her eyes?

"That's the painful thing about pets," said Mr. Dalloway; "they die. The first sorrow I can remember was for the death of a dormouse. I regret to say that I sat upon it. Still, that didn't make one any the less sorry. Here lies the duck that Samuel Johnson sat on, eh? I was big for my age."

"Then we had canaries," he continued, "a pair of ring-doves, a lemur, and at one time a martin."

"Did you live in the country?" Rachel asked him.

"We lived in the country for six months of the year. When I say 'we' I mean four sisters, a brother, and myself. There's nothing like coming of a large family. Sisters particularly are delightful."

"Dick, you were horribly spoilt!" cried Clarissa across the table.

"No, no. Appreciated," said Richard.

Rachel had other questions on the tip of her tongue; or rather one enormous question, which she did not in the least know how to put into words. The talk appeared too airy to admit of it.

"Please tell me—everything." That was what she wanted to say. He had drawn apart one little chink and showed astonishing treasures. It seemed to her incredible that a man like that should be willing to talk to her. He had sisters and pets, and once lived in the country. She stirred her tea round and round; the bubbles which swam and clustered in the cup seemed to her like the union of their minds.

The talk meanwhile raced past her, and when Richard suddenly stated in a jocular tone of voice, "I'm sure Miss Vinrace, now, has secret leanings towards Catholicism," she had no idea what to answer, and Helen could not help laughing at the start she gave.

However, breakfast was over and Mrs. Dalloway was rising. "I always think religion's like collecting beetles," she said, summing up the discussion as she went up the stairs with Helen. "One person has a passion for black beetles; another hasn't; it's no good arguing about it. What's *your* black beetle now?"

"I suppose it's my children," said Helen.

"Ah—that's different," Clarissa breathed. "Do tell me. You have a boy, haven't you? Isn't it detestable, leaving them?"

It was as though a blue shadow had fallen across a pool. Their eyes became deeper, and their voices more cordial.

Instead of joining them as they began to pace the deck, Rachel was indignant with the prosperous matrons, who made her feel outside their world and motherless, and turning back, she left them abruptly. She slammed the door of her room, and pulled out her music. It was all old music—Bach and Beethoven, Mozart and Purcell—the pages yellow, the engraving rough to the finger. In three minutes she was deep in a very difficult, very classical fugue in A, and over her face came a queer remote impersonal expression of complete absorption and anxious satisfaction. Now she stumbled; now she faltered and had to play the same bar twice over; but an invisible line seemed to string the notes together, from which rose a shape, a building. She was so far absorbed in this work, for it was really difficult to find how all these sounds should stand together, and drew upon the whole of her faculties, that she never heard a knock at the door. It was burst impulsively open, and Mrs. Dalloway stood in the room leaving the door open, so that a strip of the white deck and of the blue sea appeared through the opening. The shape of the Bach fugue crashed to the ground.

"Don't let me interrupt," Clarissa implored. "I heard you playing, and I couldn't resist. I adore Bach!"

Rachel flushed and fumbled her fingers in her lap. She stood up awkwardly.

"It's too difficult," she said.

"But you were playing quite splendidly! I ought to have stayed outside."

"No," said Rachel.

She slid *Cowper's Letters* and *Wuthering Heights* out of the arm-chair, so that Clarissa was invited to sit there.

"What a dear little room!" she said, looking round. "Oh, *Cowper's Letters!* I've never read them. Are they nice?"

"Rather dull," said Rachel.

"He wrote awfully well, didn't he?" said Clarissa; "—if one likes that kind of thing—finished his sentences and all that. *Wuthering Heights!* Ah—that's more in my line. I really couldn't exist without the Brontës! Don't you love them? Still, on the whole, I'd rather live without them than without Jane Austen."

Lightly and at random though she spoke, her manner conveyed an extraordinary degree of sympathy and desire to befriend.

"Jane Austen? I don't like Jane Austen," said Rachel.

"You monster!" Clarissa exclaimed. "I can only just forgive you. Tell me why?"

"She's so—so—well, so like a tight plait," Rachel floundered.

"Ah—I see what you mean. But I don't agree. And you won't when you're older. At your age I only liked Shelley. I can remember sobbing over him in the garden.

> He has outsoared the shadow of our night,
> Envy and calumny and hate and pain—

you remember?

> Can touch him not and torture not again
> From the contagion of the world's slow stain.

How divine!—and yet what nonsense!" She looked lightly round the room. "I always think it's *living*, not dying, that counts. I really respect some snuffy old stockbroker who's gone on adding up column after column all his days, and trotting back to his villa at Brixton with some old pug dog he worships, and a dreary little wife sitting at the end of the table, and going off to Margate for a fortnight—I assure you I know heaps like that—well, they seem to me *really* nobler than poets whom every one worships, just because they're geniuses and die young. But I don't expect *you* to agree with me!"

She pressed Rachel's shoulder.

"Um-m-m—" she went on quoting—

> Unrest which men miscall delight—

"when you're my age you'll see that the world is *crammed* with delightful things. I think young people make such a mistake about that—not letting themselves be happy. I sometimes think that happiness is the only thing that counts. I don't know you well enough to say, but I should guess you might be a little inclined to—when one's young and attractive—I'm going to say it!—*every*thing's at one's feet." She glanced round as much as to say, "not only a few stuffy books and Bach."

"I long to ask questions," she continued. "You interest me so much. If I'm impertinent, you must just box my ears."

"And I—I want to ask questions," said Rachel with such earnestness that Mrs. Dalloway had to check her smile.

"D'you mind if we walk?" she said. "The air's so delicious."

She snuffed it like a racehorse as they shut the door and stood on deck.

"Isn't it good to be alive?" she exclaimed, and drew Rachel's arm within hers.

"Look, look! How exquisite!"

The shores of Portugal were beginning to lose their substance; but the land was still the land, though at a great distance. They could distinguish the little towns that were sprinkled in the folds of the hills, and the smoke rising faintly. The towns appeared to be very small in comparison with the great purple mountains behind them.

"Honestly, though," said Clarissa, having looked, "I don't like views. They're too inhuman." They walked on.

"How odd it is!" she continued impulsively. "This time yesterday we'd never met. I was packing in a stuffy little room in the hotel. We know absolutely nothing about each other–and yet–I feel as if I *did* know you!"

"You have children–your husband was in Parliament?"

"You've never been to school, and you live–?"

"With my aunts at Richmond."

"Richmond?"

"You see, my aunts like the Park. They like the quiet."

"And you don't! I understand!" Clarissa laughed.

"I like walking in the Park alone; but not–with the dogs," she finished.

"No; and some people *are* dogs; aren't they?" said Clarissa, as if she had guessed a secret. "But not every one–oh no, not every one."

"Not every one," said Rachel, and stopped.

"I can quite imagine you walking alone," said Clarissa: "and thinking–in a little world of your own. But how you will enjoy it–some day!"

"I shall enjoy walking with a man–is that what you mean?" said Rachel, regarding Mrs. Dalloway with her large enquiring eyes.

"I wasn't thinking of a man particularly," said Clarissa. "But you will."

"No. I shall never marry," Rachel determined.

"I shouldn't be so sure of that," said Clarissa. Her sidelong glance told Rachel that she found her attractive although she was inexplicably amused.

"Why do people marry?" Rachel asked.

"That's what you're going to find out," Clarissa laughed.

Rachel followed her eyes and found that they rested for a second, on the robust figure of Richard Dalloway, who was engaged in striking a match on the sole of his boot; while Willoughby expounded something, which seemed to be of great interest to them both.

"There's nothing like it," she concluded. "Do tell me about the Ambroses. Or am I asking too many questions?"

"I find you easy to talk to," said Rachel.

The short sketch of the Ambroses was, however, somewhat perfunctory, and contained little but the fact that Mr. Ambrose was her uncle.

"Your mother's brother?"

When a name has dropped out of use, the lightest touch upon it tells. Mrs. Dalloway went on:

"Are you like your mother?"

"No; she was different," said Rachel.

She was overcome by an intense desire to tell Mrs. Dalloway things she had never told any one—things she had not realised herself until this moment.

"I am lonely," she began. "I want—" She did not know what she wanted, so that she could not finish the sentence; but her lip quivered.

But it seemed that Mrs. Dalloway was able to understand without words.

"I know," she said, actually putting one arm round Rachel's shoulder. "When I was your age I wanted too. No one understood until I met Richard. He gave me all I wanted. He's man and woman as well." Her eyes rested upon Mr. Dalloway, leaning upon the rail, still talking. "Don't think I say that because I'm his wife—I see his faults more clearly than I see any one else's. What one wants in the person one lives with is that they should keep one at one's best. I often wonder what I've done to be so happy!" she exclaimed, and a tear slid down her cheek. She wiped it away, squeezed Rachel's hand, and exclaimed:

"How good life is!" At that moment, standing out in the fresh breeze, with the sun upon the waves, and Mrs. Dalloway's hand upon her arm, it seemed indeed as if life which had been unnamed before was infinitely wonderful, and too good to be true.

Here Helen passed them, and seeing Rachel arm-in-arm with a comparative stranger, looking excited, was amused, but at the same time slightly irritated. But they were immediately joined by Richard, who had enjoyed a very interesting talk with Willoughby and was in a sociable mood.

"Observe my Panama," he said, touching the brim of his hat. "Are you aware, Miss Vinrace, how much can be done to induce fine weather by appropriate headdress? I have determined that it is a hot summer day; I warn you that nothing you can say will shake me. Therefore I am going to sit down. I advise you to follow my example." Three chairs in a row invited them to be seated.

Leaning back, Richard surveyed the waves.

"That's a very pretty blue," he said. "But there's a little too much of it. Variety is essential to a view. Thus, if you have hills you ought to have a river; if a river, hills. The best view in the world in my opinion is that from Boars Hill on a fine day—it must be a fine day, mark you—A rug?—Oh, thank you, my dear. . . . in that case you have also the advantage of associations—the Past."

"D'you want to talk, Dick, or shall I read aloud?"

Clarissa had fetched a book with the rugs.

"*Persuasion*," announced Richard, examining the volume.

"That's for Miss Vinrace," said Clarissa. "She can't bear our beloved Jane."

"That—if I may say so—is because you have not read her," said Richard. "She is incomparably the greatest female writer we possess."

"She is the greatest," he continued, "and for this reason: she does not attempt to write like a man. Every other woman does; on that account, I don't read 'em."

"Produce your instances, Miss Vinrace," he went on, joining his finger-tips. "I'm ready to be converted."

He waited, while Rachel vainly tried to vindicate her sex from the slight he put upon it.

"I'm afraid he's right," said Clarissa. "He generally is—the wretch!"

"I brought *Persuasion,*" she went on, "because I thought it was a little less threadbare than the others—though, Dick, it's no good *your* pretending to know Jane by heart, considering that she always sends you to sleep!"

"After the labours of legislation, I deserve sleep," said Richard.

"You're not to think about those guns," said Clarissa, seeing that his eye, passing over the waves, still sought the land meditatively, "or about navies, or empires, or anything." So saying she opened the book and began to read:

"'Sir Walter Elliott, of Kellynch Hall, in Somersetshire, was a man who, for his own amusement, never took up any book but the *Baronetage*'—don't you know Sir Walter?—'There he found occupation for an idle hour, and consolation in a distressed one.' She does write well, doesn't she? 'There—'" She read on in a light humorous voice. She was determined that Sir Walter should take her husband's mind off the guns of Britain, and divert him in an exquisite, quaint, sprightly, and slightly ridiculous world. After a time it appeared that the sun was sinking in that world, and the points becoming softer. Rachel looked up to see what caused the change. Richard's eyelids were closing and opening; opening and closing. A loud nasal breath announced that he no longer considered appearances, that he was sound asleep.

"Triumph!" Clarissa whispered at the end of a sentence. Suddenly she raised her hand in protest. A sailor hesitated; she gave the book to Rachel, and stepped lightly to take the message—"Mr. Grice wished to know if it was convenient," etc. She followed him. Ridley, who had prowled unheeded, started forward, stopped, and, with a gesture of disgust, strode off to his study. The sleeping politician was left in Rachel's charge. She read a sentence, and took a look at him. In sleep he looked like a coat hanging at the end of a bed; there were all the wrinkles, and the sleeves and trousers kept their shape though no longer filled out by legs and arms. You can then best judge the age and state of the coat. She looked him all over until it seemed to her that he must protest.

He was a man of forty perhaps; and here there were lines round his eyes, and there curious clefts in his cheeks. Slightly battered he appeared, but dogged and in the prime of life.

"Sisters and a dormouse and some canaries," Rachel murmured, never taking her eyes off him. "I wonder, I wonder" she ceased, her chin upon her hand, still looking at him. A bell chimed behind them, and Richard raised his head. Then he opened his eyes which wore for a second the queer look of a shortsighted person's whose spectacles are lost. It took him a moment to recover from the impropriety of having snored, and possibly grunted, before a young lady. To wake and find oneself left alone with one was also slightly disconcerting.

"I suppose I've been dozing," he said. "What's happened to everyone? Clarissa?"

"Mrs. Dalloway has gone to look at Mr. Grice's fish," Rachel replied.

"I might have guessed," said Richard. "It's a common occurrence. And how have you improved the shining hour? Have you become a convert?"

"I don't think I've read a line," said Rachel.

"That's what I always find. There are too many things to look at. I find nature very stimulating myself. My best ideas have come to me out of doors."

"When you were walking?"

"Walking—riding—yachting—I suppose the most momentous conversations of my life took place while perambulating the great court at Trinity. I was at both universities. It was a fad of my father's. He thought it broadening to the mind. I think I agree with him. I can remember—what an age ago it seems!—settling the basis of a future state with the present Secretary for India. We thought ourselves very wise. I'm not sure we weren't. We were happy, Miss Vinrace, and we were young—gifts which make for wisdom."

"Have you done what you said you'd do?" she asked.

"A searching question! I answer—Yes and No. If on the one hand I have not accomplished what I set out to accomplish—which of us does!—on the other I can fairly say this: I have not lowered my ideal."

He looked resolutely at a sea-gull, as though his ideal flew on the wings of the bird.

"But," said Rachel, "what *is* your ideal?"

"There you ask too much, Miss Vinrace," said Richard playfully.

She could only say that she wanted to know, and Richard was sufficiently amused to answer.

"Well, how shall I reply? In one word—Unity. Unity of aim, of dominion, of progress. The dispersion of the best ideas over the greatest area."

"The English?"

"I grant that the English seem, on the whole, whiter than most men, their records cleaner. But, good Lord, don't run away with the idea that I don't see the drawbacks—horrors—unmentionable things done in our very midst! I'm under no illusions. Few people, I suppose, have fewer illusions than I have. Have you ever been in a factory, Miss Vinrace!—No, I suppose not—I may say I hope not."

As for Rachel, she had scarcely walked through a poor street, and always under the escort of father, maid, or aunts.

"I was going to say that if you'd ever seen the kind of thing that's going on round you, you'd understand what it is that makes me and men like me politicians. You asked me a moment ago whether I'd done what I set out to do. Well, when I consider my life, there is one fact I admit that I'm proud of; owing to me some thousands of girls in Lancashire—and many thousands to come after them—can spend an hour every day in the open air which their mothers had to spend over their looms. I'm prouder of that, I own, than I should be of writing Keats and Shelley into the bargain!"

It became painful to Rachel to be one of those who write Keats and Shelley. She liked Richard Dalloway, and warmed as he warmed. He seemed to mean what he said.

"I know nothing!" she exclaimed.

"It's far better that you should know nothing," he said paternally, "and you wrong yourself, I'm sure. You play very nicely, I'm told, and I've no doubt you've read heaps of learned books."

Elderly banter would no longer check her.

"You talk of unity," she said. "You ought to make me understand."

"I never allow my wife to talk politics," he said seriously. "For this reason. It is impossible for human beings, constituted as they are, both to fight and to have ideals. If I have preserved mine, as I am thankful to say that in great measure I have, it is due to the fact that I have been able to come home to my wife in the evening and to find that she has spent her day in calling, music, play with the children, domestic duties—what you will; her illusions have not been destroyed. She gives me courage to go on. The strain of public life is very great," he added.

This made him appear a battered martyr, parting every day with some of the finest gold, in the service of mankind.

"I can't think," Rachel exclaimed, "how any one does it!"

"Explain, Miss Vinrace," said Richard. "This is a matter I want to clear up."

His kindness was genuine, and she determined to take the chance he gave her, although to talk to a man of such worth and authority made her heart beat.

"It seems to me like this," she began, doing her best first to recollect and then to expose her shivering private visions.

"There's an old widow in her room, somewhere, let us suppose in the suburbs of Leeds."

Richard bent his head to show that he accepted the widow.

"In London you're spending your life, talking, writing things, getting bills through, missing what seems natural. The result of it all is that she goes to her cupboard and finds a little more tea, a few lumps of sugar, or a little less tea and a newspaper. Widows all over the country I admit do this. Still, there's the mind of the widow—the affections; those you leave untouched. But you waste you own."

"If the widow goes to her cupboard and finds it bare," Richard answered, "her spiritual outlook we may admit will be affected. If I may pick holes in your philosophy, Miss Vinrace, which has its merits, I would point out that a human being is not a set of compartments, but an organism. Imagination, Miss Vinrace; use your imagination; that's where you young Liberals fail. Conceive the world as a whole. Now for your second point; when you assert that in trying to set the house in order for the benefit of the young generation I am wasting my higher capabilities, I totally disagree with you. I can conceive no more exalted aim—to be the citizen of the Empire. Look at it in this way, Miss Vinrace; conceive the state as a complicated machine; we citizens are parts of that machine; some fulfil more important duties; others (perhaps I am one of them) serve only to connect some obscure parts of the mechanism, concealed from the public eye. Yet if the meanest screw fails in its task, the proper working of the whole is imperilled."

It was impossible to combine the image of a lean black widow, gazing out of her window, and longing for some one to talk to, with the image of a vast machine, such as one sees at South Kensington, thumping, thumping, thumping. The attempt at communication had been a failure.

"We don't seem to understand each other," she said.

"Shall I say something that will make you very angry?" he replied.

"It won't," said Rachel.

"Well, then; no woman has what I may call the political instinct. You have very great virtues; I am the first, I hope, to admit that; but I have never met a woman who even saw what is meant by statesmanship. I am going to make you still more angry. I hope that I never shall meet such a woman. Now, Miss Vinrace, are we enemies for life?"

Vanity, irritation, and a thrusting desire to be understood, urged her to make another attempt.

"Under the streets, in the sewers, in the wires, in the telephones, there is something alive; is that what you mean? In things like dust-carts, and men mending roads? You feel that all the time when you walk about London, and when you turn on a tap and the water comes?"

"Certainly," said Richard. "I understand you to mean that the whole of modern society is based upon cooperative effort. If only more people would realise that, Miss Vinrace, there would be fewer of your old widows in solitary lodgings!"

Rachel considered.

"Are you a Liberal or are you a Conservative?" she asked.

"I call myself a Conservative for convenience sake," said Richard, smiling. "But there is more in common between the two parties than people generally allow."

There was a pause, which did not come on Rachel's side from any lack of things to say; as usual she could not say them, and was further confused by the fact that the time for talking probably ran short. She was haunted by absurd jumbled ideas—how, if one went back far enough, everything perhaps was intelligible; everything was in common; for the mammoths who pastured in the fields of Richmond High Street had turned into paving stones and boxes full of ribbon, and her aunts.

"Did you say you lived in the country when you were a child?" she asked.

Crude as her manners seemed to him, Richard was flattered. There could be no doubt that her interest was genuine.

"I did," he smiled.

"And what happened?" she asked. "Or do I ask too many questions?"

"I'm flattered, I assure you. But—let me see—what happened? Well, riding, lessons, sisters. There was an enchanted rubbish heap, I remember, where all kinds of queer things happened. Odd, what things impress children! I can remember the look of the place to this day. It's a fallacy to think that children are happy. They're not; they're unhappy. I've never suffered so much as I did when I was a child."

"Why?" she asked.

"I didn't get on well with my father," said Richard shortly. "He was a very able man, but hard. Well—it makes one determined not to sin in that way oneself. Children never forget injustice. They forgive heaps of things grown-up people mind; but that sin is the unpardonable sin. Mind you—I daresay I was a difficult child to manage; but when I think what I was ready to give! No, I was more sinned against than sinning. And then I went to school, where I did very fairly well; and and then, as I say, my father sent me to both universities. . . . D'you know, Miss Vinrace, you've made me think? How little, after all, one can tell anybody about one's life! Here I sit; there you sit; both, I doubt not, chock-full of the most interesting experiences, ideas, emotions; yet how communicate? I've told you what every second person you meet might tell you."

"I don't think so," she said. "It's the way of saying things, isn't it, not the things?"

"True," said Richard. "Perfectly true." He paused. "When I look back over my life—I'm forty-two—what are the great facts that stand out? What were the revelations, if I may call them so? The misery of the poor and—" (he hesitated and pitched over) "love!"

Upon that word he lowered his voice; it was a word that seemed to unveil the skies for Rachel.

"It's an odd thing to say to a young lady," he continued. "But have you any idea what—what I mean by that? No, of course not. I don't use the word in a conventional sense. I use it as young men use it. Girls are kept very ignorant, aren't they? Perhaps it's wise—perhaps—You *don't* know?"

He spoke as if he had lost consciousness of what he was saying.

"No; I don't," she said, scarcely speaking above her breath.

"Warships, Dick! Over there! Look!" Clarissa, released from Mr. Grice, appreciative of all his seaweeds, skimmed towards them, gesticulating.

She had sighted two sinister grey vessels, low in the water, and bald as bone, one closely following the other with the look of eyeless beasts seeking their prey. Consciousness returned to Richard instantly.

"By George!" he exclaimed, and stood shielding his eyes.

"Ours, Dick?" said Clarissa.

"The Mediterranean Fleet," he answered.

"The *Euphrosyne* was slowly dipping her flag. Richard raised his hat. Convulsively Clarissa squeezed Rachel's hand.

"Aren't you glad to be English!" she said.

The warships drew past, casting a curious effect of discipline and sadness upon the waters, and it was not until they were again invisible that people spoke to each other naturally. At lunch the talk was all of valour and death, and the magnificent qualities of British admirals. Clarissa quoted one poet, Willoughby quoted another. Life on board a man-of-war was splendid, so they agreed, and sailors, whenever one met them, were quite especially nice and simple.

This being so, no one liked it when Helen remarked that it seemed to her as wrong to keep sailors as to keep a Zoo, and that as for dying on a battle-field, surely it was time we ceased to praise courage—"or to write bad poetry about it," snarled Pepper.

But Helen was really wondering why Rachel, sitting silent, looked so queer and flushed.

5

She was not able to follow up her observations, however, or to come to any conclusion, for by one of those accidents which are liable to happen at sea, the whole course of their lives was now put out of order.

Even at tea the floor rose beneath their feet and pitched too low again, and at dinner the ship seemed to groan and strain as though a lash were descending. She who had been a broad-backed dray-horse, upon whose hind-quarters pierrots might waltz, became a colt in a field. The plates slanted away from the knives, and Mrs. Dalloway's face blanched for a second as she helped herself and saw the potatoes roll this way and that. Willoughby, of course, extolled the virtues of his ship, and quoted what had been said of her by experts and distinguished passengers, for he loved his own possessions. Still, dinner was uneasy, and directly the ladies were alone Clarissa owned that she would be better off in bed, and went, smiling bravely.

Next morning the storm was on them, and no politeness could ignore it. Mrs. Dalloway stayed in her room. Richard faced three meals, eating valiantly at each; but at the third, certain glazed asparagus swimming in oil finally conquered him.

"That beats me," he said, and withdrew.

"Now we are alone once more," remarked William Pepper, looking round the table; but no one was ready to engage him in talk, and the meal ended in silence.

On the following day they met—but as flying leaves meet in the air. Sick they were not; but the wind propelled them hastily into rooms, violently downstairs. They passed each other gasping on deck; they shouted across tables. They wore fur coats; and Helen was never seen without a bandanna on her head. For comfort they retreated to their cabins, where with tightly wedged feet they let the ship bounce and tumble. Their sensations were the sensations of potatoes in a sack on a galloping horse. The world outside was merely a violent grey tumult. For two days they had a perfect rest from their old emotions. Rachel had just enough consciousness to suppose herself a donkey on the summit of a moor in a hail-storm, with its coat blown into furrows; then she became a wizened tree, perpetually driven back by the salt Atlantic gale.

Helen, on the other hand, staggered to Mrs. Dalloway's door, knocked, could not be heard for the slamming of doors and the battering of wind, and entered.

There were basins, of course. Mrs. Dalloway lay half-raised on a pillow, and did not open her eyes. Then she murmured, "Oh, Dick, is that you?"

Helen shouted—for she was thrown against the washstand—"How are you?"

Clarissa opened one eye. It gave her an incredibly dissipated appearance. "Awful!" she gasped. Her lips were white inside.

Planting her feet wide, Helen contrived to pour champagne into a tumbler with a tooth-brush in it.

"Champagne," she said.

"There's a tooth-brush in it," murmured Clarissa, and smiled; it might have been the contortion of one weeping. She drank.

"Disgusting," she whispered, indicating the basins. Relics of humour still played over her face like moonshine.

"Want more?" Helen shouted. Speech was again beyond Clarissa's reach. The wind laid the ship shivering on her side. Pale agonies crossed Mrs. Dalloway in waves. When the curtains flapped, grey lights puffed across her. Between the spasms of the storm, Helen made the curtain fast, shook the pillows, stretched the bed-clothes, and smoothed the hot nostrils and forehead with cold scent.

"You *are* good!" Clarissa gasped. "Horrid mess!"

She was trying to apologise for white underclothes fallen and scattered on the floor. For one second she opened a single eye, and saw that the room was tidy.

"That's nice," she gasped.

Helen left her; far, far away she knew that she felt a kind of liking for Mrs. Dalloway. She could not help respecting her spirit and her desire, even in the throes of sickness, for a tidy bedroom. Her petticoats, however, rose above her knees.

Quite suddenly the storm relaxed its grasp. It happened at tea; the expected paroxysm of the blast gave out just as it reached its climax and dwindled away, and the ship instead of taking the usual plunge went steadily. The monotonous order of plunging and rising, roaring and relaxing, was interfered with, and every one at table looked up and felt something loosen within them. The strain was slackened and human feelings began to peep again, as they do when daylight shows at the end of a tunnel.

"Try a turn with me," Ridley called across to Rachel."

"Foolish!" cried Helen, but they went stumbling up the ladder. Choked by the wind their spirits rose with a rush, for on the skirts of all the grey tumult was a misty spot of gold. Instantly the world dropped into shape; they were no longer atoms flying in the void, but people riding a triumphant ship on the back of the sea. Wind and space were banished; the world floated like an apple in a tub, and the mind of man, which had been unmoored also, once more attached itself to the old beliefs.

Having scrambled twice round the ship and received many sound cuffs from the wind, they saw a sailor's face positively shine golden. They looked, and beheld a complete yellow circle of sun; next minute it was traversed by sailing stands of cloud, and then completely hidden. By breakfast the next morning, however, the sky was swept clean, the waves, although steep, were blue, and after their view of the strange under-world, inhabited by phantoms, people began to live among tea-pots and loaves of bread with greater zest than ever.

Richard and Clarissa, however, still remained on the borderland. She did not attempt to sit up; her husband stood on his feet, contemplated his waistcoat and trousers, shook his head, and then lay down again. The inside of his brain was still rising and falling like the sea on the stage. At four o'clock he woke from sleep and saw the sunlight make a vivid angle across the red plush curtains and the grey tweed trousers. The ordinary world outside slid into his mind, and by the time he was dressed he was an English gentleman again.

He stood beside his wife. She pulled him down to her by the lapel of his coat, kissed him, and held him fast for a minute.

"Go and get a breath of air, Dick," she said. "You look quite washed out. . . . How nice you smell! . . . And be polite to that woman. She was so kind to me."

Thereupon Mrs. Dalloway turned to the cool side of her pillow, terribly flattened but still invincible.

Richard found Helen talking to her brother-in-law, over two dishes of yellow cake and smooth bread and butter.

"You look very ill!" she exclaimed on seeing him. "Come and have some tea."

He remarked that the hands that moved about the cups were beautiful.

"I hear you've been very good to my wife," he said. "She's had an awful time of it. You came in and fed her with champagne. Were you among the saved yourself?"

"I? Oh, I haven't been sick for twenty years—sea-sick, I mean."

"There are three stages of convalescence, I always say," broke in the hearty voice of Willoughby. "The milk stage, the bread-and-butter stage, and the roast-beef stage. I should say you were at the bread-and-butter stage." He handed him the plate.

"Now, I should advise a hearty tea, then a brisk walk on deck; and by dinner-time you'll be clamouring for beef, eh?" He went off laughing, excusing himself on the score of business.

"What a splendid fellow he is!" said Richard. "Always keen on something."

"Yes," said Helen, "he's always been like that."

"This is a great undertaking of his," Richard continued. "It's a business that won't stop with ships, I should say. We shall see him in Parliament, or I'm much mistaken. He's the kind of man we want in Parliament—the man who has done things."

But Helen was not much interested in her brother-in-law.

"I expect your head's aching, isn't it?" she asked, pouring a fresh cup.

"Well, it is," said Richard. "It's humiliating to find what a slave one is to one's body in this world. D'you know, I can never work without a kettle on the hob. As often as not I don't drink tea, but I must feel that I can if I want to."

"That's very bad for you," said Helen.

"It shortens one's life; but I'm afraid, Mrs. Ambrose, we politicians must make up our minds to that at the outset. We've got to burn the candle at both ends, or—"

"You've cooked your goose!" said Helen brightly.

"We can't make you take us seriously, Mrs. Ambrose," he protested. "May I ask how you've spent your time? Reading—philosophy?" (He saw the black book.) "Metaphysics and fishing!" he exclaimed. "If I had to live again I believe I should devote myself to one or the other." He began turning the pages.

"'Good, then, is indefinable,'" he read out. "How jolly to think that's going on still! 'So far as I know there is only one ethical writer, Professor Henry Sidgwick, who has clearly recognised and stated this fact.' That's just the kind of thing we used to talk about when we were boys. I can remember arguing until five in the morning with Duffy—now Secretary for India—pacing round and round those cloisters until we decided it was too late to go to bed, and we went for a ride instead. Whether we ever came to any conclusion—that's another matter. Still, it's the arguing that counts. It's things like that that stand out in life. Nothing's been quite so vivid since. It's the philosophers, it's the scholars," he continued, "they're the people who pass the torch, who keep the light burning by which we live. Being a politician doesn't necessarily blind one to that, Mrs. Ambrose."

"No. Why should it?" said Helen. "But can you remember if your wife takes sugar?"

She lifted the tray and went off with it to Mrs. Dalloway.

Richard twisted a muffler twice round his throat and struggled up on deck. His body, which had grown white and tender in a dark room, tingled all over in the fresh air. He felt himself a man undoubtedly in the prime of life. Pride glowed in his eye as he let the wind buffet him and stood firm. With his head slightly lowered he sheered round corners, strode uphill, and met the blast. There was a collision. For a second he could not see what the body was he had run into. "Sorry." "Sorry." It was Rachel who apologised. They both laughed, too much blown about to speak. She drove open the door of her room and stepped into its calm. In order to speak to her, it was necessary that Richard should follow. They stood in a whirlpool of wind; papers began flying round in circles, the door crashed to, and they tumbled, laughing, into chairs. Richard sat upon Bach.

"My word! What a tempest!" he exclaimed.

"Fine, isn't it?" said Rachel. Certainly the struggle and wind had given her a decision she lacked; red was in her cheeks, and her hair was down.

"Oh, what fun!" he cried. "What am I sitting on? Is this your room? How jolly!" "There–sit there," she commanded. Cowper slid once more.

"How jolly to meet again," said Richard. "It seems an age. *Cowper's Letters?* . . . Bach? . . . *Wuthering Heights?* . . . Is this where you meditate on the world, and then come out and pose poor politicians with questions? In the intervals of sea-sickness I've thought a lot of our talk. I assure you, you made me think."

"I made you think! But why?"

"What solitary icebergs we are, Miss Vinrace! How little we can communicate! There are lots of things I should like to tell you about–to hear your opinion of. Have you ever read Burke?"

"Burke?" she repeated. "Who was Burke?"

"No? Well, then I shall make a point of sending you a copy. *The Speech on the French Revolution–The American Rebellion?* Which shall it be, I wonder?" He noted something in his pocket-book. "And then you must write and tell me what you think of it. This reticence–this isolation–that's what's the matter with modern life! Now, tell me about yourself. What are your interests and occupations? I should imagine that you were a person with very strong interests. Of course you are! Good God! When I think of the age we live in, with its opportunities and possibilities, the mass of things to be done and enjoyed–why haven't we ten lives instead of one? But about yourself?"

"You see, I'm a woman," said Rachel.

"I know–I know," said Richard, throwing his head back, and drawing his fingers across his eyes.

"How strange to be a woman! A young and beautiful woman," he continued sententiously, "has the whole world at her feet. That's true, Miss Vinrace. You have an inestimable power–for good or for evil. What couldn't you do–" he broke off.

"What?" asked Rachel.

"You have beauty," he said. The ship lurched. Rachel fell slightly forward. Richard took her in his arms and kissed her. Holding her tight, he kissed her passionately, so that she felt the hardness of his body and the roughness of his cheek printed upon hers. She fell back in her chair, with tremendous beats of the heart, each of which sent black waves across her eyes. He clasped his forehead in his hands.

"You tempt me," he said. The tone of his voice was terrifying. He seemed choked in fright. They were both trembling. Rachel stood up and went. Her head was cold, her knees shaking, and the physical pain of the emotion was so great that she could only keep herself moving above the great leaps of her heart. She leant upon the rail of the ship, and gradually ceased to feel, for a chill of body and mind crept over her. Far out between the waves little black and white sea-birds were riding. Rising and falling with smooth and graceful movements in the hollows of the waves they seemed singularly detached and unconcerned.

"You're peaceful," she said. She became peaceful too, at the same time possessed with a strange exultation. Life seemed to hold infinite possibilities she had never guessed at. She leant upon the rail and looked over the troubled grey waters, where the sunlight was fitfully scattered upon the crests of the waves, until she was cold and absolutely calm again. Nevertheless something wonderful had happened.

At dinner, however, she did not feel exalted, but merely uncomfortable, as if she and Richard had seen something together which is hidden in ordinary life, so that they did not like to look at each other. Richard slid his eyes over her uneasily once, and never looked at her again. Formal platitudes were manufactured with effort, but Willoughby was kindled.

"Beef for Mr. Dalloway!" he shouted. "Come now—after that walk you're at the beef stage, Dalloway!"

Wonderful masculine stories followed about Bright and Disraeli and coalition governments, wonderful stories which made the people at the dinner-table seem featureless and small. After dinner, sitting alone with Rachel under the great swinging lamp, Helen was struck by her pallor. It once more occurred to her that there was something strange in the girl's behaviour.

"You look tired. Are you tired?" she asked.

"Not tired," said Rachel. "Oh, yes, I suppose I am tired."

Helen advised bed, and she went, not seeing Richard again. She must have been very tired for she fell asleep at once, but after an hour or two of dreamless sleep, she dreamt. She dreamt that she was walking down a long tunnel, which grew so narrow by degrees that she could touch the damp bricks on either side. At length the tunnel opened and became a vault; she found herself trapped in it, bricks meeting her wherever she turned, alone with a little deformed man who squatted on the floor gibbering, with long nails. His face was pitted and like the face of an animal. The wall behind him oozed with damp, which collected into drops and slid down. Still and cold as death she lay, not daring to move, until she broke the agony by tossing herself across the bed, and woke crying "Oh!"

Light showed her the familiar things: her clothes, fallen off the chair; the water jug gleaming white; but the horror did not go at once. She felt herself pursued, so that she got up and actually locked her door. A voice moaned for her; eyes desired her. All night long barbarian men harassed the ship; they came scuffling down the passages, and stopped to snuffle at her door. She could not sleep again.

6

"That's the tragedy of life—as I always say!" said Mrs. Dalloway. "Beginning things and having to end them. Still, I'm not going to let *this* end, if you're willing." It was the morning, the sea was calm, and the ship once again was anchored not far from another shore.

She was dressed in her long fur cloak, with the veils wound around her head, and once more the rich boxes stood on top of each other so that the scene of a few days back seemed to be repeated.

"D'you suppose we shall ever meet in London?" said Ridley ironically. "You'll have forgotten all about me by the time you step out there."

He pointed to the shore of the little bay, where they could now see the separate trees with moving branches.

"How horrid you are!" she laughed. "Rachel's coming to see me anyhow—the instant you get back," she said, pressing Rachel's arm. "Now—you've no excuse!"

With a silver pencil she wrote her name and address on the flyleaf of *Persuasion*, and gave the book to Rachel. Sailors were shouldering the luggage, and people were beginning to congregate. There were Captain Cobbold, Mr. Grice, Willoughby, Helen, and an obscure grateful man in a blue jersey.

"Oh, it's time," said Clarissa. "Well, good-bye. I *do* like you," she murmured as she kissed Rachel. People in the way made it unnecessary for Richard to shake Rachel by the hand; he managed to look at her very stiffly for a second before he followed his wife down the ship's side.

The boat separating from the vessel made off towards the land, and for some minutes Helen, Ridley, and Rachel leant over the rail, watching. Once Mrs. Dalloway turned and waved; but the boat steadily grew smaller and smaller until it ceased to rise and fall, and nothing could be seen save two resolute backs.

"Well, that's over," said Ridley after a long silence. "We shall never see *them* again," he added, turning to go to his books. A feeling of emptiness and melancholy came over them; they knew in their hearts that it was over, and that they had parted for ever, and the knowledge filled them with far greater depression than the length of their acquaintance seemed to justify. Even as the boat pulled away they could feel other sights and sounds beginning to take the place of the Dalloways, and the feeling was so unpleasant that they tried to resist it. For so, too, would they be forgotten.

In much the same way as Mrs. Chailey downstairs was sweeping the withered rose-leaves off the dressing-table, so Helen was anxious to make things straight again after the visitors had gone. Rachel's obvious languor and listlessness made her an easy prey, and indeed Helen had devised a kind of trap. That something had happened she now felt pretty certain; moreover, she had come to think that they had been strangers long enough; she wished to know what the girl was like, partly of course because Rachel showed no disposition to be known. So, as they turned from the rail, she said:

"Come and talk to me instead of practising," and led the way to the sheltered side where the deck-chairs were stretched in the sun. Rachel followed her indifferently. Her mind was absorbed by Richard; by the extreme strangeness of what had happened, and by a thousand feelings of which she had not been conscious before. She made scarcely any attempt to listen to what Helen was saying, as Helen indulged in commonplaces to begin with. While Mrs. Ambrose arranged her embroidery, sucked her silk, and threaded her needle, she lay back gazing at the horizon.

"Did you like those people?" Helen asked her casually.

"Yes," she replied blankly.

"You talked to him, didn't you?"

She said nothing for a minute.

"He kissed me," she said without any change of tone.

Helen started, looked at her, but could not make out what she felt.

"M-m-m'yes," she said, after a pause. "I thought he was that kind of man."

"What kind of man?" said Rachel.

"Pompous and sentimental."

"I like him," said Rachel.

"So you really didn't mind?"

For the first time since Helen had known her Rachel's eyes lit up brightly.

"I did mind," she said vehemently. "I dreamt. I couldn't sleep."

"Tell me what happened," said Helen. She had to keep her lips from twitching as she listened to Rachel's story. It was poured out abruptly with great seriousness and no sense of humour.

"We talked about politics. He told me what he had done for the poor somewhere. I asked him all sorts of questions. He told me about his own life. The day before yesterday, after the storm, he came in to see me. It happened then, quite suddenly. He kissed me. I don't know why." As she spoke she grew flushed. "I was a good deal excited," she continued. "But I didn't mind till afterwards; when—" she paused, and saw the figure of the bloated little man again—"I became terrified."

From the look in her eyes it was evident she was again terrified. Helen was really at a loss what to say. From the little she knew of Rachel's upbringing she supposed that she had been kept entirely ignorant as to the relations of men with women. With a shyness which she felt with women and not with men she did not like to explain simply what these are. Therefore she took the other course and belittled the whole affair.

"Oh, well," she said, "He was a silly creature, and if I were you, I'd think no more about it."

"No," said Rachel, sitting bolt upright, "I shan't do that. I shall think about it all day and all night until I find out exactly what it does mean."

"Don't you ever read?" Helen asked tentatively.

"*Cowper's Letters*—that kind of thing. Father gets them for me or my Aunts."

Helen could hardly restrain herself from saying out loud what she thought of a man who brought up his daughter so that at the age of twenty-four she scarcely knew that men desired women and was terrified by a kiss. She had good reason to fear that Rachel had made herself incredibly ridiculous.

"You don't know many men?" she asked.

"Mr. Pepper," said Rachel ironically.

"So no one's ever wanted to marry you?"

"No," she answered ingenuously.

Helen reflected that as, from what she had said, Rachel certainly would think these things out, it might be as well to help her.

"You oughtn't to be frightened," she said. "It's the most natural thing in the world. Men will want to kiss you, just as they'll want to marry you. The pity is to get things out of proportion. It's like noticing the noises people make when they eat, or men spitting; or, in short, any small thing that gets on one's nerves."

Rachel seemed to be inattentive to these remarks.

"Tell me," she said suddenly, "what are those women in Piccadilly?"

"In Picadilly? They are prostituted," said Helen.

"It *is* terrifying—it *is* disgusting," Rachel asserted, as if she included Helen in the hatred.

"It is," said Helen. "But—"

"I did like him," Rachel mused, as if speaking to herself. "I wanted to talk to him; I wanted to know what he'd done. The women in Lancashire—"

It seemed to her as she recalled their talk that there was something lovable about Richard, good in their attempted friendship, and strangely piteous in the way they had parted.

The softening of her mood was apparent to Helen.

"You see," she said, "you must take things as they are; and if you want friendship with men you must run risks. Personally," she continued, breaking into a smile, "I think it's worth it; I don't mind being kissed; I'm rather jealous, I believe, that Mr. Dalloway kissed you and didn't kiss me. Though," she added, "he bored me considerably."

But Rachel did not return the smile or dismiss the whole affair, as Helen meant her to. Her mind was working very quickly, inconsistently and painfully. Helen's words hewed down great blocks which had stood there always, and the light which came in was cold. After sitting for a time with fixed eyes, she burst out:

"So that's why I can't walk alone!"

By this new light she saw her life for the first time a creeping hedged-in thing, driven cautiously between high walls, here turned aside, there plunged in darkness, made dull and crippled for ever—her life that was the only chance she had—a thousand words and actions became plain to her.

"Because men are brutes! I hate men!" she exclaimed.

"I thought you said you liked him?" said Helen.

"I liked him, and I liked being kissed," she answered, as if that only added more difficulties to her problem.

Helen was surprised to see how genuine both shock and problem were, but she could think of no way of easing the difficulty except by going on talking. She wanted to make her niece talk, and so to understand why this rather dull, kindly, plausible politician had made so deep an impression on her, for surely at the age of twenty-four this was not natural.

"And did you like Mrs. Dalloway too?" she asked.

As she spoke she saw Rachel redden; for she remembered silly things she had said, and also, it occurred to her that she treated this exquisite woman rather badly, for Mrs. Dalloway had said that she loved her husband.

"She was quite nice, but a thimble-pated creature," Helen continued. "I never heard such nonsense! Chitter-chatter-chitter-chatter—fish and the Greek alphabet—never listened to a word any one said—chock-full of idiotic theories about the way to bring up children—I'd far rather talk to him any day. He was pompous, but he did at least understand what was said to him."

The glamour insensibly faded a little both from Richard and Clarissa.

They had not been so wonderful after all, then, in the eyes of a mature person.

"It's very difficult to know what people are like," Rachel remarked, and Helen saw with pleasure that she spoke more naturally. "I suppose I was taken in."

There was little doubt about that according to Helen, but she restrained herself and said aloud:

"One has to make experiments."

"And they *were* nice," said Rachel. "They were extraordinarily interesting." She tried to recall the image of the world as a live thing that Richard had given her, with drains like nerves, and bad houses like patches of diseased skin. She recalled his watch-words—Unity—Imagination, and saw again the bubbles meeting in her tea-cup as he spoke of sisters and canaries, boyhood and his father, her small world becoming wonderfully enlarged.

"But all people don't seem to you equally interesting, do they?" asked Mrs. Ambrose.

Rachel explained that most people had hitherto been symbols; but that when they talked to one they ceased to be symbols, and became——"I could listen to them for ever!" she exclaimed. She then jumped up, disappeared downstairs for a minute, and came back with a fat red book.

"*Who's Who,*" she said, laying it upon Helen's knee and turning the pages. "It gives short lives of people—for instance: 'Sir Roland Beal; born 1852; parents from Moffatt; educated at Rugby; passed first into R.E.; married 1878 the daughter of T. Fishwick; served in the Bechuanaland Expedition 1884-85 (honourably mentioned). Clubs: United Service, Naval and Military. Recreations: an enthusiastic curler.'"

Sitting on the deck at Helen's feet she went on turning the pages and reading biographies of bankers, writers, clergymen, sailors, surgeons, judges, professors, statesmen, editors, philanthropists, merchants, and actresses; what clubs they belonged to, where they lived, what games they played, and how many acres they owned.

She became absorbed in the book.

Helen meanwhile stitched at her embroidery and thought over the things they had said. Her conclusion was that she would very much like to show her niece, if it were possible, how to live, or as she put it, how to be a reasonable person. She thought that there must be something wrong in this confusion between politics and kissing politicians, and that an elder person ought to be able to help.

"I quite agree," she said, "that people are very interesting; only—" Rachel, putting her finger between the pages, looked up enquiringly.

"Only I think you ought to discriminate," she ended. "It's a pity to be intimate with people who are—well, rather second-rate, like the Dalloways, and to find it out later."

"But how does one know?" Rachel asked.

"I really can't tell you," replied Helen candidly, after a moment's thought. "You'll have to find out for yourself. But try and—Why don't you call me Helen?" she added. "'Aunt's' a horrid name. I never liked my Aunts."

"I should like to call you Helen," Rachel answered.

"D'you think me very unsympathetic?"

Rachel reviewed the points which Helen had certainly failed to understand; they arose chiefly from the difference of nearly twenty years in age between them, which made Mrs. Ambrose appear too humorous and cool in a matter of such moment.

"No," she said. "Some things you don't understand, of course."

"Of course," Helen agreed. "So now you can go ahead and be a person on your own account," she added.

The vision of her own personality, of herself as a real everlasting thing, different from anything else, unmergeable, like the sea or the wind, flashed into Rachel's mind, and she became profoundly excited at the thought of living.

"I can be m-m-myself," she stammered, "in spite of you, in spite of the Dalloways, and Mr. Pepper, and Father, and my Aunts, in spite of these?" She swept her hand across a whole page of statesmen and soldiers.

"In spite of them all," said Helen gravely. She then put down her needle, and explained a plan which had come into her head as they talked. Instead of wandering on down the Amazons until she reached some sulphurous tropical port, where one had to lie within doors all day beating off insects with a fan, the sensible thing to do surely was to spend the season with them in their villa by the seaside, where among other advantages Mrs. Ambrose herself would be at hand to—

"After all, Rachel," she broke off, "it's silly to pretend that because there's twenty years' difference between us we therefore can't talk to each other like human beings."

"No; because we like each other," said Rachel.

"Yes," Mrs. Ambrose agreed.

That fact, together with other facts, had been made clear by their twenty minutes' talk, although how they had come to these conclusions they could not have said.

However they were come by, they were sufficiently serious to send Mrs. Ambrose a day or two later in search of her brother-in-law. She found him sitting in his room working, applying a stout blue pencil authoritatively to bundles of filmy paper. Papers lay to left and to right of him, there were great envelopes so gorged with papers that they spilt papers on to the table. Above him hung a photograph of a woman's head. The need of sitting absolutely still before a Cockney photographer had given her lips a queer little pucker, and her eyes for the same reason looked as though she thought the whole situation ridiculous. Nevertheless it was the head of an individual and interesting woman, who would no doubt have turned and laughed at Willoughby if she could have caught his eye; but when he looked up at her he sighed profoundly. In his mind this work of his, the great factories at Hull which showed like mountains at night, the ships that crossed the ocean punctually, the schemes for combining this and that and building up a solid mass of industry, was all an offering to her; he laid his success at her feet; and was always thinking how to educate his daughter so that Theresa might be glad. He was a very ambitious man; and although he had not been particularly kind to her while she lived, as Helen thought, he now believed that she watched him from Heaven, and inspired what was good in him.

Mrs. Ambrose apologised for the interruption, and asked whether she might speak to him about a plan of hers. Would he consent to leave his daughter with them when they landed, instead of taking her on up the Amazons?

"We would take great care of her," she added, "and we should really like it."

Willoughby looked very grave and carefully laid aside his papers.

"She's a good girl," he said at length. "There is a likeness?"—he nodded his head at the photograph of Theresa and sighed. Helen looked at Theresa pursing up her lips before the Cockney photographer. It suggested her in an absurd human way, and she felt an intense desire to share some joke.

"She's the only thing that's left to me," sighed Willoughby. "We go on year after year without talking about these things——" He broke off. "But it's better so. Only life's very hard."

Helen was sorry for him, and patted him on the shoulder, but she felt uncomfortable when her brother-in-law expressed his feelings, and took refuge in praising Rachel, and explaining why she thought her plan might be a good one.

"True," said Willoughby when she had done. "The social conditions are bound to be primitive. I should be out a good deal. I agreed because she wished it. And of course I have complete confidence in you. . . . You see, Helen," he continued, becoming confidential, "I want to bring her up as her mother would have wished. I don't hold with these modern views—any more than you do, eh? She's a nice quiet girl, devoted to her music—a little less of *that* would do no harm. Still, it's kept her happy, and we lead a very quiet life at Richmond. I should like her to begin to see more people. I want to take her about with me when I get home. I've half a mind to rent a house in London, leaving my sisters at Richmond, and take her to see one or two people who'd be kind to her for my sake. I'm beginning to realise," he continued, stretching himself out, "that all this is tending to Parliament, Helen. It's the only way to get things done as one wants them done. I talked to Dalloway about it. In that case, of course, I should want Rachel to be able to take more part in things. A certain amount of entertaining would be necessary—dinners, an occasional evening party. One's constituents like to be fed, I believe. In all these ways Rachel could be of great help to me. So," he wound up, "I should be very glad, if we arrange this visit (which must be upon a business footing, mind), if you could see your way to helping my girl, bringing her out—she's a little shy now—making a woman of her, the kind of woman her mother would have liked her to be," he ended, jerking his head at the photograph.

Willoughby's selfishness, though consistent as Helen saw with real affection for his daughter, made her determined to have the girl to stay with her, even if she had to promise a complete course of instruction in the feminine graces. She could not help laughing at the notion of it—Rachel a Tory hostess!—and marvelling as she left him at the astonishing ignorance of a father.

Rachel, when consulted, showed less enthusiasm than Helen could have wished. One moment she was eager, the next doubtful. Visions of a great river, now blue, now yellow in the tropical sun and crossed by bright birds, now white in the moon, now deep in shade with moving trees and canoes sliding out from the tangled banks, beset her. Helen promised a river. Then she did not want to leave her father. That feeling seemed genuine too, but in the end Helen prevailed, although when she had won her case she was beset by doubts, and more than once regretted the impulse which had entangled her with the fortunes of another human being.

7

From a distance the *Euphrosyne* looked very small. Glasses were turned upon her from the decks of great liners, and she was pronounced a tramp, a cargo-boat, or one of those wretched little passenger steamers where people rolled about among the cattle on deck. The insect-like figures of Dalloways, Ambroses, and Vinraces were also derided, both from the extreme smallness of their persons and the doubt which only strong glasses could dispel as to whether they were really live creatures or only lumps on the rigging. Mr. Pepper with all his learning had been mistaken for a cormorant, and then, as unjustly, transformed into a cow. At night, indeed, when the waltzes were swinging in the saloon, and gifted passengers reciting, the little ship—shrunk to a few beads of light out among the dark waves, and one high in air upon the mast-head—seemed something mysterious and impressive to heated partners resting from the dance. She became a ship passing in the night—an emblem of the loneliness of human life, an occasion for queer confidences and sudden appeals for sympathy.

On and on she went, by day and by night, following her path, until one morning broke and showed the land. Losing its shadow-like appearance it became first cleft and mountainous, next coloured grey and purple, next scattered with white blocks which gradually separated themselves, and then, as the progress of the ship acted upon the view like a field-glass of increasing power, became streets of houses. By nine o'clock the *Euphrosyne* had taken up her position in the middle of a great bay; she dropped her anchor; immediately, as if she were a recumbent giant requiring examination, small boats came swarming about her. She rang with cries; men jumped on to her; her deck was thumped by feet. The lonely little island was invaded from all quarters at once, and after four weeks of silence it was bewildering to hear human speech. Mrs. Ambrose alone heeded none of this stir. She was pale with suspense while the boat with mail bags was making towards them. Absorbed in her letters she did not notice that she had left the *Euphrosyne,* and felt no sadness when the ship lifted up her voice and bellowed thrice like a cow separated from its calf.

"The children are well!" she exclaimed. Mr. Pepper, who sat opposite with a great mound of bag and rug upon his knees, said, "Gratifying." Rachel, to whom the end of the voyage meant a complete change of perspective, was too much bewildered by the approach of the shore to realise what children were well or why it was gratifying. Helen went on reading.

Moving very slowly, and rearing absurdly high over each wave, the little boat was now approaching a white crescent of sand. Behind this was a deep green valley, with distinct hills on either side. On the slope of the right-hand hill white houses with brown roofs were settled, like nesting sea-birds, and at intervals cypresses striped the hill with black bars. Mountains whose sides were flushed with red, but whose crowns were bald, rose as a pinnacle, half-concealing another pinnacle behind it. The hour being still early, the whole view was exquisitely light and airy; the blues and greens of sky and tree were intense but not sultry. As they drew nearer and could distinguish details, the effect of the earth with its minute objects and colours and different forms of life was overwhelming after four weeks of the sea, and kept them silent.

"Three hundred years odd," said Mr. Pepper meditatively at length.

As nobody said, "What?" he merely extracted a bottle and swallowed a pill. The piece of information that died within him was to the effect that three hundred years ago five Elizabethan barques had anchored where the *Euphrosyne* now floated. Half-drawn up upon the beach lay an equal number of Spanish galleons, unmanned, for the country was still a virgin land behind a veil. Slipping across the water, the English sailors bore away bars of silver, bales of linen, timbers of cedar wood, golden crucifixes knobbed with emeralds. When the Spaniards came down from their drinking, a fight ensued, the two parties churning up the sand, and driving each other into the surf. The Spaniards, bloated with fine living upon the fruits of the miraculous land, fell in heaps; but the hardy Englishmen, tawny with sea-voyaging, hairy for lack of razors, with muscles like wire, fangs greedy for flesh, and fingers itching for gold, despatched the wounded, drove the dying into the sea, and soon reduced the natives to a state of superstitious wonderment. Here a settlement was made; women were imported; children grew. All seemed to favour the expansion of the British Empire, and had there been men like Richard Dalloway in the time of Charles the First, the map would undoubtedly be red where it is now an odious green. But it must be supposed that the political mind of that age lacked imagination, and, merely for want of a few thousand pounds and a few thousand men, the spark died that should have been a conflagration. From the interior came Indians with subtle poisons, naked bodies, and painted idols; from the sea came vengeful Spaniards and rapacious Portuguese; exposed to all these enemies (though the climate proved wonderfully kind and the earth abundant) the English dwindled away and all but disappeared. Somewhere about the middle of the seventeenth century a single sloop watched its season and slipped out by night, bearing within it all that was left of the great British colony, a few men, a few women, and perhaps a dozen dusky children. English history then denies all knowledge of the place. Owing to one cause and another civilisation shifted its centre to a spot some four or five hundred miles to the south, and today Santa Marina is not much larger than it was three hundred years ago. In population it is a happy compromise, for Portuguese fathers wed Indian mothers, and their children intermarry with the Spanish. Although they get their ploughs from Manchester, they make their coats from their own sheep, their silk from their own worms, and their furniture from their own cedar trees, so that in arts and industries the place is still much where it was in Elizabethan days.

The reasons which had drawn the English across the sea to found a small colony within the last ten years are not so easily described, and will never perhaps be recorded in history books. Granted facility of travel, peace, good trade, and so on, there was besides a kind of dissatisfaction among the English with the older countries and the enormous accumulations of carved stone, stained glass, and rich brown painting which they offered to the tourist. The movement in search of something new was of course infinitely small, affecting only a handful of well-to-do people. It began by a few schoolmasters serving their passage out to South America as the pursers of tramp steamers. They returned in time for the summer term, when their stories of the splendours and hardships of life at sea, the humours of sea-captains, the wonders of night and dawn, and the marvels of the place delighted outsiders, and sometimes found their way into print. The country itself taxed all their powers of description, for they said it was much bigger than Italy, and really nobler than Greece. Again, they declared that the natives were strangely beautiful, very big in stature, dark, passionate, and quick to seize the knife. The place seemed new and full of new forms of beauty, in proof of which they showed handkerchiefs which the women had worn round their heads, and primitive carvings coloured bright greens and blues. Somehow or other, as fashions do, the fashion spread; an old monastery was quickly turned into a hotel, while a famous line of steamships altered its route for the convenience of passengers.

Oddly enough it happened that the least satisfactory of Helen Ambrose's brothers had been sent out years before to make his fortune, at any rate to keep clear of race-horses, in the very spot which had now become so popular. Often, leaning upon the column in the verandah, he had watched the English ships with English schoolmasters for pursers steaming into the bay. Having at length earned enough to take a holiday, and being sick of the place, he proposed to put his villa, on the slope of the mountain, at his sister's disposal. She, too, had been a little stirred by the talk of a new world, where there was always sun and never a fog, which went on around her, and the chance, when they were planning where to spend the winter out of England, seemed too good to be missed. For these reasons she determined to accept Willoughby's offer of free passages on his ship, to place the children with their grand-parents, and to do the thing thoroughly while she was about it.

Taking seats in a carriage drawn by long-tailed horses with pheasants' feathers erect between their ears, the Ambroses, Mr. Pepper, and Rachel rattled out of the harbour. The day increased in heat as they drove up the hill. The road passed through the town, where men seemed to be beating brass and crying "Water," where the passage was blocked by mules and cleared by whips and curses, where the women walked barefoot, their heads balancing baskets, and cripples hastily displayed mutilated members; it issued among steep green fields, not so green but that the earth showed through. Great trees now shaded all but the centre of the road, and a mountain stream, so shallow and so swift that it plaited itself into strands as it ran, raced along the edge. Higher they went, until Ridley and Rachel walked behind; next they turned along a lane scattered with stones, where Mr. Pepper raised his stick and silently indicated a shrub, bearing among sparse leaves a voluminous purple blossom; and at a rickety canter the last stage of the way was accomplished.

The villa was a roomy white house, which, as is the case with most continental houses, looked to an English eye frail, ramshackle, and absurdly frivolous, more like a pagoda in a tea-garden than a place where one slept. The garden called urgently for the services of gardener. Bushes waved their branches across the paths, and the blades of grass, with spaces of earth between them, could be counted. In the circular piece of ground in front of the verandah were two cracked vases, from which red flowers drooped, with a stone fountain between them, now parched in the sun. The circular garden led to a long garden, where the gardener's shears had scarcely been, unless now and then, when he cut a bough of blossom for his beloved. A few tall trees shaded it, and round bushes with wax-like flowers mobbed their heads together in a row. A garden smoothly laid with turf, divided by thick hedges, with raised beds of bright flowers, such as we keep within walls in England, would have been out of place upon the side of this bare hill. There was no ugliness to shut out, and the villa looked straight across the shoulder of a slope, ribbed with olive trees, to the sea.

The indecency of the whole place struck Mrs. Chailey forcibly. There were no blinds to shut out the sun, nor was there any furniture to speak of for the sun to spoil. Standing in the bare stone hall, and surveying a staircase of superb breadth, but cracked and carpetless, she further ventured the opinion that there were rats, as large as terriers at home, and that if one put one's foot down with any force one would come through the floor. As for hot water—at this point her investigations left her speechless.

"Poor creature!" she murmured to the sallow Spanish servant-girl who came out with the pigs and hens to receive them, "no wonder you hardly look like a human being!" Maria accepted the compliment with an exquisite Spanish grace. In Chailey's opinion they would have done better to stay on board an English ship, but none knew better than she that her duty commanded her to stay.

When they were settled in, and in train to find daily occupation, there was some speculation as to the reasons which induced Mr. Pepper to stay, taking up his lodging in the Ambroses' house. Efforts had been made for some days before landing to impress upon him the advantages of the Amazons.

"That great stream!" Helen would begin, gazing as if she saw a visionary cascade, "I've a good mind to go with you myself, Willoughby—only I can't. Think of the sunsets and the moonrises—I believe the colours are unimaginable."

"There are wild peacocks," Rachel hazarded.

"And marvellous creatures in the water," Helen asserted.

"One might discover a new reptile," Rachel continued.

"There's certain to be a revolution, I'm told," Helen urged.

The effect of these subterfuges was a little dashed by Ridley, who, after regarding Pepper for some moments, sighed aloud, "Poor fellow!" and inwardly speculated upon the unkindness of women.

He stayed, however, in apparent contentment for six days, playing with a microscope and a notebook in one of the many sparsely furnished sitting-rooms, but on the evening of the seventh day, as they sat at dinner, he appeared more restless than usual. The dinner-table was set between two long windows which were left uncurtained by Helen's orders. Darkness fell as sharply as a knife in this climate, and the town then sprang out in circles and lines of bright dots beneath them. Buildings which never showed by day showed by night, and the sea flowed right over the land judging by the moving lights of the steamers. The sight fulfilled the same purpose as an orchestra in a London restaurant, and silence had its setting. William Pepper observed it for some time; he put on his spectacles to contemplate the scene.

"I've identified the big block to the left," he observed, and pointed with his fork at a square formed by several rows of lights.

"One should infer that they can cook vegetables," he added.

"An hotel?" said Helen.

"Once a monastery," said Mr. Pepper.

Nothing more was said then, but, the day after, Mr. Pepper returned from a midday walk, and stood silently before Helen who was reading in the verandah.

"I've taken a room over there," he said.

"You're not going?" she exclaimed.

"On the whole—yes," he remarked. "No private cook can cook vegetables."

Knowing his dislike of questions, which she to some extent shared, Helen asked no more. Still, an uneasy suspicion lurked in her mind that William was hiding a wound. She flushed to think that her words, or her husband's, or Rachel's had penetrated and stung. She was half-moved to cry, "Stop, William; explain!" and would have returned to the subject at luncheon if William had not shown himself inscrutable and chill, lifting fragments of salad on the point of his fork, with the gesture of a man pronging seaweed, detecting gravel, suspecting germs.

"If you all die of typhoid I won't be responsible!" he snapped.

"If you die of dulness, neither will I," Helen echoed in her heart.

She reflected that she had never yet asked him whether he had been in love. They had got further and further from that subject instead of drawing nearer to it, and she could not help feeling it a relief when William Pepper, with all his knowledge, his microscope, his note-books, his genuine kindliness and good sense, but a certain dryness of soul, took his departure. Also she could not help feeling it sad that friendships should end thus, although in this case to have the room empty was something of a comfort, and she tried to console herself with the reflection that one never knows how far other people feel the things they might be supposed to feel.

8

The next few months passed away, as many years can pass away, without definite events, and yet, if suddenly disturbed, it would be seen that such months or years had a character unlike others. The three months which had passed had brought them to the beginning of March. The climate had kept its promise, and the change of season from winter to spring had made very little difference, so that Helen, who was sitting in the drawing-room with a pen in her hand, could keep the windows open though a great fire of logs burnt on one side of her. Below, the sea was still blue and the roofs still brown and white, though the day was fading rapidly. It was dusk in the room, which, large and empty at all times, now appeared larger and emptier than usual. Her own figure, as she sat writing with a pad on her knee, shared the general effect of size and lack of detail, for the flames which ran along the branches, suddenly devouring little green tufts, burnt intermittently and sent irregular illuminations across her face and the plaster walls. There were no pictures on the walls but here and there boughs laden with heavy-petalled flowers spread widely against them. Of the books fallen on the bare floor and heaped upon the large table, it was only possible in this light to trace the outline.

Mrs. Ambrose was writing a very long letter. Beginning "Dear Bernard," it went on to describe what had been happening in the Villa San Gervasio during the past three months, as, for instance, that they had had the British Consul to dinner, and had been taken over a Spanish man-of-war, and had seen a great many processions and religious festivals, which were so beautiful that Mrs. Ambrose couldn't conceive why, if people must have a religion, they didn't all become Roman Catholics. They had made several expeditions though none of any length. It was worth coming if only for the sake of the flowering trees which grew wild quite near the house, and the amazing colours of sea and earth. The earth, instead of being brown, was red, purple, green. "You won't believe me," she added, "there is no colour like it in England." She adopted, indeed, a condescending tone towards that poor island, which was now advancing chilly crocuses and nipped violets in nooks, in copses, in cosy corners, tended by rosy old gardeners in mufflers, who were always touching their hats and bobbing obsequiously. She went on to deride the islanders themselves. Rumours of London all in a ferment over a General Election had reached them even out here. "It seems incredible," she went on, "that people should care whether Asquith is in or Austen Chamberlin out, and while you scream yourselves hoarse about politics you let the only people who are trying for something good starve or simply laugh at them. When have you ever encouraged a living artist? Or bought his best work? Why are you all so ugly and so servile? Here the servants are human beings. They talk to one as if they were equals. As far as I can tell there are no aristocrats."

Perhaps it was the mention of aristocrats that reminded her of Richard Dalloway and Rachel, for she ran on with the same penful to describe her niece.

"It's an odd fate that has put me in charge of a girl," she wrote, "considering that I have never got on well with women, or had much to do with them. However, I must retract some of the things that I have said against them. If they were properly educated I don't see why they shouldn't be much the same as men—as satisfactory I mean; though, of course, very different. The question is, how should one educate them. The present method seems to me abominable. This girl, though twenty-four, had never heard that men desired women, and, until I explained it, did not know how children were born. Her ignorance upon other matters as important" (here Mrs. Ambrose's letter may not be quoted) . . ."was complete. It seems to me not merely foolish but criminal to bring people up like that. Let alone the suffering to them, it explains why women are what they are—the wonder is they're no worse. I have taken it upon myself to enlighten her, and now, though still a good deal prejudiced and liable to exaggerate, she is more or less a reasonable human being. Keeping them ignorant, of course, defeats its own object, and when they begin to understand they take it all much too seriously. My brother-in-law really deserved a catastrophe—which he won't get. I now pray for a young man to come to my help; some one, I mean, who would talk to her openly, and prove how absurd most of her ideas about life are. Unluckily such men seem almost as rare as the women. The English colony certainly doesn't provide one; artists, merchants, cultivated people—they are stupid, conventional, and flirtatious. . . ." She ceased, and with her pen in her hand sat looking into the fire, making the logs into caves and mountains, for it had grown too dark to go on writing. Moreover, the house began to stir as the hour of dinner approached; she could hear the plates being chinked in the dining-room next door, and Chailey instructing the Spanish girl where to put things down in vigorous English. The bell rang; she rose, met Ridley and Rachel outside, and they all went in to dinner.

Three months had made but little difference in the appearance either of Ridley or Rachel; yet a keen observer might have thought that the girl was more definite and self-confident in her manner than before. Her skin was brown, her eyes certainly brighter, and she attended to what was said as though she might be going to contradict it. The meal began with the comfortable silence of people who are quite at their ease together. Then Ridley, leaning on his elbow and looking out of the window, observed that it was a lovely night.

"Yes," said Helen. She added, "The season's begun," looking at the lights beneath them. She asked Maria in Spanish whether the hotel was not filling up with visitors. Maria informed her with pride that there would come a time when it was positively difficult to buy eggs—the shopkeepers would not mind what prices they asked; they would get them, at any rate, from the English.

"That's an English steamer in the bay," said Rachel, looking at a triangle of lights below. "She came in early this morning."

"Then we may hope for some letters and send ours back," said Helen.

For some reason the mention of letters always made Ridley groan, and the rest of the meal passed in a brisk argument between husband and wife as to whether he was or was not wholly ignored by the entire civilised world.

"Considering the last batch," said Helen, "you deserve beating. You were asked to lecture, you were offered a degree, and some silly woman praised not only your books but your beauty—she said he was what Shelley would have been if Shelley had lived to fifty-five and grown a beard. Really, Ridley, I think you're the vainest man I know," she ended, rising from the table, "which I may tell you is saying a good deal."

Finding her letter lying before the fire she added a few lines to it, and then announced that she was going to take the letters now—Ridley must bring his—and Rachel?

"I hope you've written to your Aunts? It's high time."

The women put on cloaks and hats, and after inviting Ridley to come with them, which he emphatically refused to do, exclaiming that Rachel he expected to be a fool, but Helen surely knew better, they turned to go. He stood over the fire gazing into the depths of the looking-glass, and compressing his face into the likeness of a commander surveying a field of battle, or a martyr watching the flames lick his toes, rather than that of a secluded Professor.

Helen laid hold of his beard.

"Am I a fool?" she said.

"Let me go, Helen."

"Am I a fool?" she repeated.

"Vile woman!" he exclaimed, and kissed her.

"We'll leave you to your vanities," she called back as they went out of the door.

It was a beautiful evening, still light enough to see a long way down the road, though the stars were coming out. The pillar-box was let into a high yellow wall where the lane met the road, and having dropped the letters into it, Helen was for turning back.

"No, no," said Rachel, taking her by the wrist. "We're going to see life. You promised."

"Seeing life" was the phrase they used for their habit of strolling through the town after dark. The social life of Santa Marina was carried on almost entirely by lamp-light, which the warmth of the nights and the scents culled from flowers made pleasant enough. The young women, with their hair magnificently swept in coils, a red flower behind the ear, sat on the doorsteps, or issued out on to balconies, while the young men ranged up and down beneath, shouting up a greeting from time to time and stopping here and there to enter into amorous talk. At the open windows merchants could be seen making up the day's account, and older women lifting jars from shelf to shelf. The streets were full of people, men for the most part, who interchanged their views of the world as they walked, or gathered round the wine-tables at the street corner, where an old cripple was twanging his guitar strings, while a poor girl cried her passionate song in the gutter. The two Englishwomen excited some friendly curiosity, but no one molested them.

Helen sauntered on, observing the different people in their shabby clothes, who seemed so careless and so natural, with satisfaction.

"Just think of the Mall tonight!" she exclaimed at length. "It's the fifteenth of March. Perhaps there's a Court." She thought of the crowd waiting in the cold spring air to see the grand carriages go by. "It's very cold, if it's not raining," she said. "First there are men selling picture postcards; then there are wretched little shop-girls with round bandboxes; then there are bank clerks in tail coats; and then—any number of dressmakers. People from South Kensington drive up in a hired fly; officials have a pair of bays; earls, on the other hand, are allowed one footman to stand up behind; dukes have two, royal dukes—so I was told—have three; the king, I suppose, can have as many as he likes. And the people believe in it!"

Out here it seemed as though the people of England must be shaped in the body like the kings and queens, knights and pawns of the chess-board, so strange were their differences, so marked and so implicitly believed in.

They had to part in order to circumvent a crowd.

"They believe in God," said Rachel as they regained each other. She meant that the people in the crowd believed in Him; for she remembered the crosses with bleeding plaster figures that stood where foot-paths joined, and the inexplicable mystery of a service in a Roman Catholic church.

"We shall never understand!" she sighed.

They had walked some way and it was now night, but they could see a large iron gate a little way farther down the road on their left.

"Do you mean to go right up to the hotel?" Helen asked.

Rachel gave the gate a push; it swung open, and, seeing no one about and judging that nothing was private in this country, they walked straight on. An avenue of trees ran along the road, which was completely straight. The trees suddenly came to an end; the road turned a corner, and they found themselves confronted by a large square building. They had come out upon the broad terrace which ran round the hotel and were only a few feet distant from the windows. A row of long windows opened almost to the ground. They were all of them uncurtained, and all brilliantly lighted, so that they could see everything inside. Each window revealed a different section of the life of the hotel. They drew into one of the broad columns of shadow which separated the windows and gazed in. They found themselves just outside the dining-room. It was being swept; a waiter was eating a bunch of grapes with his leg across the corner of a table. Next door was the kitchen, where they were washing up; white cooks were dipping their arms into cauldrons, while the waiters made their meal voraciously off broken meats, sopping up the gravy with bits of crumb. Moving on, they became lost in a plantation of bushes, and then suddenly found themselves outside the drawing-room, where the ladies and gentlemen, having dined well, lay back in deep arm-chairs, occasionally speaking or turning over the pages of magazines. A thin woman was flourishing up and down the piano.

"What is a dahabeeyah, Charles?" the distinct voice of a widow, seated in an arm-chair by the window, asked her son.

It was the end of the piece, and his answer was lost in the general clearing of throats and tapping of knees.

"They're all old in this room," Rachel whispered.

Creeping on, they found that the next window revealed two men in shirt-sleeves playing billiards with two young ladies.

"He pinched my arm!" the plump young woman cried, as she missed her stroke.

"Now you two—no ragging," the young man with the red face reproved them, who was marking.

"Take care or we shall be seen," whispered Helen, plucking Rachel by the arm. Incautiously her head had risen to the middle of the window.

Turning the corner they came to the largest room in the hotel, which was supplied with four windows, and was called the Lounge, although it was really a hall. Hung with armour and native embroideries, furnished with divans and screens, which shut off convenient corners, the room was less formal than the others, and was evidently the haunt of youth. Signor Rodriguez, whom they knew to be the manager of the hotel, stood quite near them in the doorway surveying the scene—the gentlemen lounging in chairs, the couples leaning over coffee-cups, the game of cards in the centre under profuse clusters of electric light. He was congratulating himself upon the enterprise which had turned the refectory, a cold stone room with pots on trestles, into the most comfortable room in the house. The hotel was very full, and proved his wisdom in decreeing that no hotel can flourish without a lounge.

The people were scattered about in couples or parties of four, and either they were actually better acquainted, or the informal room made their manners easier. Through the open window came an uneven humming sound like that which rises from a flock of sheep pent within hurdles at dusk. The card-party occupied the centre of the foreground.

Helen and Rachel watched them play for some minutes without being able to distinguish a word. Helen was observing one of the men intently. He was a lean, somewhat cadaverous man of about her own age, whose profile was turned to them, and he was the partner of a highly-coloured girl, obviously English by birth.

Suddenly, in the strange way in which some words detach themselves from the rest, they heard him say quite distinctly—

"All you want is practice, Miss Warrington; courage and practice—one's no good without the other."

"Hughling Elliot! Of course!" Helen exclaimed. She ducked her head immediately, for at the sound of his name he looked up. The game went on for a few minutes, and was then broken up by the approach of a wheeled chair, containing a voluminous old lady who paused by the table and said—

"Better luck tonight, Susan?"

"All the luck's on our side," said a young man who until now had kept his back turned to the window. He appeared to be rather stout, and had a thick crop of hair.

"Luck, Mr. Hewet?" said his partner, a middle-aged lady with spectacles. "I assure you, Mrs. Paley, our success is due solely to our brilliant play."

"Unless I go to bed early I get practically no sleep at all," Mrs. Paley was heard to explain, as if to justify her seizure of Susan, who got up and proceeded to wheel the chair to the door.

"They'll get some one else to take my place," she said cheerfully. But she was wrong. No attempt was made to find another player, and after the young man had built three stories of a card-house, which fell down, the players strolled off in different directions.

Mr. Hewet turned his full face towards the window. They could see that he had large eyes obscured by glasses; his complexion was rosy, his lips clean-shaven; and, seen among ordinary people, it appeared to be an interesting face. He came straight towards them, but his eyes were fixed not upon the eavesdroppers but upon a spot where the curtain hung in folds.

"Asleep?" he said.

Helen and Rachel started to think that some one had been sitting near to them unobserved all the time. There were legs in the shadow. A melancholy voice issued from above them.

"Two women," it said.

A scuffling was heard on the gravel. The women had fled. They did not stop running until they felt certain that no eye could penetrate the darkness and the hotel was only a square shadow in the distance, with red holes regularly cut in it.

9

An hour passed, and the downstairs rooms at the hotel grew dim and were almost deserted, while the little box-like squares above them were brilliantly irradiated. Some forty or fifty people were going to bed. The thump of jugs set down on the floor above could be heard and the clink of china, for there was not as thick a partition between the rooms as one might wish, so Miss Allan, the elderly lady who had been playing bridge, determined, giving the wall a smart rap with her knuckles. It was only matchboard, she decided, run up to make many little rooms of one large one. Her grey petticoats slipped to the ground, and, stooping, she folded her clothes with neat, if not loving fingers, screwed her hair into a plait, wound her father's great gold watch, and opened the complete works of Wordsworth. She was reading the *Prelude*, partly because she always read the *Prelude* abroad, and partly because she was engaged in writing a short

Primer of English Literature–Beowulf to Swinburne–which would have a paragraph on Wordsworth. She was deep in the fifth book, stopping indeed to pencil a note, when a pair of boots dropped, one after another, on the floor above her. She looked up and speculated. Whose boots were they, she wondered. She then became aware of a swishing sound next door–a woman, clearly, putting away her dress. It was succeeded by a gentle tapping sound, such as that which accompanies hair-dressing. It was very difficult to keep her attention fixed upon the *Prelude*. Was it Susan Warrington tapping? She forced herself, however, to read to the end of the book, when she placed a mark between the pages, sighed contentedly, and then turned out the light.

Very different was the room through the wall, though as like in shape as one egg-box is like another. As Miss Allan read her book, Susan Warrington was brushing her hair. Ages have consecrated this hour, and the most majestic of all domestic actions, to talk of love between women; but Miss Warrington being alone could not talk; she could only look with extreme solicitude at her own face in the glass. She turned her head from side to side, tossing heavy locks now this way now that; and then withdrew a pace or two, and considered herself seriously.

"I'm nice-looking," she determined. "Not pretty–possibly," she drew herself up a little. "Yes–most people would say I was handsome."

She was really wondering what Arthur Venning would say she was. Her feeling about him was decidedly queer. She would not admit to herself that she was in love with him or that she wanted to marry him, yet she spent every minute when she was alone in wondering what he thought of her, and in comparing what they had done today with what they had done the day before.

"He didn't ask me to play, but he certainly followed me into the hall," she meditated, summing up the evening. She was thirty years of age, and owing to the number of her sisters and the seclusion of life in a country parsonage had as yet had no proposal of marriage. The hour of confidences was often a sad one, and she had been known to jump into bed, treating her hair unkindly, feeling herself overlooked by life in comparison with others. She was a big, well-made woman, the red lying upon her cheeks in patches that were too well defined, but her serious anxiety gave her a kind of beauty.

She was just about to pull back the bed-clothes when she exclaimed, "Oh, but I'm forgetting," and went to her writing-table. A brown volume lay there stamped with the figure of the year. She proceeded to write in the square ugly hand of a mature child, as she wrote daily year after year, keeping the diaries, though she seldom looked at them.

"A.M.–Talked to Mrs. H. Elliot about country neighbours. She knows the Manns; also the Selby-Carroways. How small the world is! Like her.

Read a chapter of *Miss Appleby's Adventure* to Aunt E. P.M.—Played lawn-tennis with Mr. Perrott and Evelyn M. Don't *like* Mr. P. Have a feeling that he is not 'quite,' though clever certainly. Beat them. Day splendid, view wonderful. One gets used to no trees, though much too bare at first. Cards after dinner. Aunt E. cheerful, though twingy, she says. Mem.: *ask about damp sheets.*"

She knelt in prayer, and then lay down in bed, tucking the blankets comfortably about her, and in a few minutes her breathing showed that she was asleep. With its profoundly peaceful sighs and hesitations it resembled that of a cow standing up to its knees all night through in the long grass.

A glance into the next room revealed little more than a nose, prominent above the sheets. Growing accustomed to the darkness, for the windows were open and showed grey squares with splinters of starlight, one could distinguish a lean form, terribly like the body of a dead person, the body indeed of William Pepper, asleep too. Thirty-six, thirty-seven, thirty-eight—here were three Portuguese men of business, asleep presumably, since a snore came with the regularity of a great ticking clock. Thirty-nine was a corner room, at the end of the passage, but late though it was—"One" struck gently downstairs—a line of light under the door showed that some one was still awake.

"How late you are, Hugh!" a woman, lying in bed, said in a peevish but solicitous voice. Her husband was brushing his teeth, and for some moments did not answer.

"You should have gone to sleep," he replied. "I was talking to Thornbury."

"But you know that I never can sleep when I'm waiting for you," she said.

To that he made no answer, but only remarked, "Well then, we'll turn out the light." They were silent.

The faint but penetrating pulse of an electric bell could now be heard in the corridor. Old Mrs. Paley, having woken hungry but without her spectacles, was summoning her maid to find the biscuit-box. The maid having answered the bell, drearily respectful even at this hour though muffled in a mackintosh, the passage was left in silence. Downstairs all was empty and dark; but on the upper floor a light still burnt in the room where the boots had dropped so heavily above Miss Allan's head. Here was the gentleman who, a few hours previously, in the shade of the curtain, had seemed to consist entirely of legs. Deep in an arm-chair he was reading the third volume of Gibbon's *History of the Decline and Fall of Rome* by candle light. As he read he knocked the ash automatically, now and again, from his cigarette and turned the page, while a whole procession of splendid sentences entered his capacious brow and went marching through his brain in order. It seemed likely that this process might continue for an hour or more, until the entire regiment had shifted its quarters, had not the door opened, and the young man, who was inclined to be stout, come in with large naked feet.

"Oh, Hirst, what I forgot to say was—"

"Two minutes," said Hirst, raising his finger.

He safely stowed away the last words of the paragraph.

"What was it you forgot to say?" he asked.

"D'you think you *do* make enough allowance for feelings?" asked Mr. Hewet. He had again forgotten what he had meant to say.

After intense contemplation of the immaculate Gibbon Mr. Hirst smiled at the question of his friend. He laid aside his book and considered.

"I should call yours a singularly untidy mind," he observed. "Feelings? Aren't they just what we do allow for? We put love up there, and all the rest somewhere down below." With his left hand he indicated the top of a pyramid, and with his right the base.

"But you didn't get out of bed to tell me that," he added severely.

"I got out of bed," said Hewet vaguely, "merely to talk I suppose."

"Meanwhile I shall undress," said Hirst. When naked of all but his shirt, and bent over the basin, Mr. Hirst no longer impressed one with the majesty of his intellect, but with the pathos of his young yet ugly body, for he stooped, and he was so thin that there were dark lines between the different bones of his neck and shoulders.

"Women interest me," said Hewet, who, sitting on the bed with his chin resting on his knees, paid no attention to the undressing of Mr. Hirst.

"They're so stupid," said Hirst. "You're sitting on my pyjamas."

"I suppose they *are* stupid?" Hewet wondered.

"There can't be two opinions about that, I imagine," said Hirst, hopping briskly across the room, "unless you're in love—that fat woman Warrington?" he enquired.

"Not one fat woman—all fat women," Hewet sighed.

"The women I saw tonight were not fat," said Hirst, who was taking advantage of Hewet's company to cut his toe-nails.

"Describe them," said Hewet.

"You know I can't describe things!" said Hirst. "They were much like other women, I should think. They always are."

"No; that's where we differ," said Hewet. "I say everything's different. No two people are in the least the same. Take you and me now."

"So I used to think once," said Hirst. "But now they're all types. Don't take us—take this hotel. You could draw circles round the whole lot of them, and they'd never stray outside."

("You can kill a hen by doing that"), Hewet murmured.

"Mr. Hughling Elliot, Mrs. Hughling Elliot, Miss Allan, Mr. and Mrs. Thornbury—one circle," Hirst continued. "Miss Warrington, Mr. Arthur Venning, Mr. Perrott, Evelyn M. another circle; then there are a whole lot of natives; finally ourselves."

"Are we all alone in our circle?" asked Hewet.

"Quite alone," said Hirst. "You try to get out, but you can't. You only make a mess of things by trying."

"I'm not a hen in a circle," said Hewet. "I'm a dove on a tree-top."

"I wonder if this is what they call an ingrowing toe-nail?" said Hirst, examining the big toe on his left foot.

"I flit from branch to branch," continued Hewet. "The world is profoundly pleasant." He lay back on the bed, upon his arms.

"I wonder if it's really nice to be as vague as you are?" asked Hirst, looking at him. "It's the lack of continuity—that's what's so odd bout you," he went on. "At the age of twenty-seven, which is nearly thirty, you seem to have drawn no conclusions. A party of old women excites you still as though you were three."

Hewet contemplated the angular young man who was neatly brushing the rims of his toe-nails into the fire-place in silence for a moment.

"I respect you, Hirst," he remarked.

"I envy you—some things," said Hirst. "One: your capacity for not thinking; two: people like you better than they like me. Women like you, I suppose."

"I wonder whether that isn't really what matters most?" said Hewet. Lying now flat on the bed he waved his hand in vague circles above him.

"Of course it is," said Hirst. "But that's not the difficulty. The difficulty is, isn't it, to find an appropriate object?"

"There are no female hens in your circle?" asked Hewet.

"Not the ghost of one," said Hirst.

Although they had known each other for three years Hirst had never yet heard the true story of Hewet's loves. In general conversation it was taken for granted that they were many, but in private the subject was allowed to lapse. The fact that he had money enough to do no work, and that he had left Cambridge after two terms owing to a difference with the authorities, and had then travelled and drifted, made his life strange at many points where his friends' lives were much of a piece.

"I don't see your circles—I don't see them," Hewet continued. "I see a thing like a teetotum spinning in and out—knocking into things—dashing from side to side—collecting numbers—more and more and more, till the whole place is thick with them. Round and round they go—out there, over the rim—out of sight."

His fingers showed that the waltzing teetotums had spun over the edge of the counterpane and fallen off the bed into infinity.

"Could you contemplate three weeks alone in this hotel?" asked Hirst, after a moment's pause.

Hewet proceeded to think.

"The truth of it is that one never is alone, and one never is in company," he concluded.

"Meaning?" said Hirst.

"Meaning? Oh, something about bubbles—auras—what d'you call 'em? You can't see my bubble; I can't see yours; all we see of each other is a speck, like the wick in the middle of that flame. The flame goes about with us everywhere; it's not ourselves exactly, but what we feel; the world is short, or people mainly; all kinds of people."

"A nice streaky bubble yours must be!" said Hirst.

"And supposing my bubble could run into some one else's bubble—"

"And they both burst?" put in Hirst.

"Then—then—then—" pondered Hewet, as if to himself, "it would be an e—nor—mous world," he said, stretching his arms to their full width, as though even so they could hardly clasp the billowy universe, for when he was with Hirst he always felt unusually sanguine and vague.

"I don't think you altogether as foolish as I used to, Hewet," said Hirst. "You don't know what you mean but you try to say it."

"But aren't you enjoying yourself here?" asked Hewet.

"On the whole—yes," said Hirst. "I like observing people. I like looking at things. This country is amazingly beautiful. Did you notice how the top of the mountain turned yellow tonight? Really we must take our lunch and spend the day out. You're getting disgustingly fat." He pointed at the calf of Hewet's bare leg.

"We'll get up an expedition," said Hewet energetically. "We'll ask the entire hotel. We'll hire donkeys and—"

"Oh, Lord!" said Hirst, "do shut it! I can see Miss Warrington and Miss Allan and Mrs. Elliot and the rest squatting on the stones and quacking, 'How jolly!'"

"We'll ask Venning and Perrott and Miss Murgatroyd—every one we can lay hands on," went on Hewet. "What's the name of the little old grasshopper with the eyeglasses? Pepper?—Pepper shall lead us."

"Thank God, you'll never get the donkeys," said Hirst.

"I must make a note of that," said Hewet, slowly dropping his feet to the floor. "Hirst escorts Miss Warrington; Pepper advances alone on a white ass; provisions equally distributed—or shall we hire a mule? The matrons—there's Mrs. Paley, by Jove!—share a carriage."

"That's where you'll go wrong," said Hirst. "Putting virgins among matrons."

"How long should you think that an expedition like that would take, Hirst?" asked Hewet.

"From twelve to sixteen hours I would say," said Hirst. "The time usually occupied by a first confinement."

"It will need considerable organisation," said Hewet. He was now padding softly round the room, and stopped to stir the books on the table. They lay heaped one upon another.

"We shall want some poets too," he remarked. "Not Gibbon; no; d'you happen to have *Modern Love* or John Donne? You see, I contemplate pauses when people get tired of looking at the view, and then it would be nice to read something rather difficult aloud."

"Mrs. Paley *will* enjoy herself," said Hirst.

"Mrs. Paley will enjoy it certainly," said Hewet. "It's one of the saddest things I know—the way elderly ladies cease to read poetry. And yet how appropriate this is:

> I speak as one who plumbs
> Life's dim profound,
> One who at length can sound
> Clear views and certain.
> But—after love what comes?
> A scene that lours,
> A few sad vacant hours,
> And then, the Curtain.

I daresay Mrs. Paley is the only one of us who can really understand that."

"We'll ask her," said Hirst. "Please, Hewet, if you must go to bed, draw my curtain. Few things distress me more than the moonlight."

Hewet retreated, pressing the poems of Thomas Hardy beneath his arm, and in their beds next door to each other both the young men were soon asleep.

Between the extinction of Hewet's candle and the rising of a dusky Spanish boy who was the first to survey the desolation of the hotel in the early morning, a few hours of silence intervened. One could almost hear a hundred people breathing deeply, and however wakeful and restless it would have been hard to escape sleep in the middle of so much sleep. Looking out of the windows, there was only darkness to be seen. All over the shadowed half of the world people lay prone, and a few flickering lights in empty streets marked the places where their cities were built. Red and yellow omnibuses were crowding each other in Piccadilly; sumptuous women were rocking at a standstill; but here in the darkness an owl flitted from tree to tree, and when the breeze lifted the branches the moon flashed as if it were a torch. Until all people should awake again the houseless animals were abroad, the tigers and the stags, and the elephants coming down in the darkness to drink at pools. The wind at night blowing over the hills and woods was purer and fresher than the wind by day, and the earth, robbed of detail, more mysterious than the earth coloured and divided by roads and fields. For six hours this profound beauty existed, and then as the east grew whiter and whiter the ground swam to the surface, the roads were revealed, the smoke rose and the people stirred, and the sun shone upon the windows of the hotel at Santa Marina until they were uncurtained, and the gong blaring all through the house gave notice of breakfast.

Directly breakfast was over, the ladies as usual circled vaguely, picking up papers and putting them down again, about the hall.

"And what are you going to do today?" asked Mrs. Elliot drifting up against Miss Warrington.

Mrs. Elliot, the wife of Hughling the Oxford Don, was a short woman, whose expression was habitually plaintive. Her eyes moved from thing to thing as though they never found anything sufficiently pleasant to rest upon for any length of time.

"I'm going to try to get Aunt Emma out into the town," said Susan. "She's not seen a thing yet."

"I call it so spirited of her at her age," said Mrs. Elliot, "coming all this way from her own fireside."

"Yes, we always tell her she'll die on board ship," Susan replied. "She was born on one," she added.

"In the old days," said Mrs. Elliot, "a great many people were. I always pity the poor women so! We've got a lot to complain of!" She shook her head. Her eyes wandered about the table, and she remarked irrelevantly, "The poor little Queen of Holland! Newspaper reporters practically, one may say, at her bedroom door!"

"Were you talking of the Queen of Holland?" said the pleasant voice of Miss Allan, who was searching for the thick pages of *The Times* among a litter of thin foreign sheets.

"I always envy any one who lives in such an excessively flat country," she remarked.

"How very strange!" said Mrs. Elliot. "I find a flat country so depressing."

"I'm afraid you can't be very happy here then, Miss Allan," said Susan.

"On the contrary," said Miss Allan, "I am exceedingly fond of mountains." Perceiving *The Times* at some distance, she moved off to secure it.

"Well, I must find my husband," said Mrs. Elliot, fidgeting away.

"And I must go to my aunt," said Miss Warrington, and taking up the duties of the day they moved away.

Whether the flimsiness of foreign sheets and the coarseness of their type is any proof of frivolity and ignorance, there is no doubt that English people scarce consider news read there as news, any more than a programme bought from a man in the street inspires confidence in what it says. A very respectable elderly pair, having inspected the long tables of newspapers, did not think it worth their while to read more than the headlines.

"The debate on the fifteenth should have reached us by now," Mrs. Thornbury murmured. Mr. Thornbury, who was beautifully clean and had red rubbed into his handsome worn face like traces of paint on a weather-beaten wooden figure, looked over his glasses and saw that Miss Allan had *The Times*.

The couple therefore sat themselves down in arm-chairs and waited.

"Ah, there's Mr. Hewet," said Mrs. Thornbury. "Mr. Hewet," she continued, "do come and sit by us. I was telling my husband how much you reminded me of a dear old friend of mine—Mary Umpleby. She was a most delightful woman, I assure you. She grew roses. We used to stay with her in the old days."

"No young man likes to have it said that he resembles an elderly spinster," said Mr. Thornbury.

"On the contrary," said Mr. Hewet, "I always think it a compliment to remind people of some one else. But Miss Umpleby—why did she grow roses?"

"Ah, poor thing," said Mrs. Thornbury, "that's a long story. She had gone through dreadful sorrows. At one time I think she would have lost her senses if it hadn't been for her garden. The soil was very much against her—a blessing in disguise; she had to be up at dawn—out in all weathers. And then there are creatures that eat roses. But she triumphed. She always did. She was a brave soul." She sighed deeply but at the same time with resignation.

"I did not realise that I was monopolising the paper," said Miss Allan, coming up to them.

"We were so anxious to read about the debate," said Mrs. Thornbury, accepting it on behalf of her husband.

"One doesn't realise how interesting a debate can be until one has sons in the navy. My interests are equally balanced, though; I have sons in the army too; and one son who makes speeches at the Union—my baby!"

"Hirst would know him, I expect," said Hewet.

"Mr. Hirst has such an interesting face," said Mrs. Thornbury. "But I feel one ought to be very clever to talk to him. Well, William?" she enquired, for Mr. Thornbury grunted.

"They're making a mess of it," said Mr. Thornbury. He had reached the second column of the report, a spasmodic column, for the Irish members had been brawling three weeks ago at Westminster over a question of naval efficiency. After a disturbed paragraph or two, the column of print once more ran smoothly.

"You have read it?" Mrs. Thornbury asked Miss Allan.

"No, I am ashamed to say I have only read about the discoveries in Crete," said Miss Allan.

"Oh, but I would give so much to realise the ancient world!" cried Mrs. Thornbury. "Now that we old people are alone—we're on our second honeymoon—I am really going to put myself to school again. After all we are *founded* on the past, aren't we, Mr. Hewet? My soldier son says that there is still a great deal to be learnt from Hannibal. One ought to know so much more than one does. Somehow when I read the paper, I begin with the debates first, and, before I've done, the door always opens—we're a very large party at home—and so one never does think enough about the ancients and all they've done for us. But *you* begin at the beginning, Miss Allan."

"When I think of the Greeks I think of them as naked black men," said Miss Allan, "which is quite incorrect, I'm sure."

"And you, Mr. Hirst?" said Mrs. Thornbury, perceiving that the gaunt young man was near. "I'm sure you read everything."

"I confine myself to cricket and crime," said Hirst. "The worst of coming from the upper classes," he continued, "is that one's friends are never killed in railway accidents."

Mr. Thornbury threw down the paper, and emphatically dropped his eyeglasses. The sheets fell in the middle of the group, and were eyed by them all.

"It's not gone well?" asked his wife solicitously.

Hewet picked up one sheet and read, "A lady was walking yesterday in the streets of Westminster when she perceived a cat in the window of a deserted house. The famished animal—"

"I shall be out of it anyway," Mr. Thornbury interrupted peevishly.

"Cats are often forgotten," Miss Allan remarked.

"Remember, William, the Prime Minister has reserved his answer," said Mrs. Thornbury.

"At the age of eighty, Mr. Joshua Harris of Eeles Park, Brondesbury, has had a son," said Hirst.

". . . The famished animal, which had been noticed by workmen for some days, was rescued, but—by Jove! it bit the man's hand to pieces!"

"Wild with hunger, I suppose," commented Miss Allan.

"You're all neglecting the chief advantage of being abroad," said Mr. Hughling Elliot, who had joined the group. "You might read your news in French, which is equivalent to reading no news at all."

Mr. Elliot had a profound knowledge of Coptic, which he concealed as far as possible, and quoted French phrases so exquisitely that it was hard to believe that he could also speak the ordinary tongue. He had an immense respect for the French.

"Coming?" he asked the two young men. "We ought to start before it's really hot."

"I beg of you not to walk in the heat, Hugh," his wife pleaded, giving him an angular parcel enclosing half a chicken and some raisins.

"Hewet will be our barometer," said Mr. Elliot. "He will melt before I shall."

Indeed, if so much as a drop had melted off his spare ribs, the bones would have lain bare. The ladies were left alone now, surrounding *The Times* which lay upon the floor. Miss Allan looked at her father's watch.

"Ten minutes to eleven," she observed.

"Work?" asked Mrs. Thornbury.

"Work," replied Miss Allan.

"What a fine creature she is!" murmured Mrs. Thornbury, as the square figure in its manly coat withdrew.

"And I'm sure she has a hard life," sighed Mrs. Elliot.

"Oh, it *is* a hard life," said Mrs. Thornbury. "Unmarried women—earning their livings—it's the hardest life of all."

"Yet she seems pretty cheerful," said Mrs. Elliot.

"It must be very interesting," said Mrs. Thornbury. "I envy her her knowledge."

"But that isn't what women want," said Mrs. Elliot.

"I'm afraid it's all a great many can hope to have," sighed Mrs. Thornbury. "I believe that there are more of us than ever now. Sir Harley Lethbridge was telling me only the other day how difficult it is to find boys for the navy—partly because of their teeth, it is true. And I have heard young women talk quite openly of——"

"Dreadful, dreadful!" exclaimed Mrs. Elliot. "The crown, as one may call it, of a woman's life. I, who know what it is to be childless——" she sighed and ceased.

"But we must not be hard," said Mrs. Thornbury. "The conditions are so much changed since I was a young woman."

"Surely *maternity* does not change," said Mrs. Elliot.

"In some ways we can learn a great deal from the young," said Mrs. Thornbury. "I learn so much from my own daughters."

"I believe that Hughling really doesn't mind," said Mrs. Elliot. "But then he has his work."

"Women without children can do so much for the children of others," observed Mrs. Thornbury gently.

"I sketch a great deal," said Mrs. Elliot, "but that isn't really an occupation. It's so disconcerting to find girls just beginning doing better than one does oneself! And nature's difficult—very difficult!"

"Are there not institutions—clubs—that you could help?" asked Mrs. Thornbury.

"They are so exhausting," said Mrs. Elliot. "I look strong, because of my colour; but I'm not; the youngest of eleven never is."

"If the mother is careful before," said Mrs. Thornbury judicially, "there is no reason why the size of the family should make any difference. And there is no training like the training that brothers and sisters give each other. I am sure of that. I have seen it with my own children. My eldest boy Ralph, for instance—"

But Mrs. Elliot was inattentive to the elder lady's experience, and her eyes wandered about the hall.

"My mother had two miscarriages, I know," she said suddenly. "The first because she met one of those great dancing bears—they shouldn't be allowed; the other—it was a horrid story—our cook had a child and there was a dinner party. So I put my dyspepsia down to that."

"And a miscarriage is so much worse than a confinement," Mrs. Thornbury murmured absentmindedly, adjusting her spectacles and picking up *Times*. Mrs. Elliot rose and fluttered away.

When she had heard what one of the million voices speaking in the paper had to say, and noticed that a cousin of hers had married a clergyman at Minehead—ignoring the drunken women, the golden animals of Crete, the movements of battalions, the dinners, the reforms, the fires, the indignant, the learned and benevolent, Mrs. Thornbury went upstairs to write a letter for the mail.

The paper lay directly beneath the clock, the two together seeming to represent stability in a changing world. Mr. Perrott passed through; Mr. Venning poised for a second on the edge of a table. Mrs. Paley was wheeled past. Susan followed. Mr. Venning strolled after her. Portuguese military families, their clothes suggesting late rising in untidy bedrooms, trailed across, attended by confidential nurses carrying noisy children. As midday drew on, and the sun beat straight upon the roof, an eddy of great flies droned in a circle; iced drinks were served under the palms; the long blinds were pulled down with a shriek, turning all the light yellow. The clock now had a silent hall to tick in, and an audience of four or five somnolent merchants. By degrees white figures with shady hats came in at the door, admitting a wedge of the hot summer day, and shutting it out again. After resting in the dimness for a minute, they went upstairs. Simultaneously, the clock wheezed one, and the gong sounded, beginning softly, working itself into a frenzy, and ceasing. There was a pause. Then all those who had gone upstairs came down; cripples came, planting both feet on the same step lest they should slip; prim little girls came, holding the nurse's finger; fat old men came still buttoning waistcoats. The gong had been sounded in the garden, and by degrees recumbent figures rose and strolled in to eat, since the time had come for them to feed again.

There were pools and bars of shade in the garden even at midday, where two or three visitors could lie working or talking at their ease.

Owing to the heat of the day, luncheon was generally a silent meal, when people observed their neighbors and took stock of any new faces there might be, hazarding guesses as to who they were and what they did. Mrs. Paley, although well over seventy and crippled in the legs, enjoyed her food and the peculiarities of her fellow-beings. She was seated at a small table with Susan.

"I shouldn't like to say what *she* is!" she chuckled, surveying a tall woman dressed conspicuously in white, with paint in the hollows of her cheeks, who was always late, and always attended by a shabby female follower, at which remark Susan blushed, and wondered why her aunt said such things.

Lunch went on methodically, until each of the seven courses was left in fragments and the fruit was merely a toy, to be peeled and sliced as a child destroys a daisy, petal by petal. The food served as an extinguisher upon any faint flame of the human spirit that might survive the midday heat, but Susan sat in her room afterwards, turning over and over the delightful fact that Mr. Venning had come to her in the garden, and had sat there quite half an hour while she read aloud to her aunt. Men and women sought different corners where they could lie unobserved, and from two to four it might be said without exaggeration that the hotel was inhabited by bodies without souls. Disastrous would have been the result if a fire or a death had suddenly demanded something heroic of human nature, but tragedies come in the hungry hours. Towards four o'clock the human spirit again began to lick the body, as a flame licks a black promontory of coal. Mrs. Paley felt it unseemly to open her toothless jaw so widely, though there was no one near, and Mrs. Elliot surveyed her found flushed face anxiously in the looking-glass.

Half an hour later, having removed the traces of sleep, they met each other in the hall, and Mrs. Paley observed that she was going to have her tea.

"You like your tea too, don't you?" she said, and invited Mrs. Elliot, whose husband was still out, to join her at a special table which she had placed for her under a tree.

"A little silver goes a long way in this country," she chuckled.

She sent Susan back to fetch another cup.

"They have such excellent biscuits here," she said, contemplating a plateful. "Not sweet biscuits, which I don't like—dry biscuits . . . Have you been sketching?"

"Oh, I've done two or three little daubs," said Mrs. Elliot, speaking rather louder than usual. "But it's so difficult after Oxfordshire, where there are so many trees. The light's so strong here. Some people admire it, I know, but I find it very fatiguing."

"I really don't need cooking, Susan," said Mrs. Paley, when her niece returned. "I must trouble you to move me."

Everything had to be moved. Finally the old lady was placed so that the light wavered over her, as though she were a fish in a net. Susan poured out tea, and was just remarking that they were having hot weather in Wiltshire too, when Mr. Venning asked whether he might join them.

"It's so nice to find a young man who doesn't despise tea," said Mrs. Paley, regaining her good humour. "One of my nephews the other day asked for a glass of sherry—at five o'clock! I told him he could get it at the public house round the corner, but not in my drawing room."

"I'd rather go without lunch than tea," said Mr. Venning. "That's not strictly true. I want both."

Mr. Venning was a dark young man, about thirty-two years of age, very slapdash and confident in his manner, although at this moment obviously a little excited. His friend Mr. Perrott was a barrister, and as Mr. Perrott refused to go anywhere without Mr. Venning it was necessary, when Mr. Perrott came to Santa Marina about a Company, for Mr. Venning to come too. He was a barrister also, but he loathed a profession which kept him indoors over books, and directly his widowed mother died he was going, so he confided to Susan, to take up flying seriously, and become partner in a large business for making aeroplanes. The talk rambled on. It dealt, of course, with the beauties and singularities of the place, the streets, the people, and the quantities of unowned yellow dogs.

"Don't you think it dreadfully cruel the way they treat dogs in this country?" asked Mrs. Paley.

"I'd have 'em all shot," said Mr. Venning.

"Oh, but the darling puppies," said Susan.

"Jolly little chaps," said Mr. Venning. "Look here, you've got nothing to eat." A great wedge of cake was handed Susan on the point of a trembling knife. Her hand trembled too as she took it.

"I have such a dear dog at home," said Mrs. Elliot.

"My parrot can't stand dogs," said Mrs. Paley, with the air of one making a confidence. "I always suspect that he (or she) was teased by a dog when I was abroad."

"You didn't get far this morning, Miss Warrington," said Mr. Venning.

"It was hot," she answered. Their conversation became private, owing to Mrs. Paley's deafness and the long sad history which Mrs. Elliot had embarked upon of a wire-haired terrier, white with just one black spot, belonging to an uncle of hers, which had committed suicide. "Animals do commit suicide," she sighed, as if she asserted a painful fact.

"Couldn't we explore the town this evening?" Mr. Venning suggested.

"My aunt—" Susan began.

"You deserve a holiday," he said. "You're always doing things for other people."

"But that's my life," she said, under cover of refilling the teapot.

"That's no one's life," he returned, "no young person's. You'll come?"

"I should like to come," she murmured.

At this moment Mrs. Elliot looked up and exclaimed, "Oh, Hugh! He's bringing some one," she added.

"He would like some tea," said Mrs. Paley. "Susan, run and get some cups—there are the two young men."

"We're thirsting for tea," said Mr. Elliot. "You know Mr. Ambrose, Hilda? We met on the hill."

"He dragged me in," said Ridley, "or I should have been ashamed. I'm dusty and dirty and disagreeable." He pointed to his boots which were white with dust, while a dejected flower drooping in his buttonhole, like an exhausted animal over a gate, added to the effect of length and untidiness. He was introduced to the others. Mr. Hewet and Mr. Hirst brought chairs, and tea began again, Susan pouring cascades of water from pot to pot, always cheerfully, and with the competence of long use.

"My wife's brother," Ridley explained to Hilda, whom he failed to remember, "has a house here, which he has lent us. I was sitting on a rock thinking of nothing at all when Elliot started up like a fairy in a pantomime."

"Our chicken got into the salt," Hewet said dolefully to Susan. "Nor is it true that bananas include moisture as well as sustenance.

Hirst was already drinking.

"We've been cursing you," said Ridley in answer to Mrs. Elliot's kind enquiries about his wife. "You tourists eat up all the eggs, Helen tells me. That's an eye-sore too"—he nodded his head at the hotel. "Disgusting luxury, I call it. We live with pigs in the drawing-room."

"The food is not at all what it ought to be, considering the price," said Mrs. Paley seriously. "But unless one goes to a hotel where is one to go to?"

"Stay at home," said Ridley. "I often wish I had! Everyone ought to stay at home. But, of course, they won't."

Mrs. Paley conceived a certain grudge against Ridley, who seemed to be criticising her habits after an acquaintance of five minutes.

"I believe in foreign travel myself," she stated, "if one knows one's native land, which I think I can honestly say I do. I should not allow any one to travel until they had visited Kent and Dorsetshire—Kent for the hops, and Dorsetshire for its old stone cottages. There is nothing to compare with them here."

"Yes—I always think that some people like the flat and other people like the downs," said Mrs. Elliot rather vaguely.

Hirst, who had been eating and drinking without interruption, now lit a cigarette, and observed, "Oh, but we're all agreed by this time that nature's a mistake. She's either very ugly, appallingly uncomfortable, or absolutely terrifying. I don't know which alarms me most—a cow or a tree. I once met a cow in a field by night. The creature looked at me. I assure you it turned my hair grey. It's a disgrace that the animals should be allowed to go at large."

"And what did the cow think of *him?*" Venning mumbled to Susan, who immediately decided in her own mind that Mr. Hirst was a dreadful young man, and that although he had such an air of being clever he probably wasn't as clever as Arthur, in the ways that really matter.

"Wasn't it Wilde who discovered the fact that nature makes no allowance for hip-bones?" enquired Hughling Elliot. He knew by this time exactly what scholarships and distinction Hirst enjoyed, and had formed a very high opinion of his capacities.

But Hirst merely drew his lips together very tightly and made no reply.

Ridley conjectured that it was now permissible for him to take his leave. Politeness required him to thank Mrs. Elliot for his tea, and to add, with a wave of his hand, "You must come up and see us."

The wave included both Hirst and Hewet, and Hewet answered, "I should like it immensely."

The party broke up, and Susan, who had never felt so happy in her life, was just about to start for her walk in the town with Arthur, when Mrs. Paley beckoned her back. She could not understand from the book how Double Demon patience is played; and suggested that if they sat down and worked it out together it would fill up the time nicely before dinner.

10

Among the promises which Mrs. Ambrose had made her niece should she stay was a room cut off from the rest of the house, large, private—a room in which she could play, read, think, defy the world, a fortress as well as a sanctuary. Rooms, she knew, became more like worlds than rooms at the age of twenty-four. Her judgment was correct, and when she shut the door Rachel entered an enchanted place, where the poets sang and things fell into their right proportions. Some days after the vision of the hotel by night she was sitting alone, sunk in an arm-chair, reading a brightly-covered red volume lettered on the back *Works of Henrik Ibsen.* Music was open on the piano, and books of music rose in two jagged pillars on the floor; but for the moment music was deserted.

Far from looking bored or absent-minded, her eyes were concentrated almost sternly upon the page, and from her breathing, which was slow but repressed, it could be seen that her whole body was constrained by the working of her mind. At last she shut the book sharply, lay back, and drew a deep breath, expressive of the wonder which always marks the transition from the imaginary world to the real world.

"What I want to know," she said aloud, "is this: What is the truth? What's the truth of it all?" She was speaking partly as herself, and partly as the heroine of the play she had just read. The landscape outside, because she had seen nothing but print for the space of two hours, now appeared amazingly solid and clear, but although there were men on the hill washing the trunks of olive trees with a white liquid, for the moment she herself was the most vivid thing in it—an heroic statue in the middle of the foreground, dominating the view. Ibsen's plays always left her in that condition. She acted them for days at a time, greatly to Helen's amusement; and then it would be Meredith's turn and she became Diana of the Crossways. But Helen was aware that it was not all acting, and that some sort of change was taking place in the human being. When Rachel became tired of the rigidity of her pose on the back of the chair, she turned round, slid comfortably down into it, and gazed out over the furniture through the window opposite which opened on the garden. (Her mind wandered away from Nora, but she went on thinking of things that the book suggested to her, of women and life.)

During the three months she had been here she had made up considerably, as Helen meant she should, for time spent in interminable walks round sheltered gardens, and the household gossip of her aunts. But Mrs. Ambrose would have been the first to disclaim any influence, or indeed any belief that to influence was within her power. She saw her less shy, and less serious, which was all to the good, and the violent leaps and the interminable mazes which had led to that result were usually not even guessed at by her. Talk was the medicine she trusted to, talk about everything, talk that was free, unguarded, and as candid as a habit of talking with men made natural in her own case. Nor did she encourage those habits of unselfishness and amiability founded upon insincerity which are put at so high a value in mixed households of men and women. She desired that Rachel should think, and for this reason offered books and discouraged too entire a dependence upon Bach and Beethoven and Wagner. But when Mrs. Ambrose would have suggested Defoe, Maupassant, or some spacious chronicle of family life, Rachel chose modern books, books in shiny yellow covers, books with a great deal of gilding on the back, which were tokens in her aunt's eyes of harsh wrangling and disputes about facts which had no such importance as the moderns claimed for them. But she did not interfere. Rachel read what she chose, reading with the curious literalness of one to whom written sentences are unfamiliar, and handling words as though they were made of wood, separately of great importance, and possessed of shapes like tables or chairs. In this way she came to conclusions, which had to be remodelled according to the adventures of the day, and were indeed recast as liberally as any one could desire, leaving always a small grain of belief behind them.

Ibsen was succeeded by a novel such as Mrs. Ambrose detested, whose purpose was to distribute the guilt of a woman's downfall upon the right shoulders; a purpose which was achieved, if the reader's discomfort were any proof of it. She threw the book down, looked out of the window, turned away from the window, and relapsed into an arm-chair.

The morning was hot, and the exercise of reading left her mind contracting and expanding like the main-spring of a clock, and the small noises of midday, which one can ascribe to no definite cause, in a regular rhythm. It was all very real, very big, very impersonal, and after a moment or two she began to raise her first finger and to let it fall on the arm of her chair so as to bring back to herself some consciousness of her own existence. She was next overcome by the unspeakable queerness of the fact that she should be sitting in an arm-chair, in the morning, in the middle of the world. Who were the people moving in the house—moving things from one place to another? And life, what was that? It was only a light passing over the surface and vanishing, as in time she would vanish, though the furniture in the room would remain. Her dissolution became so complete that she could not raise her finger any more, and sat perfectly still, listening and looking always at the same spot. It became stranger and stranger. She was overcome with awe that things should exist at all. . . . She forgot that she had any fingers to raise. . . . The things that existed were so immense and so desolate. . . . She continued to be conscious of these vast masses of substance for a long stretch of time, the clock still ticking in the midst of the universal silence.

"Come in," she said mechanically, for a string in her brain seemed to be pulled by a persistent knocking at the door. With great slowness the door opened and a tall human being came towards her, holding out her arm and saying:

"What am I to say to this?"

The utter absurdity of a woman coming into a room with a piece of paper in her hand amazed Rachel.

"I don't know what to answer, or who Terence Hewet is," Helen continued, in the toneless voice of a ghost. She put a paper before Rachel on which were written the incredible words:

Dear Mrs. Ambrose—

I am getting up a picnic for next Friday, when we propose to start at eleven-thirty if the weather is fine, and to make the ascent of Monte Rosa. It will take some time, but the view should be magnificent. It would give me great pleasure if you and Miss Vinrace would consent to be of the party.

Yours sincerely,
Terence Hewet

Rachel read the words aloud to make herself believe in them. For the same reason she put her hand on Helen's shoulder.

"Books—books—books," said Helen, in her absent-minded way. "More new books—I wonder what you find in them. . . ."

For the second time Rachel read the letter, but to herself. This time, instead of seeming vague as ghosts, each word was astonishingly prominent; they came out as the tops of mountains come through a mist. *Friday—eleven-thirty—Miss Vinrace.* The blood began to run in her veins; she felt her eyes brighten.

"We must go," she said, rather surprising Helen by her decision. "We must certainly go"—such was the relief of finding that things still happened, and indeed they appeared the brighter for the mist surrounding them.

"Monte Rosa—that's the mountain over there, isn't it?" said Helen; "but Hewet—who's he? One of the young men Ridley met, I suppose. Shall I say yes, then? It may be dreadfully dull."

She took the letter back and went, for the messenger was waiting for her answer.

The party which had been suggested a few nights ago in Mr. Hirst's bedroom had taken shape and was the source of great satisfaction to Mr. Hewet, who had seldom used his practical abilities, and was pleased to find them equal to the strain. His invitations had been universally accepted, which was the more encouraging as they had been issued against Hirst's advice to people who were very dull, not at all suited to each other, and sure not to come.

"Undoubtedly," he said, as he twirled and untwirled a note signed Helen Ambrose, "the gifts needed to make a great commander have been absurdly overrated. About half the intellectual effort which is needed to review a book of modern poetry has enabled me to get together seven or eight people, of opposite sexes, at the same spot at the same hour on the same day. What else is generalship, Hirst? What more did Wellington do on the field of Waterloo? It's like counting the number of pebbles of a path, tedious but not difficult."

He was sitting in his bedroom, one leg over the arm of the chair, and Hirst was writing a letter opposite. Hirst was quick to point out that all the difficulties remained.

"For instance, here are two women you've never seen. Suppose one of them suffers from mountain-sickness, as my sister does, and the other—"

"Oh, the women are for you," Hewet interrupted. "I asked them solely for your benefit. What you want, Hirst, you know, is the society of young women of your own age. You don't know how to get on with women, which is a great defect, considering that half the world consists of women."

Hirst groaned that he was quite aware of that.

But Hewet's complacency was a little chilled as he walked with Hirst to the place where a general meeting had been appointed. He wondered why on earth he had asked these people, and what one really expected to get from bunching human beings up together.

"Cows," he reflected, "draw together in a field; ships in a calm; and we're just the same when we've nothing else to do. But why do we do it?—is it to prevent ourselves from seeing to the bottom of things" (he stopped by a stream and began stirring it with his walking-stick and clouding the water with mud), "making cities and mountains and whole universes out of nothing, or do we really love each other, or do we, on the other hand, live in a state of perpetual uncertainty, knowing nothing, leaping from moment to moment as from world to world?—which is, on the whole, the view *I* incline to."

He jumped over the stream; Hirst went round and joined him, remarking that he had long ceased to look for the reason of any human action.

Half a mile further, they came to a group of plane trees and the salmon-pink farmhouse standing by the stream which had been chosen as meeting-place. It was a shady spot, lying conveniently just where the hill sprung out from the flat. Between the thin stems of the plane trees the young men could see little knots of donkeys pasturing, and a tall woman rubbing the nose of one of them, while another woman was kneeling by the stream lapping water out of her palms.

As they entered the shady place, Helen looked up and then held out her hand.

"I must introduce myself," she said. "I am Mrs. Ambrose."

Having shaken hands, she said, "That's my niece."

Rachel approached awkwardly. She held out her hand, but withdrew it. "It's all wet," she said.

Scarcely had they spoken, when the first carriage drew up.

The donkeys were quickly jerked into attention, and the second carriage arrived. By degrees the grove filled with people—the Elliots, the Thornburys, Mr. Venning and Susan, Miss Allan, Evelyn Murgatroyd, and Mr. Perrott. Mr. Hirst acted the part of hoarse energetic sheep-dog. By means of a few words of caustic Latin he had the animals marshalled, and by inclining a sharp shoulder he lifted the ladies. "What Hewet fails to understand," he remarked, "is that we must break the back of the ascent before midday." He was assisting a young lady, by name Evelyn Murgatroyd, as he spoke. She rose light as a bubble to her seat. With a feather drooping from a broad-brimmed hat, in white from top to toe, she looked like a gallant lady of the time of Charles the First leading royalist troops into action.

"Ride with me," she commanded; and, as soon as Hirst had swung himself across a mule, the two started, leading the cavalcade.

"You're not to call me Miss Murgatroyd. I hate it," she said. "My name's Evelyn. What's yours?"

"St. John," he said.

"I like that," said Evelyn. "And what's your friend's name?"

"His initials being R. S. T., we call him Monk," said Hirst.

"Oh, you're all too clever," she said. "Which way?" Pick me a branch. Let's canter."

She gave her donkey a sharp cut with a switch and started forward. The full and romantic career of Evelyn Murgatroyd is best hit off by her own words, "Call me Evelyn and I'll call you St. John." She said that on very slight provocation—her surname was enough—but although a great many young men had answered her already with considerable spirit she went on saying it and making choice of none. But her donkey stumbled to a jog-trot, and she had to ride in advance alone, for the path when it began to ascend one of the spines of the hill became narrow and scattered with stones. The cavalcade wound on like a jointed caterpillar, tufted with the white parasols of the ladies, and the panama hats of the gentlemen. At one point where the ground rose sharply, Evelyn M. jumped off, threw her reins to the native boy, and adjured St. John Hirst to dismount too. Their example was followed by those who felt the need of stretching.

"I don't see any need to get off," said Miss Allan to Mrs. Elliot just behind her, "considering the difficulty I had getting on."

"These little donkeys stand anything, *n'est-ce pas?*" Mrs. Elliot addressed the guide, who obligingly bowed his head.

"Flowers," said Helen, stooping to pick the lovely little bright flowers which grew separately here and there. "You pinch their leaves and then they smell," she said, laying one on Miss Allan's knee.

"Haven't we met before?" asked Miss Allan, looking at her.

"I was taking it for granted," Helen laughed, for in the confusion of meeting they had not been introduced.

"How sensible!" chirped Mrs. Elliot. "That's just what one would always like—only unfortunately it's not possible."

"Not possible?" said Helen. "Everything's possible. Who knows what mayn't happen before night-fall?" she continued, mocking the poor lady's timidity, who depended implicitly upon one thing following another that the mere glimpse of a world where dinner could be disregarded, or the table moved one inch from its accustomed place, filled her with fears for her own stability.

Higher and higher they went, becoming separated from the world. The world, when they turned to look back, flattened itself out, and was marked with squares of thin green and grey.

"Towns are very small," Rachel remarked, obscuring the whole of Santa Marina and its suburbs with one hand. The sea filled in all the angles of the coast smoothly, breaking in a white frill, and here and there ships were set firmly in the blue. The sea was stained with purple and green blots, and there was a glittering line upon the rim where it met the sky. The air was very clear and silent save for the sharp noise of grasshoppers and the hum of bees, which sounded loud in the ear as they shot past and vanished. The party halted and sat for a time in a quarry on the hillside.

"Amazingly clear," exclaimed St. John, identifying one cleft in the land after another.

Evelyn M. sat beside him, propping her chin on her hand. She surveyed the view with a certain look of triumph.

"D'you think Garibaldi was ever up here?" she asked Mr. Hirst. Oh, if she had been his bride! If, instead of a picnic party, this was a party of patriots, and she, red-shirted like the rest, had lain among grim men, flat on the turf, aiming her gun at the white turrets beneath them, screening her eyes to pierce through the smoke! So thinking, her foot stirred restlessly, and she exclaimed:

"I don't call this *life*, do you?"

"What do you call life?" said St. John.

"Fighting—revolution," she said, still gazing at the doomed city. "You only care for books, I know."

"You're quite wrong," said St. John.

"Explain," she urged, for there were no guns to be aimed at bodies, and she turned to another kind of warfare.

"What do I care for? People," he said.

"Well, I *am* surprised!" she exclaimed. "You look so awfully serious. Do let's be friends and tell each other what we're like. I hate being cautious, don't you?"

But St. John was decidedly cautious, as she could see by the sudden constriction of his lips, and had no intention of revealing his soul to a young lady. "The ass is eating my hat," he remarked, and stretched out for it instead of answering her. Evelyn blushed very slightly and then turned with some impetuosity upon Mr. Perrott, and when they mounted again it was Mr. Perrott who lifted her to her seat.

"When one has laid the eggs one eats the omelette," said Hughling Elliot, exquisitely in French, a hint to the rest of them that it was time to ride on again.

The midday sun which Hirst had foretold was beginning to beat down hotly. The higher they got the more of the sky appeared, until the mountain was only a small tent of earth against an enormous blue background. The English fell silent; the natives who walked beside the donkeys broke into queer wavering songs and tossed jokes from one to the other. The way grew very steep, and each rider kept his eyes fixed on the hobbling curved form of the rider and donkey directly in front of him. Rather more strain was being put upon their bodies than is quite legitimate in a party of pleasure, and Hewet overheard one or two slightly grumbling remarks.

"Expeditions in such heat are perhaps a little unwise," Mrs. Elliot murmured to Miss Allan.

But Miss Allan returned, "I always like to get to the top"; and it was true, although she was a big woman, stiff in the joints, and unused to donkey-riding, but as her holidays were few she made the most of them.

The vivacious white figure rode well in front; she had somehow possessed herself of a leafy branch and wore it round her hat like a garland. They went on for a few minutes in silence.

"The view will be wonderful," Hewet assured them, turning round in his saddle and smiling encouragement. Rachel caught his eye and smiled too. They struggled on for some time longer, nothing being heard but the clatter of hooves striving on the loose stones. Then they saw that Evelyn was off her ass, and that Mr. Perrott was standing in the attitude of a statesman in Parliament Square, stretching an arm of stone towards the view. A little to the left of them was a low ruined wall, the stump of an Elizabethan watch-tower.

"I couldn't have stood it much longer," Mrs. Elliot confided to Mrs. Thornbury, but the excitement of being at the top in another moment and seeing the view prevented any one from answering her. One after another they came out on the flat space at the top and stood overcome with wonder. Before them they beheld an immense space—grey sands running into forest, and forest merging in mountains, and mountains washed by air—the infinite distances of South America. A river ran across the plain, as flat as the land, and appearing quite as stationary. The effect of so much space was at first rather chilling. They felt themselves very small, and for some time no one said anything. Then Evelyn exclaimed, "Splendid!" She took hold of the hand that was next her; it chanced to be Miss Allan's hand.

"North—South—East—West," said Miss Allan, jerking her head slightly towards the points of the compass.

Hewet, who had gone a little in front, looked up at his guests as if to justify himself for having brought them. He observed how strangely the people standing in a row with their figures bent slightly forward and their clothes plastered by the wind to the shape of their bodies resembled naked statues. On their pedestal of earth they looked unfamiliar and noble, but in another moment they had broken their rank, and he had to see to the laying out of food. Hirst came to his help, and they handed packets of chicken and bread from one to another.

As St. John gave Helen her packet she looked him full in the face and said:

"Do you remember—two women?"

He looked at her sharply.

"I do," he answered.

"So you're the two women!" Hewet exclaimed, looking from Helen to Rachel.

"Your lights tempted us," said Helen. "We watched you playing cards, but we never knew that we were being watched."

"It was like a thing in a play," Rachel added.

"And Hirst couldn't describe you," said Hewet.

It was certainly odd to have seen Helen and to find nothing to say about her.

Hughling Elliot put up his eyeglass and grasped the situation.

"I don't know of anything more dreadful," he said, pulling at the joint of a chicken's leg, "than being seen when one isn't conscious of it. One feels sure one has been caught doing something ridiculous—looking at one's tongue in a hansom, for instance."

Now the others ceased to look at the view, and drawing together sat down in a circle round the baskets.

"And yet those little looking-glasses in hansoms have a fascination of their own," said Mrs. Thornbury. "One's features look so different when one can only see a bit of them."

"There will soon be very few hansom cabs left," said Mrs. Elliot. "And four-wheeled cabs—I assure you even at Oxford it's almost impossible to get a four-wheeled cab."

"I wonder what happens to the horses," said Susan.

"Veal pie," said Arthur.

"It's high time that horses should become extinct anyhow," said Hirst. "They're distressingly ugly, besides being vicious."

But Susan, who had been brought up to understand that the horse is the noblest of God's creatures, could not agree, and Venning thought Hirst an unspeakable ass, but was too polite not to continue the conversation.

"When they see us falling out of aeroplanes they get some of their own back, I expect," he remarked.

"You fly?" said old Mr. Thornbury, putting on his spectacles to look at him.

"I hope to, some day," said Arthur.

Here flying was discussed at length, and Mrs. Thornbury delivered an opinion which was almost a speech to the effect that it would be quite necessary in time of war, and in England we were terribly behind-hand. "If I were a young fellow," she concluded, "I should certainly qualify." It was odd to look at the little elderly lady, in her grey coat and skirt, with a sandwich in her hand, her eyes lighting up with zeal as she imagined herself a young man in an aeroplane. For some reason, however, the talk did not run easily after this, and all they said was about drink and salt and the view. Suddenly Miss Allan, who was seated with her back to the ruined wall, put down her sandwich, picked something off her neck, and remarked, "I'm covered with little creatures." It was true, and the discovery was very welcome. The ants were pouring down a glacier of loose earth heaped between the stones of the ruin—large brown ants with polished bodies. She held out one on the back of her hand for Helen to look at.

"Suppose they sting?" said Helen.

"They will not sting, but they may infest the victuals," said Miss Allan, and measures were taken at once to divert the ants from their course. At Hewet's suggestion it was decided to adopt the methods of modern warfare against an invading army. The table-cloth represented the invaded country, and round it they built barricades of baskets, set up the wine bottles in a rampart, made fortifications of bread and dug fosses of salt. When an ant got through it was exposed to a fire of bread-crumbs, until Susan pronounced that that was cruel, and rewarded those brave spirits with spoil in the shape of tongue. Playing this game they lost their stiffness, and even became unusually daring, for Mr. Perrott, who was very shy, said, "Permit me," and removed an ant from Evelyn's neck.

"It would be no laughing matter really," said Mrs. Elliot confidentially to Mrs. Thornbury, "if an ant did get between the vest and the skin."

The noise grew suddenly more clamorous, for it was discovered that a long line of ants had found their way on to the table-cloth by a back entrance, and if success could be gauged by noise, Hewet had every reason to think his party a success. Nevertheless he became, for no reason at all, profoundly depressed.

"They are not satisfactory; they are ignoble," he thought, surveying his guests from a little distance, where he was gathering together the plates. He glanced at them all, stooping and swaying and gesticulating round the table-cloth. Amiable and modest, respectable in many ways, lovable even in their contentment and desire to be kind, how mediocre they all were, and capable of what insipid cruelty to one another! There was Mrs. Thornbury, sweet but trivial in her maternal egoism; Mrs. Elliot, perpetually complaining of her lot; her husband a mere pea in a pod; and Susan—she had no self, and counted neither one way nor the other; Venning was as honest and as brutal as a schoolboy; poor old Thornbury merely trod his round like a horse in a mill; and the less one examined into Evelyn's character the better, he suspected. Yet these were the people with money, and to them rather than to others was given the management of the world. Put among them some one more vital, who cared for life or for beauty, and what an agony, what a waste would they inflict on him if he tried to share with them and not to scourge!

"There's Hirst," he concluded, coming to the figure of his friend; with his usual little frown of concentration upon his forehead he was peeling the skin off a banana. "And he's as ugly as sin." For the ugliness of St. John Hirst, and the limitations that went with it, he made the rest in some way responsible. It was their fault that he had to live alone. Then he came to Helen, attracted to her by the sound of her laugh. She was laughing at Miss Allan. "You wear combinations in this heat?" she said in a voice which was meant to be private. He liked the look of her immensely, not so much her beauty, but her largeness and simplicity, which made her stand out from the rest like a great stone woman, and he passed on in a gentler mood. His eye fell upon Rachel. She was lying back rather behind the others resting on one elbow; she might have been thinking precisely the same thoughts as Hewet himself. Her eyes were fixed rather sadly but not intently upon the row of people opposite her. Hewet crawled up to her on his knees, with a piece of bread in his hand.

"What are you looking at?" he asked.

She was a little startled, but answered directly, "Human beings."

11

One after another they rose and stretched themselves, and in a few minutes divided more or less into two separate parties. One of these parties was dominated by Hughling Elliot and Mrs. Thornbury, who, having both read the same books and considered the same questions, were now anxious to name the places beneath them and to hang upon them stores of information about navies and armies, political parties, natives and mineral products—all of which combined, they said, to prove that South America was the country of the future.

Evelyn M. listened with her bright blue eyes fixed upon the oracles.

"How it makes one long to be a man!" she exclaimed.

Mr. Perrott answered, surveying the plain, that a country with a future was a very fine thing.

"If I were you," said Evelyn, turning to him and drawing her glove vehemently through her fingers, "I'd raise a troop and conquer some great territory and make it splendid. You'd want women for that. I'd love to start life from the very beginning as it ought to be—nothing squalid—but great halls and gardens and splendid men and women. But you—you only like Law Courts!"

"And would you really be content without pretty frocks and sweets and all the things young ladies like?" asked Mr. Perrott, concealing a certain amount of pain beneath his ironical manner.

"I'm not a young lady," Evelyn flashed; she bit her underlip. "Just because I like splendid things you laugh at me. Why are there no men like Garibaldi now?" she demanded.

"Look here," said Mr. Perrott, "you don't give me a chance. You think we ought to begin things fresh. Good. But I don't see precisely—conquer a territory? They're all conquered already, aren't they?"

"It's not any territory in particular," Evelyn explained. "It's the idea, don't you see? We lead such tame lives. And I feel sure you've got splendid things in you."

Hewet saw the scars and hollows in Mr. Perrott's sagacious face relax pathetically. He could imagine the calculations which even then went on within his mind, as to whether he would be justified in asking a woman to marry him, considering that he made no more than five hundred a year at the Bar, owned no private means, and had an invalid sister to support. Mr. Perrott again knew that he was not "quite," as Susan stated in her diary; not quite a gentleman she meant, for he was the son of a grocer in Leeds, had started life with a basket on his back, and now, though practically indistinguishable from a born gentleman, showed his origin to keen eyes in an impeccable neatness of dress, lack of freedom in manner, extreme cleanliness of person, and a certain indescribable timidity and precision with his knife and fork which might be the relic of days when meat was rare, and the way of handling it by no means gingerly.

The two parties who were strolling about and losing their unity now came together, and joined each other in a long stare over the yellow and green patches of the heated landscape below. The hot air danced across it, making it impossible to see the roofs of a village on the plain distinctly. Even on the top of the mountain where a breeze played lightly, it was very hot, and the heat, the food, the immense space, and perhaps some less well-defined cause produced a comfortable drowsiness and a sense of happy relaxation in them. They did not say much, but felt no constraint in being silent.

"Suppose we go and see what's to be seen over there?" said Arthur to

Susan, and the pair walked off together, their departure certainly sending some thrill of emotion through the rest.

"An odd lot, aren't they?" said Arthur. "I thought we should never get 'em all to the top. But I'm glad we came, by Jove! I wouldn't have missed this for something."

"I don't *like* Mr. Hirst," said Susan inconsequently. "I suppose he's very clever, but why should clever people be so—I expect he's awfully nice, really," she added, instinctively qualifying what might have seemed an unkind remark.

"Hirst? Oh, he's one of these learned chaps," said Arthur indifferently. "He don't look as if he enjoyed it. You should hear him talking to Elliot. It's as much as I can do to follow 'em at all. . . . I was never good at my books."

With these sentences and the pauses that came between them they reached a little hillock, on the top of which grew several slim trees.

"D'you mind if we sit down here?" said Arthur, looking about him. "It's jolly in the shade—and the view—" They sat down, and looked straight ahead of them in silence for some time.

"But I do envy those clever chaps sometimes," Arthur remarked. "I don't suppose they ever . . ." He did not finish his sentence.

"I can't see why you should envy them," said Susan, with great sincerity.

"Odd things happen to one," said Arthur. "One goes along smoothly enough, one thing following another, and it's all very jolly and plain sailing, and you think you know all about it, and suddenly one doesn't know where one is a bit, and everything seems different from what it used to seem. Now today, coming up that path, riding behind you, I seemed to see everything as if—" he paused and plucked a piece of grass up by the roots. He scattered the little lumps of earth which were sticking to the roots—"As if it had a kind of meaning. You've made the difference to me," he jerked out, "I don't see why I shouldn't tell you. I've felt it ever since I knew you. . . . It's because I love you."

Even while they had been saying commonplace things Susan had been conscious of the excitement of intimacy, which seemed not only to lay bare something in her, but in the trees and the sky, and the progress of his speech which seemed inevitable was positively painful to her, for no human being had ever come so close to her before.

She was struck motionless as his speech went on, and her heart gave great separate leaps at the last words. She sat with her fingers curled round a stone, looking straight in front of her down the mountain over the plain. So then, it had actually happened to her, a proposal of marriage.

Arthur looked round at her; his face was oddly twisted. She was drawing her breath with such difficulty that she could hardly answer.

"You might have known." He seized her in his arms; again and again and again they clasped each other, murmuring inarticulately.

"Well," sighed Arthur, sinking back on the ground, "that's the most wonderful thing that's ever happened to me." He looked as if he were trying to put things seen in a dream beside real things.

There was a long silence.

"It's the most perfect thing in the world," Susan stated, very gently and with great conviction. It was no longer merely a proposal of marriage, but of marriage with Arthur, with whom she was in love.

In the silence that followed, holding his hand tightly in hers, she prayed to God that she might make him a good wife.

"And what will Mr. Perrott say?" she asked at the end of it.

"Dear old fellow," said Arthur who, now that the first shock was over, was relaxing into an enormous sense of pleasure and contentment. "We must be very nice to him, Susan."

He told her how hard Perrott's life had been, and how absurdly devoted he was to Arthur himself. He went on to tell her about his mother, a widow lady, of strong character. In return Susan sketched the portraits of her own family—Edith in particular, her youngest sister, whom she loved better than any one else, "except you, Arthur. . . . Arthur," she continued, "what was it that you first liked me for?"

"It was a buckle you wore one night at sea," said Arthur, after due consideration. "I remember noticing—it's an absurd thing to notice!—that you didn't take peas, because I don't either."

From this they went on to compare their more serious tastes, or rather Susan ascertained what Arthur cared about, and professed herself very fond of the same thing. They would live in London, perhaps have a cottage in the country near Susan's family, for they would find it strange without her at first. Her mind, stunned to begin with, now flew to the various changes that her engagement would make—how delightful it would be to join the ranks of the married women—no longer to hang on to groups of girls much younger than herself—to escape the long solitude of an old maid's life. Now and then her amazing good fortune overcame her, and she turned to Arthur with an exclamation of love.

They lay in each other's arms and had no notion that they were observed. Yet two figures suddenly appeared among the trees above them.

"Here's shade," began Hewet, when Rachel suddenly stopped dead. They saw a man and woman lying on the ground beneath them, rolling slightly this way and that as the embrace tightened and slackened. The man then sat upright and the woman, who now appeared to be Susan Warrington, lay back upon the ground, with her eyes shut and an absorbed look upon her face, as though she were not altogether conscious. Nor could you tell from her expression whether she was happy, or had suffered something. When Arthur again turned to her, butting her as a lamb butts a ewe, Hewet and Rachel retreated without a word. Hewet felt uncomfortably shy.

"I don't like that," said Rachel after a moment.

"I can remember not liking it either," said Hewet. "I can remember—" but he changed his mind and continued in an ordinary tone of voice, "Well, we may take it for granted that they're engaged. D'you think he'll ever fly, or will she put a stop to that?"

But Rachel was still agitated; she could not get away from the sight they had just seen. Instead of answering Hewet she persisted.

"Love's an odd thing, isn't it, making one's heart beat."

"It's so enormously important, you see," Hewet replied. "Their lives are now changed for ever."

"And it makes one sorry for them too," Rachel continued, as though she were tracing the course of her feelings. "I don't know either of them, but I could almost burst into tears. That's silly, isn't it?"

"Just because they're in love," said Hewet. "Yes," he added after a moment's consideration, "there's something horribly pathetic about it, I agree."

And now, as they had walked some way from the grove of trees, and had come to a rounded hollow very tempting to the back, they proceeded to sit down, and the impression of the lovers lost some of its force, though a certain intensity of vision, which was probably the result of the sight, remained with them. As a day upon which any emotion has been repressed is different from other days, so this day was now different, merely because they had seen other people at a crisis of their lives.

"A great encampment of tents they might be," said Hewet, looking in front of him at the mountains. "Isn't it like a water-colour too—you know the way water-colours dry in ridges all across the paper—I've been wondering what they looked like."

His eyes became dreamy, as though he were matching things, and reminded Rachel in their colour of the green flesh of a snail. She sat beside him looking at the mountains too. When it became painful to look any longer, the great size of the view seeming to enlarge her eyes beyond their natural limit, she looked at the ground; it pleased her to scrutinise this inch of the soil of South America so minutely that she noticed every grain of earth and made it into a world where she was endowed with the supreme power. She bent a blade of grass, and set an insect on the utmost tassel of it, and wondered if the insect realised his strange adventure, and thought how strange it was that she should have bent that tassel rather than any other of the million tassels.

"You've never told me you name," said Hewet suddenly. "Miss Somebody Vinrace. . . . I like to know people's Christian names."

"Rachel," she replied.

"Rachel," he repeated. "I have an aunt called Rachel, who put the life of Father Damien into verse. She is a religious fanatic—the result of the way she was brought up, down in Northamptonshire, never seeing a soul. Have you any aunts?"

"I live with them," said Rachel.

"And I wonder what they're doing now?" Hewet enquired.

"They are probably buying wool," Rachel determined. She tried to describe them. "They are small, rather pale women," she began, "very clean. We live in Richmond. They have an old dog, too, who will only eat the marrow out of bones. . . . They are always going to church. They tidy their drawers a good deal." But here she was overcome by the difficulty of describing people.

"It's impossible to believe that it's all going on still!" she exclaimed.

The sun was behind them and two long shadows suddenly lay upon the ground in front of them, one waving because it was made by a skirt, and the other stationary, because thrown by a pair of legs in trousers.

"You look very comfortable!" said Helen's voice above them.

"Hirst," said Hewet, pointing at the scissorlike shadow; he then rolled round to look up at them.

"There's room for us all here," he said.

When Hirst had seated himself comfortably, he said:

"Did you congratulate the young couple?"

It appeared that, coming to the same spot a few minutes after Hewet and Rachel, Helen and Hirst had seen precisely the same thing.

"No, we didn't congratulate them," said Hewet. "They seemed very happy."

"Well," said Hirst, pursing up his lips, "so long as I needn't marry either of them—"

"We were very much moved," said Hewet.

"I thought you would be," said Hirst. "Which was it, Monk? The thought of the immortal passions, or the thought of new-born males to keep the Roman Catholics out? I assure you," he said to Helen, "he's capable of being moved by either."

Rachel was a good deal stung by his banter, which she felt to be directed equally against them both, but she could think of no repartee.

"Nothing moves Hirst," Hewet laughed; he did not seem to be stung at all. "Unless it were a transfinite number falling in love with a finite one—I suppose such things do happen, even in mathematics."

"On the contrary," said Hirst with a touch of annoyance, "I consider myself a person of very strong passions." It was clear from the way he spoke that he meant it seriously; he spoke of course for the benefit of the ladies.

"By the way, Hirst," said Hewet, after a pause, "I have a terrible confession to make. Your book—the poems of Wordsworth, which if you remember I took off your table just as we were starting, and certainly put in my pocket here—"

"Is lost," Hirst finished for him.

"I consider that there is still a chance," Hewet urged, slapping himself to right and left, "that I never did take it after all."

"No," said Hirst. "It is here." He pointed to his breast.

"Thank God," Hewet exclaimed. "I need no longer feel as though I'd murdered a child!"

"I should think you were always losing things," Helen remarked, looking at him meditatively.

"I don't lose things," said Hewet. "I mislay them. That was the reason why Hirst refused to share a cabin with me on the voyage out."

"You came out together?" Helen enquired.

"I propose that each member of this party now gives a short biographical sketch of himself or herself," said Hirst, sitting upright. "Miss Vinrace, you come first; begin."

Rachel stated that she was twenty-four years of age, the daughter of a ship-owner, that she had never been properly educated; played the piano, had no brothers or sisters, and lived at Richmond with aunts, her mother being dead.

"Next," said Hirst, having taken in these facts; he pointed at Hewet. "I am the son of an English gentleman. I am twenty-seven," Hewet began. "My father was a fox-hunting squire. He died when I was ten in the hunting field. I can remember his body coming home, on a shutter I suppose, just as I was going down to tea, and noticing that there was jam for tea, and wondering whether I should be allowed—"

"Yes; but keep to the facts," Hirst put in.

"I was educated at Winchester and Cambridge, which I had to leave after a time. I have done a good many things since——"

"Profession?"

"None—at least——"

"Tastes?"

"Literary. I'm writing a novel."

"Brothers and sisters?"

"Three sisters, no brother, and a mother."

"Is that all we're to hear about you?" said Helen. She stated that she was very old—forty last October, and her father had been a solicitor in the city who had gone bankrupt, for which reason she had never had much education—they lived in one place after another—but an elder brother used to lend her books.

"If I were to tell you everything——" she stopped and smiled. "It would take too long," she concluded. "I married when I was thirty, and I have two children. My husband is a scholar. And now—it's your turn," she nodded at Hirst.

"You've left out a great deal," he reproved her. "My name is St. John Alaric Hirst," he began in a jaunty tone of voice. "I'm twenty-four years old. I'm the son of the Reverend Sidney Hirst, vicar of Great Wappyng in Norfolk. Oh, I got scholarships everywhere—Westminster—King's. I'm now a fellow of King's. Don't it sound dreary? Parents both alive (alas). Two brothers and one sister. I'm a very distinguished young man," he added.

"One of the three, or is it five, most distinguished men in England," Hewet remarked.

"Quite correct," said Hirst.

"That's all very interesting," said Helen after a pause. "But of course we've left out the only questions that matter. For instance, are we Christians?"

"I am not," "I am not," both the young men replied.

"I am," Rachel stated.

"You believe in a personal God?" Hirst demanded, turning round and fixing her with his eyeglasses.

"I believe—I believe," Rachel stammered, "I believe there are things we don't know about, and the world might change in a minute and anything appear."

At this Helen laughed outright. "Nonsense," she said. "You're not a Christian. You've never thought what you are.—And there are lots of other questions," she continued, "though perhaps we can't ask them yet." Although they had talked so freely they were all uncomfortably conscious that they really knew nothing about each other.

"The important questions," Hewet pondered, "the really interesting ones. I doubt that one ever does ask them."

Rachel, who was slow to accept the fact that only a very few things can be said even by people who know each other well, insisted on knowing what he meant.

"Whether we've ever been in love?" she enquired. "Is that the kind of question you mean?"

Again Helen laughed at her, benignantly strewing her with handfuls of the long tasselled grass, for she was so brave and so foolish.

"Oh, Rachel," she cried. "It's like having a puppy in the house having you with one—a puppy that brings one's underclothes down into the hall."

But again the sunny earth in front of them was crossed by fantastic wavering figures, the shadows of men and women.

"There they are!" exclaimed Mrs. Elliot. There was a touch of peevishness in her voice. "And we've had *such* a hunt to find you. Do you know what the time is?"

Mrs. Elliot and Mr. and Mrs. Thornbury now confronted them; Mrs. Elliot was holding out her watch, and playfully tapping it upon the face. Hewet was recalled to the fact that this was a party for which he was responsible, and he immediately led them back to the watch-tower, where they were to have tea before starting home again. A bright crimson scarf fluttered from the top of the wall, which Mr. Perrott and Evelyn were tying to a stone as the others came up. The heat had changed just so far that instead of sitting in the shadow they sat in the sun, which was still hot enough to paint their faces red and yellow, and to colour great sections of the earth beneath them.

"There's nothing half so nice as tea!" said Mrs. Thornbury, taking her cup.

"Nothing," said Helen. "Can't you remember as a child chopping up hay—" she spoke much more quickly than usual, and kept her eye fixed upon Mrs. Thornbury, "and pretending it was tea, and getting scolded by the nurses—why I can't imagine, except that nurses are such brutes, won't allow pepper instead of salt though there's no earthly harm in it. Weren't your nurses just the same?"

During this speech Susan came into the group, and sat down by Helen's side. A few minutes later Mr. Venning strolled up from the opposite direction. He was a little flushed, and in the mood to answer hilariously whatever was said to him.

"What have you been doing to that old chap's grave?" he asked, pointing to the red flag which floated from the top of the stones.

"We have tried to make him forget his misfortune in having died three hundred years ago," said Mr. Perrott.

"It would be awful—to be dead!" ejaculated Evelyn M.

"To be dead?" said Hewet. "I don't think it would be awful. It's quite easy to imagine. When you go to bed tonight fold your hands so—breathe slower and slower—" He lay back with his hands clasped upon his breast, and his eyes shut, "Now," he murmured in an even monotonous voice, "I shall never, never, never move again." His body, lying flat among them, did for a moment suggest death.

"This is a horrible exhibition, Mr. Hewet!" cried Mrs. Thornbury.

"More cake for us!" said Arthur.

"I assure you there's nothing horrible about it," said Hewet, sitting up and laying hands upon the cake.

"It's so natural," he repeated. "People with children should make them do that exercise every night. . . . Not that I look forward to being dead."

"And when you allude to a grave," said Mr. Thornbury, who spoke almost for the first time, "have you any authority for calling that ruin a grave? I am quite with you in refusing to accept the common interpretation which declares it to be the remains of an Elizabethan watch-tower—any more than I believe that the circular mounds or barrows which we find on the top of our English downs were camps. The antiquaries call everything a camp. I am always asking them, Well then, where do you think our ancestors kept their cattle? Half the camps in England are merely the ancient pound or barton as we call it in my part of the world. The argument that no one would keep his cattle in such exposed and inaccessible spots has no weight at all, if you reflect that in those days a man's cattle were his capital, his stock-in-trade, his daughter's dowries. Without cattle he was a serf, another man's man. . . ." His eyes slowly lost their intensity, and he muttered a few concluding words under his breath, looking curiously old and forlorn.

Hughling Elliot, who might have been expected to engage the old gentleman in argument, was absent at the moment. He now came up holding out a large square of cotton upon which a fine design was printed in pleasant bright colours that made his hand look pale.

"A bargain," he announced, laying it down on the cloth. "I've just bought it from the big man with the ear-rings. Fine, isn't it? It wouldn't suit every one, of course, but it's just the thing—isn't it, Hilda?—for Mrs. Raymond Parry."

"Mrs. Raymond Parry!" cried Helen and Mrs. Thornbury at the same moment.

They looked at each other as though a mist hitherto obscuring their faces had been blown away.

"Ah—you have been to those wonderful parties too?" Mrs. Elliot asked with interest.

Mrs. Parry's drawing-room, though thousands of miles away, behind a vast curve of water on a tiny piece of earth, came before their eyes. They who had had no solidity or anchorage before seemed to be attached to it somehow, and at once grown more substantial. Perhaps they had been in the drawing-room at the same moment; perhaps they had passed each other on the stairs; at any rate they knew some of the same people. They looked one another up and down with new interest. But they could do no more than look at each other, for there was no time to enjoy the fruits of the discovery. The donkeys were advancing, and it was advisable to begin the descent immediately, for the night fell so quickly that it would be dark before they were home again.

Accordingly, remounting in order, they filed off down the hillside. Scraps of talk came floating back from one to another. There were jokes to begin with, and laughter; some walked part of the way, and picked flowers, and sent stones bounding before them.

"Who writes the best Latin verse in your college, Hirst?" Mr. Elliot called back incongruously, and Mr. Hirst returned that he had no idea.

The dusk fell as suddenly as the natives had warned them, the hollows of the mountain on either side filling up with darkness and the path becoming so dim that it was surprising to hear the donkeys' hooves still striking on hard rock. Silence fell upon one, and then upon another, until they were all silent, their minds spilling out into the deep blue air. The way seemed shorter in the dark than in the day; and soon the lights of the town were seen on the flat far beneath them.

Suddenly some one cried, "Ah!"

In a moment the slow yellow drop rose again from the plain below; it rose, paused, opened like a flower, and fell in a shower of drops.

"Fireworks," they cried.

Another went up more quickly; and then another; they could almost hear it twist and roar.

"Some Saint's day, I suppose," said a voice. The rush and embrace of the rockets as they soared up into the air seemed like the fiery way in which lovers suddenly rose and united, leaving the crowd gazing up at them with strained white faces. But Susan and Arthur, riding down the hill, never said a word to each other, and kept accurately apart.

Then the fireworks became erratic, and soon they ceased altogether, and the rest of the journey was made almost in darkness, the mountain being a great shadow behind them, and bushes and trees little shadows which threw darkness across the road. Among the plane-trees they separated, bundling into carriages and driving off, without saying good-night, or saying it only in a half-muffled way.

It was so late that there was no time for normal conversation between their arrival at the hotel and their retirement to bed. But Hirst wandered into Hewet's room with a collar in his hand.

"Well, Hewet," he remarked, on the crest of a gigantic yawn, "that was a great success, I consider." He yawned. "But take care you're not landed with that young woman. . . . I don't really like young women. . . ."

Hewet was too much drugged by hours in the open air to make any reply. In fact every one of the party was sound asleep within ten minutes or so of each other, with the exception of Susan Warrington. She lay for a considerable time looking blankly at the wall opposite, her hands clasped above her heart, and her light burning by her side. All articulate thought had long ago deserted her; her heart seemed to have grown to the size of a sun, and to illuminate her entire body, shedding like the sun a steady tide of warmth.

"I'm happy, I'm happy, I'm happy," she repeated. "I love every one. I'm happy."

12

When Susan's engagement had been approved at home, and made public to any one who took an interest in it at the hotel—and by this time the society at the hotel was divided so as to point to invisible chalk-marks such as Mr. Hirst had described, the news was felt to justify some celebration—an expedition? That had been done already. A dance then. The advantage of a dance was that it abolished one of those long evenings which were apt to become tedious and lead to absurdly early hours in spite of bridge.

Two or three people standing under the erect body of the stuffed leopard in the hall very soon had the matter decided. Evelyn slid a pace or two this way and that, and pronounced that the floor was excellent. Signor Rodriguez informed them of an old Spaniard who fiddled at weddings—fiddled so as to make a tortoise waltz; and his daughter, although endowed with eyes as black as coal-scuttles, had the same power over the piano. If there were any so sick or so surly as to prefer sedentary occupations on the night in question to spinning and watching others spin, the drawing-room and billiard-room were theirs. Hewet made it his business to conciliate the outsiders as much as possible. To Hirst's theory of the invisible chalk-marks he would pay no attention whatever. He was treated to a snub or two, but, in reward, found obscure lonely gentlemen delighted to have this opportunity of talking to their kind, and the lady of doubtful character showed every symptom of confiding her case to him in the near future. Indeed it was made quite obvious to him that the two or three hours between dinner and bed contained an amount of unhappiness, which was really pitiable, so many people had not succeeded in making friends.

It was settled that the dance was to be on Friday, one week after the engagement, and at dinner Hewet declared himself satisfied.

"They're all coming!" he told Hirst. "Pepper!" he called, seeing William Pepper slip past in the wake of the soup with a pamphlet beneath his arm, "We're counting on you to open the ball."

"You will certainly put sleep out of the question," Pepper returned.

"You are to take the floor with Miss Allan," Hewet continued, consulting a sheet of pencilled notes.

Pepper stopped and began a discourse upon round dances, country dances, morris dances, and quadrilles, all of which are entirely superior to the bastard waltz and spurious polka which have ousted them most unjustly in contemporary popularity—when the waiters gently pushed him on to his table in the corner.

The dining-room at this moment had a certain fantastic resemblance to a farmyard scattered with grain on which bright pigeons kept descending. Almost all the ladies wore dresses which they had not yet displayed, and their hair rose in waves and scrolls so as to appear like carved wood in Gothic churches rather than hair. The dinner was shorter and less formal than usual, even the waiters seeming to be affected with the general excitement. Ten minutes before the clock struck nine the committee made a tour through the ballroom. The hall, when emptied of its furniture, brilliantly lit, adorned with flowers whose scent tinged the air, presented a wonderful appearance of ethereal gaiety.

"It's like a starlit sky on an absolutely cloudless night," Hewet murmured, looking about him, at the airy empty room.

"A heavenly floor, anyhow," Evelyn added, taking a run and sliding two or three feet along.

"What about those curtains?" asked Hirst. The crimson curtains were drawn across the long windows. "It's a perfect night outside."

"Yes, but curtains inspire confidence," Miss Allan decided. "When the ball is in full swing it will be time to draw them. We might even open the windows a little. . . . If we do it now elderly people will imagine there are draughts.

Her wisdom had come to be recognised, and held in respect. Meanwhile as they stood talking, the musicians were unwrapping their instruments, and the violin was repeating again and again a note struck upon the piano. Everything was ready to begin.

After a few minutes' pause, the father, the daughter, and the son-in-law who played the horn flourished with one accord. Like the rats who followed the piper, heads instantly appeared in the doorway. There was another flourish; and then the trio dashed spontaneously into the triumphant swing of the waltz. It was as though the room were instantly flooded with water. After a moment's hesitation first one couple, then another, leapt into mid-stream, and went round and round in the eddies. The rhythmic swish of the dancers sounded like a swirling pool. By degrees the room grew perceptibly hotter. The smell of kid gloves mingled with the strong scent of flowers. The eddies seemed to circle faster and faster, until the music wrought itself into a crash, ceased, and the circles were smashed into little separate bits. The couples struck off in different directions, leaving a thin row of elderly people stuck fast to the walls, and here and there a piece of trimming or a handkerchief or a flower lay upon the floor. There was a pause, and then the music started again, the eddies whirled, the couples circled round in them, until there was a crash, and the circles were broken up into separate bits.

When this had happened about five times, Hirst, who leant against a window-frame, like some singular gargoyle, perceived that Helen Ambrose and Rachel stood in the doorway. The crowd was such that they could not move, but he recognised them by a piece of Helen's shoulder and a glimpse of Rachel's head turning round. He made his way to them; they greeted him with relief.

"We are suffering the tortures of the damned," said Helen.

"This is my idea of hell," said Rachel.

Her eyes were bright and she looked bewildered.

Hewet and Miss Allan, who had been waltzing somewhat laboriously, paused and greeted the newcomers.

"This *is* nice," said Hewet. "But where is Mr. Ambrose?"

"Pindar," said Helen. "May a married woman who was forty in October dance? I can't stand still." She seemed to fade into Hewet, and they both dissolved in the crowd.

"We must follow suit," said Hirst to Rachel, and he took her resolutely by the elbow. Rachel, without being expert, danced well, because of a good ear for rhythm, but Hirst had no taste for music, and a few dancing lessons at Cambridge had only put him into possession of the anatomy of a waltz, without imparting any of its spirit. A single turn proved to them that their methods were incompatible; instead of fitting into each other their bones seemed to jut out in angles making smooth turning an impossibility, and cutting, moreover, into the circular progress of the other dancers.

"Shall we stop?" said Hirst. Rachel gathered from his expression that he was annoyed.

They staggered to seats in the corner, from which they had a view of the room. It was still surging, in waves of blue and yellow, striped by the black evening-clothes of the gentlemen.

"An amazing spectacle," Hirst remarked. "Do you dance much in London?" They were both breathing fast, and both a little excited, though each was determined not to show any excitement at all.

"Scarcely ever. Do you?"

"My people give a dance every Christmas."

"This isn't half a bad floor," Rachel said. Hirst did not attempt to answer her platitude. He sat quite silent, staring at the dancers. After three minutes the silence became so intolerable to Rachel that she was goaded to advance another commonplace about the beauty of the night. Hirst interrupted her ruthlessly.

"Was that all nonsense what you said the other day about being a Christian and having no education?" he asked.

"It was practically true," she replied. "But I also play the piano very well," she said, "better, I expect than any one in this room. You are the most distinguished man in England, aren't you?" she asked shyly.

"One of the three," he corrected.

Helen whirling past here tossed a fan into Rachel's lap.

"She is very beautiful," Hirst remarked.

They were again silent. Rachel was wondering whether he thought her also nice-looking; St. John was considering the immense difficulty of talking to girls who had no experience of life. Rachel had obviously never thought or felt or seen anything, and she might be intelligent or she might be just like all the rest. But Hewet's taunt rankled in his mind—"you don't know how to get on with women," and he was determined to profit by this opportunity. Her evening-clothes bestowed on her just that degree of unreality and distinction which made it romantic to speak to her, and stirred a desire to talk, which irritated him because he did not know how to begin. He glanced at her, and she seemed to him very remote and inexplicable, very young and chaste. He drew a sigh, and began.

"About books now. What have you read? Just Shakespeare and the Bible?"

"I haven't read many classics," Rachel stated. She was slightly annoyed by his jaunty and rather unnatural manner, while his masculine acquirements induced her to take a very modest view of her own power.

"D'you mean to tell me you've reached the age of twenty-four without reading Gibbon?" he demanded.

"Yes, I have," she answered.

"Mon Dieu!" he exclaimed, throwing out his hands. "You must begin tomorrow. I shall send you my copy. What I want to know is—" he looked at her critically. "You see, the problem is, can one really talk to you? Have you got a mind, or are you like the rest of your sex? You seem to me absurdly young compared with men of your age."

Rachel looked at him but said nothing.

"About Gibbon," he continued. "D'you think you'll be able to appreciate him? He's the test, of course. It's awfully difficult to tell about women," he continued, "how much, I mean, is due to lack of training, and how much is native incapacity. I don't see myself why you shouldn't understand—only I suppose you've led an absurd life until now—you've just walked in a crocodile, I suppose, with your hair down your back."

The music was again beginning. Hirst's eye wandered about the room in search of Mrs. Ambrose. With the best will in the world he was conscious that they were not getting on well together.

"I'd like awfully to lend you books," he said, buttoning his gloves, and rising from his seat. "We shall meet again. "I'm going to leave you now."

He got up and left her.

Rachel looked round. She felt herself surrounded, like a child at a party, by the faces of strangers all hostile to her, with hooked noses and sneering, indifferent eyes. She was by a window, she pushed it open with a jerk. She stepped out into the garden. Her eyes swam with tears of rage.

"Damn that man!" she exclaimed, having acquired some of Helen's words. "Damn his insolence!"

She stood in the middle of the pale square of light which the window she had opened threw upon the grass. The forms of great black trees rose massively in front of her. She stood still, looking at them, shivering slightly with anger and excitement. She heard the trampling and swinging of the dancers behind her, and the rhythmic sway of the waltz music.

"There are trees," she said aloud. Would the trees make up for St. John Hirst? She would be a Persian princess far from civilisation, riding her horse upon the mountains alone, and making her women sing to her in the evening, far from all this, from the strife and men and women—a form came out of the shadow; a little red light burnt high up in its blackness.

"Miss Vinrace, is it?" said Hewet, peering at her. "You were dancing with Hirst?"

"He's made me furious!" she cried vehemently. "No one's any right to be insolent!"

"Insolent?" Hewet repeated, taking his cigar from his mouth in surprise. "Hirst—insolent?"

"It's insolent to—" said Rachel, and stopped. She did not know exactly why she had been made so angry. With a great effort she pulled herself together.

"Oh, well," she added, the vision of Helen and her mockery before her, "I dare say I'm a fool." She made as though she were going back into the ballroom, but Hewet stopped her.

"Please explain to me," he said. "I feel sure Hirst didn't mean to hurt you."

When Rachel tried to explain, she found it very difficult. She could not say that she found the vision of herself walking in a crocodile with her hair down her back peculiarly unjust and horrible, nor could she explain why Hirst's assumption of the superiority of his nature and experience had seemed to her not only galling but terrible—as if a gate had clanged in her face. Pacing up and down the terrace beside Hewet she said bitterly:

"It's no good; we should live separate; we cannot understand each other; we only bring out what's worst."

Hewet brushed aside her generalisation as to the natures of the two sexes, for such generalisations bored him and seemed to him generally untrue. But, knowing Hirst, he guessed fairly accurately what had happened, and, though secretly much amused, was determined that Rachel should not store the incident away in her mind to take its place in the view she had of life.

"Now you'll hate him," he said, "which is wrong. Poor old Hirst—he can't help his method. And really, Miss Vinrace, he was doing his best; he was paying you a compliment—he was trying—he was trying——" he could not finish for the laughter that overcame him.

Rachel veered round suddenly and laughed out too. She saw that there was something ridiculous about Hirst, and perhaps about herself.

"It's his way of making friends, I suppose," she laughed. "Well—I shall do my part. I shall begin—'Ugly in body, repulsive in mind as you are, Mr. Hirst——'"

"Hear, hear!" cried Hewet. "That's the way to treat him. You see, Miss Vinrace, you must make allowances for Hirst. He's lived all his life in front of a looking-glass, so to speak, in a beautiful panelled room, hung with Japanese prints and lovely old chairs and tables, just one splash of colour, you know, in the right place—between the windows I think it is—and there he sits hour after hour with his toes on the fender, talking about philosophy and God and his liver and his heart and the hearts of his friends. They're all broken. You can't expect him to be at his best in a ballroom. He wants a cosy, smoky, masculine place, where he can stretch his legs out, and only speak when he's got something to say. For myself, I find it rather dreary. But I do respect it. They're all so much in earnest. They do take the serious things very seriously."

The description of Hirst's way of life interested Rachel so much that she almost forgot her private grudge against him, and her respect revived.

"They are really very clever then?" she asked.

"Of course they are. So far as brains go I think it's true what he said the other day; they're the cleverest people in England. But—you ought to take him in hand," he added. "There's a great deal more in him than's ever been got at. He wants some one to laugh at him. . . . The idea of Hirst telling you that you've had no experiences! Poor old Hirst!"

They had been pacing up and down the terrace while they talked, and now one by one the dark windows were uncurtained by an invisible hand, and panes of light fell regularly at equal intervals upon the grass. They stopped to look in at the drawing-room, and perceived Mr. Pepper writing alone at a table.

"There's Pepper writing to his aunt," said Hewet. "She must be a very remarkable old lady, eighty-five he tells me, and he takes her for walking tours in the New Forest. . . . Pepper!" he cried, rapping on the window. "Go and do your duty. Miss Allan expects you."

When they came to the windows of the ballroom, the swing of the dancers and the lilt of the music was irresistible.

"Shall we?" said Hewet, and they clasped hands and swept off magnificently into the great swirling pool. Although this was only the second time they had met, the first time they had seen a man and woman kissing each other, and the second time Mr. Hewet had found that a young woman angry is very like a child. So that when they joined hands in the dance they felt more at their ease than is usual.

It was midnight and the dance was now at its height. Servants were peeping in at the windows; the garden was sprinkled with the white shapes of couples sitting out. Mrs. Thornbury and Mrs. Elliot sat side by side under a palm tree, holding fans, handkerchiefs, and brooches deposited in their laps by flushed maidens. Occasionally they exchanged comments.

"Miss Warrington *does* look happy," said Mrs. Elliot; they both smiled; they both sighed.

"He has a great deal of character," said Mrs. Thornbury, alluding to Arthur.

"And character is what one wants," said Mrs. Elliot. "Now that young man is *clever* enough," she added, nodding at Hirst, who came past with Miss Allan on his arm.

"He does not look strong," said Mrs. Thornbury. "His complexion is not good.—Shall I tear it off?" she asked, for Rachel had stopped, conscious of a long strip trailing behind her.

"I hope you are enjoying yourselves?" Hewet asked the ladies.

"This is a very familiar position for me!" smiled Mrs. Thornbury. "I have brought out five daughters—and they all loved dancing! You love it too, Miss Vinrace?" she asked, looking at Rachel with maternal eyes. "I know I did when I was your age. How I used to beg my mother to let me stay—and now I sympathise with the poor mothers—but I sympathise with the daughters too!"

She smiled sympathetically, and at the same time rather keenly, at Rachel.

"They seem to find a great deal to say to each other," said Mrs. Elliot, looking significantly at the backs of the couple as they turned away. "Did you notice at the picnic? He was the only person who could make her utter."

"Her father is a very interesting man," said Mrs. Thornbury. "He has one of the largest shipping businesses in Hull. He made a very able reply, you remember, to Mr. Asquith at the last election. It is so interesting to find that a man of his experience is a strong Protectionist."

She would have liked to discuss politics, which interested her more than personalities, but Mrs. Elliot would only talk about the Empire in a less abstract form.

"I hear there are dreadful accounts from England about the rats," she said. "A sister-in-law, who lives at Norwich, tells me it has been quite unsafe to order poultry. The plague—you see. It attacks the rats, and through them other creatures."

"And the local authorities are not taking proper steps?" asked Mrs. Thornbury.

"That she does not say. But she describes the attitude of the educated people—who should know better—as callous in the extreme. Of course, my sister-in-law is one of those active modern women, who always takes things up, you know—the kind of woman one admires, though one does not feel, at least I do not feel—but then she has a constitution of iron."

Mrs. Elliot, brought back to the consideration of her own delicacy, here sighed.

"A very animated face," said Mrs. Thornbury, looking at Evelyn M. who had stopped near them to pin tight a scarlet flower at her breast. It would not stay, and, with a spirited gesture of impatience, she thrust it into her partner's button-hole. He was a tall melancholy youth, who received the gift as a knight might receive his lady's token.

"Very trying to the eyes," was Mrs. Eliot's next remark, after watching the yellow whirl in which so few of the whirlers had either name or character for her, for a few minutes. Bursting out of the crowd, Helen approached them, and took a vacant chair.

"May I sit by you?" she said, smiling and breathing fast. "I suppose I ought to be ashamed of myself," she went on, sitting down, "at my age."

Her beauty, now that she was flushed and animated, was more expansive than usual, and both the ladies felt the same desire to touch her.

"I *am* enjoying myself," she panted. "Movement—isn't it amazing?"

"I have always heard that nothing comes up to dancing if one is a good dancer," said Mrs. Thornbury, looking at her with a smile.

Helen swayed slightly as if she sat on wires.

"I could dance for ever!" she said. "They ought to let themselves go more!" she exclaimed. "They ought to leap and swing. Look! How they mince!"

"Have you seen those wonderful Russian dancers?" began Mrs. Elliot. But Helen saw her partner coming and rose as the moon rises. She was half round the room before they took their eyes off her, for they could not help admiring her, although they thought it a little odd that a woman of her age should enjoy dancing.

Directly Helen was left alone for a minute she was joined by St. John Hirst, who had been watching for an opportunity.

"Should you mind sitting out with me?" he asked. "I'm quite incapable of dancing." He piloted Helen to a corner which was supplied with two arm-chairs, and thus enjoyed the advantage of semi-privacy. They sat down, and for a few minutes Helen was too much under the influence of dancing to speak.

"Astonishing!" she exclaimed at last. "What sort of shape can she think her body is?" This remark was called forth by a lady who came past them, waddling rather than walking, and leaning on the arm of a stout man with globular green eyes set in a fat white face. Some support was necessary, for she was very stout, and so compressed that the upper part of her body hung considerably in advance of her feet, which could only trip in tiny steps, owing to the tightness of the skirt round her ankles. The dress itself consisted of a small piece of shiny yellow satin, adorned here and there indiscriminately with round shields of blue and green beads made to imitate hues of a peacock's breast. On the summit of a frothy castle of hair a purple plume stood erect, while her short neck was encircled by a black velvet ribbon knobbed with gems, and golden bracelets were tightly wedged into the flesh of her fat gloved arms. She had the face of an impertinent but jolly little pig, mottled red under a dusting of powder.

St. John could not join in Helen's laughter.

"It makes me sick," he declared. "The whole thing makes me sick. . . . Consider the minds of those people—their feelings. Don't you agree?"

"I always make a vow never to go to another party of any description," Helen replied, "and I always break it."

She leant back in her chair and looked laughingly at the young man. She could see that he was genuinely cross, if at the same time slightly excited.

"However," he said, resuming his jaunty tone, "I suppose one must just make up one's mind to it."

"To what?"

"There never will be more than five people in the world worth talking to."

Slowly the flush and sparkle in Helen's face died away, and she looked as quiet and as observant as usual.

"Five people?" she remarked. "I should say there were more than five."

"You've been very fortunate, then," said Hirst. "Or perhaps I've been very unfortunate." He became silent.

"Should you say I was a difficult kind of person to get on with?" he asked sharply.

"Most clever people are when they're young," Helen replied.

"And of course I am—immensely clever," said Hirst. "I'm infinitely cleverer than Hewet. It's quite possible," he continued in his curiously impersonal manner, "that I'm going to be one of the people who really matter. That's utterly different from being clever, though one can't expect one's family to see it," he added bitterly.

Helen thought herself justified in asking, "Do you find your family difficult to get on with?"

"Intolerable. . . . They want me to be a peer and a privy councillor. I've come out here partly in order to settle the matter. It's got to be settled.

Either I must go to the bar, or I must stay on in Cambridge. Of course, there are obvious drawbacks to each, but the arguments certainly do seem to me in favour of Cambridge. This kind of thing!" he waved his hand at the crowded ballroom. "Repulsive. I'm conscious of great powers of affection too. I'm not susceptible, of course, in the way Hewet is. I'm very fond of a few people. I think, for example, that there's something to be said for my mother, though she is in many ways so deplorable. . . . At Cambridge, of course, I should inevitably become the most important man in the place, but there are other reasons why I dread Cambridge—" he ceased.

"Are you finding me a dreadful bore?" he asked. He changed curiously from a friend confiding in a friend to a conventional young man at a party.

"Not in the least," said Helen. "I like it very much."

"You can't think," he exclaimed, speaking almost with emotion, "what a difference it makes finding someone to talk to! Directly I saw you I felt you might possibly understand me. I'm very fond of Hewet, but he hasn't the remotest idea what I'm like. You're the only woman I've ever met who seems to have the faintest conception of what I mean when I say a thing."

The next dance was beginning; it was the Barcarolle out of Hoffman, which made Helen beat her toe in time to it; but she felt that after such a compliment it was impossible to get up and go, and, besides being amused, she was really flattered, and the honesty of his conceit attracted her. She suspected that he was not happy, and was sufficiently feminine to wish to receive confidences.

"I'm very old," she sighed.

"The odd thing is that I don't find you old at all," he replied. "I feel as though we were exactly the same age. Moreover–" here he hesitated, but took courage from a glance at her face, "I feel as if I could talk quite plainly to you as one does to a man–about the relations between the sexes, about . . . and . . ."

In spite of his certainty a slight redness came into his face as he spoke the last two words.

She reassured him at once by the laugh with which she exclaimed, "I should hope so!"

He looked at her with real cordiality, and the lines which were drawn about his nose and lips slackened for the first time.

"Thank God!" he exclaimed. "Now we can behave like civilised human beings."

Certainly a barrier which usually stands fast had fallen, and it was possible to speak of matters which are generally only alluded to between men and women when doctors are present, or the shadow of death. In five minutes he was telling her the history of his life. It was long, for it was full of extremely elaborate incidents, which led on to a discussion of the principles on which morality is founded, and thus to several very interesting matters, which even in this ballroom had to be discussed in a whisper, lest one of the pouter pigeon ladies or resplendent merchants should overhear them, and proceed to demand that they should leave the place. When they had come to an end, or, to speak more accurately, when Helen intimated by a slight slackening of her attention that they had sat there long enough, Hirst rose, exclaiming, "So there's no reason whatever for all this mystery!"

"None, except that we are English people," she answered. She took his arm and they crossed the ball-room, making their way with difficulty between the spinning couples, who were now perceptibly dishevelled, and certainly to a critical eye by no means lovely in their shapes. The excitement of undertaking a friendship and the length of their talk, made them hungry, and they went in search of food to the dining-room, which was now full of people eating at little separate tables. In the doorway they met Rachel, going up to dance again with Arthur Venning. She was flushed and looked very happy, and Helen was struck by the fact that in this mood she was certainly more attractive than the generality of young women. She had never noticed it so clearly before.

"Enjoying yourself?" she asked, as they stopped for a second.

"Miss Vinrace," Arthur answered for her, "has just made a confession; she'd no idea that dances could be so delightful."

"Yes!" Rachel exclaimed. "I've changed my view of life completely!"

"You don't say so!" Helen mocked. They passed on.

"That's typical of Rachel," she said. "She changes her view of life about every other day. D'you know, I believe you're just the person I want," she said, as they sat down, "to help me complete her education? She's been brought up practically in a nunnery. Her father's too absurd. I've been doing what I can—but I'm too old, and I'm a woman. Why shouldn't you talk to her—explain things to her—talk to her, I mean, as you talk to me?"

"I have made one attempt already this evening," said St. John. "I rather doubt that it was successful. She seems to me so very young and inexperienced. I have promised to lend her Gibbon."

"It's not Gibbon exactly," Helen pondered. "It's the facts of life, I think—d'you see what I mean? What really goes on, what people feel, although they generally try to hide it? There's nothing to be frightened of. It's so much more beautiful than the pretences—always more interesting—always better, I should say, than *that* kind of thing."

She nodded her head at a table near them, where two girls and two young men were chaffing each other very loudly, and carrying on an arch insinuating dialogue, sprinkled with endearments, about, it seemed, a pair of stockings or a pair of legs. One of the girls was flirting a fan and pretending to be shocked, and the sight was very unpleasant, partly because it was obvious that the girls were secretly hostile to each other.

"In my old age, however," Helen sighed, "I'm coming to think that it doesn't much matter in the long run what one does: people always go their own way—nothing will ever influence them." She nodded her head at the supper party.

But St. John did not agree. He said that he thought one could really make a great deal of difference by one's point of view, books and so on, and added that few things at the present time mattered more than the enlightenment of women. He sometimes thought that almost everything was due to education.

In the ballroom, meanwhile, the dancers were being formed into squares for the lancers. Arthur and Rachel, Susan and Hewet, Miss Allan and Hughling Elliot found themselves together.

Miss Allan looked at her watch.

"Half-past one," she stated. "And I have to despatch Alexander Pope tomorrow."

"Pope!" snorted Mr. Elliot. "Who reads Pope, I should like to know? And as for reading about him— No, no, Miss Allan; be persuaded you will benefit the world much more by dancing than by writing." It was one of Mr. Elliot's affectations that nothing in the world could compare with the delights of dancing—nothing in the world was so tedious as literature. Thus he sought pathetically enough to ingratiate himself with the young, and to prove to them beyond a doubt that though married to a ninny of a wife, and rather pale and bent and careworn by his weight of learning, he was as much alive as the youngest of them all.

"It's a question of bread and butter," said Miss Allan calmly. "However, they seem to expect me." She took up her position and pointed a square black toe.

"Mr. Hewet, you bow to me." It was evident at once that Miss Allan was the only one of them who had a thoroughly sound knowledge of the figures of the dance.

After the lancers there was a waltz; after the waltz a polka; and then a terrible thing happened; the music, which had been sounding regularly with five-minute pauses, stopped suddenly. The lady with the great dark eyes began to swathe her violin in silk, and the gentleman placed his horn carefully in its case. They were surrounded by couples imploring them in English, in French, in Spanish, of one more dance, one only; it was still early. But the old man at the piano merely exhibited his watch and shook his head. He turned up the collar of his coat and produced a red silk muffler, which completely dashed his festive appearance. Strange as it seemed, the musicians were pale and heavy-eyed; they looked bored and prosaic, as if the summit of their desire was cold meat and beer, succeeded immediately by bed.

Rachel was one of those who had begged them to continue. When they refused she began turning over the sheets of dance music which lay upon the piano. The pieces were generally bound in coloured covers, with pictures on them of romantic scenes—gondoliers astride on the crescent of the moon, nuns peering through the bars of a convent window, or young women with their hair down pointing a gun at the stars. She remembered that the general effect of the music to which they had danced so gaily was one of passionate regret for dead love and the innocent years of youth; dreadful sorrows had always separated the dancers from their past happiness.

"No wonder they get sick of playing stuff like this," she remarked reading a bar or two; "they're really hymn tunes, played very fast, with bits out of Wagner and Beethoven."

"Do you play? Would you play? Anything, so long as we can dance to it!" From all sides her gift for playing the piano was insisted upon, and she had to consent. As very soon she had played the only pieces of dance music she could remember, she went on to play an air from a sonata by Mozart.

"But that's not a dance," said some one pausing by the piano.

"It is," she replied, emphatically nodding her head. "Invent the steps." Sure of her melody she marked the rhythm boldly so as to simplify the way. Helen caught the idea; seized Miss Allan by the arm, and whirled round the room, now curtseying, now spinning round, now tripping this way and that like a child skipping through a meadow.

"This is the dance for people who don't know how to dance!" she cried. The tune changed to a minuet; St. John hopped with incredible swiftness first on his left leg, then on his right; the tune flowed melodiously; Hewet, swaying his arms and holding out the tails of his coat, swam down the room in imitation of the voluptuous dreamy dance of an Indian maiden dancing before her Rajah. The tune marched; and Miss Allen advanced with skirts extended and bowed profoundly to the engaged pair. Once their feet fell in with the rhythm they showed a complete lack of selfconsciousness. From Mozart Rachel passed without stopping to old English hunting songs, carols, and hymn tunes, for, as she had observed, any good tune, with a little management, became a tune one could dance to. By degrees every person in the room was tripping and turning in pairs or alone. Mr. Pepper executed an ingenious pointed step derived from figure-skating, for which he once held some local championship; while Mrs. Thornbury tried to recall an old country dance which she had seen danced by her father's tenants in Dorsetshire in the old days. As for Mr. and Mrs. Elliot, they gallopaded round and round the room with such impetuosity that the other dancers shivered at their approach. Some people were heard to criticise the performance as a romp; to others it was the most enjoyable part of the evening.

"Now for the great round dance!" Hewet shouted. Instantly a gigantic circle was formed, the dancers holding hands and shouting out, "D'you ken John Peel," as they swung faster and faster and faster, until the strain was too great, and one link of the chain—Mrs. Thornbury—gave way, and the rest went flying across the room in all directions, to land upon the floor or the chairs or in each other's arms as seemed most convenient.

Rising from these positions, breathless and unkempt, it struck them for the first time that the electric lights pricked the air very vainly, and instinctively a great many eyes turned to the windows. Yes—there was the dawn. While they had been dancing the night had passed, and it had come. Outside, the mountains showed very pure and remote; the dew was sparkling on the grass, and the sky was flushed with blue, save for the pale yellows and pinks in the East. The dancers came crowding to the windows, pushed them open, and here and there ventured a foot upon the grass.

"How silly the poor old lights look!" said Evelyn M. in a curiously subdued tone of voice. "And ourselves; it isn't becoming." It was true; the untidy hair, and the green and yellow gems, which had seemed so festive half an hour ago, now looked cheap and slovenly. The complexions of the elder ladies suffered terribly, and, as if conscious that a cold eye had been turned upon them, they began to say good-night and to make their way up to bed.

Rachel, though robbed of her audience, had gone on playing to herself. From John Peel she passed to Bach, who was at this time the subject of her intense enthusiasm, and one by one some of the younger dancers came in from the garden and sat upon the deserted gilt chairs round the piano, the room being now so clear that they turned out the lights. As they sat and listened, their nerves were quieted; the heat and soreness of their lips, the result of incessant talking and laughing, was smoothed away. They sat very still as if they saw a building with spaces and columns succeeding each other rising in the empty space. Then they began to see themselves and their lives, and the whole of human life advancing very nobly under the direction of the music. They felt themselves ennobled, and when Rachel stopped playing they desired nothing but sleep.

Susan rose. "I think this has been the happiest night of my life!" she exclaimed. "I do adore music," she said, as she thanked Rachel. "It just seems to say all the things one can't say oneself." She gave a nervous little laugh and looked from one to another with great benignity, as though she would like to say something but could not find the words in which to express it. "Every one's been so kind—so very kind," she said. Then she too went to bed.

The party having ended in the very abrupt way in which parties do end, Helen and Rachel stood by the door with their cloaks on, looking for a carriage.

"I suppose you realise that there are no carriages left?" said St. John, who had been out to look. "You must sleep here."

"Oh, no," said Helen; "we shall walk."

"May we come too?" Hewet asked. "We can't go to bed. Imagine lying among bolsters and looking at one's washstand on a morning like this—Is that where you live?" They had begun to walk down the avenue, and he turned and pointed at the white and green villa on the hillside, which seemed to have its eyes shut.

"That's not a light burning, is it?" Helen asked anxiously.

"It's the sun," said St. John. The upper windows had each a spot of gold on them.

"I was afraid it was my husband, still reading Greek," she said. "All this time he's been editing *Pindar*."

They passed through the town and turned up the steep road, which was perfectly clear, though still unbordered by shadows. Partly because they were tired, and partly because the early light subdued them, they scarcely spoke, but breathed in the delicious fresh air, which seemed to belong to a different state of life from the air at midday. When they came to the high yellow wall, where the lane turned off from the road, Helen was for dismissing the two young men.

"You've come far enough," she said. "Go back to bed."

But they seemed unwilling to move.

"Let's sit down a moment," said Hewet. He spread his coat on the ground. "Let's sit down and consider." They sat down and looked out over the bay; it was very still, the sea was rippling faintly, and lines of green and blue were beginning to stripe it. There were no sailing boats as yet, but a steamer was anchored in the bay, looking very ghostly in the mist; it gave one unearthly cry, and then all was silent.

Rachel occupied herself in collecting one grey stone after another and building them into a little cairn; she did it very quietly and carefully.

"And so you've changed your view of life, Rachel?" said Helen.

Rachel added another stone and yawned. "I don't remember," she said, "I feel like a fish at the bottom of the sea." She yawned again. None of these people possessed any power to frighten her out here in the dawn, and she felt perfectly familiar even with Mr. Hirst.

"My brain, on the contrary," said Hirst, "is in a condition of abnormal activity." He sat in his favourite position with his arms binding his legs together and his chin resting on the top of his knees. "I see through everything—absolutely everything. Life has no more mysteries for me." He spoke with conviction, but did not appear to wish for an answer. Near though they sat, and familiar though they felt, they seemed mere shadows to each other.

"And all those people down there going to sleep," Hewet began dreamily, "thinking such different things—Miss Warrington, I suppose, is now on her knees; the Elliots are a little startled, it's not often *they* get out of breath, and they want to get to sleep as quickly as possible; then there's the poor lean young man who danced all night with Evelyn; he's putting his flower in water and asking himself, 'Is this love?'—and poor old Perrott, I daresay, can't get to sleep at all, and is reading his favourite Greek book to console himself—and the others—no, Hirst," he wound up, "I don't find it simple at all."

"I have a key," said Hirst cryptically. His chin was still upon his knees and his eyes fixed in front of him.

A silence followed. Then Helen rose and bade them good-night. "But," she said, "remember that you've got to come and see us."

They waved good-night and parted, but the two young men did not go back to the hotel; they went for a walk, during which they scarcely spoke, and never mentioned the names of the two women, who were, to a considerable extent, the subject of their thoughts. They did not wish to share their impressions. They returned to the hotel in time for breakfast.

13

There were many rooms in the villa, but one room which possessed a character of its own because the door was always shut, and no sound of music or laughter issued from it. Every one in the house was vaguely conscious that something went on behind that door, and without in the least knowing what it was, were influenced in their own thoughts by the knowledge that if the passed it the door would be shut, and if they made a noise Mr. Ambrose inside would be disturbed. Certain acts therefore possessed merit, and others were bad, so that life became more harmonious and less disconnected than it would have been had Mr. Ambrose given up editing *Pindar*, and taken to a nomad existence, in and out of every room in the house. As it was, every one was conscious that by observing certain rules, such as punctuality and quiet, by cooking well, and performing other small duties, one ode after another was satisfactorily restored to the world, and they shared the continuity of the scholar's life. Unfortunately, as age puts one barrier between human beings, and learning another, and sex a third, Mr. Ambrose in his study was some thousand miles distant from the nearest human being, who in this household was inevitably a woman. He sat hour after hour among white-leaved books, alone like an idol in an empty church, still except for the passage of his hand from one side of the sheet to another, silent save for an occasional choke, which drove him to extend his pipe a moment in the air. As he worked his way further and further into the heart of the poet, his chair became more and more deeply encircled by books, which lay open on the floor, and could only be crossed by a careful process of stepping, so delicate that his visitors generally stopped and addressed him from the outskirts.

On the morning after the dance, however, Rachel came into her uncle's room and hailed him twice, "Uncle Ridley," before he paid her any attention.

At length he looked over his spectacles.

"Well?" he asked.

"I want a book," she replied. "Gibbon's *History of the Roman Empire*. May I have it?"

She watched the lines on her uncle's face gradually rearrange themselves at her question. It had been smooth as a mask before she spoke.

"Please say that again," said her uncle, either because he had not heard or because he had not understood.

She repeated the same words and reddened slightly as she did so.

"Gibbon! What on earth d'you want him for?" he enquired.

"Somebody advised me to read it," Rachel stammered.

"But I don't travel about with a miscellaneous collection of eighteenth-century historians!" her uncle exclaimed. "Gibbon! Ten big volumes at least."

Rachel said that she was sorry to interrupt, and was turning to go.

"Stop!" cried her uncle. He put down his pipe, placed his book on one side, and rose and led her slowly round the room, holding her by the arm. "Plato," he said, laying one finger on the first of a row of small dark books, "and Jorrocks next door, which is wrong. Sophocles, Swift. You don't care for German commentators, I presume. French, then. You read French? You should read Balzac. Then we come to Wordsworth and Coleridge, Pope, Johnson, Addison, Wordsworth, Shelley, Keats. One thing leads to another. Why is Marlowe here? Mrs. Chailey, I presume. But what's the use of reading if you don't read Greek? After all, if you read Greek, you need never read anything else, pure waste of time—pure waste of time," thus speaking half to himself, with quick movements of his hands; they had come round again to the circle of books on the floor, and their progress was stopped.

"Well," he demanded, "which shall it be?"

"Balzac," said Rachel, "or have you the *Speech on the American Revolution*, Uncle Ridley?"

"*The Speech on the American Revolution?*" he asked. He looked at her very keenly again. "Another young man at the dance?"

"No. That was Mr. Dalloway," she confessed.

"Good Lord!" he flung back his head in recollection of Mr. Dalloway.

She chose for herself a volume at random, submitted it to her uncle, who, seeing that it was *La Cousine Bette*, bade her throw it away if she found it too horrible, and was about to leave him when he demanded whether she had enjoyed her dance?

He then wanted to know what people did at dances, seeing that he had only been to one thirty-five years ago, when nothing had seemed to him more meaningless and idiotic. Did they enjoy turning round and round to the screech of a fiddle? Did they talk, and say pretty things, and if so, why didn't they do it, under reasonable conditions? As for himself—he sighed and pointed at the signs of industry lying all about him, which, in spite of his sigh, filled his face with such satisfaction that his niece thought good to leave. On bestowing a kiss she was allowed to go, but not until she had bound herself to learn at any rate the Greek alphabet, and to return her French novel when done with, upon which something more suitable would be found for her.

As the rooms in which people live are apt to give off something of the same shock as their faces when seen for the first time, Rachel walked very slowly downstairs, lost in wonder at her uncle, and his books, and his neglect of dances, and his queer, utterly inexplicable, but apparently satisfactory view of life, when her eye was caught by a note with her name on it lying in the hall. The address was written in a small strong hand unknown to her, and the note, which had no beginning, ran—

> I send the first volume of Gibbon as I promised. Personally I find little to be said for the moderns, but I'm going to send you Wedekind when I've done him. Donne? Have you read Webster and all that set? I envy you reading them for the first time. Completely exhausted after last night. And you?

The flourish of initials which she took to be St. J. A. H., wound up the letter. She was very much flattered that Mr. Hirst should have remembered her, and fulfilled his promise so quickly.

There was still an hour to luncheon, and with Gibbon in one hand, and Balzac in the other she strolled out of the gate and down the little path of beaten mud between the olive trees on the slope of the hill. It was too hot for climbing hills, but along the valley there were trees and a grass path running by the river bed. In this land where the population was centred in the towns it was possible to lose sight of civilisation in a very short time, passing only an occasional farmhouse, where the women were handling red roots in the courtyard; or a little boy lying on his elbows on the hillside surrounded by a flock of black strong-smelling goats. Save for a thread of water at the bottom, the river was merely a deep channel of dry yellow stones. On the bank grew those trees which Helen had said it was worth the voyage out merely to see. April had burst their buds, and they bore large blossoms among their glossy green leaves with petals of a thick wax-like substance coloured an exquisite cream or pink or deep crimson. But filled with one of those unreasonable exultations which start generally from an unknown cause, and sweep whole countries and skies into their embrace, she walked without seeing. The night was encroaching upon the day. Her ears hummed with the tunes she had played the night before; she sang, and the singing made her walk faster and faster. She did not see distinctly where she was going, the trees and the landscape appearing only as masses of green and blue, with an occasional space of differently coloured sky. Faces of people she had seen last night came before her; she heard their voices; she stopped singing, and began saying things over again or saying things differently, or inventing things that might have been said. The constraint of being among strangers in a long silk dress made it unusually exciting to stride thus alone. Hewet, Hirst, Mr. Venning, Miss Allan, the music, the light, the dark trees in the garden, the dawn—as she walked they went surging round in her head, a tumultuous background from which the present moment, with its opportunity of doing exactly as she liked, sprung more wonderfully vivid even than the night before.

So she might have walked until she had lost all knowledge of her way, had it not been for the interruption of a tree, which, although it did not grow across her path, stopped her as effectively as if the branches had struck her in the face. It was an ordinary tree, but to her it appeared so strange that it might have been the only tree in the world. Dark was the trunk in the middle, and the branches sprang here and there, leaving jagged intervals of light between them as distinctly as if it had but that second risen from the ground. Having seen a sight that would last her for a lifetime, and for a lifetime would preserve that second, the tree once more sank into the ordinary ranks of trees, and she was able to seat herself in its shade and to pick the red flowers with the thin green leaves which were growing beneath it. She laid them side by side, flower to flower and stalk to stalk, caressing them for walking alone. Flowers and even pebbles in the earth had their own life and disposition, and brought back the feelings of a child to whom they were companions. Looking up, her eye was caught by the line of the mountains flying out energetically across the sky like the lash of a curling whip. She looked at the pale distant sky, and the high bare places on the mountain-tops lying exposed to the sun. When she sat down she had dropped her books on to the earth at her feet, and now she looked down on them lying there, so square in the grass, a tall stem bending over and tickling the smooth brown cover of Gibbon, while the mottled blue Balzac lay naked in the sun. With a feeling that to open and read would certainly be a surprising experience, she turned the historian's page and read that—

> His generals, in the early part of his reign, attempted the reduction of Aethiopia and Arabia Felix. They marched near a thousand miles to the south of the tropic; but the heat of the climate soon repelled the invaders and protected the unwarlike natives of those sequestered regions. . . . The northern countries of Europe scarcely deserved the expense and labour of conquest. The forests and morasses of Germany were filled with a hardy race of barbarians, who despised life when it was separated from freedom.

Never had any words been so vivid and so beautiful—Arabia Felix—Aethiopia. But those were not more noble than the others, hardy barbarians, forests, and morasses. They seemed to drive roads back to the very beginning of the world, on either side of which the populations of all times and countries stood in avenues, and by passing down them all knowledge would be hers, and the book of the world turned back to the very first page. Such was her excitement at the possibilities of knowledge now opening before her that she ceased to read, and a breeze turning the page, the covers of Gibbon gently ruffled and closed together. She then rose again and walked on. Slowly her mind became less confused and sought the origins of her exaltation, which were twofold and could be limited by an effort to the persons of Mr. Hirst and Mr. Hewet. Any clear analysis of them was impossible owing to the haze of wonder in which they were enveloped. She could not reason about them as about people whose feelings went by the same rule as her own did, and her mind dwelt on them with a kind of physical pleasure such as is caused by the contemplation of bright things hanging in the sun. From them all life seemed to radiate; the very words of books were steeped in radiance. She then became haunted by a suspicion which she was so reluctant to face that she welcomed a trip and stumble over the grass because thus her attention was dispersed, but in a second it had collected itself again. Unconsciously she had been walking faster and faster, her body trying to outrun her mind; but she was now on the summit of a little hillock of earth which rose above the river and displayed the valley. She was no longer able to juggle with several ideas, but must deal with the most persistent, and a kind of melancholy replaced her excitement. She sank down on to the earth clasping her knees together, and looking blankly in front of her. For some time she observed a great yellow butterfly, which was opening and closing its wings very slowly on a little flat stone.

"What is it to be in love?" she demanded, after a long silence; each word as it came into being seemed to shove itself out into an unknown sea. Hypnotised by the wings of the butterfly, and awed by the discovery of a terrible possibility in life, she sat for some time longer. When the butterfly flew away, she rose, and with her two books beneath her arm returned home again, much as a soldier prepared for battle.

14

The sun of that same day going down, dusk was saluted as usual at the hotel by an instantaneous sparkle of electric lights. The hours between dinner and bedtime were always difficult enough to kill, and the night after the dance they were further tarnished by the peevishness of dissipation. Certainly, in the opinion of Hirst and Hewet, who lay back in long arm-chairs in the middle of the hall, with their coffee-cups beside them, and their cigarettes in their hands, the evening was unusually dull, the women unusually badly dressed, the men unusually fatuous. Moreover, when the mail had been distributed half an hour ago there were no letters for either of the two young men. As every other person, practically, had received two or three plump letters from England, which they were now engaged in reading, this seemed hard, and prompted Hirst to make the caustic remark that the animals had been fed. Their silence, he said, reminded him of the silence in the lion-house when each beast holds a lump of raw meat in its paws. He went on, stimulated by this comparison, to liken some to hippopotamuses, some to canary birds, some to swine, some to parrots, and some to loathsome reptiles curled round the half-decayed bodies of sheep. The intermittent sounds—now a cough, now a horrible wheezing or throat-clearing, now a little patter of conversation—were just, he declared, what you hear if you stand in the lion-house when the bones are being mauled. But these comparisons did not rouse Hewet, who, after a careless glance round the room, fixed his eyes upon a thicket of native spears which were so ingeniously arranged as to run their points at you whichever way you approached them. He was clearly oblivious of his surroundings; whereupon Hirst, perceiving that Hewet's mind was a complete blank, fixed his attention more closely upon his fellow-creatures. He was too far from them, however, to hear what they were saying, but it pleased him to construct little theories about them from their gestures and appearance.

Mrs. Thornbury had received a great many letters. She was completely engrossed in them. When she had finished a page she handed it to her husband, or gave him the sense of what she was reading in a series of short quotations linked together by a sound at the back of her throat. "Evie writes that George has gone to Glasgow. 'He finds Mr. Chadbourne so nice to work with, and we hope to spend Christmas together, but I should not like to move Betty and Alfred any great distance (no, quite right), though it is difficult to imagine cold weather in this heat. . . . Eleanor and Roger drove over in the new trap. . . . Eleanor certainly looked more like herself than I've seen her since the winter. She has put Baby on three bottles now, which I'm sure is wise (I'm sure it is too), and so gets better nights. . . . My hair still falls out. I find it on the pillow! But I am cheered by hearing from Tottie Hall Green. . . . Muriel is in Torquay enjoying herself greatly at dances. She *is* going to show her black put after all.' . . . A line from Herbert—so busy, poor fellow! Ah! Margaret says, 'Poor old Mrs. Fairbank died on the eighth, quite suddenly in the conservatory, only a maid in the house, who hadn't the presence of mind to lift her up, which they think might have saved her, but the doctor says it might have come at any moment, and one can only feel thankful that it was in the house and not in the street (I should think so!). The pigeons have increased terribly, just as the rabbits did five years ago . . .'" While she read her husband kept nodding his head very slightly, but very steadily in sign of approval.

Near by, Miss Allan was reading her letters too. They were not altogether pleasant, as could be seen from the slight rigidity which came over her large fine face as she finished reading them and replaced them neatly in their envelopes. The lines of care and responsibility on her face made her resemble an elderly man rather than a woman. The letters brought her news of the failure of last year's fruit crop in New Zealand, which was a serious matter, for Hubert, her only brother, made his living on a fruit farm, and if it failed again, of course, he would throw up his place, come back to England, and what were they to do with him this time? The journey out here, which meant the loss of a term's work, became an extravagance and not the just and wonderful holiday due to her after fifteen years of punctual lecturing and correcting essays upon English literature. Emily, her sister, who was a teacher also, wrote: "We ought to be prepared, though I have no doubt Hubert will be more reasonable this time." And then went on in her sensible way to say that she was enjoying a very jolly time in the Lakes. "They are looking exceedingly pretty just now. I have seldom seen the trees so forward at this time of year. We have taken our lunch out several days. Old Alice is as young as ever, and asks after every one affectionately. The days pass very quickly, and term will soon be here. Political prospects *not* good, I think privately, but do not like to damp Ellen's enthusiasm. Lloyd George has taken the Bill up, but so have many before now, and we are where we are; but trust to find myself mistaken. Anyhow, we have our work cut out for us. . . . Surely Meredith lacks the *human* note one likes in W. W.?" she concluded, and went on to discuss some questions of English literature which Miss Allan had raised in her last letter.

At a little distance from Miss Allan, on a seat shaded and made semi-private by a thick clump of palm trees, Arthur and Susan were reading each other's letters. The big slashing manuscripts of hockey-playing young women in Wiltshire lay on Arthur's knee, while Susan deciphered tight little legal hands which rarely filled more than a page, and always conveyed the same impression of jocular and breezy goodwill.

"I do hope Mr. Hutchinson will like me, Arthur," she said, looking up.

"Who's your loving Flo?" asked Arthur.

"Flo Graves—the girl I told you about, who was engaged to that dreadful Mr. Vincent," said Susan. "Is Mr. Hutchinson married?" she asked.

Already her mind was busy with benevolent plans for her friends, or rather with one magnificent plan—which was simple too—they were all to get married—at once—directly she got back. Marriage, marriage that was the right thing, the only thing, the solution required by every one she knew, and a great part of her meditations was spent in tracing every instance of discomfort, loneliness, ill-health, unsatisfied ambition, restlessness, eccentricity, taking things up and dropping them again, public speaking, and philanthropic activity on the part of men and particularly on the part of women to the fact that they wanted to marry, were trying to marry, and had not succeeded in getting married. If, as she was bound to own, these symptoms sometimes persisted after marriage, she could only ascribe them to the unhappy law of nature which decreed that there was only one Arthur Venning, and only one Susan who could marry him. Her theory, of course, had the merit of being fully supported by her own case. She had been vaguely uncomfortable at home for two or three years now, and a voyage like this with her selfish old aunt, who paid her fare but treated her as servant and companion in one, was typical of the kind of thing people expected of her. Directly she became engaged, Mrs. Paley behaved with instinctive respect, positively protested when Susan as usual knelt down to lace her shoes, and appeared really grateful for an hour of Susan's company where she had been used to exact two or three as her right. She therefore foresaw a life of far greater comfort than she had been used to, and the change had already produced a great increase of warmth in her feelings towards other people.

It was close on twenty years now since Mrs. Paley had been able to lace her own shoes or even to see them, the disappearance of her feet having coincided more or less accurately with the death of her husband, a man of business, soon after which event Mrs. Paley began to grow stout. She was a selfish, independent old woman, possessed of a considerable income, which she spent upon the upkeep of a house that needed seven servants and a charwoman in Lancaster Gate, and another with a garden and carriage-horses in Surrey. Susan's engagement relieved her of the one great anxiety of her life—that her son Christopher should "entangle himself" with his cousin. Now that this familiar source of interest was removed, she felt a little low and inclined to see more in Susan than she used to. She had decided to give her a very handsome wedding present, a cheque for two hundred, two hundred and fifty, or possibly, conceivably—it depended upon the under-gardener and Huths' bill for doing up the drawing-room—three hundred pounds sterling.

She was thinking of this very question, revolving the figures, as she sat in her wheeled chair with a table spread with cards by her side. The Patience had somehow got into a muddle, and she did not like to call for Susan to help her, as Susan seemed to be busy with Arthur.

"She's every right to expect a handsome present from me, of course," she thought, looking vaguely at the leopard on its hind legs, "and I've no doubt she does! Money goes a long way with every one. The young are very selfish. If I were to die, nobody would miss me but Dakyns, and she'll be consoled by the will! However, I've got no reason to complain. . . . I can still enjoy myself. I'm not a burden to any one. . . . I like a great many things a good deal, in spite of my legs."

Being slightly depressed, however, she went on to think of the only people she had known who had not seemed to her at all selfish or fond of money, who had seemed to her somehow rather finer than the general run; people she willingly acknowledged, who were finer than she was. There were only two of them. One was her brother, who had been drowned before her eyes, the other was a girl, her greatest friend, who had died in giving birth to her first child. These things had happened some fifty years ago.

"They ought not to have died," she thought. "However, they did—and we selfish old creatures go on." The tears came to her eyes; she felt a genuine regret for them, a kind of respect for their youth and beauty, and a kind of shame for herself; but the tears did not fall; and she opened one of those innumerable novels which she used to pronounce good or bad, or pretty middling, or really wonderful. "I can't think how people come to imagine such things," she would say, taking off her spectacles and looking up with the old faded eyes, that were becoming ringed with white.

Just behind the stuffed leopard Mr. Elliot was playing chess with Mr. Pepper. He was being defeated, naturally, for Mr. Pepper scarcely took his eyes off the board, and Mr. Elliot kept leaning back in his chair and throwing out remarks to a gentleman who had only arrived the night before, a tall handsome man, with a head resembling the head of an intellectual ram. After a few remarks of a general nature had passed, they were discovering that they knew some of the same people, as indeed had been obvious from their appearance directly they saw each other.

"Ah yes, old Truefit," said Mr. Elliot. "He has a son at Oxford. I've often stayed with them. It's a lovely old Jacobean house. Some exquisite Greuzes—one or two Dutch pictures which the old boy kept in the cellars. Then there were stacks upon stacks of prints. Oh, the dirt in that house! He was a miser, you know. The boy married a daughter of Lord Pinwells. I know them too. The collecting mania tends to run in families. This chap collects buckles—men's shoe-buckles they must be, in use between the years 1580 and 1660; the dates mayn't be right, but fact's as I say. Your true collector always has some unaccountable fad of that kind. On other points he's as level-headed as a breeder of shorthorns, which is what he happens to be. Then the Pinwells, as you probably know, have their share of eccentricity too. Lady Maud, for instance—" he was interrupted here by the necessity of considering his move—"Lady Maud has a horror of cats and clergymen, and people with big front teeth. I've heard her shout across a table, 'Keep your mouth shut, Miss Smith; they're as yellow as carrots!' across a table, mind you. To me she's always been civility itself. She dabbles in literature, likes to collect a few of us in her drawing-room, but mention a clergyman, a bishop even, nay, the Archbishop himself, and she gobbles like a turkey-cock. I've been told it's a family feud—something to do with an ancestor in the reign of Charles the First. Yes," he continued, suffering check after check, "I always like to know something of the grandmothers of our fashionable young men. In my opinion they preserve all that we admire in the eighteenth century, with the advantage, in the majority of cases, that they are personally clean. Not that one would insult old Lady Barborough by calling her clean. How often d'you think, Hilda," he called out to his wife, "her ladyship takes a bath?"

"I should hardly like to say, Hugh," Mrs. Elliot tittered, "but wearing puce velvet, as she does even on the hottest August day, it somehow doesn't show."

"Pepper, you have me," said Mr. Elliot. "My chess is even worse than I remembered." He accepted his defeat with great equanimity, because he really wished to talk.

He drew his chair beside Mr. Wilfrid Flushing, the newcomer.

"Are these at all in your line?" he asked, pointing at a case in front of them, where highly polished crosses, jewels, and bits of embroidery, the work of the natives, were displayed to tempt visitors.

"Shams, all of them," said Mr. Flushing briefly. "This rug, now, isn't at all bad." He stopped and picked up a piece of the rug at their feet. "Not old, of course, but the design is quite in the right tradition. Alice, lend me your brooch. See the difference between the old work and the new."

A lady, who was reading with great concentration, unfastened her brooch and gave it to her husband without looking at him or acknowledging the tentative bow which Mr. Elliot was desirous of giving her. If she had listened, she might have been amused by the reference to old Lady Barborough, her great-aunt, but, oblivious of her surroundings, she went on reading.

The clock, which had been wheezing for some minutes like an old man preparing to cough, now struck nine. The sound slightly disturbed certain somnolent merchants, government officials, and men of independent means who were lying back in their chairs, chatting, smoking, ruminating about their affairs, with their eyes half shut; they raised their lids for an instant at the sound and then closed them again. They had the appearance of crocodiles so fully gorged by their last meal that the future of the world gives them no anxiety whatever. The only disturbance in the placid bright room was caused by a large moth which shot from light to light, whizzing over elaborate heads of hair, and causing several young women to raise their hands nervously and exclaim, "Some one ought to kill it!"

Absorbed in their own thoughts, Hewet and Hirst had not spoken for a long time.

When the clock struck, Hirst said:

"Ah, the creatures begin to stir. . . ." He watched them raise themselves, look about them, and settle down again. "What I abhor most of all," he concluded, "is the female breast. Imagine being Venning and having to get into bed with Susan! But the really repulsive thing is that they feel nothing at all—about what I do when I have a hot bath. They're gross, they're absurd, they're utterly intolerable!"

So saying, and drawing no reply from Hewet, he proceeded to think about himself, about science, about Cambridge, about the Bar, about Helen and what she thought of him, until, being very tired, he was nodding off to sleep.

Suddenly Hewet woke him up.

"How d'you know what you feel, Hirst?"

"Are you in love?" asked Hirst. He put in his eyeglass.

"Don't be a fool," said Hewet.

"Well, I'll sit down and think about it," said Hirst. "One really ought to. If these people would only think about things, the world would be a far better place for us all to live in. Are you trying to think?"

That was exactly what Hewet had been doing for the last half-hour, but he did not find Hirst sympathetic at the moment.

"I shall go for a walk," he said.

"Remember we weren't in bed last night," said Hirst with a prodigious yawn.

Hewet rose and stretched himself.

"I want to go and get a breath of air," he said.

An unusual feeling had been bothering him all the evening and forbidding him to settle into any one train of thought. It was precisely as if he had been in the middle of a talk which interested him profoundly when some one came up and interrupted him. He could not finish the talk, and the longer he sat there the more he wanted to finish it. As the talk that had been interrupted was a talk with Rachel, he had to ask himself why he felt this, and why he wanted to go on talking to her. Hirst would merely say that he was in love with her. But he was not in love with her. Did love begin in that way, with the wish to go on talking? No. It always began in his case with definite physical sensations, and these were now absent, he did not even find her physically attractive. There was something, of course, unusual about her—she was young, inexperienced, and inquisitive, they had been more open with each other than was usually possible. He always found girls interesting to talk to, and surely these were good reasons why he should wish to go on talking to her; and last night, what with the crowd and the confusion, he had only been able to begin to talk to her. What was she doing now? Lying on a sofa and looking at the ceiling, perhaps. He could imagine her doing that, and Helen in an arm-chair, with her hands on the arm of it, so—looking ahead of her, with her great big eyes—oh no, they'd be talking, of course, about the dance. But suppose Rachel was going away in a day or two, suppose this was the end of her visit, and her father had arrived in one of the steamers anchored in the bay—it was intolerable to know so little. Therefore he exclaimed, "How d'you know what you feel, Hirst?" to stop himself from thinking.

But Hirst did not help him, and the other people with their aimless movements and their unknown lives were disturbing, so that he longed for the empty darkness. The first thing he looked for when he stepped out of the hall door was the light of the Ambroses' villa. When he had definitely decided that a certain light apart from the others higher up the hill was their light, he was considerably reassured. There seemed to be at once a little stability in all this incoherence. Without any definite plan in his head, he took the turning to the right and walked through the town and came to the wall by the meeting of the roads, where he stopped. The booming of the sea was audible. The dark-blue mass of the mountains rose against the paler blue of the sky. There was no moon, but myriads of stars, and lights were anchored up and down in the dark waves of earth all round him. He had meant to go back, but the single light of the Ambroses' villa had now become three separate lights, and he was tempted to go on. He might as well make sure that Rachel was still there. Walking fast, he soon stood by the iron gate of their garden, and pushed it open; the outline of the house suddenly appeared sharply before his eyes, and the thin column of the verandah cutting across the palely lit gravel of the terrace. He hesitated. At the back of the house some one was rattling cans. He approached the front; the light on the terrace showed him that the sitting-rooms were on that side. He stood as near the light as he could by the corner of the house, the leaves of a creeper brushing his face. After a moment he could hear a voice. The voice went on steadily; it was not talking, but from the continuity of the sound it was a voice reading aloud. He crept a little closer; he crumpled the leaves together so as to stop their rustling about his ears. It might be Rachel's voice. He left the shadow and stepped into the radius of the light, and then heard a sentence spoken quite distinctly.

"And there we lived from the year 1860 to 1895, the happiest years of my parents' lives, and there in 1862 my brother Maurice was born, to the delight of his parents, as he was destined to be the delight of all who knew him."

The voice quickened, and the tone became conclusive rising slightly in pitch, as if these words were at the end of the chapter. Hewet drew back again into the shadow. There was a long silence. He could just hear chairs being moved inside. He had almost decided to go back, when suddenly two figures appeared at the window, not six feet from him.

"It was Maurice Fielding, of course, that your mother was engaged to," said Helen's voice. She spoke reflectively, looking out into the dark garden, and thinking evidently as much of the look of the night as of what she was saying.

"Mother?" said Rachel. Hewet's heart leapt, and he noticed the fact. Her voice, though low, was full of surprise.

"You didn't know that?" said Helen.

"I never knew there'd been any one else," said Rachel. She was clearly surprised, but all they said was said low and inexpressively, because they were speaking out into the cool dark night.

"More people were in love with her than with any one I've ever known," Helen stated. She had that power—she enjoyed things. She wasn't beautiful, but—I was thinking of her last night at the dance. She got on with every kind of person, and then she made it all so amazingly—funny."

It appeared that Helen was going back into the past, choosing her words deliberately, comparing Theresa with the people she had known since Theresa died.

"I don't know how she did it," she continued, and ceased, and there was a long pause, in which a little owl called first here, then there, as it moved from tree to tree in the garden.

"That's so like Aunt Lucy and Aunt Katie," said Rachel at last. "They always make out that she was very sad and very good."

"Then why, for goodness' sake, did they do nothing but criticize her when she was alive?" said Helen. Very gentle their voices sounded, as if they fell through the waves of the sea.

"If I were to die tomorrow . . ." she began.

The broken sentences had an extraordinary beauty and detachment in Hewet's ears, and a kind of mystery too, as though they were spoken by people in their sleep.

"No, Rachel," Helen's voice continued, "I'm not going to walk in the garden; it's damp—it's sure to be damp; besides, I see at least a dozen toads."

"Toads? Those are stones, Helen. Come out. It's nicer out. The flowers smell," Rachel replied.

Hewet drew still farther back. His heart was beating very quickly. Apparently Rachel tried to pull Helen out on to the terrace, and Helen resisted. There was a certain amount of scuffling, entreating, resisting, and laughter from both of them. Then a man's form appeared. Hewet could not hear what they were all saying. In a minute they had gone in; he could hear bolts grating then; there was dead silence, and all the lights went out.

He turned away, still crumpling and uncrumpling a handful of leaves which he had torn from the wall. An exquisite sense of pleasure and relief possessed him; it was all so solid and peaceful after the ball at the hotel, whether he was in love with them or not, and he was not in love with them; no, but it was good that they should be alive.

After standing still for a minute or two he turned and began to walk towards the gate. With the movement of his body, the excitement, the romance and the richness of life crowded into his brain. He shouted out a line of poetry, but the words escaped him, and he stumbled among lines and fragments of lines which had no meaning at all except for the beauty of the words. He shut the gate, and ran swinging from side to side down the hill, shouting any nonsense that came into his head. "Here am I," he cried rhythmically, as his feet pounded to the left and to the right, "plunging along, like an elephant in the jungle, stripping the branches as I go (he snatched at the twigs of a bush at the roadside), roaring innumerable words, lovely words about innumerable things, running downhill and talking nonsense aloud to myself about roads and leaves and lights and women coming out into the darkness—about women—about Rachel, about Rachel." He stopped and drew a deep breath. The night seemed immense and hospitable, and although so dark there seemed to be things moving down there in the harbour and movement out at sea. He gazed until the darkness numbed him, and then he walked on quickly, still murmuring to himself. "And I ought to be in bed, snoring and dreaming, dreaming, dreaming. Dreams and realities, dreams and realities, dreams and realities," he repeated all the way up the avenue, scarcely knowing what he said, until he reached the front door. Here he paused for a second, and collected himself before he opened the door.

His eyes were dazed, his hands very cold, and his brain excited and yet half asleep. Inside the door everything was as he had left it except that the hall was now empty. There were the chairs turning in towards each other where people had sat talking, and the empty glasses on little tables, and the newspapers scattered on the floor. As he shut the door he felt as if he were enclosed in a square box, and instantly shrivelled up. It was all very bright and very small. He stopped for a minute by the long table to find a paper which he had meant to read, but he was still too much under the influence of the dark and the fresh air to consider carefully which paper it was or where he had seen it.

As he fumbled vaguely among the papers he saw a figure cross the tail of his eye, coming downstairs. He heard the swishing sound of skirts, and to his great surprise, Evelyn M. came up to him, laid her hand on the table as if to prevent him from taking up a paper, and said:

"You're just the person I wanted to talk to." Her voice was a little unpleasant and metallic, her eyes were very bright, and she kept them fixed upon him.

"To talk to me?" he repeated. "But I'm half asleep."

"But I think you understand better than most people," she answered, and sat down on a little chair placed beside a big leather chair so that Hewet had to sit down beside her.

"Well?" he said. He yawned openly, and lit a cigarette. He could not believe that this was really happening to him. "What is it?"

"Are you really sympathetic, or is it just a pose?" she demanded.

"It's for you to say," he replied. "I'm interested, I think." He still felt numb all over and as if she was much too close to him.

"Any one can be interested!" she cried impatiently. "Your friend Mr. Hirst's interested, I daresay. however, I do believe in you. You look as if you'd got a nice sister, somehow." She paused, picking at some sequins on her knees, and then, as if she had made up her mind, she started off, "Anyhow, I'm going to ask your advice. D'you ever get into a state where you don't know your own mind? That's the state I'm in now. You see, last night at the dance Raymond Oliver—he's the tall dark boy who looks as if he had Indian blood in him, but he says he's not really—well, we were sitting out together, and he told me all about himself, how unhappy he is at home, and how he hates being out here. They've put him into some beastly mining business. He says it's beastly—I should like it, I know, but that's neither here nor there. And I felt awfully sorry for him, one couldn't help being sorry for him, and when he asked me to let him kiss me, I did. I don't see any harm in that, do you? And then this morning he said he'd thought I meant something more, and I wasn't the sort to let any one kiss me. And we talked and talked. I daresay I was very silly, but one can't help liking people when one's sorry for them. I do like him most awfully—" She paused. "So I gave him half a promise, and then, you see, there's Alfred Perrott."

"Oh, Perrott," said Hewet.

"We got to know each other on that picnic the other day," she continued. "He seemed so lonely, especially as Arthur had gone off with Susan, and one couldn't help guessing what was in his mind. So we had quite a long talk when you were looking at the ruins, and he told me all about his life, and his struggles, and how fearfully hard it had been. D'you know, he was a boy in a grocer's shop and took parcels to people's houses in a basket? That interested me awfully, because I always say it doesn't matter how you're born if you've got the right stuff in you. And he told me about his sister who's paralysed, poor girl, and one can see she's a great trial, though he's evidently very devoted to her. I must say I do admire people like that! I don't expect you do because you're so clever. Well, last night we sat out in the garden together, and I couldn't help seeing what he wanted to say, and comforting him a little, and telling him I did care—I really do—only, then, there's Raymond Oliver. What I want you to tell me is, can one be in love with two people at once, or can't one?"

She became silent, and sat with her chin on her hands, looking very intent, as if she were facing a real problem which had to be discussed between them.

"I think it depends what sort of person you are," said Hewet. He looked at her. She was small and pretty, aged perhaps twenty-eight or twenty-nine, but though dashing and sharply cut, her features expressed nothing very clearly, except a great deal of spirit and good health.

"Who are you, what are you; you see, I know nothing about you," he continued.

"Well, I was coming to that," said Evelyn M. She continued to rest her chin on her hands and to look intently ahead of her. "I'm the daughter of a mother and no father, if that interests you," she said. "It's not a very nice thing to be. It's what often happens in the country. She was a farmer's daughter, and he was rather a swell—the young man up at the great house. He never made things straight—never married her—though he allowed us quite a lot of money. His people wouldn't let him. Poor father! I can't help liking him. Mother wasn't the sort of woman who could keep him straight, anyhow. He was killed in the war. I believe his men worshipped him. They say great big troopers broke down and cried over his body on the battlefield. I wish I'd known him. Mother had all the life crushed out of her. The world–" She clenched her fist. "Oh, people can be horrid to a woman like that!" She turned upon Hewet.

"Well," she said, "d'you want to know any more about me?"

"But you?" he asked, "Who looked after you?"

"I've looked after myself mostly," she laughed. "I've had splendid friends. I do like people! That's the trouble. What would you do if you liked two people, both of them tremendously, and you couldn't tell which most?"

"I should go on liking them–I should wait and see. Why not?"

"But one has to make up one's mind," said Evelyn. "Or are you one of the people who doesn't believe in marriages and all that? Look here–this isn't fair, I do all the telling, and you tell nothing. Perhaps you're the same as your friend"–she looked at him suspiciously; "perhaps you don't like me?"

"I don't know you," said Hewet.

"I know when I like a person directly I see them! I knew I liked you the very first night at dinner. Oh dear," she continued impatiently, "what a lot of bother would be saved if only people would say the things they think straight out! I'm made like that. I can't help it."

"But don't you find it leads to difficulties?" Hewet asked.

"That's men's fault," she answered. "They always drag it in–love, I mean."

"And so you've gone on having one proposal after another," said Hewet.

"I don't suppose I've had more proposals than most women," said Evelyn, but she spoke without conviction.

"Five, six, ten?" Hewet ventured.

Evelyn seemed to intimate that perhaps ten was the right figure, but that it really was not a high one.

"I believe you're thinking me a heartless flirt," she protested. "But I don't care if you are. I don't care what any one thinks of me. Just because one's interested and likes to be friends with men, and talk to them as one talks to women, one's called a flirt."

"But Miss Murgatroyd—"

"I wish you'd call me Evelyn," she interrupted.

"After ten proposals do you honestly think that men are the same as women?"

"Honestly, honestly–how I hate that word! It's always used by prigs," cried Evelyn. "Honestly I think they ought to be. That's what's so disappointing. Every time one thinks it's not going to happen, and every time it does."

"The pursuit of Friendship," said Hewet. "The title of a comedy."

"You're horrid," she cried. "You don't care a bit really. You might be Mr. Hirst."

"Well," said Hewet, "let's consider. Let us consider—" He paused, because for the moment he could not remember what it was that they had to consider. He was far more interested in her than in her story, for as she went on speaking his numbness had disappeared, and he was conscious of a mixture of liking, pity, and distrust. "You've promised to marry both Oliver and Perrott?" he concluded.

"Not exactly promised," said Evelyn. "I can't make up my mind which I really like best. Oh how I detest modern life!" she flung off. "It must have been so much easier for the Elizabethans! I thought the other day on that mountain how I'd have liked to be one of those colonists, to cut down trees and make laws and all that, instead of fooling about with all these people who think one's just a pretty young lady. Though I'm not. I really might *do* something." She reflected in silence for a minute. Then she said:

"I'm afraid right down in my heart that Alfred Perrot *won't* do. He's not strong, is he?"

"Perhaps he couldn't cut down a tree," said Hewet. "Have you never cared for anybody?" he asked.

"I've cared for heaps of people, but not to marry them," she said. "I suppose I'm too fastidious. All my life I've wanted somebody I could look up to, somebody great and big and splendid. Most men are so small."

"What d'you mean by splendid?" Hewet asked. "People are—nothing more."

Evelyn was puzzled.

"We don't care for people because of their qualities," he tried to explain. "It's just them that we care for,"—he struck a match—"just that," he said, pointing to the flames.

"I see what you mean," she said, "but I don't agree. I do know why I care for people, and I think I'm hardly ever wrong. I see at once what they've got in them. Now I think you must be rather splendid; but not Mr. Hirst."

Hewlet shook his head.

"He's not nearly so unselfish, or so sympathetic, or so big, or so understanding," Evelyn continued.

Hewet sat silent, smoking his cigarette.

"I should hate cutting down trees," he remarked.

"I'm not trying to flirt with you, though I suppose you think I am!" Evelyn shot out. "I'd never have come to you if I'd thought you'd merely think odious things of me!" The tears came into her eyes.

"Do you never flirt?" he asked.

"Of course I don't," she protested. "Haven't I told you? I want friendship; I want to care for some one greater and nobler than I am, and if they fall in love with me it isn't my fault; I don't want it; I positively hate it."

Hewet could see that there was very little use in going on with the conversation, for it was obvious that Evelyn did not wish to say anything in particular, but to impress upon him an image of herself, being, for some reason which she would not reveal, unhappy, or insecure. He was very tired, and a pale waiter kept walking ostentatiously into the middle of the room and looking at them meaningly.

"They want to shut up," he said. "My advice is that you should tell Oliver and Perrott tomorrow that you've made up your mind that you don't mean to marry either of them. I'm certain you don't. If you change your mind you can always tell them so. They're both sensible men; they'll understand. And then all this bother will be over." He got up.

But Evelyn did not move. She sat looking up at him with her bright eager eyes, in the depths of which he thought he detected some disappointment, or dissatisfaction.

"Good-night," he said.

"There are heaps of things I want to say to you still," she said. "And I'm going to, some time. I suppose you must go to bed now?"

"Yes," said Hewet. "I'm half asleep." He left her still sitting by herself in the empty hall.

"Why is it that they *won't* be honest?" he muttered to himself as he went upstairs. Why was it that relations between different people were so unsatisfactory, so fragmentary, so hazardous, and words so dangerous that the instinct to sympathise with another human being was an instinct to be examined carefully and probably crushed? What had Evelyn really wished to say to him? What was she feeling left alone in the empty hall? The mystery of life and the unreality even of one's own sensations overcame him as he walked down the corridor which led to his room. It was dimly lighted, but sufficiently for him to see a figure in a bright dressing-gown pass swiftly in front of him, the figure of a woman crossing from one room to another.

15

Whether too slight or too vague the ties that bind people casually meeting in a hotel at midnight, they possess one advantage at least over the bonds which unite the elderly, who have lived together once and so must live for ever. Slight they may be, but vivid and genuine, merely because the power to break them is within the grasp of each, and there is no reason for continuance except a true desire that continue they shall. When two people have been married for years they seem to become unconscious of each other's bodily presence so that they move as if alone, speak aloud things which they do not expect to be answered, and in general seem to experience all the comfort of solitude without its loneliness. The joint lives of Ridley and Helen had arrived at this stage of community, and it was often necessary for one or the other to recall with an effort whether a thing had been said or only thought, shared or dreamt in private. At four o'clock in the afternoon two or three days later Mrs. Ambrose was standing brushing her hair, while her husband was in the dressing-room which opened out of her room, and occasionally, through the cascade of water—he was washing his face—she caught exclamations, "So it goes on year after year; I wish, I wish, I wish I could make an end of it," to which she paid no attention.

"It's white? Or only brown?" Thus she herself murmured, examining a hair which gleamed suspiciously among the brown. She pulled it out and laid it on the dressing-table. She was criticising her own appearance, or rather approving of it, standing a little way back from the glass and looking at her own face with superb pride and melancholy, when her husband appeared in the doorway in his shirt sleeves, his face half obscured by a towel.

"You often tell me I don't notice things," he remarked.

"Tell me if this is a white hair, then?" she replied. She laid the hair on his hand.

"There's not a white hair on your head," he exclaimed.

"Ah, Ridley, I begin to doubt," she sighed; and bowed her head under his eyes so that he might judge, but the inspection produced only a kiss where the line of parting ran, and husband and wife then proceeded to move about the room, casually murmuring.

"What was that you were saying?" Helen remarked, after an interval of conversation which no third person could have understood.

"Rachel—you ought to keep an eye upon Rachel," he observed significantly, and Helen, though she went on brushing her hair, looked at him. His observations were apt to be true.

"Young gentlemen don't interest themselves in young women's education without a motive," he remarked.

"Oh, Hirst," said Helen.

"Hirst and Hewet, they're all the same to me—all covered with spots," he replied. "He advises her to read Gibbon. Did you know that?"

Helen did not know that, but she would not allow herself inferior to her husband in powers of observation. She merely said:

"Nothing would surprise me. Even that dreadful flying man we met at the dance—even Mr. Dalloway—even—"

"I advise you to be circumspect," said Ridley. "There's Willoughby, remember—Willoughby"; he pointed at a letter.

Helen looked with a sigh at an envelope which lay upon her dressing-table. Yes, there lay Willoughby, curt, inexpressive, perpetually jocular, robbing a whole continent of mystery, enquiring after his daughter's manners and morals—hoping she wasn't a bore, and bidding them pack her off to him on board the very next ship if she were—and then grateful and affectionate with suppressed emotion, and then half a page about his own triumphs over wretched little natives who went on strike and refused to load his ships, until he roared English oaths at them, "popping my head out of the window just as I was, in my shirt sleeves. The beggars had the sense to scatter."

"If Theresa married Willoughby," she remarked, turning the page with a hairpin, "one doesn't see what's to prevent Rachel—"

But Ridley was now off on grievances of his own connected with the washing of his shirts, which somehow led to the frequent visits of Hughling Elliot, who was a bore, a pedant, a dry stick of a man, and yet Ridley couldn't simply point at the door and tell him to go. The truth of it was, they saw too many people. And so on and so on, more conjugal talk pattering softly and unintelligibly, until they were both ready to go down to tea.

The first thing that caught Helen's eye as she came downstairs was a carriage at the door, filled with skirts and feathers nodding on the tops of hats. She had only time to gain the drawing-room before two names were oddly mispronounced by the Spanish maid, and Mrs. Thornbury came in slightly in advance of Mrs. Wilfrid Flushing.

"Mrs. Wilfrid Flushing," said Mrs. Thornbury, with a wave of her hand. "A friend of our common friend Mrs. Raymond Parry."

Mrs. Flushing shook hands energetically. She was a woman of forty perhaps, very well set up and erect, splendidly robust, though not as tall as the upright carriage of her body made her appear.

She looked Helen straight in the face and said, "You have a charmin' house."

She had a strongly marked face, her eyes looked straight at you, and though naturally she was imperious in her manner she was nervous at the same time. Mrs. Thornbury acted as interpreter, making things smooth all round by a series of charming commonplace remarks.

"I've taken it upon myself, Mr. Ambrose," she said, "to promise that you will be so kind as to give Mrs. Flushing the benefit of your experience. I'm sure no one here knows the country as well as you do. No one takes such wonderful long walks. No one, I'm sure, has your encyclopaedic knowledge upon every subject. Mr. Wilfrid Flushing is a collector. He has discovered really beautiful things already. I had no notion that the peasants were so artistic–though of course in the past—"

"Not old things–new things," interrupted Mrs. Flushing curtly. "That is, if he takes my advice."

The Ambroses had not lived for many years in London without knowing something of a good many people, by name at least, and Helen remembered hearing of the Flushings. Mr. Flushing was a man who kept an old furniture shop; he had always said he would not marry because most women have red cheeks, and would not take a house because most houses have narrow staircases, and would not eat meat because most animals bleed when they are killed; and then he had married an eccentric aristocratic lady, who certainly was not pale, who looked as if she ate meat, who had forced him to do all the things he most disliked–and this then was the lady. Helen looked at her with interest. They had moved out into the garden, where the tea was laid under a tree, and Mrs. Flushing was helping herself to cherry jam. She had a peculiar jerking movement of the body when she spoke, which caused the canary-coloured plume on her hat to jerk too. Her small but finely-cut and vigorous features, together with the deep red of lips and cheeks, pointed to many generations of well-trained and well-nourished ancestors behind her.

"Nothin' that's more than twenty years old interests me," she continued. "Mouldy old pictures, dirty old books, they stick 'em in museums when they're only fit for burnin'."

"I quite agree," Helen laughed. "But my husband spends his life in digging up manuscripts which nobody wants." She was amused by Ridley's expression of startled disapproval.

"There's a clever man in London called John who paints ever so much better than the old masters," Mrs. Flushing continued. "His pictures excite me–nothin' that's old excites me."

"But even his pictures will become old," Mrs. Thornbury intervened.

"Then I'll have 'em burnt, or I'll put it in my will," said Mrs. Flushing.

"And Mrs. Flushing lived in one of the most beautiful old houses in England—Chillingley," Mrs. Thornbury explained to the rest of them.

"If I'd my way I'd burn that tomorrow," Mrs. Flushing laughed. She had a laugh like the cry of a jay, at once startling and joyless.

"What does any sane person want with those great big houses?" she demanded. "If you go downstairs after dark you're covered with black beetles, and the electric lights always goin' out. What would you do if spiders came out of the tap when you turned on the hot water?" she demanded, fixing her eye on Helen.

Mrs. Ambrose shrugged her shoulders with a smile.

"This is what I like," said Mrs. Flushing. She jerked her head at the Villa. "A little house in a garden. I had one once in Ireland. One could lie in bed in the mornin' and pick roses outside the window with one's toes."

"And the gardeners, weren't they surprised?" Mrs. Thornbury enquired.

"There were no gardeners," Mrs. Flushing chuckled. "Nobody but me and an old woman without any teeth. You know the poor in Ireland lose their teeth after they're twenty. But you wouldn't expect a politician to understand that—Arthur Balfour wouldn't understand that."

Ridley sighed that he never expected any one to understand anything, least of all politicians.

"However," he concluded, "there's one advantage I find in extreme old age—nothing matters a hang except one's food and one's digestion. All I ask is to be left alone to moulder away in solitude. It's obvious that the world's going as fast as it can to—the Nethermost Pit, and all I can do is to sit still and consume as much of my own smoke as possible." He groaned, and with a melancholy glance laid the jam on his bread, for he felt the atmosphere of this abrupt lady distinctly unsympathetic.

"I always contradict my husband when he says that," said Mrs. Thornbury sweetly. "You men! Where would you be if it weren't for the women!"

"Read the *Symposium*," said Ridley grimly.

"*Symposium?*" cried Mrs. Flushing. "That's Latin or Greek? Tell me, is there a good translation?"

"No," said Ridley. "You will have to learn Greek."

Mrs. Flushing cried, "Ah, ah, ah! I'd rather break stones in the road. I always envy the men who break stones and sit on those nice little heaps all day wearin' spectacles. I'd infinitely rather break stones than clean out poultry runs, or feed the cows, or—"

Here Rachel came up from the lower garden with a book in her hand.

"What's that book?" said Ridley, when she had shaken hands.

"It's Gibbon," said Rachel as she sat down.

"*The Decline and Fall of the Roman Empire?*" said Mrs. Thornbury. "A very wonderful book, I know. My dear father was always quoting it at us, with the result that we resolved never to read a line."

"Gibbon the historian?" enquired Mrs. Flushing. "I connect him with some of the happiest hours of my life. We used to lie in bed and read Gibbon—about the massacres of the Christians, I remember—when we were supposed to be asleep. It's no joke, I can tell you, readin' a great big book, in double columns, by a night-light, and the light that comes through a chink in the door. Then there were the moths—tiger moths, yellow moths, and horrid cockchafers. Louisa, my sister, would have the window open. I wanted it shut. We fought every night of our lives over that window. Have you ever seen a moth dyin' in a night-light?" she enquired.

Again there was an interruption. Hewet and Hirst appeared at the drawing-room window and came up to the tea-table.

Rachel's heart beat hard. She was conscious of an extraordinary intensity in everything, as though their presence stripped some cover off the surface of things; but the greetings were remarkably commonplace.

"Excuse me," said Hirst, rising from his chair directly he had sat down. He went into the drawing-room, and returned with a cushion which he placed carefully upon his seat.

"Rheumatism," he remarked, as he sat down for the second time.

"The result of the dance?" Helen enquired.

"Whenever I get at all run down I tend to be rheumatic," Hirst stated. He bent his wrist back sharply. "I hear little pieces of chalk grinding together!"

Rachel looked at him. She was amused, and yet she was respectful; if such a thing could be, the upper part of her face seemed to laugh, and the lower part to check its laughter.

Hewet picked up the book that lay on the ground.

"You like this?" he asked in an undertone.

"No, I don't like it," she replied. She had indeed been trying all the afternoon to read it, and for some reason the glory which she had perceived at first had faded, and, read as she would, she could not grasp the meaning with her mind.

"It goes round, round, round, like a roll of oil-cloth," she hazarded. Evidently she meant Hewet alone to hear her words, but Hirst demanded, "What d'you mean?"

She was instantly ashamed of her figure of speech, for she could not explain it in words of sober criticism.

"Surely it's the most perfect style, so far as style goes, that's ever been invented," he continued. "Every sentence is practically perfect, and the wit——"

"Ugly in body, repulsive in mind," she thought, instead of thinking about Gibbon's style. "Yes, but strong, searching, unyielding in mind."

She looked at his big head, a disproportionate part of which was occupied by the forehead, and at the direct, severe eyes.

"I give you up in despair," he said. He meant it lightly, but she took it seriously, and believed that her value as a human being was lessened because she did not happen to admire the style of Gibbon. The others were talking now in a group about the native villages which Mrs. Flushing ought to visit.

"I despair too," she said impetuously. "How are you going to judge people merely by their minds?"

"You agree with my spinster Aunt, I expect," said St. John in his jaunty manner, which was always irritating because it made the person he talked to appear unduly clumsy and in earnest. "'Be good, sweet maid'—I thought Mr. Kingsley and my Aunt were now obsolete."

"One can be very nice without having read a book," she asserted. Very silly and simple her words sounded, and laid her open to derision.

"Did I ever deny it?" Hirst enquired, raising his eyebrows.

Most unexpectedly Mrs. Thornbury here intervened, either because it was her mission to keep things smooth or because she had long wished to speak to Mr. Hirst, feeling as she did that young men were her sons.

"I have lived all my life with people like your Aunt, Mr. Hirst," she said, leaning forward in her chair. Her brown squirrel-like eyes became even brighter than usual. "They have never heard of Gibbon. They only care for their pheasants and their peasants. They are great big men who look so fine on horseback, as people must have done, I think, in the days of the great wars. Say what you like against them—they are animal, they are unintellectual; they don't read themselves, and they don't want others to read, but they are some of the finest and the kindest human beings on the face of the earth! You would be surprised at some of the stories I could tell. You have never guessed, perhaps, at all the romances that go on in the heart of the country. There are the people, I feel, among whom Shakespeare will be born if he is ever born again. In those old houses, up among the Downs——"

"My Aunt," Hirst interrupted, "spends her life in East Lambeth among the degraded poor. I only quoted my Aunt because she is inclined to persecute people she calls 'intellectual,' which is what I suspect Miss Vinrace of doing. It's all the fashion now. If you're clever it's always taken for granted that you're completely without sympathy, understanding, affection—all the things that really matter. Oh, you Christians! You're the most conceited, patronising, hypocritical set of old humbugs in the kingdom! Of course," he continued, "I'm the first to allow your country gentlemen great merits. For one thing, they're probably quite frank about their passions, which we are not. My father, who is a clergyman in Norfolk, says that there is hardly a squire in the country who does not——"

"But about Gibbon?" Hewet interrupted. The look of nervous tension which had come over every face was relaxed by the interruption.

"You find him monotonous, I suppose. But you know—" He opened the book, and began searching for passages to read aloud, and in a little time he found a good one which he considered suitable. But there was nothing in the world that bored Ridley more than being read aloud to, and he was besides scrupulously fastidious as to the dress and behaviour of ladies. In the space of fifteen minutes he had decided against Mrs. Flushing on the ground that her orange plume did not suit her complexion, that she spoke too loud, that she crossed her legs, and finally, when he saw her accept a cigarette that Hewet offered her, he jumped up, exclaiming something about "bar parlours," and left them. Mrs. Flushing was evidently relieved by his departure. She puffed her cigarette, stuck her legs out, and examined Helen closely as to the character and reputation of their common friend Mrs. Raymond Parry. By a series of little strategems she drove her to define Mrs. Parry as somewhat elderly, by no means beautiful, very much made up–an insolent old harridan, in short, whose parties were amusing because one met odd people; but Helen herself always pitied poor Mr. Parry, who was understood to be shut up downstairs with cases full of gems, while his wife enjoyed herself in the drawing-room. "Not that I believe what people say against her–although she hints, of course–" Upon which Mrs. Flushing cried out with delight:

"She's my first cousin! Go on–go on!"

When Mrs. Flushing rose to go she was obviously delighted with her new acquaintances. She made three or four different plans for meeting or going on an expedition, or showing Helen the things they had bought, on her way to the carriage. She included them all in a vague but magnificent invitation.

As Helen returned to the garden again, Ridley's words of warning came into her head, and she hesitated a moment and looked at Rachel sitting between Hirst and Hewet. But she could draw no conclusions, for Hewet was still reading Gibbon aloud, and Rachel, for all the expression she had, might have been a shell, and his words water rubbing against her ears, as water rubs a shell on the edge of a rock.

Hewet's voice was very pleasant. When he reached the end of the period Hewet stopped, and no one volunteered any criticism.

"I do adore the aristocracy!" Hirst exclaimed after a moment's pause. "They're so amazingly unscrupulous. None of us would dare to behave as that woman behaves."

"What I like about them," said Helen as she sat down, "is that they're so well put together. Naked, Mrs. Flushing would be superb. Dressed as she dresses, it's absurd, of course."

"Yes," said Hirst. A shade of depression crossed his face. "I've never weighed more than ten stone in my life," he said, "which is ridiculous, considering my height, and I've actually gone down in weight since we came here. I daresay that accounts for the rheumatism." Again he jerked his wrist back sharply, so that Helen might hear the grinding of the chalk stones. She could not help smiling.

"It's no laughing matter for me, I assure you," he protested. "My mother's a chronic invalid, and I'm always expecting to be told that I've got heart disease myself. Rheumatism always goes to the heart in the end."

"For goodness' sake, Hirst," Hewet protested; "one might think you were an old cripple of eighty. If it comes to that, I had an aunt who died of cancer myself, but I put a bold face on it—" He rose and began tilting his chair backwards and forwards on its hind legs. "Is any one here inclined for a walk?" he said. "There's a magnificent walk, up behind the house. You come out on to a cliff and look right down into the sea. The rocks are all red; you can see them through the water. The other day I saw a sight that fairly took my breath away—about twenty jelly-fish, semitransparent, pink, with long streamers, floating on the top of the waves."

"Sure they weren't mermaids?" said Hirst. "It's much too hot to climb uphill." He looked at Helen, who showed no signs of moving.

"Yes, it's too hot," Helen decided.

There was a short silence.

"I'd like to come," said Rachel.

"But she might have said that anyhow," Helen thought to herself as Hewet and Rachel went away together, and Helen was left alone with St. John, to St. John's obvious satisfaction.

He may have been satisfied, but his usual difficulty in deciding that one subject was more deserving of notice than another prevented him from speaking for some time. He sat staring intently at the head of a dead match, while Helen considered—so it seemed from the expression of her eyes—something not closely connected with the present moment.

At last St. John exclaimed, "Damn! Damn everything! Damn everybody!" he added. "At Cambridge there are people to talk to."

"At Cambridge there are people to talk to," Helen echoed him, rhythmically and absent-mindedly. Then she woke up. "By the way, have you settled what you're going to do—is it to be Cambridge or the Bar?"

He pursed his lips, but made no immediate answer, for Helen was still slightly inattentive. She had been thinking about Rachel and which of the two young men she was likely to fall in love with, and now sitting opposite to Hirst she thought, "He's ugly. It's a pity they're so ugly."

She did not include Hewet in this criticism; she was thinking of the clever, honest, interesting young men she knew, of whom Hirst was a good example, and wondering whether it was necessary that thought and scholarship should thus maltreat their bodies, and should thus elevate their minds to a very high tower from which the human race appeared to them like rats and mice squirming on the flat.

"And the future?" she reflected, vaguely envisaging a race of men becoming more and more like Hirst, and a race of women becoming more and more like Rachel. "Oh no," she concluded, glancing at him, "one wouldn't marry you. Well, then, the future of the race is in the hands of Susan and Arthur; no—that's dreadful. Of farm labourers; no—not of the English at all, but of Russians and Chinese." This train of thought did not satisfy her, and was interrupted by St. John, who began again:

"I wish you knew Bennett. He's the greatest man in the world."

"Bennett?" she enquired. Becoming more at ease, St. John dropped the concentrated abruptness of his manner, and explained that Bennett was a man who lived in an old windmill six miles out of Cambridge. He lived the perfect life, according to St. John, very lonely, very simple, caring only for the truth of things, always ready to talk, and extraordinarily modest, though his mind was of the greatest.

"Don't you think," said St. John, when he had done describing him, "that kind of thing makes this kind of thing rather flimsy? Did you notice at tea how poor old Hewet had to change the conversation? How they were all ready to pounce upon me because they thought I was going to say something improper? It wasn't anything, really. If Bennett had been there he'd have said exactly what he meant to say, or he'd have got up and gone. But there's something rather bad for the character in that—I mean if one hasn't got Bennett's character. It's inclined to make one bitter. Should you say that I was bitter?"

Helen did not answer, and he continued:

"Of course I am, disgustingly bitter, and it's a beastly thing to be. But the worst of me is that I'm so envious. I envy every one. I can't endure people who do things better than I do—perfectly absurd things too—waiters balancing piles of plates—even Arthur, because Susan's in love with him. I want people to like me, and they don't. It's partly my appearance, I expect," he continued, "though it's an absolute lie to say I've Jewish blood in me—as a matter of fact we've been in Norfolk, Hirst of Hirstbourne Hall, for three centuries at least. It must be awfully soothing to be like you—every one liking one at once."

"I assure you they don't," Helen laughed.

"They do," said Hirst with conviction. "In the first place, you're the most beautiful woman I've ever seen; in the second, you have an exceptionally nice nature."

If Hirst had looked at her instead of looking intently at his teacup he would have seen Helen blush, partly with pleasure, partly with an impulse of affection towards the young man who had seemed, and would seem again, so ugly and so limited. She pitied him, for she suspected that he suffered, and she was interested in him, for many of the things he said seemed to her true; she admired the morality of youth, and yet she felt imprisoned. As if her instinct were to escape to something brightly coloured and impersonal, which she could hold in her hands, she went into the house and returned with her embroidery. But he was not interested in her embroidery; he did not even look at it.

"About Miss Vinrace," he began—"oh, look here, do let's be St. John and Helen, and Rachel and Terence—what's she like? Does she reason, does she feel, or is she merely a kind of footstool?"

"Oh no," said Helen, with great decision. From her observations at tea she was inclined to doubt whether Hirst was the person to educate Rachel. She had gradually come to be interested in her niece, and fond of her; she disliked some things about her very much, she was amused by others; but she felt her, on the whole, a live if unformed human being, experimental, and not always fortunate in her experiments, but with powers of some kind, and a capacity for feeling. Somewhere in the depths of her, too, she was bound to Rachel by the indestructible if inexplicable ties of sex. "She seems vague, but she's a will of her own," she said, as if in the interval she had run through her qualities.

The embroidery, which was a matter for thought, the design being difficult and the colours wanting consideration, brought lapses into the dialogue when she seemed to be engrossed in her skeins of silk, or, with head a little drawn back and eyes narrowed, considered the effect of the whole. Thus she merely said, "Um-m-m" to St. John's next remark, "I shall ask her to go for a walk with me."

Perhaps he resented this division of attention. He sat silent watching Helen closely.

"You're absolutely happy," he proclaimed at last.

"Yes?" Helen enquired, sticking in her needle.

"Marriage, I suppose," said St. John.

"Yes," said Helen, gently drawing her needle out.

"Children?" St. John enquired.

"Yes," said Helen, sticking her needle in again. "I don't know why I'm happy," she suddenly laughed, looking him full in the face. There was a considerable pause.

"There's an abyss between us," said St. John. His voice sounded as if it issued from the depths of a cavern in the rocks. "You're infinitely simpler than I am. Women always are, of course. That's the difficulty. One never knows how a woman gets there. Supposing all the time you're thinking, 'Oh, what a morbid young man!'"

Helen sat and looked at him with her needle in her hand. From her position she saw his head in front of the dark pyramid of a magnolia-tree. With one foot raised on the rung of a chair, and her elbow out in the attitude for sewing, her own figure possessed the sublimity of a woman's of the early world, spinning the thread of fate—the sublimity possessed by many women of the present day who fall into the attitude required by scrubbing or sewing. St. John looked at her.

"I suppose you've never paid any a compliment in the course of your life," he said irrelevantly.

"I spoil Ridley rather," Helen considered.

"I'm going to ask you point blank—do you like me?"

After a certain pause, she replied, "Yes, certainly."

"Thank God!" he exclaimed. "That's one mercy. You see," he continued with emotion, "I'd rather you liked me than any one I've ever met."

"What about the five philosophers?" said Helen, with a laugh, stitching firmly and swiftly at her canvas. "I wish you'd describe them."

Hirst had no particular wish to describe them, but when he began to consider them he found himself soothed and strengthened. Far away to the other side of the world as they were, in smoky rooms, and grey medieval courts, they appeared remarkable figures, free-spoken men with whom one could be at ease; incomparably more subtle in emotion than the people here. They gave him, certainly, what no woman could give him, not Helen even. Warming at the thought of them, he went on to lay his case before Mrs. Ambrose. Should he stay on at Cambridge or should he go to the Bar? One day he thought one thing, another day another. Helen listened attentively. At last, without any preface, she pronounced her decision.

"Leave Cambridge and go to the Bar," she said. He pressed her for her reasons.

"I think you'd enjoy London more," she said. It did not seem a very subtle reason, but she appeared to think it sufficient. She looked at him against the background of flowering magnolia. There was something curious in the sight. Perhaps it was that the heavy wax-like flowers were so smooth and inarticulate, and his face—he had thrown his hat away, his hair was rumpled, he held his eye-glasses in his hand, so that a red mark appeared on either side of his nose—was so worried and garrulous. It was a beautiful bush, spreading very widely, and all the time she had sat there talking she had been noticing the patches of shade and the shape of the leaves, and the way the great white flowers sat in the midst of the green. She had noticed it half-consciously, nevertheless the pattern had become part of their talk. She laid down her sewing, and began to walk up and down the garden, and Hirst rose too and paced by her side. He was rather disturbed, uncomfortable, and full of thought. Neither of them spoke.

The sun was beginning to go down, and a change had come over the mountains, as if they were robbed of their earthly substance, and composed merely of intense blue mist. Long thin clouds of flamingo red, with edges like the edges of curled ostrich feathers, lay up and down the sky at different altitudes. The roofs of the town seemed to have sunk lower than usual; the cypresses appeared very black between the roofs, and the roofs themselves were brown and white. As usual in the evening, single cries and single bells became audible rising from beneath.

St. John stopped suddenly.

"Well, you must take the responsibility," he said. "I've made up my mind; I shall go to the Bar."

His words were very serious, almost emotional; they recalled Helen after a second's hesitation.

"I'm sure you're right," she said warmly, and shook the hand he held out. "You'll be a great man, I'm certain."

Then, as if to make him look at the scene, she swept her hand round the immense circumference of the view. From the sea, over the roofs of the town, across the crests of the mountains, over the river and the plain, and again across the crests of the mountains it swept until it reached the villa, the garden, the magnolia-tree, and the figures of Hirst and herself standing together, when it dropped to her side.

16

Hewet and Rachel had long ago reached the particular place on the edge of the cliff where, looking down into the sea, you might chance on jelly-fish and dolphins. Looking the other way, the vast expanse of land gave them a sensation which is given by no view, however extended, in England; the villages and the hills there having names, and the farthest horizon of hills as often as not dipping and showing a line of mist which is the sea; here the view was one of infinite sun-dried earth, earth pointed in pinnacles, heaped in vast barriers, earth widening and spreading away and away like the immense floor of the sea, earth chequered by day and by night, and partitioned into different lands, where famous cities were founded, and the races of men changed from dark savages to white civilised men, and back to dark savages again. Perhaps their English blood made this prospect uncomfortably impersonal and hostile to them, for having once turned their faces that way they next turned them to the sea, and for the rest of the time sat looking at the sea. The sea, though it was a thin and sparkling water here, which seemed incapable of surge or anger, eventually narrowed itself, clouded its pure tint with grey, and swirled through narrow channels and dashed in a shiver of broken waters against massive granite rocks. It was this sea that flowed up to the mouth of the Thames; and the Thames washed the roots of the city of London.

Hewet's thoughts had followed some such course as this, for the first thing he said as they stood on the edge of the cliff was—

"I'd like to be in England!"

Rachel lay down on her elbow, and parted the tall grasses which grew on the edge, so that she might have a clear view. The water was very calm; rocking up and down at the base of the cliff, and so clear that one could see the red of the stones at the bottom of it. So it had been at the birth of the world, and so it had remained ever since. Probably no human being had ever broken that water with boat or with body. Obeying some impulse, she determined to mar that eternity of peace, and threw the largest pebble she could find. It struck the water, and the ripples spread out and out. Hewet looked down too.

"It's wonderful," he said, as they widened and ceased. The freshness and the newness seemed to him wonderful. He threw a pebble next. There was scarcely any sound.

"But England," Rachel murmured in the absorbed tone of one whose eyes are concentrated upon some sight. "What d'you want with England?"

"My friends chiefly," he said, "and all the things one does."

He could look at Rachel without her noticing it. She was still absorbed in the water and the exquisitely pleasant sensations which a little depth of the sea washing over rocks suggests. He noticed that she was wearing a dress of deep blue colour, made of a soft thin cotton stuff, which clung to the shape of her body. It was a body with the angles and hollows of a young woman's body not yet developed, but in no way distorted, and thus interesting and even lovable. Raising his eyes Hewet observed her head; she had taken her hat off, and the face rested on her hand. As she looked down into the sea, her lips were slightly parted. The expression was one of childlike intentness, as if she were watching for a fish to swim past over the clear red rocks. Nevertheless her twenty-four years of life had given her a look of reserve. Her hand, which lay on the ground, the fingers curling slightly in, was well shaped and competent; the square-tipped and nervous fingers were the fingers of a musician. With something like anguish Hewet realised that, far from being unattractive, her body was very attractive to him. She looked up suddenly. Her eyes were full of eagerness and interest.

"You write novels?" she asked.

For the moment he could not think what he was saying. He was overcome with the desire to hold her in his arms.

"Oh yes," he said. "That is, I want to write them."

She would not take her large grey eyes off his face.

"Novels," she repeated. "Why do you write novels? You ought to write music. Music, you see"–she shifted her eyes, and became less desirable as her brain began to work, inflicting a certain change upon her face–"music goes straight for things. It says all there is to say at once. With writing it seems to me there's so much"–she paused for an expression, and rubbed her fingers in the earth–"scratching on the matchbox. Most of the time when I was reading Gibbon this afternoon I was horribly, oh infernally, damnably bored!" She gave a shake of laughter, looking at Hewet, who laughed too.

"*I* shan't lend you books," he remarked.

"Why is it," Rachel continued, "that I can laugh at Mr. Hirst to you, but not to his face? At tea I was completely overwhelmed, not by his ugliness–by his mind." She enclosed a circle in the air with her hands. She realised with a great sense of comfort how easily she could talk to Hewet, those thorns or ragged corners which tear the surface of some relationships being smoothed away.

"So I observed," said Hewet. "That's a thing that never ceases to amaze me." He had recovered his composure to such an extent that he could light and smoke a cigarette, and feeling her ease, became happy and easy himself.

"The respect that women, even well-educated, very able women, have for men," he went on. "I believe we must have the sort of power over you that we're said to have over horses. They see us three times as big as we are or they'd never obey us. For that very reason, I'm inclined to doubt that you'll ever do anything even when you have the vote." He looked at her reflectively. She appeared very smooth and sensitive and young. "It'll take at least six generations before you're sufficiently thick-skinned to go into law courts and business offices. Consider what a bully the ordinary man is," he continued, "the ordinary hard-working, rather ambitious solicitor or man of business with a family to bring up and a certain position to maintain. And then, of course, the daughters have to give way to the sons; the sons have to be educated; they have to bully and shove for their wives and families, and so it all comes over again. And meanwhile there are the women in the background. . . . Do you really think that the vote will do you any good?"

"The vote?" Rachel repeated. She had to visualise it as a little bit of paper which she dropped into a box before she understood his question, and looking at each other they smiled at something absurd in the question.

"Not to me," she said. "But I play the piano. . . . Are men really like that?" she asked, returning to the question that interested her. "I'm not afraid of you." She looked at him easily.

"Oh, I'm different," Hewet replied. "I've got between six and seven hundred a year of my own. And then no one takes a novelist seriously, thank heavens. There's no doubt it helps to make up for the drudgery of a profession if a man's taken very, very seriously by every one—if he gets appointments, and has offices and a title, and lots of letters after his name, and bits of ribbon and degrees. I don't grudge it 'em, though sometimes it comes over me—what an amazing concoction! What a miracle the masculine conception of life is—judges, civil servants, army, navy, Houses of Parliament, lord mayors—what a world we've made of it! Look at Hirst now. I assure you," he said, "not a day's passed since we came here without a discussion as to whether he's to stay on at Cambridge or to go to the Bar. It's his career—his sacred career. And if I've heard it twenty times, I'm sure his mother and sister have heard it five hundred times. Can't you imagine the family conclaves, and the sister told to run out and feed the rabbits because St. John must have the school-room to himself—'St. John's working,' 'St. John wants his tea brought to him.' Don't you know the kind of thing? No wonder that St. John thinks it a matter of considerable importance. It is too. He has to earn his living. But St. John's sister—" Hewet puffed in silence. "No one takes her seriously, poor dear. She feeds the rabbits."

"Yes," said Rachel. "I've fed rabbits for twenty-four years; it seems odd now." She looked meditative, and Hewet, who had been talking much at random and instinctively adopting the feminine point of view, saw that she would now talk about herself, which was what he wanted, for so they might come to know each other.

She looked back meditatively upon her past life.

"How do you spend your day?" he asked.

She meditated still. When she thought of their day it seemed to her it was cut into four pieces by their meals. These divisions were absolutely rigid, the contents of the day having to accommodate themselves within the four rigid bars. Looking back at her life, that was what she saw.

"Breakfast nine; luncheon one; tea five; dinner eight," she said.

"Well," said Hewet, "what d'you do in the morning?"

"I used to play the piano for hours and hours."

"And after luncheon?"

"Then I went shopping with one of my aunts. Or we went to see some one, or we took a message; or we did something that had to be done—the taps might be leaking. They visit the poor a good deal—old char-women with bad legs, women who want tickets for hospitals. Or I used to walk in the park by myself. And after tea people sometimes called; or in summer we sat in the garden or played croquet; in winter I read aloud, while they worked; after dinner I played the piano and they wrote letters. If father was at home we had friends of his to dinner, and about once a month we went up to the play. Every now and then we dined out; sometimes I went to a dance in London, but that was difficult because of getting back. The people we saw were old family friends, and relations, but we didn't see many people. There was the clergyman, Mr. Pepper, and the Hunts. Father generally wanted to be quiet when he came home, because he works very hard at Hull. Also my aunts aren't very strong. A house takes up a lot of time if you do it properly. Our servants were always bad, and so Aunt Lucy used to do a good deal in the kitchen, and Aunt Clara, I think, spent most of the morning dusting the drawing-room and going through the linen and silver. Then there were the dogs. They had to be exercised, besides being washed and brushed. Now Sandy's dead, but Aunt Clara has a very old cockatoo that came from India. Everything in our house," she exclaimed, "comes from somewhere! It's full of old furniture, not really old, Victorian, things mother's family had or father's family had, which they didn't like to get rid of, I suppose, though we've really no room for them. It's rather a nice house," she continued, "except that it's a little dingy—dull I should say." She called up before her eyes a vision of the drawing-room at home; it was a large oblong room, with a square window opening on the garden. Green plush chairs stood against the wall; there was a heavy carved book-case, with glass doors, and a general impression of faded sofa covers, large spaces of pale green, and baskets with pieces of wool-work dropping out of them. Photographs from old Italian masterpieces hung on the walls, and views of Venetian bridges and Swedish waterfalls which members of the family had seen years ago. There were also one or two portraits of fathers and grandmothers, and an engraving of John Stuart Mill, after the picture by Watts. It was a room without definite character, being neither typically and openly hideous, nor strenuously artistic, nor really comfortable. Rachel roused herself from the contemplation of this familiar picture.

"But this isn't very interesting for you," she said, looking up.

"Good Lord!" Hewet exclaimed. "I've never been so much interested in my life." She then realised that while she had been thinking of Richmond, his eyes had never left her face. The knowledge of this excited her.

"Go on, please go on," he urged. "Let's imagine it's a Wednesday. You're all at luncheon. You sit there, and Aunt Lucy there, and Aunt Clara here"; he arranged three pebbles on the grass between them.

"Aunt Clara carves the neck of lamb," Rachel continued. She fixed her gaze upon the pebbles. "There's a very ugly yellow china stand in front of me, called a dumb waiter, on which are three dishes, one for biscuits, one for butter, and one for cheese. There's a pot of ferns. Then there's Blanche the maid, who snuffles because of her nose. We talk—oh yes, it's Aunt Lucy's afternoon at Walworth, so we're rather quick over luncheon. She goes off. She has a purple bag, and a black notebook. Aunt Clara has what they call a G.F.S. meeting in the drawing-room on Wednesday, so I take the dogs out. I go up Richmond Hill, along the terrace, into the park. It's the 18th of April—the same day as it is here. It's spring in England. The ground is rather damp. However, I cross the road and get on to the grass and we walk along, and I sing as I always do when I'm alone, until we come to the open place where you can see the whole of London beneath you on a clear day. Hampstead Church spire there, Westminster Cathedral over there, and factory chimneys about here. There's generally a haze over the low parts of London; but it's often blue over the park when London's in a mist. It's the open place that the balloons cross going over to Hurlingham. They're pale yellow. Well, then, it smells very good, particularly if they happen to be burning wood in the keeper's lodge which is there. I could tell you now how to get from place to place, and exactly what trees you'd pass, and where you'd cross the roads. You see, I played there when I was small. Spring is good, but it's best in the autumn when the deer are barking; then it gets dusky, and I go back through the streets, and you can't see people properly; they come past very quick, you just see their faces and then they're gone—that's what I like—and no one knows in the least what you're doing—"

"But you have to be back for tea, I suppose?" Hewet checked her.

"Tea? Oh yes. Five o'clock. Then I say what I've done, and my aunts say what they've done, and perhaps some one comes in: Mrs. Hunt, let's suppose. She's an old lady with a lame leg. She has or she once had eight children; so we ask after them. They're all over the world; so we ask where they are, and sometimes they're ill, or they're stationed in a cholera district, or in some place where it only rains once in five months. Mrs. Hunt," she said with a smile, "had a son who was hugged to death by a bear."

Here she stopped and looked at Hewet to see whether he was amused by the same things that amused her. She was reassured. But she thought it necessary to apologise again; she had been talking too much.

"You can't conceive how it interests me," he said. Indeed, his cigarette had gone out, and he had to light another.

"Why does it interest you?" she asked.

"Partly because you're a woman," he replied. When he said this, Rachel, who had become oblivious of anything, and had reverted to a childlike state of interest and pleasure, lost her freedom and became self-conscious. She felt herself at once singular and under observation, as she felt with St. John Hirst. She was about to launch into an argument which would have made them both feel bitterly against each other, and to define sensations which had no such importance as words were bound to give them when Hewet led her thoughts in a different direction.

"I've often walked along the streets where people live all in a row, and one house is exactly like another house, and wondered what on earth the women were doing inside," he said. "Just consider: it's the beginning of the twentieth century, and until a few years ago no woman had ever come out by herself and said things at all. There it was going on in the background, for all those thousands of years, this curious silent unrepresented life. Of course we're always writing about women—abusing them, or jeering at them, or worshipping them; but it's never come from women themselves. I believe we still don't know in the least how they live, or what they feel, or what they do precisely. If one's a man, the only confidences one gets are from young women about their love affairs. But the lives of women of forty, of unmarried women, of working women, of women who keep shops and bring up children, of women like your aunts or Mrs. Thornbury or Miss Allan—one knows nothing whatever about them. They won't tell you. Either they're afraid, or they've got a way of treating men. It's the man's view that's represented, you see. Think of a railway train: fifteen carriages for men who want to smoke. Doesn't it make your blood boil? If I were a woman I'd blow some one's brains out. Don't you laugh at us a great deal? Don't you think it all a great humbug? You, I mean—how does it all strike you?"

His determination to know, while it gave meaning to their talk, hampered her; he seemed to press further and further, and made it appear so important. She took some time to answer, and during that time she went over and over the course of her twenty-four years, lighting now on one point, now on another—on her aunts, her mother, her father, and at last her mind fixed upon her aunts and her father, and she tried to describe them as at this distance they appeared to her.

They were very much afraid of her father. He was a great dim force in the house, by means of which they held on to the great world which is represented every morning in *The Times*. But the real life of the house was something quite different from this. It went on independently of Mr. Vinrace, and tended to hide itself from him. He was good-humoured towards them, but contemptuous. She had always taken it for granted that his point of view was just, and founded upon an ideal scale of things where the life of one person was absolutely more important than the life of another, and that in that scale they were much less importance than he was. But did she really believe that? Hewet's words made her think. She always submitted to her father, just as they did, but it was her aunts who influenced her really; her aunts who built up the fine, closely woven substance of their life at home. They were less splendid but more natural than her father was. All her rages had been against them; it was their world with its four meals, its punctuality, and servants on the stairs at half-past ten, that she examined so closely and wanted so vehemently to smash to atoms. Following these thoughts she looked up and said:

"And there's a sort of beauty in it—there they are at Richmond at this very moment building things up. They're all wrong, perhaps, but there's a sort of beauty in it," she repeated. "It's so unconscious, so modest. And yet they feel things. They do mind if people die. Old spinsters are always doing things. I don't quite know what they do. Only that was what I felt when I lived with them. It was very real."

She reviewed their little journeys to and fro, to Walworth, to charwomen with bad legs, to meetings for this and that, their minute acts of charity and unselfishness which flowered punctually from a definite view of what they ought to do, their friendships, their tastes and habits; she saw all these things like grains of sand falling, falling through innumerable days, making an atmosphere and building up a solid mass, a background. Hewet observed her as she considered this.

"Were you happy?" he demanded.

Again she had become absorbed in something else, and he called her back to an unusually vivid consciousness of herself.

"I was both," she replied. "I was happy and I was miserable. You've no conception what it's like—to be a young woman." She looked straight at him. "There are terrors and agonies," she said, keeping her eye on him as if to detect the slightest hint of laughter.

"I can believe it," he said. He returned her look with perfect sincerity.

"Women one sees in the streets," she said.

"Prostitutes?"

"Men kissing one."

He nodded his head.

"You were never told?"

She shook her head.

"And then," she began and stopped. Here came in the great space of life into which no one had ever penetrated. All that she had been saying about her father and her aunts and walks in Richmond Park, and what they did from hour to hour, was merely on the surface. Hewet was watching her. Did he demand that she should describe that also? Why did he sit so near and keep his eye on her? Why did they not have done with this searching and agony? Why did they not kiss each other simply? She wished to kiss him. But all the time she went on spinning out words.

"A girl is more lonely than a boy. No one cares in the least what she does. Nothing's expected of her. Unless one's very pretty people don't listen to what you say. . . . And that is what I like," she added energetically, as if the memory were very happy. "I like walking in Richmond Park and singing to myself and knowing it doesn't matter a damn to anybody. I like seeing things go on—as we saw you that night when you didn't see us—I love the freedom of it—it's like being the wind or the sea." She turned with a curious fling of her hands and looked at the sea. It was still very blue, dancing away as far as the eye could reach, but the light on it was yellower, and the clouds were turning flamingo red.

A feeling of intense depression crossed Hewet's mind as she spoke. It seemed plain that she would never care for one person rather than another; she was evidently quite indifferent to him; they seemed to come very near, and then they were as far apart as ever again; and her gesture as she turned away had been oddly beautiful.

"Nonsense," he said abruptly. "You like people. You like admiration. Your real grudge against Hirst is that he doesn't admire you."

She made no answer for some time. Then she said:

"That's probably true. Of course I like people—I like almost every one I've ever met."

She turned her back on the sea and regarded Hewet with friendly if critical eyes. He was good-looking in the sense that he had always had a sufficiency of beef to eat and fresh air to breathe. His head was big; the eyes were also large; though generally vague they could be forcible; and the lips were sensitive. One might account him a man of considerable passion and fitful energy, likely to be at the mercy of moods which had little relation to facts; at once tolerant and fastidious. The breadth of his forehead showed capacity for thought. The interest with which Rachel looked at him was heard in her voice.

"What novels do you write?" she asked.

"I want to write a novel about Silence," he said; "the things people don't say. But the difficulty is immense." He sighed. "However, you don't care," he continued. He looked at her almost severely. "Nobody cares. All you read a novel for is to see what sort of person the writer is, and, if you know him, which of his friends he's put in. As for the novel itself, the whole conception, the way one's seen the thing, felt about it, make it stand in relation to other things, not one in a million cares for that. And yet I sometimes wonder whether there's anything else in the whole world worth doing. These other people," he indicated the hotel, "are always wanting something they can't get. But there's an extraordinary satisfaction in writing, even in the attempt to write. What you said just now is true: one doesn't want to be things; one wants merely to be allowed to see them."

Some of the satisfaction of which he spoke came into his face as he gazed out to sea.

It was Rachel's turn now to feel depressed. As he talked of writing he had become suddenly impersonal. He might never care for any one; all that desire to know her and get at her, which she had felt pressing on her almost painfully, had completely vanished.

"Are you a good writer?" she asked.

"Yes," he said. "I'm not first-rate, of course; I'm good second-rate; about as good as Thackeray, I should say."

Rachel was amazed. For one thing it amazed her to hear Thackeray called second-rate; and then she could not widen her point of view to believe that there could be great writers in existence at the present day, or if there were, that any one she knew could be a great writer, and his self-confidence astounded her, and he became more and more remote.

"My other novel," Hewet continued, "is about a young man who is obsessed by an idea—the idea of being a gentleman. He manages to exist at Cambridge on a hundred pounds a year. He has a coat! it was once a very good coat. But the trousers—they're not so good. Well, he goes up to London, gets into good society, owing to an early-morning adventure on the banks of the Serpentine. He is led into telling lies—my idea, you see, is to show the gradual corruption of the soul—calls himself the son of some great landed proprietor in Devonshire. Meanwhile the coat becomes older and older, and he hardly dares to wear the trousers. Can't you imagine the wretched man, after some splendid evening of debauchery, contemplating these garments—hanging them over the end of the bed, arranging them now in full light, now in shade, and wondering whether they will survive him, or he will survive them? Thoughts of suicide cross his mind. He has a friend, too, a man who somehow subsists upon selling small birds, for which he sets traps in the fields near Uxbridge. They're scholars, both of them. I know one or two wretched starving creatures like that who quote Aristotle at you over a fried herring and a pint of porter. Fashionable life, too, I have to represent at some length, in order to show my hero under all circumstances. Lady Theo Bingham Bingley, whose bay mare he had the good fortune to stop, is the daughter of a very fine old Tory peer. I'm going to describe the kind of parties I once went to—the fashionable intellectuals, you know, who like to have the latest book on their tables. They give parties, river parties, parties where you play games. There's no difficulty in conceiving incidents; the difficulty is to put them into shape—not to get run away with, as Lady Theo was. It ended disastrously for her, poor woman, for the book, as I planned it, was going to end in profound and sordid respectability. Disowned by her father, she marries my hero, and they live in a snug little villa outside Croydon, in which town he is set up as a house agent. He never succeeds in becoming a real gentleman after all. That's the interesting part of it. Does it seem to you the kind of book you'd like to read?" he enquired; "or perhaps you'd like my Stuart tragedy better," he continued, without waiting for her to answer him. "My idea is that there's a certain quality of beauty in the past, which the ordinary historical novelist completely ruins by his absurd conventions. The moon becomes the Regent of the Skies. People clap spurs to their horses, and so on. I'm going to treat people as though they were exactly the same as we are. The advantage is that, detached from modern conditions, one can make them more intense and more abstract then people who live as we do."

Rachel had listened to all this with attention, but with a certain amount of bewilderment. They both sat thinking their own thoughts.

"I'm not like Hirst," said Hewet, after a pause; he spoke meditatively; "I don't see circles of chalk between people's feet. I sometimes wish I did. It seems to me so tremendously complicated and confused. One can't come to any decision at all; one's less and less capable of making judgments. D'you find that? And then one never knows what any one feels. We're all in the dark. We try to find out, but can you imagine anything more ludicrous than one person's opinion of another person? One goes along thinking one knows; but one really doesn't know."

As he said this he was leaning on his elbow arranging and rearranging in the grass the stones which had represented Rachel and her aunts at luncheon. He was speaking as much to himself as to Rachel. He was reasoning against the desire, which had returned with intensity, to take her in his arms; to have done with indirectness; to explain exactly what he felt. What he said was against his belief; all the things that were important about her he knew; he felt them in the air around them; but he said nothing; he went on arranging the stones.

"I like you; d'you like me?" Rachel suddenly observed.

"I like you immensely," Hewet replied, speaking with the relief of a person who is unexpectedly given an opportunity of saying what he wants to say. He stopped moving the pebbles.

"Mightn't we call each other Rachel and Terence?" he asked.

"Terence," Rachel repeated. "Terence—that's like the cry of an owl."

She looked up with a sudden rush of delight, and in looking at Terence with eyes widened by pleasure she was struck by the change that had come over the sky behind them. The substantial blue day had faded to a paler and more ethereal blue; the clouds were pink, far away and closely packed together; and the peace of evening had replaced the heat of the southern afternoon, in which they had started on their walk.

"It must be late!" she exclaimed.

It was nearly eight o'clock.

"But eight o'clock doesn't count here, does it?" Terence asked, as they got up and turned inland again. They began to walk rather quickly down the hill on a little path between the olive trees.

They felt more intimate because they shared the knowledge of what eight o'clock in Richmond meant. Terence walked in front, for there was not room for them side by side.

"What I want to do in writing novels is very much what you want to do when you play the piano, I expect," he began, turning and speaking over his shoulder. "We want to find out what's behind things, don't we?—

Look at the lights down there," he continued, "scattered about anyhow. Things I feel come to me like lights. . . . I want to combine them. . . . Have you ever seen fireworks that make figures? . . . I want to make figures. . . . Is that what you want to do?"

Now they were out on the road and could walk side by side.

"When I play the piano? Music is different. . . . But I see what you mean." They tried to invent theories and to make their theories agree. As Hewet had no knowledge of music, Rachel took his stick and drew figures in the thin white dust to explain how Bach wrote his fugues.

"My musical gift was ruined," he explained, as they walked on after one of these demonstrations, "by the village organist at home, who had invented a system of notation which he tried to teach me, with the result that I never got to the tune-playing at all. My mother thought music wasn't manly for boys; she wanted me to kill rats and birds—that's the worst of living in the country. We live in Devonshire. It's the loveliest place in the world. Only—it's always difficult at home when one's grown up. I'd like you to know one of my sisters. . . . Oh, here's your gate—" He pushed it open. They paused for a moment. She could not ask him to come in. She could not say that she hoped they would meet again; there was nothing to be said, and so without a word she went through the gate, and was soon invisible. Directly Hewet lost sight of her, he felt the old discomfort return, even more strongly than before. Their talk had been interrupted in the middle, just as he was beginning to say the things he wanted to say. After all, what had they been able to say? He ran his mind over the things they had said, the random, unnecessary things which had eddied round and round and used up all the time, and drawn them so close together and flung them so far apart, and left him in the end unsatisfied, ignorant still of what she felt and of what she was like. What was the use of talking, talking, merely talking?

17

It was now the height of the season, and every ship that came from England left a few people on the shores of Santa Marina who drove up to the hotel. The fact that the Ambroses had a house where one could escape momentarily from the slightly inhuman atmosphere of an hotel was a source of genuine pleasure not only to Hirst and Hewet, but to the Elliots, the Thornburys, the Flushings, Miss Allan, Evelyn M., together with other people whose identity was so little developed that the Ambroses did not discover that they possessed names. By degrees there was established a kind of correspondence between the two houses, the big and the small, so that at most hours of the day one house could guess what was going on in the other, and the words "the villa" and "the hotel" called up the idea of two separate systems of life. Acquaintances showed signs of developing into friends, for that one tie to Mrs. Parry's drawing-room had inevitably split into many other ties attached to different parts of England, and sometimes these alliances seemed cynically fragile, and sometimes painfully acute, lacking as they did the supporting background of organised English life. One night when the moon was round between the trees, Evelyn M. told Helen the story of her life, and claimed her everlasting friendship; or another occasion, merely because of a sigh, or a pause, or a word thoughtlessly dropped, poor Mrs. Elliot left the villa half in tears, vowing never again to meet the cold and scornful woman who had insulted her, and in truth, meet again they never did. It did not seem worth while to piece together so slight a friendship.

Hewet, indeed, might have found excellent material at this time up at the villa for some chapters in the novel which was to be called "Silence, or the Things People don't say." Helen and Rachel had become very silent. Having detected, as she thought, a secret, and judging that Rachel meant to keep it from her, Mrs. Ambrose respected it carefully, but from that cause, though unintentionally, a curious atmosphere of reserve grew up between them. Instead of sharing their views upon all subjects, and plunging after an idea wherever it might lead, they spoke chiefly in comment upon the people they saw, and the secret between them made itself felt in what they said even of Thornburys and Elliots. Always calm and unemotional in her judgments, Mrs. Ambrose was now inclined to be definitely pessimistic. She was not severe upon individuals so much as incredulous of the kindness of destiny, fate, what happens in the long run, and apt to insist that this was generally adverse to people in proportion as they deserved well. Even this theory she was ready to discard in favour of one which made chaos triumphant, things happening for no reason at all, and every one groping about in illusion and ignorance. With a certain pleasure she developed these views to her niece, taking a letter from home as her test: which gave good news, but might just as well have given bad. How did she know that at this very moment both her children were not lying dead, crushed by motor omnibuses? "It's happening to somebody: why shouldn't it happen to me?" she would argue, her face taking on the stoical expression of anticipated sorrow. however sincere these views may have been, they were undoubtedly called forth by the irrational state of her niece's mind. It was so fluctuating, and went so quickly from joy to despair, that it seemed necessary to confront it with some stable opinion which naturally became dark as well as stable. Perhaps Mrs. Ambrose had some idea that in leading the talk into these quarters she might discover what was in Rachel's mind, but it was difficult to judge, for sometimes she would agree with the gloomiest thing that was said, at other times she refused to listen, and rammed Helen's theories down her throat with laughter, chatter, ridicule of the wildest, and fierce bursts of anger even at what she called the "croaking of a raven in the mud."

"It's hard enough without that," she asserted.

"What's hard?" Helen demanded.

"Life," she replied, and then they both became silent.

Helen might draw her own conclusions as to why life was hard, as to why an hour later, perhaps, life was something so wonderful and vivid that the eyes of Rachel beholding it were positively exhilarating to a spectator. True to her creed, she did not attempt to interfere, although there were enough of those weak moments of depression to make it perfectly easy for a less scrupulous person to press through and know all, and perhaps Rachel was sorry that she did not choose. All these moods ran themselves into one general effect, which Helen compared to the sliding of a river, quick, quicker, quicker still, as it races to a waterfall. Her instinct was to cry out Stop! but even had there been any use in crying Stop! she would have refrained, thinking it best that things should take their way, the water racing because the earth was shaped to make it race.

It seemed that Rachel herself had no suspicion that she was watched, or that there was anything in her manner likely to draw attention to her. What had happened to her she did not know. Her mind was very much in the condition of the racing water to which Helen compared it. She wanted to see Terence; she was perpetually wishing to see him when he was not there; it was an agony to miss seeing him; agonies were strewn all about her day on account of him, but she never asked herself what this force driving through her life arose from. She thought of no result any more than a tree perpetually pressed downwards by the wind considers the result of being pressed downwards by the wind.

During the two or three weeks which had passed since their walk, half a dozen notes from him had accumulated in her drawer. She would read them, and spend the whole morning in a daze of happiness; the sunny land outside the window being no less capable of analysing its own colour and heat than she was of analysing hers. In these moods she found it impossible to read or play the piano, even to move being beyond her inclination. The time passed without her noticing it. When it was dark she was drawn to the window by the lights of the hotel. A light that went in and out was the light in Terence's window: there he sat, reading perhaps, or now he was walking up and down pulling out one book after another; and now he was seated in his chair again, and she tried to imagine what he was thinking about. The steady lights marked the rooms where Terence sat with people moving round him. Every one who stayed in the hotel had a peculiar romance and interest about them. They were not ordinary people. She would attribute wisdom to Mrs. Elliot, beauty to Susan Warrington, a splendid vitality to Evelyn M., because Terence spoke to them. As unreflecting and pervasive were the moods of depression. Her mind was as the landscape outside when dark beneath clouds and straitly lashed by wind and hail. Again she would sit passive in her chair exposed to pain, and Helen's fantastical or gloomy words were like so many darts goading her to cry out against the hardness of life. Best of all were the moods when for no reason again this stress of feeling slackened, and life went on as usual, only with a joy and colour in its events that was unknown before; they had a significance like that which she had seen in the tree: the nights were black bars separating her from the days; she would have liked to run all the days into one long continuity of sensation. Although these moods were directly or indirectly caused by the presence of Terence or the thought of him, she never said to herself that she was in love with him, or considered what was to happen if she continued to feel such things, so that Helen's image of the river sliding on to the waterfall had a great likeness to the facts, and the alarm which Helen sometimes felt was justified.

In her curious condition of unanalysed sensations she was incapable of making a plan which should have any effect upon her state of mind. She abandoned herself to the mercy of accidents, missing Terence one day, meeting him the next, receiving his letters always with a start of surprise. Any woman experienced in the progress of courtship would have come by certain opinions from all this which would have given her at least a theory to go upon; but no one had ever been in love with Rachel, and she had never been in love with any one. Moreover, none of the books she read, from *Wuthering Heights* to *Man and Superman*, and the plays of Ibsen, suggested from their analysis of love that what their heroines felt was what she was feeling now. It seemed to her that her sensations had no name.

She met Terence frequently. When they did not meet, he was apt to send a note with a book or about a book, for he had not been able after all to neglect that approach to intimacy. But sometimes he did not come or did not write for several days at a time. Again when they met their meeting might be one of inspiriting joy or of harassing despair. Over all their partings hung the sense of interruption, leaving them both unsatisfied, though ignorant that the other shared the feeling.

If Rachel was ignorant of her own feelings, she was even more completely ignorant of his. At first he moved as a god; as she came to know him better he was still the centre of light, but combined with this beauty a wonderful power of making her daring and confident of herself. She was conscious of emotions and powers which she had never suspected in herself, and of a depth in the world hitherto unknown. When she thought of their relationship she saw rather than reasoned, representing her view of what Terence felt by a picture of him drawn across the room to stand by her side. This passage across the room amounted to a physical sensation, but what it meant she did not know.

Thus the time went on, wearing a calm, bright look upon its surface. Letters came from England, letters came from Willoughby, and the days accumulated their small events which shaped the year. Superficially, three odes of Pindar were mended, Helen covered about five inches of her embroidery, and St. John completed the first two acts of a play. He and Rachel being now very good friends, he read them aloud to her, and she was so genuinely impressed by the skill of his rhythms and the variety of his adjectives, as well as by the fact that he was Terence's friend, that he began to wonder whether he was not intended for literature rather than for law. It was a time of profound thought and sudden revelations for more than one couple, and several single people.

A Sunday came, which no one in the villa with the exception of Rachel and the Spanish maid proposed to recognise. Rachel still went to church, because she had never, according to Helen, taken the trouble to think about it. Since they had celebrated the service at the hotel she went there expecting to get some pleasure from her passage across the garden and through the hall of the hotel, although it was very doubtful whether she would see Terence, or at any rate have the chance of speaking to him.

As the greater number of visitors at the hotel were English, there was almost as much difference between Sunday and Wednesday as there is in England, and Sunday appeared here as there, the mute black ghost or penitent spirit of the busy weekday. The English could not pale the sunshine, but they could in some miraculous way slow down the hours, dull the incidents, lengthen the meals, and make even the servants and pageboys wear a look of boredom and propriety. The best clothes which every one put on helped the general effect; it seemed that no lady could sit down without bending a clean starched petticoat, and no gentleman could breathe without a sudden crackle from a stiff shirt-front.

As the hands of the clock neared eleven, on this particular Sunday, various people tended to draw together in the hall, clasping little red-leaved books in their hands. The clock marked a few minutes to the hour when a stout black figure passed through the hall with a preoccupied expression, as though he would rather not recognise salutations, although aware of them, and disappeared down the corridor which led from it.

"Mr. Bax," Mrs. Thornbury whispered.

The little group of people then began to move off in the same direction as the stout black figure. Looked at in an odd way by people who made no effort to join them, they moved with one exception slowly and consciously towards the stairs. Mrs. Flushing was the exception. She came running downstairs, strode across the hall, joined the procession much out of breath, demanding of Mrs. Thornbury in an agitated whisper, "Where, where?"

"We are all going," said Mrs. Thornbury gently, and soon they were descending the stairs two by two. Rachel was among the first to descend. She did not see that Terence and Hirst came in at the rear possessed of no black volume, but of one thin book bound in light-blue cloth, which St. John carried under his arm.

The chapel was the old chapel of the monks. It was a profound cool place where they had said Mass for hundreds of years, and done penance in the cold moonlight, and worshipped old brown pictures and carved saints which stood with upraised hands of blessing in the hollows in the walls. The transition from Catholic to Protestant worship had been bridged by a time of disuse, when there were no services, and the place was used for storing jars of oil, liqueur, and deck-chairs; the hotel flourishing, some religious body had taken the place in hand, and it was now fitted out with a number of glazed yellow benches, claret-coloured footstools; it had a small pulpit, and a brass eagle carrying the Bible on its back, while the piety of different women had supplied ugly squares of carpet, and long strips of embroidery heavily wrought with monograms in gold.

As the congregation entered they were met by mild sweet chords issuing from a harmonium, where Miss Willett, concealed from view by a baize curtain, struck emphatic chords with uncertain fingers. The sound spread through the chapel as the rings of water spread from a fallen stone. The twenty or twenty-five people who composed the congregation first bowed their heads and then sat up and looked about them. It was very quiet, and the light down here seemed paler than the light above. The usual bows and smiles were dispensed with, but they recognised each other. The Lord's Prayer was read over them. As the childlike battle of voices rose, the congregation, many of whom had only met on the staircase, felt themselves pathetically united and well-disposed towards each other. As if the prayer were a torch applied to fuel, a smoke seemed to rise automatically and fill the place with the ghosts of innumerable services on innumerable Sunday mornings at home. Susan Warrington in particular was conscious of the sweetest sense of sisterhood, as she covered her face with her hands and saw slips of bent backs through the chinks between her fingers. Her emotions rose calmly and evenly, approving of herself and of life at the same time. It was all so quiet and so good. But having created this peaceful atmosphere Mr. Bax suddenly turned the page and read a psalm. Though he read it with no change of voice the mood was broken.

"Be merciful unto me, O God," he read, "for man goeth about to devour me: he is daily fighting and troubling me. . . . They daily mistake my words: all that they imagine is to do me evil. They hold all together and keep themselves close. . . . Break their teeth, O God, in their mouths; smite the jaw-bones of the lions, O Lord: let them fall away like water that runneth apace; and when they shoot their arrows let them be rooted out."

Nothing in Susan's experience at all corresponded with this, and as she had no love of language she had long ceased to attend to such remarks, although she followed them with the same kind of mechanical respect with which she heard many of Lear's speeches read aloud. Her mind was still serene and really occupied with praise of her own nature and praise of God, that is of the solemn and satisfactory order of the world.

But it could be seen from a glance at their faces that most of the others, the men in particular, felt the inconvenience of the sudden intrusion of this old savage. They looked more secular and critical as then listened to the ravings of the old black man with a cloth round his loins cursing with vehement gesture by a camp-fire in the desert. After that there was a general sound of pages being turned as if they were in class, and then they read a little bit of the Old Testament about making a well, very much as school boys translate an easy passage from the *Anabasis* when they have shut up their French grammar. Then they returned to the New Testament and the sad and beautiful figure of Christ. While Christ spoke they made another effort to fit his interpretation of life upon the lives they lived, but as they were all very different, some practical, some ambitious, some stupid, some wild and experimental, some in love, and others long past any feeling except a feeling of comfort, they did very different things with the words of Christ.

From their faces it seemed that for the most part they made no effort at all, and, recumbent as it were, accepted the ideas the words gave as representing goodness, in the same way, no doubt, as one of those industrious needlewomen had accepted the bright ugly pattern on her mat as beauty.

Whatever the reason might be, for the first time in her life, instead of slipping at once into some curious pleasant cloud of emotion, too familiar to be considered, Rachel listened critically to what was being said. By the time they had swung in an irregular way from prayer to psalm, from psalm to history, from history to poetry, and Mr. Bax was giving out his text, she was in a state of acute discomfort. Such was the discomfort she felt when forced to sit through an unsatisfactory piece of music badly played. Tantalised, enraged by the clumsy insensitiveness of the conductor, who put the stress on the wrong places, and annoyed by the vast flock of the audience tamely praising and acquiescing without knowing or caring, so she was not tantalized and enraged, only here, with eyes half-shut and lips pursed together, the atmosphere of forced solemnity increased her anger. All round her were people pretending to feel what they did not feel, while somewhere above her floated the idea which they could none of them grasp, which they pretended to grasp, always escaping out of reach, a beautiful idea, an idea like a butterfly. One after another, vast and hard and cold, appeared to her the churches all over the world where this blundering effort and misunderstanding were perpetually going on, great buildings, filled with innumerable men and women, not seeing clearly, who finally gave up the effort to see, and relapsed tamely into praise and acquiescence, half-shutting their eyes and pursing up their lips. The thought had the same sort of physical discomfort as is caused by a film of mist always coming between the eyes and the printed page. She did her best to brush away the film and to conceive something to be worshipped as the service went on, but failed, always misled by the voice of Mr. Bax saying things which misrepresented the idea, and by the patter of baaing inexpressive human voices falling round her like damp leaves. The effort was tiring and dispiriting. She ceased to listen, and fixed her eyes on the face of a woman near her, a hospital nurse, whose expression of devout attention seemed to prove that she was at any rate receiving satisfaction. But looking at her carefully she came to the conclusion that the hospital nurse was only slavishly acquiescent, and that the look of satisfaction was produced by no splendid conception of God within her. How indeed, could she conceive anything far outside her own experience, a woman with a commonplace face like hers, a little round red face, upon which trivial duties and trivial spites had drawn lines, whose weak blue eyes saw without intensity or individuality, whose features were blurred, insensitive, and callous? She was adoring something shallow and smug, clinging to it, so the obstinate mouth witnessed, with the assiduity of a limpet; nothing would tear her from her demure belief in her own virtue and the virtues of her religion. She was a limpet, with the sensitive side of her stuck to a rock, for ever dead to the rush of fresh and beautiful things past her. The face of this single worshipper became printed on Rachel's mind with an impression of keen horror, and she had it suddenly revealed to her what Helen meant and St. John meant when they proclaimed their hatred of Christianity. With the violence that now marked her feelings, she rejected all that she had implicitly believed.

Meanwhile Mr. Bax was half-way through the second lesson. She looked at him. He was a man of the world with supple lips and an agreeable manner, he was indeed a man of much kindliness and simplicity, though by no means clever, but she was not in the mood to give any one credit for such qualities, and examined him as though he were an epitome of all the vices of his service.

Right at the back of the chapel Mrs. Flushing, Hirst, and Hewet sat in a row in a very different frame of mind. Hewet was staring at the roof with his legs stuck out in front of him, for as he had never tried to make the service fit any feeling or idea of his, he was able to enjoy the beauty of the language without hindrance. His mind was occupied first with accidental things, such as the women's hair in front of him, the light on the faces, then with the words which seemed to him magnificent, and then more vaguely with the characters of the other worshippers. But when he suddenly perceived Rachel, all these thoughts were driven out of his head, and he thought only of her. The psalms, the prayers, the Litany, and the sermon were all reduced to one chanting sound which paused, and then renewed itself, a little higher or a little lower. He stared alternately at Rachel and at the ceiling, but his expression was now produced not by what he saw but by something in his mind. He was almost as painfully disturbed by his thoughts as she was by hers.

Early in the service Mrs. Flushing had discovered that she had taken up a Bible instead of a prayer-book, and, as she was sitting next to Hirst, she stole a glance over his shoulder. He was reading steadily in the thin pale-blue volume. Unable to understand, she peered closer, upon which Hirst politely laid the book before her, pointing to the first line of a Greek poem and then to the translation opposite.

"What's that?" she whispered inquisitively.

"Sappho," he replied. "The one Swinburne did—the best thing that's ever been written."

Mrs. Flushing could not resist such an opportunity. She gulped down the Ode to Aphrodite during the Litany, keeping herself with difficulty from asking when Sappho lived, and what else she wrote worth reading, and contriving to come in punctually at the end with "the forgiveness of sins, the Resurrection of the body, and the life everlastin'. Amen."

Meanwhile Hirst took out an envelope and began scribbling on the back of it. When Mr. Bax mounted the pulpit he shut up Sappho with his envelope between the pages, settled his spectacles, and fixed his gaze intently upon the clergyman. Standing in the pulpit he looked very large and fat; the light coming through the greenish unstained window-glass made his face appear smooth and white like a very large egg.

He looked round at all the faces looking mildly up at him, although some of them were the faces of men and women old enough to be his grandparents, and gave out his text with weighty significance. The argument of the sermon was that visitors to this beautiful land, although they were on a holiday, owed a duty to the natives. It did not, in truth, differ very much from a leading article upon topics of general interest in the weekly newspapers. It rambled with a kind of amiable verbosity from one heading to another, suggesting that all human beings are very much the same under their skins, illustrating this by the resemblance of the games which little Spanish boys play to the games little boys in London streets play, observing that very small things do influence people, particularly natives; in fact, a very dear friend of Mr. Bax's had told him that the success of our rule in India, that vast country, largely depended upon the strict code of politeness which the English adopted towards the natives, which led to the remark that small things were not necessarily small, and that somehow to the virtue of sympathy, which was a virtue never more needed than today, when we lived in a time of experiment and upheaval—witness the aeroplane and wireless telegraph, and there were other problems which hardly presented themselves to our fathers, but which no man who called himself a man could leave unsettled. Here Mr. Bax became more definitely clerical, if it were possible, he seemed to speak with a certain innocent craftiness, as he pointed out that all this laid a special duty upon earnest Christians. What men were inclined to say now was, "Oh, that fellow—he's a parson." What we want them to say is, "He's a good fellow"—in other words, "He is my brother." He exhorted them to keep in touch with men of the modern type; they must sympathise with their multifarious interests in order to keep before their eyes that whatever discoveries were made there was one discovery which could not be superseded, which was indeed as much of a necessity to the most successful and most brilliant of them all as it had been to their fathers. The humblest could help; the least important things had an influence (here his manner became definitely priestly and his remarks seemed to be directed to women, for indeed Mr. Bax's congregations were mainly composed of women, and he was used to assigning them their duties in his innocent clerical campaigns). Leaving more definite instruction, he passed on, and his theme broadened into a peroration for which he drew a long breath and stood very upright—"As a drop of water, detached, alone, separate from others, falling from the cloud and entering the great ocean, alters, so scientists tell us, not only the immediate spot in the ocean where it falls, but all the myriad drops which together compose the great universe of waters, and by this means alters the configuration of the globe and the lives of millions of sea creatures, and finally the lives of the men and women who seek their living upon the shores—as all this is within the compass of a single drop of water, such as any rain shower sends in millions to lose themselves in the earth, to lose themselves we say, but we know very well that the fruits of the earth could not flourish without them—so is a marvel comparable to this within the reach of each one of us, who dropping a little word or a little deed into the great universe alters it; yea, it is a solemn thought, *alters* it, for good or for evil, not for one instant, or in one vicinity, but throughout the entire race, and for all eternity." Whipping round as though to avoid applause, he continued with the same breath, but in a different tone of voice—"And now to God the Father . . ."

He gave his blessing, and then, while the solemn chords again issued from the harmonium behind the curtain, the different people began scraping and fumbling and moving very awkwardly and consciously towards the door. Half-way upstairs, at a point where the light and sounds of the upper world conflicted with the dimness and the dying hymn-tune of the under, Rachel felt a hand drop upon her shoulder.

"Miss Vinrace," Mrs. Flushing whispered peremptorily, "stay to luncheon. It's such a dismal day. They don't even give one beef for luncheon. Please stay."

Here they came out into the hall, where once more the little band was greeted with curious respectful glances by the people who had not gone to church, although their clothing made it clear that they approved of Sunday to the very verge of going to church. Rachel felt unable to stand any more of this particular atmosphere, and was about to say she must go back, when Terence passed them, drawn along in talk with Evelyn M. Rachel thereupon contented herself with saying that the people looked very respectable, which negative remark Mrs. Flushing interpreted to mean that she would stay.

"English people abroad!" she returned with a vivid flash of malice. "Ain't they awful! But we won't stay here," she continued, plucking at Rachel's arm. "Come up to my room."

She bore her past Hewet and Evelyn and the Thornburys and the Elliots. Hewet stepped forward.

"Luncheon—" he began.

"Miss Vinrace has promised to lunch with me," said Mrs. Flushing, and began to pound energetically up the staircase, as though the middle classes of England were in pursuit. She did not stop until she had slammed her bedroom door behind them.

"Well, what did you think of it?" she demanded, panting slightly.

All the disgust and horror which Rachel had been accumulating burst forth beyond her control.

"I thought it the most loathsome exhibition I'd ever seen!" she broke out. "How can they—how dare they—what do you mean by it—Mr. Bax, hospital nurses, old men, prostitutes, disgusting——"

She hit off the points she remembered as fast as she could, but she was too indignant to stop to analyse her feelings. Mrs. Flushing watched her with keen gusto as she stood ejaculating with emphatic movements of her head and hands in the middle of the room.

"Go on, go on, do go on," she laughed, clapping her hands. "It's delightful to hear you!"

"But why do you go?" Rachel demanded.

"I've been every Sunday of my life ever since I can remember," Mrs. Flushing chuckled, as though that were a reason by itself.

Rachel turned abruptly to the window. She did not know what it was that had put her into such a passion; the sight of Terence in the hall had confused her thoughts, leaving her merely indignant. She looked straight at their own villa, half-way up the side of the mountain. The most familiar view seen framed through glass has a certain unfamiliar distinction, and she grew calm as she gazed. Then she remembered that she was in the presence of some one she did not know well, and she turned and looked at Mrs. Flushing. Mrs. Flushing was still sitting on the edge of the bed, looking up, with her lips parted, so that her strong white teeth showed in two rows.

"Tell me," she said, "which d'you like best, Mr. Hewet or Mr. Hirst?"

"Mr. Hewet," Rachel replied, but her voice did not sound natural.

"Which is the one who reads Greek in church?" Mrs. Flushing demanded.

It might have been either of them and while Mrs. Flushing proceeded to describe them both, and to say that both frightened her, but one frightened her more than the other, Rachel looked for a chair. The room, of course, was one of the largest and most luxurious in the hotel. There were a great many arm-chairs and settees covered in brown holland, but each of these was occupied by a large square piece of yellow cardboard, and all the pieces of cardboard were dotted or lined with spots or dashes of bright oil paint.

"But you're not to look at those," said Mrs. Flushing as she saw Rachel's eye wander. She jumped up, and turned as many as she could, face downwards, upon the floor. Rachel, however, managed to possess herself of one of them, and, with the vanity of an artist, Mrs. Flushing demanded anxiously, "Well, well?"

"It's a hill," Rachel replied. There could be no doubt that Mrs. Flushing had represented the vigorous and abrupt fling of the earth up into the air; you could almost see the clods flying as it whirled.

Rachel passed from one to another. They were all marked by something of the jerk and decision of their maker; they were all perfectly untrained onslaughts of the brush upon some half-realised idea suggested by hill or tree; and they were all in some way characteristic of Mrs. Flushing.

"I see things movin'," Mrs. Flushing explained. "So"—she swept her hand through a yard of the air. She then took up one of the cardboards which Rachel had laid aside, seated herself on a stool, and began to flourish a stump of charcoal. While she occupied herself in strokes which seemed to serve her as speech serves others, Rachel, who was very restless, looked about her.

"Open the wardrobe," said Mrs. Flushing after a pause, speaking indistinctly because of a paint-brush in her mouth, "and look at the things."

As Rachel hesitated, Mrs. Flushing came forward, still with a paint-brush in her mouth, flung open the wings of her wardrobe, and tossed a quantity of shawls, stuffs, cloaks, embroideries, on to the bed. Rachel began to finger them. Mrs. Flushing came up once more, and dropped a quantity of beads, brooches, earrings, bracelets, tassels, and combs among the draperies. Then she went back to her stool and began to paint in silence. The stuffs were coloured and dark and pale; they made a curious swarm of lines and colours upon the counterpane, with the reddish lumps of stone and peacocks' feathers and clear pale tortoise-shell combs lying among them.

"The women wore them hundreds of years ago, they wear 'em still," Mrs. Flushing remarked. "My husband rides about and finds 'em; they don't know what they're worth, so we get 'em cheap. And we shall sell 'em to smart women in London," she chuckled, as though the thought of these ladies and their absurd appearance amused her. After painting for some minutes, she suddenly laid down her brush and fixed her eyes upon Rachel.

"I tell you what I want to do," she said. "I want to go up there and see things for myself. It's silly stayin' here with a pack of old maids as though we were at the seaside in England. I want to go up the river and see the natives in their camps. It's only a matter of ten days under canvas. My husband's done it. One would lie out under the trees at night and be towed down the river by day, and if we saw anythin' nice we'd shout out and tell 'em to stop." She rose and began piercing the bed again and again with a long golden pin, as she watched to see what effect her suggestion had upon Rachel.

"We must make up a party," she went on. "Ten people could hire a launch. Now you'll come, and Mrs. Ambrose'll come, and will Mr. Hirst and t'other gentleman come? Where's a pencil?"

She became more and more determined and excited as she evolved her plan. She sat on the edge of the bed and wrote down a list of surnames, which she invariably spelt wrong. Rachel was enthusiastic, for indeed the idea was immeasurably delightful to her. She had always had a great desire to see the river, and the name of Terence threw a lustre over the prospect, which made it almost too good to come true. She did what she could to help Mrs. Flushing by suggesting names, helping her to spell them, and counting up the days of the week upon her fingers. As Mrs. Flushing wanted to know all she could tell her about the birth and pursuits of every person she suggested, and threw in wild stories of her own as to the temperaments and habits of artists, and people of the same name who used to come to Chillingley in the old days, but were doubtless not the same, though they too were very clever men interested in Egyptology, the business took some time. At last Mrs. Flushing sought her diary for help, the method of reckoning dates on the fingers proving unsatisfactory. She opened and shut every drawer in her writing-table, and then cried furiously, "Yarmouth! Yarmouth! Drat the woman! She's always out of the way when she's wanted!"

At this moment the luncheon gong began to work itself into its midday frenzy. Mrs. Flushing rang her bell violently. The door was opened by a handsome maid who was almost as upright as her mistress.

"Oh, Yarmouth," said Mrs. Flushing, "just find my diary and see where ten days from now would bring us to, and ask the hall porter how many men 'ud be wanted to row eight people up the river for a week, and what it 'ud cost, and put it on a slip of paper and leave it on my dressing-table. Now—" she pointed at the door with a superb forefinger so that Rachel had to lead the way.

"Oh, and Yarmouth," Mrs. Flushing called back over her shoulder. "Put those things away and hang 'em in their right places, there's a good girl, or it fusses Mr. Flushin'."

To all of which Yarmouth merely replied, "Yes, ma'am."

As they entered the long dining-room it was obvious that the day was still Sunday, although the mood was slightly abating. The Flushings' table was set by the side in the window, so that Mrs. Flushing could scrutinise each figure as it entered, and her curiosity seemed to be intense.

"Old Mrs. Paley," she whispered as the wheeled chair slowly made its way through the door, Arthur pushing behind. "Thornburys" came next. "That nice woman," she nudged Rachel to look at Miss Allan. "What's her name?" The painted lady who always came in late, tripping into the room with a prepared smile as though she came out upon a stage, might well have quailed before Mrs. Flushing's stare, which expressed her steely hostility to the whole tribe of painted ladies. Next came the two young men whom Mrs. Flushing called collectively the Hirsts. They sat down opposite, across the gangway.

Mr. Flushing treated his wife with a mixture of admiration and indulgence, making up by the suavity and fluency of his speech for the abruptness of hers. While she darted and ejaculated he gave Rachel a sketch of the history of South American art. He would deal with one of his wife's exclamations, and then return as smoothly as ever to his theme. He knew very well how to make a luncheon pass agreeably, without being dull or intimate. He had formed the opinion, so he told Rachel, that wonderful treasures lay hid in the depths of the land; the things Rachel had seen were merely trifles picked up in the course of one short journey. He thought there might be giant gods hewn out of stone in the mountain-side; and colossal figures standing by themselves in the middle of vast green pasture lands, where none but natives had ever trod. Before the dawn of European art he believed that the primitive huntsmen and priests had built temples of massive stone slabs, had formed out of the dark rocks and the great cedar trees majestic figures of gods and of beasts, and symbols of the great forces, water, air, and forest among which they lived. There might be prehistoric towns, like those in Greece and Asia, standing in open places among the trees, filled with the works of this early race. Nobody had been there; scarcely anything was known. Thus talking and displaying the most picturesque of his theories, Rachel's attention was fixed upon him.

She did not see that Hewet kept looking at her across the gangway, between the figures of waiters hurrying past with plates. He was inattentive, and Hirst was finding him also very cross and disagreeable. They had touched upon all the usual topics—upon politics and literature, gossip and Christianity. They had quarrelled over the service, which was every bit as fine as Sappho, according to Hewet; so that Hirst's paganism was mere ostentation. Why go to church, he demanded, merely in order to read Sappho? Hirst observed that he had listened to every word of the sermon, as he could prove if Hewet would like a repetition of it; and he went to church in order to realise the nature of his Creator, which he had done very vividly that morning, thanks to Mr. Bax, who had inspired him to write three of the most superb lines in English literature, an invocation to the Deity.

"I wrote 'em on the back of the envelope of my aunt's last letter," he said, and pulled it from between the pages of Sappho.

"Well, let's hear them," said Hewet, slightly mollified by the prospect of a literary discussion.

"My dear Hewet, do you wish us both to be flung out of the hotel by an enraged mob of Thornburys and Elliots?" Hirst enquired. "The merest whisper would be sufficient to incriminate me for ever. God!" he broke out, "what's the use of attempting to write when the world's peopled by such damned fools? Seriously, Hewet, I advise you to give up literature. What's the good of it? There's your audience."

He nodded his head at the tables where a very miscellaneous collection of Europeans were now engaged in eating, in some cases in gnawing, the stringy foreign fowls. Hewet looked, and grew more out of temper than ever. Hirst looked too. His eyes fell upon Rachel, and he bowed to her.

"I rather think Rachel's in love with me," he remarked, as his eyes returned to his plate. "That's the worst of friendships with young women—they tend to fall in love with one."

To that Hewet made no answer whatever, and sat singularly still. Hirst did not seem to mind getting no answer, for he returned to Mr. Bax again, quoting the peroration about the drop of water; and when Hewet scarcely replied to these remarks either, he merely pursed his lips, chose a fig, and relapsed quite contentedly into his own thoughts, of which he always had a very large supply. When luncheon was over they separated, taking their cups of coffee to different parts of the hall.

From his chair beneath the palm-tree Hewet saw Rachel come out of the dining-room with the Flushings; he saw them look round for chairs, and choose three in a corner where they could go on talking in private. Mr. Flushing was now in the full tide of his discourse. He produced a sheet of paper upon which he made drawings as he went on with his talk. He saw Rachel lean over and look, pointing to this and that with her finger. Hewet unkindly compared Mr. Flushing, who was extremely well dressed for a hot climate, and rather elaborate in his manner, to a very persuasive shop-keeper. Meanwhile, as he sat looking at them, he was entangled in the Thornburys and Miss Allan, who, after hovering about for a minute or two, settled in chairs round him, holding their cups in their hands. They wanted to know whether he could tell them anything about Mr. Bax. Mr. Thornbury as usual sat saying nothing, looking vaguely ahead of him, occasionally raising his eye-glasses, as if to put them on, but always thinking better of it at the last moment, and letting them fall again. After some discussion, the ladies put it beyond a doubt that Mr. Bax was not the son of Mr. William Bax. There was a pause. Then Mrs. Thornbury remarked that she was still in the habit of saying Queen instead of King in the National Anthem. There was another pause. Then Miss Allan observed reflectively that going to church abroad always made her feel as if she had been to a sailor's funeral. There was then a very long pause, which threatened to be final, when, mercifully, a bird about the size of a magpie, but of a metallic blue colour, appeared on the section of the terrace that could be seen from where they sat. Mrs. Thornbury was led to enquire whether we should like it if all our rooks were blue—"What do *you* think, William?" she asked, touching her husband on the knee.

"If all our rooks were blue," he said—he raised his glasses; he actually placed them on his nose—"they would not live long in Wiltshire," he concluded; he dropped his glasses to his side again. The three elderly people now gazed meditatively at the bird, which was so obliging as to stay in the middle of the view for a considerable space of time, thus making it unnecessary for them to speak again. Hewet began to wonder whether he might not cross over to the Flushings' corner, when Hirst appeared from the background, slipped into a chair by Rachel's side, and began to talk to her with every appearance of familiarity. Hewet could stand it no longer. He rose, took his hat and dashed out of doors.

18

Everything he saw was distasteful to him. He hated the blue and white, the intensity and definiteness, the hum and heat of the south; the landscape seemed to him as hard and as romantic as a cardboard background on the stage, and the mountain but a wooden screen against a sheet painted blue. He walked fast in spite of the heat of the sun.

Two roads led out of the town on the eastern side; one branched off towards the Ambroses' villa, the other struck into the country, eventually reaching a village on the plain, but many footpaths, which had been stamped in the earth when it was wet, led off from it, across great dry fields, to scattered farm-houses, and the villas of rich natives. Hewet stepped off the road on to one of these, in order to avoid the hardness and heat of the main road, the dust of which was always being raised in small clouds by carts and ramshackle flies which carried parties of festive peasants, or turkeys swelling unevenly like a bundle of air balls beneath a net, or the brass bedstead and black wooden boxes of some newly wedded pair.

The exercise indeed served to clear away the superficial irritations of the morning, but he remained miserable. It seemed proved beyond a doubt that Rachel was indifferent to him, for she had scarcely looked at him, and she had talked to Mr. Flushing with just the same interest with which she talked to him. Finally, Hirst's odious words flicked his mind like a whip, and he remembered that he had left her talking to Hirst. She was at this moment talking to him, and it might be true, as he said, that she was in love with him. He went over all the evidence for this supposition—her sudden interest in Hirst's writing, her way of quoting his opinions respectfully, or with only half a laugh; her very nickname for him, "the great Man," might have some serious meaning in it. Supposing that there were an understanding between them, what would it mean to him?

"Damn it all!" he demanded, "am I in love with her?" To that he could only return himself one answer. He certainly was in love with her, if he knew what love meant. Ever since he had first seen her he had been interested and attracted, more and more interested and attracted, until he was scarcely able to think of anything except Rachel. But just as he was sliding into one of the long feasts of meditation about them both, he checked himself by asking whether he wanted to marry her? That was the real problem, for these miseries and agonies could not be endured, and it was necessary that he should make up his mind. He instantly decided that he did not want to marry any one. Partly because he was irritated by Rachel the idea of marriage irritated him. It immediately suggested the picture of two people sitting alone over the fire; the man was reading, the woman sewing. There was a second picture. He saw a man jump up, say good-night, leave the company and hasten away with the quiet secret look of one who is stealing to certain happiness. Both these pictures were very unpleasant, and even more so was a third picture, of husband and wife and friend; and the married people glancing at each other as though they were content to let something pass unquestioned, being themselves possessed of the deeper truth. Other pictures—he was walking very fast in his irritation, and they came before him without any conscious effort, like pictures on a sheet—succeeded these. Here were the worn husband and wife sitting with their children round them, very patient, tolerant, and wise. But that too, was an unpleasant picture. He tried all sorts of pictures, taking them from the lives of friends of his, for he knew many different married couples; but he saw them always, walled up in a warm firelit room. When, on the other hand, he began to think of unmarried people, he saw them active in an unlimited world; above all, standing on the same ground as the rest, without shelter or advantage. All the most individual and humane of his friends were bachelors and spinsters; indeed he was surprised to find that the women he most admired and knew best were unmarried women. Marriage seemed to be worse for them than it was for men. Leaving these general pictures he considered the people whom he had been observing lately at the hotel. He had often revolved these questions in his mind, as he watched Susan and Arthur, or Mr. and Mrs. Thornbury, or Mr. and Mrs. Elliot. He had observed how the shy happiness and surprise of the engaged couple had gradually been replaced by a comfortable, tolerant state of mind, as if they had already done with the adventure of intimacy and were taking up their parts. Susan used to pursue Arthur about with a sweater, because he had one day let slip that a brother of his had died of pneumonia. The sight amused him, but was not pleasant if you substituted Terence and Rachel for Arthur and Susan; and Arthur was far less eager to get you in a corner and talk about flying and the mechanics of aeroplanes. They would settle down. He then looked at the couples who had been married for several years. It was true that Mrs. Thornbury had a husband, and that for the most part she was wonderfully successful in bringing him into the conversation, but one could not imagine what they said to each other when they were alone. There was the same difficulty with regard to the Elliots, except that they probably bickered openly in private. They sometimes bickered in public, though these disagreements were painfully covered over by little insincerities on the part of the wife, who was afraid of public opinion, because she was much stupider than her husband, and had to make efforts to keep hold of him. There could be no doubt, he decided, that it would have been far better for the world if these couples had separated. Even the Ambroses, whom he admired and respected profoundly—in spite of all the love between them, was not their marriage too a compromise? She gave way to him; she spoilt him; she arranged things for him; she who was all truth to others was not true to her husband, was not true to her friends if they came in conflict with her husband. It was a strange and piteous flaw in her nature. Perhaps Rachel had been right, then, when she said that night in the garden, "We bring out what's worst in each other—we should live separate."

No Rachel had been utterly wrong! Every argument seemed to be against undertaking the burden of marriage until he came to Rachel's argument, which was manifestly absurd. From having been the pursued, he turned and became the pursuer. Allowing the case against marriage to lapse, he began to consider the peculiarities of character which had led to her saying that. Had she meant it? Surely one ought to know the character of the person with whom one might spend all one's life; being a novelist, let him try to discover what sort of person she was. When he was with her he could not analyse her qualities, because he seemed to know them instinctively, but when he was away from her it sometimes seemed to him that he did not know her at all. She was young, but she was also old; she had little self-confidence, and yet she was a good judge of people. She was happy; but what made her happy? If they were alone and the excitement had worn off, and they had to deal with the ordinary facts of the day, what would happen? Casting his eye upon his own character, two things appeared to him: that he was very unpunctual, and that he disliked answering notes. As far as he knew Rachel was inclined to be punctual, but he could not remember that he had ever seen her with a pen in her hand. Let him next imagine a dinner-party, say at the Crooms, and Wilson, who had taken her down, talking about the state of the Liberal party. She would say—of course she was absolutely ignorant of politics. Nevertheless she was intelligent certainly, and honest too. Her temper was uncertain—that he had noticed—and she was not domestic, and she was not easy, and she was not quiet, or beautiful, except in some dresses in some lights. But the great gift she had was that she understood what was said to her; there had never been any one like her for talking to. You could say anything—you could say everything, and yet she was never servile. Here he pulled himself up, for it seemed to him suddenly that he knew less about her than about any one. All these thoughts had occurred to him many times already; often had he tried to argue and reason; and again he had reached the old state of doubt. He did not know her, and he did not know what she felt, or whether they could live together, or whether he wanted to marry her, and yet he was in love with her.

Supposing he went to her and said (he slackened his pace and began to speak aloud, as if he were speaking to Rachel):

"I worship you, but I loathe marriage, I hate its smugness, its safety, its compromise, and the thought of you interfering in my work, hindering me; what would you answer?"

He stopped, leant against the trunk of a tree, and gazed without seeing them at some stones scattered on the bank of the dry river-bed. He saw Rachel's face distinctly, the grey eyes, the hair, the mouth; the face that could look so many things—plain, vacant, almost insignificant, or wild, passionate, almost beautiful, yet in his eyes was always the same because of the extraordinary freedom with which she looked at him, and spoke as she felt. What would she answer? What did she feel? Did she love him, or did she feel nothing at all for him or for any other man, being, as she had said that afternoon, free, like the wind or the sea?

"Oh, you're free!" he exclaimed, in exultation at the thought of her, "and I'd keep you free. We'd be free together. We'd share everything together. No happiness would be like ours. No lives would compare with ours." He opened his arms wide as if to hold her and the world in one embrace.

No longer able to consider marriage, or to weigh coolly what her nature was, or how it would be if they lived together, he dropped to the ground and sat absorbed in the thought of her, and soon tormented by the desire to be in her presence again.

19

But Hewet need not have increased his torments by imagining that Hirst was still talking to Rachel. The party very soon broke up, the Flushings going in one direction, Hirst in another, and Rachel remaining in the hall, pulling the illustrated papers about, turning from one to another, her movements expressing the unformed restless desire in her mind. She did not know whether to go or to stay, though Mrs. Flushing had commanded her to appear at tea. The hall was empty, save for Miss Willett who was playing scales with her fingers upon a sheet of sacred music, and the Carters, an opulent couple who disliked the girl, because her shoe laces were untied, and she did not look sufficiently cheery, which by some indirect process of thought led them to think that she would not like them. Rachel certainly would not have liked them, if she had seen them, for the excellent reason that Mr. Carter waxed his moustache, and Mrs. Carter wore bracelets, and they were evidently the kind of people who would not like her; but she was too much absorbed by her own restlessness to think or to look.

She was turning over the slippery pages of an American magazine, when the hall door swung, a wedge of light fell upon the floor, and a small white figure upon whom the light seemed focussed, made straight across the room to her.

"What! You here?" Evelyn exclaimed. "Just caught a glimpse of you at lunch; but you wouldn't condescend to look at *me*."

It was part of Evelyn's character that in spite of many snubs which she received or imagined, she never gave up the pursuit of people she wanted to know, and in the long run generally succeeded in knowing them and even in making them like her.

She looked round her. "I hate this place. I hate these people," she said. "I wish you'd come up to my room with me. I do want to talk to you."

As Rachel had no wish to go or to stay, Evelyn took her by the wrist and drew her out of the hall and up the stairs. As they went upstairs two steps at a time, Evelyn, who still kept hold of Rachel's hand, ejaculated broken sentences about not caring a hang what people said. "Why should one, if one knows one's right? And let 'em all go to blazes! Them's my opinions!"

She was in a state of great excitement, and the muscles of her arms were twitching nervously. It was evident that she was only waiting for the door to shut to tell Rachel all about it. Indeed, directly they were inside her room, she sat on the end of the bed and said, "I suppose you think I'm mad?"

Rachel was not in the mood to think clearly about any one's state of mind. She was however in the mood to say straight out whatever occurred to her without fear of the consequences.

"Somebody's proposed to you," she remarked.

"How on earth did you guess that?" Evelyn exclaimed, some pleasure mingling with her surprise. "Do as I look as if I'd just had a proposal?"

"You look as if you had them every day," Rachel replied.

"But I don't suppose I've had more than you've had," Evelyn laughed rather insincerely.

"I've never had one."

"But you will—lots—it's the easiest thing in the world—But that's not what's happened this afternoon exactly. It's—Oh, it's a muddle, a detestable, horrible, disgusting muddle!"

She went to the wash-stand and began sponging her cheeks with cold water; for they were burning hot. Still sponging them and trembling slightly she turned and explained in the high pitched voice of nervous excitement: "Alfred Perrott says I've promised to marry him, and I say I never did. Sinclair says he'll shoot himself if I don't marry him, and I say, 'Well, shoot yourself!' But of course he doesn't—they never do. And Sinclair got hold of me this afternoon and began bothering me to give an answer, and accusing me of flirting with Alfred Perrott, and told me I'd no heart, and was merely a Siren, oh, and quantities of pleasant things like that. So at last I said to him, 'Well, Sinclair, you've said enough now. You can just let me go.' And then he caught me and kissed me—the disgusting brute—I can still feel his nasty hairy face just there—as if he'd any right to, after what he'd said!"

She sponged a spot on her left cheek energetically.

"I've never met a man that was fit to compare with a woman!" she cried; "they've no dignity, they've no courage, they've nothing but their beastly passions and their brute strength! Would any woman have behaved like that—if a man had said he didn't want her? We've too much self-respect; we're infinitely finer than they are."

She walked about the room, dabbing her wet cheeks with a towel. Tears were now running down with the drops of cold water.

"It makes me angry," she explained, drying her eyes.

Rachel sat watching her. She did not think of Evelyn's position; she only thought that the world was full or people in torment.

"There's only one man here I really like," Evelyn continued; "Terence Hewet. One feels as if one could trust him."

At these words Rachel suffered an indescribable chill; her heart seemed to be pressed together by cold hands.

"Why?" she asked. "Why can you trust him?"

"I don't know," said Evelyn. "Don't you have feelings about people? Feelings you're absolutely certain are right? I had a long talk with Terence the other night. I felt we were really friends after that. There's something of a woman in him—" She paused as though she were thinking of very intimate things that Terence had told her, so at least Rachel interpreted her gaze.

She tried to force herself to say, "Has to be proposed to you?" but the question was too tremendous, and in another moment Evelyn was saying that the finest men were like women, and women were nobler than men—for example, one couldn't imagine a woman like Lillah Harrison thinking a mean thing or having anything base about her.

"How I'd like you to know her!" she exclaimed.

She was becoming much calmer, and her cheeks were now quite dry. Her eyes had regained their usual expression of keen vitality, and she seemed to have forgotten Alfred and Sinclair and her emotion.

"Lillah runs a home for inebriate women in the Deptford Road," she continued. "She started it, managed it, did everything off her own bat, and it's now the biggest of its kind in England. You can't think what those women are like—and their homes. But she goes among them at all hours of the day and night. I've often been with her. . . . That's what's the matter with us. . . . We don't *do* things. What do you *do?*" she demanded, looking at Rachel with a slightly ironical smile. Rachel had scarcely listened to any of this, and her expression was vacant and unhappy. She had conceived an equal dislike for Lillah Harrison and her work in the Deptford Road, and for Evelyn M. and her profusion of love affairs.

"I play," she said with an affection of stolid composure.

"That's about it!" Evelyn laughed. "We none of us do anything but play. And that's why women like Lillah Harrison, who's worth twenty of you and me, have to work themselves to the bone. But I'm tired of playing," she went on, lying flat on the bed, and raising her arms above her head. Thus stretched out, she looked more diminutive than ever.

"I'm going to do something. I've got a splendid idea. Look here, you must join. I'm sure you've got any amount of stuff in you, though you look—well, as if you'd lived all your life in a garden." She sat up, and began to explain with animation. "I belong to a club in London. It meets every Saturday, so it's called the Saturday Club. We're supposed to talk about art, but I'm sick of talking about art—what's the good of it? With all kinds of real things going on round one? It isn't as if they'd got anything to say about art, either. So what I'm going to tell 'em is that we've talked enough about art, and we'd better talk about life for a change. Questions that really matter to people's lives, the White Slave Traffic, Women Suffrage, the Insurance Bill, and so on. And when we've made up our mind what we want to do we could form ourselves into a society for doing it. . . . I'm certain that if people like ourselves were to take things in hand instead of leaving it to policemen and magistrates, we could put a stop to—prostitution"—she lowered her voice at the ugly word—"in six months. My idea is that men and women ought to join in these matters. We ought to go into Piccadilly and stop one of these poor wretches and say: 'Now, look here, I'm no better than you are, and I don't pretend to be any better, but you're doing what you know to be beastly, and I won't have you doing beastly things, because we're all the same under our skins, and if you do a beastly thing it does matter to me.' That's what Mr. Bax was saying this morning, and it's true, though you clever people—you're clever too, aren't you?—don't believe it."

When Evelyn began talking—it was a fact she often regretted—her thoughts came so quickly that she never had any time to listen to other people's thoughts. She continued without more pause than was needed for taking breath.

"I don't see why the Saturday club people shouldn't do a really great work in that way," she went on. "Of course it would want organisation, some one to give their life to it, but I'm ready to do that. My notion's to think of the human beings first and let the abstract ideas take care of themselves. What's wrong with Lillah—if there is anything wrong—is that she thinks of Temperance first and the women afterwards. Now there's one thing I'll say to my credit," she continued; "I'm not intellectual or artistic or anything of that sort, but I'm jolly human." She slipped off the bed and sat on the floor, looking up at Rachel. She searched up into her face as if she were trying to read what kind of character was concealed behind the face. She put her hand on Rachel's knee.

"It *is* being human that counts, isn't it?" she continued. "Being real, whatever Mr. Hirst may say. Are you real?"

Rachel felt much as Terence had felt that Evelyn was too close to her, and that there was something exciting in this closeness, although it was also disagreeable. She was spared the need of finding an answer to the question, for Evelyn proceeded, "Do you *believe* in anything?"

In order to put an end to the scrutiny of these bright blue eyes, and to relieve her own physical restlessness, Rachel pushed back her chair and exclaimed, "In everything!" and began to finger different objects, the books on the table, the photographs, the freshly leaved plant with the stiff bristles, which stood in a large earthenware pot in the window.

"I believe in the bed, in the photographs, in the pot, in the balcony, in the sun, in Mrs. Flushing," she remarked, still speaking recklessly, with something at the back of her mind forcing her to say the things that one usually does not say. "But I don't believe in God, I don't believe in Mr. Bax, I don't believe in the hospital nurse. I don't believe—" She took up a photograph and, looking at it, did not finish her sentence.

"That's my mother," said Evelyn, who remained sitting on the floor binding her knees together with her arms, and watching Rachel curiously.

Rachel considered the portrait. "Well, I don't much believe in her," she remarked after a time in a low tone of voice.

Mrs. Murgatroyd looked indeed as if the life had been crushed out of her; she knelt on a chair, gazing piteously from behind the body of a Pomeranian dog which she clasped to her cheek, as if for protection.

"And that's my dad," said Evelyn, for there were two photographs in one frame. The second photograph represented a handsome soldier with high regular features and a heavy black moustache; his hand rested on the hilt of his sword; there was a decided likeness between him and Evelyn.

"And it's because of them," said Evelyn, "that I'm going to help the other women. You've heard about me, I suppose? They weren't married, you see; I'm not anybody in particular. I'm not a bit ashamed of it. They loved each other anyhow, and that's more than most people can say of their parents."

Rachel sat down on the bed, with the two pictures in her hands, and compared them—the man and the woman who had, so Evelyn said, loved each other. That fact interested her more than the campaign on behalf of unfortunate women which Evelyn was once more beginning to describe. She looked again from one to the other.

"What d'you think it's like," she asked, as Evelyn paused for a minute, "being in love?"

"Have you never been in love?" Evelyn asked. "Oh no—one's only got to look at you to see that," she added. She considered. "I really was in love once," she said. She fell into reflection, her eyes losing their bright vitality and approaching something like an expression of tenderness. "It was heavenly!—while it lasted. The worst of it is it don't last, not with me. That's the bother."

She went on to consider the difficulty with Alfred and Sinclair about which she had pretended to ask Rachel's advice. But she did not want advice; she wanted intimacy. When she looked at Rachel, who was still looking at the photographs on the bed, she could not help seeing that Rachel was not thinking about her. What was she thinking about, then? Evelyn was tormented by the little spark of life in her which was always trying to work through to other people, and was always being rebuffed. Falling silent she looked at her visitor, her shoes, her stockings, the combs in her hair, all the details of her dress in short, as though by seizing every detail she might get closer to the life within.

Rachel at last put down the photographs, walked to the window and remarked, "It's odd. People talk as much about love as they do about religion."

"I wish you'd sit down and talk," said Evelyn impatiently.

Instead Rachel opened the window, which was made in two long panes, and looked down into the garden below.

"That's where we got lost the first night," she said. "It must have been in those bushes."

"They kill hens down there," said Evelyn. "They cut their heads off with a knife—disgusting! But tell me—what——"

"I'd like to explore the hotel," Rachel interrupted. She drew her head in and looked at Evelyn, who still sat on the floor.

"It's just like other hotels," said Evelyn.

That might be, although every room and passage and chair in the place had a character of its own in Rachel's eyes; but she could not bring herself to stay in one place any longer. She moved slowly towards the door.

"What is it you want?" said Evelyn. "You make me feel as if you were always thinking of something you don't say. . . . Do say it!"

But Rachel made no response to this invitation either. She stopped with her fingers on the handle of the door, as if she remembered that some sort of pronouncement was due from her.

"I suppose you'll marry one of them," she said, and then turned the handle and shut the door behind her. She walked slowly down the passage, running her hand along the wall beside her. She did not think which way she was going, and therefore walked down a passage which only led to a window and a balcony. She looked down at the kitchen premises, the wrong side of the hotel life, which was cut off from the right side by a maze of small bushes. The ground was bare, old tins were scattered about, and the bushes wore towels and aprons upon their heads to dry. Every now and then a waiter came out in a white apron and threw rubbish on to a heap. Two large women in cotton dresses were sitting on a bench with blood-smeared tin trays in front of them and yellow bodies across their knees. They were plucking the birds, and talking as they plucked. Suddenly a chicken came floundering, half flying, half running into the space, pursued by a third woman whose age could hardly be under eighty. Although wizened and unsteady on her legs she kept up the chase, egged on by the laughter of the others; her face was expressive of furious rage, and as she ran she swore in Spanish. Frightened by hand-clapping here, a napkin there, the bird ran this way and that in sharp angles, and finally fluttered straight at the old woman, who opened her scanty grey skirts to enclose it, dropped upon it in a bundle, and then holding it out cut its head off with an expression of vindictive energy and triumph combined. The blood and the ugly wriggling fascinated Rachel, so that although she knew that some one had come up behind and was standing beside her, she did not turn round until the old woman had settled down on the bench beside the others. Then she looked up sharply, because of the ugliness of what she had seen. It was Miss Allan who stood beside her.

"Not a pretty sight," said Miss Allan, "although I daresay it's really more humane than our method. . . . I don't believe you've ever been in my room," she added, and turned away as if she meant Rachel to follow her. Rachel followed, for it seemed possible that each new person might remove the mystery which burdened her.

The bedrooms at the hotel were all on the same pattern, save that some were larger and some smaller; they had a floor of dark red tiles; they had a high bed, draped in mosquito curtains; they had each a writing-table and a dressing-table, and a couple of arm-chairs. But directly a box was unpacked the rooms became very different, so that Miss Allan's room was very unlike Evelyn's room. There were no variously coloured hatpins on her dressing-table; no scent-bottles; no narrow curved pairs of scissors; no great variety of shoes and boots; no silk petticoats lying on the chairs. The room was extremely neat. There seemed to be two pairs of everything. The writing-table, however, was piled with manuscript, and a table was drawn out to stand by the arm-chair on which were two separate heaps of dark library books, in which there were many slips of paper sticking out at different degrees of thickness. Miss Allan had asked Rachel to come in out of kindness, thinking that she was waiting about with nothing to do. Moreover, she liked young women, for she had taught many of them, and having received so much hospitality from the Ambroses she was glad to be able to repay a minute part of it. She looked about accordingly for something to show her. The room did not provide much entertainment. She touched her manuscript. "Age of Chaucer; Age of Elizabeth; Age of Dryden," she reflected; "I'm glad there aren't many more ages. I'm still in the middle of the eighteenth century. Won't you sit down, Miss Vinrace? The chair, though small, is firm. . . . Euphues. The germ of the English novel," she continued, glancing at another page. "Is that the kind of thing that interests you?"

She looked at Rachel with great kindness and simplicity, as though she would do her utmost to provide anything she wished to have. This expression had a remarkable charm in a face otherwise much lined with care and thought.

"Oh no, it's music with you, isn't it?" she continued, recollecting, "and I generally find that they don't go together. Sometimes of course we have prodigies—" She was looking about her for something and now saw a jar on the mantelpiece which she reached down and gave to Rachel. "If you put your finger into this jar you may be able to extract a piece of preserved ginger. Are you a prodigy?"

But the ginger was deep and could not be reached.

"Don't bother," she said, as Miss Allan looked about for some other implement. "I daresay I shouldn't like preserved ginger."

"You've never tried?" enquired Miss Allan. "Then I consider that it is your duty to try now. Why, you may add a new pleasure to life, and as you are still young—" She wondered whether a button-hook would do. "I make it a rule to try everything," she said. "Don't you think it would be very annoying if you tasted ginger for the first time on your death-bed, and found you never liked anything so much? I should be so exceedingly annoyed that I think I should get well on that account alone."

She was now successful, and a lump of ginger emerged on the end of the button-hook. While she went to wipe the button-hook, Rachel bit the ginger and at once cried, "I must spit it out!"

"Are you sure you have really tasted it?" Miss Allan demanded.

For answer Rachel threw it out of the window.

"An experience anyhow," said Miss Allan calmly. "Let me see—I have nothing else to offer you, unless you would like to taste this." A small cupboard hung above her bed, and she took out of it a slim elegant jar filled with a bright green fluid.

"Creme de Menthe," she said. "Liqueur, you know. It looks as if I drank, doesn't it? As a matter of fact it goes to prove what an exceptionally abstemious person I am. I've had that jar for six-and-twenty years," she added, looking at it with pride, as she tipped it over, and from the height of the liquid it could be seen that the bottle was still untouched.

"Twenty-six years?" Rachel exclaimed.

Miss Allan was gratified, for she had meant Rachel to be surprised.

"When I went to Dresden six-and-twenty years ago," she said, "a certain friend of mine announced her intention of making me a present. She thought that in the event of shipwreck or accident a stimulant might be useful. However, as I had no occasion for it, I gave it back on my return. On the eve of any foreign journey the same bottle always makes its appearance, with the same note; on my return in safety it is always handed back. I consider it a kind of charm against accidents. Though I was once detained twenty-four hours by an accident to the train in front of me, I have never met with any accident myself. Yes," she continued, now addressing the bottle, "we have seen many climes and cupboards together, have we not? I intend one of these days to have a silver label made with an inscription. It is a gentleman, as you may observe, and his name is Oliver. . . . I do not think I could forgive you, Miss Vinrace, if you broke my Oliver," she said, firmly taking the bottle out of Rachel's hands and replacing it in the cupboard.

Rachel was swinging the bottle by the neck. She was interested by Miss Allan to the point of forgetting the bottle.

"Well," she exclaimed, "I do think that odd; to have had a friend for twenty-six years, and a bottle, and—to have made all those journeys."

"Not at all; I call it the reverse of odd," Miss Allan replied. "I always consider myself the most ordinary person I know. It's rather distinguished to be as ordinary as I am. I forget—are you a prodigy, or did you say you were not a prodigy?"

She smiled at Rachel very kindly. She seemed to have known and experienced so much, as she moved cumbrously about the room, that surely there must be balm for all anguish in her words, could one induce her to have recourse to them. But Miss Allan, who was now locking the cupboard door, showed no signs of breaking the reticence which had snowed her under for years. An uncomfortable sensation kept Rachel silent; on the one hand, she wished to whirl high and strike a spark out of the cool pink flesh; on the other she perceived there was nothing to be done but to drift past each other in silence.

"I'm not a prodigy. I find it very difficult to say what I mean—" she observed at length.

"It's a matter of temperament, I believe," Miss Allan helped her. "There are some people who have no difficulty; for myself I find there are a great many things I simply cannot say. But then I consider myself very slow. One of my colleagues now, knows whether she likes you or not—let me see, how does she do it?—by the way you say good-morning at breakfast. It is sometimes a matter of years before I can make up my mind. But most young people seem to find it easy?"

"Oh no," said Rachel. "It's hard!"

Miss Allan looked at Rachel quietly, saying nothing; she suspected that there were difficulties of some kind. Then she put her hand to the back of her head, and discovered that one of the grey coils of hair had come loose.

"I must ask you to be so kind as to excuse me," she said, rising, "if I do my hair. I have never yet found a satisfactory type of hairpin. I must change my dress, too, for the matter of that; and I should be particularly glad of your assistance, because there is a tiresome set of hooks which I *can* fasten for myself, but it takes from ten to fifteen minutes; whereas with your help—"

She slipped off her coat and skirt and blouse, and stood doing her hair before the glass, a massive homely figure, her petticoat being so short that she stood on a pair of thick slate-grey legs.

"People say youth is pleasant; I myself find middle age far pleasanter," she remarked, removing hair pins and combs, and taking up her brush. When it fell loose her hair only came down to her neck.

"When one was young," she continued, "things could seem so very serious if one was made that way. . . . And now my dress."

In a wonderfully short space of time her hair had been reformed in its usual loops. The upper half of her body now became dark green with black stripes on it; the skirt, however, needed hooking at various angles, and Rachel had to kneel on the floor, fitting the eyes to the hooks.

"Our Miss Johnson used to find life very unsatisfactory, I remember," Miss Allan continued. She turned her back to the light. "And then she took to breeding guinea-pigs for their spots, and became absorbed in that. I have just heard that the yellow guinea-pig has had a black baby. We had a bet of sixpence on about it. She will be very triumphant."

The skirt was fastened. She looked at herself in the glass with the curious stiffening of her face generally caused by looking in the glass.

"Am I in a fit state to encounter my fellow-beings?" she asked. "I forget which way it is—but they find black animals very rarely have coloured babies—it may be the other way round. I have had it so often explained to me that it is very stupid of me to have forgotten again."

She moved about the room acquiring small objects with quiet force, and fixing them about her—a locket, a watch and chain, a heavy gold bracelet, and the parti-coloured button of a suffrage society. Finally, completely equipped for Sunday tea, she stood before Rachel, and smiled at her kindly. She was not an impulsive woman, and her life had schooled her to restrain her tongue. At the same time, she was possessed of an amount of good-will towards others, and in particular towards the young, which often made her regret that speech was so difficult.

"Shall we descend?" she said.

She put one hand upon Rachel's shoulder, and stooping, picked up a pair of walking-shoes with the other, and placed them neatly side by side outside her door. As they walked down the passage they passed many pairs of boots and shoes, some black and some brown, all side by side, and all different, even to the way in which they lay together.

"I always think that people are so like their boots," said Miss Allan. "That is Mrs. Paley's—" but as she spoke the door opened, and Mrs. Paley rolled out in her chair, equipped also for tea.

She greeted Miss Allan and Rachel.

"I was just saying that people are so like their boots," said Miss Allan. Mrs. Paley did not hear. She repeated it more loudly still. Mrs. Paley did not hear. She repeated it a third time. Mrs. Paley heard, but she did not understand. She was apparently about to repeat it for the fourth time, when Rachel suddenly said something inarticulate, and disappeared down the corridor. This misunderstanding, which involved a complete block in the passage, seemed to her unbearable. She walked quickly and blindly in the opposite direction, and found herself at the end of a *cul de sac*. There was a window, and a table and a chair in the window, and upon the table stood a rusty inkstand, an ashtray, an old copy of a French newspaper, and a pen with a broken nib. Rachel sat down, as if to study the French newspaper, but a tear fell on the blurred French print, raising a soft blot. She lifted her head sharply, exclaiming aloud, "It's intolerable!" Looking out of the window with eyes that would have seen nothing even had they not been dazed by tears, she indulged herself at last in violent abuse of the entire day. It had been miserable from start to finish; first, the service in the chapel; then luncheon; then Evelyn; then Miss Allan; then old Mrs. Paley blocking up the passage. All day long she had been tantalized and put off. She had now reached one of those eminences, the result of some crisis, from which the world is finally displayed in its true proportions. She disliked the look of it immensely—churches, politicians, misfits, and huge impostures—men like Mr. Dalloway, men like Mr. Bax, Evelyn and her chatter, Mrs. Paley blocking up the passage. Meanwhile the steady beat of her own pulse represented the hot current of feeling that ran down beneath; beating, struggling, fretting. For the time, her own body was the source of all the life in the world, which tried to burst forth here—there—and was repressed now by Mr. Bax, now by Evelyn, now by the imposition of ponderous stupidity, the weight of the entire world. Thus tormented, she would twist her hands together, for all things were wrong, all people stupid. Vaguely seeing that there were people down in the garden beneath she represented them as aimless masses of matter, floating hither and thither, without aim except to impede her. What were they doing, those other people in the world?

"Nobody knows," she said. The force of her rage was beginning to spend itself, and the vision of the world which had been so vivid became dim.

"It's a dream," she murmured. She considered the rusty inkstand, the pen, the ash-tray, and the old French newspaper. These small and worthless objects seemed to her to represent human lives.

"We're asleep and dreaming," she repeated. But the possibility which now suggested itself that one of the shapes might be the shape of Terence roused her from her melancholy lethargy. She became as restless as she had been before she sat down. She was no longer able to see the world as a town laid out beneath her. It was covered instead by a haze of feverish red mist. She had returned to the state in which she had been all day. Thinking was no escape. Physical movement was the only refuge, in and out of rooms, in and out of people's minds, seeking she knew not what. Therefore she rose, pushed back the table, and went downstairs. She went out of the hall door, and, turning the corner of the hotel, found herself among the people whom she had seen from the window. But owing to the broad sunshine after shaded passages, and to the substance of living people after dreams, the group appeared with startling intensity, as though the dusty surface had been peeled off everything, leaving only the reality and the instant. It had the look of a vision printed on the dark at night. White and grey and purple figures were scattered on the green, round wicker tables, in the middle the flame of the tea-urn made the air waver like a faulty sheet of glass, a massive green tree stood over them as if it were a moving force held at rest. As she approached, she could hear Evelyn's voice repeating monotonously, "Here then—here—good doggie, come here"; for a moment nothing seemed to happen; it all stood still, and then she realised that one of the figures was Helen Ambrose; and the dust again began to settle.

The group indeed had come together in a miscellaneous way; one tea-table joining to another tea-table, and deck-chairs serving to connect two groups. But even at a distance it could be seen that Mrs. Flushing, upright and imperious, dominated the party. She was talking vehemently to Helen across the table.

"Ten days under canvas," she was saying. "No comforts. If you want comforts, don't come. But I may tell you, if you don't come you'll regret it all your life. You say yes?"

At this moment Mrs. Flushing caught sight of Rachel.

"Ah, there's your niece. She's promised. You're coming, aren't you?" Having adopted the plan, she pursued it with the energy of a child.

Rachel took her part with eagerness.

"Of course I'm coming. So are you, Helen. And Mr. Pepper too." As she sat she realised that she was surrounded by people she knew, but that Terence was not among them. From various angles people began saying what they thought of the proposed expedition. According to some it would be hot, but the nights would be cold; according to others, the difficulties would lie rather in getting a boat, and in speaking the language. Mrs. Flushing disposed of all objections, whether due to man or due to nature, by announcing that her husband would settle all that.

Meanwhile Mr. Flushing quietly explained to Helen that the expedition was really a simple matter; it took five days at the outside; and the place—a native village—was certainly well worth seeing before she returned to England. Helen murmured ambiguously, and did not commit herself to one answer rather than to another.

The tea-party, however, included too many different kinds of people for general conversation to flourish; and from Rachel's point of view possessed the great advantage that it was quite unnecessary for her to talk. Over there Susan and Arthur were explaining to Mrs. Paley that an expedition had been proposed; and Mrs. Paley having grasped the fact, gave the advice of an old traveller that they should take nice canned vegetables, fur cloaks, and insect powder. She leant over to Mrs. Flushing and whispered something which from the twinkle in her eyes probably had reference to bugs. Then Helen was reciting "Toll for the Brave" to St. John Hirst, in order apparently to win a sixpence which lay upon the table; while Mr. Hughling Elliot imposed silence upon his section of the audience by his fascinating anecdote of Lord Curzon and the undergraduate's bicycle. Mrs. Thornbury was trying to remember the name of a man who might have been another Garibaldi, and had written a book which they ought to read; and Mr. Thornbury recollected that he had a pair of binoculars at anybody's service. Miss Allan meanwhile murmured with the curious intimacy which a spinster often achieves with dogs, to the fox-terrier which Evelyn had at last induced to come over to them. Little particles of dust or blossom fell on the plates now and then when the branches sighed above. Rachel seemed to see and hear a little of everything, much as a river feels the twigs that fall into it and sees the sky above, but her eyes were too vague for Evelyn's liking. She came across, and sat on the ground at Rachel's feet.

"Well?" she asked suddenly. "What are you thinking about?"

"Miss Warrington," Rachel replied rashly, because she had to say something. She did indeed see Susan murmuring to Mrs. Elliot, while Arthur stared at her with complete confidence in his own love. Both Rachel and Evelyn then began to listen to what Susan was saying.

"There's the ordering and the dogs and the garden, and the children coming to be taught," her voice proceeded rhythmically as if checking the list, "and my tennis, and the village, and letters to write for father, and a thousand little things that don't sound much; but I never have a moment to myself, and when I got to bed, I'm so sleepy I'm off before my head touches the pillow. Besides I like to be a great deal with my Aunts—I'm a great bore, aren't I, Aunt Emma?" (she smiled at old Mrs. Paley, who with head slightly drooped was regarding the cake with speculative affection), "and father has to be very careful about chills in winter which means a great deal of running about, because he won't look after himself, any more than you will, Arthur! So it all mounts up!"

Her voice mounted too, in a mild ecstasy of satisfaction with her life and her own nature. Rachel suddenly took a violent dislike to Susan, ignoring all that was kindly, modest, and even pathetic about her. She appeared insincere and cruel; she saw her grown stout and prolific, the kind blue eyes now shallow and watery, the bloom of the cheeks congealed to a network of dry red canals.

Helen turned to her. "Did you go to church?" she asked. She had won her sixpence and seemed making ready to go.

"Yes," said Rachel. "For the last time," she added.

In preparing to put on her gloves, Helen dropped one.

"You're not going?" Evelyn asked, taking hold of one glove as if to keep them.

"It's high time we went," said Helen. "Don't you see how silent every one's getting—?"

A silence had fallen upon them all, caused partly by one of the accidents of talk, and partly because they saw some one approaching. Helen could not see who it was, but keeping her eyes fixed upon Rachel observed something which made her say to herself, "So it's Hewet." She drew on her gloves with a curious sense of the significance of the moment. Then she rose, for Mrs. Flushing had seen Hewet too, and was demanding information about rivers and boats which showed that the whole conversation would now come over again.

Rachel followed her, and they walked in silence down the avenue. In spite of what Helen had seen and understood, the feeling that was uppermost in her mind was now curiously perverse; if she went on this expedition, she would not be able to have a bath, the effort appeared to her to be great and disagreeable.

"It's so unpleasant, being cooped up with people one hardly knows," she remarked. "People who mind being seen naked."

"You don't mean to go?" Rachel asked.

The intensity with which this was spoken irritated Mrs. Ambrose.

"I don't mean to go, and I don't mean not to go," she replied. She became more and more casual and indifferent.

"After all, I daresay we've seen all there is to be seen; and there's the bother of getting there, and whatever they may say it's bound to be vilely uncomfortable."

For some time Rachel made no reply; but every sentence Helen spoke increased her bitterness. At last she broke out—

"Thank God, Helen, I'm not like you! I sometimes think you don't think or feel or care to do anything but exist! You're like Mr. Hirst. You see that things are bad, and you pride yourself on saying so. It's what you call being honest; as a matter of fact it's being lazy, being dull, being nothing. You don't help; you put an end to things."

Helen smiled as if she rather enjoyed the attack.

"Well?" she enquired.

"It seems to me bad—that's all," Rachel replied.

"Quite likely," said Helen.

At any other time Rachel would probably have been silenced by her Aunt's candour; but this afternoon she was not in the mood to be silenced by any one. A quarrel would be welcome.

"You're only half alive," she continued.

"Is that because I didn't accept Mr. Flushing's invitation?" Helen asked, "or do you always think that?"

At the moment it appeared to Rachel that she had always seen the same faults in Helen, from the very first night on board the *Euphrosyne*, in spite of her beauty, in spite of her magnanimity and their love.

"Oh, it's only what's the matter with every one!" she exclaimed. "No one feels—no one does anything but hurt. I tell you, Helen, the world's bad. It's an agony, living, wanting——"

Here she tore a handful of leaves from a bush and crushed them to control herself.

"The lives of these people," she tried to explain, the aimlessness, the way they live. One goes from one to another, and it's all the same. One never gets what one wants out of any of them."

Her emotional state and her confusion would have made her an easy prey if Helen had wished to argue or had wished to draw confidences. But instead of talking she fell into a profound silence as they walked on. Aimless, trivial, meaningless, oh no—what she had seen at tea made it impossible for her to believe that. The little jokes, the chatter, the inanities of the afternoon had shrivelled up before her eyes. Underneath the likings and spites, the comings together and partings, great things were happening—terrible things, because they were so great. Her sense of safety was shaken, as if beneath twigs and dead leaves she had seen the movement of a snake. It seemed to her that a moment's respite was allowed, a moment's make-believe, and then again the profound and reasonless law asserted itself, moulding them all to its liking, making and destroying.

She looked at Rachel walking beside her, still crushing the leaves in her fingers and absorbed in her own thoughts. She was in love, and she pitied her profoundly. But she roused herself from these thoughts and apologised. "I'm very sorry," she said, "but if I'm dull, it's my nature, and it can't be helped." If it was a natural defect, however, she found an easy remedy, for she went on to say that she thought Mr. Flushing's scheme a very good one, only needing a little consideration, which it appeared she had given it by the time they reached home. By that time they had settled that if anything more was said, they would accept the invitation.

20

When considered in detail by Mr. Flushing and Mrs. Ambrose the expedition proved neither dangerous nor difficult. They found also that it was not even unusual. Every year at this season English people made parties which steamed a short way up the river, landed, and looked at the native village, bought a certain number of things from the natives, and returned again without damage done to mind or body. When it was discovered that six people really wished the same thing the arrangements were soon carried out.

Since the time of Elizabeth very few people had seen the river, and nothing has been done to change its appearance from what it was to the eyes of the Elizabethan voyagers. The time of Elizabeth was only distant from the present time by a moment of space compared with the ages which had passed since the water had run between those banks, and the green thickets swarmed there, and the small trees had grown to huge wrinkled trees in solitude. Changing only with the change of the sun and the clouds, the waving green mass had stood there for century after century, and the water had run between its banks ceaselessly, sometimes washing away earth and sometimes the branches of trees, while in other parts of the world one town had risen upon the ruins of another town, and the men in the towns had become more and more articulate and unlike each other. A few miles of this river were visible from the top of the mountain where some weeks before the party from the hotel had picnicked. Susan and Arthur had seen it as they kissed each other, and Terence and Rachel as they sat talking about Richmond, and Evelyn and Perrott as they strolled about, imagining that they were great captains sent to colonise the world. They had seen the broad blue mark across the sand where it flowed into the sea, and the green cloud of trees mass themselves about it farther up, and finally hide its waters altogether from sight. At intervals for the first twenty miles or so houses were scattered on the bank; by degrees the houses became huts, and, later still, there was neither hut nor house, but trees and grass, which were seen only by hunters, explorers, or merchants, marching or sailing, but making no settlement.

By leaving Santa Marina early in the morning, driving twenty miles and riding eight, the party, which was composed finally of six English people, reached the river-side as the night fell. They came cantering through the trees—Mr. and Mrs. Flushing, Helen Ambrose, Rachel, Terence, and St. John. The tired little horses then stopped automatically, and the English dismounted. Mrs. Flushing strode to the river-bank in high spirits. The day had been long and hot, but she had enjoyed the speed and the open air; she had left the hotel which she hated, and she found the company to her liking. The river was swirling past in the darkness; they could just distinguish the smooth moving surface of the water, and the air was full of the sound of it. They stood in an empty space in the midst of great tree-trunks, and out there a little green light moving slightly up and down showed them where the steamer lay in which they were to embark.

When they all stood upon its deck they found that it was a very small boat which throbbed gently beneath them for a few minutes, and then shoved smoothly through the water. They seemed to be driving into the heart of the night, for the trees closed in front of them, and they could hear all round them the rustling of leaves. The great darkness had the usual effect of taking away all desire for communication by making their words sound thin and small; and, after walking round the deck three or four times, they clustered together, yawning deeply, and looking at the same spot of deep gloom on the banks. Murmuring very low in the rhythmical tone of one oppressed by the air, Mrs. Flushing began to wonder where they were to sleep, for they could not sleep downstairs, they could not sleep in a doghole smelling of oil, they could not sleep on deck, they could not sleep—She yawned profoundly. It was as Helen had foreseen; the question of nakedness had risen already, although they were half asleep, and almost invisible to each other. With St. John's help she stretched an awning, and persuaded Mrs. Flushing that she could take off her clothes behind this, and that no one would notice if by chance some part of her which had been concealed for forty-five years was laid bare to the human eye. Mattresses were thrown down, rugs provided, and the three women lay near each other in the soft open air.

The gentlemen, having smoked a certain number of cigarettes, dropped the glowing ends into the river, and looked for a time at the ripples wrinkling the black water beneath them, undressed too, and lay down at the other end of the boat. They were very tired, and curtained from each other by the darkness. The light from one lantern fell upon a few ropes, a few planks of the deck, and the rail of the boat, but beyond that there was unbroken darkness, no light reached their faces, or the trees which were massed on the sides of the river.

Soon Wilfrid Flushing slept, and Hirst slept. Hewet alone lay awake looking straight up into the sky. The gentle motion and the black shapes that were drawn ceaselessly across his eyes had the effect of making it impossible for him to think. Rachel's presence so near him lulled thought asleep. Being so near him, only a few paces off at the other end of the boat, she made it as impossible for him to think about her as it would have been impossible to see her if she had stood quite close to him, her forehead against his forehead. In some strange way the boat became identified with himself, and just as it would have been useless for him to get up and steer the boat, so was it useless for him to struggle any longer with the irresistible force of his own feelings. He was drawn on and on away from all he knew, slipping over barriers and past landmarks into unknown waters as the boat glided over the smooth surface of the river. In profound peace, enveloped in deeper unconsciousness than had been his for many nights, he lay on deck watching the tree-tops change their position slightly against the sky, and arch themselves, and sink and tower huge, until he passed from seeing them into dreams where he lay beneath the shadow of the vast trees, looking up into the sky.

When they woke next morning they had gone a considerable way up the river; on the right was a high yellow bank of sand tufted with trees, on the left a swamp quivering with long reeds and tall bamboos on the top of which, swaying slightly, perched vivid green and yellow birds. The morning was hot and still. After breakfast they drew chairs together and sat in an irregular semicircle in the bow. An awning above their heads protected them from the heat of the sun, and the breeze which the boat made aired them softly. Mrs. Flushing was already dotting and striping her canvas, her head jerking this way and that with the action of a bird nervously picking up grain; the others had books or pieces of paper or embroidery on their knees, at which they looked fitfully and again looked at the river ahead. At one point Hewet read part of a poem aloud, but the number of moving things entirely vanquished his words. He ceased to read, and no one spoke. They moved on under the shelter of the trees. There was now a covey of red birds feeding on one of the little islets to the left, or again a blue-green parrot flew shrieking from tree to tree. As they moved on the country grew wilder and wilder. The trees and the undergrowth seemed to be strangling each other near the ground in a multitudinous wrestle; while here and there a splendid tree towered high above the swarm, shaking its thin green umbrellas lightly in the upper air. Hewet looked at his books again. The morning was peaceful as the night had been, only it was very strange because he could see it was light, and he could see Rachel and hear her voice and be near to her. He felt as if he were waiting, as if somehow he were stationary among things that passed over him and around him, voices, people's bodies, birds, only Rachel too was waiting with him. He looked at her sometimes as if she must know that they were waiting together, and being drawn on together, without being able to offer any resistance. Again he read from his book:

> Whoever you are holding me now in your hand,
> Without one thing all will be useless.

A bird gave a wild laugh, a monkey chuckled a malicious question, and, as fire fades in the hot sunshine, his words flickered and went out.

By degrees as the river narrowed, and the high sandbanks fell to level ground thickly grown with trees, the sounds of the forest could be heard. It echoed like a hall. There were sudden cries; and then long spaces of silence, such as there are in a cathedral when a boy's voice has ceased and the echo of it still seems to haunt about the remote places of the roof. Once Mr. Flushing rose and spoke to a sailor, and even announced that some time after luncheon the steamer would stop, and they could walk a little way through the forest.

"There are tracks all through the trees there," he explained. "We're no distance from civilisation yet."

He scrutinised his wife's painting. Too polite to praise it openly, he contented himself with cutting off one half of the picture with one hand, and giving a flourish in the air with the other.

"God!" Hirst exclaimed, staring straight ahead. "Don't you think it's amazingly beautiful?"

"Beautiful?" Helen enquired. It seemed a strange little word, and Hirst and herself both so small that she forgot to answer him.

Hewet felt that he must speak.

"That's where the Elizabethans got their style," he mused, staring into the profusion of leaves and blossoms and prodigious fruits.

"Shakespeare? I hate Shakespeare!" Mrs. Flushing exclaimed; and Wilfrid returned admiringly, "I believe you're the only person who dares to say that, Alice." But Mrs. Flushing went on painting. She did not appear to attach much value to her husband's compliment, and painted steadily, sometimes muttering a half-audible word or groan.

The morning was now very hot.

"Look at Hirst!" Mr. Flushing whispered. His sheet of paper had slipped on to the deck, his head lay back, and he drew a long snoring breath.

Terence picked up the sheet of paper and spread it out before Rachel. It was a continuation of the poem on God which he had begun in the chapel, and it was so indecent that Rachel did not understand half of it although she saw that it was indecent. Hewet began to fill in words where Hirst had left spaces, but he soon ceased; his pencil rolled on deck. Gradually they approached nearer and nearer to the bank on the right-hand side, so that the light which covered them became definitely green, falling through a shade of green leaves, and Mrs. Flushing set aside her sketch and stared ahead of her in silence. Hirst woke up; they were then called to luncheon, and while they ate it, the steamer came to a standstill a little way out from the bank. The boat which was towed behind them was brought to the side, and the ladies were helped into it.

For protection against boredom, Helen put a book of memoirs beneath her arm, and Mrs. Flushing her paint-box, and, thus equipped, they allowed themselves to be set on shore on the verge of the forest.

They had not strolled more than a few hundred yards along the track which ran parallel with the river before Helen professed to find it was unbearably hot. The river breeze had ceased, and a hot steamy atmosphere, thick with scents, came from the forest.

"I shall sit down here," she announced, pointing to the trunk of a tree which had fallen long ago and was now laced across and across by creepers and thong-like brambles. She seated herself, opened her parasol, and looked at the river which was barred by the stems of trees. She turned her back to the trees which disappeared in black shadow behind her.

"I quite agree," said Mrs. Flushing, and proceeded to undo her paint-box. Her husband strolled about to select an interesting point of view for her. Hirst cleared a space on the ground by Helen's side, and seated himself with great deliberation, as if he did not mean to move until he had talked to her for a long time. Terence and Rachel were left standing by themselves without occupation. Terence saw that the time had come as it was fated to come, but although he realised this he was completely calm and master of himself. He chose to stand for a few moments talking to Helen, and persuading her to leave her seat. Rachel joined him too in advising her to come with them.

"Of all the people I've ever met," he said, "you're the least adventurous. You might be sitting on green chairs in Hyde Park. Are you going to sit there the whole afternoon? Aren't you going to walk?"

"Oh, no," said Helen, "one's only got to use one's eye. There's everything here—everything," she repeated in a drowsy tone of voice. "What will you gain by walking?"

"You'll be hot and disagreeable by tea-time, we shall be cool and sweet," put in Hirst. Into his eyes as he looked up at them had come yellow and green reflections from the sky and the branches, robbing them of their intentness, and he seemed to think what he did not say. It was thus taken for granted by them both that Terence and Rachel proposed to walk into the woods together; with one look at each other they turned away.

"Good-bye!" cried Rachel.

"Good-by. Beware of snakes," Hirst replied. He settled himself still more comfortably under the shade of the fallen tree and Helen's figure. As they went, Mr. Flushing called after them, "We must start in an hour. Hewet, please remember that. An hour."

Whether made by man, or for some reason preserved by nature, there was a wide pathway striking through the forest at right angles to the river. It resembled a drive in an English forest, save that tropical bushes with their sword-like leaves grew at the side, and the ground was covered with an unmarked springy moss instead of grass, starred with little yellow flowers. As they passed into the depths of the forest the light grew dimmer, and the noises of the ordinary world were replaced by those creaking and sighing sounds which suggest to the traveller in a forest that he is walking at the bottom of the sea. The path narrowed and turned; it was hedged in by dense creepers which knotted tree to tree, and burst here and there into star-shaped crimson blossoms. The sighing and creaking up above were broken every now and then by the jarring cry of some startled animal. The atmosphere was close and the air came at them in languid puffs of scent. The vast green light was broken here and there by a round of pure yellow sunlight which fell through some gap in the immense umbrella of green above, and in these yellow spaces crimson and black butterflies were circling and settling. Terence and Rachel hardly spoke.

Not only did the silence weigh upon them, but they were both unable to frame any thoughts. There was something between them which had to be spoken of. One of them had to begin, but which of them was it to be? Then Hewet picked up a red fruit and threw it as high as he could. When it dropped, he would speak. They heard the flapping of great wings; they heard the fruit go pattering through the leaves and eventually fall with a thud. The silence was again profound.

"Does this frighten you?" Terence asked when the sound of the fruit falling had completely died away.

"No," she answered. "I like it."

She repeated "I like it." She was walking fast, and holding herself more erect than usual. There was another pause.

"You like being with me?" Terence asked.

"Yes, with you," she replied.

He was silent for a moment. Silence seemed to have fallen upon the world.

"That is what I have felt ever since I knew you," he replied. "We are happy together." He did not seem to be speaking, or she to be hearing.

"Very happy," she answered.

They continued to walk for some time in silence. Their steps unconsciously quickened.

"We love each other," Terence said.

"We love each other," she repeated.

The silence was then broken by their voices which joined in tones of strange unfamiliar sound which formed no words. Faster and faster they walked; simultaneously they stopped, clasped each other in their arms, then releasing themselves, dropped to the earth. They sat side by side. Sounds stood out from the background making a bridge across their silence; they heard the swish of the trees and some beast croaking in a remote world.

"We love each other," Terence repeated, searching into her face. Their faces were both very pale and quiet, and they said nothing. He was afraid to kiss her again. By degrees she drew close to him, and rested against him. In this position they sat for some time. She said "Terence" once; he answered "Rachel."

"Terrible—terrible," she murmured after another pause, but in saying this she was thinking as much of the persistent churning of the water as of her own feeling. On and on it went in the distance, the senseless and cruel churning of the water. She observed that the tears were running down Terence's cheeks.

The next movement was on his part. A very long time seemed to have passed. He took out his watch.

"Flushing said an hour. We've been gone more than half an hour."

"And it takes that to get back," said Rachel. She raised herself very slowly. When she was standing up she stretched her arms and drew a deep breath, half a sigh, half a yawn. She appeared to be very tired. Her cheeks were white. "Which way?" she asked.

"There," said Terence.

They began to walk back down the mossy path again. The sighing and creaking continued far overhead, and the jarring cries of animals. The butterflies were circling still in the patches of yellow sunlight. At first Terence was certain of his way, but as they walked he became doubtful. They had to stop to consider, and then to return and start once more, for although he was certain of the direction of the river he was not certain of striking the point where they had left the others. Rachel followed him, stopping where he stopped, turning where he turned, ignorant of the way, ignorant why he stopped or why he turned.

"I don't want to be late," he said, "because—" He put a flower into her hand and her fingers closed upon it quietly. "We're so late—so late—so horribly late," he repeated as if he were talking in his sleep. "Ah—this is right. We turn here."

They found themselves again in the broad path, like the drive in the

English forest, where they had started when they left the others. They walked on in silence as people walking in their sleep, and were oddly conscious now and again of the mass of their bodies. Then Rachel exclaimed suddenly, "Helen!"

In the sunny space at the edge of the forest they saw Helen still sitting on the tree-trunk, her dress showing very white in the sun, with Hirst still propped on his elbow by her side. They stopped instinctively. At the sight of other people they could not go on. They stood hand in hand for a minute or two in silence. They could not bear to face other people.

"But we must go on," Rachel insisted at last, in the curious dull tone of voice in which they had both been speaking, and with a great effort they forced themselves to cover the short distance which lay between them and the pair sitting on the tree-trunk.

As they approached, Helen turned round and looked at them. She looked at them for some time without speaking, and when they were close to her she said quietly:

"Did you meet Mr. Flushing? He has gone to find you. He thought you must be lost, though I told him you weren't lost."

Hirst half turned round and threw his head back so that he looked at the branches crossing themselves in the air above him.

"Well, was it worth the effort?" he enquired dreamily.

Hewet sat down on the grass by his side and began to fan himself.

Rachel had balanced herself near Helen on the end of the tree trunk.

"Very hot," she said.

"You look exhausted anyhow," said Hirst.

"It's fearfully close in those trees," Helen remarked, picking up her book and shaking it free from the dried blades of grass which had fallen between the leaves. Then they were all silent, looking at the river swirling past in front of them between the trunks of the trees until Mr. Flushing interrupted them. He broke out of the trees a hundred yards to the left, exclaiming sharply:

"Ah, so you found the way after all. But it's late—much later than we arranged, Hewet."

He was slightly annoyed, and in his capacity as leader of the expedition, inclined to be dictatorial. He spoke quickly, using curiously sharp, meaningless words.

"Being late wouldn't matter normally, of course," he said, "but when it's a question of keeping the men up to time——"

He gathered them together and made them come down to the river-bank, where the boat was waiting to row them out to the steamer.

The heat of the day was going down, and over their cups of tea the Flushings tended to become communicative. It seemed to Terence as he listened to them talking, that existence now went on in two different layers. Here were the Flushings talking, talking somewhere high up in the air above him, and he and Rachel had dropped to the bottom of the world together. But with something of a child's directness, Mrs. Flushing had also the instinct which leads a child to suspect what its elders wish to keep hidden. She fixed Terence with her vivid blue eyes and addressed herself to him in particular. What would he do, she wanted to know, if the boat ran upon a rock and sank.

"Would you care for anythin' but savin' yourself? Should I? No, no," she laughed, "not one scrap—don't tell me. There's only two creatures the ordinary woman cares about," she continued, "her child and her dog; and I don't believe it's even two with men. One reads a lot about love—that's why poetry's so dull. But what happens in real life, he? It ain't love!" she cried.

Terence murmured something unintelligible. Mr. Flushing, however, had recovered his urbanity. He was smoking a cigarette, and he now answered his wife.

"You must always remember, Alice," he said, "that your upbringing was very unnatural—unusual, I should say. They had no mother," he explained, dropping something of the formality of his tone; "and a father—he was a very delightful man, I've no doubt, but he cared only for racehorses and Greek statues. Tell them about the bath, Alice."

"In the stable-yard," said Mrs. Flushing. "Covered with ice in winter. We had to get in; if we didn't, we were whipped. The strong ones lived—the others died. What you call survival of the fittest—a most excellent plan, I daresay, if you've thirteen children!"

"And all this going on in the heart of England, in the nineteenth century!" Mr. Flushing exclaimed, turning to Helen.

"I'd treat my children just the same if I had any," said Mrs. Flushing.

Every word sounded quite distinctly in Terence's ears; but what were they saying, and who were they talking to, and who were they, these fantastic people, detached somewhere high up in the air? Now that they had drunk their tea, they rose and leant over the bow of the boat. The sun was going down, and the water was dark and crimson. The river had widened again, and they were passing a little island set like a dark wedge in the middle of the stream. Two great white birds with red lights on them stood there on stilt-like legs, and the beach of the island was unmarked, save by the skeleton print of birds' feet. The branches of the trees on the bank looked more twisted and angular than ever, and the green of the leaves was lurid and splashed with gold. Then Hirst began to talk, leaning over the bow.

"It makes one awfully queer, don't you find?" he complained. "These trees get on one's nerves—it's all so crazy. God's undoubtedly mad. What sane person could have conceived a wilderness like this, and peopled it with apes and alligators? I should go mad if I lived here—raving mad."

Terence attempted to answer him, but Mrs. Ambrose replied instead. She bade him look at the way things massed themselves—look at the amazing colours, look at the shapes of the trees. She seemed to be protecting Terence from the approach of the others.

"Yes," said Mr. Flushing. "And in my opinion," he continued, "the absence of population to which Hirst objects is precisely the significant touch. You must admit, Hirst, that a little Italian town even would vulgarise the whole scene, would detract from the vastness—the sense of elemental grandeur." He swept his hands towards the forest, and paused for a moment, looking at the great green mass, which was now falling silent. "I own it makes us seem pretty small—us, not them." He nodded his head at a sailor who leant over the side spitting into the river. "And that, I think, is what my wife feels, the essential superiority of the peasant——"

Under cover of Mr. Flushing's words, which continued now gently reasoning with St. John and persuading him, Terence drew Rachel to the side, pointing ostensibly to a great gnarled tree-trunk which had fallen and lay half in the water. He wished, at any rate, to be near her, but he found that he could say nothing. They could hear Mr. Flushing flowing on, now about his wife, now about art, now about the future of the country, little meaningless words floating high in air. As it was becoming cold he began to pace the deck with Hirst. Fragments of their talk came out distinctly as they passed—art, emotion, truth, reality.

"Is it true, or is it a dream?" Rachel murmured, when they had passed.

"It's true, it's true," he replied.

But the breeze freshened, and there was a general desire for movement. When the party rearranged themselves under cover of rugs and cloaks, Terence and Rachel were at opposite ends of the circle, and could not speak to each other. But as the dark descended, the words of the others seemed to curl up and vanish as the ashes of burnt paper, and left them sitting perfectly silent at the bottom of the world. Occasional starts of exquisite joy ran through them, and then they were peaceful again.

21

Thanks to Mr. Flushing's discipline, the right stages of the river were reached at the right hours, and when next morning after breakfast the chairs were again drawn out in a semicircle in the bow, the launch was within a few miles of the native camp which was the limit of the journey. Mr. Flushing, as he sat down, advised them to keep their eyes fixed on the left bank, where they would soon pass a clearing, and in that clearing, was a hut where Mackenzie, the famous explorer, had died of fever some ten years ago, almost within reach of civilisation—Mackenzie, he repeated, the man who went farther inland than any one's been yet. Their eyes turned that way obediently. The eyes of Rachel saw nothing. Yellow and green shapes did, it is true, pass before them, but she only knew that one was large and another small; she did not know that they were trees. These directions to look here and there irritated her, as interruptions irritate a person absorbed in thought, although she was not thinking of anything. She was annoyed with all that was said, and with the aimless movements of people's bodies, because they seemed to interfere with her and to prevent her from speaking to Terence. Very soon Helen saw her staring moodily at a coil of rope, and making no effort to listen. Mr. Flushing and St. John were engaged in more or less continuous conversation about the future of the country from a political point of view, and the degree to which it had been explored; the others, with their legs stretched out, or chins poised on the hands, gazed in silence.

Mrs. Ambrose looked and listened obediently enough, but inwardly she was prey to an uneasy mood not readily to be ascribed to any one cause. Looking on shore as Mr. Flushing bade her, she thought the country very beautiful, but also sultry and alarming. She did not like to feel herself the victim of unclassified emotions, and certainly as the launch slipped on and on, in the hot morning sun, she felt herself unreasonably moved. Whether the unfamiliarity of the forest was the cause of it, or something less definite, she could not determine. Her mind left the scene and occupied itself with anxieties for Ridley, for her children, for far-off things, such as old age and poverty and death. Hirst, too, was depressed. He had been looking forward to this expedition as to a holiday, for, once away from the hotel, surely wonderful things would happen, instead of which nothing happened, and here they were as uncomfortable, as restrained, as self-conscious as ever. That, of course, was what came of looking forward to anything; one was always disappointed. He blamed Wilfrid Flushing, who was so well dressed and so formal; he blamed Hewet and

Rachel. Why didn't they talk? He looked at them sitting silent and self-absorbed, and the sight annoyed him. He supposed that they were engaged, or about to become engaged, but instead of being in the least romantic or exciting, that was as dull as everything else; it annoyed him, too, to think that they were in love. He drew close to Helen and began to tell her how uncomfortable his night had been, lying on the deck, sometimes too hot, sometimes too cold, and the stars so bright that he couldn't get to sleep. He had lain awake all night thinking, and when it was light enough to see, he had written twenty lines of his poem on God, and the awful thing was that he'd practically proved the fact that God did not exist. He did not see that he was teasing her, and he went on to wonder what would happen if God did exist—"an old gentleman in a beard and a long blue dressing gown, extremely testy and disagreeable as he's bound to be? Can you suggest a rhyme? God, rod, sod—all used; any others?"

Although he spoke much as usual, Helen could have seen, had she looked, that he was also impatient and disturbed. But she was not called upon to answer, for Mr. Flushing now exclaimed "There!" They looked at the hut on the bank, a desolate place with a large rent in the roof, and the ground round it yellow, scarred with fires and scattered with rusty open tins.

"Did they find his dead body there?" Mrs. Flushing exclaimed, leaning forward in her eagerness to see the spot where the explorer had died.

"They found his body and his skins and a notebook," her husband replied. But the boat had soon carried them on and left the place behind.

It was so hot that they scarcely moved, except now to change a foot, or, again, to strike a match. Their eyes, concentrated upon the bank, were full of the same green reflections, and their lips were slightly pressed together as though the sights they were passing gave rise to thoughts, save that Hirst's lips moved intermittently as half consciously he sought rhymes for God. Whatever the thoughts of the others, no one said anything for a considerable space. They had grown so accustomed to the wall of trees on either side that they looked up with a start when the light suddenly widened out and the trees came to an end.

"It almost reminds one of an English park," said Mr. Flushing.

Indeed no change could have been greater. On both banks of the river lay an open lawn-like space, grass covered and planted, for the gentleness and order of the place suggested human care, with graceful trees on the top of little mounds. As far as they could gaze, this lawn rose and sank with the undulating motion of an old English park. The change of scene naturally suggested a change of position, grateful to most of them. They rose and leant over the rail.

"It might be Arundel or Windsor," Mr. Flushing continued, "if you cut down that bush with the yellow flowers; and, by Jove, look!"

Rows of brown backs paused for a moment and then leapt with a motion as if they were springing over waves out of sight.

For a moment no one of them could believe that they had really seen live animals in the open—a herd of wild deer, and the sight aroused a childlike excitement in them, dissipating their gloom.

"I've never in my life seen anything bigger than a hare!" Hirst exclaimed with genuine excitement. "What an ass I was not to bring my Kodak!"

Soon afterwards the launch came gradually to a standstill, and the captain explained to Mr. Flushing that it would be pleasant for the passengers if they now went for a stroll on shore; if they chose to return within an hour, he would take them on to the village; if they chose to walk—it was only a mile or two farther on—he would meet them at the landing-place.

The matter being settled, they were once more put on shore: the sailors, producing raisins and tobacco, leant upon the rail and watched the six English, whose coats and dresses looked so strange upon the green, wander off. A joke that was by no means proper set them all laughing, and then they turned round and lay at their ease upon the deck.

Directly they landed, Terence and Rachel drew together slightly in advance of the others.

"Thank God!" Terence exclaimed, drawing a long breath. "At last we're alone."

"And if we keep ahead we can talk," said Rachel.

Nevertheless, although their position some yards in advance of the others made it possible for them to say anything they chose, they were both silent.

"You love me?" Terence asked at length, breaking the silence painfully. To speak or to be silent was equally an effort, for when they were silent they were keenly conscious of each other's presence, and yet words were either too trivial or too large.

She murmured inarticulately, ending, "And you?"

"Yes, yes," he replied; but there were so many things to be said, and now that they were alone it seemed necessary to bring themselves still more near, and to surmount a barrier which had grown up since they had last spoken. It was difficult, frightening even, oddly embarrassing. At one moment he was clear-sighted, and, at the next, confused.

"Now I'm going to begin at the beginning," he said resolutely. "I'm going to tell you what I ought to have told you before. In the first place, I've never been in love with other women, but I've had other women. Then I've great faults. I'm very lazy, I'm moody—" He persisted, in spite of her exclamation, "You've got to know the worst of me. I'm lustful. I'm overcome by a sense of futility—incompetence. I ought never to have asked you to marry me, I expect. I'm a bit of a snob; I'm ambitious—"

"Oh, our faults!" she cried. "What do they matter?" Then she demanded, "Am I in love—is this being in love—are we to marry each other?"

Overcome by the charm of her voice and her presence, he exclaimed, "Oh, you're free, Rachel. To you, time will make no difference, or marriage or—"

The voices of the others behind them kept floating, now farther, now nearer, and Mrs. Flushing's laugh rose clearly by itself.

"Marriage?" Rachel repeated.

The shouts were renewed behind, warning them that they were bearing too far to the left. Improving their course, he continued, "Yes, marriage." The feeling that they could not be united until she knew all about him made him again endeavour to explain.

"All that's been bad in me, the things I've put up with—the second best—"

She murmured, considered her own life, but could not describe how it looked to her now.

"And the loneliness!" he continued. A vision of walking with her through the streets of London came before his eyes. "We will go for walks together," he said. The simplicity of the idea relieved them, and for the first time they laughed. They would have liked had they dared to take each other by the hand, but the consciousness of eyes fixed on them from behind had not yet deserted them.

"Books, people, sights—Mrs. Nutt, Greeley, Hutchinson," Hewet murmured.

With every word the mist which had enveloped them, making them seem unreal to each other, since the previous afternoon melted a little further, and their contact became more and more natural. Up through the sultry southern landscape they saw the world they knew appear clearer and more vividly than it had ever appeared before As upon that occasion at the hotel when she had sat in the window, the world once more arranged itself beneath her gaze very vividly and in its true proportions. She glanced curiously at Terence from time to time, observing his grey coat and his purple tie; observing the man with whom she was to spend the rest of her life.

After one of these glances she murmured, "Yes, I'm in love. There's no doubt; I'm in love with you."

Nevertheless, they remained uncomfortably apart; drawn so close together, as she spoke, that there seemed no division between them, and the next moment separate and far away again. Feeling this painfully, she exclaimed, "It will be a fight."

But as she looked at him she perceived from the shape of his eyes, the lines about his mouth, and other peculiarities that he pleased her, and she added:

"Where I want to fight, you have compassion. You're finer than I am; you're much finer."

He returned her glance and smiled, perceiving, much as she had done, the very small individual things about her which made her delightful to him. She was his for ever. This barrier being surmounted, innumerable delights lay before them both.

"I'm not finer," he answered. "I'm only older, lazier; a man, not a woman."

"A man," she repeated, and a curious sense of possession coming over her, it struck her that she might now touch him; she put out her hand and lightly touched his cheek. His fingers followed where hers had been, and the touch of his hand upon his face brought back the overpowering sense of unreality. This body of his was unreal; the whole world was unreal.

"What's happened?" he began. "Why did I ask you to marry me? How did it happen?"

"Did you ask me to marry you?" she wondered. They faded far away from each other, and neither of them could remember what had been said.

"We sat upon the ground," he recollected.

"We sat upon the ground," she confirmed him. The recollection of sitting upon the ground, such as it was, seemed to unite them again, and they walked on in silence, their minds sometimes working with difficulty and sometimes ceasing to work, their eyes alone perceiving the things round them. Now he would attempt again to tell her his faults, and why he loved her; and she would describe what she had felt at this time or at that time, and together they would interpret her feeling. So beautiful was the sound of their voices that by degrees they scarcely listened to the words they framed. Long silences came between their words, which were no longer silences of struggle and confusion but refreshing silences, in which trivial thoughts moved easily. They began to speak naturally of ordinary things, of the flowers and the trees, how they grew there so red, like garden flowers at home, and there bent and crooked like the arm of a twisted old man.

Very gently and quietly, almost as if it were the blood singing in her veins, or the water of the stream running over stones, Rachel became conscious of a new feeling within her. She wondered for a moment what it was, and then said to herself, with a little surprise at recognising in her own person so famous a thing:

"This is happiness, I suppose." And aloud to Terence she spoke, "This is happiness."

On the heels of her words he answered, "This is happiness," upon which they guessed that the feeling had sprung in both of them the same time. They began therefore to describe how this felt and that felt, how like it was and yet how different; for they were very different.

Voices crying behind them never reached through the waters in which they were now sunk. The repetition of Hewet's name in short, dissevered syllables was to them the crack of a dry branch or the laughter of a bird. The grasses and breezes sounding and murmuring all round them, they never noticed that the swishing of the grasses grew louder and louder, and did not cease with the lapse of the breeze. A hand dropped abrupt as iron on Rachel's shoulder; it might have been a bolt from heaven. She fell beneath it, and the grass whipped across her eyes and filled her mouth and ears. Through the waving stems she saw a figure, large and shapeless against the sky. Helen was upon her. Rolled this way and that, now seeing only forests of green, and now the high blue heaven; she was speechless and almost without sense. At last she lay still, all the grasses shaken round her and before her by her panting. Over her loomed two great heads, the heads of a man and woman, of Terence and Helen.

Both were flushed, both laughing, and the lips were moving; they came together and kissed in the air above her. Broken fragments of speech came down to her on the ground. She thought she heard them speak of love and then of marriage. Raising herself and sitting up, she too realised Helen's soft body, the strong and hospitable arms, and happiness swelling and breaking in one vast wave. When this fell away, and the grasses once more lay low, and the sky became horizontal, and the earth rolled out flat on each side, and the trees stood upright, she was the first to perceive a little row of human figures standing patiently in the distance. For the moment she could not remember who they were.

"Who are they?" she asked, and then recollected.

Falling into line behind Mr. Flushing, they were careful to leave at least three yards' distance between the toe of his boot and the rim of her skirt.

He led them across a stretch of green by the river-bank and then through a grove of trees, and bade them remark the signs of human habitation, the blackened grass, the charred tree-stumps, and there, through the trees, strange wooden nests, drawn together in an arch where the trees drew apart, the village which was the goal of their journey.

Stepping cautiously, they observed the women, who were squatting on the ground in triangular shapes, moving their hands, either plaiting straw or in kneading something in bowls. But when they had looked for a moment undiscovered, they were seen, and Mr. Flushing, advancing into the centre of the clearing, was engaged in talk with a lean majestic man, whose bones and hollows at once made the shapes of the Englishman's body appear ugly and unnatural. The women took no notice of the strangers, except that their hands paused for a moment and their long narrow eyes slid round and fixed upon them with the motionless inexpensive gaze of those removed from each other far far beyond the plunge of speech. Their hands moved again, but the stare continued. It followed them as they walked, as they peered into the huts where they could distinguish guns leaning in the corner, and bowls upon the floor, and stacks of rushes; in the dusk the solemn eyes of babies regarded them, and old women stared out too. As they sauntered about, the stare followed them, passing over their legs, their bodies, their heads, curiously not without hostility, like the crawl of a winter fly. As she drew apart her shawl and uncovered her breast to the lips of her baby, the eyes of a woman never left their faces, although they moved uneasily under her stare, and finally turned away, rather than stand there looking at her any longer. When sweetmeats were offered them, they put out great red hands to take them, and felt themselves treading cumbrously like tight-coated soldiers among these soft instinctive people. But soon the life of the village took no notice of them; they had become absorbed in it. The women's hands became busy again with the straw; their eyes dropped. If they moved, it was to fetch something from the hut, or to catch a straying child, or to cross the space with a jar balanced on their heads; if they spoke, it was to cry some harsh unintelligible cry. Voices rose when a child was beaten, and fell again; voices rose in song, which slid up a little way and down a little way, and settled again upon the same low and melancholy note. Seeking each other, Terence and Rachel drew together under a tree. Peaceful, and even beautiful at first, the sight of the women, who had given up looking at them, made them now feel very cold and melancholy.

"Well," Terence sighed at length, "it makes us seem insignificant, doesn't it?"

Rachel agreed. So it would go on for ever and ever, she said, those women sitting under the trees, the trees and the river. They turned away and began to walk through the trees, leaning, without fear of discovery, upon each other's arms. They had not gone far before they began to assure each other once more that they were in love, were happy, were content; but why was it so painful being in love, why was there so much pain in happiness?

The sight of the village indeed affected them all curiously though all differently. St. John had left the others and was walking slowly down to the river, absorbed in his own thoughts, which were bitter and unhappy, for he felt himself alone; and Helen, standing by herself in the sunny space among the native women, was exposed to presentiments of disaster. The cries of the senseless beasts rang in her ears high and low in the air, as they ran from tree-trunk to tree-top. How small the little figures looked wandering through the trees! She became acutely conscious of the little limbs, the thin veins, the delicate flesh of men and women, which breaks so easily and lets the life escape compared with these great trees and deep waters. A falling branch, a foot that slips, and the earth has crushed them or the water drowned them. Thus thinking, she kept her eyes anxiously fixed upon the lovers, as if by doing so she could protect them from their fate. Turning, she found the Flushings by her side.

They were talking about the things they had bought and arguing whether they were really old, and whether there were not signs here and there of European influence. Helen was appealed to. She was made to look at a brooch, and then at a pair of ear-rings. But all the time she blamed them for having come on this expedition, for having ventured too far and exposed themselves. Then she roused herself and tried to talk, but in a few moments she caught herself seeing a picture of a boat upset on the river in England, at midday. It was morbid, she knew, to imagine such things; nevertheless she sought out the figures of the others between the trees, and whenever she saw them she kept her eyes fixed on them, so that she might be able to protect them from disaster.

But when the sun went down and the steamer turned and began to steam back towards civilisation, again her fears were calmed. In the semi-darkness the chairs on deck and the people sitting in them were angular shapes, the mouth being indicated by a tiny burning spot, and the arm by the same spot moving up or down as the cigar or cigarette was lifted to and from the lips. Words crossed the darkness, but, not knowing where they fell, seemed to lack energy and substance. Deep sights proceeded regularly, although with some attempt at suppression, from the large white mound which represented the person of Mrs. Flushing. The day had been long and very hot, and now that all the colours were blotted out the cool night air seemed to press soft fingers upon the eyelids, sealing them down. Some philosophical remark directed, apparently, at St. John Hirst missed its aim, and hung so long suspended in the air until it was engulfed by a yawn, that it was considered dead, and this gave the signal for stirring of legs and murmurs about sleep. The white mound moved, finally lengthened itself and disappeared, and after a few turns and paces St. John and Mr. Flushing withdrew, leaving the three chairs still occupied by three silent bodies. The light which came from a lamp high on the mast and a sky pale with stars left them with shapes but without features; but even in this darkness the withdrawal of the others made them feel each other very near, for they were all thinking of the same thing. For some time no one spoke, then Helen said with a sigh, "So you're both very happy?"

As if washed by the air her voice sounded more spiritual and softer than usual. Voices at a little distance answered her, "Yes."

Through the darkness she was looking at them both, and trying to distinguish him. What was there for her to say? Rachel had passed beyond her guardianship. A voice might reach her ears, but never again would it carry as far as it had carried twenty-four hours ago. Nevertheless, speech seemed to be due from her before she went to bed. She wished to speak, but she felt strangely old and depressed.

"D'you realise what you're doing?" she demanded. "She's young, you're both young; and marriage—" Here she ceased. They begged her, however, to continue, with such earnestness in their voices, as if they only craved advice, that she was led to add:

"Marriage! well, it's not easy."

"That's what we want to know," they answered, and she guessed that now they were looking at each other.

"It depends on both of you," she stated. Her face was turned towards Terence, and although he could hardly see her, he believed that her words really covered a genuine desire to know more about him. He raised himself from his semi-recumbent position and proceeded to tell her what she wanted to know. He spoke as lightly as he could in order to take away her depression.

"I'm twenty-seven, and I've about seven hundred a year," he began. "My temper is good on the whole, and health excellent, though Hirst detects a gouty tendency. Well, then, I think I'm very intelligent." He paused as if for confirmation.

Helen agreed.

"Though, unfortunately, rather lazy. I intend to allow Rachel to be a fool if she wants to, and—Do you find me on the whole satisfactory in other respects?" he asked shyly.

"Yes, I like what I know of you," Helen replied.

"But then—one knows so little."

"We shall live in London," he continued, "and—" With one voice they suddenly enquired whether she did not think them the happiest people that she had ever known.

"Hush," she checked them, "Mrs. Flushing, remember. She's behind us."

Then they fell silent, and Terence and Rachel felt instinctively that their happiness had made her sad, and, while they were anxious to go on talking about themselves, they did not like to.

"We've talked too much about ourselves," Terence said. "Tell us——"

"Yes, tell us——" Rachel echoed. They were both in the mood to believe that every one was capable of saying something very profound.

"What can I tell you?" Helen reflected, speaking more to herself in a rambling style than as a prophetess delivering a message. She forced herself to speak.

"After all, though I scold Rachel, I'm not much wiser myself. I'm older, of course, I'm half-way through, and you're just beginning. It's puzzling—sometimes, I think, disappointing; the great things aren't as great, perhaps, as one expects—but it's interesting—— Oh, yes, you're certain to find it interesting—— And so it goes on," they became conscious here of the procession of dark trees into which, as far as they could see, Helen was now looking, "and there are pleasures where one doesn't expect them (you must write to your father), and you'll be very happy, I've no doubt. But I must go to bed, and if you are sensible you will follow in ten minutes, and so," she rose and stood before them, almost featureless and very large, "Good-night." She passed behind the curtain.

After sitting in silence for the greater part of the ten minutes she allowed them, they rose and hung over the rail. Beneath them the smooth black water slipped away very fast and silently. The spark of a cigarette vanished behind them. "A beautiful voice," Terence murmured.

Rachel assented. Helen had a beautiful voice.

After a silence she asked, looking up into the sky, "Are we on the deck of a steamer on a river in South America? Am I Rachel, are you Terence?"

The great black world lay round them. As they were drawn smoothly along it seemed possessed of immense thickness and endurance. They could discern pointed tree-tops and blunt rounded tree-tops. Raising their eyes above the trees, they fixed them on the stars and the pale border of sky above the trees. The little points of frosty light infinitely far away drew their eyes and held them fixed, so that it seemed as if they stayed a long time and fell a great distance when once more they realised their hands grasping the rail and their separate bodies standing side by side.

"You'd forgotten completely about me," Terence reproached her, taking her arm and beginning to pace the deck, "and I never forget you."

"Oh, no," she whispered, she had not forgotten, only the stars—the night—the dark——

"You're like a bird half asleep in its nest, Rachel. You're asleep. You're talking in your sleep."

Half asleep, and murmuring broken words, they stood in the angle made by the bow of the boat. It slipped on down the river. Now a bell struck on the bridge, and they heard the lapping of water as it rippled away on either side, and once a bird startled in its sleep creaked, flew on to the next tree, and was silent again. The darkness poured down profusely, and left them with scarcely any feeling of life, except that they were standing there together in the darkness.

22

The darkness fell, but rose again, and as each day spread widely over the earth and parted them from the strange day in the forest when they had been forced to tell each other what they wanted, this wish of theirs was revealed to other people, and in the process became slightly strange to themselves. Apparently it was not anything unusual that had happened; it was that they had become engaged to marry each other. The world, which consisted for the most part of the hotel and the villa, expressed itself glad on the whole that two people should marry, and allowed them to see that they were not expected to take part in the work which has to be done in order that the world shall go on, but might absent themselves for a time. They were accordingly left alone until they felt the silence as if, playing in a vast church, the door had been shut on them. They were driven to walk alone, and sit alone, to visit secret places where the flowers had never been picked and the trees were solitary. In solitude they could express those beautiful but too vast desires which were so oddly uncomfortable to the ears of other men and women—desires for a world, such as their own world which contained two people seemed to them to be, where people knew each other intimately and thus judged each other by what was good, and never quarrelled, because that was waste of time.

They would talk of such questions among books, or out in the sun, or sitting in the shade of a tree undisturbed. They were no longer embarrassed, or half-choked with meaning which could not express itself; they were not afraid of each other, or, like travellers down a twisting river, dazzled with sudden beauties when the corner is turned; the unexpected happened, but even the ordinary was lovable, and in many ways preferable to the ecstatic and mysterious, for it was refreshingly solid, and called out effort, and effort under such circumstances was not effort but delight.

While Rachel played the piano, Terence sat near her, engaged, as far as the occasional writing of a word in pencil testified, in shaping the world as it appeared to him now that he and Rachel were going to be married. It was different certainly. The book called *Silence* would not now be the same book that it would have been. He would then put down his pencil and stare in front of him, and wonder in what respects the world was different—it had, perhaps, more solidity, more coherence, more importance, greater depth. Why, even the earth sometimes seemed to him very deep; not carved into hills and cities and fields, but heaped in great masses. He would look out of the window for ten minutes at a time; but no, he did not care for the earth swept of human beings. He liked human beings—he liked them, he suspected, better than Rachel did. There she was, swaying enthusiastically over her music, quite forgetful of him—but he liked that quality in her. He liked the impersonality which it produced in her. At last, having written down a series of little sentences, with notes of interrogation attached to them, he observed aloud, "'Women—under the heading Women I've written:

"'Not really vainer than men. Lack of self-confidence at the base of most serious faults. Dislike of own sex traditional, or founded on fact? Every woman not so much a rake at heart, as an optimist, because they don't think.' What do you say, Rachel?" He paused with his pencil in his hand and a sheet of paper on his knee.

Rachel said nothing. Up and up the steep spiral of a very late Beethoven sonata she climbed, like a person ascending a ruined staircase, energetically at first, then more laboriously advancing her feet with effort until she could go no higher and returned with a run to begin at the very bottom again.

"'Again, it's the fashion now to say that women are more practical and less idealistic than men, also that they have considerable organising ability but no sense of honour'—query, what is meant by masculine term, honour?—what corresponds to it in your sex? Eh?"

Attacking her staircase once more, Rachel again neglected this opportunity of revealing the secrets of her sex. She had, indeed, advanced so far in the pursuit of wisdom that she allowed these secrets to rest undisturbed; it seemed to be reserved for a later generation to discuss them philosophically.

Crashing down a final chord with her left hand, she exclaimed at last, swinging round upon him:

"No, Terence, it's no good; here am I, the best musician in South America, not to speak of Europe and Asia, and I can't play a note because of you in the room interrupting me every other second."

"You don't seem to realise that that's what I've been aiming at for the last half-hour," he remarked. "I've no objection to nice simple tunes—indeed, I find them very helpful to my literary composition, but that kind of thing is merely like an unfortunate old dog going round on its hind legs in the rain."

He began turning over the little sheets of note-paper which were scattered on the table, conveying the congratulations of their friends.

"'—all possible wishes for all possible happiness,'" he read; "correct, but not very vivid, are they?"

"They're sheer nonsense!" Rachel exclaimed. "Think of words compared with sounds!" she continued. "Think of novels and plays and histories—" Perched on the edge of the table, she stirred the red and yellow volumes contemptuously. She seemed to herself to be in a position where she could despise all human learning. Terence looked at them too.

"God, Rachel, you do read trash!" he exclaimed. "And you're behind the times too, my dear. No one dreams of reading this kind of thing now—antiquated problem plays, harrowing descriptions of life in the east end—oh, no, we've exploded all that. Read poetry, Rachel, poetry, poetry, poetry!"

Picking up one of the books, he began to read aloud, his intention being to satirise the short sharp bark of the writer's English; but she paid no attention, and after an interval of meditation exclaimed:

"Does it ever seem to you, Terence, that the world is composed entirely of vast blocks of matter, and that we're nothing but patches of light—" she looked at the soft spots of sun wavering over the carpet and up the wall—"like that?"

"No," said Terence, "I feel solid; immensely solid; the legs of my chair might be rooted in the bowels of the earth. But at Cambridge, I can remember, there were times when one fell into ridiculous states of semi-coma about five o'clock in the morning. Hirst does now, I expect—oh, no, Hirst wouldn't."

Rachel continued, "The day your note came, asking us to go on the picnic, I was sitting where you're sitting now, thinking that; I wonder if I could think that again? I wonder if the world's changed? and if so, when it'll stop changing, and which is the real world?"

"When I first saw you," he began, "I thought you were like a creature who'd lived all its life among pearls and old bones. Your hands were wet, d'you remember, and you never said a word until I gave you a bit of bread, and then you said, 'Human Beings!'"

"And I thought you—a prig," she recollected. "No; that's not quite it. There were the ants who stole the tongue, and I thought you and St. John were like those ants—very big, very ugly, very energetic, with all your virtues on your backs. However, when I talked to you I liked you——"

"You fell in love with me," he corrected her. "You were in love with me all the time, only you didn't know it."

"No, I never fell in love with you," she asserted.

"Rachel—what a lie—didn't you sit here looking at my window—didn't you wander about the hotel like an owl in the sun——?"

"No," she repeated, "I never fell in love, if falling in love is what people say it is, and it's the world that tells the lies and I tell the truth. Oh, what lies—what lies!"

She crumpled together a handful of letters from Evelyn M., from Mr. Pepper, from Mrs. Thornbury and Miss Allan, and Susan Warrington. It was strange, considering how very different these people were, that they used almost the same sentences when they wrote to congratulate her upon her engagement.

That any one of these people had ever felt what she felt, or could ever feel it, or had even the right to pretend for a single second that they were capable of feeling it, appalled her much as the church service had done, much as the face of the hospital nurse had done; and if they didn't feel a thing why did they go and pretend to? The simplicity and arrogance and hardness of her youth, now concentrated into a single spark as it was by her love of him, puzzled Terence; being engaged had not that effect on him; the world was different, but not in that way; he still wanted the things he had always wanted, and in particular he wanted the companionship of other people more than ever perhaps. He took the letters out of her hand, and protested:

"Of course they're absurd, Rachel; of course they say things just because other people say them, but even so, what a nice woman Miss Allan is; you can't deny that; and Mrs. Thornbury too; she's got too many children I grant you, but if half-a-dozen of them had gone to the bad instead of rising infallibly to the tops of their trees—hasn't she a kind of beauty—of elemental simplicity as Flushing would say? Isn't she rather like a large old tree murmuring in the moonlight, or a river going on and on and on? By the way, Ralph's been made governor of the Carroway Islands—the youngest governor in the service; very good, isn't it?"

But Rachel was at present unable to conceive that the vast majority of the affairs of the world went on unconnected by a single thread with her own destiny.

"I won't have eleven children," she asserted; "I won't have the eyes of an old woman. She looks at one up and down, up and down, as if one were a horse."

"We must have a son and we must have a daughter," said Terence, putting down the letters, "because, let alone the inestimable advantage of being our children, they'd be so well brought up." They went on to sketch an outline of the ideal education—how their daughter should be required from infancy to gaze at a large square of cardboard painted blue, to suggest thoughts of infinity, for women were grown too practical; and their son—he should be taught to laugh at great men, that is, at distinguished successful men, at men who wore ribands and rose to the tops of their trees. He should in no way resemble (Rachel added) St. John Hirst.

At this Terence professed the greatest admiration for St. John Hirst. Dwelling upon his good qualities he became seriously convinced of them; he had a mind like a torpedo, he declared, aimed at falsehood. Where should we all be without him and his like? Choked in weeds; Christians, bigots—why, Rachel herself, would be a slave with a fan to sing songs to men when they felt drowsy.

"But you'll never see it!" he exclaimed; "because with all your virtues you don't, and you never will, care with every fibre of your being for the pursuit of truth! You've no respect for facts, Rachel; you're essentially feminine."

She did not trouble to deny it, nor did she think good to produce the one unanswerable argument against the merits which Terence admired. St. John Hirst said that she was in love with him; she would never forgive that; but the argument was not one to appeal to a man.

"But I like him," she said, and she thought to herself that she also pitied him, as one pities those unfortunate people who are outside the warm mysterious globe full of changes and miracles in which we ourselves move about; she thought that it must be very dull to be St. John Hirst.

She summed up what she felt about him by saying that she would not kiss him supposing he wished it, which was not likely.

As if some apology were due to Hirst for the kiss which she then bestowed upon him, Terence protested:

"And compared with Hirst I'm a perfect Zany."

The clock here struck twelve instead of eleven.

"We're wasting the morning—I ought to be writing my book, and you ought to be answering these."

"We've only got twenty-one whole mornings left," said Rachel. "And my father'll be here in a day or two."

However, she drew a pen and paper towards her and began to write laboriously,

"My dear Evelyn—"

Terence, meanwhile, read a novel which some one else had written, a process which he found essential to the composition of his own. For a considerable time nothing was to be heard but the ticking of the clock and the fitful scratch of Rachel's pen, as she produced phrases which bore a considerable likeness to those which she had condemned. She was struck by it herself, for she stopped writing and looked up; looked at Terence deep in the arm-chair, looked at the different pieces of furniture, at her bed in the corner, at the window-pane which showed the branches of a tree filled in with sky, heard the clock ticking, and was amazed at the gulf which lay between all that and her sheet of paper. Would there ever be a time when the world was one and indivisible? Even with Terence himself—how far apart they could be, how little she knew what was passing in his brain now! She then finished her sentence, which was awkward and ugly, and stated that they were "both very happy, and going to be married in the autumn probably and hope to live in London, where we hope you will come and see us when we get back." Choosing "affectionately," after some further speculation, rather than sincerely, she signed the letter and was doggedly beginning on another when Terence remarked, quoting from his book:

"Listen to this, Rachel. 'It is probable that Hugh' (he's the hero, a literary man), 'had not realised at the time of his marriage, any more than the young man of parts and imagination usually does realise, the nature of the gulf which separates the needs and desires of the male from the needs and desires of the female. . . . At first they had been very happy. The walking tour in Switzerland had been a time of jolly companionship and stimulating revelations for both of them. Betty had proved herself the ideal comrade. . . . They had shouted *Love in the Valley* to each other across the snowy slopes of the Riffelhorn' (and so on, and so on—I'll skip the descriptions). . . . 'But in London, after the boy's birth, all was changed. Betty was an admirable mother; but it did not take her long to find out that motherhood, as that function is understood by the mother of the upper middle classes, did not absorb the whole of her energies. She was young and strong, with healthy limbs and a body and brain that called urgently for exercise. . . .' (In short she began to give tea-parties.) . . . 'Coming in late from this singular talk with old Bob Murphy in his smoky, book-lined room, where the two men had each unloosened his soul to the other, with the sound of the traffic humming in his ears, and the foggy London sky slung tragically across his mind . . . he found women's hats dotted about among his papers. Women's wraps and absurd little feminine shoes and umbrellas were in the hall. . . . Then the bills began to come in. . . . He tried to speak frankly to her. He found her lying on the great polar-bear skin in their bedroom, half-undressed, for they were dining with the Greens in Wilton Crescent, the ruddy firelight making the diamonds wink and twinkle on her bare arms and in the delicious curve of her breast—a vision of adorable femininity. He forgave her all.' (Well, this goes from bad to worse, and finally about fifty pages later, Hugh takes a week-end ticket to Swanage and 'has it out with himself on the downs above Corfe.' . . . Here there's fifteen pages or so which we'll skip. The conclusion is . . .) 'They were different. Perhaps, in the far future, when generations of men had struggled and failed as he must now struggle and fail, woman would be, indeed, what she now made a pretence of being—the friend and companion—not the enemy and parasite of man.'

"The end of it is, you see, Hugh went back to his wife, poor fellow. It was his duty, as a married man. Lord, Rachel," he concluded, "will it be like that when we're married?"

Instead of answering him she asked,

"Why don't people write about the things they do feel?"

"Ah, that's the difficulty!" he sighed, tossing the book away.

"Well, then, what will it be like when we're married? What are the things people do feel?"

She seemed doubtful.

"Sit on the floor and let me look at you," he commanded. Resting her chin on his knee, she looked straight at him.

He examined her curiously.

"You're not beautiful," he began, "but I like your face. I like the way your hair grows down in a point, and your eyes too—they never see anything. Your mouth's too big, and your cheeks would be better if they had more colour in them. But what I like about your face is that it makes one wonder what the devil you're thinking about—it makes me want to do that—" He clenched his fist and shook it so near her that she started back, "because now you look as if you'd blow my brains out. There are moments," he continued, "when, if we stood on a rock together, you'd throw me into the sea."

Hypnotised by the force of his eyes in hers, she repeated, "If we stood on a rock together——"

To be flung into the sea, to be washed hither and thither, and driven about the roots of the world—the idea was incoherently delightful. She sprang up, and began moving about the room, bending and thrusting aside the chairs and tables as if she were indeed striking through the waters. He watched her with pleasure; she seemed to be cleaving a passage for herself, and dealing triumphantly with the obstacles which would hinder their passage through life.

"It does seem possible!" he exclaimed, "though I've always thought it the most unlikely thing in the world—I shall be in love with you all my life, and our marriage will be the most exciting thing that's ever been done! We'll never have a moment's peace—" He caught her in his arms as she passed him, and they fought for mastery, imagining a rock, and the sea heaving beneath them. At last she was thrown to the floor, where she lay gasping, and crying for mercy.

"I'm a mermaid! I can swim," she cried, "so the game's up." Her dress was torn across, and peace being established, she fetched a needle and thread and began to mend the tear.

"And now," she said, "be quiet and tell me about the world; tell me about everything that's ever happened, and I'll tell you—let me see, what can I tell you?—I'll tell you about Miss Montgomerie and the river party. She was left, you see, with one foot in the boat, and the other on shore."

They had spent much time already in thus filling out for the other the course of their past lives, and the characters of their friends and relations, so that very soon Terence knew not only what Rachel's aunts might be expected to say upon every occasion, but also how their bedrooms were furnished, and what kind of bonnets they wore. He could sustain a conversation between Mrs. Hunt and Rachel, and carry on a tea-party including the Rev. William Johnson and Miss Macquoid, the Christian Scientists, with remarkable likeness to the truth. But he had known many more people, and was far more highly skilled in the art of narrative than Rachel was, whose experiences were, for the most part, of a curiously childlike and humorous kind, so that it generally fell to her lot to listen and ask questions.

He told her not only what had happened, but what he had thought and felt, and sketched for her portraits which fascinated her of what other men and women might be supposed to be thinking and feeling, so that she became very anxious to go back to England, which was full of people, where she could merely stand in the streets and look at them. According to him, too, there was an order, a pattern which made life reasonable, or if that word was foolish, made it of deep interest anyhow, for sometimes it seemed possible to understand why things happened as they did. Nor were people so solitary and uncommunicative as she believed. She should look for vanity—for vanity was a common quality—first in herself, and then in Helen, in Ridley, in St. John, they all had their share of it—and she would find it in ten people out of every twelve she met; and once linked together by one such tie she would find them not separate and formidable, but practically indistinguishable, and she would come to love them when she found that they were like herself. If she denied this, she must defend her belief that human beings were as various as the beasts at the Zoo, which had stripes and manes, and horns and humps; and so, wrestling over the entire list of their acquaintances, and diverging into anecdote and theory and speculation, they came to know each other. The hours passed quickly, and seemed to them full to leaking-point. After a night's solitude they were always ready to begin again.

The virtues which Mrs. Ambrose had once believed to exist in free talk between men and women did in truth exist for both of them, although not quite in the measure she prescribed. Far more than upon the nature of sex they dwelt upon the nature of poetry, but it was true that talk which had no boundaries deepened and enlarged the strangely small bright view of a girl. In return for what he could tell her she brought him such curiosity and sensitiveness of perception, that he was led to doubt whether any gift bestowed by much reading and living was quite the equal of that for pleasure and pain. What would experience give her after all, except a kind of ridiculous formal balance, like that of a drilled dog in the street? He looked at her face and wondered how it would look in twenty years' time, when the eyes had dulled, and the forehead wore those little persistent wrinkles which seem to show that the middle-aged are facing something hard which the young do not see? What would the hard thing be for them, he wondered? Then his thoughts turned to their life in England.

The thought of England was delightful, for together they would see the old things freshly; it would be England in June, and there would be

June nights in the country; and the nightingales singing in the lanes, into which they could steal when the room grew hot; and there would be English meadows gleaming with water and set with stolid cows, and clouds dipping low and trailing across the green hills. As he sat in the room with her, he wished very often to be back again in the thick of life, doing things with Rachel.

He crossed to the window and exclaimed, "Lord, how good it is to think of lanes, muddy lanes, with brambles and nettles, you know, and real grass fields, and farmyards with pigs and cows, and men walking beside carts with pitchforks—there's nothing to compare with that here—look at the stony red earth, and the bright blue sea, and the glaring white houses—how tired one gets of it! And the air, without a stain or a wrinkle. I'd give anything for a sea mist."

Rachel, too, had been thinking of the English country: the flat land rolling away to the sea, and the woods and the long straight roads, where one can walk for miles without seeing any one, and the great church towers and the curious houses clustered in the valleys, and the birds, and the dusk, and the rain falling against the windows.

"But London, London's the place," Terence continued. They looked together at the carpet, as though London itself were to be seen there lying on the floor, with all its spires and pinnacles pricking through the smoke.

"On the whole, what I should like best at this moment," Terence pondered, "would be to find myself walking down Kingsway, by those big placards, you know, and turning into the Strand. Perhaps I might go and look over Waterloo Bridge for a moment. Then I'd go along the Strand past the shops with all the new books in them, and through the little archway into the Temple. I always like the quiet after the uproar. You hear your own footsteps suddenly quite loud. The Temple's very pleasant. I think I should go and see if I could find dear old Hodgkin—the man who writes books about Van Eyck, you know. When I left England he was very sad about his tame magpie. He suspected that a man had poisoned it. And then Russell lives on the next staircase. I think you'd like him. He's a passion for Handel. Well, Rachel," he concluded, dismissing the vision of London, "we shall be doing that together in six weeks' time, and it'll be the middle of June then—and June in London—my God! how pleasant it all is!"

"And we're certain to have it too," she said. "It isn't as if we were expecting a great deal—only to walk about and look at things."

"Only a thousand a year and perfect freedom," he replied. "How many people in London d'you think have that?"

"And now you've spoilt it," she complained. "Now we've got to think of the horrors." She looked grudgingly at the novel which had once caused her perhaps an hour's discomfort, so that she had never opened it again, but kept it on her table, and looked at it occasionally, as some medieval monk kept a skull, or a crucifix to remind him of the frailty of the body.

"Is it true, Terence," she demanded, "that women die with bugs crawling across their faces?"

"I think it's very probable," he said. "But you must admit, Rachel, that we so seldom think of anything but ourselves that an occasional twinge is really rather pleasant."

Accusing him of an affection of cynicism which was just as bad as sentimentality itself, she left her position by his side and knelt upon the window sill, twisting the curtain tassels between her fingers. A vague sense of dissatisfaction filled her.

"What's so detestable in this country," she exclaimed, "is the blue—always blue sky and blue sea. It's like a curtain—all the things one wants are on the other side of that. I want to know what's going on behind it. I hate these divisions, don't you, Terence? One person all in the dark about another person. Now I liked the Dalloways," she continued, "and they're gone. I shall never see them again. Just by going on a ship we cut ourselves off entirely from the rest of the world. I want to see England there—London there—all sorts of people—why shouldn't one? why should one be shut up all by oneself in a room?"

While she spoke thus half to herself and with increasing vagueness, because her eye was caught by a ship that had just come into the bay, she did not see that Terence had ceased to stare contentedly in front of him, and was looking at her keenly and with dissatisfaction. She seemed to be able to cut herself adrift from him, and to pass away to unknown places where she had no need of him. The thought roused his jealousy.

"I sometimes think you're not in love with me and never will be," he said energetically. She started and turned round at his words.

"I don't satisfy you in the way you satisfy me," he continued. "There's something I can't get hold of in you. You don't want me as I want you—you're always wanting something else."

He began pacing up and down the room.

"Perhaps I ask too much," he went on. "Perhaps it isn't really possible to have what I want. Men and women are too different. You can't understand—you don't understand——"

He came up to where she stood looking at him in silence.

It seemed to her now that what he was saying was perfectly true, and that she wanted many more things than the love of one human being—the sea, the sky. She turned again the looked at the distant blue, which was so smooth and serene where the sky met the sea; she could not possibly want only one human being.

"Or is it only this damnable engagement?" he continued. "Let's be married here, before we go back—or is it too great a risk? Are we sure we want to marry each other?"

They began pacing up and down the room, but although they came very near each other in their pacing, they took care not to touch each other. The hopelessness of their position overcame them both. They were impotent; they could never love each other sufficiently to overcome all these barriers, and they could never be satisfied with less. Realising this with intolerable keenness she stopped in front of him and exclaimed:

"Let's break it off, then."

The words did more to unite them than any amount of argument. As if they stood on the edge of a precipice they clung together. They knew that they could not separate; painful and terrible it might be, but they were joined for ever. They lapsed into silence, and after a time crept together in silence. Merely to be so close soothed them, and sitting side by side the divisions disappeared, and it seemed as if the world were once more solid and entire, and as if, in some strange way, they had grown larger and stronger.

It was long before they moved, and when they moved it was with great reluctance. They stood together in front of the looking-glass, and with a brush tried to make themselves look as if they had been feeling nothing all the morning, neither pain nor happiness. But it chilled them to see themselves in the glass, for instead of being vast and indivisible they were really very small and separate, the size of the glass leaving a large space for the reflection of other things.

23

But no brush was able to efface completely the expression of happiness, so that Mrs. Ambrose could not treat them when they came downstairs as if they had spent the morning in a way that could be discussed naturally. This being so, she joined in the world's conspiracy to consider them for the time incapacitated from the business of life, struck by their intensity of feeling into enmity against life, and almost succeeded in dismissing them from her thoughts.

She reflected that she had done all that it was necessary to do in practical matters. She had written a great many letters, and had obtained Willoughby's consent. She had dwelt so often upon Mr. Hewet's prospects, his profession, his birth, appearance, and temperament, that she had almost forgotten what he was really like. When she refreshed herself by a look at him, she used to wonder again what he was like, and then, concluding that they were happy at any rate, thought no more about it.

She might more profitably consider what would happen in three years' time, or what might have happened if Rachel had been left to explore the world under her father's guidance. The result, she was honest enough to own, might have been better—who knows? She did not disguise from herself that Terence had faults. She was inclined to think him too easy and tolerant, just as he was inclined to think her perhaps a trifle hard—no, it was rather that she was uncompromising. In some ways she found St. John preferable; but then, of course, he would never have suited Rachel. Her friendship with St. John was established, for although she fluctuated between irritation and interest in a way that did credit to the candour of her disposition, she liked his company on the whole. He took her outside this little world of love and emotion. He had a grasp of facts. Supposing, for instance, that England made a sudden move towards some unknown port on the coast of Morocco, St. John knew what was at the back of it, and to hear him engaged with her husband in argument about finance and the balance of power, gave her an odd sense of stability. She respected their arguments without always listening to them, much as she respected a solid brick wall, or one of those immense municipal buildings which, although they compose the greater part of our cities, have been built day after day and year after year by unknown hands. She liked to sit and listen, and even felt a little elated when the engaged couple, after showing their profound lack of interest, slipped from the room, and were seen pulling flowers to pieces in the garden. It was not that she was jealous of them, but she did undoubtedly envy them their great unknown future that lay before them. Slipping from one such thought to another, she was at the dining-room with fruit in her hands. Sometimes she stopped to straighten a candle stooping with the heat, or disturbed some too rigid arrangement of the chairs. She had reason to suspect that Chailey had been balancing herself on the top of a ladder with a wet duster during their absence, and the room had never been quite like itself since. Returning from the dining-room for the third time, she perceived that one of the arm-chairs was now occupied by St. John. He lay back in it, with his eyes half shut, looking, as he always did, curiously buttoned up in a neat grey suit and fenced against the exuberance of a foreign climate which might at any moment proceed to take liberties with him. Her eyes rested on him gently and then passed on over his head. Finally she took the chair opposite.

"I didn't want to come here," he said at last, "but I was positively driven to it. . . . Evelyn M.," he groaned.

He sat up, and began to explain with mock solemnity how the detestable woman was set upon marrying him.

"She pursues me about the place. This morning she appeared in the smoking-room. All I could do was to seize my hat and fly. I didn't want to come, but I couldn't stay and face another meal with her."

"Well, we must make the best of it," Helen replied philosophically. It was very hot, and they were indifferent to any amount of silence, so that they lay back in their chairs waiting for something to happen. The bell rang for luncheon, but there was no sound of movement in the house. Was there any news? Helen asked; anything in the papers? St. John shook his head. O yes, he had a letter from home, a letter from his mother, describing the suicide of the parlour-maid. She was called Susan Jane, and she came into the kitchen one afternoon, and said that she wanted cook to keep her money for her; she had twenty pounds in gold. Then she went out to buy herself a hat. She came in at half-past five and said that she had taken poison. They had only just time to get her into bed and call a doctor before she died.

"Well?" Helen enquired.

"There'll have to be an inquest," said St. John.

Why had she done it? He shrugged his shoulders. Why do people kill themselves? Why do the lower orders do any of the things they do do? Nobody knows. They sat in silence.

"The bell's run fifteen minutes and they're not down," said Helen at length.

When they appeared, St. John explained why it had been necessary for him to come to luncheon. He imitated Evelyn's enthusiastic tone as she confronted him in the smoking-room. "She thinks there can be nothing *quite* so thrilling as mathematics, so I've lent her a large work in two volumes. It'll be interesting to see what she makes of it."

Rachel could now afford to laugh at him. She reminded him of Gibbon; she had the first volume somewhere still; if he were undertaking the education of Evelyn, that surely was the test; or she had heard that Burke, upon the American Rebellion—Evelyn ought to read them both simultaneously. When St. John had disposed of her argument and had satisfied his hunger, he proceeded to tell them that the hotel was seething with scandals, some of the most appalling kind, which had happened in their absence; he was indeed much given to the study of his kind.

"Evelyn M., for example—but that was told me in confidence."

"Nonsense!" Terence interposed.

"You've heard about poor Sinclair, too?"

"Oh, yes, I've heard about Sinclair. He's retired to his mine with a revolver. He writes to Evelyn daily that he's thinking of committing suicide. I've assured her that he's never been so happy in his life, and, on the whole, she's inclined to agree with me."

"But then she's entangled herself with Perrott," St. John continued; "and I have reason to think, from something I saw in the passage, that everything isn't as it should be between Arthur and Susan. There's a young female lately arrived from Manchester. A very good thing if it were broken off, in my opinion. Their married life is something too horrible to contemplate. Oh, and I distinctly heard old Mrs. Paley rapping out the most fearful oaths as I passed her bedroom door. It's supposed that she tortures her maid in private—it's practically certain she does. One can tell it from the look in her eyes."

"When you're eighty and the gout tweezes you, you'll be swearing like a trooper," Terence remarked. "You'll be very fat, very testy, very disagreeable. Can't you imagine him—bald as a coot, with a pair of sponge-bag trousers, a little spotted tie, and a corporation?"

After a pause Hirst remarked that the worst infamy had still to be told. He addressed himself to Helen.

"They've hoofed out the prostitute. One night while we were away that old numskull Thornbury was doddering about the passages very late. (Nobody seems to have asked him what *he* was up to.) He saw the Signora Lola Mendoza, as she calls herself, cross the passage in her nightgown. He communicated his suspicions next morning to Elliot, with the result that Rodriguez went to the woman and gave her twenty-four hours in which to clear out of the place. No one seems to have enquired into the truth of the story, or to have asked Thornbury and Elliot what business it was of theirs; they had it entirely their own way. I propose that we should all sign a Round Robin, go to Rodriguez in a body, and insist upon a full enquiry. Something's got to be done, don't you agree?"

Hewet remarked that there could be no doubt as to the lady's profession.

"Still," he added, "it's a great shame, poor woman; only I don't see what's to be done—"

"I quite agree with you, St. John," Helen burst out. "It's monstrous. The hypocritical smugness of the English makes my blood boil. A man who's made a fortune in trade as Mr. Thornbury has is bound to be twice as bad as any prostitute."

She respected St. John's morality, which she took far more seriously than any one else did, and now entered into a discussion with him as to the steps that were to be taken to enforce their peculiar view of what was right. The argument led to some profoundly gloomy statements of a general nature. Who were they, after all—what authority had they—what power against the mass of superstition and ignorance? It was the English, of course; there must be something wrong in the English blood. Directly you met an English person, of the middle classes, you were conscious of an indefinable sensation of loathing; directly you saw the brown crescent of houses above Dover, the same thing came over you. But unfortunately St. John added, you couldn't trust these foreigners—

They were interrupted by sounds of strife at the further end of the table. Rachel appealed to her aunt.

"Terence says we must go to tea with Mrs. Thornbury because she's been so kind, but I don't see it; in fact, I'd rather have my right hand sawn in pieces—just imagine! the eyes of all those women!"

"Fiddlesticks, Rachel," Terence replied. "Who wants to look at you? You're consumed with vanity! You're a monster of conceit! Surely, Helen, you ought to have taught her by this time that she's a person of no conceivable importance whatever—not beautiful, or well dressed, or conspicuous for elegance or intellect, or deportment. A more ordinary sight than you are," he concluded, "except for the tear across your dress has never been seen. However, stay at home if you want to. I'm going."

She appealed again to her aunt. It wasn't the being looked at, she explained, but the things people were sure to say. The women in particular. She liked women, but where emotion was concerned they were as flies on a lump of sugar. They would be certain to ask her questions. Evelyn M. would say: "Are you in love? Is it nice being in love?" And Mrs. Thornbury—her eyes would go up and down, up and down—she shuddered at the thought of it. Indeed, the retirement of their life since their engagement had made her so sensitive, that she was not exaggerating her case.

She found an ally in Helen, who proceeded to expound her views of the human race, as she regarded with complacency the pyramid of variegated fruits in the centre of the table. It wasn't that they were cruel, or meant to hurt, or even stupid exactly; but she had always found that the ordinary person had so little emotion in his own life that the scent of it in the lives of others was like the scent of blood in the nostrils of a bloodhound. Warming to the theme, she continued:

"Directly anything happens—it may be a marriage, or a birth, or a death—on the whole they prefer it to be a death—every one wants to see you. They insist upon seeing you. They've got nothing to say; they don't care a rap for you; but you've got to go to lunch or to tea or to dinner, and if you don't you're damned. It's the smell of blood," she continued; "I don't blame 'em; only they shan't have mind if I know it!"

She looked about her as if she had called up a legion of human beings, all hostile and all disagreeable, who encircled the table, with mouths gaping for blood, and made it appear a little island of neutral country in the midst of the enemy's country.

Her words roused her husband, who had been muttering rhythmically to himself, surveying his guests and his food and his wife with eyes that were now melancholy and now fierce, according to the fortunes of the lady in his ballad. He cut Helen short with a protest. He hated even the semblance of cynicism in women. "Nonsense, nonsense," he remarked abruptly.

Terence and Rachel glanced at each other across the table, which meant that when they were married they would not behave like that. The entrance of Ridley into the conversation had a strange effect. It became at once more formal and more polite. It would have been impossible to talk quite easily of anything that came into their heads, and to say the word prostitute as simply as any other word. The talk now turned upon literature and politics, and Ridley told stories of the distinguished people he had known in his youth. Such talk was of the nature of an art, and the personalities and informalities of the young were silenced. As they rose to go, Helen stopped for a moment, leaning her elbows on the table.

"You've all been sitting here," she said, "for almost an hour, and you haven't noticed my figs, or my flowers, or the way the light comes through, or anything. I haven't been listening, because I've been looking at you. You looked very beautiful; I wish you'd go on sitting for ever."

She led the way to the drawing-room, where she took up her embroidery, and began again to dissuade Terence from walking down to the hotel in this heat. But the more she dissuaded, the more he was determined to go. He became irritated and obstinate. There were moments when they almost disliked each other. He wanted other people; he wanted Rachel, to see them with him. He suspected that Mrs. Ambrose would now try to dissuade her from going. He was annoyed by all this space and shade and beauty, and Hirst, recumbent, drooping a magazine from his wrist.

"I'm going," he repeated. "Rachel needn't come unless she wants to."

"If you go, Hewet, I wish you'd make enquiries about the prostitute," said Hirst. "Look here," he added, "I'll walk half the way with you."

Greatly to their surprise he raised himself, looked at his watch, and remarked that, as it was now half an hour since luncheon, the gastric juices had had sufficient time to secrete; he was trying a system, he explained, which involved short spells of exercise interspaced by longer intervals of rest.

"I shall be back at four," he remarked to Helen, "when I shall lie down on the sofa and relax all my muscles completely."

"So you're going, Rachel?" Helen asked. "You won't stay with me?"

She smiled, but she might have been sad.

Was she sad, or was she really laughing? Rachel could not tell, and she felt for the moment very uncomfortable between Helen and Terence. Then she turned away, saying merely that she would go with Terence, on condition that he did all the talking.

A narrow border of shadow ran along the road, which was broad enough for two, but not broad enough for three. St. John therefore dropped a little behind the pair, and the distance between them increased by degrees. Walking with a view to digestion, and with one eye upon his watch, he looked from time to time at the pair in front of him. They seemed to be so happy, so intimate, although they were walking side by side much as other people walk. They turned slightly toward each other now and then, and said something which he thought must be something very private. They were really disputing about Helen's character, and Terence was trying to explain why it was that she annoyed him so much sometimes. But St. John thought that they were saying things which they did not want him to hear, and was led to think of his own isolation. These people were happy, and in some ways he despised them for being made happy so simply, and in other ways he envied them. He was much more remarkable than they were, but he was not happy. People never liked him; he doubted sometimes whether even Helen liked him. To be simple, to be able to say simply what one felt, without the terrific self-consciousness which possessed him, and showed him his own face and words perpetually in a mirror, that would be worth almost any other gift, for it made one happy. Happiness, happiness, what was happiness? He was never happy. He saw too clearly the little vices and deceits and flaws of life, and, seeing them, it seemed to him honest to take notice of them. That was the reason, no doubt, why people generally disliked him, and complained that he was heartless and bitter. Certainly they never told him the things he wanted to be told, that he was nice and kind, and that they liked him. But it was true that half the sharp things that he said about them were said because he was unhappy or hurt himself. But he admitted that he had very seldom told any one that he cared for them, and when he had been demonstrative, he had generally regretted it afterwards. His feelings about Terence and Rachel were so complicated that he had never yet been able to bring himself to say that he was glad that they were going to be married. He saw their faults so clearly, and the inferior nature of a great deal of their feeling for each other, and he expected that their love would not last. He looked at them again, and, very strangely, for he was so used to thinking that he seldom saw anything, the look of them filled him with a simple emotion of affection in which there were some traces of pity also. What, after all, did people's faults matter in comparison with what was good in them? He resolved that he would now tell them what he felt. He quickened his pace and came up with them just as they reached the corner where the lane joined the main road. They stood still and began to laugh at him, and to ask him whether the gastric juices—but he stopped them and began to speak very quickly and stiffly.

"D'you remember the morning after the dance?" he demanded. "It was here we sat, and you talked nonsense, and Rachel made little heaps of stones. I, on the other hand, had the whole meaning of life revealed to me in a flash." He paused for a second, and drew his lips together in a tight little purse. "Love," he said. "It seems to me to explain everything. So, on the whole, I'm very glad that you two are going to be married." He then turned round abruptly, without looking at them, and walked back to the villa. He felt both exalted and ashamed of himself for having thus said what he felt. Probably they were laughing at him, probably they thought him a fool, and, after all, had he really said what he felt?

It was true that they laughed when he was gone; but the dispute about Helen which had become rather sharp, ceased, and they became peaceful and friendly.

24

They reached the hotel rather early in the afternoon, so that most people were still lying down, or sitting speechless in their bedrooms, and Mrs. Thornbury, although she had asked them to tea, was nowhere to be seen. They sat down, therefore, in the shady hall, which was almost empty, and full of the light swishing sounds of air going to and fro in a large empty space. Yes, this arm-chair was the same arm-chair in which Rachel had sat that afternoon when Evelyn came up, and this was the magazine she had been looking at, and this the very picture, a picture of New York by lamplight. How odd it seemed—nothing had changed.

By degrees a certain number of people began to come down the stairs and to pass through the hall, and in this dim light their figures possessed a sort of grace and beauty, although they were all unknown people. Sometimes they went straight through and out into the garden by the swing door, sometimes they stopped for a few minutes and bent over the tables and began turning over the newspapers. Terence and Rachel sat watching them through their half-closed eyelids—the Johnsons, the Parkers, the Baileys, the Simmons', the Lees, the Morleys, the Campbells, the Gardiners. Some were dressed in white flannels and were carrying racquets under their arms, some were short, some tall, some were only children, and some perhaps were servants, but they all had their standing, their reason for following each other through the hall, their money, their position, whatever it might be. Terence soon gave up looking at them, for he was tired; and, closing his eyes, he fell half asleep in his chair. Rachel watched the people for some time longer; she was fascinated by the certainty and the grace of their movements, and by the inevitable way in which they seemed to follow each other, and loiter and pass on and disappear. But after a time her thoughts wandered, and she began to think of the dance, which had been held in this room, only then the room itself looked quite different. Glancing round, she could hardly believe that it was the same room. It had looked so bare and so bright and formal on that night when they came into it out of the darkness; it had been filled, too, with little red, excited faces, always moving, and people so brightly dressed and so animated that they did not seem in the least like real people, nor did you feel that you could talk to them. And now the room was dim and quiet, and beautiful silent people passed through it, to whom you could go and say anything you liked. She felt herself amazingly secure as she sat in her arm-chair, and able to review not only the night of the dance, but the entire past, tenderly and humorously, as if she had been turning in a fog for a long time, and could now see exactly where she had turned. For the methods by which she had reached her present position, seemed to her very strange, and the strangest thing about them was that she had not known where they were leading her. That was the strange thing, that one did not know where one was going, or what one wanted, and followed blindly, suffering so much in secret, always unprepared and amazed and knowing nothing; but one thing led to another and by degrees something had formed itself out of nothing, and so one reached at last this calm, this quiet, this certainty, and it was this process that people called living. Perhaps, then, every one really knew as she knew now where they were going; and things formed themselves into a pattern not only for her, but for them, and in that pattern lay satisfaction and meaning. When she looked back she could see that a meaning of some kind was apparent in the lives of her aunts, and in the brief visit of the Dalloways whom she would never see again, and in the life of her father.

The sound of Terence, breathing deep in his slumber, confirmed her in her calm. She was not sleepy although she did not see anything very distinctly, but although the figures passing through the hall became vaguer and vaguer, she believed that they all knew exactly where they were going, and the sense of their certainty filled her with comfort. For the moment she was as detached and disinterested as if she had no longer any lot in life, and she thought that she could now accept anything that came to her without being perplexed by the form in which it appeared. What was there to frighten or to perplex in the prospect of life? Why should this insight ever again desert her? The world was in truth so large, so hospitable, and after all it was so simple. "Love," St. John had said, "that seems to explain it all." Yes, but it was not the love of man for woman, of

Terence for Rachel. Although they sat so close together, they had ceased to be little separate bodies; they had ceased to struggle and desire one another. There seemed to be peace between them. It might be love, but it was not the love of man for woman.

Through her half-closed eyelids she watched Terence lying back in his chair, and she smiled as she saw how big his mouth was, and his chin so small, and his nose curved like a switchback with a knob at the end. Naturally, looking like that he was lazy, and ambitious, and full of moods and faults. She remembered their quarrels, and in particular how they had been quarreling about Helen that very afternoon, and she thought how often they would quarrel in the thirty, or forty, or fifty years in which they would be living in the same house together, catching trains together, and getting annoyed because they were so different. But all this was superficial, and had nothing to do with the life that went on beneath the eyes and the mouth and the chin, for that life was independent of her, and independent of everything else. So too, although she was going to marry him and to live with him for thirty, or forty, or fifty years, and to quarrel, and to be so close to him, she was independent of him; she was independent of everything else. Nevertheless, as St. John said, it was love that made her understand this, for she had never felt this independence, this calm, and this certainty until she fell in love with him, and perhaps this too was love. She wanted nothing else.

For perhaps two minutes Miss Allan had been standing at a little distance looking at the couple lying back so peacefully in their arm-chairs. She could not make up her mind whether to disturb them or not, and then, seeming to recollect something, she came across the hall. The sound of her approach woke Terence, who sat up and rubbed his eyes. He heard Miss Allan talking to Rachel.

"Well," she was saying, "this is very nice. It is very nice indeed. Getting engaged seems to be quite the fashion. It cannot often happen that two couples who have never seen each other before meet in the same hotel and decide to get married." Then she paused and smiled, and seemed to have nothing more to say, so that Terence rose and asked her whether it was true that she had finished her book. Some one had said that she had really finished it. Her face lit up; she turned to him with a livelier expression than usual.

"Yes, I think I can fairly say I have finished it," she said. "That is, omitting Swinburne—Beowulf to Browning—I rather like the two B's myself. Beowulf to Browning," she repeated, "I think that is the kind of title which might catch one's eye on a railway bookstall."

She was indeed very proud that she had finished her book, for no one knew what an amount of determination had gone to the making of it. Also she thought that it was a good piece of work, and, considering what anxiety she had been in about her brother while she wrote it, she could not resist telling them a little more about it.

"I must confess," she continued, "that if I had known how many classics there are in English literature, and how verbose the best of them contrive to be, I should never have undertaken the work. They only allow one seventy thousand words, you see."

"Only seventy thousand words!" Terence exclaimed.

"Yes, and one has to say something about everybody," Miss Allan added. "That is what I find so difficult, saying something different about everybody." Then she thought that she had said enough about herself, and she asked whether they had come down to join the tennis tournament. "The young people are very keen about it. It begins again in half an hour."

Her gaze rested benevolently upon them both, and, after a momentary pause, she remarked, looking at Rachel as if she had remembered something that would serve to keep her distinct from other people:

"You're the remarkable person who doesn't like ginger." But the kindness of the smile in her rather worn and courageous face made them feel that although she would scarcely remember them as individuals, she had laid upon them the burden of the new generation.

"And in that I quite agree with her," said a voice behind; Mrs. Thornbury had overheard the last few words about not liking ginger. "It's associated in my mind with a horrid old aunt of ours (poor thing, she suffered dreadfully, so it isn't fair to call her horrid) who used to give it to us when we were small, and we never had the courage to tell her we didn't like it. We just had to put it out in the shrubbery—she had a big house near Bath."

They began moving slowly across the hall, when they were stopped by the impact of Evelyn, who dashed into them, as though in running downstairs to catch them her legs had got beyond her control.

"Well," she exclaimed, with her usual enthusiasm, seizing Rachel by the arm, "I call this splendid! I guessed it was going to happen from the very beginning! I saw you two were made for each other. Now you've just got to tell me all about it—when's it to be, where are you going to live—are you both tremendously happy?"

But the attention of the group was diverted to Mrs. Elliot, who was passing them with her eager but uncertain movement, carrying in her hands a plate and an empty hot-water bottle. She would have passed them, but Mrs. Thornbury went up and stopped her.

"Thank you, Hughling's better," she replied, in answer to Mrs. Thornbury's enquiry, "but he's not an easy patient. He wants to know what his temperature is, and if I tell him he gets anxious, and if I don't tell him he suspects. You know what men are when they're ill! And of course there are none of the proper appliances, and, though he seems very willing and anxious to help" (here she lowered her voice mysteriously), "one can't feel that Dr. Rodriguez is the same as a proper doctor. If you would come and see him, Mr. Hewet," she added, "I know it would cheer him up—lying there in bed all day—and the flies—But I must go and find Angelo—the food here—of course, with an invalid, one wants things particularly nice." And she hurried past them in search of the head waiter. The worry of nursing her husband had fixed a plaintive frown upon her forehead; she was pale and looked unhappy and more than usually inefficient, and her eyes wandered more vaguely than ever from point to point.

"Poor thing!" Mrs. Thornbury exclaimed. She told them that for some days Hughling Elliot had been ill, and the only doctor available was the brother of the proprietor, or so the proprietor said, whose right to the title of doctor was not above suspicion.

"I know how wretched it is to be ill in a hotel," Mrs. Thornbury remarked, once more leading the way with Rachel to the garden. "I spent six weeks on my honeymoon in having typhoid at Venice," she continued. "But even so, I look back upon them as some of the happiest weeks in my life. Ah, yes," she said, taking Rachel's arm, "you think yourself happy now, but it's nothing to the happiness that comes afterwards. And I assure you I could find it in my heart to envy you young people! You've a much better time than we had, I may tell you. When I look back upon it, I can hardly believe how things have changed. When we were engaged I wasn't allowed to go for walks with William alone—some one had always to be in the room with us—I really believe I had to show my parents all his letters!—though they were very fond of him too. Indeed, I may say they looked upon him as their own son. It amuses me," she continued, "to think how strict they were to us, when I see how they spoil their grandchildren!"

The table was laid under the tree again, and taking her place before the teacups, Mrs. Thornbury beckoned and nodded until she had collected quite a number of people, Susan and Arthur and Mr. Pepper, who were strolling about, waiting for the tournament to begin. A murmuring tree, a river brimming in the moonlight, Terence's words came back to Rachel as she sat drinking the tea and listening to the words which flowed on so lightly, so kindly, and with such silvery smoothness. This long life and all these children had left her very smooth; they seemed to have rubbed away the marks of individuality, and to have left only what was old and maternal.

"And the things you young people are going to see!" Mrs. Thornbury continued. She included them all in her forecast, she included them all in her maternity, although the party comprised William Pepper and Miss Allan, both of whom might have been supposed to have seen a fair share of the panorama. "When I see how the world has changed in my lifetime," she went on, "I can set no limit to what may happen in the next fifty years. Ah, no, Mr. Pepper, I don't agree with you in the least," she laughed, interrupting his gloomy remark about things going steadily from bad to worse. "I know I ought to feel that, but I don't, I'm afraid. They're going to be much better people than we were. Surely everything goes to prove that. All round me I see women, young women, women with household cares of every sort, going out and doing things that we should not have thought it possible to do."

Mr. Pepper thought her sentimental and irrational like all old women, but her manner of treating him as if he were a cross old baby baffled him and charmed him, and he could only reply to her with a curious grimace which was more a smile than a frown.

"And they remain women," Mrs. Thornbury added. "They give a great deal to their children."

As she said this she smiled slightly in the direction of Susan and Rachel. They did not like to be included in the same lot, but they both smiled a little self-consciously, and Arthur and Terence glanced at each other too. She made them feel that they were all in the same boat together, and they looked at the women they were going to marry and compared them. It was inexplicable how any one could wish to marry Rachel, incredible that any one should be ready to spend his life with Susan; but singular though the other's taste must be, they bore each other no ill-will on account of it; indeed, they liked each other rather the better for the eccentricity of their choice.

"I really must congratulate you," Susan remarked, as she leant across the table for the jam.

There seemed to be no foundation for St. John's gossip about Arthur and Susan. Sunburnt and vigorous they sat side by side, with their racquets across their knees, not saying much but smiling slightly all the time. Through the thin white clothes which they wore, it was possible to see the lines of their bodies and legs, the beautiful curves of their muscles, his leanness and her flesh, and it was natural to think of the firm-fleshed sturdy children that would be theirs. Their faces had too little shape in them to be beautiful, but they had clear eyes and an appearance of great health and power of endurance, for it seemed as if the blood would never cease to run in his veins, or to lie deeply and calmly in her cheeks. Their eyes at the present moment were brighter than usual, and wore the peculiar expression of pleasure and self-confidence which is seen in the eyes of athletes, for they had been playing tennis, and they were both first-rate at the game.

Evelyn had not spoken, but she had been looking from Susan to Rachel. Well—they had both made up their minds very easily, they had done in a very few weeks what it sometimes seemed to her that she would never be able to do. Although they were so different, she thought that she could see in each the same look of satisfaction and completion, the same calmness of manner, and the same slowness of movement. It was that slowness, that confidence, that content which she hated, she thought to herself. They moved so slowly because they were not single but double, and Susan was attached to Arthur, and Rachel to Terence, and for the sake of this one man they had renounced all other men, and movement, and the real things of life. Love was all very well, and those snug domestic houses, with the kitchen below and the nursery above, which were so secluded and self-contained, like little islands in the torrents of the world; but the real things were surely the things that happened, the causes, the wars, the ideals, which happened in the great world outside, and went so independently of these women, turning so quietly and beautifully towards the men. She looked at them sharply. Of course they were happy and content, but there must be better things than that. Surely one could get nearer to life, one could get more out of life, one could enjoy more and feel more than they would ever do. Rachel in particular looked so young—what could she know of life? She became restless, and getting up, crossed over to sit beside Rachel. She reminded her that she had promised to join her club.

"The bother is," she went on, "that I mayn't be able to start work seriously till October. I've just had a letter from a friend of mine whose brother is in business in Moscow. They want me to stay with them, and as they're in the thick of all the conspiracies and anarchists, I've a good mind to stop on my way home. It sounds too thrilling." She wanted to make Rachel see how thrilling it was. "My friend knows a girl of fifteen who's been sent to Siberia for life merely because they caught her addressing a letter to an anarchist. And the letter wasn't from her, either. I'd give all I have in the world to help on a revolution against the Russian government, and it's bound to come."

She looked from Rachel to Terence. They were both a little touched by the sight of her remembering how lately they had been listening to evil words about her, and Terence asked her what her scheme was, and she explained that she was going to found a club—a club for doing things, really doing them. She became very animated, as she talked on and on, for she professed herself certain that if once twenty people—no, ten would be enough if they were keen—set about doing things instead of talking about doing them, they could abolish almost every evil that exists. It was brains that were needed. If only people with brains—of course they would want a room, a nice room, in Bloomsbury preferably, where they could meet once a week. . . .

As she talked Terence could see the traces of fading youth in her face, the lines that were being drawn by talk and excitement round her mouth and eyes, but he did not pity her; looking into those bright, rather hard, and very courageous eyes, he saw that she did not pity herself, or feel any desire to exchange her own life for the more refined and orderly lives of people like himself and St. John, although, as the years went by, the fight would become harder and harder. Perhaps, though, she would settle down; perhaps, after all, she would marry Perrott. While his mind was half occupied with what she was saying, he thought of her probable destiny, the light clouds of tobacco smoke serving to obscure his face from her eyes.

Terence smoked and Arthur smoked and Evelyn smoked, so that the air was full of the mist and fragrance of good tobacco. In the intervals when no one spoke, they heard far off the low murmur of the sea, as the waves quietly broke and spread the beach with a film of water, and withdrew to break again. The cool green light fell through the leaves of the tree, and there were soft crescents and diamonds of sunshine upon the plates and the tablecloth. Mrs. Thornbury, after watching them all for a time in silence, began to ask Rachel kindly questions—When did they all go back? Oh, they expected her father. She must want to see her father—there would be a great deal to tell him, and (she looked sympathetically at Terence) he would be so happy, she felt sure. Years ago, she continued, it might have been ten or twenty years ago, she remembered meeting Mr. Vinrace at a party, and, being so much struck by his face, which was so unlike the ordinary face one sees at a party, that she had asked who he was, and she was told that it was Mr. Vinrace, and she had always remembered the name—an uncommon name—and he had a lady with him, a very sweet-looking woman, but it was one of those dreadful London crushes, where you don't talk—you only look at each other—and although she had shaken hands with Mr. Vinrace, she didn't think they had said anything. She sighed very slightly, remembering the past.

Then she turned to Mr. Pepper, who had become very dependent on her, so that he always chose a seat near her, and attended to what she was saying, although he did not often make any remark of his own.

"You who know everything, Mr. Pepper," she said, "tell us how did those wonderful French ladies manage their salons? Did we ever do anything of the same kind in England, or do you think that there is some reason why we cannot do it in England?"

Mr. Pepper was pleased to explain very accurately why there has never been an English salon. There were three reasons, and they were very good ones, he said. As for himself, when he went to a party, as one was sometimes obliged to, from a wish not to give offence—his niece, for example, had been married the other day—he walked into the middle of the room, said "Ha! ha!" as loud as ever he could, considered that he had done his duty, and walked away again. Mrs. Thornbury protested. She was going to give a party directly she got back, and they were all to be invited, and she should set people to watch Mr. Pepper, and if she heard that he had been caught saying "Ha! ha!" she would—she would do something very dreadful indeed to him. Arthur Venning suggested that what she must do was to rig up something in the nature of a surprise—a portrait, for example, of a nice old lady in a lace cap, concealing a bath of cold water, which at a signal could be sprung on Pepper's head; or they'd have a chair which shot him twenty feet high directly he sat on it.

Susan laughed. She had done her tea; she was feeling very well contented, partly because she had been playing tennis brilliantly, and then every one was so nice; she was beginning to find it so much easier to talk, and to hold her own even with quite clever people, for somehow clever people did not frighten her any more. Even Mr. Hirst, whom she had disliked when she first met him, really wasn't disagreeable; and, poor man, he always looked so ill; perhaps he was in love; perhaps he had been in love with Rachel—she really shouldn't wonder; or perhaps it was Evelyn—she was of course very attractive to men. Leaning forward, she went on with the conversation. She said that she thought that the reason why parties were so dull was mainly because gentlemen will not dress: even in London, she stated, it struck her very much how people don't think it necessary to dress in the evening, and of course if they don't dress in London they won't dress in the country. It was really quite a treat at Christmas-time when there were the Hunt balls, and the gentlemen wore nice red coats, but Arthur didn't care for dancing, so she supposed that they wouldn't go even to the ball in their little country town. She didn't think that people who were fond of one sport often care for another, although her father was an exception. But then he was an exception in every way—such a gardener, and he knew all about birds and animals, and of course he was simply adored by all the old women in the village, and at the same time what he really liked best was a book. You always knew where to find him if he were wanted; he would be in his study with a book. Very likely it would be an old, old book, some fusty old thing that no one else would dream of reading. She used to tell him that he would have made a first-rate old bookworm if only he hadn't had a family of six to support, and six children, she added, charmingly confident of universal sympathy, didn't leave one much time for being a bookworm.

Still talking about her father, of whom she was very proud, she rose, for Arthur upon looking at his watch found that it was time they went back again to the tennis court. The others did not move.

"They're very happy!" said Mrs. Thornbury, looking benignantly after them. Rachel agreed; they seemed to be so certain of themselves; they seemed to know exactly what they wanted.

"D'you think they *are* happy?" Evelyn murmured to Terence in an undertone, and she hoped that he would say that he did not think them happy; but, instead, he said that they must go too—go home, for they were always being late for meals, and Mrs. Ambrose, who was very stern and particular, didn't like that. Evelyn laid hold of Rachel's skirt and protested. Why should they go? It was still early, and she had so many things to say to them.

"No," said Terence, "we must go, because we walk so slowly. We stop and look at things, and we talk."

"What d'you talk about?" Evelyn enquired, upon which he laughed and said that they talked about everything.

Mrs. Thornbury went with them to the gate, trailing very slowly and gracefully across the grass and the gravel, and talking all the time about flowers and birds. She told them that she had taken up the study of botany since her daughter married, and it was wonderful what a number of flowers there were which she had never seen, although she had lived in the country all her life and she was now seventy-two. It was a good thing to have some occupation which was quite independent of other people, she said, when one got old. But the odd thing was that one never felt old. She always felt that she was twenty-five, not a day more or a day less, but, of course, one couldn't expect other people to agree to that.

"It must be very wonderful to be twenty-five, and not merely to imagine that you're twenty-five," she said, looking from one to the other with her smooth, bright glance. "It must be very wonderful, very wonderful indeed." She stood talking to them at the gate for a long time; she seemed reluctant that they should go.

25

The afternoon was very hot, so hot that the breaking of the waves on the shore sounded like the repeated sigh of some exhausted creature, and even on the terrace under an awning the bricks were hot, and the air danced perpetually over the short dry grass. The red flowers in the stone basins were drooping with the heat, and the white blossoms which had been so smooth and thick only a few weeks ago were now dry, and their edges were curled and yellow. Only the stiff and hostile plants of the south, whose fleshy leaves seemed to be grown upon spines, still remained standing upright and defied the sun to beat them down. It was too hot to talk, and it was not easy to find any book that would withstand the power of the sun. Many books had been tried and then let fall, and now Terence was reading Milton aloud, because he said the words of Milton had substance and shape, so that it was not necessary to understand what he was saying; one could merely listen to his words; one could almost handle them.

> There is a gentle nymph not far from hence,

he read,

> That with moist curb sways the smooth Severn stream.
> Sabrina is her name, a virgin pure;
> Whilom she was the daughter of Locrine,
> That had the sceptre from his father Brute.

The words, in spite of what Terence had said, seemed to be laden with meaning, and perhaps it was for this reason that it was painful to listen to them; they sounded strange; they meant different things from what they usually meant. Rachel at any rate could not keep her attention fixed upon them, but went off upon curious trains of thought suggested by words such as "curb" and "Locrine" and "Brute," which brought unpleasant sights before her eyes, independently of their meaning. Owing to the heat and the dancing air the garden too looked strange—the trees were either too near or too far, and her head almost certainly ached. She was not quite certain, and therefore she did not know, whether to tell Terence now, or to let him go on reading. She decided that she would wait until he came to the end of a stanza, and if by that time she had turned her head this way and that, and it ached in every position undoubtedly, she would say very calmly that her head ached.

> Sabrina fair,
> Listen where thou art sitting
> Under the glassy, cool, translucent wave,
> In twisted braids of lilies knitting
> The loose train of thy amber dropping hair,
> Listen for dear honour's sake,
> Goddess of the silver lake,
> Listen and save!

But her head ached; it ached whichever way she turned it.

She sat up and said as she had determined, "My head aches so that I shall go indoors."

He was half-way through the next verse, but he dropped the book instantly.

"Your head aches?" he repeated.

For a few moments they sat looking at one another in silence, holding each other's hands. During this time his sense of dismay and catastrophe were almost physically painful; all round him he seemed to hear the shiver of broken glass which, as it fell to earth, left him sitting in the open air. But at the end of two minutes, noticing that she was not sharing his dismay, but was only rather more languid and heavy-eyed than usual, he recovered, fetched Helen, and asked her to tell him what they had better do, for Rachel had a headache.

Mrs. Ambrose was not discomposed, but advised that she should go to bed, and added that she must expect her head to ache if she sat up to all hours and went out in the heat, but a few hours in bed would cure it completely. Terence was unreasonably reassured by her words, as he had been unreasonably depressed the moment before. Helen's sense seemed to have much in common with the ruthless good sense of nature, which avenged rashness by a headache, and, like nature's good sense, might be depended upon.

Rachel went to bed; she lay in the dark, it seemed to her, for a very long time, but at length, waking from a transparent kind of sleep, she saw the windows white in front of her, and recollected that some time before she had gone to bed with a headache, and that Helen had said it would be gone when she woke. She supposed, therefore, that she was now quite well again. At the same time the wall of her room was painfully white, and curved slightly, instead of being straight and flat. Turning her eyes to the window, she was not reassured by what she saw there. The movement of the blind as it filled with air and blew slowly out, drawing the cord with a little trailing sound along the floor, seemed to her terrifying, as if it were the movement of an animal in the room. She shut her eyes, and the pulse in her head beat so strongly that each thump seemed to tread upon a nerve, piercing her forehead with a little stab of pain. It might not be the same headache, but she certainly had a headache. She turned from side to side, in the hope that the coolness of the sheets would cure her, and that when she next opened her eyes to look the room would be as usual. After a considerable number of vain experiments, she resolved to put the matter beyond a doubt. She got out of bed and stood upright, holding on to the brass ball at the end of the bedstead. Ice-cold at first, it soon became as hot as the palm of her hand, and as the pains in her head and body and the instability of the floor proved that it would be far more intolerable to stand and walk than to lie in bed, she got into bed again; but though the change was refreshing at first, the discomfort of bed was soon as great as the discomfort of standing up. She accepted the idea that she would have to stay in bed all day long, and as she laid her head on the pillow, relinquished the happiness of the day.

When Helen came in an hour or two later, suddenly stopped her cheerful words, looked startled for a second and then unnaturally calm, the fact that she was ill was put beyond a doubt. It was confirmed when the whole household knew of it, when the song that some one was singing in the garden stopped suddenly, and when Maria, as she brought water, slipped past the bed with averted eyes. There was all the morning to get through, and then all the afternoon, and at intervals she made an effort to cross over into the ordinary world, but she found that her heat and discomfort had put a gulf between her world and the ordinary world which she could not bridge. At one point the door opened, and Helen came in with a little dark man who had—it was the chief thing she noticed about him—very hairy hands. She was drowsy and intolerably hot, and as he seemed shy and obsequious she scarcely troubled to answer him, although she understood that he was a doctor. At another point the door opened and Terence came in very gently, smiling too steadily, as she realised, for it to be natural. He sat down and talked to her, stroking her hands until it became irksome to her to lie any more in the same position and she turned round, and when she looked up again Helen was beside her and Terence had gone. It did not matter; she would see him tomorrow when things would be ordinary again. Her chief occupation during the day was to try to remember how the lines went:

Under the glassy, cool, translucent wave,
In twisted braids of lilies knitting
The loose train of thy amber dropping hair;

and the effort worried her because the adjectives persisted in getting into the wrong places.

The second day did not differ very much from the first day, except that her bed had become very important, and the world outside, when she tried to think of it, appeared distinctly further off. The glassy, cool, translucent wave was almost visible before her, curling up at the end of the bed, and as it was refreshingly cool she tried to keep her mind fixed upon it. Helen was here, and Helen was there all day long; sometimes she said that it was lunchtime, and sometimes that it was teatime; but by the next day all landmarks were obliterated, and the outer world was so far away that the different sounds, such as the sounds of people moving overhead, could only be ascribed to their cause by a great effort of memory. The recollection of what she had felt, or of what she had been doing and thinking three days before, had faded entirely. On the other hand, every object in the room, and the bed itself, and her own body with its various limbs and their different sensations were more and more important each day. She was completely cut off, and unable to communicate with the rest of the world, isolated alone with her body.

Hours and hours would pass thus, without getting any further through the morning, or again a few minutes would lead from broad daylight to the depths of the night. One evening when the room appeared very dim, either because it was evening or because the blinds were drawn, Helen said to her, "Some one is going to sit here tonight. You won't mind?"

Opening her eyes, Rachel saw not only Helen but a nurse in spectacles, whose face vaguely recalled something that she had once seen. She had seen her in the chapel. "Nurse McInnis," said Helen, and the nurse smiled steadily as they all did, and said that she did not find many people who were frightened of her. After waiting for a moment they both disappeared, and having turned on her pillow Rachel woke to find herself in the midst of one of those interminable nights which do not end at twelve, but go on into the double figures—thirteen, fourteen, and so on until they reach the twenties, and then the thirties, and then the forties. She realised that there is nothing to prevent nights from doing this if they choose. At a great distance an elderly woman sat with her head bent down; Rachel raised herself slightly and saw with dismay that she was playing cards by the light of a candle which stood in the hollow of a newspaper. The sight had something inexplicably sinister about it, and she was terrified and cried out, upon which the woman laid down her cards and came across the room, shading the candle with her hands. Coming nearer and nearer across the great space of the room, she stood at last above Rachel's head and said, "Not asleep? Let me make you comfortable."

She put down the candle and began to arrange the bedclothes. It struck Rachel that a woman who sat playing cards in a cavern all night long would have very cold hands, and she shrunk from the touch of them.

"Why, there's a toe all the way down there!" the woman said, proceeding to tuck in the bedclothes. Rachel did not realise that the toe was hers.

"You must try and lie still," she proceeded, "because if you lie still you will be less hot, and if you toss about you will make yourself more hot, and we don't want you to be any hotter than you are." She stood looking down upon Rachel for an enormous length of time.

"And the quieter you lie the sooner you will be well," she repeated.

Rachel kept her eyes fixed upon the peaked shadow on the ceiling, and all her energy was concentrated upon the desire that this shadow should move. But the shadow and the woman seemed to be eternally fixed above her. She shut her eyes. When she opened them again several more hours had passed, but the night still lasted interminably. The woman was still playing cards, only she sat now in a tunnel under a river, and the light stood in a little archway in the wall above her. She cried "Terence!" and the peaked shadow again moved across the ceiling, as the woman with an enormous slow movement rose, and they both stood still above her.

"It's just as difficult to keep you in bed as it was to keep Mr. Forrest in bed," the woman said, "and he was such a tall gentleman."

In order to get rid of this terrible stationary sight Rachel again shut her eyes, and found herself walking through a tunnel under the Thames, where there were little deformed women sitting in archways playing cards, while the bricks of which the wall was made oozed with damp, which collected into drops and slid down the wall. But the little old women became Helen and Nurse McInnis after a time, standing in the window together whispering, whispering incessantly.

Meanwhile outside her room the sounds, the movements, and the lives of the other people in the house went on in the ordinary light of the sun, throughout the usual succession of hours. When, on the first day of her illness, it became clear that she would not be absolutely well, for her temperature was very high, until Friday, that day being Tuesday, Terence was filled with resentment, not against her, but against the force outside them which was separating them. He counted up the number of days that would almost certainly be spoilt for them. He realised, with an odd mixture of pleasure and annoyance, that, for the first time in his life, he was so dependent upon another person that his happiness was in her keeping. The days were completely wasted upon trifling, immaterial things, for after three weeks of such intimacy and intensity all the usual occupations were unbearably flat and beside the point. The least intolerable occupation was to talk to St. John about Rachel's illness, and to discuss every symptom and its meaning, and, when this subject was exhausted, to discuss illness of all kinds, and what caused them, and what cured them.

Twice every day he went in to sit with Rachel, and twice every day the same thing happened. On going into her room, which was not very dark, where the music was lying about as usual, and her books and letters, his spirits rose instantly. When he saw her he felt completely reassured. She did not look very ill. Sitting by her side he would tell her what he had been doing, using his natural voice to speak to her, only a few tones lower down than usual; but by the time he had sat there for five minutes he was plunged into the deepest gloom. She was not the same; he could not bring them back to their old relationship; but although he knew that it was foolish he could not prevent himself from endeavouring to bring her back, to make her remember, and when this failed he was in despair. He always concluded as he left her room that it was worse to see her than not to see her, but by degrees, as the day wore on, the desire to see her returned and became almost too great to be borne.

On Thursday morning when Terence went into her room he felt the usual increase of confidence. She turned round and made an effort to remember certain facts from the world that was so many millions of miles away.

"You have come up from the hotel?" she asked.

"No; I'm staying here for the present," he said. "We've just had luncheon," he continued, "and the mail has come in. There's a bundle of letters for you—letters from England."

Instead of saying, as he meant her to say, that she wished to see them, she said nothing for some time.

"You see, there they go, rolling off the edge of the hill," she said suddenly.

"Rolling, Rachel? What do you see rolling? There's nothing rolling."

"The old woman with the knife," she replied, not speaking to Terence in particular, and looking past him. As she appeared to be looking at a vase on the shelf opposite, he rose and took it down.

"Now they can't roll any more," he said cheerfully. Nevertheless she lay gazing at the same spot, and paid him no further attention although he spoke to her. He became so profoundly wretched that he could not endure to sit with her, but wandered about until he found St. John, who was reading *The Times* in the verandah. He laid it aside patiently, and heard all that Terence had to say about delirium. He was very patient with Terence. He treated him like a child.

By Friday it could not be denied that the illness was no longer an attack that would pass off in a day or two; it was a real illness that required a good deal of organisation, and engrossed the attention of at least five people, but there was no reason to be anxious. Instead of lasting five days it was going to last ten days. Rodriguez was understood to say that there were well-known varieties of this illness. Rodriguez appeared to think that they were treating the illness with undue anxiety. His visits were always marked by the same show of confidence, and in his interviews with Terence he always waved aside his anxious and minute questions with a kind of flourish which seemed to indicate that they were all taking it much too seriously. He seemed curiously unwilling to sit down.

"A high temperature," he said, looking furtively about the room, and appearing to be more interested in the furniture and in Helen's embroidery than in anything else. "In this climate you must expect a high temperature. You need not be alarmed by that. It is the pulse we go by" (he tapped his own hairy wrist), "and the pulse continues excellent."

Thereupon he bowed and slipped out. The interview was conducted laboriously upon both sides in French, and this, together with the fact that he was optimistic, and that Terence respected the medical profession from hearsay, made him less critical than he would have been had he encountered the doctor in any other capacity. Unconsciously he took Rodriguez' side against Helen, who seemed to have taken an unreasonable prejudice against him.

When Saturday came it was evident that the hours of the day must be more strictly organised than they had been. St. John offered his services; he said that he had nothing to do, and that he might as well spend the day at the villa if he could be of use. As if they were starting on a difficult expedition together, they parcelled out their duties between them, writing out an elaborate scheme of hours upon a large sheet of paper which was pinned to the drawing-room door. Their distance from the town, and the difficulty of procuring rare things with unknown names from the most unexpected places, made it necessary to think very carefully, and they found it unexpectedly difficult to do the simple but practical things that were required of them, as if they, being very tall, were asked to stoop down and arrange minute grains of sand in a pattern on the ground.

It was St. John's duty to fetch what was needed from the town, so that Terence would sit all through the long hot hours alone in the drawing-room, near the open door, listening for any movement upstairs, or call from Helen. He always forgot to pull down the blinds, so that he sat in bright sunshine, which worried him without his knowing what was the cause of it. The room was terribly stiff and uncomfortable. There were hats in the chairs, and medicine bottles among the books. He tried to read, but good books were too good, and bad books were too bad, and the only thing he could tolerate was the newspaper, which with its news of London, and the movements of real people who were giving dinner-parties and making speeches, seemed to give a little background of reality to what was otherwise mere nightmare. Then, just as his attention was fixed on the print, a soft call would come from Helen, or Mrs. Chailey would bring in something which was wanted upstairs, and he would run up very quietly in his socks, and put the jug on the little table which stood crowded with jugs and cups outside the bedroom door; or if he could catch Helen for a moment he would ask, "How is she?"

"Rather restless. . . . On the whole, quieter, I think."

The answer would be one or the other.

As usual she seemed to reserve something which she did not say, and Terence was conscious that they disagreed, and, without saying it aloud, were arguing against each other. But she was too hurried and pre-occupied to talk.

The strain of listening and the effort of making practical arrangements and seeing that things worked smoothly, absorbed all Terence's power. Involved in this long dreary nightmare, he did not attempt to think what it amounted to. Rachel was ill; that was all; he must see that there was medicine and milk, and that things were ready when they were wanted. Thought had ceased; life itself had come to a standstill. Sunday was rather worse than Saturday had been, simply because the strain was a little greater every day, although nothing else had changed. The separate feelings of pleasure, interest, and pain, which combine to make up the ordinary day, were merged in one long-drawn sensation of sordid misery and profound boredom. He had never been so bored since he was shut up in the nursery alone as a child. The vision of Rachel as she was now, confused and heedless, had almost obliterated the vision of her as she had been once long ago; he could hardly believe that they had ever been happy, or engaged to be married, for what were feelings, what was there to be felt? Confusion covered every sight and person, and he seemed to see St. John, Ridley, and the stray people who came up now and then from the hotel to enquire, through a mist; the only people who were not hidden in this mist were Helen and Rodriguez, because they could tell him something definite about Rachel.

Nevertheless the day followed the usual forms. At certain hours they went into the dining-room, and when they sat round the table they talked about indifferent things. St. John usually made it his business to start the talk and to keep it from dying out.

"I've discovered the way to get Sancho past the white house," said St. John on Sunday at luncheon. "You crackle a piece of paper in his ear, then he bolts for about a hundred yards, but he goes on quite well after that."

"Yes, but he wants corn. You should see that he has corn."

"I don't think much of the stuff they give him; and Angelo seems a dirty little rascal."

There was then a long silence. Ridley murmured a few lines of poetry under his breath, and remarked, as if to conceal the fact that he had done so, "Very hot today."

"Two degrees higher than it was yesterday," said St. John. "I wonder where these nuts come from," he observed, taking a nut out of the plate, turning it over in his fingers, and looking at it curiously.

"London, I should think," said Terence, looking at the nut too.

"A competent man of business could make a fortune here in no time," St. John continued. "I suppose the heat does something funny to people's brains. Even the English go a little queer. Anyhow they're hopeless people to deal with. They kept me three-quarters of an hour waiting at the chemist's this morning, for no reason whatever."

There was another long pause. Then Ridley enquired, "Rodriguez seems satisfied?"

"Quite," said Terence with decision. "It's just got to run its course." Whereupon Ridley heaved a deep sigh. He was genuinely sorry for every one, but at the same time he missed Helen considerably, and was a little aggrieved by the constant presence of the two young men.

They moved back into the drawing-room.

"Look here, Hirst," said Terence, "there's nothing to be done for two hours." He consulted the sheet pinned to the door. "You go and lie down. I'll wait here. Chailey sits with Rachel while Helen has her luncheon."

It was asking a good deal of Hirst to tell him to go without waiting for a sight of Helen. These little glimpses of Helen were the only respites from strain and boredom, and very often they seemed to make up for the discomfort of the day, although she might not have anything to tell them. However, as they were on an expedition together, he had made up his mind to obey.

Helen was very late in coming down. She looked like a person who has been sitting for a long time in the dark. She was pale and thinner, and the expression of her eyes was harassed but determined. She ate her luncheon quickly, and seemed indifferent to what she was doing. She brushed aside Terence's enquiries, and at last, as if he had not spoken, she looked at him with a slight frown and said:

"We can't go on like this, Terence. Either you've got to find another doctor, or you must tell Rodriguez to stop coming, and I'll manage for myself. It's no use for him to say that Rachel's better; she's not better; she's worse."

Terence suffered a terrific shock, like that which he had suffered when Rachel said, "My head aches." He stilled it by reflecting that Helen was overwrought, and he was upheld in this opinion by his obstinate sense that she was opposed to him in the argument.

"Do you think she's in danger?" he asked.

"No one can go on being as ill as that day after day—" Helen replied. She looked at him, and spoke as if she felt some indignation with somebody.

"Very well, I'll talk to Rodriguez this afternoon," he replied.

Helen went upstairs at once.

Nothing now could assuage Terence's anxiety. He could not read, nor could he sit still, and his sense of security was shaken, in spite of the fact that he was determined that Helen was exaggerating, and that Rachel was not very ill. But he wanted a third person to confirm him in his belief.

Directly Rodriguez came down he demanded, "Well, how is she? Do you think her worse?"

"There is no reason for anxiety, I tell you—none," Rodriguez replied in his execrable French, smiling uneasily, and making little movements all the time as if to get away.

Hewet stood firmly between him and the door. He was determined to see for himself what kind of man he was. His confidence in the man vanished as he looked at him and saw his insignificance, his dirty appearance, his shiftiness, and his unintelligent, hairy face. It was strange that he had never seen this before.

"You won't object, of course, if we ask you to consult another doctor?" he continued.

At this the little man became openly incensed.

"Ah!" he cried. "You have not confidence in me? You object to my treatment? You wish me to give up the case?"

"Not at all," Terence replied, "but in serious illness of this kind—"

Rodriguez shrugged his shoulders.

"It is not serious, I assure you. You are overanxious. The young lady is not seriously ill, and I am a doctor. The lady of course is frightened," he sneered. "I understand that perfectly."

"The name and address of the doctor is—?" Terence continued.

"There is no other doctor," Rodriguez replied sullenly. "Every one has confidence in me. Look! I will show you."

He took out a packet of old letters and began turning them over as if in search of one that would confute Terence's suspicions. As he searched, he began to tell a story about an English lord who had trusted him—a great English lord, whose name he had, unfortunately, forgotten.

"There is no other doctor in the place," he concluded, still turning over the letters.

"Never mind," said Terence shortly. "I will make enquiries for myself."

Rodriguez put the letters back in his pocket.

"Very well," he remarked. "I have no objection."

He lifted his eyebrows, shrugged his shoulders, as if to repeat that they took the illness much too seriously and that there was no other doctor, and slipped out, leaving behind him an impression that he was conscious that he was distrusted, and that his malice was aroused.

After this Terence could no longer stay downstairs. He went up, knocked at Rachel's door, and asked Helen whether he might see her for a few minutes. He had not seen her yesterday. She made no objection, and went and sat at a table in the window.

Terence sat down by the bedside. Rachel's face was changed. She looked as though she were entirely concentrated upon the effort of keeping alive. Her lips were drawn, and her cheeks were sunken and flushed, though without colour. Her eyes were not entirely shut, the lower half of the white part showing, not as if she saw, but as if they remained open because she was too much exhausted to close them. She opened them completely when he kissed her. But she only saw an old woman slicing a man's head off with a knife.

"There it falls!" she murmured. She then turned to Terence and asked him anxiously some question about a man with mules, which he could not understand. "Why doesn't he come? Why doesn't he come?" she repeated. He was appalled to think of the dirty little man downstairs in connection with illness like this, and turning instinctively to Helen, but she was doing something at a table in the window, and did not seem to realise how great the shock to him must be. He rose to go, for he could not endure to listen any longer; his heart beat quickly and painfully with anger and misery. As he passed Helen she asked him in the same weary, unnatural, but determined voice to fetch her more ice, and to have the jug outside filled with fresh milk.

When he had done these errands he went to find Hirst. Exhausted and very hot, St. John had fallen asleep on a bed, but Terence woke him without scruple.

"Helen thinks she's worse," he said. "There's no doubt she's frightfully ill. Rodriguez is useless. We must get another doctor."

"But there is no other doctor," said Hirst drowsily, sitting up and rubbing his eyes.

"Don't be a damned fool!" Terence exclaimed. "Of course there's another doctor, and, if there isn't, you've got to find one. It ought to have been done days ago. I'm going down to saddle the horse." He could not stay still in one place.

In less than ten minutes St. John was riding to the town in the scorching heat in search of a doctor, his orders being to find one and bring him back if he had to be fetched in a special train.

"We ought to have done it days ago," Hewet repeated angrily.

When he went back into the drawing-room he found that Mrs. Flushing was there, standing very erect in the middle of the room, having arrived, as people did in these days, by the kitchen or through the garden unannounced.

"She's better?" Mrs. Flushing enquired abruptly; they did not attempt to shake hands.

"No," said Terence. "If anything, they think she's worse."

Mrs. Flushing seemed to consider for a moment or two, looking straight at Terence all the time.

"Let me tell you," she said, speaking in nervous jerks, "it's always about the seventh day one begins to get anxious. I daresay you've been sittin' here worryin' by yourself. You think she's bad, but any one comin' with a fresh eye would see she was better. Mr. Elliot's had fever; he's all right now," she threw out. "It wasn't anythin' she caught on the expedition. What's it matter—a few days' fever? My brother had fever for twenty-six days once. And in a week or two he was up and about. We gave him nothin' but milk and arrowroot—"

Here Mrs. Chailey came in with a message.

"I'm wanted upstairs," said Terence.

"You see—she'll be better," Mrs. Flushing jerked out as he left the room. Her anxiety to persuade Terence was very great, and when he left her without saying anything she felt dissatisfied and restless; she did not like to stay, but she could not bear to go. She wandered from room to room looking for some one to talk to, but all the rooms were empty.

Terence went upstairs, stood inside the door to take Helen's directions, looked over at Rachel, but did not attempt to speak to her. She appeared vaguely conscious of his presence, but it seemed to disturb her, and she turned, so that she lay with her back to him.

For six days indeed she had been oblivious of the world outside, because it needed all her attention to follow the hot, red, quick sights which passed incessantly before her eyes. She knew that it was of enormous importance that she should attend to these sights and grasp their meaning, but she was always being just too late to hear or see something which would explain it all. For this reason, the faces—Helen's face, the nurse's, Terence's, the doctor's—which occasionally forced themselves very close to her, were worrying because they distracted her attention and she might miss the clue. However, on the fourth afternoon she was suddenly unable to keep Helen's face distinct from the sights themselves; her lips widened as she bent down over the bed, and she began to gabble unintelligibly like the rest. The sights were all concerned in some plot, some adventure, some escape. The nature of what they were doing changed incessantly, although there was always a reason behind it, which she must endeavour to grasp. Now they were among trees and savages, now they were on the sea, now they were on the tops of high towers; now they jumped; now they flew. But just as the crisis was about to happen, something invariably slipped in her brain, so that the whole effort had to begin over again. The heat was suffocating. At last the faces went further away; she fell into a deep pool of sticky water, which eventually closed over her head. She saw nothing and heard nothing but a faint booming sound, which was the sound of the sea rolling over her head. While all her tormentors thought that she was dead, she was not dead, but curled up at the bottom of the sea. There she lay, sometimes seeing darkness, sometimes light, while every now and then some one turned her over at the bottom of the sea.

After St. John had spent some hours in the heat of the sun wrangling with evasive and very garrulous natives, he extracted the information that there was a doctor, a French doctor, who was at present away on a holiday in the hills. It was quite impossible, so they said, to find him. With his experience of the country, St. John thought it unlikely that a telegram would either be sent or received; but having reduced the distance of the hill town, in which he was staying, from a hundred miles to thirty miles, and having hired a carriage and horses, he started at once to fetch the doctor himself. He succeeded in finding him, and eventually forced the unwilling man to leave his young wife and return forthwith. They reached the villa at midday on Tuesday.

Terence came out to receive them, and St. John was struck by the fact that he had grown perceptibly thinner in the interval; he was white too; his eyes looked strange. But the curt speech and the sulky masterful manner of Dr. Lesage impressed them both favourably, although at the same time it was obvious that he was very much annoyed at the whole affair. Coming downstairs he gave his directions emphatically, but it never occurred to him to give an opinion either because of the presence of Rodriguez who was now obsequious as well as malicious, or because he took it for granted that they knew already what was to be known.

"Of course," he said with a shrug of his shoulders, when Terence asked him, "Is she very ill?"

They were both conscious of a certain sense of relief when Dr. Lesage was gone, leaving explicit directions, and promising another visit in a few hours' time; but, unfortunately, the rise of their spirits led them to talk more than usual, and in talking they quarrelled. They quarrelled about a road, the Portsmouth Road. St. John said that it is macadamised where it passes Hindhead, and Terence knew as well as he knew his own name that it is not macadamised at that point. In the course of the argument they said some very sharp things to each other, and the rest of the dinner was eaten in silence, save for an occasional half-stifled reflection from Ridley.

When it grew dark and the lamps were brought in, Terence felt unable to control his irritation any longer. St. John went to bed in a state of complete exhaustion, bidding Terence good-night with rather more affection than usual because of their quarrel, and Ridley retired to his books. Left alone, Terence walked up and down the room; he stood at the open window.

The lights were coming out one after another in the town beneath, and it was very peaceful and cool in the garden, so that he stepped out on to the terrace. As he stood there in the darkness, able only to see the shapes of trees through the fine grey light, he was overcome by a desire to escape, to have done with this suffering, to forget that Rachel was ill. He allowed himself to lapse into forgetfulness of everything. As if a wind that had been raging incessantly suddenly fell asleep, the fret and strain and anxiety which had been pressing on him passed away. He seemed to stand in an unvexed space of air, on a little island by himself; he was free and immune from pain. It did not matter whether Rachel was well or ill; it did not matter whether they were apart or together; nothing mattered—nothing mattered. The waves beat on the shore far away, and the soft wind passed through the branches of the trees, seeming to encircle him with peace and security, with dark and nothingness. Surely the world of strife and fret and anxiety was not the real world, but this was the real world, the world that lay beneath the superficial world, so that, whatever happened, one was secure. The quiet and peace seemed to lap his body in a fine cool sheet, soothing every nerve; his mind seemed once more to expand, and become natural.

But when he had stood thus for a time a noise in the house roused him; he turned instinctively and went into the drawing-room. The sight of the lamp-lit room brought back so abruptly all that he had forgotten that he stood for a moment unable to move. He remembered everything, the hour, the minute even, what point they had reached, and what was to come. He cursed himself for making believe for a minute that things were different from what they are. The night was now harder to face than ever.

Unable to stay in the empty drawing-room, he wandered out and sat on the stairs half-way up to Rachel's room. He longed for some one to talk to, but Hirst was asleep, and Ridley was asleep; there was no sound in Rachel's room. The only sound in the house was the sound of Chailey moving in the kitchen. At last there was a rustling on the stairs overhead, and Nurse McInnis came down fastening the links in her cuffs, in preparation for the night's watch. Terence rose and stopped her. He had scarcely spoken to her, but it was possible that she might confirm him in the belief which still persisted in his own mind that Rachel was not seriously ill. He told her in a whisper that Dr. Lesage had been and what he had said.

"Now, Nurse," he whispered, "please tell me your opinion. Do you consider that she is very seriously ill? Is she in any danger?"

"The doctor has said—" she began.

"Yes, but I want your opinion. You have had experience of many cases like this?"

"I could not tell you more than Dr. Lesage, Mr. Hewet," she replied cautiously, as though her words might be used against her. "The case is serious, but you may feel quite certain that we are doing all we can for Miss Vinrace." She spoke with some professional self-approbation. But she realised perhaps that she did not satisfy the young man, who still blocked her way, for she shifted her feet slightly upon the stair and looked out of the window where they could see the moon over the sea.

"If you ask me," she began in a curiously stealthy tone, "I never like May for my patients."

"May?" Terence repeated.

"It may be a fancy, but I don't like to see anybody fall ill in May," she continued. "Things seem to go wrong in May. Perhaps it's the moon. They say the moon affects the brain, don't they, Sir?"

He looked at her but he could not answer her; like all the others, when one looked at her she seemed to shrivel beneath one's eyes and become worthless, malicious, and untrustworthy.

She slipped past him and disappeared.

Though he went to his room he was unable even to take his clothes off. For a long time he paced up and down, and then leaning out of the window gazed at the earth which lay so dark against the paler blue of the sky. With a mixture of fear and loathing he looked at the slim black cypress trees which were still visible in the garden, and heard the unfamiliar creaking and grating sounds which show that the earth is still hot. All these sights and sounds appeared sinister and full of hostility and foreboding; together with the natives and the nurse and the doctor and the terrible force of the illness itself they seemed to be in conspiracy against him. They seemed to join together in their effort to extract the greatest possible amount of suffering from him. He could not get used to his pain, it was a revelation to him. He had never realised before that underneath every action, underneath the life of every day, pain lies, quiescent, but ready to devour; he seemed to be able to see suffering, as if it were a fire, curling up over the edges of all action, eating away the lives of men and women. He thought for the first time with understanding of words which had before seemed to him empty: the struggle of life; the hardness of life. Now he knew for himself that life is hard and full of suffering. He looked at the scattered lights in the town beneath, and thought of Arthur and Susan, or Evelyn and Perrott venturing out unwittingly, and by their happiness laying themselves open to suffering such as this. How did they dare to love each other, he wondered; how had he himself dared to live as he had lived, rapidly and carelessly, passing from one thing to another, loving Rachel as he had loved her? Never again would he feel secure; he would never believe in the stability of life, or forget what depths of pain lie beneath small happiness and feelings of content and safety. It seemed to him as he looked back that their happiness had never been so great as his pain was now. There had always been something imperfect in their happiness, something they had wanted and had not been able to get. It had been fragmentary and incomplete, because they were so young and had not known what they were doing.

The light of his candle flickered over the boughs of a tree outside the window, and as the branch swayed in the darkness there came before his mind a picture of all the world that lay outside his window; he thought of the immense river and the immense forest, the vast stretches of dry earth and the plains of the sea that encircled the earth; from the sea the sky rose steep and enormous, and the air washed profoundly between the sky and the sea. How vast and dark it must be tonight, lying exposed to the wind; and in all this great space it was curious to think how few the towns were, and how small little rings of light, or single glow-worms he figured them, scattered here and there, among the swelling uncultivated folds of the world. And in those towns were little men and women, tiny men and women. Oh, it was absurd, when one thought of it, to sit here in a little room suffering and caring. What did anything matter? Rachel, a tiny creature, lay ill beneath him, and here in his little room he suffered on her account. The nearness of their bodies in this vast universe, and the minuteness of their bodies, seemed to him absurd and laughable. Nothing mattered, he repeated; they had no power, no hope. He leant on the window-sill, thinking, until he almost forgot the time and the place. Nevertheless, although he was convinced that it was absurd and laughable, and that they were small and hopeless, he never lost the sense that these thoughts somehow formed part of a life which he and Rachel would live together.

Owing perhaps to the change of doctor, Rachel appeared to be rather better next day. Terribly pale and worn though Helen looked, there was a slight lifting of the cloud which had hung all these days in her eyes.

"She talked to me," she said voluntarily. "She asked me what day of the week it was, like herself."

Then suddenly, without any warning or any apparent reason, the tears formed in her eyes and rolled steadily down her cheeks. She cried with scarcely any attempt at movement of her features, and without any attempt to stop herself, as if she did not know that she was crying. In spite of the relief which her words gave him, Terence was dismayed by the sight; had everything given way? Were there no limits to the power of this illness? Would everything go down before it? Helen had always seemed to him strong and determined, and now she was like a child. He took her in his arms, and she clung to him like a child, crying softly and quietly upon his shoulder. Then she roused herself and wiped her tears away; it was silly to behave like that, she said; very silly, she repeated, when there could be no doubt that Rachel was better. She asked Terence to forgive her for her folly. She stopped at the door and came back and kissed him without saying anything.

On this day indeed Rachel was conscious of what went on round her. She had come to the surface of the dark, sticky pool, and a wave seemed to bear her up and down with it; she had ceased to have any will of her own; she lay on the top of the wave conscious of some pain, but chiefly of weakness. The wave was replaced by the side of a mountain. Her body became a drift of melting snow, above which her knees rose in huge peaked mountains of bare bone. It was true that she saw Helen and saw her room, but everything had become very pale and semi-transparent. Sometimes she could see through the wall in front of her. Sometimes when Helen went away she seemed to go so far that Rachel's eyes could hardly follow her. The room also had an odd power of expanding, and though she pushed her voice out as far as possible until sometimes it became a bird and flew away, she thought it doubtful whether it ever reached the person she was talking to. There were immense intervals or chasms, for things still had the power to appear visibly before her, between one moment and the next; it sometimes took an hour for Helen to raise her arm, pausing long between each jerky movement, and pour out medicine. Helen's form stooping to raise her in bed appeared of gigantic size, and came down upon her like the ceiling falling. But for long spaces of time she would merely lie conscious of her body floating on the top of the bed and her mind driven to some remote corner of her body, or escaped and gone flitting round the room. All sights were something of an effort, but the sight of Terence was the greatest effort, because he forced her to join mind to body in the desire to remember something. She did not wish to remember; it troubled her when people tried to disturb her loneliness; she wished to be alone. She wished for nothing else in the world.

Although she had cried, Terence observed Helen's greater hopefulness with something like triumph; in the argument between them she had made the first sign of admitting herself in the wrong. He waited for Dr. Lesage to come down that afternoon with considerable anxiety, but with the same certainty at the back of his mind that he would in time force them all to admit that they were in the wrong.

As usual, Dr. Lesage was sulky in his manner and very short in his answers. To Terence's demand, "She seems to be better?" he replied, looking at him in an odd way, "She has a chance of life."

The door shut and Terence walked across to the window. He leant his forehead against the pane.

"Rachel," he repeated to himself. "She has a chance of life. Rachel."

How could they say these things of Rachel? Had any one yesterday seriously believed that Rachel was dying? They had been engaged for four weeks. A fortnight ago she had been perfectly well. What could fourteen days have done to bring her from that state to this? To realise what they meant by saying that she had a chance of life was beyond him, knowing as he did that they were engaged. He turned, still enveloped in the same dreary mist, and walked towards the door. Suddenly he saw it all. He saw the room and the garden, and the trees moving in the air, they could go on without her; she could die. For the first time since she fell ill he remembered exactly what she looked like and the way in which they cared for each other. The immense happiness of feeling her close to him mingled with a more intense anxiety than he had felt yet. He could not let her die; he could not live without her. But after a momentary struggle, the curtain fell again, and he saw nothing and felt nothing clearly. It was all going on—going on still, in the same way as before. Save for a physical pain when his heart beat, and the fact that his fingers were icy cold, he did not realise that he was anxious about anything. Within his mind he seemed to feel nothing about Rachel or about any one or anything in the world. He went on giving orders, arranging with Mrs. Chailey, writing out lists, and every now and then he went upstairs and put something quietly on the table outside Rachel's door. That night Dr. Lesage seemed to be less sulky than usual. He stayed voluntarily for a few moments, and, addressing St. John and Terence equally, as if he did not remember which of them was engaged to the young lady, said, "I consider that her condition tonight is very grave."

Neither of them went to bed or suggested that the other should go to bed. They sat in the drawing-room playing picquet with the door open. St. John made up a bed upon the sofa, and when it was ready insisted that Terence should lie upon it. They began to quarrel as to who should lie on the sofa and who should lie upon a couple of chairs covered with rugs. St. John forced Terence at last to lie down upon the sofa.

"Don't be a fool, Terence," he said. "You'll only get ill if you don't sleep."

"Old fellow," he began, as Terence still refused, and stopped abruptly, fearing sentimentality; he found that he was on the verge of tears.

He began to say what he had long been wanting to say, that he was sorry for Terence, that he cared for him, that he cared for Rachel. Did she know how much he cared for her—had she said anything, asked perhaps? He was very anxious to say this, but he refrained, thinking that it was a selfish question after all, and what was the use of bothering Terence to talk about such things? He was already half asleep. But St. John could not sleep at once. If only, he thought to himself, as he lay in the darkness, something would happen—if only this strain would come to an end. He did not mind what happened, so long as the succession of these hard and dreary days was broken; he did not mind if she died. He felt himself disloyal in not minding it, but it seemed to him that he had no feelings left.

All night long there was no call or movement, except the opening and shutting of the bedroom door once. By degrees the light returned into the untidy room. At six the servants began to move; at seven they crept downstairs into the kitchen; and half an hour later the day began again.

Nevertheless it was not the same as the days that had gone before, although it would have been hard to say in what the difference consisted. Perhaps it was that they seemed to be waiting for something. There were certainly fewer things to be done than usual. People drifted through the drawing-room—Mr. Flushing, Mr. and Mrs. Thornbury. They spoke very apologetically in low tones, refusing to sit down, but remaining for a considerable time standing up, although the only thing they had to say was, "Is there anything we can do?" and there was nothing they could do.

Feeling oddly detached from it all, Terence remembered how Helen had said that whenever anything happened to you this was how people behaved. Was she right, or was she wrong? He was too little interested to frame an opinion of his own. He put things away in his mind, as if one of these days he would think about them, but not now. The mist of unreality had deepened and deepened until it had produced a feeling of numbness all over his body. Was it his body? Were those really his own hands?

This morning also for the first time Ridley found it impossible to sit alone in his room. He was very uncomfortable downstairs, and, as he did not know what was going on, constantly in the way; but he would not leave the drawing-room. Too restless to read, and having nothing to do, he began to pace up and down reciting poetry in an undertone. Occupied in various ways—now in undoing parcels, now in uncorking bottles, now in writing directions, the sound of Ridley's song and the beat of his pacing worked into the minds of Terence and St. John all the morning as a half comprehended refrain.

They wrestled up, they wrestled down,
They wrestled sore and still:
The fiend who blinds the eyes of men,
That night he had his will.

Like stags full spent, among the bent
They dropped awhile to rest——

"Oh, it's intolerable!" Hirst exclaimed, and then checked himself, as if it were a breach of their agreement. Again and again Terence would creep half-way up the stairs in case he might be able to glean news of Rachel. But the only news now was of a very fragmentary kind; she had drunk something; she had slept a little; she seemed quieter. In the same way, Dr. Lesage confined himself to talking about details, save once when he volunteered the information that he had just been called in to ascertain, by severing a vein in the wrist, that an old lady of eighty-five was really dead. She had a horror of being buried alive.

"It is a horror," he remarked, "that we generally find in the very old, and seldom in the young." They both expressed their interest in what he told them; it seemed to them very strange. Another strange thing about the day was that the luncheon was forgotten by all of them until it was late in the afternoon, and then Mrs. Chailey waited on them, and looked strange too, because she wore a stiff print dress, and her sleeves were rolled up above her elbows. She seemed as oblivious of her appearance, however, as if she had been called out of her bed by a midnight alarm of fire, and she had forgotten, too, her reserve and her composure; she talked to them quite familiarly as if she had nursed them and held them naked on her knee. She assured them over and over again that it was their duty to eat.

The afternoon, being thus shortened, passed more quickly than they expected. Once Mrs. Flushing opened the door, but on seeing them shut it again quickly; once Helen came down to fetch something, but she stopped as she left the room to look at a letter addressed to her. She stood for a moment turning it over, and the extraordinary and mournful beauty of her attitude struck Terence in the way things struck him now—

as something to be put away in his mind and to be thought about afterwards. They scarcely spoke, the argument between them seeming to be suspended or forgotten.

Now that the afternoon sun had left the front of the house, Ridley paced up and down the terrace repeating stanzas of a long poem, in a subdued but suddenly sonorous voice. Fragments of the poem were wafted in at the open window as he passed and repassed.

> Peor and Baalim
> Forsake their Temples dim,
> With that twice batter'd God of Palestine
> And mooned Astaroth–

The sound of these words were strangely discomforting to both the young men, but they had to be borne. As the evening drew on and the red light of the sunset glittered far away on the sea, the same sense of desperation attacked both Terence and St. John at the thought that the day was nearly over, and that another night was at hand. The appearance of one light after another in the town beneath them produced in Hirst a repetition of his terrible and disgusting desire to break down and sob. Then the lamps were brought in by Chailey. She explained that Maria, in opening a bottle, had been so foolish as to cut her arm badly, but she had bound it up; it was unfortunate when there was so much work to be done. Chailey herself limped because of the rheumatism in her feet, but it appeared to her mere waste of time to take any notice of the unruly flesh of servants. The evening went on. Dr. Lesage arrived unexpectedly, and stayed upstairs a very long time. He came down once and drank a cup of coffee.

"She is very ill," he said in answer to Ridley's question. All the annoyance had by this time left his manner, he was grave and formal, but at the same time it was full of consideration, which had not marked it before. He went upstairs again. The three men sat together in the drawing-room. Ridley was quite quiet now, and his attention seemed to be thoroughly awakened. Save for little half-voluntary movements and exclamations that were stifled at once, they waited in complete silence. It seemed as if they were at last brought together face to face with something definite.

It was nearly eleven o'clock when Dr. Lesage again appeared in the room. He approached them very slowly, and did not speak at once. He looked first at St. John and then at Terence, and said to Terence, "Mr. Hewet, I think you should go upstairs now."

Terence rose immediately, leaving the others seated with Dr. Lesage standing motionless between them.

Chailey was in the passage outside, repeating over and over again, "It's wicked–it's wicked."

Terence paid her no attention; he heard what she was saying, but it conveyed no meaning to his mind. All the way upstairs he kept saying to himself, "This has not happened to me. It is not possible that this has happened to me."

He looked curiously at his own hand on the banisters. The stairs were very steep, and it seemed to take him a long time to surmount them. Instead of feeling keenly, as he knew that he ought to feel, he felt nothing at all. When he opened the door he saw Helen sitting by the bedside. There were shaded lights on the table, and the room, though it seemed to be full of a great many things, was very tidy. There was a faint and not unpleasant smell of disinfectants. Helen rose and gave up her chair to him in silence. As they passed each other their eyes met in a peculiar level glance, he wondered at the extraordinary clearness of his eyes, and at the deep calm and sadness that dwelt in them. He sat down by the bedside, and a moment afterwards heard the door shut gently behind her. He was alone with Rachel, and a faint reflection of the sense of relief that they used to feel when they were left alone possessed him. He looked at her. He expected to find some terrible change in her, but there was none. She looked indeed very thin, and, as far as he could see, very tired, but she was the same as she had always been. Moreover, she saw him and knew him. She smiled at him and said, "Hullo, Terence."

The curtain which had been drawn between them for so long vanished immediately.

"Well, Rachel," he replied in his usual voice, upon which she opened her eyes quite widely and smiled with her familiar smile. He kissed her and took her hand.

"It's been wretched without you," he said.

She still looked at him and smiled, but soon a slight look of fatigue or perplexity came into her eyes and she shut them again.

"But when we're together we're perfectly happy," he said. He continued to hold her hand.

The light being dim, it was impossible to see any change in her face. An immense feeling of peace came over Terence, so that he had no wish to move or to speak. The terrible torture and unreality of the last days were over, and he had come out now into perfect certainty and peace. His mind began to work naturally again and with great ease. The longer he sat there the more profoundly was he conscious of the peace invading every corner of his soul. Once he held his breath and listened acutely; she was still breathing; he went on thinking for some time; they seemed to be thinking together; he seemed to be Rachel as well as himself; and then he listened again; no, she had ceased to breathe. So much the better—this was death. It was nothing; it was to cease to breathe. It was happiness, it was perfect happiness. They had now what they had always wanted to have, the union which had been impossible while they lived. Unconscious whether he thought the words or spoke them aloud, he said, "No two people have ever been so happy as we have been. No one has ever loved as we have loved."

It seemed to him that their complete union and happiness filled the room with rings eddying more and more widely. He had no wish in the world left unfulfilled. They possessed what could never be taken from them.

He was not conscious that any one had come into the room, but later, moments later, or hours later perhaps, he felt an arm behind him. The arms were round him. He did not want to have arms round him, and the mysterious whispering voices annoyed him. He laid Rachel's hand, which was now cold, upon the counterpane, and rose from his chair, and walked across to the window. The windows were uncurtained, and showed the moon, and a long silver pathway upon the surface of the waves.

"Why," he said, in his ordinary tone of voice, "look at the moon. There's a halo round the moon. We shall have rain tomorrow."

The arms, whether they were the arms of man or of woman, were round him again; they were pushing him gently towards the door. He turned of his own accord and walked steadily in advance of the arms, conscious of a little amusement at the strange way in which people behaved merely because some one was dead. He would go if they wished it, but nothing they could do would disturb his happiness.

As he saw the passage outside the room, and the table with the cups and the plates, it suddenly came over him that here was a world in which he would never see Rachel again.

"Rachel! Rachel!" he shrieked, trying to rush back to her. But they prevented him, and pushed him down the passage and into a bedroom far from her room. Downstairs they could hear the thud of his feet on the floor, as he struggled to break free; and twice they heard him shout, "Rachel, Rachel!"

26

For two or three hours longer the moon poured its light through the empty air. Unbroken by clouds it fell straightly, and lay almost like a chill white frost over the sea and the earth. During these hours the silence was not broken, and the only movement was caused by the movement of trees and branches which stirred slightly, and then the shadows that lay across the white spaces of the land moved too. In this profound silence one sound only was audible, the sound of a slight but continuous breathing which never ceased, although it never rose and never fell. It continued after the birds had begun to flutter from branch to branch, and could be heard behind the first thin notes of their voices. It continued all through the hours when the east whitened, and grew red, and a faint blue tinged the sky, but when the sun rose it ceased, and gave place to other sounds.

The first sounds that were heard were little inarticulate cries, the cries, it seemed, of children or of the very poor, of people who were very weak or in pain. But when the sun was above the horizon, the air which had been thin and pale grew every moment richer and warmer, and the sounds of life became bolder and more full of courage and authority. By degrees the smoke began to ascend in wavering breaths over the houses, and these slowly thickened, until they were as round and straight as columns, and instead of striking upon pale white blinds, the sun shone upon dark windows, beyond which there was depth and space.

The sun had been up for many hours, and the great dome of air was warmed through and glittering with thin gold threads of sunlight, before any one moved in the hotel. White and massive it stood in the early light, half asleep with its blinds down.

At about half-past nine Miss Allan came very slowly into the hall, and walked very slowly to the table where the morning papers were laid, but she did not put out her hand to take one; she stood still, thinking, with her head a little sunk upon her shoulders. She looked curiously old, and from the way in which she stood, a little hunched together and very massive, you could see what she would be like when she was really old, how she would sit day after day in her chair looking placidly in front of her. Other people began to come into the room, and to pass her, but she did not speak to any of them or even look at them, and at last, as if it were necessary to do something, she sat down in a chair, and looked quietly and fixedly in front of her. She felt very old this morning, and useless too, as if her life had been a failure, as if it had been hard and laborious to no purpose. She did not want to go on living, and yet she knew that she would. She was so strong that she would live to be a very old woman. She would probably live to be eighty, and as she was now fifty, that left thirty years more for her to live. She turned her hands over and over in her lap and looked at them curiously; her old hands, that had done so much work for her. There did not seem to be much point in it all; one went on, of course one went on. . . . She looked up to see Mrs. Thornbury standing beside her, with lines drawn upon her forehead, and her lips parted as if she were about to ask a question.

Miss Allan anticipated her.

"Yes," she said. "She died this morning, very early, about three o'clock."

Mrs. Thornbury made a little exclamation, drew her lips together, and the tears rose in her eyes. Through them she looked at the hall which was now laid with great breadths of sunlight, and at the careless, casual groups of people who were standing beside the solid arm-chairs and tables. They looked to her unreal, or as people look who remain unconscious that some great explosion is about to take place beside them. But there was no explosion, and they went on standing by the chairs and the tables. Mrs. Thornbury no longer saw them, but, penetrating through them as though they were without substance, she saw the house, the people in the house, the room, the bed in the room, and the figure of the dead lying still in the dark beneath the sheets. She could almost see the dead. She could almost hear the voices of the mourners.

"They expected it?" she asked at length.

Miss Allan could only shake her head.

"I know nothing," she replied, "except what Mrs. Flushing's maid told me. She died early this morning."

The two women looked at each other with a quiet significant gaze, and then, feeling oddly dazed, and seeking she did not know exactly what, Mrs. Thornbury went slowly upstairs and walked quietly along the passages, touching the wall with her fingers as if to guide herself. Housemaids were passing briskly from room to room, but Mrs. Thornbury avoided them; she hardly saw them; they seemed to her to be in another world. She did not even look up directly when Evelyn stopped her. It was evident that Evelyn had been lately in tears, and when she looked at Mrs. Thornbury she began to cry again. Together they drew into the hollow of a window, and stood there in silence. Broken words formed themselves at last among Evelyn's sobs. "It was wicked," she sobbed, "it was cruel—they were so happy."

Mrs. Thornbury patted her on the shoulder.

"It seems hard—very hard," she said. She paused and looked out over the slope of the hill at the Ambroses' villa; the windows were blazing in the sun, and she thought how the soul of the dead had passed from those windows. Something had passed from the world. It seemed to her strangely empty.

"And yet the older one grows," she continued, her eyes regaining more than their usual brightness, "the more certain one becomes that there is a reason. How could one go on if there were no reason?" she asked.

She asked the question of some one, but she did not ask it of Evelyn. Evelyn's sobs were becoming quieter. "There must be a reason," she said. "It can't only be an accident. For it was an accident—it need never have happened."

Mrs. Thornbury sighed deeply.

"But we must not let ourselves think of that," she added, "and let us hope that they don't either. Whatever they had done it might have been the same. These terrible illnesses—"

"There's no reason—I don't believe there's any reason at all!" Evelyn broke out, pulling the blind down and letting it fly back with a little snap.

"Why should these things happen? Why should people suffer? I honestly believe," she went on, lowering her voice slightly, "that Rachel's in Heaven, but Terence. . . ."

"What's the good of it all?" she demanded.

Mrs. Thornbury shook her head slightly but made no reply, and pressing Evelyn's hand she went on down the passage. Impelled by a strong desire to hear something, although she did not know exactly what there was to hear, she was making her way to the Flushings' room. As she opened their door she felt that she had interrupted some argument between husband and wife. Mrs. Flushing was sitting with her back to the light, and Mr. Flushing was standing near her, arguing and trying to persuade her of something.

"Ah, here is Mrs. Thornbury," he began with some relief in his voice. "You have heard, of course. My wife feels that she was in some way responsible. She urged poor Miss Vinrace to come on the expedition. I'm sure you will agree with me that it is most unreasonable to feel that. We don't even know—in fact I think it most unlikely—that she caught her illness there. These diseases—Besides, she was set on going. She would have gone whether you asked her or not, Alice."

"Don't, Wilfrid," said Mrs. Flushing, neither moving nor taking her eyes off the spot on the floor upon which they rested. "What's the use of talking? What's the use—?" She ceased.

"I was coming to ask you," said Mrs. Thornbury, addressing Wilfrid, for it was useless to speak to his wife. "Is there anything you think that one could do? Has the father arrived? Could one go and see?"

The strongest wish in her being at this moment was to be able to do something for the unhappy people—to see them—to assure them—to help them. It was dreadful to be so far away from them. But Mr. Flushing shook his head; he did not think that now—later perhaps one might be able to help. Here Mrs. Flushing rose stiffly, turned her back to them, and walked to the dressing-room opposite. As she walked, they could see her breast slowly rise and slowly fall. But her grief was silent. She shut the door behind her.

When she was alone by herself she clenched her fists together, and began beating the back of a chair with them. She was like a wounded animal. She hated death; she was furious, outraged, indignant with death, as if it were a living creature. She refused to relinquish her friends to death. She would not submit to dark and nothingness. She began to pace up and down, clenching her hands, and making no attempt to stop the quick tears which raced down her cheeks. She sat still at last, but she did not submit. She looked stubborn and strong when she had ceased to cry.

In the next room, meanwhile, Wilfrid was talking to Mrs. Thornbury with greater freedom now that his wife was not sitting there.

"That's the worst of these places," he said. "People will behave as though they were in England, and they're not. I've no doubt myself that Miss Vinrace caught the infection up at the villa itself. She probably ran risks a dozen times a day that might have given her the illness. It's absurd to say she caught it with us."

If he had not been sincerely sorry for them he would have been annoyed. "Pepper tells me," he continued, "that he left the house because he thought them so careless. He says they never washed their vegetables properly. Poor people! It's a fearful price to pay. But it's only what I've seen over and over again—people seem to forget that these things happen, and then they do happen, and they're surprised."

Mrs. Thornbury agreed with him that they had been very careless, and that there was no reason whatever to think that she had caught the fever on the expedition; and after talking about other things for a short time, she left him and went sadly along the passage to her own room. There must be some reason why such things happen, she thought to herself, as she shut the door. Only at first it was not easy to understand what it was. It seemed so strange—so unbelievable. Why, only three weeks ago—only a fortnight ago, she had seen Rachel; when she shut her eyes she could almost see her now, the quiet, shy girl who was going to be married. She thought of all that she would have missed had she died at Rachel's age, the children, the married life, the unimaginable depths and miracles that seemed to her, as she looked back, to have lain about her, day after day, and year after year. The stunned feeling, which had been making it difficult for her to think, gradually gave way to a feeling of the opposite nature; she thought very quickly and very clearly, and, looking back over all her experiences, tried to fit them into a kind of order. There was undoubtedly much suffering, much struggling, but, on the whole, surely there was a balance of happiness—surely order did prevail. Nor were the deaths of young people really the saddest things in life—they were saved so much; they kept so much. The dead—she called to mind those who had died early, accidentally—were beautiful; she often dreamt of the dead. And in time Terence himself would come to feel——She got up and began to wander restlessly about the room.

For an old woman of her age she was very restless, and for one of her clear, quick mind she was unusually perplexed. She could not settle to anything, so that she was relieved when the door opened. She went up to her husband, took him in her arms, and kissed him with unusual intensity, and then as they sat down together she began to pat him and question him as if he were a baby, an old, tired, querulous baby. She did not tell him about Miss Vinrace's death, for that would only disturb him, and he was put out already. She tried to discover why he was uneasy. Politics again? What were those horrid people doing? She spent the whole morning in discussing politics with her husband, and by degrees she became deeply interested in what they were saying. But every now and then what she was saying seemed to her oddly empty of meaning.

At luncheon it was remarked by several people that the visitors at the hotel were beginning to leave; there were fewer every day. There were only forty people at luncheon, instead of the sixty that there had been. So old Mrs. Paley computed, gazing about her with her faded eyes, as she took her seat at her own table in the window. Her party generally consisted of Mr. Perrott as well as Arthur and Susan, and today Evelyn was lunching with them also.

She was unusually subdued. Having noticed that her eyes were red, and guessing the reason, the others took pains to keep up an elaborate conversation between themselves. She suffered it to go on for a few minutes, leaning both elbows on the table, and leaving her soup untouched, when she exclaimed suddenly, "I don't know how you feel, but I can simply think of nothing else!"

The gentlemen murmured sympathetically, and looked grave.

Susan replied, "Yes—isn't it perfectly awful? When you think what a nice girl she was—only just engaged, and this need never have happened—it seems too tragic." She looked at Arthur as though he might be able to help her with something more suitable.

"Hard lines," said Arthur briefly. "But it was a foolish thing to do—to go up that river." He shook his head. "They should have known better. You can't expect Englishwomen to stand roughing it as the natives do who've been acclimatised. I'd half a mind to warn them at tea that day when it was being discussed. But it's no good saying these sort of things—it only puts people's backs up—it never makes any difference."

Old Mrs. Paley, hitherto contented with her soup, here intimated, by raising one hand to her ear, that she wished to know what was being said.

"You heard, Aunt Emma, that poor Miss Vinrace has died of the fever," Susan informed her gently. She could not speak of death loudly or even in her usual voice, so that Mrs. Paley did not catch a word. Arthur came to the rescue.

"Miss Vinrace is dead," he said very distinctly.

Mrs. Paley merely bent a little towards him and asked, "Eh?"

"Miss Vinrace is dead," he repeated. It was only by stiffening all the muscles round his mouth that he could prevent himself from bursting into laughter, and forced himself to repeat for the third time, "Miss Vinrace. . . . She's dead."

Let alone the difficulty of hearing the exact words, facts that were outside her daily experience took some time to reach Mrs. Paley's consciousness. A weight seemed to rest upon her brain, impeding, though not damaging its action. She sat vague-eyed for at least a minute before she realised what Arthur meant.

"Dead?" she said vaguely. "Miss Vinrace dead? Dear me . . . that's very sad. But I don't at the moment remember which she was. We seem to have made so many new acquaintances here." She looked at Susan for help. "A tall dark girl, who just missed being handsome, with a high colour?"

"No," Susan interposed. "She was—" then she gave it up in despair. There was no use in explaining that Mrs. Paley was thinking of the wrong person.

"She ought not to have died," Mrs. Paley continued. "She looked so strong. But people will drink the water. I can never make out why. It seems such a simple thing to tell them to put a bottle of Seltzer water in your bedroom. That's all the precaution I've ever taken, and I've been in every part of the world, I may say—Italy a dozen times over. . . . But young people always think they know better, and then they pay the penalty. Poor thing—I am very sorry for her." But the difficulty of peering into a dish of potatoes and helping herself engrossed her attention.

Arthur and Susan both secretly hoped that the subject was now disposed of, for there seemed to them something unpleasant in this discussion. But Evelyn was not ready to let it drop. Why would people never talk about the things that mattered?

"I don't believe you care a bit!" she said, turning savagely upon Mr. Perrott, who had sat all this time in silence.

"I? Oh, yes, I do," he answered awkwardly, but with obvious sincerity. Evelyn's questions made him too feel uncomfortable.

"It seems so inexplicable," Evelyn continued. "Death, I mean. Why should she be dead, and not you or I? It was only a fortnight ago that she was here with the rest of us. What d'you believe?" she demanded of Mr. Perrott. "D'you believe that things go on, that she's still somewhere—or d'you think it's simply a game—we crumble up to nothing when we die? I'm positive Rachel's not dead."

Mr. Perrott would have said almost anything that Evelyn wanted him to say, but to assert that he believed in the immortality of the soul was not in his power. He sat silent, more deeply wrinkled than usual, crumbling his bread.

Lest Evelyn should next ask him what he believed, Arthur, after making a pause equivalent to a full stop, started a completely different topic.

"Supposing," he said, "a man were to write and tell you that he wanted five pounds because he had known your grandfather, what would you do? It was this way. My grandfather—"

"Invented a stove," said Evelyn. "I know all about that. We had one in the conservatory to keep the plants warm."

"Didn't know I was so famous," said Arthur. "Well," he continued, determined at all costs to spin his story out at length, "the old chap, being about the second best inventor of his day, and a capable lawyer too, died, as they always do, without making a will. Now Fielding, his clerk, with how much justice I don't know, always claimed that he meant to do something for him. The poor old boy's come down in the world through trying inventions on his own account, lives in Penge over a tobacconist's shop. I've been to see him there. The question is—must I stump up or not? What does the abstract spirit of justice require, Perrott? Remember, I didn't benefit under my grandfather's will, and I've no way of testing the truth of the story."

"I don't know much about the abstract spirit of justice," said Susan, smiling complacently at the others, "but I'm certain of one thing—he'll get his five pounds!"

As Mr. Perrott proceeded to deliver an opinion, and Evelyn insisted that he was much too stingy, like all lawyers, thinking of the letter and not of the spirit, while Mrs. Paley required to be kept informed between the courses as to what they were all saying, the luncheon passed with no interval of silence, and Arthur congratulated himself upon the tact with which the discussion had been smoothed over.

As they left the room it happened that Mrs. Paley's wheeled chair ran into the Elliots, who were coming through the door, as she was going out. Brought thus to a standstill for a moment, Arthur and Susan congratulated Hughling Elliot upon his convalescence—he was down, cadaverous enough, for the first time—and Mr. Perrott took occasion to say a few words in private to Evelyn.

"Would there be any chance of seeing you this afternoon, about three-thirty say? I shall be in the garden, by the fountain."

The block dissolved before Evelyn answered. But as she left them in the hall, she looked at him brightly and said, "Half-past three, did you say? That'll suit me."

She ran upstairs with the feeling of spiritual exaltation and quickened life which the prospect of an emotional scene always aroused in her. That Mr. Perrott was again about to propose to her, she had no doubt, and she was aware that on this occasion she ought to be prepared with a definite answer, for she was going away in three days' time. But she could not bring her mind to bear upon the question. To come to a decision was very difficult to her, because she had a natural dislike of anything final and done with; she liked to go on and on—always on and on. She was leaving, and, therefore, she occupied herself in laying her clothes out side by side upon the bed. She observed that some were very shabby. She took the photograph of her father and mother, and, before she laid it away in her box, she held it for a minute in her hand. Rachel had looked at it. Suddenly the keen feeling of some one's personality, which things that they have owned or handled sometimes preserves, overcame her; she felt Rachel in the room with her; it was as if she were on a ship at sea, and the life of the day was as unreal as the land in the distance. But by degrees the feeling of Rachel's presence passed away, and she could no longer realise her, for she had scarcely known her. But this momentary sensation left her depressed and fatigued. What had she done with her life? What future was there before her? What was make-believe, and what was real? Were these proposals and intimacies and adventures real, or was the contentment which she had seen on the faces of Susan and Rachel more real than anything she had ever felt?

She made herself ready to go downstairs, absentmindedly, but her fingers were so well trained that they did the work of preparing her almost of their own accord. When she was actually on the way downstairs, the blood began to circle through her body of its own accord too, for her mind felt very dull.

Mr. Perrott was waiting for her. Indeed, he had gone straight into the garden after luncheon, and had been walking up and down the path for more than half an hour, in a state of acute suspense.

"I'm late as usual!" she exclaimed, as she caught sight of him. "Well, you must forgive me; I had to pack up. . . . My word! It looks stormy! And that's a new steamer in the bay, isn't it?"

She looked at the bay, in which a steamer was just dropping anchor, the smoke still hanging about it, while a swift black shudder ran through the waves. "One's quite forgotten what rain looks like," she added.

But Mr. Perrott paid no attention to the steamer or to the weather.

"Miss Murgatroyd," he began with his usual formality, "I asked you to come here from a very selfish motive, I fear. I do not think you need to be assured once more of my feelings; but, as you are leaving so soon, I felt that I could not let you go without asking you to tell me—have I any reason to hope that you will ever come to care for me?"

He was very pale, and seemed unable to say any more.

The little gush of vitality which had come into Evelyn as she ran downstairs had left her, and she felt herself impotent. There was nothing for her to say; she felt nothing. Now that he was actually asking her, in his elderly gentle words, to marry him, she felt less for him than she had ever felt before.

"Let's sit down and talk it over," she said rather unsteadily.

Mr. Perrott followed her to a curved green seat under a tree. They looked at the fountain in front of them, which had long ceased to play. Evelyn kept looking at the fountain instead of thinking of what she was saying; the fountain without any water seemed to be the type of her own being.

"Of course I care for you," she began, rushing her words out in a hurry; "I should be a brute if I didn't. I think you're quite one of the nicest people I've ever known, and one of the finest too. But I wish . . . I wish you didn't care for me in that way. Are you sure you do?" For the moment she honestly desired that he should say no.

"Quite sure," said Mr. Perrott.

"You see, I'm not as simple as most women," Evelyn continued. "I think I want more. I don't know exactly what I feel."

He sat by her, watching her and refraining from speech.

"I sometimes think I haven't got it in me to care very much for one person only. Some one else would make you a better wife. I can imagine you very happy with some one else."

"If you think that there is any chance that you will come to care for me, I am quite content to wait," said Mr. Perrott.

"Well—there's no hurry, is there?" said Evelyn. "Suppose I thought it over and wrote and told you when I get back? I'm going to Moscow; I'll write from Moscow."

But Mr. Perrott persisted.

"You cannot give me any kind of idea. I do not ask for a date . . . that would be most unreasonable." He paused, looking down at the gravel path.

As she did not immediately answer, he went on.

"I know very well that I am not—that I have not much to offer you either in myself or in my circumstances. And I forget; it cannot seem the miracle to you that it does to me. Until I met you I had gone on in my own quiet way—we are both very quiet people, my sister and I—quite content with my lot. My friendship with Arthur was the most important thing in my life. Now that I know you, all that has changed. You seem to put such a spirit into everything. Life seems to hold so many possibilities that I had never dreamt of."

"That's splendid!" Evelyn exclaimed, grasping his hand. "Now you'll go back and start all kinds of things and make a great name in the world; and we'll go on being friends, whatever happens . . . we'll be great friends, won't we?"

"Evelyn!" he moaned suddenly, and took her in his arms, and kissed her. She did not resent it, although it made little impression on her.

As she sat upright again, she said, "I never see why one shouldn't go on being friends—though some people do. And friendships do make a difference, don't they? They are the kind of things that matter in one's life?"

He looked at her with a bewildered expression as if he did not really understand what she was saying. With a considerable effort he collected himself, stood up, and said, "Now I think I have told you what I feel, and I will only add that I can wait as long as ever you wish."

Left alone, Evelyn walked up and down the path. What did matter than? What was the meaning of it all?

27

All that evening the clouds gathered, until they closed entirely over the blue of the sky. They seemed to narrow the space between earth and heaven, so that there was no room for the air to move in freely; and the waves, too, lay flat, and yet rigid, as if they were restrained. The leaves on the bushes and trees in the garden hung closely together, and the feeling of pressure and restraint was increased by the short chirping sounds which came from birds and insects.

So strange were the lights and the silence that the busy hum of voices which usually filled the dining-room at meal times had distinct gaps in it, and during these silences the clatter of the knives upon plates became audible. The first roll of thunder and the first heavy drop striking the pane caused a little stir.

"It's coming!" was said simultaneously in many different languages.

There was then a profound silence, as if the thunder had withdrawn into itself. People had just begun to eat again, when a gust of cold air came through the open windows, lifting tablecloths and skirts, a light flashed, and was instantly followed by a clap of thunder right over the hotel. The rain swished with it, and immediately there were all those sounds of windows being shut and doors slamming violently which accompany a storm.

The room grew suddenly several degrees darker, for the wind seemed to be driving waves of darkness across the earth. No one attempted to eat for a time, but sat looking out at the garden, with their forks in the air. The flashes now came frequently, lighting up faces as if they were going to be photographed, surprising them in tense and unnatural expressions. The clap followed close and violently upon them. Several women half rose from their chairs and then sat down again, but dinner was continued uneasily with eyes upon the garden. The bushes outside were ruffled and whitened, and the wind pressed upon them so that they seemed to stoop to the ground. The waiters had to press dishes upon the diners' notice; and the diners had to draw the attention of waiters, for they were all absorbed in looking at the storm. As the thunder showed no signs of withdrawing, but seemed massed right overhead, while the lightning aimed straight at the garden every time, an uneasy gloom replaced the first excitement.

Finishing the meal very quickly, people congregated in the hall, where they felt more secure than in any other place because they could retreat far from the windows, and although they heard the thunder, they could not see anything. A little boy was carried away sobbing in the arms of his mother.

While the storm continued, no one seemed inclined to sit down, but they collected in little groups under the central skylight, where they stood in a yellow atmosphere, looking upwards. Now and again their faces became white, as the lightning flashed, and finally a terrific crash came, making the panes of the skylight lift at the joints.

"Ah!" several voices exclaimed at the same moment.

"Something struck," said a man's voice.

The rain rushed down. The rain seemed now to extinguish the lightning and the thunder, and the hall became almost dark.

After a minute or two, when nothing was heard but the rattle of water upon the glass, there was a perceptible slackening of the sound, and then the atmosphere became lighter.

"It's over," said another voice.

At a touch, all the electric lights were turned on, and revealed a crowd of people all standing, all looking with rather strained faces up at the skylight, but when they saw each other in the artificial light they turned at once and began to move away. For some minutes the rain continued to rattle upon the skylight, and the thunder gave another shake or two; but it was evident from the clearing of the darkness and the light drumming of the rain upon the roof, that the great confused ocean of air was travelling away from them, and passing high over head with its clouds and its rods of fire, out to sea. The building, which had seemed so small in the tumult of the storm, now became as square and spacious as usual.

As the storm drew away, the people in the hall of the hotel sat down; and with a comfortable sense of relief, began to tell each other stories about great storms, and produced in many cases their occupations for the evening. The chess-board was brought out, and Mr. Elliot, who wore a stock instead of a collar as a sign of convalescence, but was otherwise much as usual, challenged Mr. Pepper to a final contest. Round them gathered a group of ladies with pieces of needlework, or in default of needlework, with novels, to superintend the game, much as if they were in charge of two small boys playing marbles. Every now and then they looked at the board and made some encouraging remark to the gentlemen.

Mrs. Paley just round the corner had her cards arranged in long ladders before her, with Susan sitting near to sympathise but not to correct, and the merchants and the miscellaneous people who had never been discovered to possess names were stretched in their arm-chairs with their newspapers on their knees. The conversation in these circumstances was very gentle, fragmentary, and intermittent, but the room was full of the indescribable stir of life. Every now and then the moth, which was now grey of wing and shiny of thorax, whizzed over their heads, and hit the lamps with a thud.

A young woman put down her needlework and exclaimed, "Poor creature! it would be kinder to kill it." But nobody seemed disposed to rouse himself in order to kill the moth. They watched it dash from lamp to lamp, because they were comfortable, and had nothing to do.

On the sofa, beside the chess-players, Mrs. Elliot was imparting a new stitch in knitting to Mrs. Thornbury, so that their heads came very near together, and were only to be distinguished by the old lace cap which Mrs. Thornbury wore in the evening. Mrs. Elliot was an expert at knitting, and disclaimed a compliment to that effect with evident pride.

"I suppose we're all proud of something," she said, "and I'm proud of my knitting. I think things like that run in families. We all knit well. I had an uncle who knitted his own socks to the day of his death—and he did it better than any of his daughters, dear old gentleman. Now I wonder that you, Miss Allan, who use your eyes so much, don't take up knitting in the evenings. You'd find it such a relief, I should say—such a rest to the eyes—and the bazaars are so glad of things." Her voice dropped into the smooth half-conscious tone of the expert knitter; the words came gently one after another. "As much as I do I can always dispose of, which is a comfort, for then I feel that I am not wasting my time—"

Miss Allan, being thus addressed, shut her novel and observed the others placidly for a time. At last she said, "It is surely not natural to leave your wife because she happens to be in love with you. But that—as far as I can make out—is what the gentleman in my story does."

"Tut, tut, that doesn't sound good—no, that doesn't sound at all natural," murmured the knitters in their absorbed voices.

"Still, it's the kind of book people call very clever," Miss Allan added.

"*Maternity*—by Michael Jessop—I presume," Mr. Elliot put in, for he could never resist the temptation of talking while he played chess.

"D'you know," said Mrs. Elliot, after a moment, "I don't think people *do* write good novels now—not as good as they used to, anyhow."

No one took the trouble to agree with her or to disagree with her. Arthur Venning who was strolling about, sometimes looking at the game, sometimes reading a page of a magazine, looked at Miss Allan, who was half asleep, and said humorously, "A penny for your thoughts, Miss Allan."

The others looked up. They were glad that he had not spoken to them. But Miss Allan replied without any hesitation, "I was thinking of my imaginary uncle. Hasn't every one got an imaginary uncle?" she continued. "I have one—a most delightful old gentleman. He's always giving me things. Sometimes it's a gold watch; sometimes it's a carriage and pair; sometimes it's a beautiful little cottage in the New Forest; sometimes it's a ticket to the place I most want to see."

She set them all thinking vaguely of the things they wanted. Mrs. Elliot knew exactly what she wanted; she wanted a child; and the usual little pucker deepened on her brow.

"We're such lucky people," she said, looking at her husband. "We really have no wants." She was apt to say this, partly in order to convince herself, and partly in order to convince other people. But she was prevented from wondering how far she carried conviction by the entrance of Mr. and Mrs. Flushing, who came through the hall and stopped by the chess-board. Mrs. Flushing looked wilder than ever. A great strand of black hair looped down across her brow, her cheeks were whipped a dark blood red, and drops of rain made wet marks upon them.

Mr. Flushing explained that they had been on the roof watching the storm.

"It was a wonderful sight," he said. "The lightning went right out over the sea, and lit up the waves and the ships far away. You can't think how wonderful the mountains looked too, with the lights on them, and the great masses of shadow. It's all over now."

He slid down into a chair, becoming interested in the final struggle of the game.

"And you go back tomorrow?" said Mrs. Thornbury, looking at Mrs. Flushing.

"Yes," she replied.

"And indeed one is not sorry to go back," said Mrs. Elliot, assuming an air of mournful anxiety, "after all this illness."

"Are you afraid of dyin'?" Mrs. Flushing demanded scornfully.

"I think we are all afraid of that," said Mrs. Elliot with dignity.

"I suppose we're all cowards when it comes to the point," said Mrs. Flushing, rubbing her cheek against the back of the chair. "I'm sure I am."

"Not a bit of it!" said Mr. Flushing, turning round, for Mr. Pepper took a very long time to consider his move. "It's not cowardly to wish to live, Alice. It's the very reverse of cowardly. Personally, I'd like to go on for a hundred years—granted, of course, that I had the full use of my faculties. Think of all the things that are bound to happen!"

"That is what I feel," Mrs. Thornbury rejoined. "The changes, the improvements, the inventions—and beauty. D'you know I feel sometimes that I couldn't bear to die and cease to see beautiful things about me?"

"It would certainly be very dull to die before they have discovered whether there is life in Mars," Miss Allan added.

"Do you really believe there's life in Mars?" asked Mrs. Flushing, turning to her for the first time with keen interest. "Who tells you that? Some one who knows? D'you know a man called—?"

Here Mrs. Thornbury laid down her knitting, and a look of extreme solicitude came into her eyes.

"There is Mr. Hirst," she said quietly.

St. John had just come through the swing door. He was rather blown about by the wind, and his cheeks looked terribly pale, unshorn, and cavernous. After taking off his coat he was going to pass straight through the hall and up to his room, but he could not ignore the presence of so many people he knew, especially as Mrs. Thornbury rose and went up to him, holding out her hand. But the shock of the warm lamp-lit room, together with the sight of so many cheerful human beings sitting together at their ease, after the dark walk in the rain, and the long days of strain and horror, overcame him completely. He looked at Mrs. Thornbury and could not speak.

Every one was silent. Mr. Pepper's hand stayed upon his Knight. Mrs. Thornbury somehow moved him to a chair, sat herself beside him, and with tears in her own eyes said gently, "You have done everything for your friend."

Her action set them all talking again as if they had never stopped, and Mr. Pepper finished the move with his Knight.

"There was nothing to be done," said St. John. He spoke very slowly. "It seems impossible—"

He drew his hand across his eyes as if some dream came between him and the others and prevented him from seeing where he was.

"And that poor fellow," said Mrs. Thornbury, the tears falling again down her cheeks.

"Impossible," St. John repeated.

"Did he have the consolation of knowing—?" Mrs. Thornbury began very tentatively.

But St. John made no reply. He lay back in his chair, half-seeing the others, half-hearing what they said. He was terribly tired, and the light and warmth, the movements of the hands, and the soft communicative voices soothed him; they gave him a strange sense of quiet and relief. As he sat there, motionless, this feeling of relief became a feeling of profound happiness. Without any sense of disloyalty to Terence and Rachel he ceased to think about either of them. The movements and the voices seemed to draw together from different parts of the room, and to combine themselves into a pattern before his eyes; he was content to sit silently watching the pattern build itself up, looking at what he hardly saw.

The game was really a good one, and Mr. Pepper and Mr. Elliot were becoming more and more set upon the struggle. Mrs. Thornbury, seeing that St. John did not wish to talk, resumed her knitting.

"Lightning again!" Mrs. Flushing suddenly exclaimed. A yellow light flashed across the blue window, and for a second they saw the green trees outside. She strode to the door, pushed it open, and stood half out in the open air.

But the light was only the reflection of the storm which was over. The rain had ceased, the heavy clouds were blown away, and the air was thin and clear, although vapourish mists were being driven swiftly across the moon. The sky was once more a deep and solemn blue, and the shape of the earth was visible at the bottom of the air, enormous, dark, and solid, rising into the tapering mass of the mountain, and pricked here and there on the slopes by the tiny lights of villas. The driving air, the drone of the trees, and the flashing light which now and again spread a broad illumination over the earth filled Mrs. Flushing with exultation. Her breasts rose and fell.

"Splendid! Splendid!" she muttered to herself. Then she turned back into the hall and exclaimed in a peremptory voice, "Come outside and see, Wilfrid; it's wonderful."

Some half-stirred; some rose; some dropped their balls of wool and began to stoop to look for them.

"To bed—to bed," said Miss Allan.

"It was the move with your Queen that gave it away, Pepper," exclaimed Mr. Elliot triumphantly, sweeping the pieces together and standing up. He had won the game.

"What? Pepper beaten at last? I congratulate you!" said Arthur Venning, who was wheeling old Mrs. Paley to bed.

All these voices sounded gratefully in St. John's ears as he lay half-asleep, and yet vividly conscious of everything around him. Across his eyes passed a procession of objects, black and indistinct, the figures of people picking up their books, their cards, their balls of wool, their work-baskets, and passing him one after another on their way to bed.

NIGHT AND DAY

1

It was a Sunday evening in October, and in common with many other young ladies of her class, Katharine Hilbery was pouring out tea. Perhaps a fifth part of her mind was thus occupied, and the remaining parts leapt over the little barrier of day which interposed between Monday morning and this rather subdued moment, and played with the things one does voluntarily and normally in the daylight. But although she was silent, she was evidently mistress of a situation which was familiar enough to her, and inclined to let it take its way for the six hundredth time, perhaps, without bringing into play any of her unoccupied faculties. A single glance was enough to show that Mrs. Hilbery was so rich in the gifts which make tea-parties of elderly distinguished people successful, that she scarcely needed any help from her daughter, provided that the tiresome business of tea-cups and bread and butter was discharged for her.

Considering that the little party had been seated round the tea-table for less than twenty minutes, the animation observable on their faces, and the amount of sound they were producing collectively, were very creditable to the hostess. It suddenly came into Katharine's mind that if some one opened the door at this moment he would think that they were enjoying themselves; he would think, "What an extremely nice house to come into!" and instinctively she laughed, and said something to increase the noise, for the credit of the house presumably, since she herself had not been feeling exhilarated. At the very same moment, rather to her amusement, the door was flung open, and a young man entered the room. Katharine, as she shook hands with him, asked him, in her own mind, "Now, do you think we're enjoying ourselves enormously?" . . . "Mr. Denham, mother," she said aloud, for she saw that her mother had forgotten his name.

That fact was perceptible to Mr. Denham also, and increased the awkwardness which inevitably attends the entrance of a stranger into a room full of people much at their ease, and all launched upon sentences. At the same time, it seemed to Mr. Denham as if a thousand softly padded doors had closed between him and the street outside. A fine mist, the etherealized essence of the fog, hung visibly in the wide and rather empty space of the drawing-room, all silver where the candles were grouped on the tea-table, and ruddy again in the firelight. With the omnibuses and cabs still running in his head, and his body still tingling with his quick walk along the streets and in and out of traffic and foot-passengers, this drawing-room seemed very remote and still; and the faces of the elderly people were mellowed, at some distance from each other, and had a bloom on them owing to the fact that the air in the drawing-room was thickened by blue grains of mist. Mr. Denham had come in as Mr. Fortescue, the eminent novelist, reached the middle of a very long sentence. He kept this suspended while the newcomer sat down, and Mrs. Hilbery deftly joined the severed parts by leaning towards him and remarking:

"Now, what would you do if you were married to an engineer, and had to live in Manchester, Mr. Denham?"

"Surely she could learn Persian," broke in a thin, elderly gentleman. "Is there no retired schoolmaster or man of letters in Manchester with whom she could read Persian?"

"A cousin of ours has married and gone to live in Manchester," Katharine explained. Mr. Denham muttered something, which was indeed all that was required of him, and the novelist went on where he had left off. Privately, Mr. Denham cursed himself very sharply for having exchanged the freedom of the street for this sophisticated drawing-room, where, among other disagreeables, he certainly would not appear at his best. He glanced round him, and saw that, save for Katharine, they were all over forty, the only consolation being that Mr. Fortescue was a considerable celebrity, so that tomorrow one might be glad to have met him.

"Have you ever been to Manchester?" he asked Katharine.

"Never," she replied.

"Why do you object to it, then?"

Katharine stirred her tea, and seemed to speculate, so Denham thought, upon the duty of filling somebody else's cup, but she was really wondering how she was going to keep this strange young man in harmony with the rest. She observed that he was compressing his teacup, so that there was danger lest the thin china might cave inwards. She could see that he was nervous; one would expect a bony young man with his face slightly reddened by the wind, and his hair not altogether smooth, to be nervous in such a party. Further, he probably disliked this kind of thing, and had come out of curiosity, or because her father had invited him—anyhow, he would not be easily combined with the rest.

"I should think there would be no one to talk to in Manchester," she replied at random. Mr. Fortescue had been observing her for a moment or two, as novelists are inclined to observe, and at this remark he smiled, and made it the text for a little further speculation.

"In spite of a slight tendency to exaggeration, Katharine decidedly hits the mark," he said, and lying back in his chair, with his opaque contemplative eyes fixed on the ceiling, and the tips of his fingers pressed together, he depicted, first the horrors of the streets of Manchester, and then the bare, immense moors on the outskirts of the town, and then the scrubby little house in which the girl would live, and then the professors and the miserable young students devoted to the more strenuous works of our younger dramatists, who would visit her, and how her appearance would change by degrees, and how she would fly to London, and how Katharine would have to lead her about, as one leads an eager dog on a chain, past rows of clamorous butchers' shops, poor dear creature.

"Oh, Mr. Fortescue," exclaimed Mrs. Hilbery, as he finished, "I had just written to say how I envied her! I was thinking of the big gardens and the dear old ladies in mittens, who read nothing but the *Spectator*, and snuff the candles. Have they *all* disappeared? I told her she would find the nice things of London without the horrid streets that depress one so."

"There is the University," said the thin gentleman, who had previously insisted upon the existence of people knowing Persian.

"I know there are moors there, because I read about them in a book the other day," said Katharine.

"I am grieved and amazed at the ignorance of my family," Mr. Hilbery remarked. He was an elderly man, with a pair of oval, hazel eyes which were rather bright for his time of life, and relieved the heaviness of his face. He played constantly with a little green stone attached to his watch-chain, thus displaying long and very sensitive fingers, and had a habit of moving his head hither and thither very quickly without altering the position of his large and rather corpulent body, so that he seemed to be providing himself incessantly with food for amusement and reflection with the least possible expenditure of energy. One might suppose that he had passed the time of life when his ambitions were personal, or that he had gratified them as far as he was likely to do, and now employed his considerable acuteness rather to observe and reflect than to attain any result.

Katharine, so Denham decided, while Mr. Fortescue built up another rounded structure of words, had a likeness to each of her parents, but these elements were rather oddly blended. She had the quick, impulsive movements of her mother, the lips parting often to speak, and closing again; and the dark oval eyes of her father brimming with light upon a basis of sadness, or, since she was too young to have acquired a sorrowful point of view, one might say that the basis was not sadness so much as a spirit given to contemplation and self-control. Judging by her hair, her coloring, and the shape of her features, she was striking, if not actually beautiful. Decision and composure stamped her, a combination of qualities that produced a very marked character, and one that was not calculated to put a young man, who scarcely knew her, at his ease. For the rest, she was tall; her dress was of some quiet color, with old yellow-tinted lace for ornament, to which the spark of an ancient jewel gave its one red gleam. Denham noticed that, although silent, she kept sufficient control of the situation to answer immediately her mother appealed to her for help, and yet it was obvious to him that she attended only with the surface skin of her mind. It struck him that her position at the tea-table, among all these elderly people, was not without its difficulties, and he checked his inclination to find her, or her attitude, generally antipathetic to him. The talk had passed over Manchester, after dealing with it very generously.

"Would it be the Battle of Trafalgar or the Spanish Armada, Katharine?" her mother demanded.

"Trafalgar, mother."

"Trafalgar, of course! How stupid of me! Another cup of tea, with a thin slice of lemon in it, and then, dear Mr. Fortescue, please explain my absurd little puzzle. One can't help believing gentlemen with Roman noses, even if one meets them in omnibuses."

Mr. Hilbery here interposed so far as Denham was concerned, and talked a great deal of sense about the solicitors' profession, and the changes which he had seen in his lifetime. Indeed, Denham properly fell to his lot, owing to the fact that an article by Denham upon some legal matter, published by Mr. Hilbery in his Review, had brought them acquainted. But when a moment later Mrs. Sutton Bailey was announced, he turned to her, and Mr. Denham found himself sitting silent, rejecting possible things to say, beside Katharine, who was silent too. Being much about the same age and both under thirty, they were prohibited from the use of a great many convenient phrases which launch conversation into smooth waters. They were further silenced by Katharine's rather malicious determination not to help this young man, in whose upright and resolute bearing she detected something hostile to her surroundings, by any of the usual feminine amenities. They therefore sat silent, Denham controlling his desire to say something abrupt and explosive, which should shock her into life. But Mrs. Hilbery was immediately sensitive to any silence in the drawing-room, as of a dumb note in a sonorous scale, and leaning across the table she observed, in the curiously tentative detached manner which always gave her phrases the likeness of butterflies flaunting from one sunny spot to another, "D'you know, Mr. Denham, you remind me so much of dear Mr. Ruskin. . . . Is it his tie, Katharine, or his hair, or the way he sits in his chair? Do tell me, Mr. Denham, are you an admirer of Ruskin? Some one, the other day, said to me, 'Oh, no, we don't read Ruskin, Mrs. Hilbery.' What *do* you read, I wonder?—for you can't spend all your time going up in aeroplanes and burrowing into the bowels of the earth."

She looked benevolently at Denham, who said nothing articulate, and then at Katharine, who smiled but said nothing either, upon which Mrs. Hilbery seemed possessed by a brilliant idea, and exclaimed:

"I'm sure Mr. Denham would like to see our things, Katharine. I'm sure he's not like that dreadful young man, Mr. Ponting, who told me that he considered it our duty to live exclusively in the present. After all, what *is* the present? Half of it's the past, and the better half, too, I should say," she added, turning to Mr. Fortescue.

Denham rose, half meaning to go, and thinking that he had seen all that there was to see, but Katharine rose at the same moment, and saying, "Perhaps you would like to see the pictures," led the way across the drawing-room to a smaller room opening out of it.

The smaller room was something like a chapel in a cathedral, or a grotto in a cave, for the booming sound of the traffic in the distance suggested the soft surge of waters, and the oval mirrors, with their silver surface, were like deep pools trembling beneath starlight. But the comparison to a religious temple of some kind was the more apt of the two, for the little room was crowded with relics.

As Katharine touched different spots, lights sprang here and there, and revealed a square mass of red-and-gold books, and then a long skirt in blue-and-white paint lustrous behind glass, and then a mahogany writing-table, with its orderly equipment, and, finally, a picture above the table, to which special illumination was accorded. When Katharine had touched these last lights, she stood back, as much as to say, "There!" Denham found himself looked down upon by the eyes of the great poet, Richard Alardyce, and suffered a little shock which would have led him, had he been wearing a hat, to remove it. The eyes looked at him out of the mellow pinks and yellows of the paint with divine friendliness, which embraced him, and passed on to contemplate the entire world. The paint had so faded that very little but the beautiful large eyes were left, dark in the surrounding dimness.

Katharine waited as though for him to receive a full impression, and then she said:

"This is his writing-table. He used this pen," and she lifted a quill pen and laid it down again. The writing-table was splashed with old ink, and the pen disheveled in service. There lay the gigantic gold-rimmed spectacles, ready to his hand, and beneath the table was a pair of large, worn slippers, one of which Katharine picked up, remarking:

"I think my grandfather must have been at least twice as large as any one is nowadays. This," she went on, as if she knew what she had to say by heart, "is the original manuscript of the 'Ode to Winter.' The early poems are far less corrected than the later. Would you like to look at it?"

While Mr. Denham examined the manuscript, she glanced up at her grandfather, and, for the thousandth time, fell into a pleasant dreamy state in which she seemed to be the companion of those giant men, of their own lineage, at any rate, and the insignificant present moment was put to shame. That magnificent ghostly head on the canvas, surely, never beheld all the trivialities of a Sunday afternoon, and it did not seem to matter what she and this young man said to each other, for they were only small people.

"This is a copy of the first edition of the poems," she continued, without considering the fact that Mr. Denham was still occupied with the manuscript, "which contains several poems that have not been reprinted, as well as corrections." She paused for a minute, and then went on, as if these spaces had all been calculated.

"That lady in blue is my great-grandmother, by Millington. Here is my uncle's walking-stick—he was Sir Richard Warburton, you know, and rode with Havelock to the Relief of Lucknow. And then, let me see—oh, that's the original Alardyce, 1697, the founder of the family fortunes, with his wife. Some one gave us this bowl the other day because it has their crest and initials. We think it must have been given them to celebrate their silver wedding-day."

Here she stopped for a moment, wondering why it was that Mr. Denham said nothing. Her feeling that he was antagonistic to her, which had lapsed while she thought of her family possessions, returned so keenly that she stopped in the middle of her catalog and looked at him. Her mother, wishing to connect him reputably with the great dead, had compared him with Mr. Ruskin; and the comparison was in Katharine's mind, and led her to be more critical of the young man than was fair, for a young man paying a call in a tail-coat is in a different element altogether from a head seized at its climax of expressiveness, gazing immutably from behind a sheet of glass, which was all that remained to her of Mr. Ruskin. He had a singular face—a face built for swiftness and decision rather than for massive contemplation; the forehead broad, the nose long and formidable, the lips clean-shaven and at once dogged and sensitive, the cheeks lean, with a deeply running tide of red blood in them. His eyes, expressive now of the usual masculine impersonality and authority, might reveal more subtle emotions under favorable circumstances, for they were large, and of a clear, brown color; they seemed unexpectedly to hesitate and speculate; but Katharine only looked at him to wonder whether his face would not have come nearer the standard of her dead heroes if it had been adorned with side-whiskers. In his spare build and thin, though healthy, cheeks, she saw tokens of an angular and acrid soul. His voice, she noticed, had a slight vibrating or creaking sound in it, as he laid down the manuscript and said:

"You must be very proud of your family, Miss Hilbery."

"Yes, I am," Katharine answered, and she added, "Do you think there's anything wrong in that?"

"Wrong? How should it be wrong? It must be a bore, though, showing your things to visitors," he added reflectively.

"Not if the visitors like them."

"Isn't it difficult to live up to your ancestors?" he proceeded.

"I dare say I shouldn't try to write poetry," Katharine replied.

"No. And that's what I should hate. I couldn't bear my grandfather to cut me out. And, after all," Denham went on, glancing round him satirically, as Katharine thought, "it's not your grandfather only. You're cut out all the way round. I suppose you come of one of the most distinguished families in England. There are the Warburtons and the Mannings—and you're related to the Otways, aren't you? I read it all in some magazine," he added.

"The Otways are my cousins," Katharine replied.

"Well," said Denham, in a final tone of voice, as if his argument were proved.

"Well," said Katharine, "I don't see that you've proved anything."

Denham smiled, in a peculiarly provoking way. He was amused and gratified to find that he had the power to annoy his oblivious, supercilious hostess, if he could not impress her; though he would have preferred to impress her.

He sat silent, holding the precious little book of poems unopened in his hands, and Katharine watched him, the melancholy or contemplative expression deepening in her eyes as her annoyance faded. She appeared to be considering many things. She had forgotten her duties.

"Well," said Denham again, suddenly opening the little book of poems, as though he had said all that he meant to say or could, with propriety, say. He turned over the pages with great decision, as if he were judging the book in its entirety, the printing and paper and binding, as well as the poetry, and then, having satisfied himself of its good or bad quality, he placed it on the writing-table, and examined the malacca cane with the gold knob which had belonged to the soldier.

"But aren't you proud of your family?" Katharine demanded.

"No," said Denham. "We've never done anything to be proud of—unless you count paying one's bills a matter for pride."

"That sounds rather dull," Katharine remarked.

"You would think us horribly dull," Denham agreed.

"Yes, I might find you dull, but I don't think I should find you ridiculous," Katharine added, as if Denham had actually brought that charge against her family.

"No—because we're not in the least ridiculous. We're a respectable middle-class family, living at Highgate."

"We don't live at Highgate, but we're middle class too, I suppose."

Denham merely smiled, and replacing the malacca cane on the rack, he drew a sword from its ornamental sheath.

"That belonged to Clive, so we say," said Katharine, taking up her duties as hostess again automatically.

"Is it a lie?" Denham inquired.

"It's a family tradition. I don't know that we can prove it."

"You see, we don't have traditions in our family," said Denham.

"You sound very dull," Katharine remarked, for the second time.

"Merely middle class," Denham replied.

"You pay your bills, and you speak the truth. I don't see why you should despise us."

Mr. Denham carefully sheathed the sword which the Hilberys said belonged to Clive.

"I shouldn't like to be you; that's all I said," he replied, as if he were saying what he thought as accurately as he could.

"No, but one never would like to be any one else."

"I should. I should like to be lots of other people."

"Then why not us?" Katharine asked.

Denham looked at her as she sat in her grandfather's arm-chair, drawing her great-uncle's malacca cane smoothly through her fingers, while her background was made up equally of lustrous blue-and-white paint, and crimson books with gilt lines on them. The vitality and composure of her attitude, as of a bright-plumed bird poised easily before further flights, roused him to show her the limitations of her lot. So soon, so easily, would he be forgotten.

"You'll never know anything at first hand," he began, almost savagely. "It's all been done for you. You'll never know the pleasure of buying things after saving up for them, or reading books for the first time, or making discoveries."

"Go on," Katharine observed, as he paused, suddenly doubtful, when he heard his voice proclaiming aloud these facts, whether there was any truth in them.

"Of course, I don't know how you spend your time," he continued, a little stiffly, "but I suppose you have to show people round. You are writing a life of your grandfather, aren't you? And this kind of thing"—he nodded towards the other room, where they could hear bursts of cultivated laughter—"must take up a lot of time."

She looked at him expectantly, as if between them they were decorating a small figure of herself, and she saw him hesitating in the disposition of some bow or sash.

"You've got it very nearly right," she said, "but I only help my mother. I don't write myself."

"Do you do anything yourself?" he demanded.

"What do you mean?" she asked. "I don't leave the house at ten and come back at six."

"I don't mean that."

Mr. Denham had recovered his self-control; he spoke with a quietness which made Katharine rather anxious that he should explain himself, but at the same time she wished to annoy him, to waft him away from her on some light current of ridicule or satire, as she was wont to do with these intermittent young men of her father's.

"Nobody ever does do anything worth doing nowadays," she remarked. "You see"—she tapped the volume of her grandfather's poems—"we don't even print as well as they did, and as for poets or painters or novelists—there are none; so, at any rate, I'm not singular."

"No, we haven't any great men," Denham replied. "I'm very glad that we haven't. I hate great men. The worship of greatness in the nineteenth century seems to me to explain the worthlessness of that generation."

Katharine opened her lips and drew in her breath, as if to reply with equal vigor, when the shutting of a door in the next room withdrew her attention, and they both became conscious that the voices, which had been rising and falling round the tea-table, had fallen silent; the light, even, seemed to have sunk lower. A moment later Mrs. Hilbery appeared in the doorway of the ante-room. She stood looking at them with a smile of expectancy on her face, as if a scene from the drama of the younger generation were being played for her benefit. She was a remarkable-looking woman, well advanced in the sixties, but owing to the lightness of her frame and the brightness of her eyes she seemed to have been wafted over the surface of the years without taking much harm in the passage. Her face was shrunken and aquiline, but any hint of sharpness was dispelled by the large blue eyes, at once sagacious and innocent, which seemed to regard the world with an enormous desire that it should behave itself nobly, and an entire confidence that it could do so, if it would only take the pains.

Certain lines on the broad forehead and about the lips might be taken to suggest that she had known moments of some difficulty and perplexity in the course of her career, but these had not destroyed her trustfulness, and she was clearly still prepared to give every one any number of fresh chances and the whole system the benefit of the doubt. She wore a great resemblance to her father, and suggested, as he did, the fresh airs and open spaces of a younger world.

"Well," she said, "how do you like our things, Mr. Denham?"

Mr. Denham rose, put his book down, opened his mouth, but said nothing, as Katharine observed, with some amusement.

Mrs. Hilbery handled the book he had laid down.

"There are some books that *live*," she mused. "They are young with us, and they grow old with us. Are you fond of poetry, Mr. Denham? But what an absurd question to ask! The truth is, dear Mr. Fortescue has almost tired me out. He is so eloquent and so witty, so searching and so profound that, after half an hour or so, I feel inclined to turn out all the lights. But perhaps he'd be more wonderful than ever in the dark. What d'you think, Katharine? Shall we give a little party in complete darkness? There'd have to be bright rooms for the bores. . . ."

Here Mr. Denham held out his hand.

"But we've any number of things to show you!" Mrs. Hilbery exclaimed, taking no notice of it. "Books, pictures, china, manuscripts, and the very chair that Mary Queen of Scots sat in when she heard of Darnley's murder. I must lie down for a little, and Katharine must change her dress (though she's wearing a very pretty one), but if you don't mind being left alone, supper will be at eight. I dare say you'll write a poem of your own while you're waiting. Ah, how I love the firelight! Doesn't our room look charming?"

She stepped back and bade them contemplate the empty drawing-room, with its rich, irregular lights, as the flames leapt and wavered.

"Dear things!" she exclaimed. "Dear chairs and tables! How like old friends they are—faithful, silent friends. Which reminds me, Katharine, little Mr. Anning is coming tonight, and Tite Street, and Cadogan Square. . . . Do remember to get that drawing of your great-uncle glazed. Aunt Millicent remarked it last time she was here, and I know how it would hurt me to see *my* father in a broken glass."

It was like tearing through a maze of diamond-glittering spiders' webs to say good-bye and escape, for at each movement Mrs. Hilbery remembered something further about the villainies of picture-framers or the delights of poetry, and at one time it seemed to the young man that he would be hypnotized into doing what she pretended to want him to do, for he could not suppose that she attached any value whatever to his presence. Katharine, however, made an opportunity for him to leave, and for that he was grateful to her, as one young person is grateful for the understanding of another.

2

The young man shut the door with a sharper slam than any visitor had used that afternoon, and walked up the street at a great pace, cutting the air with his walking-stick. He was glad to find himself outside that drawing-room, breathing raw fog, and in contact with unpolished people who only wanted their share of the pavement allowed them. He thought that if he had had Mr. or Mrs. or Miss Hilbery out here he would have made them, somehow, feel his superiority, for he was chafed by the memory of halting awkward sentences which had failed to give even the young woman with the sad, but inwardly ironical eyes a hint of his force. He tried to recall the actual words of his little outburst, and unconsciously supplemented them by so many words of greater expressiveness that the irritation of his failure was somewhat assuaged. Sudden stabs of the unmitigated truth assailed him now and then, for he was not inclined by nature to take a rosy view of his conduct, but what with the beat of his foot upon the pavement, and the glimpse which half-drawn curtains offered him of kitchens, dining-rooms, and drawing-rooms, illustrating with mute power different scenes from different lives, his own experience lost its sharpness.

His own experience underwent a curious change. His speed slackened, his head sank a little towards his breast, and the lamplight shone now and again upon a face grown strangely tranquil. His thought was so absorbing that when it became necessary to verify the name of a street, he looked at it for a time before he read it; when he came to a crossing, he seemed to have to reassure himself by two or three taps, such as a blind man gives, upon the curb; and, reaching the Underground station, he blinked in the bright circle of light, glanced at his watch, decided that he might still indulge himself in darkness, and walked straight on.

And yet the thought was the thought with which he had started. He was still thinking about the people in the house which he had left; but instead of remembering, with whatever accuracy he could, their looks and sayings, he had consciously taken leave of the literal truth. A turn of the street, a firelit room, something monumental in the procession of the lamp-posts, who shall say what accident of light or shape had suddenly changed the prospect within his mind, and led him to murmur aloud:

"She'll do. . . . Yes, Katharine Hilbery'll do. . . . I'll take Katharine Hilbery."

As soon as he had said this, his pace slackened, his head fell, his eyes became fixed. The desire to justify himself, which had been so urgent, ceased to torment him, and, as if released from constraint, so that they worked without friction or bidding, his faculties leapt forward and fixed, as a matter of course, upon the form of Katharine Hilbery. It was marvellous how much they found to feed upon, considering the destructive nature of Denham's criticism in her presence. The charm, which he had tried to disown, when under the effect of it, the beauty, the character, the aloofness, which he had been determined not to feel, now possessed him wholly; and when, as happened by the nature of things, he had exhausted his memory, he went on with his imagination. He was conscious of what he was about, for in thus dwelling upon Miss Hilbery's qualities, he showed a kind of method, as if he required this vision of her for a particular purpose. He increased her height, he darkened her hair; but physically there was not much to change in her. His most daring liberty was taken with her mind, which, for reasons of his own, he desired to be exalted and infallible, and of such independence that it was only in the case of Ralph Denham that it swerved from its high, swift flight, but where he was concerned, though fastidious at first, she finally swooped from her eminence to crown him with her approval. These delicious details, however, were to be worked out in all their ramifications at his leisure; the main point was that Katharine Hilbery would do; she would do for weeks, perhaps for months. In taking her he had provided himself with something the lack of which had left a bare place in his mind for a considerable time. He gave a sigh of satisfaction; his consciousness of his actual position somewhere in the neighborhood of Knightsbridge returned to him, and he was soon speeding in the train towards Highgate.

Although thus supported by the knowledge of his new possession of considerable value, he was not proof against the familiar thoughts which the suburban streets and the damp shrubs growing in front gardens and the absurd names painted in white upon the gates of those gardens suggested to him. His walk was uphill, and his mind dwelt gloomily upon the house which he approached, where he would find six or seven brothers and sisters, a widowed mother, and, probably, some aunt or uncle sitting down to an unpleasant meal under a very bright light. Should he put in force the threat which, two weeks ago, some such gathering had wrung from him—the terrible threat that if visitors came on Sunday he should dine alone in his room? A glance in the direction of Miss Hilbery determined him to make his stand this very night, and accordingly, having let himself in, having verified the presence of Uncle Joseph by means of a bowler hat and a very large umbrella, he gave his orders to the maid, and went upstairs to his room.

He went up a great many flights of stairs, and he noticed, as he had very seldom noticed, how the carpet became steadily shabbier, until it ceased altogether, how the walls were discolored, sometimes by cascades of damp, and sometimes by the outlines of picture-frames since removed, how the paper flapped loose at the corners, and a great flake of plaster had fallen from the ceiling. The room itself was a cheerless one to return to at this inauspicious hour. A flattened sofa would, later in the evening, become a bed; one of the tables concealed a washing apparatus; his clothes and boots were disagreeably mixed with books which bore the gilt of college arms; and, for decoration, there hung upon the wall photographs of bridges and cathedrals and large, unprepossessing groups of insufficiently clothed young men, sitting in rows one above another upon stone steps. There was a look of meanness and shabbiness in the furniture and curtains, and nowhere any sign of luxury or even of a cultivated taste, unless the cheap classics in the book-case were a sign of an effort in that direction. The only object that threw any light upon the character of the room's owner was a large perch, placed in the window to catch the air and sun, upon which a tame and, apparently, decrepit rook hopped dryly from side to side. The bird, encouraged by a scratch behind the ear, settled upon Denham's shoulder. He lit his gas-fire and settled down in gloomy patience to await his dinner. After sitting thus for some minutes a small girl popped her head in to say,

"Mother says, aren't you coming down, Ralph? Uncle Joseph—"

"They're to bring my dinner up here," said Ralph, peremptorily; whereupon she vanished, leaving the door ajar in her haste to be gone. After Denham had waited some minutes, in the course of which neither he nor the rook took their eyes off the fire, he muttered a curse, ran downstairs, intercepted the parlor-maid, and cut himself a slice of bread and cold meat. As he did so, the dining-room door sprang open, a voice exclaimed "Ralph!" but Ralph paid no attention to the voice, and made off upstairs with his plate. He set it down in a chair opposite him, and ate with a ferocity that was due partly to anger and partly to hunger. His mother, then, was determined not to respect his wishes; he was a person of no importance in his own family; he was sent for and treated as a child. He reflected, with a growing sense of injury, that almost every one of his actions since opening the door of his room had been won from the grasp of the family system. By rights, he should have been sitting downstairs in the drawing-room describing his afternoon's adventures, or listening to the afternoon's adventures of other people; the room itself, the gas-fire, the arm-chair—all had been fought for; the wretched bird, with half its feathers out and one leg lamed by a cat, had been rescued under protest; but what his family most resented, he reflected, was his wish for privacy. To dine alone, or to sit alone after dinner, was flat rebellion, to be fought with every weapon of underhand stealth or of open appeal. Which did he dislike most—deception or tears? But, at any rate, they could not rob him of his thoughts; they could not make him say where he had been or whom he had seen. That was his own affair; that, indeed, was a step entirely in the right direction, and, lighting his pipe, and cutting up the remains of his meal for the benefit of the rook, Ralph calmed his rather excessive irritation and settled down to think over his prospects.

This particular afternoon was a step in the right direction, because it was part of his plan to get to know people beyond the family circuit, just as it was part of his plan to learn German this autumn, and to review legal books for Mr. Hilbery's *Critical Review.* He had always made plans since he was a small boy; for poverty, and the fact that he was the eldest son of a large family, had given him the habit of thinking of spring and summer, autumn and winter, as so many stages in a prolonged campaign. Although he was still under thirty, this forecasting habit had marked two semicircular lines above his eyebrows, which threatened, at this moment, to crease into their wonted shapes. But instead of settling down to think, he rose, took a small piece of cardboard marked in large letters with the word OUT, and hung it upon the handle of his door. This done, he sharpened a pencil, lit a reading-lamp and opened his book. But still he hesitated to take his seat. He scratched the rook, he walked to the window; he parted the curtains, and looked down upon the city which lay, hazily luminous, beneath him. He looked across the vapors in the direction of Chelsea; looked fixedly for a moment, and then returned to his chair. But the whole thickness of some learned counsel's treatise upon Torts did not screen him satisfactorily. Through the pages he saw a drawing-room, very empty and spacious; he heard low voices, he saw women's figures, he could even smell the scent of the cedar log which flamed in the grate. His mind relaxed its tension, and seemed to be giving out now what it had taken in unconsciously at the time. He could remember Mr. Fortescue's exact words, and the rolling emphasis with which he delivered them, and he began to repeat what Mr. Fortescue had said, in Mr. Fortescue's own manner, about Manchester. His mind then began to wander about the house, and he wondered whether there were other rooms like the drawing-room, and he thought, inconsequently, how beautiful the bathroom must be, and how leisurely it was—the life of these well-kept people, who were, no doubt, still sitting in the same room, only they had changed their clothes, and little Mr. Anning was there, and the aunt who would mind if the glass of her father's picture was broken. Miss Hilbery had changed her dress ("although she's wearing such a pretty one," he heard her mother say), and she was talking to Mr. Anning, who was well over forty, and bald into the bargain, about books. How peaceful and spacious it was; and the peace possessed him so completely that his muscles slackened, his book drooped from his hand, and he forgot that the hour of work was wasting minute by minute.

He was roused by a creak upon the stair. With a guilty start he composed himself, frowned and looked intently at the fifty-sixth page of his volume. A step paused outside his door, and he knew that the person, whoever it might be, was considering the placard, and debating whether to honor its decree or not. Certainly, policy advised him to sit still in autocratic silence, for no custom can take root in a family unless every breach of it is punished severely for the first six months or so. But Ralph was conscious of a distinct wish to be interrupted, and his disappointment was perceptible when he heard the creaking sound rather farther down the stairs, as if his visitor had decided to withdraw. He rose, opened the door with unnecessary abruptness, and waited on the landing. The person stopped simultaneously half a flight downstairs.

"Ralph?" said a voice, inquiringly.

"Joan?"

"I was coming up, but I saw your notice."

"Well, come along in, then." He concealed his desire beneath a tone as grudging as he could make it.

Joan came in, but she was careful to show, by standing upright with one hand upon the mantelpiece, that she was only there for a definite purpose, which discharged, she would go.

She was older than Ralph by some three or four years. Her face was round but worn, and expressed that tolerant but anxious good humor which is the special attribute of elder sisters in large families. Her pleasant brown eyes resembled Ralph's, save in expression, for whereas he seemed to look straightly and keenly at one object, she appeared to be in the habit of considering everything from many different points of view. This made her appear his elder by more years than existed in fact between them. Her gaze rested for a moment or two upon the rook. She then said, without any preface:

"It's about Charles and Uncle John's offer. . . . Mother's been talking to me. She says she can't afford to pay for him after this term. She says she'll have to ask for an overdraft as it is."

"That's simply not true," said Ralph.

"No. I thought not. But she won't believe me when I say it."

Ralph, as if he could foresee the length of this familiar argument, drew up a chair for his sister and sat down himself.

"I'm not interrupting?" she inquired.

Ralph shook his head, and for a time they sat silent. The lines curved themselves in semicircles above their eyes.

"She doesn't understand that one's got to take risks," he observed, finally.

"I believe mother would take risks if she knew that Charles was the sort of boy to profit by it."

"He's got brains, hasn't he?" said Ralph. His tone had taken on that shade of pugnacity which suggested to his sister that some personal grievance drove him to take the line he did. She wondered what it might be, but at once recalled her mind, and assented.

"In some ways he's fearfully backward, though, compared with what you were at his age. And he's difficult at home, too. He makes Molly slave for him."

Ralph made a sound which belittled this particular argument. It was plain to Joan that she had struck one of her brother's perverse moods, and he was going to oppose whatever his mother said. He called her "she," which was a proof of it. She sighed involuntarily, and the sigh annoyed Ralph, and he exclaimed with irritation:

"It's pretty hard lines to stick a boy into an office at seventeen!"

"Nobody *wants* to stick him into an office," she said.

She, too, was becoming annoyed. She had spent the whole of the afternoon discussing wearisome details of education and expense with her mother, and she had come to her brother for help, encouraged, rather irrationally, to expect help by the fact that he had been out somewhere, she didn't know and didn't mean to ask where, all the afternoon.

Ralph was fond of his sister, and her irritation made him think how unfair it was that all these burdens should be laid on her shoulders.

"The truth is," he observed gloomily, "that I ought to have accepted Uncle John's offer. I should have been making six hundred a year by this time."

"I don't think that for a moment," Joan replied quickly, repenting of her annoyance. "The question, to my mind, is, whether we couldn't cut down our expenses in some way."

"A smaller house?"

"Fewer servants, perhaps."

Neither brother nor sister spoke with much conviction, and after reflecting for a moment what these proposed reforms in a strictly economical household meant, Ralph announced very decidedly:

"It's out of the question."

It was out of the question that she should put any more household work upon herself. No, the hardship must fall on him, for he was determined that his family should have as many chances of distinguishing themselves as other families had—as the Hilberys had, for example. He believed secretly and rather defiantly, for it was a fact not capable of proof, that there was something very remarkable about his family.

"If mother won't run risks——"

"You really can't expect her to sell out again."

"She ought to look upon it as an investment; but if she won't, we must find some other way, that's all."

A threat was contained in this sentence, and Joan knew, without asking, what the threat was. In the course of his professional life, which now extended over six or seven years, Ralph had saved, perhaps, three or four hundred pounds. Considering the sacrifices he had made in order to put by this sum it always amazed Joan to find that he used it to gamble with, buying shares and selling them again, increasing it sometimes, sometimes diminishing it, and always running the risk of losing every penny of it in a day's disaster. But although she wondered, she could not help loving him the better for his odd combination of Spartan self-control and what appeared to her romantic and childish folly. Ralph interested her more than any one else in the world, and she often broke off in the middle of one of these economic discussions, in spite of their gravity, to consider some fresh aspect of his character.

"I think you'd be foolish to risk your money on poor old Charles," she observed. "Fond as I am of him, he doesn't seem to me exactly brilliant. . . . Besides, why should you be sacrificed?"

"My dear Joan," Ralph exclaimed, stretching himself out with a gesture of impatience, "don't you see that we've all got to be sacrificed? What's the use of denying it? What's the use of struggling against it? So it always has been, so it always will be. We've got no money and we never shall have any money. We shall just turn round in the mill every day of our lives until we drop and die, worn out, as most people do, when one comes to think of it."

Joan looked at him, opened her lips as if to speak, and closed them again. Then she said, very tentatively:

"Aren't you happy, Ralph?"

"No. Are you? Perhaps I'm as happy as most people, though. God knows whether I'm happy or not. What is happiness?"

He glanced with half a smile, in spite of his gloomy irritation, at his sister. She looked, as usual, as if she were weighing one thing with another, and balancing them together before she made up her mind.

"Happiness," she remarked at length enigmatically, rather as if she were sampling the word, and then she paused. She paused for a considerable space, as if she were considering happiness in all its bearings. "Hilda was here today," she suddenly resumed, as if they had never mentioned happiness. "She brought Bobbie—he's a fine boy now." Ralph observed, with an amusement that had a tinge of irony in it, that she was now going to sidle away quickly from this dangerous approach to intimacy on to topics of general and family interest. Nevertheless, he reflected, she was the only one of his family with whom he found it possible to discuss happiness, although he might very well have discussed happiness with Miss Hilbery at their first meeting. He looked critically at Joan, and wished that she did not look so provincial or suburban in her high green dress with the faded trimming, so patient, and almost resigned. He began to wish to tell her about the Hilberys in order to abuse them, for in the miniature battle which so often rages between two quickly following impressions of life, the life of the Hilberys was getting the better of the life of the Denhams in his mind, and he wanted to assure himself that there was some quality in which Joan infinitely surpassed Miss Hilbery. He should have felt that his own sister was more original, and had greater vitality than Miss Hilbery had; but his main impression of Katharine now was of a person of great vitality and composure; and at the moment he could not perceive what poor dear Joan had gained from the fact that she was the granddaughter of a man who kept a shop, and herself earned her own living. The infinite dreariness and sordidness of their life oppressed him in spite of his fundamental belief that, as a family, they were somehow remarkable.

"Shall you talk to mother?" Joan inquired. "Because, you see, the thing's got to be settled, one way or another. Charles must write to Uncle John if he's going there."

Ralph sighed impatiently.

"I suppose it doesn't much matter either way," he exclaimed. "He's doomed to misery in the long run."

A slight flush came into Joan's cheek.

"You know you're talking nonsense," she said. "It doesn't hurt any one to have to earn their own living. I'm very glad I have to earn mine."

Ralph was pleased that she should feel this, and wished her to continue, but he went on, perversely enough.

"Isn't that only because you've forgotten how to enjoy yourself? You never have time for anything decent—"

"As for instance?"

"Well, going for walks, or music, or books, or seeing interesting people. You never do anything that's really worth doing any more than I do."

"I always think you could make this room much nicer, if you liked," she observed.

"What does it matter what sort of room I have when I'm forced to spend all the best years of my life drawing up deeds in an office?"

"You said two days ago that you found the law so interesting."

"So it is if one could afford to know anything about it."

("That's Herbert only just going to bed now," Joan interposed, as a door on the landing slammed vigorously. "And then he won't get up in the morning.")

Ralph looked at the ceiling, and shut his lips closely together. Why, he wondered, could Joan never for one moment detach her mind from the details of domestic life? It seemed to him that she was getting more and more enmeshed in them, and capable of shorter and less frequent flights into the outer world, and yet she was only thirty-three.

"D'you ever pay calls now?" he asked abruptly.

"I don't often have the time. Why do you ask?"

"It might be a good thing, to get to know new people, that's all."

"Poor Ralph!" said Joan suddenly, with a smile. "You think your sister's getting very old and very dull–that's it, isn't it?"

"I don't think anything of the kind," he said stoutly, but he flushed. "But you lead a dog's life, Joan. When you're not working in an office, you're worrying over the rest of us. And I'm not much good to you, I'm afraid."

Joan rose, and stood for a moment warming her hands, and, apparently, meditating as to whether she should say anything more or not. A feeling of great intimacy united the brother and sister, and the semicircular lines above their eyebrows disappeared. No, there was nothing more to be said on either side. Joan brushed her brother's head with her hand as she passed him, murmured good night, and left the room. For some minutes after she had gone Ralph lay quiescent, resting his head on his hand, but gradually his eyes filled with thought, and the line reappeared on his brow, as the pleasant impression of companionship and ancient sympathy waned, and he was left to think on alone.

After a time he opened his book, and read on steadily, glancing once or twice at his watch, as if he had set himself a task to be accomplished in a certain measure of time. Now and then he heard voices in the house, and the closing of bedroom doors, which showed that the building, at the top of which he sat, was inhabited in every one of its cells. When midnight struck, Ralph shut his book, and with a candle in his hand, descended to the ground floor, to ascertain that all lights were extinct and all doors locked. It was a threadbare, well-worn house that he thus examined, as if the inmates had grazed down all luxuriance and plenty to the verge of decency; and in the night, bereft of life, bare places and ancient blemishes were unpleasantly visible. Katharine Hilbery, he thought, would condemn it off-hand.

3

Denham had accused Katharine Hilbery of belonging to one of the most distinguished families in England, and if any one will take the trouble to consult Mr. Galton's "Hereditary Genius," he will find that this assertion is not far from the truth. The Alardyces, the Hilberys, the Millingtons, and the Otways seem to prove that intellect is a possession which can be tossed from one member of a certain group to another almost indefinitely, and with apparent certainty that the brilliant gift will be safely caught and held by nine out of ten of the privileged race. They had been conspicuous judges and admirals, lawyers and servants of the State for some years before the richness of the soil culminated in the rarest flower that any family can boast, a great writer, a poet eminent among the poets of England, a Richard Alardyce; and having produced him, they proved once more the amazing virtues of their race by proceeding unconcernedly again with their usual task of breeding distinguished men. They had sailed with Sir John Franklin to the North Pole, and ridden with Havelock to the Relief of Lucknow, and when they were not lighthouses firmly based on rock for the guidance of their generation, they were steady, serviceable candles, illuminating the ordinary chambers of daily life. Whatever profession you looked at, there was a Warburton or an Alardyce, a Millington or a Hilbery somewhere in authority and prominence.

It may be said, indeed, that English society being what it is, no very great merit is required, once you bear a well-known name, to put you into a position where it is easier on the whole to be eminent than obscure. And if this is true of the sons, even the daughters, even in the nineteenth century, are apt to become people of importance—philanthropists and educationalists if they are spinsters, and the wives of distinguished men if they marry. It is true that there were several lamentable exceptions to this rule in the Alardyce group, which seems to indicate that the cadets of such houses go more rapidly to the bad than the children of ordinary fathers and mothers, as if it were somehow a relief to them. But, on the whole, in these first years of the twentieth century, the Alardyces and their relations were keeping their heads well above water. One finds them at the tops of professions, with letters after their names; they sit in luxurious public offices, with private secretaries attached to them; they write solid books in dark covers, issued by the presses of the two great universities, and when one of them dies the chances are that another of them writes his biography.

Now the source of this nobility was, of course, the poet, and his immediate descendants, therefore, were invested with greater luster than the collateral branches. Mrs. Hilbery, in virtue of her position as the only child of the poet, was spiritually the head of the family, and Katharine, her daughter, had some superior rank among all the cousins and connections, the more so because she was an only child. The Alardyces had married and intermarried, and their offspring were generally profuse, and had a way of meeting regularly in each other's houses for meals and family celebrations which had acquired a semi-sacred character, and were as regularly observed as days of feasting and fasting in the Church.

In times gone by, Mrs. Hilbery had known all the poets, all the novelists, all the beautiful women and distinguished men of her time. These being now either dead or secluded in their infirm glory, she made her house a meeting-place for her own relations, to whom she would lament the passing of the great days of the nineteenth century, when every department of letters and art was represented in England by two or three illustrious names. Where are their successors? she would ask, and the absence of any poet or painter or novelist of the true caliber at the present day was a text upon which she liked to ruminate, in a sunset mood of benignant reminiscence, which it would have been hard to disturb had there been need. But she was far from visiting their inferiority upon the younger generation. She welcomed them very heartily to her house, told them her stories, gave them sovereigns and ices and good advice, and weaved round them romances which had generally no likeness to the truth.

The quality of her birth oozed into Katharine's consciousness from a dozen different sources as soon as she was able to perceive anything. Above her nursery fireplace hung a photograph of her grandfather's tomb in Poets' Corner, and she was told in one of those moments of grown-up confidence which are so tremendously impressive to the child's mind, that he was buried there because he was a "good and great man." Later, on an anniversary, she was taken by her mother through the fog in a hansom cab, and given a large bunch of bright, sweet-scented flowers to lay upon his tomb. The candles in the church, the singing and the booming of the organ, were all, she thought, in his honor. Again and again she was brought down into the drawing-room to receive the blessing of some awful distinguished old man, who sat, even to her childish eye, somewhat apart, all gathered together and clutching a stick, unlike an ordinary visitor in her father's own arm-chair, and her father himself was there, unlike himself, too, a little excited and very polite. These formidable old creatures used to take her in their arms, look very keenly in her eyes, and then to bless her, and tell her that she must mind and be a good girl, or detect a look in her face something like Richard's as a small boy. That drew down upon her her mother's fervent embrace, and she was sent back to the nursery very proud, and with a mysterious sense of an important and unexplained state of things, which time, by degrees, unveiled to her.

There were always visitors—uncles and aunts and cousins "from India," to be reverenced for their relationship alone, and others of the solitary and formidable class, whom she was enjoined by her parents to "remember all your life." By these means, and from hearing constant talk of great men and their works, her earliest conceptions of the world included an august circle of beings to whom she gave the names of Shakespeare, Milton, Wordsworth, Shelley, and so on, who were, for some reason, much more nearly akin to the Hilberys than to other people. They made a kind of boundary to her vision of life, and played a considerable part in determining her scale of good and bad in her own small affairs. Her descent from one of these gods was no surprise to her, but matter for satisfaction, until, as the years wore on, the privileges of her lot were taken for granted, and certain drawbacks made themselves very manifest. Perhaps it is a little depressing to inherit not lands but an example of intellectual and spiritual virtue; perhaps the conclusiveness of a great ancestor is a little discouraging to those who run the risk of comparison with him. It seems as if, having flowered so splendidly, nothing now remained possible but a steady growth of good, green stalk and leaf. For these reasons, and for others, Katharine had her moments of despondency. The glorious past, in which men and women grew to unexampled size, intruded too much upon the present, and dwarfed it too consistently, to be altogether encouraging to one forced to make her experiment in living when the great age was dead.

She was drawn to dwell upon these matters more than was natural, in the first place owing to her mother's absorption in them, and in the second because a great part of her time was spent in imagination with the dead, since she was helping her mother to produce a life of the great poet. When Katharine was seventeen or eighteen—that is to say, some ten years ago—her mother had enthusiastically announced that now, with a daughter to help her, the biography would soon be published. Notices to this effect found their way into the literary papers, and for some time Katharine worked with a sense of great pride and achievement.

Lately, however, it had seemed to her that they were making no way at all, and this was the more tantalizing because no one with the ghost of a literary temperament could doubt but that they had materials for one of the greatest biographies that has ever been written. Shelves and boxes bulged with the precious stuff. The most private lives of the most interesting people lay furled in yellow bundles of close-written manuscript. In addition to this Mrs. Hilbery had in her own head as bright a vision of that time as now remained to the living, and could give those flashes and thrills to the old words which gave them almost the substance of flesh. She had no difficulty in writing, and covered a page every morning as instinctively as a thrush sings, but nevertheless, with all this to urge and inspire, and the most devout intention to accomplish the work, the book still remained unwritten. Papers accumulated without much furthering their task, and in dull moments Katharine had her doubts whether they would ever produce anything at all fit to lay before the public. Where did the difficulty lie? Not in their materials, alas! nor in their ambitions, but in something more profound, in her own inaptitude, and above all, in her mother's temperament. Katharine would calculate that she had never known her write for more than ten minutes at a time. Ideas came to her chiefly when she was in motion. She liked to perambulate the room with a duster in her hand, with which she stopped to polish the backs of already lustrous books, musing and romancing as she did so. Suddenly the right phrase or the penetrating point of view would suggest itself, and she would drop her duster and write ecstatically for a few breathless moments; and then the mood would pass away, and the duster would be sought for, and the old books polished again. These spells of inspiration never burnt steadily, but flickered over the gigantic mass of the subject as capriciously as a will-o'-the-wisp, lighting now on this point, now on that. It was as much as Katharine could do to keep the pages of her mother's manuscript in order, but to sort them so that the sixteenth year of Richard Alardyce's life succeeded the fifteenth was beyond her skill. And yet they were so brilliant, these paragraphs, so nobly phrased, so lightning-like in their illumination, that the dead seemed to crowd the very room. Read continuously, they produced a sort of vertigo, and set her asking herself in despair what on earth she was to do with them? Her mother refused, also, to face the radical questions of what to leave in and what to leave out. She could not decide how far the public was to be told the truth about the poet's separation from his wife. She drafted passages to suit either case, and then liked each so well that she could not decide upon the rejection of either.

But the book must be written. It was a duty that they owed the world, and to Katharine, at least, it meant more than that, for if they could not between them get this one book accomplished they had no right to their privileged position. Their increment became yearly more and more unearned. Besides, it must be established indisputably that her grandfather was a very great man.

By the time she was twenty-seven, these thoughts had become very familiar to her. They trod their way through her mind as she sat opposite her mother of a morning at a table heaped with bundles of old letters and well supplied with pencils, scissors, bottles of gum, india-rubber bands, large envelopes, and other appliances for the manufacture of books. Shortly before Ralph Denham's visit, Katharine had resolved to try the effect of strict rules upon her mother's habits of literary composition. They were to be seated at their tables every morning at ten o'clock, with a clean-swept morning of empty, secluded hours before them. They were to keep their eyes fast upon the paper, and nothing was to tempt them to speech, save at the stroke of the hour when ten minutes for relaxation were to be allowed them. If these rules were observed for a year, she made out on a sheet of paper that the completion of the book was certain, and she laid her scheme before her mother with a feeling that much of the task was already accomplished. Mrs. Hilbery examined the sheet of paper very carefully. Then she clapped her hands and exclaimed enthusiastically:

"Well done, Katharine! What a wonderful head for business you've got! Now I shall keep this before me, and every day I shall make a little mark in my pocketbook, and on the last day of all—let me think, what shall we do to celebrate the last day of all? If it weren't the winter we could take a jaunt to Italy. They say Switzerland's very lovely in the snow, except for the cold. But, as you say, the great thing is to finish the book. Now let me see——"

When they inspected her manuscripts, which Katharine had put in order, they found a state of things well calculated to dash their spirits, if they had not just resolved on reform. They found, to begin with, a great variety of very imposing paragraphs with which the biography was to open; many of these, it is true, were unfinished, and resembled triumphal arches standing upon one leg, but, as Mrs. Hilbery observed, they could be patched up in ten minutes, if she gave her mind to it. Next, there was an account of the ancient home of the Alardyces, or rather, of spring in Suffolk, which was very beautifully written, although not essential to the story. However, Katharine had put together a string of names and dates, so that the poet was capably brought into the world, and his ninth year was reached without further mishap. After that, Mrs. Hilbery wished, for sentimental reasons, to introduce the recollections of a very fluent old lady, who had been brought up in the same village, but these Katharine decided must go. It might be advisable to introduce here a sketch of contemporary poetry contributed by Mr. Hilbery, and thus terse and learned and altogether out of keeping with the rest, but Mrs. Hilbery was of opinion that it was too bare, and made one feel altogether like a good little girl in a lecture-room, which was not at all in keeping with her father. It was put on one side. Now came the period of his early manhood, when various affairs of the heart must either be concealed or revealed; here again Mrs. Hilbery was of two minds, and a thick packet of manuscript was shelved for further consideration.

Several years were now altogether omitted, because Mrs. Hilbery had found something distasteful to her in that period, and had preferred to dwell upon her own recollections as a child. After this, it seemed to Katharine that the book became a wild dance of will-o'-the-wisps, without form or continuity, without coherence even, or any attempt to make a narrative. Here were twenty pages upon her grandfather's taste in hats, an essay upon contemporary china, a long account of a summer day's expedition into the country, when they had missed their train, together with fragmentary visions of all sorts of famous men and women, which seemed to be partly imaginary and partly authentic. There were, moreover, thousands of letters, and a mass of faithful recollections contributed by old friends, which had grown yellow now in their envelopes, but must be placed somewhere, or their feelings would be hurt. So many volumes had been written about the poet since his death that she had also to dispose of a great number of misstatements, which involved minute researches and much correspondence. Sometimes Katharine brooded, half crushed, among her papers; sometimes she felt that it was necessary for her very existence that she should free herself from the past; at others, that the past had completely displaced the present, which, when one resumed life after a morning among the dead, proved to be of an utterly thin and inferior composition.

The worst of it was that she had no aptitude for literature. She did not like phrases. She had even some natural antipathy to that process of self-examination, that perpetual effort to understand one's own feeling, and express it beautifully, fitly, or energetically in language, which constituted so great a part of her mother's existence. She was, on the contrary, inclined to be silent; she shrank from expressing herself even in talk, let alone in writing. As this disposition was highly convenient in a family much given to the manufacture of phrases, and seemed to argue a corresponding capacity for action, she was, from her childhood even, put in charge of household affairs. She had the reputation, which nothing in her manner contradicted, of being the most practical of people. Ordering meals, directing servants, paying bills, and so contriving that every clock ticked more or less accurately in time, and a number of vases were always full of fresh flowers was supposed to be a natural endowment of hers, and, indeed, Mrs. Hilbery often observed that it was poetry the wrong side out. From a very early age, too, she had to exert herself in another capacity; she had to counsel and help and generally sustain her mother. Mrs. Hilbery would have been perfectly well able to sustain herself if the world had been what the world is not. She was beautifully adapted for life in another planet. But the natural genius she had for conducting affairs there was of no real use to her here. Her watch, for example, was a constant source of surprise to her, and at the age of sixty-five she was still amazed at the ascendancy which rules and reasons exerted over the lives of other people. She had never learnt her lesson, and had constantly to be punished for her ignorance. But as that ignorance was combined with a fine natural insight which saw deep whenever it saw at all, it was not possible to write Mrs. Hilbery off among the dunces; on the contrary, she had a way of seeming the wisest person in the room. But, on the whole, she found it very necessary to seek support in her daughter.

Katharine, thus, was a member of a very great profession which has, as yet, no title and very little recognition, although the labor of mill and factory is, perhaps, no more severe and the results of less benefit to the world. She lived at home. She did it very well, too. Any one coming to the house in Cheyne Walk felt that here was an orderly place, shapely, controlled—a place where life had been trained to show to the best advantage, and, though composed of different elements, made to appear harmonious and with a character of its own. Perhaps it was the chief triumph of Katharine's art that Mrs. Hilbery's character predominated. She and Mr. Hilbery appeared to be a rich background for her mother's more striking qualities.

Silence being, thus, both natural to her and imposed upon her, the only other remark that her mother's friends were in the habit of making about it was that it was neither a stupid silence nor an indifferent silence. But to what quality it owed its character, since character of some sort it had, no one troubled themselves to inquire. It was understood that she was helping her mother to produce a great book. She was known to manage the household. She was certainly beautiful. That accounted for her satisfactorily. But it would have been a surprise, not only to other people but to Katharine herself, if some magic watch could have taken count of the moments spent in an entirely different occupation from her ostensible one. Sitting with faded papers before her, she took part in a series of scenes such as the taming of wild ponies upon the American prairies, or the conduct of a vast ship in a hurricane round a black promontory of rock, or in others more peaceful, but marked by her complete emancipation from her present surroundings and, needless to say, by her surpassing ability in her new vocation. When she was rid of the pretense of paper and pen, phrase-making and biography, she turned her attention in a more legitimate direction, though, strangely enough, she would rather have confessed her wildest dreams of hurricane and prairie than the fact that, upstairs, alone in her room, she rose early in the morning or sat up late at night to . . . work at mathematics. No force on earth would have made her confess that. Her actions when thus engaged were furtive and secretive, like those of some nocturnal animal. Steps had only to sound on the staircase, and she slipped her paper between the leaves of a great Greek dictionary which she had purloined from her father's room for this purpose. It was only at night, indeed, that she felt secure enough from surprise to concentrate her mind to the utmost.

Perhaps the unwomanly nature of the science made her instinctively wish to conceal her love of it. But the more profound reason was that in her mind mathematics were directly opposed to literature. She would not have cared to confess how infinitely she preferred the exactitude, the star-like impersonality, of figures to the confusion, agitation, and vagueness of the finest prose. There was something a little unseemly in thus opposing the tradition of her family; something that made her feel wrong-headed, and thus more than ever disposed to shut her desires away from view and cherish them with extraordinary fondness. Again and again she was thinking of some problem when she should have been thinking of her grandfather. Waking from these trances, she would see that her mother, too, had lapsed into some dream almost as visionary as her own, for the people who played their parts in it had long been numbered among the dead. But, seeing her own state mirrored in her mother's face, Katharine would shake herself awake with a sense of irritation. Her mother was the last person she wished to resemble, much though she admired her. Her common sense would assert itself almost brutally, and Mrs. Hilbery, looking at her with her odd sidelong glance, that was half malicious and half tender, would liken her to "your wicked old Uncle Judge Peter, who used to be heard delivering sentence of death in the bathroom. Thank Heaven, Katharine, I've not a drop of *him* in me!"

4

At about nine o'clock at night, on every alternate Wednesday, Miss Mary Datchet made the same resolve, that she would never again lend her rooms for any purposes whatsoever. Being, as they were, rather large and conveniently situated in a street mostly dedicated to offices off the Strand, people who wished to meet, either for purposes of enjoyment, or to discuss art, or to reform the State, had a way of suggesting that Mary had better be asked to lend them her rooms. She always met the request with the same frown of well-simulated annoyance, which presently dissolved in a kind of half-humorous, half-surly shrug, as of a large dog tormented by children who shakes his ears. She would lend her room, but only on condition that all the arrangements were made by her. This fortnightly meeting of a society for the free discussion of everything entailed a great deal of moving, and pulling, and ranging of furniture against the wall, and placing of breakable and precious things in safe places. Miss Datchet was quite capable of lifting a kitchen table on her back, if need were, for although well-proportioned and dressed becomingly, she had the appearance of unusual strength and determination.

She was some twenty-five years of age, but looked older because she earned, or intended to earn, her own living, and had already lost the look of the irresponsible spectator, and taken on that of the private in the army of workers. Her gestures seemed to have a certain purpose, the muscles round eyes and lips were set rather firmly, as though the senses had undergone some discipline, and were held ready for a call on them. She had contracted two faint lines between her eyebrows, not from anxiety but from thought, and it was quite evident that all the feminine instincts of pleasing, soothing, and charming were crossed by others in no way peculiar to her sex. For the rest she was brown-eyed, a little clumsy in movement, and suggested country birth and a descent from respectable hard-working ancestors, who had been men of faith and integrity rather than doubters or fanatics.

At the end of a fairly hard day's work it was certainly something of an effort to clear one's room, to pull the mattress off one's bed, and lay it on the floor, to fill a pitcher with cold coffee, and to sweep a long table clear for plates and cups and saucers, with pyramids of little pink biscuits between them; but when these alterations were effected, Mary felt a lightness of spirit come to her, as if she had put off the stout stuff of her working hours and slipped over her entire being some vesture of thin, bright silk. She knelt before the fire and looked out into the room. The light fell softly, but with clear radiance, through shades of yellow and blue paper, and the room, which was set with one or two sofas resembling grassy mounds in their lack of shape, looked unusually large and quiet. Mary was led to think of the heights of a Sussex down, and the swelling green circle of some camp of ancient warriors. The moonlight would be falling there so peacefully now, and she could fancy the rough pathway of silver upon the wrinkled skin of the sea.

"And here we are," she said, half aloud, half satirically, yet with evident pride, "talking about art."

She pulled a basket containing balls of differently colored wools and a pair of stockings which needed darning towards her, and began to set her fingers to work; while her mind, reflecting the lassitude of her body, went on perversely, conjuring up visions of solitude and quiet, and she pictured herself laying aside her knitting and walking out on to the down, and hearing nothing but the sheep cropping the grass close to the roots, while the shadows of the little trees moved very slightly this way and that in the moonlight, as the breeze went through them. But she was perfectly conscious of her present situation, and derived some pleasure from the reflection that she could rejoice equally in solitude, and in the presence of the many very different people who were now making their way, by divers paths, across London to the spot where she was sitting.

As she ran her needle in and out of the wool, she thought of the various stages in her own life which made her present position seem the culmination of successive miracles. She thought of her clerical father in his country parsonage, and of her mother's death, and of her own determination to obtain education, and of her college life, which had merged, not so very long ago, in the wonderful maze of London, which still seemed to her, in spite of her constitutional level-headedness, like a vast electric light, casting radiance upon the myriads of men and women who crowded round it. And here she was at the very center of it all, that center which was constantly in the minds of people in remote Canadian forests and on the plains of India, when their thoughts turned to England. The nine mellow strokes, by which she was now apprised of the hour, were a message from the great clock at Westminster itself. As the last of them died away, there was a firm knocking on her own door, and she rose and opened it. She returned to the room, with a look of steady pleasure in her eyes, and she was talking to Ralph Denham, who followed her.

"Alone?" he said, as if he were pleasantly surprised by that fact.

"I am sometimes alone," she replied.

"But you expect a great many people," he added, looking round him. "It's like a room on the stage. Who is it tonight?"

"William Rodney, upon the Elizabethan use of metaphor. I expect a good solid paper, with plenty of quotations from the classics."

Ralph warmed his hands at the fire, which was flapping bravely in the grate, while Mary took up her stocking again.

"I suppose you are the only woman in London who darns her own stockings," he observed.

"I'm only one of a great many thousands really," she replied, "though I must admit that I was thinking myself very remarkable when you came in. And now that you're here I don't think myself remarkable at all. How horrid of you! But I'm afraid you're much more remarkable than I am. You've done much more than I've done."

"If that's your standard, you've nothing to be proud of," said Ralph grimly.

"Well, I must reflect with Emerson that it's being and not doing that matters," she continued.

"Emerson?" Ralph exclaimed, with derision. "You don't mean to say you read Emerson?"

"Perhaps it wasn't Emerson; but why shouldn't I read Emerson?" she asked, with a tinge of anxiety.

"There's no reason that I know of. It's the combination that's odd—books and stockings. The combination is very odd." But it seemed to recommend itself to him. Mary gave a little laugh, expressive of happiness, and the particular stitches that she was now putting into her work appeared to her to be done with singular grace and felicity. She held out the stocking and looked at it approvingly.

"You always say that," she said. "I assure you it's a common 'combination,' as you call it, in the houses of the clergy. The only thing that's odd about me is that I enjoy them both—Emerson and the stocking."

A knock was heard, and Ralph exclaimed:

"Damn those people! I wish they weren't coming!"

"It's only Mr. Turner, on the floor below," said Mary, and she felt grateful to Mr. Turner for having alarmed Ralph, and for having given a false alarm.

"Will there be a crowd?" Ralph asked, after a pause.

"There'll be the Morrises and the Crashaws, and Dick Osborne, and Septimus, and all that set. Katharine Hilbery is coming, by the way, so William Rodney told me."

"Katharine Hilbery!" Ralph exclaimed.

"You know her?" Mary asked, with some surprise.

"I went to a tea-party at her house."

Mary pressed him to tell her all about it, and Ralph was not at all unwilling to exhibit proofs of the extent of his knowledge. He described the scene with certain additions and exaggerations which interested Mary very much.

"But, in spite of what you say, I do admire her," she said. "I've only seen her once or twice, but she seems to me to be what one calls a 'personality.'"

"I didn't mean to abuse her. I only felt that she wasn't very sympathetic to me."

"They say she's going to marry that queer creature Rodney."

"Marry Rodney? Then she must be more deluded than I thought her."

"Now that's my door, all right," Mary exclaimed, carefully putting her wools away, as a succession of knocks reverberated unnecessarily, accompanied by a sound of people stamping their feet and laughing. A moment later the room was full of young men and women, who came in with a peculiar look of expectation, exclaimed "Oh!" when they saw Denham, and then stood still, gaping rather foolishly.

The room very soon contained between twenty and thirty people, who found seats for the most part upon the floor, occupying the mattresses, and hunching themselves together into triangular shapes. They were all young and some of them seemed to make a protest by their hair and dress, and something somber and truculent in the expression of their faces, against the more normal type, who would have passed unnoticed in an omnibus or an underground railway. It was notable that the talk was confined to groups, and was, at first, entirely spasmodic in character, and muttered in undertones as if the speakers were suspicious of their fellow-guests.

Katharine Hilbery came in rather late, and took up a position on the floor, with her back against the wall. She looked round quickly, recognized about half a dozen people, to whom she nodded, but failed to see Ralph, or, if so, had already forgotten to attach any name to him. But in a second these heterogeneous elements were all united by the voice of Mr. Rodney, who suddenly strode up to the table, and began very rapidly in high-strained tones:

"In undertaking to speak of the Elizabethan use of metaphor in poetry——"

All the different heads swung slightly or steadied themselves into a position in which they could gaze straight at the speaker's face, and the same rather solemn expression was visible on all of them. But, at the same time, even the faces that were most exposed to view, and therefore most tautly under control, disclosed a sudden impulsive tremor which, unless directly checked, would have developed into an outburst of laughter. The first sight of Mr. Rodney was irresistibly ludicrous. He was very red in the face, whether from the cool November night or nervousness, and every movement, from the way he wrung his hands to the way he jerked his head to right and left, as though a vision drew him now to the door, now to the window, bespoke his horrible discomfort under the stare of so many eyes. He was scrupulously well dressed, and a pearl in the center of his tie seemed to give him a touch of aristocratic opulence. But the rather prominent eyes and the impulsive stammering manner, which seemed to indicate a torrent of ideas intermittently pressing for utterance and always checked in their course by a clutch of nervousness, drew no pity, as in the case of a more imposing personage, but a desire to laugh, which was, however, entirely lacking in malice. Mr. Rodney was evidently so painfully conscious of the oddity of his appearance, and his very redness and the starts to which his body was liable gave such proof of his own discomfort, that there was something endearing in this ridiculous susceptibility, although most people would probably have echoed Denham's private exclamation, "Fancy marrying a creature like that!"

His paper was carefully written out, but in spite of this precaution Mr. Rodney managed to turn over two sheets instead of one, to choose the wrong sentence where two were written together, and to discover his own handwriting suddenly illegible. When he found himself possessed of a coherent passage, he shook it at his audience almost aggressively, and then fumbled for another. After a distressing search a fresh discovery would be made, and produced in the same way, until, by means of repeated attacks, he had stirred his audience to a degree of animation quite remarkable in these gatherings. Whether they were stirred by his enthusiasm for poetry or by the contortions which a human being was going through for their benefit, it would be hard to say. At length Mr. Rodney sat down impulsively in the middle of a sentence, and, after a pause of bewilderment, the audience expressed its relief at being able to laugh aloud in a decided outburst of applause.

Mr. Rodney acknowledged this with a wild glance round him, and, instead of waiting to answer questions, he jumped up, thrust himself through the seated bodies into the corner where Katharine was sitting, and exclaimed, very audibly:

"Well, Katharine, I hope I've made a big enough fool of myself even for you! It was terrible! terrible! terrible!"

"Hush! You must answer their questions," Katharine whispered, desiring, at all costs, to keep him quiet. Oddly enough, when the speaker was no longer in front of them, there seemed to be much that was suggestive in what he had said. At any rate, a pale-faced young man with sad eyes was already on his feet, delivering an accurately worded speech with perfect composure. William Rodney listened with a curious lifting of his upper lip, although his face was still quivering slightly with emotion.

"Idiot!" he whispered. "He's misunderstood every word I said!"

"Well then, answer him," Katharine whispered back.

"No, I shan't! They'd only laugh at me. Why did I let you persuade me that these sort of people care for literature?" he continued.

There was much to be said both for and against Mr. Rodney's paper. It had been crammed with assertions that such-and-such passages, taken liberally from English, French, and Italian, are the supreme pearls of literature. Further, he was fond of using metaphors which, compounded in the study, were apt to sound either cramped or out of place as he delivered them in fragments. Literature was a fresh garland of spring flowers, he said, in which yew-berries and the purple nightshade mingled with the various tints of the anemone; and somehow or other this garland encircled marble brows. He had read very badly some very beautiful quotations. But through his manner and his confusion of language there had emerged some passion of feeling which, as he spoke, formed in the majority of the audience a little picture or an idea which each now was eager to give expression to. Most of the people there proposed to spend their lives in the practice either of writing or painting, and merely by looking at them it could be seen that, as they listened to Mr. Purvis first, and then to Mr. Greenhalgh, they were seeing something done by these gentlemen to a possession which they thought to be their own. One person after another rose, and, as with an ill-balanced axe, attempted to hew out his conception of art a little more clearly, and sat down with the feeling that, for some reason which he could not grasp, his strokes had gone awry. As they sat down they turned almost invariably to the person sitting next them, and rectified and continued what they had just said in public. Before long, therefore, the groups on the mattresses and the groups on the chairs were all in communication with each other, and Mary Datchet, who had begun to darn stockings again, stooped down and remarked to Ralph:

"That was what I call a first-rate paper."

Both of them instinctively turned their eyes in the direction of the reader of the paper. He was lying back against the wall, with his eyes apparently shut, and his chin sunk upon his collar. Katharine was turning over the pages of his manuscript as if she were looking for some passage that had particularly struck her, and had a difficulty in finding it.

"Let's go and tell him how much we liked it," said Mary, thus suggesting an action which Ralph was anxious to take, though without her he would have been too proud to do it, for he suspected that he had more interest in Katharine than she had in him.

"That was a very interesting paper," Mary began, without any shyness, seating herself on the floor opposite to Rodney and Katharine. "Will you lend me the manuscript to read in peace?"

Rodney, who had opened his eyes on their approach, regarded her for a moment in suspicious silence.

"Do you say that merely to disguise the fact of my ridiculous failure?" he asked.

Katharine looked up from her reading with a smile.

"He says he doesn't mind what we think of him," she remarked. "He says we don't care a rap for art of any kind."

"I asked her to pity me, and she teases me!" Rodney exclaimed.

"I don't intend to pity you, Mr. Rodney," Mary remarked, kindly, but firmly. "When a paper's a failure, nobody says anything, whereas now, just listen to them!"

The sound, which filled the room, with its hurry of short syllables, its sudden pauses, and its sudden attacks, might be compared to some animal hubbub, frantic and inarticulate.

"D'you think that's all about my paper?" Rodney inquired, after a moment's attention, with a distinct brightening of expression.

"Of course it is," said Mary. "It was a very suggestive paper."

She turned to Denham for confirmation, and he corroborated her.

"It's the ten minutes after a paper is read that proves whether it's been a success or not," he said. "If I were you, Rodney, I should be very pleased with myself."

This commendation seemed to comfort Mr. Rodney completely, and he began to bethink him of all the passages in his paper which deserved to be called "suggestive."

"Did you agree at all, Denham, with what I said about Shakespeare's later use of imagery? I'm afraid I didn't altogether make my meaning plain."

Here he gathered himself together, and by means of a series of frog-like jerks, succeeded in bringing himself close to Denham.

Denham answered him with the brevity which is the result of having another sentence in the mind to be addressed to another person. He wished to say to Katharine: "Did you remember to get that picture glazed before your aunt came to dinner?" but, besides having to answer Rodney, he was not sure that the remark, with its assertion of intimacy, would not strike Katharine as impertinent. She was listening to what some one in another group was saying. Rodney, meanwhile, was talking about the Elizabethan dramatists.

He was a curious-looking man since, upon first sight, especially if he chanced to be talking with animation, he appeared, in some way, ridiculous; but, next moment, in repose, his face, with its large nose, thin cheeks and lips expressing the utmost sensibility, somehow recalled a Roman head bound with laurel, cut upon a circle of semi-transparent reddish stone. It had dignity and character. By profession a clerk in a Government office, he was one of those martyred spirits to whom literature is at once a source of divine joy and of almost intolerable irritation. Not content to rest in their love of it, they must attempt to practise it themselves, and they are generally endowed with very little facility in composition. They condemn whatever they produce. Moreover, the violence of their feelings is such that they seldom meet with adequate sympathy, and being rendered very sensitive by their cultivated perceptions, suffer constant slights both to their own persons and to the thing they worship. But Rodney could never resist making trial of the sympathies of any one who seemed favorably disposed, and Denham's praise had stimulated his very susceptible vanity.

"You remember the passage just before the death of the Duchess?" he continued, edging still closer to Denham, and adjusting his elbow and knee in an incredibly angular combination. Here, Katharine, who had been cut off by these maneuvers from all communication with the outer world, rose, and seated herself upon the window-sill, where she was joined by Mary Datchet. The two young women could thus survey the whole party. Denham looked after them, and made as if he were tearing handfuls of grass up by the roots from the carpet. But as it fell in accurately with his conception of life that all one's desires were bound to be frustrated, he concentrated his mind upon literature, and determined, philosophically, to get what he could out of that.

Katharine was pleasantly excited. A variety of courses was open to her. She knew several people slightly, and at any moment one of them might rise from the floor and come and speak to her; on the other hand, she might select somebody for herself, or she might strike into Rodney's discourse, to which she was intermittently attentive. She was conscious of Mary's body beside her, but, at the same time, the consciousness of being both of them women made it unnecessary to speak to her. But Mary, feeling, as she had said, that Katharine was a "personality," wished so much to speak to her that in a few moments she did.

"They're exactly like a flock of sheep, aren't they?" she said, referring to the noise that rose from the scattered bodies beneath her.

Katharine turned and smiled.

"I wonder what they're making such a noise about?" she said.

"The Elizabethans, I suppose."

"No, I don't think it's got anything to do with the Elizabethans. There! Didn't you hear them say, 'Insurance Bill'?"

"I wonder why men always talk about politics?" Mary speculated. "I suppose, if we had votes, we should, too."

"I dare say we should. And you spend your life in getting us votes, don't you?"

"I do," said Mary, stoutly. "From ten to six every day I'm at it."

Katharine looked at Ralph Denham, who was now pounding his way through the metaphysics of metaphor with Rodney, and was reminded of his talk that Sunday afternoon. She connected him vaguely with Mary.

"I suppose you're one of the people who think we should all have professions," she said, rather distantly, as if feeling her way among the phantoms of an unknown world.

"Oh dear no," said Mary at once.

"Well, I think I do," Katharine continued, with half a sigh. "You will always be able to say that you've done something, whereas, in a crowd like this, I feel rather melancholy."

"In a crowd? Why in a crowd?" Mary asked, deepening the two lines between her eyes, and hoisting herself nearer to Katharine upon the window-sill.

"Don't you see how many different things these people care about? And I want to beat them down—I only mean," she corrected herself, "that I want to assert myself, and it's difficult, if one hasn't a profession."

Mary smiled, thinking that to beat people down was a process that should present no difficulty to Miss Katharine Hilbery. They knew each other so slightly that the beginning of intimacy, which Katharine seemed to initiate by talking about herself, had something solemn in it, and they were silent, as if to decide whether to proceed or not. They tested the ground.

"Ah, but I want to trample upon their prostrate bodies!" Katharine announced, a moment later, with a laugh, as if at the train of thought which had led her to this conclusion.

"One doesn't necessarily trample upon people's bodies because one runs an office," Mary remarked.

"No. Perhaps not," Katharine replied. The conversation lapsed, and Mary saw Katharine looking out into the room rather moodily with closed lips, the desire to talk about herself or to initiate a friendship having, apparently, left her. Mary was struck by her capacity for being thus easily silent, and occupied with her own thoughts. It was a habit that spoke of loneliness and a mind thinking for itself. When Katharine remained silent Mary was slightly embarrassed.

"Yes, they're very like sheep," she repeated, foolishly.

"And yet they are very clever—at least," Katharine added, "I suppose they have all read Webster."

"Surely you don't think that a proof of cleverness? I've read Webster, I've read Ben Jonson, but I don't think myself clever—not exactly, at least."

"I think you must be very clever," Katharine observed.

"Why? Because I run an office?"

"I wasn't thinking of that. I was thinking how you live alone in this room, and have parties."

Mary reflected for a second.

"It means, chiefly, a power of being disagreeable to one's own family, I think. I have that, perhaps. I didn't want to live at home, and I told my father. He didn't like it. . . . But then I have a sister, and you haven't, have you?"

"No, I haven't any sisters."

"You are writing a life of your grandfather?" Mary pursued.

Katharine seemed instantly to be confronted by some familiar thought from which she wished to escape. She replied, "Yes, I am helping my mother," in such a way that Mary felt herself baffled, and put back again into the position in which she had been at the beginning of their talk. It seemed to her that Katharine possessed a curious power of drawing near and receding, which sent alternate emotions through her far more quickly than was usual, and kept her in a condition of curious alertness. Desiring to classify her, Mary bethought her of the convenient term "egoist."

"She's an egoist," she said to herself, and stored that word up to give to Ralph one day when, as it would certainly fall out, they were discussing Miss Hilbery.

"Heavens, what a mess there'll be tomorrow morning!" Katharine exclaimed. "I hope you don't sleep in this room, Miss Datchet?"

Mary laughed.

"What are you laughing at?" Katharine demanded.

"I won't tell you."

"Let me guess. You were laughing because you thought I'd changed the conversation?"

"No."

"Because you think—" She paused.

"If you want to know, I was laughing at the way you said Miss Datchet."

"Mary, then. Mary, Mary, Mary."

So saying, Katharine drew back the curtain in order, perhaps, to conceal the momentary flush of pleasure which is caused by coming perceptibly nearer to another person.

"Mary Datchet," said Mary. "It's not such an imposing name as Katharine Hilbery, I'm afraid."

They both looked out of the window, first up at the hard silver moon, stationary among a hurry of little grey-blue clouds, and then down upon the roofs of London, with all their upright chimneys, and then below them at the empty moonlit pavement of the street, upon which the joint of each paving-stone was clearly marked out. Mary then saw Katharine raise her eyes again to the moon, with a contemplative look in them, as though she were setting that moon against the moon of other nights, held in memory. Some one in the room behind them made a joke about stargazing, which destroyed their pleasure in it, and they looked back into the room again.

Ralph had been watching for this moment, and he instantly produced his sentence.

"I wonder, Miss Hilbery, whether you remembered to get that picture glazed?" His voice showed that the question was one that had been prepared.

"Oh, you idiot!" Mary exclaimed, very nearly aloud, with a sense that Ralph had said something very stupid. So, after three lessons in Latin grammar, one might correct a fellow student, whose knowledge did not embrace the ablative of "mensa."

"Picture—what picture?" Katharine asked. "Oh, at home, you mean—that Sunday afternoon. Was it the day Mr. Fortescue came? Yes, I think I remembered it."

The three of them stood for a moment awkwardly silent, and then Mary left them in order to see that the great pitcher of coffee was properly handled, for beneath all her education she preserved the anxieties of one who owns china.

Ralph could think of nothing further to say; but could one have stripped off his mask of flesh, one would have seen that his will-power was rigidly set upon a single object—that Miss Hilbery should obey him. He wished her to stay there until, by some measures not yet apparent to him, he had conquered her interest. These states of mind transmit themselves very often without the use of language, and it was evident to Katharine that this young man had fixed his mind upon her. She instantly recalled her first impressions of him, and saw herself again proffering family relics. She reverted to the state of mind in which he had left her that Sunday afternoon. She supposed that he judged her very severely. She argued naturally that, if this were the case, the burden of the conversation should rest with him. But she submitted so far as to stand perfectly still, her eyes upon the opposite wall, and her lips very nearly closed, though the desire to laugh stirred them slightly.

"You know the names of the stars, I suppose?" Denham remarked, and from the tone of his voice one might have thought that he grudged Katharine the knowledge he attributed to her.

She kept her voice steady with some difficulty.

"I know how to find the Pole star if I'm lost."

"I don't suppose that often happens to you."

"No. Nothing interesting ever happens to me," she said.

"I think you make a system of saying disagreeable things, Miss Hilbery," he broke out, again going further than he meant to. "I suppose it's one of the characteristics of your class. They never talk seriously to their inferiors."

Whether it was that they were meeting on neutral ground tonight, or whether the carelessness of an old grey coat that Denham wore gave an ease to his bearing that he lacked in conventional dress, Katharine certainly felt no impulse to consider him outside the particular set in which she lived.

"In what sense are you my inferior?" she asked, looking at him gravely, as though honestly searching for his meaning. The look gave him great pleasure. For the first time he felt himself on perfectly equal terms with a woman whom he wished to think well of him, although he could not have explained why her opinion of him mattered one way or another. Perhaps, after all, he only wanted to have something of her to take home to think about. But he was not destined to profit by his advantage.

"I don't think I understand what you mean," Katharine repeated, and then she was obliged to stop and answer some one who wished to know whether she would buy a ticket for an opera from them, at a reduction. Indeed, the temper of the meeting was now unfavorable to separate conversation; it had become rather debauched and hilarious, and people who scarcely knew each other were making use of Christian names with apparent cordiality, and had reached that kind of gay tolerance and general friendliness which human beings in England only attain after sitting together for three hours or so, and the first cold blast in the air of the street freezes them into isolation once more. Cloaks were being flung round the shoulders, hats swiftly pinned to the head; and Denham had the mortification of seeing Katharine helped to prepare herself by the ridiculous Rodney. It was not the convention of the meeting to say good-bye, or necessarily even to nod to the person with whom one was talking; but, nevertheless, Denham was disappointed by the completeness with which Katharine parted from him, without any attempt to finish her sentence. She left with Rodney.

5

Denham had no conscious intention of following Katharine, but, seeing her depart, he took his hat and ran rather more quickly down the stairs than he would have done if Katharine had not been in front of him. He overtook a friend of his, by name Harry Sandys, who was going the same way, and they walked together a few paces behind Katharine and Rodney.

The night was very still, and on such nights, when the traffic thins away, the walker becomes conscious of the moon in the street, as if the curtains of the sky had been drawn apart, and the heaven lay bare, as it does in the country. The air was softly cool, so that people who had been sitting talking in a crowd found it pleasant to walk a little before deciding to stop an omnibus or encounter light again in an underground railway. Sandys, who was a barrister with a philosophic tendency, took out his pipe, lit it, murmured "hum" and "ha," and was silent. The couple in front of them kept their distance accurately, and appeared, so far as Denham could judge by the way they turned towards each other, to be talking very constantly. He observed that when a pedestrian going the opposite way forced them to part they came together again directly afterwards. Without intending to watch them he never quite lost sight of the yellow scarf twisted round Katharine's head, or the light overcoat which made Rodney look fashionable among the crowd. At the Strand he supposed that they would separate, but instead they crossed the road, and took their way down one of the narrow passages which lead through ancient courts to the river. Among the crowd of people in the big thoroughfares Rodney seemed merely to be lending Katharine his escort, but now, when passengers were rare and the footsteps of the couple were distinctly heard in the silence, Denham could not help picturing to himself some change in their conversation. The effect of the light and shadow, which seemed to increase their height, was to make them mysterious and significant, so that Denham had no feeling of irritation with Katharine, but rather a half-dreamy acquiescence in the course of the world. Yes, she did very well to dream about—but Sandys had suddenly begun to talk. He was a solitary man who had made his friends at college and always addressed them as if they were still undergraduates arguing in his room, though many months or even years had passed in some cases between the last sentence and the present one. The method was a little singular, but very restful, for it seemed to ignore completely all accidents of human life, and to span very deep abysses with a few simple words.

On this occasion he began, while they waited for a minute on the edge of the Strand:

"I hear that Bennett has given up his theory of truth."

Denham returned a suitable answer, and he proceeded to explain how this decision had been arrived at, and what changes it involved in the philosophy which they both accepted. Meanwhile Katharine and Rodney drew further ahead, and Denham kept, if that is the right expression for an involuntary action, one filament of his mind upon them, while with the rest of his intelligence he sought to understand what Sandys was saying.

As they passed through the courts thus talking, Sandys laid the tip of his stick upon one of the stones forming a time-worn arch, and struck it meditatively two or three times in order to illustrate something very obscure about the complex nature of one's apprehension of facts. During the pause which this necessitated, Katharine and Rodney turned the corner and disappeared. For a moment Denham stopped involuntarily in his sentence, and continued it with a sense of having lost something.

Unconscious that they were observed, Katharine and Rodney had come out on the Embankment. When they had crossed the road, Rodney slapped his hand upon the stone parapet above the river and exclaimed:

"I promise I won't say another word about it, Katharine! But do stop a minute and look at the moon upon the water."

Katharine paused, looked up and down the river, and snuffed the air.

"I'm sure one can smell the sea, with the wind blowing this way," she said.

They stood silent for a few moments while the river shifted in its bed, and the silver and red lights which were laid upon it were torn by the current and joined together again. Very far off up the river a steamer hooted with its hollow voice of unspeakable melancholy, as if from the heart of lonely mist-shrouded voyagings.

"Ah!" Rodney cried, striking his hand once more upon the balustrade, "why can't one say how beautiful it all is? Why am I condemned for ever, Katharine, to feel what I can't express? And the things I can give there's no use in my giving. Trust me, Katharine," he added hastily, "I won't speak of it again. But in the presence of beauty–look at the iridescence round the moon!–one feels–one feels–Perhaps if you married me–I'm half a poet, you see, and I can't pretend not to feel what I do feel. If I could write–ah, that would be another matter. I shouldn't bother you to marry me then, Katharine."

He spoke these disconnected sentences rather abruptly, with his eyes alternately upon the moon and upon the stream.

"But for me I suppose you would recommend marriage?" said Katharine, with her eyes fixed on the moon.

"Certainly I should. Not for you only, but for all women. Why, you're nothing at all without it; you're only half alive; using only half your faculties; you must feel that for yourself. That is why——" Here he stopped himself, and they began to walk slowly along the Embankment, the moon fronting them.

> With how sad steps she climbs the sky,
> How silently and with how wan a face,

Rodney quoted.

"I've been told a great many unpleasant things about myself tonight," Katharine stated, without attending to him. "Mr. Denham seems to think it his mission to lecture me, though I hardly know him. By the way, William, you know him; tell me, what is he like?"

William drew a deep sigh.

"We may lecture you till we're blue in the face——"

"Yes–but what's he like?"

"And we write sonnets to your eyebrows, you cruel practical creature. Denham?" he added, as Katharine remained silent. "A good fellow, I should think. He cares, naturally, for the right sort of things, I expect. But you mustn't marry him, though. He scolded you, did he—what did he say?"

"What happens with Mr. Denham is this: He comes to tea. I do all I can to put him at his ease. He merely sits and scowls at me. Then I show him our manuscripts. At this he becomes really angry, and tells me I've no business to call myself a middle-class woman. So we part in a huff; and next time we meet, which was tonight, he walks straight up to me, and says, 'Go to the Devil!' That's the sort of behavior my mother complains of. I want to know, what does it mean?"

She paused and, slackening her steps, looked at the lighted train drawing itself smoothly over Hungerford Bridge.

"It means, I should say, that he finds you chilly and unsympathetic."

Katharine laughed with round, separate notes of genuine amusement.

"It's time I jumped into a cab and hid myself in my own house," she exclaimed.

"Would your mother object to my being seen with you? No one could possibly recognize us, could they?" Rodney inquired, with some solicitude.

Katharine looked at him, and perceiving that his solicitude was genuine, she laughed again, but with an ironical note in her laughter.

"You may laugh, Katharine, but I can tell you that if any of your friends saw us together at this time of night they would talk about it, and I should find that very disagreeable. But why do you laugh?"

"I don't know. Because you're such a queer mixture, I think. You're half poet and half old maid."

"I know I always seem to you highly ridiculous. But I can't help having inherited certain traditions and trying to put them into practice."

"Nonsense, William. You may come of the oldest family in Devonshire, but that's no reason why you should mind being seen alone with me on the Embankment."

"I'm ten years older than you are, Katharine, and I know more of the world than you do."

"Very well. Leave me and go home."

Rodney looked back over his shoulder and perceived that they were being followed at a short distance by a taxicab, which evidently awaited his summons. Katharine saw it, too, and exclaimed:

"Don't call that cab for me, William. I shall walk."

"Nonsense, Katharine; you'll do nothing of the kind. It's nearly twelve o'clock, and we've walked too far as it is."

Katharine laughed and walked on so quickly that both Rodney and the taxicab had to increase their pace to keep up with her.

"Now, William," she said, "if people see me racing along the Embankment like this they *will* talk. You had far better say good-night, if you don't want people to talk."

At this William beckoned, with a despotic gesture, to the cab with one hand, and with the other he brought Katharine to a standstill.

"Don't let the man see us struggling, for God's sake!" he murmured. Katharine stood for a moment quite still.

"There's more of the old maid in you than the poet," she observed briefly.

William shut the door sharply, gave the address to the driver, and turned away, lifting his hat punctiliously high in farewell to the invisible lady.

He looked back after the cab twice, suspiciously, half expecting that she would stop it and dismount; but it bore her swiftly on, and was soon out of sight. William felt in the mood for a short soliloquy of indignation, for Katharine had contrived to exasperate him in more ways than one.

"Of all the unreasonable, inconsiderate creatures I've ever known, she's the worst!" he exclaimed to himself, striding back along the Embankment. "Heaven forbid that I should ever make a fool of myself with her again. Why, I'd sooner marry the daughter of my landlady than Katharine Hilbery! She'd leave me not a moment's peace—and she'd never understand me—never, never, never!"

Uttered aloud and with vehemence so that the stars of Heaven might hear, for there was no human being at hand, these sentiments sounded satisfactorily irrefutable. Rodney quieted down, and walked on in silence, until he perceived some one approaching him, who had something, either in his walk or his dress, which proclaimed that he was one of William's acquaintances before it was possible to tell which of them he was. It was Denham who, having parted from Sandys at the bottom of his staircase, was now walking to the Tube at Charing Cross, deep in the thoughts which his talk with Sandys had suggested. He had forgotten the meeting at Mary Datchet's rooms, he had forgotten Rodney, and metaphors and Elizabethan drama, and could have sworn that he had forgotten Katharine Hilbery, too, although that was more disputable. His mind was scaling the highest pinnacles of its alps, where there was only starlight and the untrodden snow. He cast strange eyes upon Rodney, as they encountered each other beneath a lamp-post.

"Ha!" Rodney exclaimed.

If he had been in full possession of his mind, Denham would probably have passed on with a salutation. But the shock of the interruption made him stand still, and before he knew what he was doing, he had turned and was walking with Rodney in obedience to Rodney's invitation to come to his rooms and have something to drink. Denham had no wish to drink with Rodney, but he followed him passively enough. Rodney was gratified by this obedience. He felt inclined to be communicative with this silent man, who possessed so obviously all the good masculine qualities in which Katharine now seemed lamentably deficient.

"You do well, Denham," he began impulsively, "to have nothing to do with young women. I offer you my experience—if one trusts them one invariably has cause to repent. Not that I have any reason at this moment," he added hastily, "to complain of them. It's a subject that crops up now and again for no particular reason. Miss Datchet, I dare say, is one of the exceptions. Do you like Miss Datchet?"

These remarks indicated clearly enough that Rodney's nerves were in a state of irritation, and Denham speedily woke to the situation of the world as it had been one hour ago. He had last seen Rodney walking with Katharine. He could not help regretting the eagerness with which his mind returned to these interests, and fretted him with the old trivial anxieties. He sank in his own esteem. Reason bade him break from Rodney, who clearly tended to become confidential, before he had utterly lost touch with the problems of high philosophy. He looked along the road, and marked a lamp-post at a distance of some hundred yards, and decided that he would part from Rodney when they reached this point.

"Yes, I like Mary; I don't see how one could help liking her," he remarked cautiously, with his eye on the lamp-post.

"Ah, Denham, you're so different from me. You never give yourself away. I watched you this evening with Katharine Hilbery. My instinct is to trust the person I'm talking to. That's why I'm always being taken in, I suppose."

Denham seemed to be pondering this statement of Rodney's, but, as a matter of fact, he was hardly conscious of Rodney and his revelations, and was only concerned to make him mention Katharine again before they reached the lamp-post.

"Who's taken you in now?" he asked. "Katharine Hilbery?"

Rodney stopped and once more began beating a kind of rhythm, as if he were marking a phrase in a symphony, upon the smooth stone balustrade of the Embankment.

"Katharine Hilbery," he repeated, with a curious little chuckle. "No, Denham, I have no illusions about that young woman. I think I made that plain to her tonight. But don't run away with a false impression," he continued eagerly, turning and linking his arm through Denham's, as though to prevent him from escaping; and, thus compelled, Denham passed the monitory lamp-post, to which, in passing, he breathed an excuse, for how could he break away when Rodney's arm was actually linked in his? "You must not think that I have any bitterness against her—far from it. It's not altogether her fault, poor girl. She lives, you know, one of those odious, self-centered lives—at least, I think them odious for a woman—feeding her wits upon everything, having control of everything, getting far too much her own way at home—spoilt, in a sense, feeling that every one is at her feet, and so not realizing how she hurts—that is, how rudely she behaves to people who haven't all her advantages. Still, to do her justice, she's no fool," he added, as if to warn Denham not to take any liberties. "She has taste. She has sense. She can understand you when you talk to her. But she's a woman, and there's an end of it," he added, with another little chuckle, and dropped Denham's arm.

"And did you tell her all this tonight?" Denham asked.

"Oh dear me, no. I should never think of telling Katharine the truth about herself. That wouldn't do at all. One has to be in an attitude of adoration in order to get on with Katharine.

"Now I've learnt that she's refused to marry him why don't I go home?" Denham thought to himself. But he went on walking beside Rodney, and for a time they did not speak, though Rodney hummed snatches of a tune out of an opera by Mozart. A feeling of contempt and liking combine very naturally in the mind of one to whom another has just spoken unpremeditatedly, revealing rather more of his private feelings than he intended to reveal. Denham began to wonder what sort of person Rodney was, and at the same time Rodney began to think about Denham.

"You're a slave like me, I suppose?" he asked.

"A solicitor, yes."

"I sometimes wonder why we don't chuck it. Why don't you emigrate, Denham? I should have thought that would suit you."

"I've a family."

"I'm often on the point of going myself. And then I know I couldn't live without this"—and he waved his hand towards the City of London, which wore, at this moment, the appearance of a town cut out of gray-blue cardboard, and pasted flat against the sky, which was of a deeper blue.

"There are one or two people I'm fond of, and there's a little good music, and a few pictures, now and then—just enough to keep one dangling about here. Ah, but I couldn't live with savages! Are you fond of books? Music? Pictures? D'you care at all for first editions? I've got a few nice things up here, things I pick up cheap, for I can't afford to give what they ask."

They had reached a small court of high eighteenth-century houses, in one of which Rodney had his rooms. They climbed a very steep staircase, through whose uncurtained windows the moonlight fell, illuminating the banisters with their twisted pillars, and the piles of plates set on the window-sills, and jars half-full of milk. Rodney's rooms were small, but the sitting-room window looked out into a courtyard, with its flagged pavement, and its single tree, and across to the flat red-brick fronts of the opposite houses, which would not have surprised Dr. Johnson, if he had come out of his grave for a turn in the moonlight. Rodney lit his lamp, pulled his curtains, offered Denham a chair, and, flinging the manuscript of his paper on the Elizabethan use of Metaphor on to the table, exclaimed:

"Oh dear me, what a waste of time! But it's over now, and so we may think no more about it."

He then busied himself very dexterously in lighting a fire, producing glasses, whisky, a cake, and cups and saucers. He put on a faded crimson dressing-gown, and a pair of red slippers, and advanced to Denham with a tumbler in one hand and a well-burnished book in the other.

"The Baskerville Congreve," said Rodney, offering it to his guest. "I couldn't read him in a cheap edition."

When he was seen thus among his books and his valuables, amiably anxious to make his visitor comfortable, and moving about with something of the dexterity and grace of a Persian cat, Denham relaxed his critical attitude, and felt more at home with Rodney than he would have done with many men better known to him. Rodney's room was the room of a person who cherishes a great many personal tastes, guarding them from the rough blasts of the public with scrupulous attention. His papers and his books rose in jagged mounds on table and floor, round which he skirted with nervous care lest his dressing-gown might disarrange them ever so slightly. On a chair stood a stack of photographs of statues and pictures, which it was his habit to exhibit, one by one, for the space of a day or two. The books on his shelves were as orderly as regiments of soldiers, and the backs of them shone like so many bronze beetle-wings; though, if you took one from its place you saw a shabbier volume behind it, since space was limited. An oval Venetian mirror stood above the fireplace, and reflected duskily in its spotted depths the faint yellow and crimson of a jarful of tulips which stood among the letters and pipes and cigarettes upon the mantelpiece. A small piano occupied a corner of the room, with the score of "Don Giovanni" open upon the bracket.

"Well, Rodney," said Denham, as he filled his pipe and looked about him, "this is all very nice and comfortable."

Rodney turned his head half round and smiled, with the pride of a proprietor, and then prevented himself from smiling.

"Tolerable," he muttered.

"But I dare say it's just as well that you have to earn your own living."

"If you mean that I shouldn't do anything good with leisure if I had it, I dare say you're right. But I should be ten times as happy with my whole day to spend as I liked."

"I doubt that," Denham replied.

They sat silent, and the smoke from their pipes joined amicably in a blue vapor above their heads.

"I could spend three hours every day reading Shakespeare," Rodney remarked. "And there's music and pictures, let alone the society of the people one likes."

"You'd be bored to death in a year's time."

"Oh, I grant you I should be bored if I did nothing. But I should write plays."

"H'm!"

"I should write plays," he repeated. "I've written three-quarters of one already, and I'm only waiting for a holiday to finish it. And it's not bad—no, some of it's really rather nice."

The question arose in Denham's mind whether he should ask to see this play, as, no doubt, he was expected to do. He looked rather stealthily at Rodney, who was tapping the coal nervously with a poker, and quivering almost physically, so Denham thought, with desire to talk about this play of his, and vanity unrequited and urgent. He seemed very much at Denham's mercy, and Denham could not help liking him, partly on that account.

"Well, . . . will you let me see the play?" Denham asked, and Rodney looked immediately appeased, but, nevertheless, he sat silent for a moment, holding the poker perfectly upright in the air, regarding it with his rather prominent eyes, and opening his lips and shutting them again.

"Do you really care for this kind of thing?" he asked at length, in a different tone of voice from that in which he had been speaking. And, without waiting for an answer, he went on, rather querulously: "Very few people care for poetry. I dare say it bores you."

"Perhaps," Denham remarked.

"Well, I'll lend it you," Rodney announced, putting down the poker.

As he moved to fetch the play, Denham stretched a hand to the bookcase beside him, and took down the first volume which his fingers touched. It happened to be a small and very lovely edition of Sir Thomas Browne, containing the "Urn Burial," the "Hydriotaphia," and the "Garden of Cyrus," and, opening it at a passage which he knew very nearly by heart, Denham began to read and, for some time, continued to read.

Rodney resumed his seat, with his manuscript on his knee, and from time to time he glanced at Denham, and then joined his finger-tips and crossed his thin legs over the fender, as if he experienced a good deal of pleasure. At length Denham shut the book, and stood, with his back to the fireplace, occasionally making an inarticulate humming sound which seemed to refer to Sir Thomas Browne. He put his hat on his head, and stood over Rodney, who still lay stretched back in his chair, with his toes within the fender.

"I shall look in again some time," Denham remarked, upon which Rodney held up his hand, containing his manuscript, without saying anything except—"If you like."

Denham took the manuscript and went. Two days later he was much surprised to find a thin parcel on his breakfastplate, which, on being opened, revealed the very copy of Sir Thomas Browne which he had studied so intently in Rodney's rooms. From sheer laziness he returned no thanks, but he thought of Rodney from time to time with interest, disconnecting him from Katharine, and meant to go round one evening and smoke a pipe with him. It pleased Rodney thus to give away whatever his friends genuinely admired. His library was constantly being diminished.

6

Of all the hours of an ordinary working week-day, which are the pleasantest to look forward to and to look back upon? If a single instance is of use in framing a theory, it may be said that the minutes between nine-twenty-five and nine-thirty in the morning had a singular charm for Mary Datchet. She spent them in a very enviable frame of mind; her contentment was almost unalloyed. High in the air as her flat was, some beams from the morning sun reached her even in November, striking straight at curtain, chair, and carpet, and painting there three bright, true spaces of green, blue, and purple, upon which the eye rested with a pleasure which gave physical warmth to the body.

There were few mornings when Mary did not look up, as she bent to lace her boots, and as she followed the yellow rod from curtain to breakfast-table she usually breathed some sigh of thankfulness that her life provided her with such moments of pure enjoyment. She was robbing no one of anything, and yet, to get so much pleasure from simple things, such as eating one's breakfast alone in a room which had nice colors in it, clean from the skirting of the boards to the corners of the ceiling, seemed to suit her so thoroughly that she used at first to hunt about for some one to apologize to, or for some flaw in the situation. She had now been six months in London, and she could find no flaw, but that, as she invariably concluded by the time her boots were laced, was solely and entirely due to the fact that she had her work. Every day, as she stood with her dispatch-box in her hand at the door of her flat, and gave one look back into the room to see that everything was straight before she left, she said to herself that she was very glad that she was going to leave it all, that to have sat there all day long, in the enjoyment of leisure, would have been intolerable.

Out in the street she liked to think herself one of the workers who, at this hour, take their way in rapid single file along all the broad pavements of the city, with their heads slightly lowered, as if all their effort were to follow each other as closely as might be; so that Mary used to figure to herself a straight rabbit-run worn by their unswerving feet upon the pavement. But she liked to pretend that she was indistinguishable from the rest, and that when a wet day drove her to the Underground or omnibus, she gave and took her share of crowd and wet with clerks and typists and commercial men, and shared with them the serious business of winding-up the world to tick for another four-and-twenty hours.

Thus thinking, on the particular morning in question, she made her away across Lincoln's Inn Fields and up Kingsway, and so through Southampton Row until she reached her office in Russell Square. Now and then she would pause and look into the window of some bookseller or flower shop, where, at this early hour, the goods were being arranged, and empty gaps behind the plate glass revealed a state of undress. Mary felt kindly disposed towards the shopkeepers, and hoped that they would trick the midday public into purchasing, for at this hour of the morning she ranged herself entirely on the side of the shopkeepers and bank clerks, and regarded all who slept late and had money to spend as her enemy and natural prey. And directly she had crossed the road at Holborn, her thoughts all came naturally and regularly to roost upon her work, and she forgot that she was, properly speaking, an amateur worker, whose services were unpaid, and could hardly be said to wind the world up for its daily task, since the world, so far, had shown very little desire to take the boons which Mary's society for woman's suffrage had offered it.

She was thinking all the way up Southampton Row of notepaper and foolscap, and how an economy in the use of paper might be effected (without, of course, hurting Mrs. Seal's feelings), for she was certain that the great organizers always pounce, to begin with, upon trifles like these, and build up their triumphant reforms upon a basis of absolute solidity; and, without acknowledging it for a moment, Mary Datchet was determined to be a great organizer, and had already doomed her society to reconstruction of the most radical kind. Once or twice lately, it is true, she had started, broad awake, before turning into Russell Square, and denounced herself rather sharply for being already in a groove, capable, that is, of thinking the same thoughts every morning at the same hour, so that the chestnut-colored brick of the Russell Square houses had some curious connection with her thoughts about office economy, and served also as a sign that she should get into trim for meeting Mr. Clacton, or Mrs. Seal, or whoever might be beforehand with her at the office. Having no religious belief, she was the more conscientious about her life, examining her position from time to time very seriously, and nothing annoyed her more than to find one of these bad habits nibbling away unheeded at the precious substance. What was the good, after all, of being a woman if one didn't keep fresh, and cram one's life with all sorts of views and experiments? Thus she always gave herself a little shake, as she turned the corner, and, as often as not, reached her own door whistling a snatch of a Somersetshire ballad.

The suffrage office was at the top of one of the large Russell Square houses, which had once been lived in by a great city merchant and his family, and was now let out in slices to a number of societies which displayed assorted initials upon doors of ground glass, and kept, each of them, a typewriter which clicked busily all day long. The old house, with its great stone staircase, echoed hollowly to the sound of typewriters and of errand-boys from ten to six. The noise of different typewriters already at work, disseminating their views upon the protection of native races, or the value of cereals as foodstuffs, quickened Mary's steps, and she always ran up the last flight of steps which led to her own landing, at whatever hour she came, so as to get her typewriter to take its place in competition with the rest.

She sat herself down to her letters, and very soon all these speculations were forgotten, and the two lines drew themselves between her eyebrows, as the contents of the letters, the office furniture, and the sounds of activity in the next room gradually asserted their sway upon her. By eleven o'clock the atmosphere of concentration was running so strongly in one direction that any thought of a different order could hardly have survived its birth more than a moment or so. The task which lay before her was to organize a series of entertainments, the profits of which were to benefit the society, which drooped for want of funds. It was her first attempt at organization on a large scale, and she meant to achieve something remarkable. She meant to use the cumbrous machine to pick out this, that, and the other interesting person from the muddle of the world, and to set them for a week in a pattern which must catch the eyes of Cabinet Ministers, and the eyes once caught, the old arguments were to be delivered with unexampled originality. Such was the scheme as a whole; and in contemplation of it she would become quite flushed and excited, and have to remind herself of all the details that intervened between her and success.

The door would open, and Mr. Clacton would come in to search for a certain leaflet buried beneath a pyramid of leaflets. He was a thin, sandy-haired man of about thirty-five, spoke with a Cockney accent, and had about him a frugal look, as if nature had not dealt generously with him in any way, which, naturally, prevented him from dealing generously with other people. When he had found his leaflet, and offered a few jocular hints upon keeping papers in order, the typewriting would stop abruptly, and Mrs. Seal would burst into the room with a letter which needed explanation in her hand. This was a more serious interruption than the other, because she never knew exactly what she wanted, and half a dozen requests would bolt from her, no one of which was clearly stated. Dressed in plum-colored velveteen, with short, gray hair, and a face that seemed permanently flushed with philanthropic enthusiasm, she was always in a hurry, and always in some disorder. She wore two crucifixes, which got themselves entangled in a heavy gold chain upon her breast, and seemed to Mary expressive of her mental ambiguity. Only her vast enthusiasm and her worship of Miss Markham, one of the pioneers of the society, kept her in her place, for which she had no sound qualification.

So the morning wore on, and the pile of letters grew, and Mary felt, at last, that she was the center ganglion of a very fine network of nerves which fell over England, and one of these days, when she touched the heart of the system, would begin feeling and rushing together and emitting their splendid blaze of revolutionary fireworks—for some such metaphor represents what she felt about her work, when her brain had been heated by three hours of application.

Shortly before one o'clock Mr. Clacton and Mrs. Seal desisted from their labors, and the old joke about luncheon, which came out regularly at this hour, was repeated with scarcely any variation of words. Mr. Clacton patronized a vegetarian restaurant; Mrs. Seal brought sandwiches, which she ate beneath the plane-trees in Russell Square; while Mary generally went to a gaudy establishment, upholstered in red plush, near by, where, much to the vegetarian's disapproval, you could buy steak, two inches thick, or a roast section of fowl, swimming in a pewter dish.

"The bare branches against the sky do one so much *good*," Mrs. Seal asserted, looking out into the Square.

"But one can't lunch off trees, Sally," said Mary.

"I confess I don't know how you manage it, Miss Datchet," Mr. Clacton remarked. "I should sleep all the afternoon, I know, if I took a heavy meal in the middle of the day."

"What's the very latest thing in literature?" Mary asked, good-humoredly pointing to the yellow-covered volume beneath Mr. Clacton's arm, for he invariably read some new French author at lunch-time, or squeezed in a visit to a picture gallery, balancing his social work with an ardent culture of which he was secretly proud, as Mary had very soon divined.

So they parted and Mary walked away, wondering if they guessed that she really wanted to get away from them, and supposing that they had not quite reached that degree of subtlety. She bought herself an evening paper, which she read as she ate, looking over the top of it again and again at the queer people who were buying cakes or imparting their secrets, until some young woman whom she knew came in, and she called out, "Eleanor, come and sit by me," and they finished their lunch together, parting on the strip of pavement among the different lines of traffic with a pleasant feeling that they were stepping once more into their separate places in the great and eternally moving pattern of human life.

But, instead of going straight back to the office today, Mary turned into the British Museum, and strolled down the gallery with the shapes of stone until she found an empty seat directly beneath the gaze of the Elgin marbles. She looked at them, and seemed, as usual, borne up on some wave of exaltation and emotion, by which her life at once became solemn and beautiful—an impression which was due as much, perhaps, to the solitude and chill and silence of the gallery as to the actual beauty of the statues. One must suppose, at least, that her emotions were not purely esthetic, because, after she had gazed at the Ulysses for a minute or two, she began to think about Ralph Denham. So secure did she feel with these silent shapes that she almost yielded to an impulse to say "I am in love with you" aloud. The presence of this immense and enduring beauty made her almost alarmingly conscious of her desire, and at the same time proud of a feeling which did not display anything like the same proportions when she was going about her daily work.

She repressed her impulse to speak aloud, and rose and wandered about rather aimlessly among the statues until she found herself in another gallery devoted to engraved obelisks and winged Assyrian bulls, and her emotion took another turn. She began to picture herself traveling with Ralph in a land where these monsters were couchant in the sand. "For," she thought to herself, as she gazed fixedly at some information printed behind a piece of glass, "the wonderful thing about you is that you're ready for anything; you're not in the least conventional, like most clever men."

And she conjured up a scene of herself on a camel's back, in the desert, while Ralph commanded a whole tribe of natives.

"That is what you can do," she went on, moving on to the next statue. "You always make people do what you want."

A glow spread over her spirit, and filled her eyes with brightness. Nevertheless, before she left the Museum she was very far from saying, even in the privacy of her own mind, "I am in love with you," and that sentence might very well never have framed itself. She was, indeed, rather annoyed with herself for having allowed such an ill-considered breach of her reserve, weakening her powers of resistance, she felt, should this impulse return again. For, as she walked along the street to her office, the force of all her customary objections to being in love with any one overcame her.

She did not want to marry at all. It seemed to her that there was something amateurish in bringing love into touch with a perfectly straightforward friendship, such as hers was with Ralph, which, for two years now, had based itself upon common interests in impersonal topics, such as the housing of the poor, or the taxation of land values.

But the afternoon spirit differed intrinsically from the morning spirit. Mary found herself watching the flight of a bird, or making drawings of the branches of the plane-trees upon her blotting-paper. People came in to see Mr. Clacton on business, and a seductive smell of cigarette smoke issued from his room. Mrs. Seal wandered about with newspaper cuttings, which seemed to her either "quite splendid" or "really too bad for words." She used to paste these into books, or send them to her friends, having first drawn a broad bar in blue pencil down the margin, a proceeding which signified equally and indistinguishably the depths of her reprobation or the heights of her approval.

About four o'clock on that same afternoon Katharine Hilbery was walking up Kingsway. The question of tea presented itself. The street lamps were being lit already, and as she stood still for a moment beneath one of them, she tried to think of some neighboring drawing-room where there would be firelight and talk congenial to her mood. That mood, owing to the spinning traffic and the evening veil of unreality, was ill-adapted to her home surroundings. Perhaps, on the whole, a shop was the best place in which to preserve this queer sense of heightened existence. At the same time she wished to talk. Remembering Mary Datchet and her repeated invitations, she crossed the road, turned into Russell Square, and peered about, seeking for numbers with a sense of adventure that was out of all proportion to the deed itself. She found herself in a dimly lighted hall, unguarded by a porter, and pushed open the first swing door. But the office-boy had never heard of Miss Datchet. Did she belong to the S.R.F.R.? Katharine shook her head with a smile of dismay. A voice from within shouted, "No. The S.G.S.—top floor."

Katharine mounted past innumerable glass doors, with initials on them, and became steadily more and more doubtful of the wisdom of her venture. At the top she paused for a moment to breathe and collect herself. She heard the typewriter and formal professional voices inside, not belonging, she thought, to any one she had ever spoken to. She touched the bell, and the door was opened almost immediately by Mary herself. Her face had to change its expression entirely when she saw Katharine.

"You!" she exclaimed. "We thought you were the printer." Still holding the door open, she called back, "No, Mr. Clacton, it's not Penningtons. I should ring them up again—double three double eight, Central. Well, this is a surprise. Come in," she added. "You're just in time for tea."

The light of relief shone in Mary's eyes. The boredom of the afternoon was dissipated at once, and she was glad that Katharine had found them in a momentary press of activity, owing to the failure of the printer to send back certain proofs.

The unshaded electric light shining upon the table covered with papers dazed Katharine for a moment. After the confusion of her twilight walk, and her random thoughts, life in this small room appeared extremely concentrated and bright. She turned instinctively to look out of the window, which was uncurtained, but Mary immediately recalled her.

"It was very clever of you to find your way," she said, and Katharine wondered, as she stood there, feeling, for the moment, entirely detached and unabsorbed, why she had come. She looked, indeed, to Mary's eyes strangely out of place in the office. Her figure in the long cloak, which took deep folds, and her face, which was composed into a mask of sensitive apprehension, disturbed Mary for a moment with a sense of the presence of some one who was of another world, and, therefore, subversive of her world. She became immediately anxious that Katharine should be impressed by the importance of her world, and hoped that neither Mrs. Seal nor Mr. Clacton would appear until the impression of importance had been received. But in this she was disappointed. Mrs. Seal burst into the room holding a kettle in her hand, which she set upon the stove, and then, with inefficient haste, she set light to the gas, which flared up, exploded, and went out.

"Always the way, always the way," she muttered. "Kit Markham is the only person who knows how to deal with the thing."

Mary had to go to her help, and together they spread the table, and apologized for the disparity between the cups and the plainness of the food.

"If we had known Miss Hilbery was coming, we should have bought a cake," said Mary, upon which Mrs. Seal looked at Katharine for the first time, suspiciously, because she was a person who needed cake.

Here Mr. Clacton opened the door, and came in, holding a typewritten letter in his hand, which he was reading aloud.

"Salford's affiliated," he said.

"Well done, Salford!" Mrs. Seal exclaimed enthusiastically, thumping the teapot which she held upon the table, in token of applause.

"Yes, these provincial centers seem to be coming into line at last," said Mr. Clacton, and then Mary introduced him to Miss Hilbery, and he asked her, in a very formal manner, if she were interested "in our work."

"And the proofs still not come?" said Mrs. Seal, putting both her elbows on the table, and propping her chin on her hands, as Mary began to pour out tea. "It's too bad—too bad. At this rate we shall miss the country post. Which reminds me, Mr. Clacton, don't you think we should circularize the provinces with Partridge's last speech? What? You've not read it? Oh, it's the best thing they've had in the House this Session. Even the Prime Minister——"

But Mary cut her short.

"We don't allow shop at tea, Sally," she said firmly. "We fine her a penny each time she forgets, and the fines go to buying a plum cake," she explained, seeking to draw Katharine into the community. She had given up all hope of impressing her.

"I'm sorry, I'm sorry," Mrs. Seal apologized. "It's my misfortune to be an enthusiast," she said, turning to Katharine. "My father's daughter could hardly be anything else. I think I've been on as many committees as most people. Waifs and Strays, Rescue Work, Church Work, C. O. S.–local branch–besides the usual civic duties which fall to one as a householder. But I've given them all up for our work here, and I don't regret it for a second," she added. "This is the root question, I feel; until women have votes——"

"It'll be sixpence, at least, Sally," said Mary, bringing her fist down on the table. "And we're all sick to death of women and their votes."

Mrs. Seal looked for a moment as though she could hardly believe her ears, and made a deprecating "tut-tut-tut" in her throat, looking alternately at Katharine and Mary, and shaking her head as she did so. Then she remarked, rather confidentially to Katharine, with a little nod in Mary's direction:

"She's doing more for the cause than any of us. She's giving her youth–for, alas! when I was young there were domestic circumstances——" she sighed, and stopped short.

Mr. Clacton hastily reverted to the joke about luncheon, and explained how Mrs. Seal fed on a bag of biscuits under the trees, whatever the weather might be, rather, Katharine thought, as though Mrs. Seal were a pet dog who had convenient tricks.

"Yes, I took my little bag into the square," said Mrs. Seal, with the self-conscious guilt of a child owning some fault to its elders. "It was really very sustaining, and the bare boughs against the sky do one so much *good.* But I shall have to give up going into the square," she proceeded, wrinkling her forehead. "The injustice of it! Why should I have a beautiful square all to myself, when poor women who need rest have nowhere at all to sit?" She looked fiercely at Katharine, giving her short locks a little shake. "It's dreadful what a tyrant one still is, in spite of all one's efforts. One tries to lead a decent life, but one can't. Of course, directly one thinks of it, one sees that *all* squares should be open to *every one.* Is there any society with that object, Mr. Clacton? If not, there should be, surely."

"A most excellent object," said Mr. Clacton in his professional manner. "At the same time, one must deplore the ramification of organizations, Mrs. Seal. So much excellent effort thrown away, not to speak of pounds, shillings, and pence. Now how many organizations of a philanthropic nature do you suppose there are in the City of London itself, Miss Hilbery?" he added, screwing his mouth into a queer little smile, as if to show that the question had its frivolous side.

Katharine smiled, too. Her unlikeness to the rest of them had, by this time, penetrated to Mr. Clacton, who was not naturally observant, and he was wondering who she was; this same unlikeness had subtly stimulated Mrs. Seal to try and make a convert of her. Mary, too, looked at her almost as if she begged her to make things easy. For Katharine had shown no disposition to make things easy. She had scarcely spoken, and her silence, though grave and even thoughtful, seemed to Mary the silence of one who criticizes.

"Well, there are more in this house than I'd any notion of," she said. "On the ground floor you protect natives, on the next you emigrate women and tell people to eat nuts—"

"Why do you say that '*we*' do these things?" Mary interposed, rather sharply. "We're not responsible for all the cranks who choose to lodge in the same house with us."

Mr. Clacton cleared his throat and looked at each of the young ladies in turn. He was a good deal struck by the appearance and manner of Miss Hilbery, which seemed to him to place her among those cultivated and luxurious people of whom he used to dream. Mary, on the other hand, was more of his own sort, and a little too much inclined to order him about. He picked up crumbs of dry biscuit and put them into his mouth with incredible rapidity.

"You don't belong to our society, then?" said Mrs. Seal.

"No, I'm afraid I don't," said Katharine, with such ready candor that Mrs. Seal was nonplussed, and stared at her with a puzzled expression, as if she could not classify her among the varieties of human beings known to her.

"But surely—" she began.

"Mrs. Seal is an enthusiast in these matters," said Mr. Clacton, almost apologetically. "We have to remind her sometimes that others have a right to their views even if they differ from our own. . . . *Punch* has a very funny picture this week, about a Suffragist and an agricultural laborer. Have you seen this week's *Punch*, Miss Datchet?"

Mary laughed, and said "No."

Mr. Clacton then told them the substance of the joke, which, however, depended a good deal for its success upon the expression which the artist had put into the people's faces. Mrs. Seal sat all the time perfectly grave. Directly he had done speaking she burst out:

"But surely, if you care about the welfare of your sex at all, you must wish them to have the vote?"

"I never said I didn't wish them to have the vote," Katharine protested.

"Then why aren't you a member of our society?" Mrs. Seal demanded.

Katharine stirred her spoon round and round, stared into the swirl of the tea, and remained silent. Mr. Clacton, meanwhile, framed a question which, after a moment's hesitation, he put to Katharine.

"Are you in any way related, I wonder, to the poet Alardyce? His daughter, I believe, married a Mr. Hilbery."

"Yes; I'm the poet's granddaughter," said Katharine, with a little sigh, after a pause; and for a moment they were all silent.

"The poet's granddaughter!" Mrs. Seal repeated, half to herself, with a shake of her head, as if that explained what was otherwise inexplicable.

The light kindled in Mr. Clacton's eye.

"Ah, indeed. That interests me very much," he said. "I owe a great debt to your grandfather, Miss Hilbery. At one time I could have repeated the greater part of him by heart. But one gets out of the way of reading poetry, unfortunately. You don't remember him, I suppose?"

A sharp rap at the door made Katharine's answer inaudible. Mrs. Seal looked up with renewed hope in her eyes, and exclaiming:

"The proofs at last!" ran to open the door. "Oh, it's only Mr. Denham!" she cried, without any attempt to conceal her disappointment. Ralph, Katharine supposed, was a frequent visitor, for the only person he thought it necessary to greet was herself, and Mary at once explained the strange fact of her being there by saying:

"Katharine has come to see how one runs an office."

Ralph felt himself stiffen uncomfortably, as he said:

"I hope Mary hasn't persuaded you that she knows how to run an office?"

"What, doesn't she?" said Katharine, looking from one to the other.

At these remarks Mrs. Seal began to exhibit signs of discomposure, which displayed themselves by a tossing movement of her head, and, as Ralph took a letter from his pocket, and placed his finger upon a certain sentence, she forestalled him by exclaiming in confusion:

"Now, I know what you're going to say, Mr. Denham! But it was the day Kit Markham was here, and she upsets one so—with her wonderful vitality, always thinking of something new that we ought to be doing and aren't—and I was conscious at the time that my dates were mixed. It had nothing to do with Mary at all, I assure you."

"My dear Sally, don't apologize," said Mary, laughing. "Men are such pedants—they don't know what things matter, and what things don't."

"Now, Denham, speak up for our sex," said Mr. Clacton in a jocular manner, indeed, but like most insignificant men he was very quick to resent being found fault with by a woman, in argument with whom he was fond of calling himself "a mere man." He wished, however, to enter into a literary conservation with Miss Hilbery, and thus let the matter drop.

"Doesn't it seem strange to you, Miss Hilbery," he said, "that the French, with all their wealth of illustrious names, have no poet who can compare with your grandfather? Let me see. There's Chénier and Hugo and Alfred de Musset—wonderful men, but, at the same time, there's a richness, a freshness about Alardyce——"

Here the telephone bell rang, and he had to absent himself with a smile and a bow which signified that, although literature is delightful, it is not work. Mrs. Seal rose at the same time, but remained hovering over the table, delivering herself of a tirade against party government. "For if I were to tell you what I know of back-stairs intrigue, and what can be done by the power of the purse, you wouldn't credit me, Mr. Denham, you wouldn't, indeed. Which is why I feel that the only work for my father's daughter—for he was one of the pioneers, Mr. Denham, and on his tombstone I had that verse from the Psalms put, about the sowers and the seed. . . . And what wouldn't I give that he should be alive now, seeing what we're going to see——" but reflecting that the glories of the future depended in part upon the activity of her typewriter, she bobbed her head, and hurried back to the seclusion of her little room, from which immediately issued sounds of enthusiastic, but obviously erratic, composition.

Mary made it clear at once, by starting a fresh topic of general interest, that though she saw the humor of her colleague, she did not intend to have her laughed at.

"The standard of morality seems to me frightfully low," she observed reflectively, pouring out a second cup of tea, "especially among women who aren't well educated. They don't see that small things matter, and that's where the leakage begins, and then we find ourselves in difficulties—I very nearly lost my temper yesterday," she went on, looking at Ralph with a little smile, as though he knew what happened when she lost her temper. "It makes me very angry when people tell me lies—doesn't it make you angry?" she asked Katharine.

"But considering that every one tells lies," Katharine remarked, looking about the room to see where she had put down her umbrella and her parcel, for there was an intimacy in the way in which Mary and Ralph addressed each other which made her wish to leave them. Mary, on the other hand, was anxious, superficially at least, that Katharine should stay and so fortify her in her determination not to be in love with Ralph.

Ralph, while lifting his cup from his lips to the table, had made up his mind that if Miss Hilbery left, he would go with her.

"I don't think that I tell lies, and I don't think that Ralph tells lies, do you, Ralph?" Mary continued.

Katharine laughed, with more gayety, as it seemed to Mary, than she could properly account for. What was she laughing at? At them, presumably. Katharine had risen, and was glancing hither and thither, at the presses and the cupboards, and all the machinery of the office, as if she included them all in her rather malicious amusement, which caused Mary to keep her eyes on her straightly and rather fiercely, as if she were a gay-plumed, mischievous bird, who might light on the topmost bough and pick off the ruddiest cherry, without any warning. Two women less like each other could scarcely be imagined, Ralph thought, looking from one to the other. Next moment, he too, rose, and nodding to Mary, as Katharine said good-bye, opened the door for her, and followed her out.

Mary sat still and made no attempt to prevent them from going. For a second or two after the door had shut on them her eyes rested on the door with a straightforward fierceness in which, for a moment, a certain degree of bewilderment seemed to enter; but, after a brief hesitation, she put down her cup and proceeded to clear away the tea-things.

The impulse which had driven Ralph to take this action was the result of a very swift little piece of reasoning, and thus, perhaps, was not quite so much of an impulse as it seemed. It passed through his mind that if he missed this chance of talking to Katharine, he would have to face an enraged ghost, when he was alone in his room again, demanding an explanation of his cowardly indecision. It was better, on the whole, to risk present discomfiture than to waste an evening bandying excuses and constructing impossible scenes with this uncompromising section of himself. For ever since he had visited the Hilberys he had been much at the mercy of a phantom Katharine, who came to him when he sat alone, and answered him as he would have her answer, and was always beside him to crown those varying triumphs which were transacted almost every night, in imaginary scenes, as he walked through the lamplit streets home from the office. To walk with Katharine in the flesh would either feed that phantom with fresh food, which, as all who nourish dreams are aware, is a process that becomes necessary from time to time, or refine it to such a degree of thinness that it was scarcely serviceable any longer; and that, too, is sometimes a welcome change to a dreamer. And all the time Ralph was well aware that the bulk of Katharine was not represented in his dreams at all, so that when he met her he was bewildered by the fact that she had nothing to do with his dream of her.

When, on reaching the street, Katharine found that Mr. Denham proceeded to keep pace by her side, she was surprised and, perhaps, a little annoyed. She, too, had her margin of imagination, and tonight her activity in this obscure region of the mind required solitude. If she had had her way, she would have walked very fast down the Tottenham Court Road, and then sprung into a cab and raced swiftly home. The view she had had of the inside of an office was of the nature of a dream to her. Shut off up there, she compared Mrs. Seal, and Mary Datchet, and Mr. Clacton to enchanted people in a bewitched tower, with the spiders' webs looping across the corners of the room, and all the tools of the necromancer's craft at hand; for so aloof and unreal and apart from the normal world did they seem to her, in the house of innumerable typewriters, murmuring their incantations and concocting their drugs, and flinging their frail spiders' webs over the torrent of life which rushed down the streets outside.

She may have been conscious that there was some exaggeration in this fancy of hers, for she certainly did not wish to share it with Ralph. To him, she supposed, Mary Datchet, composing leaflets for Cabinet Ministers among her typewriters, represented all that was interesting and genuine; and, accordingly, she shut them both out from all share in the crowded street, with its pendant necklace of lamps, its lighted windows, and its throng of men and women, which exhilarated her to such an extent that she very nearly forgot her companion. She walked very fast, and the effect of people passing in the opposite direction was to produce a queer dizziness both in her head and in Ralph's, which set their bodies far apart. But she did her duty by her companion almost unconsciously.

"Mary Datchet does that sort of work very well. . . . She's responsible for it, I suppose?"

"Yes. The others don't help at all. . . . Has she made a convert of you?"

"Oh no. That is, I'm a convert already."

"But she hasn't persuaded you to work for them?"

"Oh dear no—that wouldn't do at all."

So they walked on down the Tottenham Court Road, parting and coming together again, and Ralph felt much as though he were addressing the summit of a poplar in a high gale of wind.

"Suppose we get on to that omnibus?" he suggested.

Katharine acquiesced, and they climbed up, and found themselves alone on top of it.

"But which way are you going?" Katharine asked, waking a little from the trance into which movement among moving things had thrown her.

"I'm going to the Temple," Ralph replied, inventing a destination on the spur of the moment. He felt the change come over her as they sat down and the omnibus began to move forward. He imagined her contemplating the avenue in front of them with those honest sad eyes which seemed to set him at such a distance from them. But the breeze was blowing in their faces; it lifted her hat for a second, and she drew out a pin and stuck it in again—a little action which seemed, for some reason, to make her rather more fallible. Ah, if only her hat would blow off, and leave her altogether disheveled, accepting it from his hands!

"This is like Venice," she observed, raising her hand. "The motor-cars, I mean, shooting about so quickly, with their lights."

"I've never seen Venice," he replied. "I keep that and some other things for my old age."

"What are the other things?" she asked.

"There's Venice and India and, I think, Dante, too."

She laughed.

"Think of providing for one's old age! And would you refuse to see Venice if you had the chance?"

Instead of answering her, he wondered whether he should tell her something that was quite true about himself; and as he wondered, he told her.

"I've planned out my life in sections ever since I was a child, to make it last longer. You see, I'm always afraid that I'm missing something—"

"And so am I!" Katharine exclaimed. "But, after all," she added, "why should you miss anything?"

"Why? Because I'm poor, for one thing," Ralph rejoined. "You, I suppose, can have Venice and India and Dante every day of your life."

She said nothing for a moment, but rested one hand, which was bare of glove, upon the rail in front of her, meditating upon a variety of things, of which one was that this strange young man pronounced Dante as she was used to hearing it pronounced, and another, that he had, most unexpectedly, a feeling about life that was familiar to her. Perhaps, then, he was the sort of person she might take an interest in, if she came to know him better, and as she had placed him among those whom she would never want to know better, this was enough to make her silent. She hastily recalled her first view of him, in the little room where the relics were kept, and ran a bar through half her impressions, as one cancels a badly written sentence, having found the right one.

"But to know that one might have things doesn't alter the fact that one hasn't got them," she said, in some confusion. "How could I go to India, for example? Besides," she began impulsively, and stopped herself. Here the conductor came round, and interrupted them. Ralph waited for her to resume her sentence, but she said no more.

"I have a message to give your father," he remarked. "Perhaps you would give it him, or I could come—"

"Yes, do come," Katharine replied.

"Still, I don't see why you shouldn't go to India," Ralph began, in order to keep her from rising, as she threatened to do.

But she got up in spite of him, and said good-bye with her usual air of decision, and left him with a quickness which Ralph connected now with all her movements. He looked down and saw her standing on the pavement edge, an alert, commanding figure, which waited its season to cross, and then walked boldly and swiftly to the other side. That gesture and action would be added to the picture he had of her, but at present the real woman completely routed the phantom one.

7

And little Augustus Pelham said to me, 'It's the younger generation knocking at the door,' and I said to him, 'Oh, but the younger generation comes in without knocking, Mr. Pelham.' Such a feeble little joke, wasn't it, but down it went into his notebook all the same."

"Let us congratulate ourselves that we shall be in the grave before that work is published," said Mr. Hilbery.

The elderly couple were waiting for the dinner-bell to ring and for their daughter to come into the room. Their arm-chairs were drawn up on either side of the fire, and each sat in the same slightly crouched position, looking into the coals, with the expressions of people who have had their share of experiences and wait, rather passively, for something to happen. Mr. Hilbery now gave all his attention to a piece of coal which had fallen out of the grate, and to selecting a favorable position for it among the lumps that were burning already. Mrs. Hilbery watched him in silence, and the smile changed on her lips as if her mind still played with the events of the afternoon.

When Mr. Hilbery had accomplished his task, he resumed his crouching position again, and began to toy with the little green stone attached to his watch-chain. His deep, oval-shaped eyes were fixed upon the flames, but behind the superficial glaze seemed to brood an observant and whimsical spirit, which kept the brown of the eye still unusually vivid. But a look of indolence, the result of skepticism or of a taste too fastidious to be satisfied by the prizes and conclusions so easily within his grasp, lent him an expression almost of melancholy. After sitting thus for a time, he seemed to reach some point in his thinking which demonstrated its futility, upon which he sighed and stretched his hand for a book lying on the table by his side.

Directly the door opened he closed the book, and the eyes of father and mother both rested on Katharine as she came towards them. The sight seemed at once to give them a motive which they had not had before. To them she appeared, as she walked towards them in her light evening dress, extremely young, and the sight of her refreshed them, were it only because her youth and ignorance made their knowledge of the world of some value.

"The only excuse for you, Katharine, is that dinner is still later than you are," said Mr. Hilbery, putting down his spectacles.

"I don't mind her being late when the result is so charming," said Mrs. Hilbery, looking with pride at her daughter. "Still, I don't know that I *like* your being out so late, Katharine," she continued. "You took a cab, I hope?"

Here dinner was announced, and Mr. Hilbery formally led his wife downstairs on his arm. They were all dressed for dinner, and, indeed, the prettiness of the dinner-table merited that compliment. There was no cloth upon the table, and the china made regular circles of deep blue upon the shining brown wood. In the middle there was a bowl of tawny red and yellow chrysanthemums, and one of pure white, so fresh that the narrow petals were curved backwards into a firm white ball. From the surrounding walls the heads of three famous Victorian writers surveyed this entertainment, and slips of paper pasted beneath them testified in the great man's own handwriting that he was yours sincerely or affectionately or for ever. The father and daughter would have been quite content, apparently, to eat their dinner in silence, or with a few cryptic remarks expressed in a shorthand which could not be understood by the servants. But silence depressed Mrs. Hilbery, and far from minding the presence of maids, she would often address herself to them, and was never altogether unconscious of their approval or disapproval of her remarks. In the first place she called them to witness that the room was darker than usual, and had all the lights turned on.

"That's more cheerful," she exclaimed. "D'you know, Katharine, that ridiculous goose came to tea with me? Oh, how I wanted you! He tried to make epigrams all the time, and I got so nervous, expecting them, you know, that I spilt the tea—and he made an epigram about that!"

"Which ridiculous goose?" Katharine asked her father.

"Only one of my geese, happily, makes epigrams—Augustus Pelham, of course," said Mrs. Hilbery.

"I'm not sorry that I was out," said Katharine.

"Poor Augustus!" Mrs. Hilbery exclaimed. "But we're all too hard on him. Remember how devoted he is to his tiresome old mother."

"That's only because she is his mother. Any one connected with himself—"

"No, no, Katharine—that's too bad. That's—what's the word I mean, Trevor, something long and Latin—the sort of word you and Katharine know—"

Mr. Hilbery suggested "cynical."

"Well, that'll do. I don't believe in sending girls to college, but I should teach them that sort of thing. It makes one feel so dignified, bringing out these little allusions, and passing on gracefully to the next topic. But I don't know what's come over me—I actually had to ask Augustus the name of the lady Hamlet was in love with, as you were out, Katharine, and Heaven knows what he mayn't put down about me in his diary."

"I wish," Katharine started, with great impetuosity, and checked herself. Her mother always stirred her to feel and think quickly, and then she remembered that her father was there, listening with attention.

"What is it you wish?" he asked, as she paused.

He often surprised her, thus, into telling him what she had not meant to tell him; and then they argued, while Mrs. Hilbery went on with her own thoughts.

"I wish mother wasn't famous. I was out at tea, and they would talk to me about poetry."

"Thinking you must be poetical, I see—and aren't you?"

"Who's been talking to you about poetry, Katharine?" Mrs. Hilbery demanded, and Katharine was committed to giving her parents an account of her visit to the Suffrage office.

"They have an office at the top of one of the old houses in Russell Square. I never saw such queer-looking people. And the man discovered I was related to the poet, and talked to me about poetry. Even Mary Datchet seems different in that atmosphere."

"Yes, the office atmosphere is very bad for the soul," said Mr. Hilbery.

"I don't remember any offices in Russell Square in the old days, when Mamma lived there," Mrs. Hilbery mused, "and I can't fancy turning one of those noble great rooms into a stuffy little Suffrage office. Still, if the clerks read poetry there must be something nice about them."

"No, because they don't read it as we read it," Katharine insisted.

"But it's nice to think of them reading your grandfather, and not filling up those dreadful little forms all day long," Mrs. Hilbery persisted, her notion of office life being derived from some chance view of a scene behind the counter at her bank, as she slipped the sovereigns into her purse.

"At any rate, they haven't made a convert of Katharine, which was what I was afraid of," Mr. Hilbery remarked.

"Oh no," said Katharine very decidedly, "I wouldn't work with them for anything."

"It's curious," Mr. Hilbery continued, agreeing with his daughter, "how the sight of one's fellow-enthusiasts always chokes one off. They show up the faults of one's cause so much more plainly than one's antagonists. One can be enthusiastic in one's study, but directly one comes into touch with the people who agree with one, all the glamor goes. So I've always found," and he proceeded to tell them, as he peeled his apple, how he committed himself once, in his youthful days, to make a speech at a political meeting, and went there ablaze with enthusiasm for the ideals of his own side; but while his leaders spoke, he became gradually converted to the other way of thinking, if thinking it could be called, and had to feign illness in order to avoid making a fool of himself—an experience which had sickened him of public meetings.

Katharine listened and felt as she generally did when her father, and to some extent her mother, described their feelings, that she quite understood and agreed with them, but, at the same time, saw something which they did not see, and always felt some disappointment when they fell short of her vision, as they always did. The plates succeeded each other swiftly and noiselessly in front of her, and the table was decked for dessert, and as the talk murmured on in familiar grooves, she sat there, rather like a judge, listening to her parents, who did, indeed, feel it very pleasant when they made her laugh.

Daily life in a house where there are young and old is full of curious little ceremonies and pieties, which are discharged quite punctually, though the meaning of them is obscure, and a mystery has come to brood over them which lends even a superstitious charm to their performance. Such was the nightly ceremony of the cigar and the glass of port, which were placed on the right hand and on the left hand of Mr. Hilbery, and simultaneously Mrs. Hilbery and Katharine left the room. All the years they had lived together they had never seen Mr. Hilbery smoke his cigar or drink his port, and they would have felt it unseemly if, by chance, they had surprised him as he sat there. These short, but clearly marked, periods of separation between the sexes were always used for an intimate postscript to what had been said at dinner, the sense of being women together coming out most strongly when the male sex was, as if by some religious rite, secluded from the female. Katharine knew by heart the sort of mood that possessed her as she walked upstairs to the drawing-room, her mother's arm in hers; and she could anticipate the pleasure with which, when she had turned on the lights, they both regarded the drawing-room, fresh swept and set in order for the last section of the day, with the red parrots swinging on the chintz curtains, and the arm-chairs warming in the blaze. Mrs. Hilbery stood over the fire, with one foot on the fender, and her skirts slightly raised.

"Oh, Katharine," she exclaimed, "how you've made me think of Mamma and the old days in Russell Square! I can see the chandeliers, and the green silk of the piano, and Mamma sitting in her cashmere shawl by the window, singing till the little ragamuffin boys outside stopped to listen. Papa sent me in with a bunch of violets while he waited round the corner.

It must have been a summer evening. That was before things were hopeless. . . ."

As she spoke an expression of regret, which must have come frequently to cause the lines which now grew deep round the lips and eyes, settled on her face. The poet's marriage had not been a happy one. He had left his wife, and after some years of a rather reckless existence, she had died, before her time. This disaster had led to great irregularities of education, and, indeed, Mrs. Hilbery might be said to have escaped education altogether. But she had been her father's companion at the season when he wrote the finest of his poems. She had sat on his knee in taverns and other haunts of drunken poets, and it was for her sake, so people said, that he had cured himself of his dissipation, and become the irreproachable literary character that the world knows, whose inspiration had deserted him. As Mrs. Hilbery grew old she thought more and more of the past, and this ancient disaster seemed at times almost to prey upon her mind, as if she could not pass out of life herself without laying the ghost of her parent's sorrow to rest.

Katharine wished to comfort her mother, but it was difficult to do this satisfactorily when the facts themselves were so much of a legend. The house in Russell Square, for example, with its noble rooms, and the magnolia-tree in the garden, and the sweet-voiced piano, and the sound of feet coming down the corridors, and other properties of size and romance—had they any existence? Yet why should Mrs. Alardyce live all alone in this gigantic mansion, and, if she did not live alone, with whom did she live? For its own sake, Katharine rather liked this tragic story, and would have been glad to hear the details of it, and to have been able to discuss them frankly. But this it became less and less possible to do, for though Mrs. Hilbery was constantly reverting to the story, it was always in this tentative and restless fashion, as though by a touch here and there she could set things straight which had been crooked these sixty years. Perhaps, indeed, she no longer knew what the truth was.

"If they'd lived now," she concluded, "I feel it wouldn't have happened. People aren't so set upon tragedy as they were then. If my father had been able to go round the world, or if she'd had a rest cure, everything would have come right. But what could I do? And then they had bad friends, both of them, who made mischief. Ah, Katharine, when you marry, be quite, quite sure that you love your husband!"

The tears stood in Mrs. Hilbery's eyes.

While comforting her, Katharine thought to herself, "Now this is what Mary Datchet and Mr. Denham don't understand. This is the sort of position I'm always getting into. How simple it must be to live as they do!" for all the evening she had been comparing her home and her father and mother with the Suffrage office and the people there.

"But, Katharine," Mrs. Hilbery continued, with one of her sudden changes of mood, "though, Heaven knows, I don't want to see you married, surely if ever a man loved a woman, William loves you. And it's a nice, rich-sounding name too—Katharine Rodney, which, unfortunately, doesn't mean that he's got any money, because he hasn't."

The alteration of her name annoyed Katharine, and she observed, rather sharply, that she didn't want to marry any one.

"It's very dull that you can only marry one husband, certainly," Mrs. Hilbery reflected. "I always wish that you could marry everybody who wants to marry you. Perhaps they'll come to that in time, but meanwhile I confess that dear William——" But here Mr. Hilbery came in, and the more solid part of the evening began. This consisted in the reading aloud by Katharine from some prose work or other, while her mother knitted scarves intermittently on a little circular frame, and her father read the newspaper, not so attentively but that he could comment humorously now and again upon the fortunes of the hero and the heroine. The Hilberys subscribed to a library, which delivered books on Tuesdays and Fridays, and Katharine did her best to interest her parents in the works of living and highly respectable authors; but Mrs. Hilbery was perturbed by the very look of the light, gold-wreathed volumes, and would make little faces as if she tasted something bitter as the reading went on; while Mr. Hilbery would treat the moderns with a curious elaborate banter such as one might apply to the antics of a promising child. So this evening, after five pages or so of one of these masters, Mrs. Hilbery protested that it was all too clever and cheap and nasty for words.

"Please, Katharine, read us something *real.*"

Katharine had to go to the bookcase and choose a portly volume in sleek, yellow calf, which had directly a sedative effect upon both her parents. But the delivery of the evening post broke in upon the periods of Henry Fielding, and Katharine found that her letters needed all her attention.

8

She took her letters up to her room with her, having persuaded her mother to go to bed directly Mr. Hilbery left them, for so long as she sat in the same room as her mother, Mrs. Hilbery might, at any moment, ask for a sight of the post. A very hasty glance through many sheets had shown

Katharine that, by some coincidence, her attention had to be directed to many different anxieties simultaneously. In the first place, Rodney had written a very full account of his state of mind, which was illustrated by a sonnet, and he demanded a reconsideration of their position, which agitated Katharine more than she liked. Then there were two letters which had to be laid side by side and compared before she could make out the truth of their story, and even when she knew the facts she could not decide what to make of them; and finally she had to reflect upon a great many pages from a cousin who found himself in financial difficulties, which forced him to the uncongenial occupation of teaching the young ladies of Bungay to play upon the violin.

But the two letters which each told the same story differently were the chief source of her perplexity. She was really rather shocked to find it definitely established that her own second cousin, Cyril Alardyce, had lived for the last four years with a woman who was not his wife, who had borne him two children, and was now about to bear him another. This state of things had been discovered by Mrs. Milvain, her aunt Celia, a zealous inquirer into such matters, whose letter was also under consideration. Cyril, she said, must be made to marry the woman at once; and Cyril, rightly or wrongly, was indignant with such interference with his affairs, and would not own that he had any cause to be ashamed of himself. Had he any cause to be ashamed of himself, Katharine wondered; and she turned to her aunt again.

"Remember," she wrote, in her profuse, emphatic statement, "that he bears your grandfather's name, and so will the child that is to be born. The poor boy is not so much to blame as the woman who deluded him, thinking him a gentleman, which he *is*, and having money, which he has *not*."

"What would Ralph Denham say to this?" thought Katharine, beginning to pace up and down her bedroom. She twitched aside the curtains, so that, on turning, she was faced by darkness, and looking out, could just distinguish the branches of a plane-tree and the yellow lights of some one else's windows.

"What would Mary Datchet and Ralph Denham say?" she reflected, pausing by the window, which, as the night was warm, she raised, in order to feel the air upon her face, and to lose herself in the nothingness of night. But with the air the distant humming sound of far-off crowded thoroughfares was admitted to the room. The incessant and tumultuous hum of the distant traffic seemed, as she stood there, to represent the thick texture of her life, for her life was so hemmed in with the progress of other lives that the sound of its own advance was inaudible. People like Ralph and Mary, she thought, had it all their own way, and an empty space before them, and, as she envied them, she cast her mind out to imagine an empty land where all this petty intercourse of men and women, this life made up of the dense crossings and entanglements of men and women, had no existence whatever. Even now, alone, at night, looking out into the shapeless mass of London, she was forced to remember that there was one point and here another with which she had some connection. William Rodney, at this very moment, was seated in a minute speck of light somewhere to the east of her, and his mind was occupied, not with his book, but with her. She wished that no one in the whole world would think of her. However, there was no way of escaping from one's fellow-beings, she concluded, and shut the window with a sigh, and returned once more to her letters.

She could not doubt but that William's letter was the most genuine she had yet received from him. He had come to the conclusion that he could not live without her, he wrote. He believed that he knew her, and could give her happiness, and that their marriage would be unlike other marriages. Nor was the sonnet, in spite of its accomplishment, lacking in passion, and Katharine, as she read the pages through again, could see in what direction her feelings ought to flow, supposing they revealed themselves. She would come to feel a humorous sort of tenderness for him, a zealous care for his susceptibilities, and, after all, she considered, thinking of her father and mother, what is love?

Naturally, with her face, position, and background, she had experience of young men who wished to marry her, and made protestations of love, but, perhaps because she did not return the feeling, it remained something of a pageant to her. Not having experience of it herself, her mind had unconsciously occupied itself for some years in dressing up an image of love, and the marriage that was the outcome of love, and the man who inspired love, which naturally dwarfed any examples that came her way. Easily, and without correction by reason, her imagination made pictures, superb backgrounds casting a rich though phantom light upon the facts in the foreground. Splendid as the waters that drop with resounding thunder from high ledges of rock, and plunge downwards into the blue depths of night, was the presence of love she dreamt, drawing into it every drop of the force of life, and dashing them all asunder in the superb catastrophe in which everything was surrendered, and nothing might be reclaimed. The man, too, was some magnanimous hero, riding a great horse by the shore of the sea. They rode through forests together, they galloped by the rim of the sea. But waking, she was able to contemplate a perfectly loveless marriage, as the thing one did actually in real life, for possibly the people who dream thus are those who do the most prosaic things.

At this moment she was much inclined to sit on into the night, spinning her light fabric of thoughts until she tired of their futility, and went to her mathematics; but, as she knew very well, it was necessary that she should see her father before he went to bed. The case of Cyril Alardyce must be discussed, her mother's illusions and the rights of the family attended to. Being vague herself as to what all this amounted to, she had to take counsel with her father. She took her letters in her hand and went downstairs. It was past eleven, and the clocks had come into their reign, the grandfather's clock in the hall ticking in competition with the small clock on the landing. Mr. Hilbery's study ran out behind the rest of the house, on the ground floor, and was a very silent, subterranean place, the sun in daytime casting a mere abstract of light through a skylight upon his books and the large table, with its spread of white papers, now illumined by a green reading-lamp. Here Mr. Hilbery sat editing his review, or placing together documents by means of which it could be proved that Shelley had written "of" instead of "and," or that the inn in which Byron had slept was called the "Nag's Head" and not the "Turkish Knight," or that the Christian name of Keats's uncle had been John rather than Richard, for he knew more minute details about these poets than any man in England, probably, and was preparing an edition of Shelley which scrupulously observed the poet's system of punctuation. He saw the humor of these researches, but that did not prevent him from carrying them out with the utmost scrupulosity.

He was lying back comfortably in a deep arm-chair smoking a cigar, and ruminating the fruitful question as to whether Coleridge had wished to marry Dorothy Wordsworth, and what, if he had done so, would have been the consequences to him in particular, and to literature in general. When Katharine came in he reflected that he knew what she had come for, and he made a pencil note before he spoke to her. Having done this, he saw that she was reading, and he watched her for a moment without saying anything. She was reading "Isabella and the Pot of Basil," and her mind was full of the Italian hills and the blue daylight, and the hedges set with little rosettes of red and white roses. Feeling that her father waited for her, she sighed and said, shutting her book:

"I've had a letter from Aunt Celia about Cyril, father. . . . It seems to be true—about his marriage. What are we to do?"

"Cyril seems to have been behaving in a very foolish manner," said Mr. Hilbery, in his pleasant and deliberate tones.

Katharine found some difficulty in carrying on the conversation, while her father balanced his finger-tips so judiciously, and seemed to reserve so many of his thoughts for himself.

"He's about done for himself, I should say," he continued. Without saying anything, he took Katharine's letters out of her hand, adjusted his eyeglasses, and read them through.

At length he said "Humph!" and gave the letters back to her.

"Mother knows nothing about it," Katharine remarked. "Will you tell her?"

"I shall tell your mother. But I shall tell her that there is nothing whatever for us to do."

"But the marriage?" Katharine asked, with some diffidence.

Mr. Hilbery said nothing, and stared into the fire.

"What in the name of conscience did he do it for?" he speculated at last, rather to himself than to her.

Katharine had begun to read her aunt's letter over again, and she now quoted a sentence. "Ibsen and Butler. . . . He has sent me a letter full of quotations—nonsense, though clever nonsense."

"Well, if the younger generation want to carry on its life on those lines, it's none of our affair," he remarked.

"But isn't it our affair, perhaps, to make them get married?" Katharine asked rather wearily.

"Why the dickens should they apply to me?" her father demanded with sudden irritation.

"Only as the head of the family—"

"But I'm not the head of the family. Alfred's the head of the family. Let them apply to Alfred," said Mr. Hilbery, relapsing again into his armchair. Katharine was aware that she had touched a sensitive spot, however, in mentioning the family.

"I think, perhaps, the best thing would be for me to go and see them," she observed.

"I won't have you going anywhere near them," Mr. Hilbery replied with unwonted decision and authority. "Indeed, I don't understand why they've dragged you into the business at all—I don't see that it's got anything to do with you."

"I've always been friends with Cyril," Katharine observed.

"But did he ever tell you anything about this?" Mr. Hilbery asked rather sharply.

Katharine shook her head. She was, indeed, a good deal hurt that Cyril had not confided in her—did he think, as Ralph Denham or Mary Datchet might think, that she was, for some reason, unsympathetic—hostile even?

"As to your mother," said Mr. Hilbery, after a pause, in which he seemed to be considering the color of the flames, "you had better tell her the facts. She'd better know the facts before every one begins to talk about it, though why Aunt Celia thinks it necessary to come, I'm sure I don't know. And the less talk there is the better."

Granting the assumption that gentlemen of sixty who are highly cultivated, and have had much experience of life, probably think of many things which they do not say, Katharine could not help feeling rather puzzled by her father's attitude, as she went back to her room. What a distance he was from it all! How superficially he smoothed these events into a semblance of decency which harmonized with his own view of life! He never wondered what Cyril had felt, nor did the hidden aspects of the case tempt him to examine into them. He merely seemed to realize, rather languidly, that Cyril had behaved in a way which was foolish, because other people did not behave in that way. He seemed to be looking through a telescope at little figures hundreds of miles in the distance.

Her selfish anxiety not to have to tell Mrs. Hilbery what had happened made her follow her father into the hall after breakfast the next morning in order to question him.

"Have you told mother?" she asked. Her manner to her father was almost stern, and she seemed to hold endless depths of reflection in the dark of her eyes.

Mr. Hilbery sighed.

"My dear child, it went out of my head." He smoothed his silk hat energetically, and at once affected an air of hurry. "I'll send a note round from the office. . . . I'm late this morning, and I've any amount of proofs to get through."

"That wouldn't do at all," Katharine said decidedly. "She must be told—you or I must tell her. We ought to have told her at first."

Mr. Hilbery had now placed his hat on his head, and his hand was on the door-knob. An expression which Katharine knew well from her childhood, when he asked her to shield him in some neglect of duty, came into his eyes; malice, humor, and irresponsibility were blended in it. He nodded his head to and fro significantly, opened the door with an adroit movement, and stepped out with a lightness unexpected at his age. He waved his hand once to his daughter, and was gone. Left alone, Katharine could not help laughing to find herself cheated as usual in domestic bargainings with her father, and left to do the disagreeable work which belonged, by rights, to him.

9

Katharine disliked telling her mother about Cyril's misbehavior quite as much as her father did, and for much the same reasons. They both shrank, nervously, as people fear the report of a gun on the stage, from all that would have to be said on this occasion. Katharine, moreover, was unable to decide what she thought of Cyril's misbehavior. As usual, she saw something which her father and mother did not see, and the effect of that something was to suspend Cyril's behavior in her mind without any qualification at all. They would think whether it was good or bad; to her it was merely a thing that had happened.

When Katharine reached the study, Mrs. Hilbery had already dipped her pen in the ink.

"Katharine," she said, lifting it in the air, "I've just made out such a queer, strange thing about your grandfather. I'm three years and six months older than he was when he died. I couldn't very well have been his mother, but I might have been his elder sister, and that seems to me such a pleasant fancy. I'm going to start quite fresh this morning, and get a lot done."

She began her sentence, at any rate, and Katharine sat down at her own table, untied the bundle of old letters upon which she was working, smoothed them out absent-mindedly, and began to decipher the faded script. In a minute she looked across at her mother, to judge her mood. Peace and happiness had relaxed every muscle in her face; her lips were parted very slightly, and her breath came in smooth, controlled inspirations like those of a child who is surrounding itself with a building of bricks, and increasing in ecstasy as each brick is placed in position. So Mrs. Hilbery was raising round her the skies and trees of the past with every stroke of her pen, and recalling the voices of the dead. Quiet as the room was, and undisturbed by the sounds of the present moment, Katharine could fancy that here was a deep pool of past time, and that she and her mother were bathed in the light of sixty years ago. What could the present give, she wondered, to compare with the rich crowd of gifts bestowed by the past? Here was a Thursday morning in process of manufacture; each second was minted fresh by the clock upon the mantelpiece. She strained her ears and could just hear, far off, the hoot of a motor-car and the rush of wheels coming nearer and dying away again, and the voices of men crying old iron and vegetables in one of the poorer streets at the back of the house. Rooms, of course, accumulate their suggestions, and any room in which one has been used to carry on any particular occupation gives off memories of moods, of ideas, of postures that have been seen in it; so that to attempt any different kind of work there is almost impossible.

Katharine was unconsciously affected, each time she entered her mother's room, by all these influences, which had had their birth years ago, when she was a child, and had something sweet and solemn about them, and connected themselves with early memories of the cavernous glooms and sonorous echoes of the Abbey where her grandfather lay buried. All the books and pictures, even the chairs and tables, had belonged to him, or had reference to him; even the china dogs on the mantelpiece and the little shepherdesses with their sheep had been bought by him for a penny a piece from a man who used to stand with a tray of toys in Kensington High Street, as Katharine had often heard her mother tell. Often she had sat in this room, with her mind fixed so firmly on those vanished figures that she could almost see the muscles round their eyes and lips, and had given to each his own voice, with its tricks of accent, and his coat and his cravat. Often she had seemed to herself to be moving among them, an invisible ghost among the living, better acquainted with them than with her own friends, because she knew their secrets and possessed a divine foreknowledge of their destiny. They had been so unhappy, such muddlers, so wrong-headed, it seemed to her. She could have told them what to do, and what not to do. It was a melancholy fact that they would pay no heed to her, and were bound to come to grief in their own antiquated way. Their behavior was often grotesquely irrational; their conventions monstrously absurd; and yet, as she brooded upon them, she felt so closely attached to them that it was useless to try to pass judgment upon them. She very nearly lost consciousness that she was a separate being, with a future of her own. On a morning of slight depression, such as this, she would try to find some sort of clue to the muddle which their old letters presented; some reason which seemed to make it worth while to them; some aim which they kept steadily in view—but she was interrupted.

Mrs. Hilbery had risen from her table, and was standing looking out of the window at a string of barges swimming up the river.

Katharine watched her. Suddenly Mrs. Hilbery turned abruptly, and exclaimed:

"I really believe I'm bewitched! I only want three sentences, you see, something quite straightforward and commonplace, and I can't find 'em."

She began to pace up and down the room, snatching up her duster; but she was too much annoyed to find any relief, as yet, in polishing the backs of books.

"Besides," she said, giving the sheet she had written to Katharine, "I don't believe this'll do. Did your grandfather ever visit the Hebrides, Katharine?" She looked in a strangely beseeching way at her daughter. "My mind got running on the Hebrides, and I couldn't help writing a little description of them. Perhaps it would do at the beginning of a chapter. Chapters often begin quite differently from the way they go on, you know." Katharine read what her mother had written. She might have been a schoolmaster criticizing a child's essay. Her face gave Mrs. Hilbery, who watched it anxiously, no ground for hope.

"It's very beautiful," she stated, "but, you see, mother, we ought to go from point to point—"

"Oh, I know," Mrs. Hilbery exclaimed. "And that's just what I can't do. Things keep coming into my head. It isn't that I don't know everything and feel everything (who did know him, if I didn't?), but I can't put it down, you see. There's a kind of blind spot," she said, touching her forehead, "there. And when I can't sleep o' nights, I fancy I shall die without having done it."

From exultation she had passed to the depths of depression which the imagination of her death aroused. The depression communicated itself to Katharine. How impotent they were, fiddling about all day long with papers! And the clock was striking eleven and nothing done! She watched her mother, now rummaging in a great brass-bound box which stood by her table, but she did not go to her help. Of course, Katharine reflected, her mother had now lost some paper, and they would waste the rest of the morning looking for it. She cast her eyes down in irritation, and read again her mother's musical sentences about the silver gulls, and the roots of little pink flowers washed by pellucid streams, and the blue mists of hyacinths, until she was struck by her mother's silence. She raised her eyes. Mrs. Hilbery had emptied a portfolio containing old photographs over her table, and was looking from one to another.

"Surely, Katharine," she said, "the men were far handsomer in those days than they are now, in spite of their odious whiskers? Look at old John Graham, in his white waistcoat—look at Uncle Harley. That's Peter the manservant, I suppose. Uncle John brought him back from India."

Katharine looked at her mother, but did not stir or answer. She had suddenly become very angry, with a rage which their relationship made silent, and therefore doubly powerful and critical. She felt all the unfairness of the claim which her mother tacitly made to her time and sympathy, and what Mrs. Hilbery took, Katharine thought bitterly, she wasted. Then, in a flash, she remembered that she had still to tell her about Cyril's misbehavior. Her anger immediately dissipated itself; it broke like some wave that has gathered itself high above the rest; the waters were resumed into the sea again, and Katharine felt once more full of peace and solicitude, and anxious only that her mother should be protected from pain. She crossed the room instinctively, and sat on the arm of her mother's chair. Mrs. Hilbery leant her head against her daughter's body.

"What is nobler," she mused, turning over the photographs, "than to be a woman to whom every one turns, in sorrow or difficulty? How have the young women of your generation improved upon that, Katharine? I can see them now, sweeping over the lawns at Melbury House, in their flounces and furbelows, so calm and stately and imperial (and the monkey and the little black dwarf following behind), as if nothing mattered in the world but to be beautiful and kind. But they did more than we do, I sometimes think. They *were,* and that's better than doing. They seem to me like ships, like majestic ships, holding on their way, not shoving or pushing, not fretted by little things, as we are, but taking their way, like ships with white sails."

Katharine tried to interrupt this discourse, but the opportunity did not come, and she could not forbear to turn over the pages of the album in which the old photographs were stored. The faces of these men and women shone forth wonderfully after the hubbub of living faces, and seemed, as her mother had said, to wear a marvelous dignity and calm, as if they had ruled their kingdoms justly and deserved great love. Some were of almost incredible beauty, others were ugly enough in a forcible way, but none were dull or bored or insignificant. The superb stiff folds of the crinolines suited the women; the cloaks and hats of the gentlemen seemed full of character. Once more Katharine felt the serene air all round her, and seemed far off to hear the solemn beating of the sea upon the shore. But she knew that she must join the present on to this past.

Mrs. Hilbery was rambling on, from story to story.

"That's Janie Mannering," she said, pointing to a superb, white-haired dame, whose satin robes seemed strung with pearls. "I must have told you how she found her cook drunk under the kitchen table when the Empress was coming to dinner, and tucked up her velvet sleeves (she always dressed like an Empress herself), cooked the whole meal, and appeared in the drawing-room as if she'd been sleeping on a bank of roses all day. She could do anything with her hands—they all could—make a cottage or embroider a petticoat.

"And that's Queenie Colquhoun," she went on, turning the pages, "who took her coffin out with her to Jamaica, packed with lovely shawls and bonnets, because you couldn't get coffins in Jamaica, and she had a horror of dying there (as she did), and being devoured by the white ants. And there's Sabine, the loveliest of them all; ah! it was like a star rising when she came into the room. And that's Miriam, in her coachman's cloak, with all the little capes on, and she wore great top-boots underneath. You young people may say you're unconventional, but you're nothing compared with her."

Turning the page, she came upon the picture of a very masculine, handsome lady, whose head the photographer had adorned with an imperial crown.

"Ah, you wretch!" Mrs. Hilbery exclaimed, "what a wicked old despot you were, in your day! How we all bowed down before you! 'Maggie,' she used to say, 'if it hadn't been for me, where would you be now?' And it was true; she brought them together, you know. She said to my father, 'Marry her,' and he did; and she said to poor little Clara, 'Fall down and worship him,' and she did; but she got up again, of course. What else could one expect? She was a mere child—eighteen—and half dead with fright, too. But that old tyrant never repented. She used to say that she had given them three perfect months, and no one had a right to more; and I sometimes think, Katharine, that's true, you know. It's more than most of us have, only we have to pretend, which was a thing neither of them could ever do. I fancy," Mrs. Hilbery mused, "that there was a kind of sincerity in those days between men and women which, with all your outspokenness, you haven't got."

Katharine again tried to interrupt. But Mrs. Hilbery had been gathering impetus from her recollections, and was now in high spirits.

"They must have been good friends at heart," she resumed, "because she used to sing his songs. Ah, how did it go?" and Mrs. Hilbery, who had a very sweet voice, trolled out a famous lyric of her father's which had been set to an absurdly and charmingly sentimental air by some early Victorian composer.

"It's the vitality of them!" she concluded, striking her fist against the table. "That's what we haven't got! We're virtuous, we're earnest, we go to meetings, we pay the poor their wages, but we don't live as they lived. As often as not, my father wasn't in bed three nights out of the seven, but always fresh as paint in the morning. I hear him now, come singing up the stairs to the nursery, and tossing the loaf for breakfast on his sword-stick, and then off we went for a day's pleasuring—Richmond, Hampton Court, the Surrey Hills. Why shouldn't we go, Katharine? It's going to be a fine day."

At this moment, just as Mrs. Hilbery was examining the weather from the window, there was a knock at the door. A slight, elderly lady came in, and was saluted by Katharine, with very evident dismay, as "Aunt Celia!" She was dismayed because she guessed why Aunt Celia had come. It was certainly in order to discuss the case of Cyril and the woman who was not his wife, and owing to her procrastination Mrs. Hilbery was quite unprepared. Who could be more unprepared? Here she was, suggesting that all three of them should go on a jaunt to Blackfriars to inspect the site of Shakespeare's theater, for the weather was hardly settled enough for the country.

To this proposal Mrs. Milvain listened with a patient smile, which indicated that for many years she had accepted such eccentricities in her sister-in-law with bland philosophy. Katharine took up her position at some distance, standing with her foot on the fender, as though by so doing she could get a better view of the matter. But, in spite of her aunt's presence, how unreal the whole question of Cyril and his morality appeared! The difficulty, it now seemed, was not to break the news gently to Mrs. Hilbery, but to make her understand it. How was one to lasso her mind, and tether it to this minute, unimportant spot? A matter-of-fact statement seemed best.

"I think Aunt Celia has come to talk about Cyril, mother," she said rather brutally. "Aunt Celia has discovered that Cyril is married. He has a wife and children."

"No, he is *not* married," Mrs. Milvain interposed, in low tones, addressing herself to Mrs. Hilbery. "He has two children, and another on the way."

Mrs. Hilbery looked from one to the other in bewilderment.

"We thought it better to wait until it was proved before we told you," Katharine added.

"But I met Cyril only a fortnight ago at the National Gallery!" Mrs. Hilbery exclaimed. "I don't believe a word of it," and she tossed her head with a smile on her lips at Mrs. Milvain, as though she could quite understand her mistake, which was a very natural mistake, in the case of a childless woman, whose husband was something very dull in the Board of Trade.

"I didn't *wish* to believe it, Maggie," said Mrs. Milvain. "For a long time I *couldn't* believe it. But now I've seen, and I *have* to believe it."

"Katharine," Mrs. Hilbery demanded, "does your father know of this?"

Katharine nodded.

"Cyril married!" Mrs. Hilbery repeated. "And never telling us a word, though we've had him in our house since he was a child—noble William's son! I can't believe my ears!"

Feeling that the burden of proof was laid upon her, Mrs. Milvain now proceeded with her story. She was elderly and fragile, but her childlessness seemed always to impose these painful duties on her, and to revere the family, and to keep it in repair, had now become the chief object of her life. She told her story in a low, spasmodic, and somewhat broken voice.

"I have suspected for some time that he was not happy. There were new lines on his face. So I went to his rooms, when I knew he was engaged at the poor men's college. He lectures there—Roman law, you know, or it may be Greek. The landlady said Mr. Alardyce only slept there about once a fortnight now. He looked so ill, she said. She had seen him with a young person. I suspected something directly. I went to his room, and there was an envelope on the mantelpiece, and a letter with an address in Seton Street, off the Kennington Road."

Mrs. Hilbery fidgeted rather restlessly, and hummed fragments of her tune, as if to interrupt.

"I went to Seton Street," Aunt Celia continued firmly. "A very low place—lodging-houses, you know, with canaries in the window. Number seven just like all the others. I rang, I knocked; no one came. I went down the area. I am certain I saw some one inside—children—a cradle. But no reply—no reply." She sighed, and looked straight in front of her with a glazed expression in her half-veiled blue eyes.

"I stood in the street," she resumed, "in case I could catch a sight of one of them. It seemed a very long time. There were rough men singing in the public-house round the corner. At last the door opened, and some one—it must have been the woman herself—came right past me. There was only the pillar-box between us."

"And what did she look like?" Mrs. Hilbery demanded.

"One could see how the poor boy had been deluded," was all that Mrs. Milvain vouchsafed by way of description.

"Poor thing!" Mrs. Hilbery exclaimed.

"Poor *Cyril!*" Mrs. Milvain said, laying a slight emphasis upon Cyril.

"But they've got nothing to live upon," Mrs. Hilbery continued. "If he'd come to us like a man," she went on, "and said, 'I've been a fool,' one would have pitied him; one would have tried to help him. There's nothing so disgraceful after all—But he's been going about all these years, pretending, letting one take it for granted, that he was single. And the poor deserted little wife——"

"She is *not* his wife," Aunt Celia interrupted.

"I've never heard anything so detestable!" Mrs. Hilbery wound up, striking her fist on the arm of her chair. As she realized the facts she became thoroughly disgusted, although, perhaps, she was more hurt by the concealment of the sin than by the sin itself. She looked splendidly roused and indignant; and Katharine felt an immense relief and pride in her mother. It was plain that her indignation was very genuine, and that her mind was as perfectly focused upon the facts as any one could wish—more so, by a long way, than Aunt Celia's mind, which seemed to be timidly circling, with a morbid pleasure, in these unpleasant shades. She and her mother together would take the situation in hand, visit Cyril, and see the whole thing through.

"We must realize Cyril's point of view first," she said, speaking directly to her mother, as if to a contemporary, but before the words were out of her mouth, there was more confusion outside, and Cousin Caroline, Mrs. Hilbery's maiden cousin, entered the room. Although she was by birth an Alardyce, and Aunt Celia a Hilbery, the complexities of the family relationship were such that each was at once first and second cousin to the other, and thus aunt and cousin to the culprit Cyril, so that his misbehavior was almost as much Cousin Caroline's affair as Aunt Celia's. Cousin Caroline was a lady of very imposing height and circumference, but in spite of her size and her handsome trappings, there was something exposed and unsheltered in her expression, as if for many summers her thin red skin and hooked nose and reduplication of chins, so much resembling the profile of a cockatoo, had been bared to the weather; she was, indeed, a single lady; but she had, it was the habit to say, "made a life for herself," and was thus entitled to be heard with respect.

"This unhappy business," she began, out of breath as she was. "If the train had not gone out of the station just as I arrived, I should have been with you before. Celia has doubtless told you. You will agree with me, Maggie. He must be made to marry her at once for the sake of the children—"

"But does he refuse to marry her?" Mrs. Hilbery inquired, with a return of her bewilderment.

"He has written an absurd perverted letter, all quotations," Cousin Caroline puffed. "He thinks he's doing a very fine thing, where we only see the folly of it. . . . The girl's every bit as infatuated as he is—for which I blame him."

"*She* entangled *him*," Aunt Celia intervened, with a very curious smoothness of intonation, which seemed to convey a vision of threads weaving and interweaving a close, white mesh round their victim.

"It's no use going into the rights and wrongs of the affair now, Celia," said Cousin Caroline with some acerbity, for she believed herself the only practical one of the family, and regretted that, owing to the slowness of the kitchen clock, Mrs. Milvain had already confused poor dear Maggie with her own incomplete version of the facts. "The mischief's done, and very ugly mischief too. Are we to allow the third child to be born out of wedlock? (I am sorry to have to say these things before you, Katharine.) He will bear your name, Maggie—your father's name, remember."

"But let us hope it will be a girl," said Mrs. Hilbery.

Katharine, who had been looking at her mother constantly, while the chatter of tongues held sway, perceived that the look of straightforward indignation had already vanished; her mother was evidently casting about in her mind for some method of escape, or bright spot, or sudden illumination which should show to the satisfaction of everybody that all had happened, miraculously but incontestably, for the best.

"It's detestable—quite detestable!" she repeated, but in tones of no great assurance; and then her face lit up with a smile which, tentative at first, soon became almost assured. "Nowadays, people don't think so badly of these things as they used to do," she began. "It will be horribly uncomfortable for them sometimes, but if they are brave, clever children, as they will be, I dare say it'll make remarkable people of them in the end. Robert Browning used to say that every great man has Jewish blood in him, and we must try to look at it in that light. And, after all, Cyril has acted on principle. One may disagree with his principle, but, at least, one can respect it—like the French Revolution, or Cromwell cutting the King's head off. Some of the most terrible things in history have been done on principle," she concluded.

"I'm afraid I take a very different view of principle," Cousin Caroline remarked tartly.

"Principle!" Aunt Celia repeated, with an air of deprecating such a word in such a connection. "I will go tomorrow and see him," she added.

"But why should you take these disagreeable things upon yourself, Celia?" Mrs. Hilbery interposed, and Cousin Caroline thereupon protested with some further plan involving sacrifice of herself.

Growing weary of it all, Katharine turned to the window, and stood among the folds of the curtain, pressing close to the window-pane, and gazing disconsolately at the river much in the attitude of a child depressed by the meaningless talk of its elders. She was much disappointed in her mother—and in herself too. The little tug which she gave to the blind, letting it fly up to the top with a snap, signified her annoyance. She was very angry, and yet impotent to give expression to her anger, or know with whom she was angry. How they talked and moralized and made up stories to suit their own version of the becoming, and secretly praised their own devotion and tact! No; they had their dwelling in a mist, she decided; hundreds of miles away—away from what? "Perhaps it would be better if I married William," she thought suddenly, and the thought appeared to loom through the mist like solid ground. She stood there, thinking of her own destiny, and the elder ladies talked on, until they had talked themselves into a decision to ask the young woman to luncheon, and tell her, very friendlily, how such behavior appeared to women like themselves, who knew the world. And then Mrs. Hilbery was struck by a better idea.

10

Messrs. Grateley and Hooper, the solicitors in whose firm Ralph Denham was clerk, had their office in Lincoln's Inn Fields, and there Ralph Denham appeared every morning very punctually at ten o'clock. His punctuality, together with other qualities, marked him out among the clerks for success, and indeed it would have been safe to wager that in ten years' time or so one would find him at the head of his profession, had it not been for a peculiarity which sometimes seemed to make everything about him uncertain and perilous. His sister Joan had already been disturbed by his love of gambling with his savings. Scrutinizing him constantly with the eye of affection, she had become aware of a curious perversity in his temperament which caused her much anxiety, and would have caused her still more if she had not recognized the germs of it in her own nature. She could fancy Ralph suddenly sacrificing his entire career for some fantastic imagination; some cause or idea or even (so her fancy ran) for some woman seen from a railway train, hanging up clothes in a back yard. When he had found this beauty or this cause, no force, she knew, would avail to restrain him from pursuit of it. She suspected the East also, and always fidgeted herself when she saw him with a book of Indian travels in his hand, as though he were sucking contagion from the page. On the other hand, no common love affair, had there been such a thing, would have caused her a moment's uneasiness where Ralph was concerned. He was destined in her fancy for something splendid in the way of success or failure, she knew not which.

And yet nobody could have worked harder or done better in all the recognized stages of a young man's life than Ralph had done, and Joan had to gather materials for her fears from trifles in her brother's behavior which would have escaped any other eye. It was natural that she should be anxious. Life had been so arduous for all of them from the start that she could not help dreading any sudden relaxation of his grasp upon what he held, though, as she knew from inspection of her own life, such sudden impulse to let go and make away from the discipline and the drudgery was sometimes almost irresistible. But with Ralph, if he broke away, she knew that it would be only to put himself under harsher constraint; she figured him toiling through sandy deserts under a tropical sun to find the source of some river or the haunt of some fly; she figured him living by the labor of his hands in some city slum, the victim of one of those terrible theories of right and wrong which were current at the time; she figured him prisoner for life in the house of a woman who had seduced him by her misfortunes. Half proudly, and wholly anxiously, she framed such thoughts, as they sat, late at night, talking together over the gas-stove in Ralph's bedroom.

It is likely that Ralph would not have recognized his own dream of a future in the forecasts which disturbed his sister's peace of mind. Certainly, if any one of them had been put before him he would have rejected it with a laugh, as the sort of life that held no attractions for him. He could not have said how it was that he had put these absurd notions into his sister's head. Indeed, he prided himself upon being well broken into a life of hard work, about which he had no sort of illusions. His vision of his own future, unlike many such forecasts, could have been made public at any moment without a blush; he attributed to himself a strong brain, and conferred on himself a seat in the House of Commons at the age of fifty, a moderate fortune, and, with luck, an unimportant office in a Liberal Government. There was nothing extravagant in a forecast of that kind, and certainly nothing dishonorable. Nevertheless, as his sister guessed, it needed all Ralph's strength of will, together with the pressure of circumstances, to keep his feet moving in the path which led that way. It needed, in particular, a constant repetition of a phrase to the effect that he shared the common fate, found it best of all, and wished for no other; and by repeating such phrases he acquired punctuality and habits of work, and could very plausibly demonstrate that to be a clerk in a solicitor's office was the best of all possible lives, and that other ambitions were vain.

But, like all beliefs not genuinely held, this one depended very much upon the amount of acceptance it received from other people, and in private, when the pressure of public opinion was removed, Ralph let himself swing very rapidly away from his actual circumstances upon strange voyages which, indeed, he would have been ashamed to describe. In these dreams, of course, he figured in noble and romantic parts, but self-glorification was not the only motive of them. They gave outlet to some spirit which found no work to do in real life, for, with the pessimism which his lot forced upon him, Ralph had made up his mind that there was no use for what, contemptuously enough, he called dreams, in the world which we inhabit. It sometimes seemed to him that this spirit was the most valuable possession he had; he thought that by means of it he could set flowering waste tracts of the earth, cure many ills, or raise up beauty where none now existed; it was, too, a fierce and potent spirit which would devour the dusty books and parchments on the office wall with one lick of its tongue, and leave him in a minute standing in nakedness, if he gave way to it. His endeavor, for many years, had been to control the spirit, and at the age of twenty-nine he thought he could pride himself upon a life rigidly divided into the hours of work and those of dreams; the two lived side by side without harming each other. As a matter of fact, this effort at discipline had been helped by the interests of a difficult profession, but the old conclusion to which Ralph had come when he left college still held sway in his mind, and tinged his views with the melancholy belief that life for most people compels the exercise of the lower gifts and wastes the precious ones, until it forces us to agree that there is little virtue, as well as little profit, in what once seemed to us the noblest part of our inheritance.

Denham was not altogether popular either in his office or among his family. He was too positive, at this stage of his career, as to what was right and what wrong, too proud of his self-control, and, as is natural in the case of persons not altogether happy or well suited in their conditions, too apt to prove the folly of contentment, if he found any one who confessed to that weakness. In the office his rather ostentatious efficiency annoyed those who took their own work more lightly, and, if they foretold his advancement, it was not altogether sympathetically. Indeed, he appeared to be rather a hard and self-sufficient young man, with a queer temper, and manners that were uncompromisingly abrupt, who was consumed with a desire to get on in the world, which was natural, these critics thought, in a man of no means, but not engaging.

The young men in the office had a perfect right to these opinions, because Denham showed no particular desire for their friendship. He liked them well enough, but shut them up in that compartment of life which was devoted to work. Hitherto, indeed, he had found little difficulty in arranging his life as methodically as he arranged his expenditure, but about this time he began to encounter experiences which were not so easy to classify. Mary Datchet had begun this confusion two years ago by bursting into laughter at some remark of his, almost the first time they met. She could not explain why it was. She thought him quite astonishingly odd. When he knew her well enough to tell her how he spent Monday and Wednesday and Saturday, she was still more amused; she laughed till he laughed, too, without knowing why. It seemed to her very odd that he should know as much about breeding bulldogs as any man in England; that he had a collection of wild flowers found near London; and his weekly visit to old Miss Trotter at Ealing, who was an authority upon the science of Heraldry, never failed to excite her laughter. She wanted to know everything, even the kind of cake which the old lady supplied on these occasions; and their summer excursions to churches in the neighborhood of London for the purpose of taking rubbings of the brasses became most important festivals, from the interest she took in them. In six months she knew more about his odd friends and hobbies than his own brothers and sisters knew, after living with him all his life; and Ralph found this very pleasant, though disordering, for his own view of himself had always been profoundly serious.

Certainly it was very pleasant to be with Mary Datchet and to become, directly the door was shut, quite a different sort of person, eccentric and lovable, with scarcely any likeness to the self most people knew. He became less serious, and rather less dictatorial at home, for he was apt to hear Mary laughing at him, and telling him, as she was fond of doing, that he knew nothing at all about anything. She made him, also, take an interest in public questions, for which she had a natural liking; and was in process of turning him from Tory to Radical, after a course of public meetings, which began by boring him acutely, and ended by exciting him even more than they excited her.

But he was reserved; when ideas started up in his mind, he divided them automatically into those he could discuss with Mary, and those he must keep for himself. She knew this and it interested her, for she was accustomed to find young men very ready to talk about themselves, and had come to listen to them as one listens to children, without any thought of herself. But with Ralph, she had very little of this maternal feeling, and, in consequence, a much keener sense of her own individuality.

Late one afternoon Ralph stepped along the Strand to an interview with a lawyer upon business. The afternoon light was almost over, and already streams of greenish and yellowish artificial light were being poured into an atmosphere which, in country lanes, would now have been soft with the smoke of wood fires; and on both sides of the road the shop windows were full of sparkling chains and highly polished leather cases, which stood upon shelves made of thick plate-glass. None of these different objects was seen separately by Denham, but from all of them he drew an impression of stir and cheerfulness. Thus it came about that he saw Katharine Hilbery coming towards him, and looked straight at her, as if she were only an illustration of the argument that was going forward in his mind. In this spirit he noticed the rather set expression in her eyes, and the slight, half-conscious movement of her lips, which, together with her height and the distinction of her dress, made her look as if the scurrying crowd impeded her, and her direction were different from theirs. He noticed this calmly; but suddenly, as he passed her, his hands and knees began to tremble, and his heart beat painfully. She did not see him, and went on repeating to herself some lines which had stuck to her memory: "It's life that matters, nothing but life—the process of discovering—the everlasting and perpetual process, not the discovery itself at all." Thus occupied, she did not see Denham, and he had not the courage to stop her. But immediately the whole scene in the Strand wore that curious look of order and purpose which is imparted to the most heterogeneous things when music sounds; and so pleasant was this impression that he was very glad that he had not stopped her, after all. It grew slowly fainter, but lasted until he stood outside the barrister's chambers.

When his interview with the barrister was over, it was too late to go back to the office. His sight of Katharine had put him queerly out of tune for a domestic evening. Where should he go? To walk through the streets of London until he came to Katharine's house, to look up at the windows and fancy her within, seemed to him possible for a moment; and then he rejected the plan almost with a blush as, with a curious division of consciousness, one plucks a flower sentimentally and throws it away, with a blush, when it is actually picked. No, he would go and see Mary Datchet. By this time she would be back from her work.

To see Ralph appear unexpectedly in her room threw Mary for a second off her balance. She had been cleaning knives in her little scullery, and when she had let him in she went back again, and turned on the cold-water tap to its fullest volume, and then turned it off again. "Now," she thought to herself, as she screwed it tight, "I'm not going to let these silly ideas come into my head. . . . Don't you think Mr. Asquith deserves to be hanged?" she called back into the sitting-room, and when she joined him, drying her hands, she began to tell him about the latest evasion on the part of the Government with respect to the Women's Suffrage Bill. Ralph did not want to talk about politics, but he could not help respecting Mary for taking such an interest in public questions. He looked at her as she leant forward, poking the fire, and expressing herself very clearly in phrases which bore distantly the taint of the platform, and he thought, "How absurd Mary would think me if she knew that I almost made up my mind to walk all the way to Chelsea in order to look at Katharine's windows. She wouldn't understand it, but I like her very much as she is."

For some time they discussed what the women had better do; and as Ralph became genuinely interested in the question, Mary unconsciously let her attention wander, and a great desire came over her to talk to Ralph about her own feelings; or, at any rate, about something personal, so that she might see what he felt for her; but she resisted this wish. But she could not prevent him from feeling her lack of interest in what he was saying, and gradually they both became silent. One thought after another came up in Ralph's mind, but they were all, in some way, connected with Katharine, or with vague feelings of romance and adventure such as she inspired. But he could not talk to Mary about such thoughts; and he pitied her for knowing nothing of what he was feeling. "Here," he thought, "is where we differ from women; they have no sense of romance."

"Well, Mary," he said at length, "why don't you say something amusing?"

His tone was certainly provoking, but, as a general rule, Mary was not easily provoked. This evening, however, she replied rather sharply:

"Because I've got nothing amusing to say, I suppose."

Ralph thought for a moment, and then remarked:

"You work too hard. I don't mean your health," he added, as she laughed scornfully, "I mean that you seem to me to be getting wrapped up in your work."

"And is that a bad thing?" she asked, shading her eyes with her hand.

"I think it is," he returned abruptly.

"But only a week ago you were saying the opposite." Her tone was defiant, but she became curiously depressed. Ralph did not perceive it, and took this opportunity of lecturing her, and expressing his latest views upon the proper conduct of life. She listened, but her main impression was that he had been meeting some one who had influenced him. He was telling her that she ought to read more, and to see that there were other points of view as deserving of attention as her own. Naturally, having last seen him as he left the office in company with Katharine, she attributed the change to her; it was likely that Katharine, on leaving the scene which she had so clearly despised, had pronounced some such criticism, or suggested it by her own attitude. But she knew that Ralph would never admit that he had been influenced by anybody.

"You don't read enough, Mary," he was saying. "You ought to read more poetry."

It was true that Mary's reading had been rather limited to such works as she needed to know for the sake of examinations; and her time for reading in London was very little. For some reason, no one likes to be told that they do not read enough poetry, but her resentment was only visible in the way she changed the position of her hands, and in the fixed look in her eyes. And then she thought to herself, "I'm behaving exactly as I said I wouldn't behave," whereupon she relaxed all her muscles and said, in her reasonable way:

"Tell me what I ought to read, then."

Ralph had unconsciously been irritated by Mary, and he now delivered himself of a few names of great poets which were the text for a discourse upon the imperfection of Mary's character and way of life.

"You live with your inferiors," he said, warming unreasonably, as he knew, to his text. "And you get into a groove because, on the whole, it's rather a pleasant groove. And you tend to forget what you're there for. You've the feminine habit of making much of details. You don't see when things matter and when they don't. And that's what's the ruin of all these organizations. That's why the Suffragists have never done anything all these years. What's the point of drawing-room meetings and bazaars? You want to have ideas, Mary; get hold of something big; never mind making mistakes, but don't niggle. Why don't you throw it all up for a year, and travel?—see something of the world. Don't be content to live with half a dozen people in a backwater all your life. But you won't," he concluded.

"I've rather come to that way of thinking myself—about myself, I mean," said Mary, surprising him by her acquiescence. "I should like to go somewhere far away."

For a moment they were both silent. Ralph then said:

"But look here, Mary, you haven't been taking this seriously, have you?" His irritation was spent, and the depression, which she could not keep out of her voice, made him feel suddenly with remorse that he had been hurting her.

"You won't go away, will you?" he asked. And as she said nothing, he added, "Oh no, don't go away."

"I don't know exactly what I mean to do," she replied. She hovered on the verge of some discussion of her plans, but she received no encouragement. He fell into one of his queer silences, which seemed to Mary, in spite of all her precautions, to have reference to what she also could not prevent herself from thinking about—their feeling for each other and their relationship. She felt that the two lines of thought bored their way in long, parallel tunnels which came very close indeed, but never ran into each other.

When he had gone, and he left her without breaking his silence more than was needed to wish her good night, she sat on for a time, reviewing what he had said. If love is a devastating fire which melts the whole being into one mountain torrent, Mary was no more in love with Denham than she was in love with her poker or her tongs. But probably these extreme passions are very rare, and the state of mind thus depicted belongs to the very last stages of love, when the power to resist has been eaten away, week by week or day by day. Like most intelligent people, Mary was something of an egoist, to the extent, that is, of attaching great importance to what she felt, and she was by nature enough of a moralist to like to make certain, from time to time, that her feelings were creditable to her. When Ralph left her she thought over her state of mind, and came to the conclusion that it would be a good thing to learn a language—say Italian or German. She then went to a drawer, which she had to unlock, and took from it certain deeply scored manuscript pages. She read them through, looking up from her reading every now and then and thinking very intently for a few seconds about Ralph. She did her best to verify all the qualities in him which gave rise to emotions in her; and persuaded herself that she accounted reasonably for them all. Then she looked back again at her manuscript, and decided that to write grammatical English prose is the hardest thing in the world. But she thought about herself a great deal more than she thought about grammatical English prose or about Ralph Denham, and it may therefore be disputed whether she was in love, or, if so, to which branch of the family her passion belonged.

11

"It's life that matters, nothing but life—the process of discovering, the everlasting and perpetual process," said Katharine, as she passed under the archway, and so into the wide space of King's Bench Walk, "not the discovery itself at all." She spoke the last words looking up at Rodney's windows, which were a semilucent red color, in her honor, as she knew. He had asked her to tea with him. But she was in a mood when it is almost physically disagreeable to interrupt the stride of one's thought, and she walked up and down two or three times under the trees before approaching his staircase. She liked getting hold of some book which neither her father or mother had read, and keeping it to herself, and gnawing its contents in privacy, and pondering the meaning without sharing her thoughts with any one, or having to decide whether the book was a good one or a bad one. This evening she had twisted the words of Dostoevsky to suit her mood—a fatalistic mood—to proclaim that the process of discovery was life, and that, presumably, the nature of one's goal mattered not at all. She sat down for a moment upon one of the seats; felt herself carried along in the swirl of many things; decided, in her sudden way, that it was time to heave all this thinking overboard, and rose, leaving a fishmonger's basket on the seat behind her. Two minutes later her rap sounded with authority upon Rodney's door.

"Well, William," she said, "I'm afraid I'm late."

It was true, but he was so glad to see her that he forgot his annoyance. He had been occupied for over an hour in making things ready for her, and he now had his reward in seeing her look right and left, as she slipped her cloak from her shoulders, with evident satisfaction, although she said nothing. He had seen that the fire burnt well; jam-pots were on the table, tin covers shone in the fender, and the shabby comfort of the room was extreme. He was dressed in his old crimson dressing-gown, which was faded irregularly, and had bright new patches on it, like the paler grass which one finds on lifting a stone. He made the tea, and Katharine drew off her gloves, and crossed her legs with a gesture that was rather masculine in its ease. Nor did they talk much until they were smoking cigarettes over the fire, having placed their teacups upon the floor between them.

They had not met since they had exchanged letters about their relationship. Katharine's answer to his protestation had been short and sensible. Half a sheet of notepaper contained the whole of it, for she merely had to say that she was not in love with him, and so could not marry him, but their friendship would continue, she hoped, unchanged. She had added a postscript in which she stated, "I like your sonnet very much."

So far as William was concerned, this appearance of ease was assumed. Three times that afternoon he had dressed himself in a tail-coat, and three times he had discarded it for an old dressing-gown; three times he had placed his pearl tie-pin in position, and three times he had removed it again, the little looking-glass in his room being the witness of these changes of mind. The question was, which would Katharine prefer on this particular afternoon in December? He read her note once more, and the postscript about the sonnet settled the matter. Evidently she admired most the poet in him; and as this, on the whole, agreed with his own opinion, he decided to err, if anything, on the side of shabbiness. His demeanor was also regulated with premeditation; he spoke little, and only on impersonal matters; he wished her to realize that in visiting him for the first time alone she was doing nothing remarkable, although, in fact, that was a point about which he was not at all sure.

Certainly Katharine seemed quite unmoved by any disturbing thoughts; and if he had been completely master of himself, he might, indeed, have complained that she was a trifle absent-minded. The ease, the familiarity of the situation alone with Rodney, among teacups and candles, had more effect upon her than was apparent. She asked to look at his books, and then at his pictures. It was while she held photograph from the Greek in her hands that she exclaimed, impulsively, if incongruously:

"My oysters! I had a basket," she explained, "and I've left it somewhere. Uncle Dudley dines with us tonight. What in the world have I done with them?"

She rose and began to wander about the room. William rose also, and stood in front of the fire, muttering, "Oysters, oysters—your basket of oysters!" but though he looked vaguely here and there, as if the oysters might be on the top of the bookshelf, his eyes returned always to Katharine. She drew the curtain and looked out among the scanty leaves of the plane-trees.

"I had them," she calculated, "in the Strand; I sat on a seat. Well, never mind," she concluded, turning back into the room abruptly, "I dare say some old creature is enjoying them by this time."

"I should have thought that you never forgot anything," William remarked, as they settled down again.

"That's part of the myth about me, I know," Katharine replied.

"And I wonder," William proceeded, with some caution, "what the truth about you is? But I know this sort of thing doesn't interest you," he added hastily, with a touch of peevishness.

"No; it doesn't interest me very much," she replied candidly.

"What shall we talk about then?" he asked.

She looked rather whimsically round the walls of the room.

"However we start, we end by talking about the same thing—about poetry, I mean. I wonder if you realize, William, that I've never read even Shakespeare? It's rather wonderful how I've kept it up all these years."

"You've kept it up for ten years very beautifully, as far as I'm concerned," he said.

"Ten years? So long as that?"

"And I don't think it's always bored you," he added.

She looked into the fire silently. She could not deny that the surface of her feeling was absolutely unruffled by anything in William's character; on the contrary, she felt certain that she could deal with whatever turned up. He gave her peace, in which she could think of things that were far removed from what they talked about. Even now, when he sat within a yard of her, how easily her mind ranged hither and thither! Suddenly a picture presented itself before her, without any effort on her part as pictures will, of herself in these very rooms; she had come in from a lecture, and she held a pile of books in her hand, scientific books, and books about mathematics and astronomy which she had mastered. She put them down on the table over there. It was a picture plucked from her life two or three years hence, when she was married to William; but here she checked herself abruptly.

She could not entirely forget William's presence, because, in spite of his efforts to control himself, his nervousness was apparent. On such occasions his eyes protruded more than ever, and his face had more than ever the appearance of being covered with a thin crackling skin, through which every flush of his volatile blood showed itself instantly. By this time he had shaped so many sentences and rejected them, felt so many impulses and subdued them, that he was a uniform scarlet.

"You may say you don't read books," he remarked, "but, all the same, you know about them. Besides, who wants you to be learned? Leave that to the poor devils who've got nothing better to do. You–you–ahem!–"

"Well, then, why don't you read me something before I go?" said Katharine, looking at her watch.

"Katharine, you've only just come! Let me see now, what have I got to show you?" He rose, and stirred about the papers on his table, as if in doubt; he then picked up a manuscript, and after spreading it smoothly upon his knee, he looked up at Katharine suspiciously. He caught her smiling.

"I believe you only ask me to read out of kindness," he burst out. "Let's find something else to talk about. Who have you been seeing?"

"I don't generally ask things out of kindness," Katharine observed; "however, if you don't want to read, you needn't."

William gave a queer snort of exasperation, and opened his manuscript once more, though he kept his eyes upon her face as he did so. No face could have been graver or more judicial.

"One can trust you, certainly, to say unpleasant things," he said, smoothing out the page, clearing his throat, and reading half a stanza to himself. "Ahem! The Princess is lost in the wood, and she hears the sound of a horn. (This would all be very pretty on the stage, but I can't get the effect here.) Anyhow, Sylvano enters, accompanied by the rest of the gentlemen of Gratian's court. I begin where he soliloquizes." He jerked his head and began to read.

Although Katharine had just disclaimed any knowledge of literature, she listened attentively. At least, she listened to the first twenty-five lines attentively, and then she frowned. Her attention was only aroused again when Rodney raised his finger–a sign, she knew, that the meter was about to change.

His theory was that every mood has its meter. His mastery of meters was very great; and, if the beauty of a drama depended upon the variety of measures in which the personages speak, Rodney's plays must have challenged the works of Shakespeare. Katharine's ignorance of Shakespeare did not prevent her from feeling fairly certain that plays should not produce a sense of chill stupor in the audience, such as overcame her as the lines flowed on, sometimes long and sometimes short, but always delivered with the same lilt of voice, which seemed to nail each line firmly on to the same spot in the hearer's brain. Still, she reflected, these sorts of skill are almost exclusively masculine; women neither practice them nor know how to value them; and one's husband's proficiency in this direction might legitimately increase one's respect for him, since mystification is no bad basis for respect. No one could doubt that William was a scholar. The reading ended with the finish of the Act; Katharine had prepared a little speech.

"That seems to me extremely well written, William; although, of course, I don't know enough to criticize in detail."

"But it's the skill that strikes you—not the emotion?"

"In a fragment like that, of course, the skill strikes one most."

"But perhaps—have you time to listen to one more short piece? the scene between the lovers? There's some real feeling in that, I think. Denham agrees that it's the best thing I've done."

"You've read it to Ralph Denham?" Katharine inquired, with surprise. "He's a better judge than I am. What did he say?"

"My dear Katharine," Rodney exclaimed, "I don't ask you for criticism, as I should ask a scholar. I dare say there are only five men in England whose opinion of my work matters a straw to me. But I trust you where feeling is concerned. I had you in my mind often when I was writing those scenes. I kept asking myself, 'Now is this the sort of thing Katharine would like?' I always think of you when I'm writing, Katharine, even when it's the sort of thing you wouldn't know about. And I'd rather—yes, I really believe I'd rather—you thought well of my writing than any one in the world."

This was so genuine a tribute to his trust in her that Katharine was touched.

"You think too much of me altogether, William," she said, forgetting that she had not meant to speak in this way.

"No, Katharine, I don't," he replied, replacing his manuscript in the drawer. "It does me good to think of you."

So quiet an answer, followed as it was by no expression of love, but merely by the statement that if she must go he would take her to the Strand, and would, if she could wait a moment, change his dressing-gown for a coat, moved her to the warmest feeling of affection for him that she had yet experienced. While he changed in the next room, she stood by the bookcase, taking down books and opening them, but reading nothing on their pages.

She felt certain that she would marry Rodney. How could one avoid it? How could one find fault with it? Here she sighed, and, putting the thought of marriage away, fell into a dream state, in which she became another person, and the whole world seemed changed. Being a frequent visitor to that world, she could find her way there unhesitatingly. If she had tried to analyze her impressions, she would have said that there dwelt the realities of the appearances which figure in our world; so direct, powerful, and unimpeded were her sensations there, compared with those called forth in actual life. There dwelt the things one might have felt, had there been cause; the perfect happiness of which here we taste the fragment; the beauty seen here in flying glimpses only. No doubt much of the furniture of this world was drawn directly from the past, and even from the England of the Elizabethan age. However the embellishment of this imaginary world might change, two qualities were constant in it. It was a place where feelings were liberated from the constraint which the real world puts upon them; and the process of awakenment was always marked by resignation and a kind of stoical acceptance of facts. She met no acquaintance there, as Denham did, miraculously transfigured; she played no heroic part. But there certainly she loved some magnanimous hero, and as they swept together among the leaf-hung trees of an unknown world, they shared the feelings which came fresh and fast as the waves on the shore. But the sands of her liberation were running fast; even through the forest branches came sounds of Rodney moving things on his dressing-table; and Katharine woke herself from this excursion by shutting the cover of the book she was holding, and replacing it in the bookshelf.

"William," she said, speaking rather faintly at first, like one sending a voice from sleep to reach the living. "William," she repeated firmly, "if you still want me to marry you, I will."

Perhaps it was that no man could expect to have the most momentous question of his life settled in a voice so level, so toneless, so devoid of joy or energy. At any rate William made no answer. She waited stoically. A moment later he stepped briskly from his dressing-room, and observed that if she wanted to buy more oysters he thought he knew where they could find a fishmonger's shop still open. She breathed deeply a sigh of relief.

Extract from a letter sent a few days later by Mrs. Hilbery to her sister-in-law, Mrs. Milvain:

" . . . How stupid of me to forget the name in my telegram. Such a nice, rich, English name, too, and, in addition, he has all the graces of intellect; he has read literally *everything.* I tell Katharine, I shall always put him on my right side at dinner, so as to have him by me when people begin talking about characters in Shakespeare. They won't be rich, but they'll be very, very happy. I was sitting in my room late one night, feeling that nothing nice would ever happen to me again, when I heard Katharine outside in the passage, and I thought to myself, 'Shall I call her in?' and then I thought (in that hopeless, dreary way one does think, with the fire going out and one's birthday just over), 'Why should I lay my troubles on *her?*' But my little self-control had its reward, for next moment she tapped at the door and came in, and sat on the rug, and though we neither of us said anything, I felt so happy all of a second that I couldn't help crying, 'Oh, Katharine, when you come to my age, how I hope you'll have a daughter, too!' You know how silent Katharine is. She was so silent, for such a long time, that in my foolish, nervous state I dreaded something, I don't quite know what. And then she told me how, after all, she had made up her mind. She had written. She expected him tomorrow. At first I wasn't glad at all. I didn't want her to marry any one; but when she said, 'It will make no difference. I shall always care for you and father most,' then I saw how selfish I was, and I told her she must give him everything, everything, everything! I told her I should be thankful to come second. But why, when everything's turned out just as one always hoped it would turn out, why then can one do nothing but cry, nothing but feel a desolate old woman whose life's been a failure, and now is nearly over, and age is so cruel? But Katharine said to me, 'I am happy. I'm very happy.' And then I thought, though it all seemed so desperately dismal at the time, Katharine had said she was happy, and I should have a son, and it would all turn out so much more wonderfully than I could possibly imagine, for though the sermons don't say so, I do believe the world is meant for us to be happy in. She told me that they would live quite near us, and see us every day; and she would go on with the Life, and we should finish it as we had meant to. And, after all, it would be far more horrid if she didn't marry—or suppose she married some one we couldn't endure? Suppose she had fallen in love with some one who was married already?

"And though one never thinks any one good enough for the people one's fond of, he has the kindest, truest instincts, I'm sure, and though he seems nervous and his manner is not commanding, I only think these things because it's Katharine. And now I've written this, it comes over me that, of course, all the time, Katharine has what he hasn't. She does command, she isn't nervous; it comes naturally to her to rule and control. It's time that she should give all this to some one who will need her when we aren't there, save in our spirits, for whatever people say, I'm sure I shall come back to this wonderful world where one's been so happy and so miserable, where, even now, I seem to see myself stretching out my hands for another present from the great Fairy Tree whose boughs are still hung with enchanting toys, though they are rarer now, perhaps, and between the branches one sees no longer the blue sky, but the stars and the tops of the mountains.

"One doesn't know any more, does one? One hasn't any advice to give one's children. One can only hope that they will have the same vision and the same power to believe, without which life would be so meaningless. That is what I ask for Katharine and her husband."

12

"Is Mr. Hilbery at home, or Mrs. Hilbery?" Denham asked, of the parlormaid in Chelsea, a week later.

"No, sir. But Miss Hilbery is at home," the girl answered.

Ralph had anticipated many answers, but not this one, and now it was unexpectedly made plain to him that it was the chance of seeing Katharine that had brought him all the way to Chelsea on pretence of seeing her father.

He made some show of considering the matter, and was taken upstairs to the drawing-room. As upon that first occasion, some weeks ago, the door closed as if it were a thousand doors softly excluding the world; and once more Ralph received an impression of a room full of deep shadows, firelight, unwavering silver candle flames, and empty spaces to be crossed before reaching the round table in the middle of the room, with its frail burden of silver trays and china teacups. But this time Katharine was there by herself; the volume in her hand showed that she expected no visitors.

Ralph said something about hoping to find her father.

"My father is out," she replied. "But if you can wait, I expect him soon."

It might have been due merely to politeness, but Ralph felt that she received him almost with cordiality. Perhaps she was bored by drinking tea and reading a book all alone; at any rate, she tossed the book on to a sofa with a gesture of relief.

"Is that one of the moderns whom you despise?" he asked, smiling at the carelessness of her gesture.

"Yes," she replied. "I think even you would despise him."

"Even I?" he repeated. "Why even I?"

"You said you liked modern things; I said I hated them."

This was not a very accurate report of their conversation among the relics, perhaps, but Ralph was flattered to think that she remembered anything about it.

"Or did I confess that I hated all books?" she went on, seeing him look up with an air of inquiry. "I forget—"

"Do you hate all books?" he asked.

"It would be absurd to say that I hate all books when I've only read ten, perhaps; but—" Here she pulled herself up short.

"Well?"

"Yes, I do hate books," she continued. "Why do you want to be for ever talking about your feelings? That's what I can't make out. And poetry's all about feelings—novels are all about feelings."

She cut a cake vigorously into slices, and providing a tray with bread and butter for Mrs. Hilbery, who was in her room with a cold, she rose to go upstairs.

Ralph held the door open for her, and then stood with clasped hands in the middle of the room. His eyes were bright, and, indeed, he scarcely knew whether they beheld dreams or realities. All down the street and on the doorstep, and while he mounted the stairs, his dream of Katharine possessed him; on the threshold of the room he had dismissed it, in order to prevent too painful a collision between what he dreamt of her and what she was. And in five minutes she had filled the shell of the old dream with the flesh of life; looked with fire out of phantom eyes. He glanced about him with bewilderment at finding himself among her chairs and tables; they were solid, for he grasped the back of the chair in which Katharine had sat; and yet they were unreal; the atmosphere was that of a dream. He summoned all the faculties of his spirit to seize what the minutes had to give him; and from the depths of his mind there rose unchecked a joyful recognition of the truth that human nature surpasses, in its beauty, all that our wildest dreams bring us hints of.

Katharine came into the room a moment later. He stood watching her come towards him, and thought her more beautiful and strange than his dream of her; for the real Katharine could speak the words which seemed to crowd behind the forehead and in the depths of the eyes, and the commonest sentence would be flashed on by this immortal light. And she overflowed the edges of the dream; he remarked that her softness was like that of some vast snowy owl; she wore a ruby on her finger.

"My mother wants me to tell you," she said, "that she hopes you have begun your poem. She says every one ought to write poetry. . . . All my relations write poetry," she went on. "I can't bear to think of it sometimes—because, of course, it's none of it any good. But then one needn't read it—"

"You don't encourage me to write a poem," said Ralph.

"But you're not a poet, too, are you?" she inquired, turning upon him with a laugh.

"Should I tell you if I were?"

"Yes. Because I think you speak the truth," she said, searching him for proof of this apparently, with eyes now almost impersonally direct. It would be easy, Ralph thought, to worship one so far removed, and yet of so straight a nature; easy to submit recklessly to her, without thought of future pain.

"Are you a poet?" she demanded. He felt that her question had an unexplained weight of meaning behind it, as if she sought an answer to a question that she did not ask.

"No. I haven't written any poetry for years," he replied. "But all the same, I don't agree with you. I think it's the only thing worth doing."

"Why do you say that?" she asked, almost with impatience, tapping her spoon two or three times against the side of her cup.

"Why?" Ralph laid hands on the first words that came to mind. "Because, I suppose, it keeps an ideal alive which might die otherwise."

A curious change came over her face, as if the flame of her mind were subdued; and she looked at him ironically and with the expression which he had called sad before, for want of a better name for it.

"I don't know that there's much sense in having ideals," she said.

"But you have them," he replied energetically. "Why do we call them ideals? It's a stupid word. Dreams, I mean—"

She followed his words with parted lips, as though to answer eagerly when he had done; but as he said, "Dreams, I mean," the door of the drawing-room swung open, and so remained for a perceptible instant. They both held themselves silent, her lips still parted.

Far off, they heard the rustle of skirts. Then the owner of the skirts appeared in the doorway, which she almost filled, nearly concealing the figure of a very much smaller lady who accompanied her.

"My aunts!" Katharine murmured, under her breath. Her tone had a hint of tragedy in it, but no less, Ralph thought, than the situation required. She addressed the larger lady as Aunt Millicent; the smaller was Aunt Celia, Mrs. Milvain, who had lately undertaken the task of marrying Cyril to his wife. Both ladies, but Mrs. Cosham (Aunt Millicent) in particular, had that look of heightened, smoothed, incarnadined existence which is proper to elderly ladies paying calls in London about five o'clock in the afternoon. Portraits by Romney, seen through glass, have something of their pink, mellow look, their blooming softness, as of apricots hanging upon a red wall in the afternoon sun. Mrs. Cosham was so appareled with hanging muffs, chains, and swinging draperies that it was impossible to detect the shape of a human being in the mass of brown and black which filled the arm-chair. Mrs. Milvain was a much slighter figure; but the same doubt as to the precise lines of her contour filled Ralph, as he regarded them, with dismal foreboding. What remark of his would ever reach these fabulous and fantastic characters?—for there was something fantastically unreal in the curious swayings and noddings of Mrs. Cosham, as if her equipment included a large wire spring. Her voice had a high-pitched, cooing note, which prolonged words and cut them short until the English language seemed no longer fit for common purposes. In a moment of nervousness, so Ralph thought, Katharine had turned on innumerable electric lights. But Mrs. Cosham had gained impetus (perhaps her swaying movements had that end in view) for sustained speech; and she now addressed Ralph deliberately and elaborately.

"I come from Woking, Mr. Popham. You may well ask me, why Woking? and to that I answer, for perhaps the hundredth time, because of the sunsets. We went there for the sunsets, but that was five-and-twenty years ago. Where are the sunsets now? Alas! There is no sunset now nearer than the South Coast." Her rich and romantic notes were accompanied by a wave of a long white hand, which, when waved, gave off a flash of diamonds, rubies, and emeralds. Ralph wondered whether she more resembled an elephant, with a jeweled head-dress, or a superb cockatoo, balanced insecurely upon its perch, and pecking capriciously at a lump of sugar.

"Where are the sunsets now?" she repeated. "Do you find sunsets now, Mr. Popham?"

"I live at Highgate," he replied.

"At Highgate? Yes, Highgate has its charms; your Uncle John lived at Highgate," she jerked in the direction of Katharine. She sank her head upon her breast, as if for a moment's meditation, which past, she looked up and observed: "I dare say there are very pretty lanes in Highgate. I can recollect walking with your mother, Katharine, through lanes blossoming with wild hawthorn. But where is the hawthorn now? You remember that exquisite description in De Quincey, Mr. Popham?—but I forget, you, in your generation, with all your activity and enlightenment, at which I can only marvel"—here she displayed both her beautiful white hands—"do not read De Quincey. You have your Belloc, your Chesterton, your Bernard Shaw—why should you read De Quincey?"

"But I do read De Quincey," Ralph protested, "more than Belloc and Chesterton, anyhow."

"Indeed!" exclaimed Mrs. Cosham, with a gesture of surprise and relief mingled. "You are, then, a *rara avis* in your generation. I am delighted to meet anyone who reads De Quincey."

Here she hollowed her hand into a screen, and, leaning towards Katharine, inquired, in a very audible whisper, "Does your friend *write?*"

"Mr. Denham," said Katharine, with more than her usual clearness and firmness, "writes for the Review. He is a lawyer."

"The clean-shaven lips, showing the expression of the mouth! I recognize them at once. I always feel at home with lawyers, Mr. Denham—"

"They used to come about so much in the old days," Mrs. Milvain interposed, the frail, silvery notes of her voice falling with the sweet tone of an old bell.

"You say you live at Highgate," she continued. "I wonder whether you happen to know if there is an old house called Tempest Lodge still in existence—an old white house in a garden?"

Ralph shook his head, and she sighed.

"Ah, no; it must have been pulled down by this time, with all the other old houses. There were such pretty lanes in those days. That was how your uncle met your Aunt Emily, you know," she addressed Katharine. "They walked home through the lanes."

"A sprig of May in her bonnet," Mrs. Cosham ejaculated, reminiscently.

"And next Sunday he had violets in his buttonhole. And that was how we guessed."

Katharine laughed. She looked at Ralph. His eyes were meditative, and she wondered what he found in this old gossip to make him ponder so contentedly. She felt, she hardly knew why, a curious pity for him.

"Uncle John—yes, 'poor John,' you always called him. Why was that?" she asked, to make them go on talking, which, indeed, they needed little invitation to do.

"That was what his father, old Sir Richard, always called him. Poor John, or the fool of the family," Mrs. Milvain hastened to inform them. "The other boys were so brilliant, and he could never pass his examinations, so they sent him to India—a long voyage in those days, poor fellow. You had your own room, you know, and you did it up. But he will get his knighthood and a pension, I believe," she said, turning to Ralph, "only it is not England."

"No," Mrs. Cosham confirmed her, "it is not England. In those days we thought an Indian Judgeship about equal to a county-court judgeship at home. His Honor—a pretty title, but still, not at the top of the tree. However," she sighed, "if you have a wife and seven children, and people nowadays very quickly forget your father's name—well, you have to take what you can get," she concluded.

"And I fancy," Mrs. Milvain resumed, lowering her voice rather confidentially, "that John would have done more if it hadn't been for his wife, your Aunt Emily. She was a very good woman, devoted to him, of course, but she was not ambitious for him, and if a wife isn't ambitious for her husband, especially in a profession like the law, clients soon get to know of it. In our young days, Mr. Denham, we used to say that we knew which of our friends would become judges, by looking at the girls they married. And so it was, and so, I fancy, it always will be. I don't think," she added, summing up these scattered remarks, "that any man is really happy unless he succeeds in his profession."

Mrs. Cosham approved of this sentiment with more ponderous sagacity from her side of the tea-table, in the first place by swaying her head, and in the second by remarking:

"No, men are not the same as women. I fancy Alfred Tennyson spoke the truth about that as about many other things. How I wish he'd lived to write 'The Prince'—a sequel to 'The Princess'! I confess I'm almost tired of Princesses. We want some one to show us what a good man can be. We have Laura and Beatrice, Antigone and Cordelia, but we have no heroic man. How do you, as a poet, account for that, Mr. Denham?"

"I'm not a poet," said Ralph good-humoredly. "I'm only a solicitor."

"But you write, too?" Mrs. Cosham demanded, afraid lest she should be balked of her priceless discovery, a young man truly devoted to literature.

"In my spare time," Denham reassured her.

"In your spare time!" Mrs. Cosham echoed. "That is a proof of devotion, indeed." She half closed her eyes, and indulged herself in a fascinating picture of a briefless barrister lodged in a garret, writing immortal novels by the light of a farthing dip. But the romance which fell upon the figures of great writers and illumined their pages was no false radiance in her case. She carried her pocket Shakespeare about with her, and met life fortified by the words of the poets. How far she saw Denham, and how far she confused him with some hero of fiction, it would be hard to say. Literature had taken possession even of her memories. She was matching him, presumably, with certain characters in the old novels, for she came out, after a pause, with:

"Um—um—Pendennis—Warrington—I could never forgive Laura," she pronounced energetically, "for not marrying George, in spite of everything. George Eliot did the very same thing; and Lewes was a little frog-faced man, with the manner of a dancing master. But Warrington, now, had everything in his favor; intellect, passion, romance, distinction, and the connection was a mere piece of undergraduate folly. Arthur, I confess, has always seemed to me a bit of a fop; I can't imagine how Laura married him. But you say you're a solicitor, Mr. Denham. Now there are one or two things I should like to ask you—about Shakespeare——" She drew out her small, worn volume with some difficulty, opened it, and shook it in the air. "They say, nowadays, that Shakespeare was a lawyer. They say, that accounts for his knowledge of human nature. There's a fine example for you, Mr. Denham. Study your clients, young man, and the world will be the richer one of these days, I have no doubt. Tell me, how do we come out of it, now; better or worse than you expected?"

Thus called upon to sum up the worth of human nature in a few words, Ralph answered unhesitatingly:

"Worse, Mrs. Cosham, a good deal worse. I'm afraid the ordinary man is a bit of a rascal—"

"And the ordinary woman?"

"No, I don't like the ordinary woman either—"

Ah, dear me, I've no doubt that's very true, very true." Mrs. Cosham sighed. "Swift would have agreed with you, anyhow—" She looked at him, and thought that there were signs of distinct power in his brow. He would do well, she thought, to devote himself to satire.

"Charles Lavington, you remember, was a solicitor," Mrs. Milvain interposed, rather resenting the waste of time involved in talking about fictitious people when you might be talking about real people. "But you wouldn't remember him, Katharine."

"Mr. Lavington? Oh, yes, I do," said Katharine, waking from other thoughts with her little start. "The summer we had a house near Tenby. I remember the field and the pond with the tadpoles, and making haystacks with Mr. Lavington."

"She is right. There *was* a pond with tadpoles," Mrs. Cosham corroborated. "Millais made studies of it for 'Ophelia.' Some say that is the best picture he ever painted—"

"And I remember the dog chained up in the yard, and the dead snakes hanging in the toolhouse."

"It was at Tenby that you were chased by the bull," Mrs. Milvain continued. "But that you couldn't remember, though it's true you were a wonderful child. Such eyes she had, Mr. Denham! I used to say to her father, 'She's watching us, and summing us all up in her little mind.' And they had a nurse in those days," she went on, telling her story with charming solemnity to Ralph, "who was a good woman, but engaged to a sailor. When she ought to have been attending to the baby, her eyes were on the sea. And Mrs. Hilbery allowed this girl–Susan her name was–to have him to stay in the village. They abused her goodness, I'm sorry to say, and while they walked in the lanes, they stood the perambulator alone in a field where there was a bull. The animal became enraged by the red blanket in the perambulator, and Heaven knows what might have happened if a gentleman had not been walking by in the nick of time, and rescued Katharine in his arms!"

"I think the bull was only a cow, Aunt Celia," said Katharine.

"My darling, it was a great red Devonshire bull, and not long after it gored a man to death and had to be destroyed. And your mother forgave Susan—a thing I could never have done."

"Maggie's sympathies were entirely with Susan and the sailor, I am sure," said Mrs. Cosham, rather tartly. "My sister-in-law," she continued, "has laid her burdens upon Providence at every crisis in her life, and Providence, I must confess, has responded nobly, so far—"

"Yes," said Katharine, with a laugh, for she liked the rashness which irritated the rest of the family. "My mother's bulls always turn into cows at the critical moment."

"Well," said Mrs. Milvain, "I'm glad you have some one to protect you from bulls now."

"I can't imagine William protecting any one from bulls," said Katharine.

It happened that Mrs. Cosham had once more produced her pocket volume of Shakespeare, and was consulting Ralph upon an obscure passage in "Measure for Measure." He did not at once seize the meaning of what Katharine and her aunt were saying; William, he supposed, referred to some small cousin, for he now saw Katharine as a child in a pinafore; but, nevertheless, he was so much distracted that his eye could hardly follow the words on the paper. A moment later he heard them speak distinctly of an engagement ring.

"I like rubies," he heard Katharine say.

> To be imprison'd in the viewless winds,
> And blown with restless violence round about
> The pendant world. . . .

Mrs. Cosham intoned; at the same instant "Rodney" fitted itself to "William" in Ralph's mind. He felt convinced that Katharine was engaged to Rodney. His first sensation was one of violent rage with her for having deceived him throughout the visit, fed him with pleasant old wives' tales, let him see her as a child playing in a meadow, shared her youth with him, while all the time she was a stranger entirely, and engaged to marry Rodney.

But was it possible? Surely it was not possible. For in his eyes she was still a child. He paused so long over the book that Mrs. Cosham had time to look over his shoulder and ask her niece:

"And have you settled upon a house yet, Katharine?"

This convinced him of the truth of the monstrous idea. He looked up at once and said:

"Yes, it's a difficult passage."

His voice had changed so much, he spoke with such curtness and even with such contempt, that Mrs. Cosham looked at him fairly puzzled. Happily she belonged to a generation which expected uncouthness in its men, and she merely felt convinced that this Mr. Denham was very, very clever. She took back her Shakespeare, as Denham seemed to have no more to say, and secreted it once more about her person with the infinitely pathetic resignation of the old.

"Katharine's engaged to William Rodney," she said, by way of filling in the pause; "a very old friend of ours. He has a wonderful knowledge of literature, too—wonderful." She nodded her head rather vaguely. "You should meet each other."

Denham's one wish was to leave the house as soon as he could; but the elderly ladies had risen, and were proposing to visit Mrs. Hilbery in her bedroom, so that any move on his part was impossible. At the same time, he wished to say something, but he knew not what, to Katharine alone. She took her aunts upstairs, and returned, coming towards him once more with an air of innocence and friendliness that amazed him.

"My father will be back," she said. "Won't you sit down?" and she laughed, as if now they might share a perfectly friendly laugh at the tea-party.

But Ralph made no attempt to seat himself.

"I must congratulate you," he said. "It was news to me." He saw her face change, but only to become graver than before.

"My engagement?" she asked. "Yes, I am going to marry William Rodney."

Ralph remained standing with his hand on the back of a chair in absolute silence. Abysses seemed to plunge into darkness between them. He looked at her, but her face showed that she was not thinking of him. No regret or consciousness of wrong disturbed her.

"Well, I must go," he said at length.

She seemed about to say something, then changed her mind and said merely:

"You will come again, I hope. We always seem"—she hesitated—"to be interrupted."

He bowed and left the room.

Ralph strode with extreme swiftness along the Embankment. Every muscle was taut and braced as if to resist some sudden attack from outside. For the moment it seemed as if the attack were about to be directed against his body, and his brain thus was on the alert, but without understanding. Finding himself, after a few minutes, no longer under observation, and no attack delivered, he slackened his pace, the pain spread all through him, took possession of every governing seat, and met with scarcely any resistance from powers exhausted by their first effort at defence. He took his way languidly along the river embankment, away from home rather than towards it. The world had him at its mercy. He made no pattern out of the sights he saw. He felt himself now, as he had often fancied other people, adrift on the stream, and far removed from control of it, a man with no grasp upon circumstances any longer. Old battered men loafing at the doors of public-houses now seemed to be his fellows, and he felt, as he supposed them to feel, a mingling of envy and hatred towards those who passed quickly and certainly to a goal of their own. They, too, saw things very thin and shadowy, and were wafted about by the lightest breath of wind. For the substantial world, with its prospect of avenues leading on and on to the invisible distance, had slipped from him, since Katharine was engaged. Now all his life was visible, and the straight, meager path had its ending soon enough. Katharine was engaged, and she had deceived him, too. He felt for corners of his being untouched by his disaster; but there was no limit to the flood of damage; not one of his possessions was safe now. Katharine had deceived him; she had mixed herself with every thought of his, and reft of her they seemed false thoughts which he would blush to think again. His life seemed immeasurably impoverished.

He sat himself down, in spite of the chilly fog which obscured the farther bank and left its lights suspended upon a blank surface, upon one of the riverside seats, and let the tide of disillusionment sweep through him. For the time being all bright points in his life were blotted out; all prominences leveled. At first he made himself believe that Katharine had treated him badly, and drew comfort from the thought that, left alone, she would recollect this, and think of him and tender him, in silence, at any rate, an apology. But this grain of comfort failed him after a second or two, for, upon reflection, he had to admit that Katharine owed him nothing. Katharine had promised nothing, taken nothing; to her his dreams had meant nothing. This, indeed, was the lowest pitch of his despair. If the best of one's feelings means nothing to the person most concerned in those feelings, what reality is left us? The old romance which had warmed his days for him, the thoughts of Katharine which had painted every hour, were now made to appear foolish and enfeebled. He rose, and looked into the river, whose swift race of dun-colored waters seemed the very spirit of futility and oblivion.

"In what can one trust, then?" he thought, as he leant there. So feeble and insubstantial did he feel himself that he repeated the word aloud.

"In what can one trust? Not in men and women. Not in one's dreams about them. There's nothing—nothing, nothing left at all."

Now Denham had reason to know that he could bring to birth and keep alive a fine anger when he chose. Rodney provided a good target for that emotion. And yet at the moment, Rodney and Katharine herself seemed disembodied ghosts. He could scarcely remember the look of them. His mind plunged lower and lower. Their marriage seemed of no importance to him. All things had turned to ghosts; the whole mass of the world was insubstantial vapor, surrounding the solitary spark in his mind, whose burning point he could remember, for it burnt no more. He had once cherished a belief, and Katharine had embodied this belief, and she did so no longer. He did not blame her; he blamed nothing, nobody; he saw the truth. He saw the dun-colored race of waters and the blank shore. But life is vigorous; the body lives, and the body, no doubt, dictated the reflection, which now urged him to movement, that one may cast away the forms of human beings, and yet retain the passion which seemed inseparable from their existence in the flesh. Now this passion burnt on his horizon, as the winter sun makes a greenish pane in the west through thinning clouds. His eyes were set on something infinitely far and remote; by that light he felt he could walk, and would, in future, have to find his way. But that was all there was left to him of a populous and teeming world.

13

The lunch hour in the office was only partly spent by Denham in the consumption of food. Whether fine or wet, he passed most of it pacing the gravel paths in Lincoln's Inn Fields. The children got to know his figure, and the sparrows expected their daily scattering of bread-crumbs. No doubt, since he often gave a copper and almost always a handful of bread, he was not as blind to his surroundings as he thought himself.

He thought that these winter days were spent in long hours before white papers radiant in electric light; and in short passages through fog-dimmed streets. When he came back to his work after lunch he carried in his head a picture of the Strand, scattered with omnibuses, and of the purple shapes of leaves pressed flat upon the gravel, as if his eyes had always been bent upon the ground. His brain worked incessantly, but his thought was attended with so little joy that he did not willingly recall it; but drove ahead, now in this direction, now in that; and came home laden with dark books borrowed from a library.

Mary Datchet, coming from the Strand at lunch-time, saw him one day taking his turn, closely buttoned in an overcoat, and so lost in thought that he might have been sitting in his own room.

She was overcome by something very like awe by the sight of him; then she felt much inclined to laugh, although her pulse beat faster. She passed him, and he never saw her. She came back and touched him on the shoulder.

"Gracious, Mary!" he exclaimed. "How you startled me!"

"Yes. You looked as if you were walking in your sleep," she said. "Are you arranging some terrible love affair? Have you got to reconcile a desperate couple?"

"I wasn't thinking about my work," Ralph replied, rather hastily. "And, besides, that sort of thing's not in my line," he added, rather grimly.

The morning was fine, and they had still some minutes of leisure to spend. They had not met for two or three weeks, and Mary had much to say to Ralph; but she was not certain how far he wished for her company. However, after a turn or two, in which a few facts were communicated, he suggested sitting down, and she took the seat beside him. The sparrows came fluttering about them, and Ralph produced from his pocket the half of a roll saved from his luncheon. He threw a few crumbs among them.

"I've never seen sparrows so tame," Mary observed, by way of saying something.

"No," said Ralph. "The sparrows in Hyde Park aren't as tame as this. If we keep perfectly still, I'll get one to settle on my arm."

Mary felt that she could have forgone this display of animal good temper, but seeing that Ralph, for some curious reason, took a pride in the sparrows, she bet him sixpence that he would not succeed.

"Done!" he said; and his eye, which had been gloomy, showed a spark of light. His conversation was now addressed entirely to a bald cock-sparrow, who seemed bolder than the rest; and Mary took the opportunity of looking at him. She was not satisfied; his face was worn, and his expression stern. A child came bowling its hoop through the concourse of birds, and Ralph threw his last crumbs of bread into the bushes with a snort of impatience.

"That's what always happens—just as I've almost got him," he said. "Here's your sixpence, Mary. But you've only got it thanks to that brute of a boy. They oughtn't to be allowed to bowl hoops here——"

"Oughtn't to be allowed to bowl hoops! My dear Ralph, what nonsense!"

"You always say that," he complained; "and it isn't nonsense. What's the point of having a garden if one can't watch birds in it? The street does all right for hoops. And if children can't be trusted in the streets, their mothers should keep them at home."

Mary made no answer to this remark, but frowned.

She leant back on the seat and looked about her at the great houses breaking the soft gray-blue sky with their chimneys.

"Ah, well," she said, "London's a fine place to live in. I believe I could sit and watch people all day long. I like my fellow-creatures. . . ."

Ralph sighed impatiently.

"Yes, I think so, when you come to know them," she added, as if his disagreement had been spoken.

"That's just when I don't like them," he replied. "Still, I don't see why you shouldn't cherish that illusion, if it pleases you." He spoke without much vehemence of agreement or disagreement. He seemed chilled.

"Wake up, Ralph! You're half asleep!" Mary cried, turning and pinching his sleeve. "What have you been doing with yourself? Moping? Working? Despising the world, as usual?"

As he merely shook his head, and filled his pipe, she went on:

"It's a bit of a pose, isn't it?"

"Not more than most things," he said.

"Well," Mary remarked, "I've a great deal to say to you, but I must go on–we have a committee." She rose, but hesitated, looking down upon him rather gravely. "You don't look happy, Ralph," she said. "Is it anything, or is it nothing?"

He did not immediately answer her, but rose, too, and walked with her towards the gate. As usual, he did not speak to her without considering whether what he was about to say was the sort of thing that he could say to her.

"I've been bothered," he said at length. "Partly by work, and partly by family troubles. Charles has been behaving like a fool. He wants to go out to Canada as a farmer—"

"Well, there's something to be said for that," said Mary; and they passed the gate, and walked slowly round the Fields again, discussing difficulties which, as a matter of fact, were more or less chronic in the Denham family, and only now brought forward to appease Mary's sympathy, which, however, soothed Ralph more than he was aware of. She made him at least dwell upon problems which were real in the sense that they were capable of solution; and the true cause of his melancholy, which was not susceptible to such treatment, sank rather more deeply into the shades of his mind.

Mary was attentive; she was helpful. Ralph could not help feeling grateful to her, the more so, perhaps, because he had not told her the truth about his state; and when they reached the gate again he wished to make some affectionate objection to her leaving him. But his affection took the rather uncouth form of expostulating with her about her work.

"What d'you want to sit on a committee for?" he asked. "It's waste of your time, Mary."

"I agree with you that a country walk would benefit the world more," she said. "Look here," she added suddenly, "why don't you come to us at Christmas? It's almost the best time of year."

"Come to you at Disham?" Ralph repeated.

"Yes. We won't interfere with you. But you can tell me later," she said, rather hastily, and then started off in the direction of Russell Square. She had invited him on the impulse of the moment, as a vision of the country came before her; and now she was annoyed with herself for having done so, and then she was annoyed at being annoyed.

"If I can't face a walk in a field alone with Ralph," she reasoned, "I'd better buy a cat and live in a lodging at Ealing, like Sally Seal—and he won't come. Or did he mean that he *would* come?"

She shook her head. She really did not know what he had meant. She never felt quite certain; but now she was more than usually baffled. Was he concealing something from her? His manner had been odd; his deep absorption had impressed her; there was something in him that she had not fathomed, and the mystery of his nature laid more of a spell upon her than she liked. Moreover, she could not prevent herself from doing now what she had often blamed others of her sex for doing—from endowing her friend with a kind of heavenly fire, and passing her life before it for his sanction.

Under this process, the committee rather dwindled in importance; the Suffrage shrank; she vowed she would work harder at the Italian language; she thought she would take up the study of birds. But this program for a perfect life threatened to become so absurd that she very soon caught herself out in the evil habit, and was rehearsing her speech to the committee by the time the chestnut-colored bricks of Russell Square came in sight. Indeed, she never noticed them. She ran upstairs as usual, and was completely awakened to reality by the sight of Mrs. Seal, on the landing outside the office, inducing a very large dog to drink water out of a tumbler.

"Miss Markham has already arrived," Mrs. Seal remarked, with due solemnity, "and this is her dog."

"A very fine dog, too," said Mary, patting him on the head.

"Yes. A magnificent fellow," Mrs. Seal agreed. "A kind of St. Bernard, she tells me—so like Kit to have a St. Bernard. And you guard your mistress well, don't you, Sailor? You see that wicked men don't break into her larder when she's out at *her* work—helping poor souls who have lost their way. . . . But we're late—we must begin!" and scattering the rest of the water indiscriminately over the floor, she hurried Mary into the committee-room.

14

Mr. Clacton was in his glory. The machinery which he had perfected and controlled was now about to turn out its bi-monthly product, a committee meeting; and his pride in the perfect structure of these assemblies was great. He loved the jargon of committee-rooms; he loved the way in which the door kept opening as the clock struck the hour, in obedience to a few strokes of his pen on a piece of paper; and when it had opened sufficiently often, he loved to issue from his inner chamber with documents in his hands, visibly important, with a preoccupied expression on his face that might have suited a Prime Minister advancing to meet his Cabinet. By his orders the table had been decorated beforehand with six sheets of blotting-paper, with six pens, six ink-pots, a tumbler and a jug of water, a bell, and, in deference to the taste of the lady members, a vase of hardy chrysanthemums. He had already surreptitiously straightened the sheets of blotting-paper in relation to the ink-pots, and now stood in front of the fire engaged in conversation with Miss Markham. But his eye was on the door, and when Mary and Mrs. Seal entered, he gave a little laugh and observed to the assembly which was scattered about the room:

"I fancy, ladies and gentlemen, that we are ready to commence."

So speaking, he took his seat at the head of the table, and arranging one bundle of papers upon his right and another upon his left, called upon Miss Datchet to read the minutes of the previous meeting. Mary obeyed. A keen observer might have wondered why it was necessary for the secretary to knit her brows so closely over the tolerably matter-of-fact statement before her. Could there be any doubt in her mind that it had been resolved to circularize the provinces with Leaflet No. 3, or to issue a statistical diagram showing the proportion of married women to spinsters in New Zealand; or that the net profits of Mrs. Hipsley's Bazaar had reached a total of five pounds eight shillings and twopence half-penny?

Could any doubt as to the perfect sense and propriety of these statements be disturbing her? No one could have guessed, from the look of her, that she was disturbed at all. A pleasanter and saner woman than Mary Datchet was never seen within a committee-room. She seemed a compound of the autumn leaves and the winter sunshine; less poetically speaking, she showed both gentleness and strength, an indefinable promise of soft maternity blending with her evident fitness for honest labor. Nevertheless, she had great difficulty in reducing her mind to obedience; and her reading lacked conviction, as if, as was indeed the case, she had lost the power of visualizing what she read. And directly the list was completed, her mind floated to Lincoln's Inn Fields and the fluttering wings of innumerable sparrows. Was Ralph still enticing the bald-headed cock-sparrow to sit upon his hand? Had he succeeded? Would he ever succeed? She had meant to ask him why it is that the sparrows in Lincoln's Inn Fields are tamer than the sparrows in Hyde Park—perhaps it is that the passers-by are rarer, and they come to recognize their benefactors. For the first half-hour of the committee meeting, Mary had thus to do battle with the skeptical presence of Ralph Denham, who threatened to have it all his own way. Mary tried half a dozen methods of ousting him. She raised her voice, she articulated distinctly, she looked firmly at Mr. Clacton's bald head, she began to write a note. To her annoyance, her pencil drew a little round figure on the blotting-paper, which, she could not deny, was really a bald-headed cock-sparrow. She looked again at Mr. Clacton; yes, he was bald, and so are cock-sparrows. Never was a secretary tormented by so many unsuitable suggestions, and they all came, alas! with something ludicrously grotesque about them, which might, at any moment, provoke her to such flippancy as would shock her colleagues for ever. The thought of what she might say made her bite her lips, as if her lips would protect her.

But all these suggestions were but flotsam and jetsam cast to the surface by a more profound disturbance, which, as she could not consider it at present, manifested its existence by these grotesque nods and beckonings. Consider it, she must, when the committee was over. Meanwhile, she was behaving scandalously; she was looking out of the window, and thinking of the color of the sky, and of the decorations on the Imperial Hotel, when she ought to have been shepherding her colleagues, and pinning them down to the matter in hand. She could not bring herself to attach more weight to one project than to another. Ralph had said—she could not stop to consider what he had said, but he had somehow divested the proceedings of all reality. And then, without conscious effort, by some trick of the brain, she found herself becoming interested in some scheme for organizing a newspaper campaign. Certain articles were to be written; certain editors approached. What line was it advisable to take? She found herself strongly disapproving of what Mr. Clacton was saying. She committed herself to the opinion that now was the time to strike hard. Directly she had said this, she felt that she had turned upon Ralph's ghost; and she became more and more in earnest, and anxious to bring the others round to her point of view. Once more, she knew exactly and indisputably what is right and what is wrong. As if emerging from a mist, the old foes of the public good loomed ahead of her—capitalists, newspaper proprietors, anti-suffragists, and, in some ways most pernicious of all, the masses who take no interest one way or another—among whom, for the time being, she certainly discerned the features of Ralph Denham.

Indeed, when Miss Markham asked her to suggest the names of a few friends of hers, she expressed herself with unusual bitterness:

"My friends think all this kind of thing useless." She felt that she was really saying that to Ralph himself.

"Oh, they're that sort, are they?" said Miss Markham, with a little laugh; and with renewed vigor their legions charged the foe.

Mary's spirits had been low when she entered the committee-room; but now they were considerably improved. She knew the ways of this world; it was a shapely, orderly place; she felt convinced of its right and its wrong; and the feeling that she was fit to deal a heavy blow against her enemies warmed her heart and kindled her eye. In one of those flights of fancy, not characteristic of her but tiresomely frequent this afternoon, she envisaged herself battered with rotten eggs upon a platform, from which Ralph vainly begged her to descend. But——

"What do I matter compared with the cause?" she said, and so on. Much to her credit, however teased by foolish fancies, she kept the surface of her brain moderate and vigilant, and subdued Mrs. Seal very tactfully more than once when she demanded, "Action!—everywhere!—at once!" as became her father's daughter.

The other members of the committee, who were all rather elderly people, were a good deal impressed by Mary, and inclined to side with her and against each other, partly, perhaps, because of her youth. The feeling that she controlled them all filled Mary with a sense of power; and she felt that no work can equal in importance, or be so exciting as, the work of making other people do what you want them to do. Indeed, when she had won her point she felt a slight degree of contempt for the people who had yielded to her.

The committee now rose, gathered together their papers, shook them straight, placed them in their attache-cases, snapped the locks firmly together, and hurried away, having, for the most part, to catch trains, in order to keep other appointments with other committees, for they were all busy people. Mary, Mrs. Seal, and Mr. Clacton were left alone; the room was hot and untidy, the pieces of pink blotting-paper were lying at different angles upon the table, and the tumbler was half full of water, which some one had poured out and forgotten to drink.

Mrs. Seal began preparing the tea, while Mr. Clacton retired to his room to file the fresh accumulation of documents. Mary was too much excited even to help Mrs. Seal with the cups and saucers. She flung up the window and stood by it, looking out. The street lamps were already lit; and through the mist in the square one could see little figures hurrying across the road and along the pavement, on the farther side. In her absurd mood of lustful arrogance, Mary looked at the little figures and thought, "If I liked I could make you go in there or stop short; I could make you walk in single file or in double file; I could do what I liked with you." Then Mrs. Seal came and stood by her.

"Oughtn't you to put something round your shoulders, Sally?" Mary asked, in rather a condescending tone of voice, feeling a sort of pity for the enthusiastic ineffective little woman. But Mrs. Seal paid no attention to the suggestion.

"Well, did you enjoy yourself?" Mary asked, with a little laugh.

Mrs. Seal drew a deep breath, restrained herself, and then burst out, looking out, too, upon Russell Square and Southampton Row, and at the passers-by, "Ah, if only one could get every one of those people into this room, and make them understand for five minutes! But they *must* see the truth some day. . . . If only one could *make* them see it. . . ."

Mary knew herself to be very much wiser than Mrs. Seal, and when Mrs. Seal said anything, even if it was what Mary herself was feeling, she automatically thought of all that there was to be said against it. On this occasion her arrogant feeling that she could direct everybody dwindled away.

"Let's have our tea," she said, turning back from the window and pulling down the blind. "It was a good meeting—didn't you think so, Sally?" she let fall, casually, as she sat down at the table. Surely Mrs. Seal must realize that Mary had been extraordinarily efficient?

"But we go at such a snail's pace," said Sally, shaking her head impatiently.

At this Mary burst out laughing, and all her arrogance was dissipated.

"You can afford to laugh," said Sally, with another shake of her head, "but I can't. I'm fifty-five, and I dare say I shall be in my grave by the time we get it—if we ever do."

"Oh, no, you won't be in your grave," said Mary, kindly.

"It'll be such a great day," said Mrs. Seal, with a toss of her locks. "A great day, not only for us, but for civilization. That's what I feel, you know, about these meetings. Each one of them is a step onwards in the great march—humanity, you know. We do want the people after us to have a better time of it—and so many don't see it. I wonder how it is that they don't see it?"

She was carrying plates and cups from the cupboard as she spoke, so that her sentences were more than usually broken apart. Mary could not help looking at the odd little priestess of humanity with something like admiration. While she had been thinking about herself, Mrs. Seal had thought of nothing but her vision.

"You mustn't wear yourself out, Sally, if you want to see the great day," she said, rising and trying to take a plate of biscuits from Mrs. Seal's hands.

"My dear child, what else is my old body good for?" she exclaimed, clinging more tightly than before to her plate of biscuits. "Shouldn't I be proud to give everything I have to the cause?—for I'm not an intelligence like you. There were domestic circumstances—I'd like to tell you one of these days—so I say foolish things. I lose my head, you know. You don't. Mr. Clacton doesn't. It's a great mistake, to lose one's head. But my heart's in the right place. And I'm so glad Kit has a big dog, for I didn't think her looking well."

They had their tea, and went over many of the points that had been raised in the committee rather more intimately than had been possible then; and they all felt an agreeable sense of being in some way behind the scenes; of having their hands upon strings which, when pulled, would completely change the pageant exhibited daily to those who read the newspapers. Although their views were very different, this sense united them and made them almost cordial in their manners to each other.

Mary, however, left the tea-party rather early, desiring both to be alone, and then to hear some music at the Queen's Hall. She fully intended to use her loneliness to think out her position with regard to Ralph; but although she walked back to the Strand with this end in view, she found her mind uncomfortably full of different trains of thought. She started one and then another. They seemed even to take their color from the street she happened to be in. Thus the vision of humanity appeared to be in some way connected with Bloomsbury, and faded distinctly by the time she crossed the main road; then a belated organ-grinder in Holborn set her thoughts dancing incongruously; and by the time she was crossing the great misty square of Lincoln's Inn Fields, she was cold and depressed again, and horribly clear-sighted. The dark removed the stimulus of human companionship, and a tear actually slid down her cheek, accompanying a sudden conviction within her that she loved Ralph, and that he didn't love her. All dark and empty now was the path where they had walked that morning, and the sparrows silent in the bare trees. But the lights in her own building soon cheered her; all these different states of mind were submerged in the deep flood of desires, thoughts, perceptions, antagonisms, which washed perpetually at the base of her being, to rise into prominence in turn when the conditions of the upper world were favorable. She put off the hour of clear thought until Christmas, saying to herself, as she lit her fire, that it is impossible to think anything out in London; and, no doubt, Ralph wouldn't come at Christmas, and she would take long walks into the heart of the country, and decide this question and all the others that puzzled her. Meanwhile, she thought, drawing her feet up on to the fender, life was full of complexity; life was a thing one must love to the last fiber of it.

She had sat there for five minutes or so, and her thoughts had had time to grow dim, when there came a ring at her bell. Her eye brightened;

she felt immediately convinced that Ralph had come to visit her. Accordingly, she waited a moment before opening the door; she wanted to feel her hands secure upon the reins of all the troublesome emotions which the sight of Ralph would certainly arouse. She composed herself unnecessarily, however, for she had to admit, not Ralph, but Katharine and William Rodney. Her first impression was that they were both extremely well dressed. She felt herself shabby and slovenly beside them, and did not know how she should entertain them, nor could she guess why they had come. She had heard nothing of their engagement. But after the first disappointment, she was pleased, for she felt instantly that Katharine was a personality, and, moreover, she need not now exercise her self-control.

"We were passing and saw a light in your window, so we came up," Katharine explained, standing and looking very tall and distinguished and rather absent-minded.

"We have been to see some pictures," said William. "Oh, dear," he exclaimed, looking about him, "this room reminds me of one of the worst hours in my existence—when I read a paper, and you all sat round and jeered at me. Katharine was the worst. I could feel her gloating over every mistake I made. Miss Datchet was kind. Miss Datchet just made it possible for me to get through, I remember."

Sitting down, he drew off his light yellow gloves, and began slapping his knees with them. His vitality was pleasant, Mary thought, although he made her laugh. The very look of him was inclined to make her laugh. His rather prominent eyes passed from one young woman to the other, and his lips perpetually formed words which remained unspoken.

"We have been seeing old masters at the Grafton Gallery," said Katharine, apparently paying no attention to William, and accepting a cigarette which Mary offered her. She leant back in her chair, and the smoke which hung about her face seemed to withdraw her still further from the others.

"Would you believe it, Miss Datchet," William continued, "Katharine doesn't like Titian. She doesn't like apricots, she doesn't like peaches, she doesn't like green peas. She likes the Elgin marbles, and gray days without any sun. She's a typical example of the cold northern nature. I come from Devonshire——"

Had they been quarreling, Mary wondered, and had they, for that reason, sought refuge in her room, or were they engaged, or had Katharine just refused him? She was completely baffled.

Katharine now reappeared from her veil of smoke, knocked the ash from her cigarette into the fireplace, and looked, with an odd expression of solicitude, at the irritable man.

"Perhaps, Mary," she said tentatively, "you wouldn't mind giving us some tea? We did try to get some, but the shop was so crowded, and in the next one there was a band playing; and most of the pictures, at any rate, were very dull, whatever you may say, William." She spoke with a kind of guarded gentleness.

Mary, accordingly, retired to make preparations in the pantry.

"What in the world are they after?" she asked of her own reflection in the little looking-glass which hung there. She was not left to doubt much longer, for, on coming back into the sitting-room with the tea-things, Katharine informed her, apparently having been instructed so to do by William, of their engagement.

"William," she said, "thinks that perhaps you don't know. We are going to be married."

Mary found herself shaking William's hand, and addressing her congratulations to him, as if Katharine were inaccessible; she had, indeed, taken hold of the tea-kettle.

"Let me see," Katharine said, "one puts hot water into the cups first, doesn't one? You have some dodge of your own, haven't you, William, about making tea?"

Mary was half inclined to suspect that this was said in order to conceal nervousness, but if so, the concealment was unusually perfect. Talk of marriage was dismissed. Katharine might have been seated in her own drawing-room, controlling a situation which presented no sort of difficulty to her trained mind. Rather to her surprise, Mary found herself making conversation with William about old Italian pictures, while Katharine poured out tea, cut cake, kept William's plate supplied, without joining more than was necessary in the conversation. She seemed to have taken possession of Mary's room, and to handle the cups as if they belonged to her. But it was done so naturally that it bred no resentment in Mary; on the contrary, she found herself putting her hand on Katharine's knee, affectionately, for an instant. Was there something maternal in this assumption of control? And thinking of Katharine as one who would soon be married, these maternal airs filled Mary's mind with a new tenderness, and even with awe. Katharine seemed very much older and more experienced than she was.

Meanwhile Rodney talked. If his appearance was superficially against him, it had the advantage of making his solid merits something of a surprise. He had kept notebooks; he knew a great deal about pictures. He could compare different examples in different galleries, and his authoritative answers to intelligent questions gained not a little, Mary felt, from the smart taps which he dealt, as he delivered them, upon the lumps of coal. She was impressed.

"Your tea, William," said Katharine gently.

He paused, gulped it down, obediently, and continued.

And then it struck Mary that Katharine, in the shade of her broad-brimmed hat, and in the midst of the smoke, and in the obscurity of her character, was, perhaps, smiling to herself, not altogether in the maternal spirit. What she said was very simple, but her words, even "Your tea, William," were set down as gently and cautiously and exactly as the feet of a Persian cat stepping among China ornaments. For the second time that day Mary felt herself baffled by something inscrutable in the character of a person to whom she felt herself much attracted. She thought that if she were engaged to Katharine, she, too, would find herself very soon using those fretful questions with which William evidently teased his bride. And yet Katharine's voice was humble.

"I wonder how you find the time to know all about pictures as well as books?" she asked.

"How do I find the time?" William answered, delighted, Mary guessed, at this little compliment. "Why, I always travel with a notebook. And I ask my way to the picture gallery the very first thing in the morning. And then I meet men, and talk to them. There's a man in my office who knows all about the Flemish school. I was telling Miss Datchet about the Flemish school. I picked up a lot of it from him—it's a way men have—Gibbons, his name is. You must meet him. We'll ask him to lunch. And this not caring about art," he explained, turning to Mary, "it's one of Katharine's poses, Miss Datchet. Did you know she posed? She pretends that she's never read Shakespeare. And why should she read Shakespeare, since she *is* Shakespeare—Rosalind, you know," and he gave his queer little chuckle. Somehow this compliment appeared very old-fashioned and almost in bad taste. Mary actually felt herself blush, as if he had said "the sex" or "the ladies." Constrained, perhaps, by nervousness, Rodney continued in the same vein.

"She knows enough—enough for all decent purposes. What do you women want with learning, when you have so much else—everything, I should say—everything. Leave us something, eh, Katharine?"

"Leave you something?" said Katharine, apparently waking from a brown study. "I was thinking we must be going——"

"Is it tonight that Lady Ferrilby dines with us? No, we mustn't be late," said Rodney, rising. "D'you know the Ferrilbys, Miss Datchet? They own Trantem Abbey," he added, for her information, as she looked doubtful. "And if Katharine makes herself very charming tonight, perhaps'll lend it to us for the honeymoon."

"I agree that may be a reason. Otherwise she's a dull woman," said Katharine. "At least," she added, as if to qualify her abruptness, "I find it difficult to talk to her."

"Because you expect every one else to take all the trouble. I've seen her sit silent a whole evening," he said, turning to Mary, as he had frequently done already. "Don't you find that, too? Sometimes when we're alone,

I've counted the time on my watch"—here he took out a large gold watch, and tapped the glass—"the time between one remark and the next. And once I counted ten minutes and twenty seconds, and then, if you'll believe me, she only said 'Um!'"

"I'm sure I'm sorry," Katharine apologized. "I know it's a bad habit, but then, you see, at home——"

The rest of her excuse was cut short, so far as Mary was concerned, by the closing of the door. She fancied she could hear William finding fresh fault on the stairs. A moment later, the door-bell rang again, and Katharine reappeared, having left her purse on a chair. She soon found it, and said, pausing for a moment at the door, and speaking differently as they were alone:

"I think being engaged is very bad for the character." She shook her purse in her hand until the coins jingled, as if she alluded merely to this example of her forgetfulness. But the remark puzzled Mary; it seemed to refer to something else; and her manner had changed so strangely, now that William was out of hearing, that she could not help looking at her for an explanation. She looked almost stern, so that Mary, trying to smile at her, only succeeded in producing a silent stare of interrogation.

As the door shut for the second time, she sank on to the floor in front of the fire, trying, now that their bodies were not there to distract her, to piece together her impressions of them as a whole. And, though priding herself, with all other men and women, upon an infallible eye for character, she could not feel at all certain that she knew what motives inspired Katharine Hilbery in life. There was something that carried her on smoothly, out of reach—something, yes, but what?—something that reminded Mary of Ralph. Oddly enough, he gave her the same feeling, too, and with him, too, she felt baffled. Oddly enough, for no two people, she hastily concluded, were more unlike. And yet both had this hidden impulse, this incalculable force—this thing they cared for and didn't talk about—oh, what was it?

15

The village of Disham lies somewhere on the rolling piece of cultivated ground in the neighborhood of Lincoln, not so far inland but that a sound, bringing rumors of the sea, can be heard on summer nights or when the winter storms fling the waves upon the long beach. So large is the church, and in particular the church tower, in comparison with the little street of cottages which compose the village, that the traveler is apt to cast his mind back to the Middle Ages, as the only time when so much piety could have been kept alive. So great a trust in the Church can surely not belong to our day, and he goes on to conjecture that every one of the villagers has reached the extreme limit of human life. Such are the reflections of the superficial stranger, and his sight of the population, as it is represented by two or three men hoeing in a turnip-field, a small child carrying a jug, and a young woman shaking a piece of carpet outside her cottage door, will not lead him to see anything very much out of keeping with the Middle Ages in the village of Disham as it is today. These people, though they seem young enough, look so angular and so crude that they remind him of the little pictures painted by monks in the capital letters of their manuscripts. He only half understands what they say, and speaks very loud and clearly, as though, indeed, his voice had to carry through a hundred years or more before it reached them. He would have a far better chance of understanding some dweller in Paris or Rome, Berlin or Madrid, than these countrymen of his who have lived for the last two thousand years not two hundred miles from the City of London.

The Rectory stands about half a mile beyond the village. It is a large house, and has been growing steadily for some centuries round the great kitchen, with its narrow red tiles, as the Rector would point out to his guests on the first night of their arrival, taking his brass candlestick, and bidding them mind the steps up and the steps down, and notice the immense thickness of the walls, the old beams across the ceiling, the staircases as steep as ladders, and the attics, with their deep, tent-like roofs, in which swallows bred, and once a white owl. But nothing very interesting or very beautiful had resulted from the different additions made by the different rectors.

The house, however, was surrounded by a garden, in which the Rector took considerable pride. The lawn, which fronted the drawing-room windows, was a rich and uniform green, unspotted by a single daisy, and on the other side of it two straight paths led past beds of tall, standing flowers to a charming grassy walk, where the Rev. Wyndham Datchet would pace up and down at the same hour every morning, with a sundial to measure the time for him. As often as not, he carried a book in his hand, into which he would glance, then shut it up, and repeat the rest of the ode from memory. He had most of Horace by heart, and had got into the habit of connecting this particular walk with certain odes which he repeated duly, at the same time noting the condition of his flowers, and stooping now and again to pick any that were withered or overblown. On wet days, such was the power of habit over him, he rose from his chair at the same hour, and paced his study for the same length of time, pausing now and then to straighten some book in the bookcase, or alter the position of the two brass crucifixes standing upon cairns of serpentine stone upon the mantelpiece. His children had a great respect for him, credited him with far more learning than he actually possessed, and saw that his habits were not interfered with, if possible. Like most people who do things methodically, the Rector himself had more strength of purpose and power of self-sacrifice than of intellect or of originality. On cold and windy nights he rode off to visit sick people, who might need him, without a murmur; and by virtue of doing dull duties punctually, he was much employed upon committees and local Boards and Councils; and at this period of his life (he was sixty-eight) he was beginning to be commiserated by tender old ladies for the extreme leanness of his person, which, they said, was worn out upon the roads when it should have been resting before a comfortable fire. His elder daughter, Elizabeth, lived with him and managed the house, and already much resembled him in dry sincerity and methodical habit of mind; of the two sons one, Richard, was an estate agent, the other, Christopher, was reading for the Bar. At Christmas, naturally, they met together; and for a month past the arrangement of the Christmas week had been much in the mind of mistress and maid, who prided themselves every year more confidently upon the excellence of their equipment. The late Mrs. Datchet had left an excellent cupboard of linen, to which Elizabeth had succeeded at the age of nineteen, when her mother died, and the charge of the family rested upon the shoulders of the eldest daughter. She kept a fine flock of yellow chickens, sketched a little, certain rose-trees in the garden were committed specially to her care; and what with the care of the house, the care of the chickens, and the care of the poor, she scarcely knew what it was to have an idle minute. An extreme rectitude of mind, rather than any gift, gave her weight in the family. When Mary wrote to say that she had asked Ralph Denham to stay with them, she added, out of deference to Elizabeth's character, that he was very nice, though rather queer, and had been overworking himself in London. No doubt Elizabeth would conclude that Ralph was in love with her, but there could be no doubt either that not a word of this would be spoken by either of them, unless, indeed, some catastrophe made mention of it unavoidable.

Mary went down to Disham without knowing whether Ralph intended to come; but two or three days before Christmas she received a telegram from Ralph, asking her to take a room for him in the village. This was followed by a letter explaining that he hoped he might have his meals with them; but quiet, essential for his work, made it necessary to sleep out.

Mary was walking in the garden with Elizabeth, and inspecting the roses, when the letter arrived.

"But that's absurd," said Elizabeth decidedly, when the plan was explained to her. "There are five spare rooms, even when the boys are here. Besides, he wouldn't get a room in the village. And he oughtn't to work if he's overworked."

"But perhaps he doesn't want to see so much of us," Mary thought to herself, although outwardly she assented, and felt grateful to Elizabeth for supporting her in what was, of course, her desire. They were cutting roses at the time, and laying them, head by head, in a shallow basket.

"If Ralph were here, he'd find this very dull," Mary thought, with a little shiver of irritation, which led her to place her rose the wrong way in the basket. Meanwhile, they had come to the end of the path, and while Elizabeth straightened some flowers, and made them stand upright within their fence of string, Mary looked at her father, who was pacing up and down, with his hand behind his back and his head bowed in meditation. Obeying an impulse which sprang from some desire to interrupt this methodical marching, Mary stepped on to the grass walk and put her hand on his arm.

"A flower for your buttonhole, father," she said, presenting a rose.

"Eh, dear?" said Mr. Datchet, taking the flower, and holding it at an angle which suited his bad eyesight, without pausing in his walk.

"Where does this fellow come from? One of Elizabeth's roses—I hope you asked her leave. Elizabeth doesn't like having her roses picked without her leave, and quite right, too."

He had a habit, Mary remarked, and she had never noticed it so clearly before, of letting his sentences tail away in a continuous murmur, whereupon he passed into a state of abstraction, presumed by his children to indicate some train of thought too profound for utterance.

"What?" said Mary, interrupting, for the first time in her life, perhaps, when the murmur ceased. He made no reply. She knew very well that he wished to be left alone, but she stuck to his side much as she might have stuck to some sleep-walker, whom she thought it right gradually to awaken. She could think of nothing to rouse him with except:

"The garden's looking very nice, father."

"Yes, yes, yes," said Mr. Datchet, running his words together in the same abstracted manner, and sinking his head yet lower upon his breast. And suddenly, as they turned their steps to retrace their way, he jerked out:

"The traffic's very much increased, you know. More rolling-stock needed already. Forty trucks went down yesterday by the 12.15—counted them myself. They've taken off the 9.3, and given us an 8.30 instead—suits the business men, you know. You came by the old 3.10 yesterday, I suppose?"

She said "Yes," as he seemed to wish for a reply, and then he looked at his watch, and made off down the path towards the house, holding the rose at the same angle in front of him. Elizabeth had gone round to the side of the house, where the chickens lived, so that Mary found herself alone, holding Ralph's letter in her hand. She was uneasy. She had put off the season for thinking things out very successfully, and now that Ralph was actually coming, the next day, she could only wonder how her family would impress him. She thought it likely that her father would discuss the train service with him; Elizabeth would be bright and sensible, and always leaving the room to give messages to the servants. Her brothers had already said that they would give him a day's shooting. She was content to leave the problem of Ralph's relations to the young men obscure, trusting that they would find some common ground of masculine agreement. But what would he think of *her*? Would he see that she was different from the rest of the family? She devised a plan for taking him to her sitting-room, and artfully leading the talk towards the English poets, who now occupied prominent places in her little bookcase. Moreover, she might give him to understand, privately, that she, too, thought her family a queer one—queer, yes, but not dull. That was the rock past which she was bent on steering him. And she thought how she would draw his attention to Edward's passion for Jorrocks, and the enthusiasm which led Christopher to collect moths and butterflies though he was now twenty-two. Perhaps Elizabeth's sketching, if the fruits were invisible, might lend color to the general effect which she wished to produce of a family, eccentric and limited, perhaps, but not dull. Edward, she perceived, was rolling the lawn, for the sake of exercise; and the sight of him, with pink cheeks, bright little brown eyes, and a general resemblance to a clumsy young cart-horse in its winter coat of dusty brown hair, made Mary violently ashamed of her ambitious scheming. She loved him precisely as he was; she loved them all; and as she walked by his side, up and down, and down and up, her strong moral sense administered a sound drubbing to the vain and romantic element aroused in her by the mere thought of Ralph. She felt quite certain that, for good or for bad, she was very like the rest of her family.

Sitting in the corner of a third-class railway carriage, on the afternoon of the following day, Ralph made several inquiries of a commercial traveler in the opposite corner. They centered round a village called Lampsher, not three miles, he understood, from Lincoln; was there a big house in Lampsher, he asked, inhabited by a gentleman of the name of Otway?

The traveler knew nothing, but rolled the name of Otway on his tongue, reflectively, and the sound of it gratified Ralph amazingly. It gave him an excuse to take a letter from his pocket in order to verify the address.

"Stogdon House, Lampsher, Lincoln," he read out.

"You'll find somebody to direct you at Lincoln," said the man; and Ralph had to confess that he was not bound there this very evening.

"I've got to walk over from Disham," he said, and in the heart of him could not help marveling at the pleasure which he derived from making a bagman in a train believe what he himself did not believe. For the letter, though signed by Katharine's father, contained no invitation or warrant for thinking that Katharine herself was there; the only fact it disclosed was that for a fortnight this address would be Mr. Hilbery's address. But when he looked out of the window, it was of her he thought; she, too, had seen these gray fields, and, perhaps, she was there where the trees ran up a slope, and one yellow light shone now, and then went out again, at the foot of the hill. The light shone in the windows of an old gray house, he thought. He lay back in his corner and forgot the commercial traveler altogether. The process of visualizing Katharine stopped short at the old gray manor-house; instinct warned him that if he went much further with this process reality would soon force itself in; he could not altogether neglect the figure of William Rodney. Since the day when he had heard from Katharine's lips of her engagement, he had refrained from investing his dream of her with the details of real life. But the light of the late afternoon glowed green behind the straight trees, and became a symbol of her. The light seemed to expand his heart. She brooded over the gray fields, and was with him now in the railway carriage, thoughtful, silent, and infinitely tender; but the vision pressed too close, and must be dismissed, for the train was slackening. Its abrupt jerks shook him wide awake, and he saw Mary Datchet, a sturdy russet figure, with a dash of scarlet about it, as the carriage slid down the platform. A tall youth who accompanied her shook him by the hand, took his bag, and led the way without uttering one articulate word.

Never are voices so beautiful as on a winter's evening, when dusk almost hides the body, and they seem to issue from nothingness with a note of intimacy seldom heard by day. Such an edge was there in Mary's voice when she greeted him. About her seemed to hang the mist of the winter hedges, and the clear red of the bramble leaves. He felt himself at once stepping on to the firm ground of an entirely different world, but he did not allow himself to yield to the pleasure of it directly. They gave him his choice of driving with Edward or of walking home across the fields with Mary—not a shorter way, they explained, but Mary thought it a nicer way. He decided to walk with her, being conscious, indeed, that he got comfort from her presence. What could be the cause of her cheerfulness, he wondered, half ironically, and half enviously, as the pony-cart started briskly away, and the dusk swam between their eyes and the tall form of Edward, standing up to drive, with the reins in one hand and the whip in the other. People from the village, who had been to the market town, were climbing into their gigs, or setting off home down the road together in little parties. Many salutations were addressed to Mary, who shouted back, with the addition of the speaker's name. But soon she led the way over a stile, and along a path worn slightly darker than the dim green surrounding it. In front of them the sky now showed itself of a reddish-yellow, like a slice of some semilucent stone behind which a lamp burnt, while a fringe of black trees with distinct branches stood against the light, which was obscured in one direction by a hump of earth, in all other directions the land lying flat to the very verge of the sky. One of the swift and noiseless birds of the winter's night seemed to follow them across the field, circling a few feet in front of them, disappearing and returning again and again.

Mary had gone this walk many hundred times in the course of her life, generally alone, and at different stages the ghosts of past moods would flood her mind with a whole scene or train of thought merely at the sight of three trees from a particular angle, or at the sound of the pheasant clucking in the ditch. But tonight the circumstances were strong enough to oust all other scenes; and she looked at the field and the trees with an involuntary intensity as if they had no such associations for her.

"Well, Ralph," she said, "this is better than Lincoln's Inn Fields, isn't it? Look, there's a bird for you! Oh, you've brought glasses, have you? Edward and Christopher mean to make you shoot. Can you shoot? I shouldn't think so—"

"Look here, you must explain," said Ralph. "Who are these young men? Where am I staying?"

"You are staying with us, of course," she said boldly. "Of course, you're staying with us—you don't mind coming, do you?"

"If I had, I shouldn't have come," he said sturdily. They walked on in silence; Mary took care not to break it for a time. She wished Ralph to feel, as she thought he would, all the fresh delights of the earth and air. She was right. In a moment he expressed his pleasure, much to her comfort.

"This is the sort of country I thought you'd live in, Mary," he said, pushing his hat back on his head, and looking about him. "Real country. No gentlemen's seats."

He snuffed the air, and felt more keenly than he had done for many weeks the pleasure of owning a body.

"Now we have to find our way through a hedge," said Mary. In the gap of the hedge Ralph tore up a poacher's wire, set across a hole to trap a rabbit.

"It's quite right that they should poach," said Mary, watching him tugging at the wire. "I wonder whether it was Alfred Duggins or Sid Rankin? How can one expect them not to, when they only make fifteen shillings a week? Fifteen shillings a week," she repeated, coming out on the other side of the hedge, and running her fingers through her hair to rid herself of a bramble which had attached itself to her. "I could live on fifteen shillings a week—easily."

"Could you?" said Ralph. "I don't believe you could," he added.

"Oh yes. They have a cottage thrown in, and a garden where one can grow vegetables. It wouldn't be half bad," said Mary, with a soberness which impressed Ralph very much.

"But you'd get tired of it," he urged.

"I sometimes think it's the only thing one would never get tired of," she replied.

The idea of a cottage where one grew one's own vegetables and lived on fifteen shillings a week, filled Ralph with an extraordinary sense of rest and satisfaction.

"But wouldn't it be on the main road, or next door to a woman with six squalling children, who'd always be hanging her washing out to dry across your garden?"

"The cottage I'm thinking of stands by itself in a little orchard."

"And what about the Suffrage?" he asked, attempting sarcasm.

"Oh, there are other things in the world besides the Suffrage," she replied, in an off-hand manner which was slightly mysterious.

Ralph fell silent. It annoyed him that she should have plans of which he knew nothing; but he felt that he had no right to press her further. His mind settled upon the idea of life in a country cottage. Conceivably, for he could not examine into it now, here lay a tremendous possibility; a solution of many problems. He struck his stick upon the earth, and stared through the dusk at the shape of the country.

"D'you know the points of the compass?" he asked.

"Well, of course," said Mary. "What d'you take me for?—a Cockney like you?" She then told him exactly where the north lay, and where the south.

"It's my native land, this," she said. "I could smell my way about it blindfold."

As if to prove this boast, she walked a little quicker, so that Ralph found it difficult to keep pace with her. At the same time, he felt drawn to her as he had never been before; partly, no doubt, because she was more independent of him than in London, and seemed to be attached firmly to a world where he had no place at all. Now the dusk had fallen to such an extent that he had to follow her implicitly, and even lean his hand on her shoulder when they jumped a bank into a very narrow lane. And he felt curiously shy of her when she began to shout through her hands at a spot of light which swung upon the mist in a neighboring field. He shouted, too, and the light stood still.

"That's Christopher, come in already, and gone to feed his chickens," she said.

She introduced him to Ralph, who could see only a tall figure in gaiters, rising from a fluttering circle of soft feathery bodies, upon whom the light fell in wavering discs, calling out now a bright spot of yellow, now one of greenish-black and scarlet. Mary dipped her hand in the bucket he carried, and was at once the center of a circle also; and as she cast her grain she talked alternately to the birds and to her brother, in the same clucking, half-inarticulate voice, as it sounded to Ralph, standing on the outskirts of the fluttering feathers in his black overcoat.

He had removed his overcoat by the time they sat round the dinner-table, but nevertheless he looked very strange among the others. A country life and breeding had preserved in them all a look which Mary hesitated to call either innocent or youthful, as she compared them, now sitting round in an oval, softly illuminated by candlelight; and yet it was something of the kind, yes, even in the case of the Rector himself. Though superficially marked with lines, his face was a clear pink, and his blue eyes had the long-sighted, peaceful expression of eyes seeking the turn of the road, or a distant light through rain, or the darkness of winter. She looked at Ralph. He had never appeared to her more concentrated and full of purpose; as if behind his forehead were massed so much experience that he could choose for himself which part of it he would display and which part he would keep to himself. Compared with that dark and stern countenance, her brothers' faces, bending low over their soup-plates, were mere circles of pink, unmolded flesh.

"You came by the 3.10, Mr. Denham?" said the Reverend Wyndham Datchet, tucking his napkin into his collar, so that almost the whole of his body was concealed by a large white diamond. "They treat us very well, on the whole. Considering the increase of traffic, they treat us very well indeed. I have the curiosity sometimes to count the trucks on the goods' trains, and they're well over fifty—well over fifty, at this season of the year."

The old gentleman had been roused agreeably by the presence of this attentive and well-informed young man, as was evident by the care with which he finished the last words in his sentences, and his slight exaggeration in the number of trucks on the trains. Indeed, the chief burden of the talk fell upon him, and he sustained it tonight in a manner which caused his sons to look at him admiringly now and then; for they felt shy of Denham, and were glad not to have to talk themselves. The store of information about the present and past of this particular corner of Lincolnshire which old Mr. Datchet produced really surprised his children, for though they knew of its existence, they had forgotten its extent, as they might have forgotten the amount of family plate stored in the plate-chest, until some rare celebration brought it forth.

After dinner, parish business took the Rector to his study, and Mary proposed that they should sit in the kitchen.

"It's not the kitchen really," Elizabeth hastened to explain to her guest, "but we call it so—"

"It's the nicest room in the house," said Edward.

"It's got the old rests by the side of the fireplace, where the men hung their guns," said Elizabeth, leading the way, with a tall brass candlestick in her hand, down a passage. "Show Mr. Denham the steps, Christopher. . . . When the Ecclesiastical Commissioners were here two years ago they said this was the most interesting part of the house. These narrow bricks prove that it is five hundred years old—five hundred years, I think—they may have said six." She, too, felt an impulse to exaggerate the age of the bricks, as her father had exaggerated the number of trucks. A big lamp hung down from the center of the ceiling and, together with a fine log fire, illuminated a large and lofty room, with rafters running from wall to wall, a floor of red tiles, and a substantial fireplace built up of those narrow red bricks which were said to be five hundred years old. A few rugs and a sprinkling of arm-chairs had made this ancient kitchen into a sitting-room. Elizabeth, after pointing out the gun-racks, and the hooks for smoking hams, and other evidence of incontestable age, and explaining that Mary had had the idea of turning the room into a sitting-room—otherwise it was used for hanging out the wash and for the men to change in after shooting—considered that she had done her duty as hostess, and sat down in an upright chair directly beneath the lamp, beside a very long and narrow oak table. She placed a pair of horn spectacles upon her nose, and drew towards her a basketful of threads and wools. In a few minutes a smile came to her face, and remained there for the rest of the evening.

"Will you come out shooting with us tomorrow?" said Christopher, who had, on the whole, formed a favorable impression of his sister's friend.

"I won't shoot, but I'll come with you," said Ralph.

"Don't you care about shooting?" asked Edward, whose suspicions were not yet laid to rest.

"I've never shot in my life," said Ralph, turning and looking him in the face, because he was not sure how this confession would be received.

"You wouldn't have much chance in London, I suppose," said Christopher. "But won't you find it rather dull—just watching us?"

"I shall watch birds," Ralph replied, with a smile.

"I can show you the place for watching birds," said Edward, "if that's what you like doing. I know a fellow who comes down from London about this time every year to watch them. It's a great place for the wild geese and the ducks. I've heard this man say that it's one of the best places for birds in the country."

"It's about the best place in England," Ralph replied. They were all gratified by this praise of their native county; and Mary now had the pleasure of hearing these short questions and answers lose their undertone of suspicious inspection, so far as her brothers were concerned, and develop into a genuine conversation about the habits of birds which afterwards turned to a discussion as to the habits of solicitors, in which it was scarcely necessary for her to take part. She was pleased to see that her brothers liked Ralph, to the extent, that is, of wishing to secure his good opinion. Whether or not he liked them it was impossible to tell from his kind but experienced manner. Now and then she fed the fire with a fresh log, and as the room filled with the fine, dry heat of burning wood, they all, with the exception of Elizabeth, who was outside the range of the fire, felt less and less anxious about the effect they were making, and more and more inclined for sleep. At this moment a vehement scratching was heard on the door.

"Piper!—oh, damn!—I shall have to get up," murmured Christopher.

"It's not Piper, it's Pitch," Edward grunted.

"All the same, I shall have to get up," Christopher grumbled. He let in the dog, and stood for a moment by the door, which opened into the garden, to revive himself with a draught of the black, starlit air.

"Do come in and shut the door!" Mary cried, half turning in her chair.

"We shall have a fine day tomorrow," said Christopher with complacency, and he sat himself on the floor at her feet, and leant his back against her knees, and stretched out his long stockinged legs to the fire—all signs that he felt no longer any restraint at the presence of the stranger. He was the youngest of the family, and Mary's favorite, partly because his character resembled hers, as Edward's character resembled Elizabeth's. She made her knees a comfortable rest for his head, and ran her fingers through his hair.

"I should like Mary to stroke my head like that," Ralph thought to himself suddenly, and he looked at Christopher, almost affectionately, for calling forth his sister's caresses. Instantly he thought of Katharine, the thought of her being surrounded by the spaces of night and the open air; and Mary, watching him, saw the lines upon his forehead suddenly deepen. He stretched out an arm and placed a log upon the fire, constraining himself to fit it carefully into the frail red scaffolding, and also to limit his thoughts to this one room.

Mary had ceased to stroke her brother's head; he moved it impatiently between her knees, and, much as though he were a child, she began once more to part the thick, reddish-colored locks this way and that. But a far stronger passion had taken possession of her soul than any her brother could inspire in her, and, seeing Ralph's change of expression, her hand almost automatically continued its movements, while her mind plunged desperately for some hold upon slippery banks.

16

Into that same black night, almost, indeed, into the very same layer of starlit air, Katharine Hilbery was now gazing, although not with a view to the prospects of a fine day for duck shooting on the morrow. She was walking up and down a gravel path in the garden of Stogdon House, her sight of the heavens being partially intercepted by the light leafless hoops of a pergola. Thus a spray of clematis would completely obscure Cassiopeia, or blot out with its black pattern myriads of miles of the Milky Way. At the end of the pergola, however, there was a stone seat, from which the sky could be seen completely swept clear of any earthly interruption, save to the right, indeed, where a line of elm-trees was beautifully sprinkled with stars, and a low stable building had a full drop of quivering silver just issuing from the mouth of the chimney. It was a moonless night, but the light of the stars was sufficient to show the outline of the young woman's form, and the shape of her face gazing gravely, indeed almost sternly, into the sky. She had come out into the winter's night, which was mild enough, not so much to look with scientific eyes upon the stars, as to shake herself free from certain purely terrestrial discontents. Much as a literary person in like circumstances would begin, absent-mindedly, pulling out volume after volume, so she stepped into the garden in order to have the stars at hand, even though she did not look at them. Not to be happy, when she was supposed to be happier than she would ever be again—that, as far as she could see, was the origin of a discontent which had begun almost as soon as she arrived, two days before, and seemed now so intolerable that she had left the family party, and come out here to consider it by herself. It was not she who thought herself unhappy, but her cousins, who thought it for her. The house was full of cousins, much of her age, or even younger, and among them they had some terribly bright eyes. They seemed always on the search for something between her and Rodney, which they expected to find, and yet did not find; and when they searched, Katharine became aware of wanting what she had not been conscious of wanting in London, alone with William and her parents. Or, if she did not want it, she missed it. And this state of mind depressed her, because she had been accustomed always to give complete satisfaction, and her self-love was now a little ruffled. She would have liked to break through the reserve habitual to her in order to justify her engagement to some one whose opinion she valued. No one had spoken a word of criticism, but they left her alone with William; not that that would have mattered, if they had not left her alone so politely; and, perhaps, that would not have mattered if they had not seemed so queerly silent, almost respectful, in her presence, which gave way to criticism, she felt, out of it.

Looking now and then at the sky, she went through the list of her cousins' names: Eleanor, Humphrey, Marmaduke, Silvia, Henry, Cassandra, Gilbert, and Mostyn–Henry, the cousin who taught the young ladies of Bungay to play upon the violin, was the only one in whom she could confide, and as she walked up and down beneath the hoops of the pergola, she did begin a little speech to him, which ran something like this:

"To begin with, I'm very fond of William. You can't deny that. I know him better than any one, almost. But why I'm marrying him is, partly, I admit–I'm being quite honest with you, and you mustn't tell any one–partly because I want to get married. I want to have a house of my own. It isn't possible at home. It's all very well for you, Henry; you can go your own way. I have to be there always. Besides, you know what our house is. You wouldn't be happy either, if you didn't do something. It isn't that I haven't the time at home–it's the atmosphere."

Here, presumably, she imagined that her cousin, who had listened with his usual intelligent sympathy, raised his eyebrows a little, and interposed:

"Well, but what do you want to do?"

Even in this purely imaginary dialogue, Katharine found it difficult to confide her ambition to an imaginary companion.

"I should like," she began, and hesitated quite a long time before she forced herself to add, with a change of voice, "to study mathematics–to know about the stars."

Henry was clearly amazed, but too kind to express all his doubts; he only said something about the difficulties of mathematics, and remarked that very little was known about the stars.

Katharine thereupon went on with the statement of her case.

"I don't care much whether I ever get to know anything–but I want to work out something in figures–something that hasn't got to do with human beings. I don't want people particularly. In some ways, Henry, I'm a humbug–I mean, I'm not what you all take me for. I'm not domestic, or very practical or sensible, really. And if I could calculate things, and use a telescope, and have to work out figures, and know to a fraction where I was wrong, I should be perfectly happy, and I believe I should give William all he wants."

Having reached this point, instinct told her that she had passed beyond the region in which Henry's advice could be of any good; and, having rid her mind of its superficial annoyance, she sat herself upon the stone seat, raised her eyes unconsciously and thought about the deeper questions which she had to decide, she knew, for herself. Would she, indeed, give William all he wanted? In order to decide the question, she ran her mind rapidly over her little collection of significant sayings, looks, compliments, gestures, which had marked their intercourse during the last day or two. He had been annoyed because a box, containing some clothes specially chosen by him for her to wear, had been taken to the wrong station, owing to her neglect in the matter of labels. The box had arrived in the nick of time, and he had remarked, as she came downstairs on the first night, that he had never seen her look more beautiful. She outshone all her cousins. He had discovered that she never made an ugly movement; he also said that the shape of her head made it possible for her, unlike most women, to wear her hair low. He had twice reproved her for being silent at dinner; and once for never attending to what he said. He had been surprised at the excellence of her French accent, but he thought it was selfish of her not to go with her mother to call upon the Middletons, because they were old family friends and very nice people. On the whole, the balance was nearly even; and, writing down a kind of conclusion in her mind which finished the sum for the present, at least, she changed the focus of her eyes, and saw nothing but the stars.

Tonight they seemed fixed with unusual firmness in the blue, and flashed back such a ripple of light into her eyes that she found herself thinking that tonight the stars were happy. Without knowing or caring more for Church practices than most people of her age, Katharine could not look into the sky at Christmas time without feeling that, at this one season, the Heavens bend over the earth with sympathy, and signal with immortal radiance that they, too, take part in her festival. Somehow, it seemed to her that they were even now beholding the procession of kings and wise men upon some road on a distant part of the earth. And yet, after gazing for another second, the stars did their usual work upon the mind, froze to cinders the whole of our short human history, and reduced the human body to an ape-like, furry form, crouching amid the brushwood of a barbarous clod of mud. This stage was soon succeeded by another, in which there was nothing in the universe save stars and the light of stars; as she looked up the pupils of her eyes so dilated with starlight that the whole of her seemed dissolved in silver and spilt over the ledges of the stars for ever and ever indefinitely through space. Somehow simultaneously, though incongruously, she was riding with the magnanimous hero upon the shore or under forest trees, and so might have continued were it not for the rebuke forcibly administered by the body, which, content with the normal conditions of life, in no way furthers any attempt on the part of the mind to alter them. She grew cold, shook herself, rose, and walked towards the house.

By the light of the stars, Stogdon House looked pale and romantic, and about twice its natural size. Built by a retired admiral in the early years of the nineteenth century, the curving bow windows of the front, now filled with reddish-yellow light, suggested a portly three-decker, sailing seas where those dolphins and narwhals who disport themselves upon the edges of old maps were scattered with an impartial hand. A semicircular flight of shallow steps led to a very large door, which Katharine had left ajar. She hesitated, cast her eyes over the front of the house, marked that a light burnt in one small window upon an upper floor, and pushed the door open. For a moment she stood in the square hall, among many horned skulls, sallow globes, cracked oil-paintings, and stuffed owls, hesitating, it seemed, whether she should open the door on her right, through which the stir of life reached her ears. Listening for a moment, she heard a sound which decided her, apparently, not to enter; her uncle, Sir Francis, was playing his nightly game of whist; it appeared probable that he was losing.

She went up the curving stairway, which represented the one attempt at ceremony in the otherwise rather dilapidated mansion, and down a narrow passage until she came to the room whose light she had seen from the garden. Knocking, she was told to come in. A young man, Henry Otway, was reading, with his feet on the fender. He had a fine head, the brow arched in the Elizabethan manner, but the gentle, honest eyes were rather skeptical than glowing with the Elizabethan vigor. He gave the impression that he had not yet found the cause which suited his temperament.

He turned, put down his book, and looked at her. He noticed her rather pale, dew-drenched look, as of one whose mind is not altogether settled in the body. He had often laid his difficulties before her, and guessed, in some ways hoped, that perhaps she now had need of him. At the same time, she carried on her life with such independence that he scarcely expected any confidence to be expressed in words.

"You have fled, too, then?" he said, looking at her cloak. Katharine had forgotten to remove this token of her star-gazing.

"Fled?" she asked. "From whom d'you mean? Oh, the family party. Yes, it was hot down there, so I went into the garden."

"And aren't you very cold?" Henry inquired, placing coal on the fire, drawing a chair up to the grate, and laying aside her cloak. Her indifference to such details often forced Henry to act the part generally taken by women in such dealings. It was one of the ties between them.

"Thank you, Henry," she said. "I'm not disturbing you?"

"I'm not here. I'm at Bungay," he replied. "I'm giving a music lesson to Harold and Julia. That was why I had to leave the table with the ladies—I'm spending the night there, and I shan't be back till late on Christmas Eve."

"How I wish—" Katharine began, and stopped short. "I think these parties are a great mistake," she added briefly, and sighed.

"Oh, horrible!" he agreed; and they both fell silent.

Her sigh made him look at her. Should he venture to ask her why she sighed? Was her reticence about her own affairs as inviolable as it had often been convenient for rather an egoistical young man to think it? But since her engagement to Rodney, Henry's feeling towards her had become rather complex; equally divided between an impulse to hurt her and an impulse to be tender to her; and all the time he suffered a curious irritation from the sense that she was drifting away from him for ever upon unknown seas. On her side, directly Katharine got into his presence, and the sense of the stars dropped from her, she knew that any intercourse between people is extremely partial; from the whole mass of her feelings, only one or two could be selected for Henry's inspection, and therefore she sighed. Then she looked at him, and their eyes meeting, much more seemed to be in common between them than had appeared possible. At any rate they had a grandfather in common; at any rate there was a kind of loyalty between them sometimes found between relations who have no other cause to like each other, as these two had.

"Well, what's the date of the wedding?" said Henry, the malicious mood now predominating.

"I think some time in March," she replied.

"And afterwards?" he asked.

"We take a house, I suppose, somewhere in Chelsea."

"It's very interesting," he observed, stealing another look at her.

She lay back in her arm-chair, her feet high upon the side of the grate, and in front of her, presumably to screen her eyes, she held a newspaper from which she picked up a sentence or two now and again. Observing this, Henry remarked:

"Perhaps marriage will make you more human."

At this she lowered the newspaper an inch or two, but said nothing. Indeed, she sat quite silent for over a minute.

"When you consider things like the stars, our affairs don't seem to matter very much, do they?" she said suddenly.

"I don't think I ever do consider things like the stars," Henry replied. "I'm not sure that that's not the explanation, though," he added, now observing her steadily.

"I doubt whether there is an explanation," she replied rather hurriedly, not clearly understanding what he meant.

"What? No explanation of anything?" he inquired, with a smile.

"Oh, things happen. That's about all," she let drop in her casual, decided way.

"That certainly seems to explain some of your actions," Henry thought to himself.

"One thing's about as good as another, and one's got to do something," he said aloud, expressing what he supposed to be her attitude, much in her accent. Perhaps she detected the imitation, for looking gently at him, she said, with ironical composure:

"Well, if you believe that your life must be simple, Henry."

"But I don't believe it," he said shortly.

"No more do I," she replied.

"What about the stars?" he asked a moment later. "I understand that you rule your life by the stars?"

She let this pass, either because she did not attend to it, or because the tone was not to her liking.

Once more she paused, and then she inquired:

"But do *you* always understand why you do everything? Ought one to understand? People like my mother understand," she reflected. "Now I must go down to them, I suppose, and see what's happening."

"What could be happening?" Henry protested.

"Oh, they may want to settle something," she replied vaguely, putting her feet on the ground, resting her chin on her hands, and looking out of her large dark eyes contemplatively at the fire.

"And then there's William," she added, as if by an afterthought.

Henry very nearly laughed, but restrained himself.

"Do they know what coals are made of, Henry?" she asked, a moment later.

"Mares' tails, I believe," he hazarded.

"Have you ever been down a coal-mine?" she went on.

"Don't let's talk about coal-mines, Katharine," he protested. "We shall probably never see each other again. When you're married—"

Tremendously to his surprise, he saw the tears stand in her eyes.

"Why do you all tease me?" she said. "It isn't kind."

Henry could not pretend that he was altogether ignorant of her meaning, though, certainly, he had never guessed that she minded the teasing. But before he knew what to say, her eyes were clear again, and the sudden crack in the surface was almost filled up.

"Things aren't easy, anyhow," she stated.

Obeying an impulse of genuine affection, Henry spoke.

"Promise me, Katharine, that if I can ever help you, you will let me."

She seemed to consider, looking once more into the red of the fire, and decided to refrain from any explanation.

"Yes, I promise that," she said at length, and Henry felt himself gratified by her complete sincerity, and began to tell her now about the coal-mine, in obedience to her love of facts.

They were, indeed, descending the shaft in a small cage, and could hear the picks of the miners, something like the gnawing of rats, in the earth beneath them, when the door was burst open, without any knocking.

"Well, here you are!" Rodney exclaimed. Both Katharine and Henry turned round very quickly and rather guiltily. Rodney was in evening dress. It was clear that his temper was ruffled.

"That's where you've been all the time," he repeated, looking at Katharine.

"I've only been here about ten minutes," she replied.

"My dear Katharine, you left the drawing-room over an hour ago."

She said nothing.

"Does it very much matter?" Henry asked.

Rodney found it hard to be unreasonable in the presence of another man, and did not answer him.

"They don't like it," he said. "It isn't kind to old people to leave them alone—although I've no doubt it's much more amusing to sit up here and talk to Henry."

"We were discussing coal-mines," said Henry urbanely.

"Yes. But we were talking about much more interesting things before that," said Katharine.

From the apparent determination to hurt him with which she spoke, Henry thought that some sort of explosion on Rodney's part was about to take place.

"I can quite understand that," said Rodney, with his little chuckle, leaning over the back of his chair and tapping the woodwork lightly with his fingers. They were all silent, and the silence was acutely uncomfortable to Henry, at least.

"Was it very dull, William?" Katharine suddenly asked, with a complete change of tone and a little gesture of her hand.

"Of course it was dull," William said sulkily.

"Well, you stay and talk to Henry, and I'll go down," she replied.

She rose as she spoke, and as she turned to leave the room, she laid her hand, with a curiously caressing gesture, upon Rodney's shoulder. Instantly Rodney clasped her hand in his, with such an impulse of emotion that Henry was annoyed, and rather ostentatiously opened a book.

"I shall come down with you," said William, as she drew back her hand, and made as if to pass him.

"Oh no," she said hastily. "You stay here and talk to Henry."

"Yes, do," said Henry, shutting up his book again. His invitation was polite, without being precisely cordial. Rodney evidently hesitated as to the course he should pursue, but seeing Katharine at the door, he exclaimed:

"No. I want to come with you."

She looked back, and said in a very commanding tone, and with an expression of authority upon her face:

"It's useless for you to come. I shall go to bed in ten minutes. Good night."

She nodded to them both, but Henry could not help noticing that her last nod was in his direction. Rodney sat down rather heavily.

His mortification was so obvious that Henry scarcely liked to open the conversation with some remark of a literary character. On the other hand, unless he checked him, Rodney might begin to talk about his feelings, and irreticence is apt to be extremely painful, at any rate in prospect. He therefore adopted a middle course; that is to say, he wrote a note upon the fly-leaf of his book, which ran, "The situation is becoming most uncomfortable." This he decorated with those flourishes and decorative borders which grow of themselves upon these occasions; and as he did so, he thought to himself that whatever Katharine's difficulties might be, they did not justify her behavior. She had spoken with a kind of brutality which suggested that, whether it is natural or assumed, women have a peculiar blindness to the feelings of men.

The penciling of this note gave Rodney time to recover himself. Perhaps, for he was a very vain man, he was more hurt that Henry had seen him rebuffed than by the rebuff itself. He was in love with Katharine, and vanity is not decreased but increased by love; especially, one may hazard, in the presence of one's own sex. But Rodney enjoyed the courage which springs from that laughable and lovable defect, and when he had mastered his first impulse, in some way to make a fool of himself, he drew inspiration from the perfect fit of his evening dress. He chose a cigarette, tapped it on the back of his hand, displayed his exquisite pumps on the edge of the fender, and summoned his self-respect.

"You've several big estates round here, Otway," he began. "Any good hunting? Let me see, what pack would it be? Who's your great man?"

"Sir William Budge, the sugar king, has the biggest estate. He bought out poor Stanham, who went bankrupt."

"Which Stanham would that be? Verney or Alfred?"

"Alfred. . . . I don't hunt myself. You're a great huntsman, aren't you? You have a great reputation as a horseman, anyhow," he added, desiring to help Rodney in his effort to recover his complacency.

"Oh, I love riding," Rodney replied. "Could I get a horse down here? Stupid of me! I forgot to bring any clothes. I can't imagine, though, who told you I was anything of a rider?"

To tell the truth, Henry labored under the same difficulty; he did not wish to introduce Katharine's name, and, therefore, he replied vaguely that he had always heard that Rodney was a great rider. In truth, he had heard very little about him, one way or another, accepting him as a figure often to be found in the background at his aunt's house, and inevitably, though inexplicably, engaged to his cousin.

"I don't care much for shooting," Rodney continued; "but one has to do it, unless one wants to be altogether out of things. I dare say there's some very pretty country round here. I stayed once at Bolham Hall. Young Cranthorpe was up with you, wasn't he? He married old Lord Bolham's daughter. Very nice people—in their way."

"I don't mix in that society," Henry remarked, rather shortly. But Rodney, now started on an agreeable current of reflection, could not resist the temptation of pursuing it a little further. He appeared to himself as a man who moved easily in very good society, and knew enough about the true values of life to be himself above it.

"Oh, but you should," he went on. "It's well worth staying there, anyhow, once a year. They make one very comfortable, and the women are ravishing."

"The women?" Henry thought to himself, with disgust. "What could any woman see in you?" His tolerance was rapidly becoming exhausted, but he could not help liking Rodney nevertheless, and this appeared to him strange, for he was fastidious, and such words in another mouth would have condemned the speaker irreparably. He began, in short, to wonder what kind of creature this man who was to marry his cousin might be. Could any one, except a rather singular character, afford to be so ridiculously vain?

"I don't think I should get on in that society," he replied. "I don't think I should know what to say to Lady Rose if I met her."

"I don't find any difficulty," Rodney chuckled. "You talk to them about their children, if they have any, or their accomplishments—painting, gardening, poetry—they're so delightfully sympathetic. Seriously, you know I think a woman's opinion of one's poetry is always worth having. Don't ask them for their reasons. Just ask them for their feelings. Katharine, for example——"

"Katharine," said Henry, with an emphasis upon the name, almost as if he resented Rodney's use of it, "Katharine is very unlike most women."

"Quite," Rodney agreed. "She is——" He seemed about to describe her, and he hesitated for a long time. "She's looking very well," he stated, or rather almost inquired, in a different tone from that in which he had been speaking. Henry bent his head.

"But, as a family, you're given to moods, eh?"

"Not Katharine," said Henry, with decision.

"Not Katharine," Rodney repeated, as if he weighed the meaning of the words. "No, perhaps you're right. But her engagement has changed her. Naturally," he added, "one would expect that to be so." He waited for Henry to confirm this statement, but Henry remained silent.

"Katharine has had a difficult life, in some ways," he continued. "I expect that marriage will be good for her. She has great powers."

"Great," said Henry, with decision.

"Yes—but now what direction d'you think they take?"

Rodney had completely dropped his pose as a man of the world, and seemed to be asking Henry to help him in a difficulty.

"I don't know," Henry hesitated cautiously.

"D'you think children—a household—that sort of thing—d'you think that'll satisfy her? Mind, I'm out all day."

"She would certainly be very competent," Henry stated.

"Oh, she's wonderfully competent," said Rodney. "But—I get absorbed in my poetry. Well, Katharine hasn't got that. She admires my poetry, you know, but that wouldn't be enough for her?"

"No," said Henry. He paused. "I think you're right," he added, as if he were summing up his thoughts. "Katharine hasn't found herself yet. Life isn't altogether real to her yet—I sometimes think——"

"Yes?" Rodney inquired, as if he were eager for Henry to continue. "That is what I——" he was going on, as Henry remained silent, but the sentence was not finished, for the door opened, and they were interrupted by Henry's younger brother Gilbert, much to Henry's relief, for he had already said more than he liked.

17

When the sun shone, as it did with unusual brightness that Christmas week, it revealed much that was faded and not altogether well-kept-up in Stogdon House and its grounds. In truth, Sir Francis had retired from service under the Government of India with a pension that was not adequate, in his opinion, to his services, as it certainly was not adequate to his ambitions. His career had not come up to his expectations, and although he was a very fine, white-whiskered, mahogany-colored old man to look at, and had laid down a very choice cellar of good reading and good stories, you could not long remain ignorant of the fact that some thunder-storm had soured them; he had a grievance. This grievance dated back to the middle years of the last century, when, owing to some official intrigue, his merits had been passed over in a disgraceful manner in favor of another, his junior.

The rights and wrongs of the story, presuming that they had some existence in fact, were no longer clearly known to his wife and children;

but this disappointment had played a very large part in their lives, and had poisoned the life of Sir Francis much as a disappointment in love is said to poison the whole life of a woman. Long brooding on his failure, continual arrangement and rearrangement of his deserts and rebuffs, had made Sir Francis much of an egoist, and in his retirement his temper became increasingly difficult and exacting.

His wife now offered so little resistance to his moods that she was practically useless to him. He made his daughter Eleanor into his chief confidante, and the prime of her life was being rapidly consumed by her father. To her he dictated the memoirs which were to avenge his memory, and she had to assure him constantly that his treatment had been a disgrace. Already, at the age of thirty-five, her cheeks were whitening as her mother's had whitened, but for her there would be no memories of Indian suns and Indian rivers, and clamor of children in a nursery; she would have very little of substance to think about when she sat, as Lady Otway now sat, knitting white wool, with her eyes fixed almost perpetually upon the same embroidered bird upon the same fire-screen. But then Lady Otway was one of the people for whom the great make-believe game of English social life has been invented; she spent most of her time in pretending to herself and her neighbors that she was a dignified, important, much-occupied person, of considerable social standing and sufficient wealth. In view of the actual state of things this game needed a great deal of skill; and, perhaps, at the age she had reached—she was over sixty—she played far more to deceive herself than to deceive any one else. Moreover, the armor was wearing thin; she forgot to keep up appearances more and more.

The worn patches in the carpets, and the pallor of the drawing-room, where no chair or cover had been renewed for some years, were due not only to the miserable pension, but to the wear and tear of twelve children, eight of whom were sons. As often happens in these large families, a distinct dividing-line could be traced, about half-way in the succession, where the money for educational purposes had run short, and the six younger children had grown up far more economically than the elder. If the boys were clever, they won scholarships, and went to school; if they were not clever, they took what the family connection had to offer them. The girls accepted situations occasionally, but there were always one or two at home, nursing sick animals, tending silkworms, or playing the flute in their bedrooms. The distinction between the elder children and the younger corresponded almost to the distinction between a higher class and a lower one, for with only a haphazard education and insufficient allowances, the younger children had picked up accomplishments, friends, and points of view which were not to be found within the walls of a public school or of a Government office. Between the two divisions there was considerable hostility, the elder trying to patronize the younger, the younger refusing to respect the elder; but one feeling united them and instantly closed any risk of a breach—their common belief in the superiority of their own family to all others. Henry was the eldest of the younger group, and their leader; he bought strange books and joined odd societies; he went without a tie for a whole year, and had six shirts made of black flannel. He had long refused to take a seat either in a shipping office or in a tea-merchant's warehouse; and persisted, in spite of the disapproval of uncles and aunts, in practicing both violin and piano, with the result that he could not perform professionally upon either. Indeed, for thirty-two years of life he had nothing more substantial to show than a manuscript book containing the score of half an opera. In this protest of his, Katharine had always given him her support, and as she was generally held to be an extremely sensible person, who dressed too well to be eccentric, he had found her support of some use. Indeed, when she came down at Christmas she usually spent a great part of her time in private conferences with Henry and with Cassandra, the youngest girl, to whom the silkworms belonged. With the younger section she had a great reputation for common sense, and for something that they despised but inwardly respected and called knowledge of the world—that is to say, of the way in which respectable elderly people, going to their clubs and dining out with ministers, think and behave. She had more than once played the part of ambassador between Lady Otway and her children. That poor lady, for instance, consulted her for advice when, one day, she opened Cassandra's bedroom door on a mission of discovery, and found the ceiling hung with mulberry-leaves, the windows blocked with cages, and the tables stacked with home-made machines for the manufacture of silk dresses.

"I wish you could help her to take an interest in something that other people are interested in, Katharine," she observed, rather plaintively, detailing her grievances. "It's all Henry's doing, you know, giving up her parties and taking to these nasty insects. It doesn't follow that if a man can do a thing a woman may too."

The morning was sufficiently bright to make the chairs and sofas in Lady Otway's private sitting-room appear more than usually shabby, and the gallant gentlemen, her brothers and cousins, who had defended the Empire and left their bones on many frontiers, looked at the world through a film of yellow which the morning light seemed to have drawn across their photographs. Lady Otway sighed, it may be at the faded relics, and turned, with resignation, to her balls of wool, which, curiously and characteristically, were not an ivory-white, but rather a tarnished yellow-white. She had called her niece in for a little chat. She had always trusted her, and now more than ever, since her engagement to Rodney, which seemed to Lady Otway extremely suitable, and just what one would wish for one's own daughter. Katharine unwittingly increased her reputation for wisdom by asking to be given knitting-needles too.

"It's so very pleasant," said Lady Otway, "to knit while one's talking. And now, my dear Katharine, tell me about your plans."

The emotions of the night before, which she had suppressed in such a way as to keep her awake till dawn, had left Katharine a little jaded, and thus more matter-of-fact than usual. She was quite ready to discuss her plans—houses and rents, servants and economy—without feeling that they concerned her very much. As she spoke, knitting methodically meanwhile, Lady Otway noted, with approval, the upright, responsible bearing of her niece, to whom the prospect of marriage had brought some gravity most becoming in a bride, and yet, in these days, most rare. Yes, Katharine's engagement had changed her a little.

"What a perfect daughter, or daughter-in-law!" she thought to herself, and could not help contrasting her with Cassandra, surrounded by innumerable silkworms in her bedroom.

"Yes," she continued, glancing at Katharine, with the round, greenish eyes which were as inexpressive as moist marbles, "Katharine is like the girls of my youth. We took the serious things of life seriously." But just as she was deriving satisfaction from this thought, and was producing some of the hoarded wisdom which none of her own daughters, alas! seemed now to need, the door opened, and Mrs. Hilbery came in, or rather, did not come in, but stood in the doorway and smiled, having evidently mistaken the room.

"I never *shall* know my way about this house!" she exclaimed. "I'm on my way to the library, and I don't want to interrupt. You and Katharine were having a little chat?"

The presence of her sister-in-law made Lady Otway slightly uneasy. How could she go on with what she was saying in Maggie's presence? for she was saying something that she had never said, all these years, to Maggie herself.

"I was telling Katharine a few little commonplaces about marriage," she said, with a little laugh. "Are none of my children looking after you, Maggie?"

"Marriage," said Mrs. Hilbery, coming into the room, and nodding her head once or twice, "I always say marriage is a school. And you don't get the prizes unless you go to school. Charlotte has won all the prizes," she added, giving her sister-in-law a little pat, which made Lady Otway more uncomfortable still. She half laughed, muttered something, and ended on a sigh.

"Aunt Charlotte was saying that it's no good being married unless you submit to your husband," said Katharine, framing her aunt's words into a far more definite shape than they had really worn; and when she spoke thus she did not appear at all old-fashioned. Lady Otway looked at her and paused for a moment.

"Well, I really don't advise a woman who wants to have things her own way to get married," she said, beginning a fresh row rather elaborately.

Mrs. Hilbery knew something of the circumstances which, as she thought, had inspired this remark. In a moment her face was clouded with sympathy which she did not quite know how to express.

"What a shame it was!" she exclaimed, forgetting that her train of thought might not be obvious to her listeners. "But, Charlotte, it would have been much worse if Frank had disgraced himself in any way. And it isn't what our husbands *get*, but what they *are*. I used to dream of white horses and palanquins, too; but still, I like the ink-pots best. And who knows?" she concluded, looking at Katharine, "your father may be made a baronet tomorrow."

Lady Otway, who was Mr. Hilbery's sister, knew quite well that, in private, the Hilberys called Sir Francis "that old Turk," and though she did not follow the drift of Mrs. Hilbery's remarks, she knew what prompted them.

"But if you can give way to your husband," she said, speaking to Katharine, as if there were a separate understanding between them, "a happy marriage is the happiest thing in the world."

"Yes," said Katharine, "but—" She did not mean to finish her sentence, she merely wished to induce her mother and her aunt to go on talking about marriage, for she was in the mood to feel that other people could help her if they would. She went on knitting, but her fingers worked with a decision that was oddly unlike the smooth and contemplative sweep of Lady Otway's plump hand. Now and then she looked swiftly at her mother, then at her aunt. Mrs. Hilbery held a book in her hand, and was on her way, as Katharine guessed, to the library, where another paragraph was to be added to that varied assortment of paragraphs, the Life of Richard Alardyce. Normally, Katharine would have hurried her mother downstairs, and seen that no excuse for distraction came her way. Her attitude towards the poet's life, however, had changed with other changes; and she was content to forget all about her scheme of hours. Mrs. Hilbery was secretly delighted. Her relief at finding herself excused manifested itself in a series of sidelong glances of sly humor in her daughter's direction, and the indulgence put her in the best of spirits. Was she to be allowed merely to sit and talk? It was so much pleasanter to sit in a nice room filled with all sorts of interesting odds and ends which she hadn't looked at for a year, at least, than to seek out one date which contradicted another in a dictionary.

"We've all had perfect husbands," she concluded, generously forgiving Sir Francis all his faults in a lump. "Not that I think a bad temper is really a fault in a man. I don't mean a bad temper," she corrected herself, with a glance obviously in the direction of Sir Francis. "I should say a quick, impatient temper. Most, in fact *all* great men have had bad tempers—except your grandfather, Katharine," and here she sighed, and suggested that, perhaps, she ought to go down to the library.

"But in the ordinary marriage, is it necessary to give way to one's husband?" said Katharine, taking no notice of her mother's suggestion, blind even to the depression which had now taken possession of her at the thought of her own inevitable death.

"I should say yes, certainly," said Lady Otway, with a decision most unusual for her.

"Then one ought to make up one's mind to that before one is married," Katharine mused, seeming to address herself.

Mrs. Hilbery was not much interested in these remarks, which seemed to have a melancholy tendency, and to revive her spirits she had recourse to an infallible remedy—she looked out of the window.

"Do look at that lovely little blue bird!" she exclaimed, and her eye looked with extreme pleasure at the soft sky. at the trees, at the green fields visible behind those trees, and at the leafless branches which surrounded the body of the small blue tit. Her sympathy with nature was exquisite.

"Most women know by instinct whether they can give it or not," Lady Otway slipped in quickly, in rather a low voice, as if she wanted to get this said while her sister-in-law's attention was diverted. "And if not—well then, my advice would be—don't marry."

"Oh, but marriage is the happiest life for a woman," said Mrs. Hilbery, catching the word marriage, as she brought her eyes back to the room again. Then she turned her mind to what she had said.

"It's the most *interesting* life," she corrected herself. She looked at her daughter with a look of vague alarm. It was the kind of maternal scrutiny which suggests that, in looking at her daughter a mother is really looking at herself. She was not altogether satisfied; but she purposely made no attempt to break down the reserve which, as a matter of fact, was a quality she particularly admired and depended upon in her daughter. But when her mother said that marriage was the most interesting life, Katharine felt, as she was apt to do suddenly, for no definite reason, that they understood each other, in spite of differing in every possible way. Yet the wisdom of the old seems to apply more to feelings which we have in common with the rest of the human race than to our feelings as individuals, and Katharine knew that only some one of her own age could follow her meaning. Both these elderly women seemed to her to have been content with so little happiness, and at the moment she had not sufficient force to feel certain that their version of marriage was the wrong one. In London, certainly, this temperate attitude toward her own marriage had seemed to her just. Why had she now changed? Why did it now depress her? It never occurred to her that her own conduct could be anything of a puzzle to her mother, or that elder people are as much affected by the young as the young are by them. And yet it was true that love—passion—whatever one chose to call it, had played far less part in Mrs. Hilbery's life than might have seemed likely, judging from her enthusiastic and imaginative temperament. She had always been more interested by other things. Lady Otway, strange though it seemed, guessed more accurately at Katharine's state of mind than her mother did.

"Why don't we all live in the country?" exclaimed Mrs. Hilbery, once more looking out of the window. "I'm sure one would think such beautiful things if one lived in the country. No horrid slum houses to depress one, no trams or motor-cars; and the people all looking so plump and cheerful. Isn't there some little cottage near you, Charlotte, which would do for us, with a spare room, perhaps, in case we asked a friend down? And we should save so much money that we should be able to travel——"

"Yes. You would find it very nice for a week or two, no doubt," said Lady Otway. "But what hour would you like the carriage this morning?" she continued, touching the bell.

"Katharine shall decide," said Mrs. Hilbery, feeling herself unable to prefer one hour to another. "And I was just going to tell you, Katharine, how, when I woke this morning, everything seemed so clear in my head that if I'd had a pencil I believe I could have written quite a long chapter. When we're out on our drive I shall find us a house. A few trees round it, and a little garden, a pond with a Chinese duck, a study for your father, a study for me, and a sitting room for Katharine, because then she'll be a married lady."

At this Katharine shivered a little, drew up to the fire, and warmed her hands by spreading them over the topmost peak of the coal. She wished to bring the talk back to marriage again, in order to hear Aunt Charlotte's views, but she did not know how to do this.

"Let me look at your engagement-ring, Aunt Charlotte," she said, noticing her own.

She took the cluster of green stones and turned it round and round, but she did not know what to say next.

"That poor old ring was a sad disappointment to me when I first had it," Lady Otway mused. "I'd set my heart on a diamond ring, but I never liked to tell Frank, naturally. He bought it at Simla."

Katharine turned the ring round once more, and gave it back to her aunt without speaking. And while she turned it round her lips set themselves firmly together, and it seemed to her that she could satisfy William as these women had satisfied their husbands; she could pretend to like emeralds when she preferred diamonds. Having replaced her ring, Lady Otway remarked that it was chilly, though not more so than one must expect at this time of year. Indeed, one ought to be thankful to see the sun at all, and she advised them both to dress warmly for their drive. Her aunt's stock of commonplaces, Katharine sometimes suspected, had been laid in on purpose to fill silences with, and had little to do with her private thoughts. But at this moment they seemed terribly in keeping with her own conclusions, so that she took up her knitting again and listened, chiefly with a view to confirming herself in the belief that to be engaged to marry some one with whom you are not in love is an inevitable step in a world where the existence of passion is only a traveller's story brought from the heart of deep forests and told so rarely that wise people doubt whether the story can be true. She did her best to listen to her mother asking for news of John, and to her aunt replying with the authentic history of Hilda's engagement to an officer in the Indian Army, but she cast her mind alternately towards forest paths and starry blossoms, and towards pages of neatly written mathematical signs. When her mind took this turn her marriage seemed no more than an archway through which it was necessary to pass in order to have her desire. At such times the current of her nature ran in its deep narrow channel with great force and with an alarming lack of consideration for the feelings of others. Just as the two elder ladies had finished their survey of the family prospects, and Lady Otway was nervously anticipating some general statement as to life and death from her sister-in-law, Cassandra burst into the room with the news that the carriage was at the door.

"Why didn't Andrews tell me himself?" said Lady Otway, peevishly, blaming her servants for not living up to her ideals.

When Mrs. Hilbery and Katharine arrived in the hall, ready dressed for their drive, they found that the usual discussion was going forward as to the plans of the rest of the family. In token of this, a great many doors were opening and shutting, two or three people stood irresolutely on the stairs, now going a few steps up, and now a few steps down, and Sir Francis himself had come out from his study, with the *Times* under his arm, and a complaint about noise and draughts from the open door which, at least, had the effect of bundling the people who did not want to go into the carriage, and sending those who did not want to stay back to their rooms. It was decided that Mrs. Hilbery, Katharine, Rodney, and Henry should drive to Lincoln, and any one else who wished to go should follow on bicycles or in the pony-cart. Every one who stayed at Stogdon House had to make this expedition to Lincoln in obedience to Lady Otway's conception of the right way to entertain her guests, which she had imbibed from reading in fashionable papers of the behavior of Christmas parties in ducal houses. The carriage horses were both fat and aged, still they matched; the carriage was shaky and uncomfortable, but the Otway arms were visible on the panels. Lady Otway stood on the topmost step, wrapped in a white shawl, and waved her hand almost mechanically until they had turned the corner under the laurel-bushes, when she retired indoors with a sense that she had played her part, and a sigh at the thought that none of her children felt it necessary to play theirs.

The carriage bowled along smoothly over the gently curving road. Mrs. Hilbery dropped into a pleasant, inattentive state of mind, in which she was conscious of the running green lines of the hedges, of the swelling ploughland, and of the mild blue sky, which served her, after the first five minutes, for a pastoral background to the drama of human life; and then she thought of a cottage garden, with the flash of yellow daffodils against blue water; and what with the arrangement of these different prospects, and the shaping of two or three lovely phrases, she did not notice that the young people in the carriage were almost silent. Henry, indeed, had been included against his wish, and revenged himself by observing Katharine and Rodney with disillusioned eyes; while Katharine was in a state of gloomy self-suppression which resulted in complete apathy. When Rodney spoke to her she either said "Hum!" or assented so listlessly that he addressed his next remark to her mother. His deference was agreeable to her, his manners were exemplary; and when the church towers and factory chimneys of the town came into sight, she roused herself, and recalled memories of the fair summer of 1853, which fitted in harmoniously with what she was dreaming of the future.

18

But other passengers were approaching Lincoln meanwhile by other roads on foot. A county town draws the inhabitants of all vicarages, farms, country houses, and wayside cottages, within a radius of ten miles at least, once or twice a week to its streets; and among them, on this occasion, were Ralph Denham and Mary Datchet. They despised the roads, and took their way across the fields; and yet, from their appearance, it did not seem as if they cared much where they walked so long as the way did not actually trip them up. When they left the Vicarage, they had begun an argument which swung their feet along so rhythmically in time with it that they covered the ground at over four miles an hour, and saw nothing of the hedgerows, the swelling plowland, or the mild blue sky. What they saw were the Houses of Parliament and the Government Offices in Whitehall. They both belonged to the class which is conscious of having lost its birthright in these great structures and is seeking to build another kind of lodging for its own notion of law and government. Purposely, perhaps, Mary did not agree with Ralph; she loved to feel her mind in conflict with his, and to be certain that he spared her female judgment no ounce of his male muscularity. He seemed to argue as fiercely with her as if she were his brother. They were alike, however, in believing that it behooved them to take in hand the repair and reconstruction of the fabric of England. They agreed in thinking that nature has not been generous in the endowment of our councilors. They agreed, unconsciously, in a mute love for the muddy field through which they tramped, with eyes narrowed close by the concentration of their minds. At length they drew breath, let the argument fly away into the limbo of other good arguments, and, leaning over a gate, opened their eyes for the first time and looked about them. Their feet tingled with warm blood and their breath rose in steam around them. The bodily exercise made them both feel more direct and less self-conscious than usual, and Mary, indeed, was overcome by a sort of light-headedness which made it seem to her that it mattered very little what happened next. It mattered so little, indeed, that she felt herself on the point of saying to Ralph:

"I love you; I shall never love anybody else. Marry me or leave me; think what you like of me—I don't care a straw." At the moment, however, speech or silence seemed immaterial, and she merely clapped her hands together, and looked at the distant woods with the rust-like bloom on their brown, and the green and blue landscape through the steam of her own breath. It seemed a mere toss-up whether she said, "I love you," or whether she said, "I love the beech-trees," or only "I love—I love."

"Do you know, Mary," Ralph suddenly interrupted her, "I've made up my mind."

Her indifference must have been superficial, for it disappeared at once. Indeed, she lost sight of the trees, and saw her own hand upon the topmost bar of the gate with extreme distinctness, while he went on:

"I've made up my mind to chuck my work and live down here. I want you to tell me about that cottage you spoke of. However, I suppose there'll be no difficulty about getting a cottage, will there?" He spoke with an assumption of carelessness as if expecting her to dissuade him.

She still waited, as if for him to continue; she was convinced that in some roundabout way he approached the subject of their marriage.

"I can't stand the office any longer," he proceeded. "I don't know what my family will say; but I'm sure I'm right. Don't you think so?"

"Live down here by yourself?" she asked.

"Some old woman would do for me, I suppose," he replied. "I'm sick of the whole thing," he went on, and opened the gate with a jerk. They began to cross the next field walking side by side.

"I tell you, Mary, it's utter destruction, working away, day after day, at stuff that doesn't matter a damn to any one. I've stood eight years of it, and I'm not going to stand it any longer. I suppose this all seems to you mad, though?"

By this time Mary had recovered her self-control.

"No. I thought you weren't happy," she said.

"Why did you think that?" he asked, with some surprise.

"Don't you remember that morning in Lincoln's Inn Fields?" she asked.

"Yes," said Ralph, slackening his pace and remembering Katharine and her engagement, the purple leaves stamped into the path, the white paper radiant under the electric light, and the hopelessness which seemed to surround all these things.

"You're right, Mary," he said, with something of an effort, "though I don't know how you guessed it."

She was silent, hoping that he might tell her the reason of his unhappiness, for his excuses had not deceived her.

"I was unhappy—very unhappy," he repeated. Some six weeks separated him from that afternoon when he had sat upon the Embankment watching his visions dissolve in mist as the waters swam past and the sense of his desolation still made him shiver. He had not recovered in the least from that depression. Here was an opportunity for making himself face it, as he felt that he ought to; for, by this time, no doubt, it was only a sentimental ghost, better exorcised by ruthless exposure to such an eye as Mary's, than allowed to underlie all his actions and thoughts as had been the case ever since he first saw Katharine Hilbery pouring out tea. He must begin, however, by mentioning her name, and this he found it impossible to do. He persuaded himself that he could make an honest statement without speaking her name; he persuaded himself that his feeling had very little to do with her.

"Unhappiness is a state of mind," he said, "by which I mean that it is not necessarily the result of any particular cause."

This rather stilted beginning did not please him, and it became more and more obvious to him that, whatever he might say, his unhappiness had been directly caused by Katharine.

"I began to find my life unsatisfactory," he started afresh. "It seemed to me meaningless." He paused again, but felt that this, at any rate, was true, and that on these lines he could go on.

"All this money-making and working ten hours a day in an office, what's it *for?* When one's a boy, you see, one's head is so full of dreams that it doesn't seem to matter what one does. And if you're ambitious, you're all right; you've got a reason for going on. Now my reasons ceased to satisfy me. Perhaps I never had any. That's very likely now I come to think of it. (What reason is there for anything, though?) Still, it's impossible, after a certain age, to take oneself in satisfactorily. And I know what carried me on"—for a good reason now occurred to him—"I wanted to be the savior of my family and all that kind of thing. I wanted them to get on in the world. That was a lie, of course—a kind of self-glorification, too. Like most people, I suppose, I've lived almost entirely among delusions, and now I'm at the awkward stage of finding it out. I want another delusion to go on with. That's what my unhappiness amounts to, Mary."

There were two reasons that kept Mary very silent during this speech, and drew curiously straight lines upon her face. In the first place, Ralph made no mention of marriage; in the second, he was not speaking the truth.

"I don't think it will be difficult to find a cottage," she said, with cheerful hardness, ignoring the whole of this statement. "You've got a little money, haven't you? Yes," she concluded, "I don't see why it shouldn't be a very good plan."

They crossed the field in complete silence. Ralph was surprised by her remark and a little hurt, and yet, on the whole, rather pleased. He had convinced himself that it was impossible to lay his case truthfully before Mary, and, secretly, he was relieved to find that he had not parted with his dream to her. She was, as he had always found her, the sensible, loyal friend, the woman he trusted; whose sympathy he could count upon, provided he kept within certain limits. He was not displeased to find that those limits were very clearly marked. When they had crossed the next hedge she said to him:

"Yes, Ralph, it's time you made a break. I've come to the same conclusion myself. Only it won't be a country cottage in my case; it'll be America. America!" she cried. "That's the place for me! They'll teach me something about organizing a movement there, and I'll come back and show you how to do it."

If she meant consciously or unconsciously to belittle the seclusion and security of a country cottage, she did not succeed; for Ralph's determination was genuine. But she made him visualize her in her own character, so that he looked quickly at her, as she walked a little in front of him across the plowed field; for the first time that morning he saw her independently of him or of his preoccupation with Katharine. He seemed to see her marching ahead, a rather clumsy but powerful and independent figure, for whose courage he felt the greatest respect.

"Don't go away, Mary!" he exclaimed, and stopped.

"That's what you said before, Ralph," she returned, without looking at him. "You want to go away yourself and you don't want me to go away. That's not very sensible, is it?"

"Mary," he cried, stung by the remembrance of his exacting and dictatorial ways with her, "what a brute I've been to you!"

It took all her strength to keep the tears from springing, and to thrust back her assurance that she would forgive him till Doomsday if he chose. She was preserved from doing so only by a stubborn kind of respect for herself which lay at the root of her nature and forbade surrender, even in moments of almost overwhelming passion. Now, when all was tempest and high-running waves, she knew of a land where the sun shone clear upon Italian grammars and files of docketed papers. Nevertheless, from the skeleton pallor of that land and the rocks that broke its surface, she knew that her life there would be harsh and lonely almost beyond endurance. She walked steadily a little in front of him across the plowed field. Their way took them round the verge of a wood of thin trees standing at the edge of a steep fold in the land. Looking between the tree-trunks, Ralph saw laid out on the perfectly flat and richly green meadow at the bottom of the hill a small gray manor-house, with ponds, terraces, and clipped hedges in front of it, a farm building or so at the side, and a screen of fir-trees rising behind, all perfectly sheltered and self-sufficient. Behind the house the hill rose again, and the trees on the farther summit stood upright against the sky, which appeared of a more intense blue between their trunks. His mind at once was filled with a sense of the actual presence of Katharine; the gray house and the intense blue sky gave him the feeling of her presence close by. He leant against a tree, forming her name beneath his breath:

"Katharine, Katharine," he said aloud, and then, looking round, saw Mary walking slowly away from him, tearing a long spray of ivy from the trees as she passed them. She seemed so definitely opposed to the vision he held in his mind that he returned to it with a gesture of impatience.

"Katharine, Katharine," he repeated, and seemed to himself to be with her. He lost his sense of all that surrounded him; all substantial things—the hour of the day, what we have done and are about to do, the presence of other people and the support we derive from seeing their belief in a common reality—all this slipped from him. So he might have felt if the earth had dropped from his feet, and the empty blue had hung all round him, and the air had been steeped in the presence of one woman. The chirp of a robin on the bough above his head awakened him, and his awakenment was accompanied by a sigh. Here was the world in which he had lived; here the plowed field, the high road yonder, and Mary, stripping ivy from the trees. When he came up with her he linked his arm through hers and said:

"Now, Mary, what's all this about America?"

There was a brotherly kindness in his voice which seemed to her magnanimous, when she reflected that she had cut short his explanations and shown little interest in his change of plan. She gave him her reasons for thinking that she might profit by such a journey, omitting the one reason which had set all the rest in motion. He listened attentively, and made no attempt to dissuade her. In truth, he found himself curiously eager to make certain of her good sense, and accepted each fresh proof of it with satisfaction, as though it helped him to make up his mind about something. She forgot the pain he had caused her, and in place of it she became conscious of a steady tide of well-being which harmonized very aptly with the tramp of their feet upon the dry road and the support of his arm. The comfort was the more glowing in that it seemed to be the reward of her determination to behave to him simply and without attempting to be other than she was. Instead of making out an interest in the poets, she avoided them instinctively, and dwelt rather insistently upon the practical nature of her gifts.

In a practical way she asked for particulars of his cottage, which hardly existed in his mind, and corrected his vagueness.

"You must see that there's water," she insisted, with an exaggeration of interest. She avoided asking him what he meant to do in this cottage, and, at last, when all the practical details had been thrashed out as much as possible, he rewarded her by a more intimate statement.

"One of the rooms," he said, "must be my study, for, you see, Mary, I'm going to write a book." Here he withdrew his arm from hers, lit his pipe, and they tramped on in a sagacious kind of comradeship, the most complete they had attained in all their friendship.

"And what's your book to be about?" she said, as boldly as if she had never come to grief with Ralph in talking about books. He told her unhesitatingly that he meant to write the history of the English village from Saxon days to the present time. Some such plan had lain as a seed in his mind for many years; and now that he had decided, in a flash, to give up his profession, the seed grew in the space of twenty minutes both tall and lusty. He was surprised himself at the positive way in which he spoke. It was the same with the question of his cottage. That had come into existence, too, in an unromantic shape—a square white house standing just off the high road, no doubt, with a neighbor who kept a pig and a dozen squalling children; for these plans were shorn of all romance in his mind, and the pleasure he derived from thinking of them was checked directly it passed a very sober limit. So a sensible man who has lost his chance of some beautiful inheritance might tread out the narrow bounds of his actual dwelling-place, and assure himself that life is supportable within its demesne, only one must grow turnips and cabbages, not melons and pomegranates. Certainly Ralph took some pride in the resources of his mind, and was insensibly helped to right himself by Mary's trust in him. She wound her ivy spray round her ash-plant, and for the first time for many days, when alone with Ralph, set no spies upon her motives, sayings, and feelings, but surrendered herself to complete happiness.

Thus talking, with easy silences and some pauses to look at the view over the hedge and to decide upon the species of a little gray-brown bird slipping among the twigs, they walked into Lincoln, and after strolling up and down the main street, decided upon an inn where the rounded window suggested substantial fare, nor were they mistaken. For over a hundred and fifty years hot joints, potatoes, greens, and apple puddings had been served to generations of country gentlemen, and now, sitting at a table in the hollow of the bow window, Ralph and Mary took their share of this perennial feast. Looking across the joint, half-way through the meal, Mary wondered whether Ralph would ever come to look quite like the other people in the room. Would he be absorbed among the round pink faces, pricked with little white bristles, the calves fitted in shiny brown leather, the black-and-white check suits, which were sprinkled about in the same room with them? She half hoped so; she thought that it was only in his mind that he was different. She did not wish him to be too different from other people. The walk had given him a ruddy color, too, and his eyes were lit up by a steady, honest light, which could not make the simplest farmer feel ill at ease, or suggest to the most devout of clergymen a disposition to sneer at his faith. She loved the steep cliff of his forehead, and compared it to the brow of a young Greek horseman, who reins his horse back so sharply that it half falls on its haunches. He always seemed to her like a rider on a spirited horse. And there was an exaltation to her in being with him, because there was a risk that he would not be able to keep to the right pace among other people. Sitting opposite him at the little table in the window, she came back to that state of careless exaltation which had overcome her when they halted by the gate, but now it was accompanied by a sense of sanity and security, for she felt that they had a feeling in common which scarcely needed embodiment in words. How silent he was! leaning his forehead on his hand, now and then, and again looking steadily and gravely at the backs of the two men at the next table, with so little self-consciousness that she could almost watch his mind placing one thought solidly upon the top of another; she thought that she could feel him thinking, through the shade of her fingers, and she could anticipate the exact moment when he would put an end to his thought and turn a little in his chair and say:

"Well, Mary—?" inviting her to take up the thread of thought where he had dropped it.

And at that very moment he turned just so, and said:

"Well, Mary?" with the curious touch of diffidence which she loved in him.

She laughed, and she explained her laugh on the spur of the moment by the look of the people in the street below. There was a motor-car with an old lady swathed in blue veils, and a lady's maid on the seat opposite, holding a King Charles's spaniel; there was a country-woman wheeling a perambulator full of sticks down the middle of the road; there was a bailiff in gaiters discussing the state of the cattle market with a dissenting minister–so she defined them.

She ran over this list without any fear that her companion would think her trivial. Indeed, whether it was due to the warmth of the room or to the good roast beef, or whether Ralph had achieved the process which is called making up one's mind, certainly he had given up testing the good sense, the independent character, the intelligence shown in her remarks. He had been building one of those piles of thought, as ramshackle and fantastic as a Chinese pagoda, half from words let fall by gentlemen in gaiters, half from the litter in his own mind, about duck shooting and legal history, about the Roman occupation of Lincoln and the relations of country gentlemen with their wives, when, from all this disconnected rambling, there suddenly formed itself in his mind the idea that he would ask Mary to marry him. The idea was so spontaneous that it seemed to shape itself of its own accord before his eyes. It was then that he turned round and made use of his old, instinctive phrase:

"Well, Mary—?"

As it presented itself to him at first, the idea was so new and interesting that he was half inclined to address it, without more ado, to Mary herself. His natural instinct to divide his thoughts carefully into two different classes before he expressed them to her prevailed. But as he watched her looking out of the window and describing the old lady, the woman with the perambulator, the bailiff and the dissenting minister, his eyes filled involuntarily with tears. He would have liked to lay his head on her shoulder and sob, while she parted his hair with her fingers and soothed him and said:

"There, there. Don't cry! Tell me why you're crying—"; and they would clasp each other tight, and her arms would hold him like his mother's. He felt that he was very lonely, and that he was afraid of the other people in the room.

"How damnable this all is!" he exclaimed abruptly.

"What are you talking about?" she replied, rather vaguely, still looking out of the window.

He resented this divided attention more than, perhaps, he knew, and he thought how Mary would soon be on her way to America.

"Mary," he said, "I want to talk to you. Haven't we nearly done? Why don't they take away these plates?"

Mary felt his agitation without looking at him; she felt convinced that she knew what it was that he wished to say to her.

"They'll come all in good time," she said; and felt it necessary to display her extreme calmness by lifting a salt-cellar and sweeping up a little heap of bread-crumbs.

"I want to apologize," Ralph continued, not quite knowing what he was about to say, but feeling some curious instinct which urged him to commit himself irrevocably, and to prevent the moment of intimacy from passing.

"I think I've treated you very badly. That is, I've told you lies. Did you guess that I was lying to you? Once in Lincoln's Inn Fields and again today on our walk. I am a liar, Mary. Did you know that? Do you think you do know me?"

"I think I do," she said.

At this point the waiter changed their plates.

"It's true I don't want you to go to America," he said, looking fixedly at the table-cloth. "In fact, my feelings towards you seem to be utterly and damnably bad," he said energetically, although forced to keep his voice low.

"If I weren't a selfish beast I should tell you to have nothing more to do with me. And yet, Mary, in spite of the fact that I believe what I'm saying, I also believe that it's good we should know each other—the world being what it is, you see——" and by a nod of his head he indicated the other occupants of the room, "for, of course, in an ideal state of things, in a decent community even, there's no doubt you shouldn't have anything to do with me—seriously, that is."

"You forget that I'm not an ideal character, either," said Mary, in the same low and very earnest tones, which, in spite of being almost inaudible, surrounded their table with an atmosphere of concentration which was quite perceptible to the other diners, who glanced at them now and then with a queer mixture of kindness, amusement, and curiosity.

"I'm much more selfish than I let on, and I'm worldly a little—more than you think, anyhow. I like bossing things—perhaps that's my greatest fault. I've none of your passion for—" here she hesitated, and glanced at him, as if to ascertain what his passion was for—"for the truth," she added, as if she had found what she sought indisputably.

"I've told you I'm a liar," Ralph repeated obstinately.

"Oh, in little things, I dare say," she said impatiently. "But not in real ones, and that's what matters. I dare say I'm more truthful than you are in small ways. But I could never care"—she was surprised to find herself speaking the word, and had to force herself to speak it out—"for any one who was a liar in that way. I love the truth a certain amount—a considerable amount—

but not in the way you love it." Her voice sank, became inaudible, and wavered as if she could scarcely keep herself from tears.

"Good heavens!" Ralph exclaimed to himself. "She loves me! Why did I never see it before? She's going to cry; no, but she can't speak."

The certainty overwhelmed him so that he scarcely knew what he was doing; the blood rushed to his cheeks, and although he had quite made up his mind to ask her to marry him, the certainty that she loved him seemed to change the situation so completely that he could not do it. He did not dare to look at her. If she cried, he did not know what he should do. It seemed to him that something of a terrible and devastating nature had happened. The waiter changed their plates once more.

In his agitation Ralph rose, turned his back upon Mary, and looked out of the window. The people in the street seemed to him only a dissolving and combining pattern of black particles; which, for the moment, represented very well the involuntary procession of feelings and thoughts which formed and dissolved in rapid succession in his own mind. At one moment he exulted in the thought that Mary loved him; at the next, it seemed that he was without feeling for her; her love was repulsive to him. Now he felt urged to marry her at once; now to disappear and never see her again. In order to control this disorderly race of thought he forced himself to read the name on the chemist's shop directly opposite him; then to examine the objects in the shop windows, and then to focus his eyes exactly upon a little group of women looking in at the great windows of a large draper's shop. This discipline having given him at least a superficial control of himself, he was about to turn and ask the waiter to bring the bill, when his eye was caught by a tall figure walking quickly along the opposite pavement—a tall figure, upright, dark, and commanding, much detached from her surroundings. She held her gloves in her left hand, and the left hand was bare. All this Ralph noticed and enumerated and recognized before he put a name to the whole—Katharine Hilbery. She seemed to be looking for somebody. Her eyes, in fact, scanned both sides of the street, and for one second were raised directly to the bow window in which Ralph stood; but she looked away again instantly without giving any sign that she had seen him. This sudden apparition had an extraordinary effect upon him. It was as if he had thought of her so intensely that his mind had formed the shape of her, rather than that he had seen her in the flesh outside in the street. And yet he had not been thinking of her at all. The impression was so intense that he could not dismiss it, nor even think whether he had seen her or merely imagined her. He sat down at once, and said, briefly and strangely, rather to himself than to Mary:

"That was Katharine Hilbery."

"Katharine Hilbery? What do you mean?" she asked, hardly understanding from his manner whether he had seen her or not.

"Katharine Hilbery," he repeated. "But she's gone now."

"Katharine Hilbery!" Mary thought, in an instant of blinding revelation; "I've always known it was Katharine Hilbery!" She knew it all now.

After a moment of downcast stupor, she raised her eyes, looked steadily at Ralph, and caught his fixed and dreamy gaze leveled at a point far beyond their surroundings, a point that she had never reached in all the time that she had known him. She noticed the lips just parted, the fingers loosely clenched, the whole attitude of rapt contemplation, which fell like a veil between them. She noticed everything about him; if there had been other signs of his utter alienation she would have sought them out, too, for she felt that it was only by heaping one truth upon another that she could keep herself sitting there, upright. The truth seemed to support her; it struck her, even as she looked at his face, that the light of truth was shining far away beyond him; the light of truth, she seemed to frame the words as she rose to go, shines on a world not to be shaken by our personal calamities.

Ralph handed her her coat and her stick. She took them, fastened the coat securely, grasped the stick firmly. The ivy spray was still twisted about the handle; this one sacrifice, she thought, she might make to sentimentality and personality, and she picked two leaves from the ivy and put them in her pocket before she disencumbered her stick of the rest of it. She grasped the stick in the middle, and settled her fur cap closely upon her head, as if she must be in trim for a long and stormy walk. Next, standing in the middle of the road, she took a slip of paper from her purse, and read out loud a list of commissions entrusted to her—fruit, butter, string, and so on; and all the time she never spoke directly to Ralph or looked at him.

Ralph heard her giving orders to attentive, rosy-checked men in white aprons, and in spite of his own preoccupation, he commented upon the determination with which she made her wishes known. Once more he began, automatically, to take stock of her characteristics. Standing thus, superficially observant and stirring the sawdust on the floor meditatively with the toe of his boot, he was roused by a musical and familiar voice behind him, accompanied by a light touch upon his shoulder.

"I'm not mistaken? Surely Mr. Denham? I caught a glimpse of your coat through the window, and I felt sure that I knew your coat. Have you seen Katharine or William? I'm wandering about Lincoln looking for the ruins."

It was Mrs. Hilbery; her entrance created some stir in the shop; many people looked at her.

"First of all, tell me where I am," she demanded, but, catching sight of the attentive shopman, she appealed to him. "The ruins—my party is waiting for me at the ruins. The Roman ruins—or Greek, Mr. Denham? Your town has a great many beautiful things in it, but I wish it hadn't so many ruins. I never saw such delightful little pots of honey in my life—are they made by your own bees? Please give me one of those little pots, and tell me how I shall find my way to the ruins."

"And now," she continued, having received the information and the pot of honey, having been introduced to Mary, and having insisted that they should accompany her back to the ruins, since in a town with so many turnings, such prospects, such delightful little half-naked boys dabbling in pools, such Venetian canals, such old blue china in the curiosity shops, it was impossible for one person all alone to find her way to the ruins. "Now," she exclaimed, "please tell me what you're doing here, Mr. Denham—for you *are* Mr. Denham, aren't you?" she inquired, gazing at him with a sudden suspicion of her own accuracy. "The brilliant young man who writes for the Review, I mean? Only yesterday my husband was telling me he thought you one of the cleverest young men he knew. Certainly, you've been the messenger of Providence to me, for unless I'd seen you I'm sure I should never have found the ruins at all."

They had reached the Roman arch when Mrs. Hilbery caught sight of her own party, standing like sentinels facing up and down the road so as to intercept her if, as they expected, she had got lodged in some shop.

"I've found something much better than ruins!" she exclaimed. "I've found two friends who told me how to find you, which I could never have done without them. They must come and have tea with us. What a pity that we've just had luncheon." Could they not somehow revoke that meal?

Katharine, who had gone a few steps by herself down the road, and was investigating the window of an ironmonger, as if her mother might have got herself concealed among mowing-machines and garden-shears, turned sharply on hearing her voice, and came towards them. She was a great deal surprised to see Denham and Mary Datchet. Whether the cordiality with which she greeted them was merely that which is natural to a surprise meeting in the country, or whether she was really glad to see them both, at any rate she exclaimed with unusual pleasure as she shook hands:

"I never knew you lived here. Why didn't you say so, and we could have met? And are you staying with Mary?" she continued, turning to Ralph. "What a pity we didn't meet before."

Thus confronted at a distance of only a few feet by the real body of the woman about whom he had dreamt so many million dreams, Ralph stammered; he made a clutch at his self-control; the color either came to his cheeks or left them, he knew not which; but he was determined to face her and track down in the cold light of day whatever vestige of truth there might be in his persistent imaginations. He did not succeed in saying anything. It was Mary who spoke for both of them. He was struck dumb by finding that Katharine was quite different, in some strange way, from his memory, so that he had to dismiss his old view in order to accept the new one. The wind was blowing her crimson scarf across her face; the wind had already loosened her hair, which looped across the corner of one of the large, dark eyes which, so he used to think, looked sad; now they looked bright with the brightness of the sea struck by an unclouded ray; everything about her seemed rapid, fragmentary, and full of a kind of racing speed. He realized suddenly that he had never seen her in the daylight before.

Meanwhile, it was decided that it was too late to go in search of ruins as they had intended; and the whole party began to walk towards the stables where the carriage had been put up.

"Do you know," said Katharine, keeping slightly in advance of the rest with Ralph, "I thought I saw you this morning, standing at a window. But I decided that it couldn't be you. And it must have been you all the same."

"Yes, I thought I saw you—but it wasn't you," he replied.

This remark, and the rough strain in his voice, recalled to her memory so many difficult speeches and abortive meetings that she was jerked directly back to the London drawing-room, the family relics, and the tea-table; and at the same time recalled some half-finished or interrupted remark which she had wanted to make herself or to hear from him—she could not remember what it was.

"I expect it was me," she said. "I was looking for my mother. It happens every time we come to Lincoln. In fact, there never was a family so unable to take care of itself as ours is. Not that it very much matters, because some one always turns up in the nick of time to help us out of our scrapes. Once I was left in a field with a bull when I was a baby—but where did we leave the carriage? Down that street or the next? The next, I think." She glanced back and saw that the others were following obediently, listening to certain memories of Lincoln upon which Mrs. Hilbery had started. "But what are you doing here?" she asked.

"I'm buying a cottage. I'm going to live here—as soon as I can find a cottage, and Mary tells me there'll be no difficulty about that."

"But," she exclaimed, almost standing still in her surprise, "you will give up the Bar, then?" It flashed across her mind that he must already be engaged to Mary.

"The solicitor's office? Yes. I'm giving that up."

"But why?" she asked. She answered herself at once, with a curious change from rapid speech to an almost melancholy tone. "I think you're very wise to give it up. You will be much happier."

At this very moment, when her words seemed to be striking a path into the future for him, they stepped into the yard of an inn, and there beheld the family coach of the Otways, to which one sleek horse was already attached, while the second was being led out of the stable door by the hostler.

"I don't know what one means by happiness," he said briefly, having to step aside in order to avoid a groom with a bucket. "Why do you think I shall be happy? I don't expect to be anything of the kind. I expect to be rather less unhappy. I shall write a book and curse my charwoman—if happiness consists in that. What do you think?"

She could not answer because they were immediately surrounded by other members of the party—by Mrs. Hilbery, and Mary, Henry Otway, and William.

Rodney went up to Katharine immediately and said to her:

"Henry is going to drive home with your mother, and I suggest that they should put us down half-way and let us walk back."

Katharine nodded her head. She glanced at him with an oddly furtive expression.

"Unfortunately we go in opposite directions, or we might have given you a lift," he continued to Denham. His manner was unusually peremptory; he seemed anxious to hasten the departure, and Katharine looked at him from time to time, as Denham noticed, with an expression half of inquiry, half of annoyance. She at once helped her mother into her cloak, and said to Mary:

"I want to see you. Are you going back to London at once? I will write." She half smiled at Ralph, but her look was a little overcast by something she was thinking, and in a very few minutes the Otway carriage rolled out of the stable yard and turned down the high road leading to the village of Lampsher.

The return drive was almost as silent as the drive from home had been in the morning; indeed, Mrs. Hilbery leant back with closed eyes in her corner, and either slept or feigned sleep, as her habit was in the intervals between the seasons of active exertion, or continued the story which she had begun to tell herself that morning.

About two miles from Lampsher the road ran over the rounded summit of the heath, a lonely spot marked by an obelisk of granite, setting forth the gratitude of some great lady of the eighteenth century who had been set upon by highwaymen at this spot and delivered from death just as hope seemed lost. In summer it was a pleasant place, for the deep woods on either side murmured, and the heather, which grew thick round the granite pedestal, made the light breeze taste sweetly; in winter the sighing of the trees was deepened to a hollow sound, and the heath was as gray and almost as solitary as the empty sweep of the clouds above it.

Here Rodney stopped the carriage and helped Katharine to alight. Henry, too, gave her his hand, and fancied that she pressed it very slightly in parting as if she sent him a message. But the carriage rolled on immediately, without wakening Mrs. Hilbery, and left the couple standing by the obelisk. That Rodney was angry with her and had made this opportunity for speaking to her, Katharine knew very well; she was neither glad nor sorry that the time had come, nor, indeed, knew what to expect, and thus remained silent. The carriage grew smaller and smaller upon the dusky road, and still Rodney did not speak. Perhaps, she thought, he waited until the last sign of the carriage had disappeared beneath the curve of the road and they were left entirely alone. To cloak their silence she read the writing on the obelisk, to do which she had to walk completely round it. She was murmuring a word to two of the pious lady's thanks above her breath when Rodney joined her. In silence they set out along the cart-track which skirted the verge of the trees.

To break the silence was exactly what Rodney wished to do, and yet could not do to his own satisfaction. In company it was far easier to approach Katharine; alone with her, the aloofness and force of her character checked all his natural methods of attack. He believed that she had behaved very badly to him, but each separate instance of unkindness seemed too petty to be advanced when they were alone together.

"There's no need for us to race," he complained at last; upon which she immediately slackened her pace, and walked too slowly to suit him. In desperation he said the first thing he thought of, very peevishly and without the dignified prelude which he had intended.

"I've not enjoyed my holiday."

"No?"

"No. I shall be glad to get back to work again."

"Saturday, Sunday, Monday—there are only three days more," she counted.

"No one enjoys being made a fool of before other people," he blurted out, for his irritation rose as she spoke, and got the better of his awe of her, and was inflamed by that awe.

"That refers to me, I suppose," she said calmly.

"Every day since we've been here you've done something to make me appear ridiculous," he went on. "Of course, so long as it amuses you, you're welcome; but we have to remember that we are going to spend our lives together. I asked you, only this morning, for example, to come out and take a turn with me in the garden. I was waiting for you ten minutes, and you never came. Every one saw me waiting. The stable-boys saw me. I was so ashamed that I went in. Then, on the drive you hardly spoke to me. Henry noticed it. Every one notices it. . . . You find no difficulty in talking to Henry, though."

She noted these various complaints and determined philosophically to answer none of them, although the last stung her to considerable irritation. She wished to find out how deep his grievance lay.

"None of these things seem to me to matter," she said.

"Very well, then. I may as well hold my tongue," he replied.

"In themselves they don't seem to me to matter; if they hurt you, of course they matter," she corrected herself scrupulously. Her tone of consideration touched him, and he walked on in silence for a space.

"And we might be so happy, Katharine!" he exclaimed impulsively, and drew her arm through his. She withdrew it directly.

"As long as you let yourself feel like this we shall never be happy," she said.

The harshness, which Henry had noticed, was again unmistakable in her manner. William flinched and was silent. Such severity, accompanied by something indescribably cold and impersonal in her manner, had constantly been meted out to him during the last few days, always in the company of others. He had recouped himself by some ridiculous display of vanity which, as he knew, put him still more at her mercy. Now that he was alone with her there was no stimulus from outside to draw his attention from his injury. By a considerable effort of self-control he forced himself to remain silent, and to make himself distinguish what part of his pain was due to vanity, what part to the certainty that no woman really loving him could speak thus.

"What do I feel about Katharine?" he thought to himself. It was clear that she had been a very desirable and distinguished figure, the mistress of her little section of the world; but more than that, she was the person of all others who seemed to him the arbitress of life, the woman whose judgment was naturally right and steady, as his had never been in spite of all his culture. And then he could not see her come into a room without a sense of the flowing of robes, of the flowering of blossoms, of the purple waves of the sea, of all things that are lovely and mutable on the surface but still and passionate in their heart.

"If she were callous all the time and had only led me on to laugh at me I couldn't have felt that about her," he thought. "I'm not a fool, after all. I can't have been utterly mistaken all these years. And yet, when she speaks to me like that! The truth of it is," he thought, "that I've got such despicable faults that no one could help speaking to me like that. Katharine is quite right. And yet those are not my serious feelings, as she knows quite well. How can I change myself? What would make her care for me?" He was terribly tempted here to break the silence by asking Katharine in what respects he could change himself to suit her; but he sought consolation instead by running over the list of his gifts and acquirements, his knowledge of Greek and Latin, his knowledge of art and literature, his skill in the management of meters, and his ancient west-country blood. But the feeling that underlay all these feelings and puzzled him profoundly and kept him silent was the certainty that he loved Katharine as sincerely as he had it in him to love any one. And yet she could speak to him like that! In a sort of bewilderment he lost all desire to speak, and would quite readily have taken up some different topic of conversation if Katharine had started one. This, however, she did not do.

He glanced at her, in case her expression might help him to understand her behavior. As usual, she had quickened her pace unconsciously, and was now walking a little in front of him; but he could gain little information from her eyes, which looked steadily at the brown heather, or from the lines drawn seriously upon her forehead. Thus to lose touch with her, for he had no idea what she was thinking, was so unpleasant to him that he began to talk about his grievances again, without, however, much conviction in his voice.

"If you have no feeling for me, wouldn't it be kinder to say so to me in private?"

"Oh, William," she burst out, as if he had interrupted some absorbing train of thought, "how you go on about feelings! Isn't it better not to talk so much, not to be worrying always about small things that don't really matter?"

"That's the question precisely," he exclaimed. "I only want you to tell me that they don't matter. There are times when you seem indifferent to everything. I'm vain, I've a thousand faults; but you know they're not everything; you know I care for you."

"And if I say that I care for you, don't you believe me?"

"Say it, Katharine! Say it as if you meant it! Make me feel that you care for me!"

She could not force herself to speak a word. The heather was growing dim around them, and the horizon was blotted out by white mist. To ask her for passion or for certainty seemed like asking that damp prospect for fierce blades of fire, or the faded sky for the intense blue vault of June.

He went on now to tell her of his love for her, in words which bore, even to her critical senses, the stamp of truth; but none of this touched her, until, coming to a gate whose hinge was rusty, he heaved it open with his shoulder, still talking and taking no account of his effort. The virility of this deed impressed her; and yet, normally, she attached no value to the power of opening gates. The strength of muscles has nothing to do on the face of it with the strength of affections; nevertheless, she felt a sudden concern for this power running to waste on her account, which, combined with a desire to keep possession of that strangely attractive masculine power, made her rouse herself from her torpor.

Why should she not simply tell him the truth—which was that she had accepted him in a misty state of mind when nothing had its right shape or size? that it was deplorable, but that with clearer eyesight marriage was out of the question? She did not want to marry any one. She wanted to go away by herself, preferably to some bleak northern moor, and there study mathematics and the science of astronomy. Twenty words would explain the whole situation to him. He had ceased to speak; he had told her once more how he loved her and why. She summoned her courage, fixed her eyes upon a lightning-splintered ash-tree, and, almost as if she were reading a writing fixed to the trunk, began:

"I was wrong to get engaged to you. I shall never make you happy. I have never loved you."

"Katharine!" he protested.

"No, never," she repeated obstinately. "Not rightly. Don't you see, I didn't know what I was doing?"

"You love some one else?" he cut her short.

"Absolutely no one."

"Henry?" he demanded.

"Henry? I should have thought, William, even you—"

"There is some one," he persisted. "There has been a change in the last few weeks. You owe it to me to be honest, Katharine."

"If I could, I would," she replied.

"Why did you tell me you would marry me, then?" he demanded.

Why, indeed? A moment of pessimism, a sudden conviction of the undeniable prose of life, a lapse of the illusion which sustains youth midway between heaven and earth, a desperate attempt to reconcile herself with facts—she could only recall a moment, as of waking from a dream, which now seemed to her a moment of surrender. But who could give reasons such as these for doing what she had done? She shook her head very sadly.

"But you're not a child—you're not a woman of moods," Rodney persisted. "You couldn't have accepted me if you hadn't loved me!" he cried.

A sense of her own misbehavior, which she had succeeded in keeping from her by sharpening her consciousness of Rodney's faults, now swept over her and almost overwhelmed her. What were his faults in comparison with the fact that he cared for her? What were her virtues in comparison with the fact that she did not care for him? In a flash the conviction that not to care is the uttermost sin of all stamped itself upon her inmost thought; and she felt herself branded for ever.

He had taken her arm, and held her hand firmly in his, nor had she the force to resist what now seemed to her his enormously superior strength. Very well; she would submit, as her mother and her aunt and most women, perhaps, had submitted; and yet she knew that every second of such submission to his strength was a second of treachery to him.

"I did say I would marry you, but it was wrong," she forced herself to say, and she stiffened her arm as if to annul even the seeming submission of that separate part of her; "for I don't love you, William; you've noticed it, every one's noticed it; why should we go on pretending? When I told you I loved you, I was wrong. I said what I knew to be untrue."

As none of her words seemed to her at all adequate to represent what she felt, she repeated them, and emphasized them without realizing the effect that they might have upon a man who cared for her. She was completely taken aback by finding her arm suddenly dropped; then she saw his face most strangely contorted; was he laughing, it flashed across her? In another moment she saw that he was in tears. In her bewilderment at this apparition she stood aghast for a second. With a desperate sense that this horror must, at all costs, be stopped, she then put her arms about him, drew his head for a moment upon her shoulder, and led him on, murmuring words of consolation, until he heaved a great sigh. They held fast to each other; her tears, too, ran down her cheeks; and were both quite silent. Noticing the difficulty with which he walked, and feeling the same extreme lassitude in her own limbs, she proposed that they should rest for a moment where the bracken was brown and shriveled beneath an oak-tree. He assented. Once more he gave a great sigh, and wiped his eyes with a childlike unconsciousness, and began to speak without a trace of his previous anger. The idea came to her that they were like the children in the fairy tale who were lost in a wood, and with this in her mind she noticed the scattering of dead leaves all round them which had been blown by the wind into heaps, a foot or two deep, here and there.

"When did you begin to feel this, Katharine?" he said; "for it isn't true to say that you've always felt it. I admit I was unreasonable the first night when you found that your clothes had been left behind. Still, where's the fault in that? I could promise you never to interfere with your clothes again. I admit I was cross when I found you upstairs with Henry. Perhaps I showed it too openly. But that's not unreasonable either when one's engaged. Ask your mother. And now this terrible thing——" He broke off, unable for the moment to proceed any further. "This decision you say you've come to—have you discussed it with any one? Your mother, for example, or Henry?"

"No, no, of course not," she said, stirring the leaves with her hand. "But you don't understand me, William——"

"Help me to understand you——"

"You don't understand, I mean, my real feelings; how could you? I've only now faced them myself. But I haven't got the sort of feeling—love, I mean—I don't know what to call it"—she looked vaguely towards the horizon sunk under mist—"but, anyhow, without it our marriage would be a farce——"

"How a farce?" he asked. "But this kind of analysis is disastrous!" he exclaimed.

"I should have done it before," she said gloomily.

"You make yourself think things you don't think," he continued, becoming demonstrative with his hands, as his manner was. "Believe me, Katharine, before we came here we were perfectly happy. You were full of plans for our house—the chair-covers, don't you remember?—like any other woman who is about to be married. Now, for no reason whatever, you begin to fret about your feeling and about my feeling, with the usual result. I assure you, Katharine, I've been through it all myself. At one time I was always asking myself absurd questions which came to nothing either. What you want, if I may say so, is some occupation to take you out of yourself when this morbid mood comes on. If it hadn't been for my poetry, I assure you, I should often have been very much in the same state myself. To let you into a secret," he continued, with his little chuckle, which now sounded almost assured, "I've often gone home from seeing you in such a state of nerves that I had to force myself to write a page or two before I could get you out of my head. Ask Denham; he'll tell you how he met me one night; he'll tell you what a state he found me in."

Katharine started with displeasure at the mention of Ralph's name. The thought of the conversation in which her conduct had been made a subject for discussion with Denham roused her anger; but, as she instantly felt, she had scarcely the right to grudge William any use of her name, seeing what her fault against him had been from first to last. And yet Denham! She had a view of him as a judge. She figured him sternly weighing instances of her levity in this masculine court of inquiry into feminine morality and gruffly dismissing both her and her family with some half-sarcastic, half-tolerant phrase which sealed her doom, as far as he was concerned, for ever. Having met him so lately, the sense of his character was strong in her. The thought was not a pleasant one for a proud woman, but she had yet to learn the art of subduing her expression. Her eyes fixed upon the ground, her brows drawn together, gave William a very fair picture of the resentment that she was forcing herself to control. A certain degree of apprehension, occasionally culminating in a kind of fear, had always entered into his love for her, and had increased, rather to his surprise, in the greater intimacy of their engagement. Beneath her steady, exemplary surface ran a vein of passion which seemed to him now perverse, now completely irrational, for it never took the normal channel of glorification of him and his doings; and, indeed, he almost preferred the steady good sense, which had always marked their relationship, to a more romantic bond. But passion she had, he could not deny it, and hitherto he had tried to see it employed in his thoughts upon the lives of the children who were to be born to them.

"She will make a perfect mother—a mother of sons," he thought; but seeing her sitting there, gloomy and silent, he began to have his doubts on this point. "A farce, a farce," he thought to himself. "She said that our marriage would be a farce," and he became suddenly aware of their situation, sitting upon the ground, among the dead leaves, not fifty yards from the main road, so that it was quite possible for some one passing to see and recognize them. He brushed off his face any trace that might remain of that unseemly exhibition of emotion. But he was more troubled by Katharine's appearance, as she sat rapt in thought upon the ground, than by his own; there was something improper to him in her self-forgetfulness. A man naturally alive to the conventions of society, he was strictly conventional where women were concerned, and especially if the women happened to be in any way connected with him. He noticed with distress the long strand of dark hair touching her shoulder and two or three dead beech-leaves attached to her dress; but to recall her mind in their present circumstances to a sense of these details was impossible. She sat there, seeming unconscious of everything. He suspected that in her silence she was reproaching herself; but he wished that she would think of her hair and of the dead beech-leaves, which were of more immediate importance to him than anything else. Indeed, these trifles drew his attention strangely from his own doubtful and uneasy state of mind; for relief, mixing itself with pain, stirred up a most curious hurry and tumult in his breast, almost concealing his first sharp sense of bleak and overwhelming disappointment. In order to relieve this restlessness and close a distressingly ill-ordered scene, he rose abruptly and helped Katharine to her feet. She smiled a little at the minute care with which he tidied her and yet, when he brushed the dead leaves from his own coat, she flinched, seeing in that action the gesture of a lonely man.

"William," she said, "I will marry you. I will try to make you happy."

19

The afternoon was already growing dark when the two other wayfarers, Mary and Ralph Denham, came out on the high road beyond the outskirts of Lincoln. The high road, as they both felt, was better suited to this return journey than the open country, and for the first mile or so of the way they spoke little. In his own mind Ralph was following the passage of the Otway carriage over the heath; he then went back to the five or ten minutes that he had spent with Katharine, and examined each word with the care that a scholar displays upon the irregularities of an ancient text. He was determined that the glow, the romance, the atmosphere of this meeting should not paint what he must in future regard as sober facts. On her side Mary was silent, not because her thoughts took much handling, but because her mind seemed empty of thought as her heart of feeling. Only Ralph's presence, as she knew, preserved this numbness, for she could foresee a time of loneliness when many varieties of pain would beset her. At the present moment her effort was to preserve what she could of the wreck of her self-respect, for such she deemed that momentary glimpse of her love so involuntarily revealed to Ralph. In the light of reason it did not much matter, perhaps, but it was her instinct to be careful of that vision of herself which keeps pace so evenly beside every one of us, and had been damaged by her confession. The gray night coming down over the country was kind to her; and she thought that one of these days she would find comfort in sitting upon the earth, alone, beneath a tree. Looking through the darkness, she marked the swelling ground and the tree. Ralph made her start by saying abruptly:

"What I was going to say when we were interrupted at lunch was that if you go to America I shall come, too. It can't be harder to earn a living there than it is here. However, that's not the point. The point is, Mary, that I want to marry you. Well, what do you say?" He spoke firmly, waited for no answer, and took her arm in his. "You know me by this time, the good and the bad," he went on. "You know my tempers. I've tried to let you know my faults. Well, what do you say, Mary?"

She said nothing, but this did not seem to strike him.

"In most ways, at least in the important ways, as you said, we know each other and we think alike. I believe you are the only person in the world I could live with happily. And if you feel the same about me—as you do, don't you, Mary?—we should make each other happy." Here he paused, and seemed to be in no hurry for an answer; he seemed, indeed, to be continuing his own thoughts.

"Yes, but I'm afraid I couldn't do it," Mary said at last. The casual and rather hurried way in which she spoke, together with the fact that she was saying the exact opposite of what he expected her to say, baffled him so much that he instinctively loosened his clasp upon her arm and she withdrew it quietly.

"You couldn't do it?" he asked.

"No, I couldn't marry you," she replied.

"You don't care for me?"

She made no answer.

"Well, Mary," he said, with a curious laugh, "I must be an arrant fool, for I thought you did." They walked for a minute or two in silence, and suddenly he turned to her, looked at her, and exclaimed: "I don't believe you, Mary. You're not telling me the truth."

"I'm too tired to argue, Ralph," she replied, turning her head away from him. "I ask you to believe what I say. I can't marry you; I don't want to marry you."

The voice in which she stated this was so evidently the voice of one in some extremity of anguish that Ralph had no course but to obey her. And as soon as the tone of her voice had died out, and the surprise faded from his mind, he found himself believing that she had spoken the truth, for he had but little vanity, and soon her refusal seemed a natural thing to him. He slipped through all the grades of despondency until he reached a bottom of absolute gloom. Failure seemed to mark the whole of his life; he had failed with Katharine, and now he had failed with Mary. Up at once sprang the thought of Katharine, and with it a sense of exulting freedom, but this he checked instantly. No good had ever come to him from Katharine; his whole relationship with her had been made up of dreams; and as he thought of the little substance there had been in his dreams he began to lay the blame of the present catastrophe upon his dreams.

"Haven't I always been thinking of Katharine while I was with Mary? I might have loved Mary if it hadn't been for that idiocy of mine. She cared for me once, I'm certain of that, but I tormented her so with my humors that I let my chances slip, and now she won't risk marrying me. And this is what I've made of my life—nothing, nothing, nothing."

The tramp of their boots upon the dry road seemed to asseverate nothing, nothing, nothing. Mary thought that this silence was the silence of relief; his depression she ascribed to the fact that he had seen Katharine and parted from her, leaving her in the company of William Rodney. She could not blame him for loving Katharine, but that, when he loved another, he should ask her to marry him—that seemed to her the cruellest treachery. Their old friendship and its firm base upon indestructible qualities of character crumbled, and her whole past seemed foolish, herself weak and credulous, and Ralph merely the shell of an honest man. Oh, the past—so much made up of Ralph; and now, as she saw, made up of something strange and false and other than she had thought it. She tried to recapture a saying she had made to help herself that morning, as Ralph paid the bill for luncheon; but she could see him paying the bill more vividly than she could remember the phrase. Something about truth was in it; how to see the truth is our great chance in this world.

"If you don't want to marry me," Ralph now began again, without abruptness, with diffidence rather, "there is no need why we should cease to see each other, is there? Or would you rather that we should keep apart for the present?"

"Keep apart? I don't know—I must think about it."

"Tell me one thing, Mary," he resumed; "have I done anything to make you change your mind about me?"

She was immensely tempted to give way to her natural trust in him, revived by the deep and now melancholy tones of his voice, and to tell him of her love, and of what had changed it. But although it seemed likely that she would soon control her anger with him, the certainty that he did not love her, confirmed by every word of his proposal, forbade any freedom of speech. To hear him speak and to feel herself unable to reply, or constrained in her replies, was so painful that she longed for the time when she should be alone. A more pliant woman would have taken this chance of an explanation, whatever risks attached to it; but to one of Mary's firm and resolute temperament there was degradation in the idea of self-abandonment; let the waves of emotion rise ever so high, she could not shut her eyes to what she conceived to be the truth. Her silence puzzled Ralph. He searched his memory for words or deeds that might have made her think badly of him. In his present mood instances came but too quickly, and on top of them this culminating proof of his baseness—that he had asked her to marry him when his reasons for such a proposal were selfish and half-hearted.

"You needn't answer," he said grimly. "There are reasons enough, I know. But must they kill our friendship, Mary? Let me keep that, at least."

"Oh," she thought to herself, with a sudden rush of anguish which threatened disaster to her self-respect, "it has come to this—to this—when I could have given him everything!"

"Yes, we can still be friends," she said, with what firmness she could muster.

"I shall want your friendship," he said. He added, "If you find it possible, let me see you as often as you can. The oftener the better. I shall want your help."

She promised this, and they went on to talk calmly of things that had no reference to their feelings—a talk which, in its constraint, was infinitely sad to both of them.

One more reference was made to the state of things between them late that night, when Elizabeth had gone to her room, and the two young men had stumbled off to bed in such a state of sleep that they hardly felt the floor beneath their feet after a day's shooting.

Mary drew her chair a little nearer to the fire, for the logs were burning low, and at this time of night it was hardly worth while to replenish them. Ralph was reading, but she had noticed for some time that his eyes instead of following the print were fixed rather above the page with an intensity of gloom that came to weigh upon her mind. She had not weakened in her resolve not to give way, for reflection had only made her more bitterly certain that, if she gave way, it would be to her own wish and not to his. But she had determined that there was no reason why he should suffer if her reticence were the cause of his suffering. Therefore, although she found it painful, she spoke:

"You asked me if I had changed my mind about you, Ralph," she said. "I think there's only one thing. When you asked me to marry you, I don't think you meant it. That made me angry—for the moment. Before, you'd always spoken the truth."

Ralph's book slid down upon his knee and fell upon the floor. He rested his forehead on his hand and looked into the fire. He was trying to recall the exact words in which he had made his proposal to Mary.

"I never said I loved you," he said at last.

She winced; but she respected him for saying what he did, for this, after all, was a fragment of the truth which she had vowed to live by.

"And to me marriage without love doesn't seem worth while," she said.

"Well, Mary, I'm not going to press you," he said. "I see you don't want to marry me. But love—don't we all talk a great deal of nonsense about it? What does one mean? I believe I care for you more genuinely than nine men out of ten care for the women they're in love with. It's only a story one makes up in one's mind about another person, and one knows all the time it isn't true. Of course one knows; why, one's always taking care not to destroy the illusion. One takes care not to see them too often, or to be alone with them for too long together. It's a pleasant illusion, but if you're thinking of the risks of marriage, it seems to me that the risk of marrying a person you're in love with is something colossal."

"I don't believe a word of that, and what's more you don't, either," she replied with anger. "However, we don't agree; I only wanted you to understand." She shifted her position, as if she were about to go. An instinctive desire to prevent her from leaving the room made Ralph rise at this point and begin pacing up and down the nearly empty kitchen, checking his desire, each time he reached the door, to open it and step out into the garden. A moralist might have said that at this point his mind should have been full of self-reproach for the suffering he had caused. On the contrary, he was extremely angry, with the confused impotent anger of one who finds himself unreasonably but efficiently frustrated. He was trapped by the illogicality of human life. The obstacles in the way of his desire seemed to him purely artificial, and yet he could see no way of removing them. Mary's words, the tone of her voice even, angered him, for she would not help him. She was part of the insanely jumbled muddle of a world which impedes the sensible life. He would have liked to slam the door or break the hind legs of a chair, for the obstacles had taken some such curiously substantial shape in his mind.

"I doubt that one human being ever understands another," he said, stopping in his march and confronting Mary at a distance of a few feet.

"Such damned liars as we all are, how can we? But we can try. If you don't want to marry me, don't; but the position you take up about love, and not seeing each other—isn't that mere sentimentality? You think I've behaved very badly," he continued, as she did not speak. "Of course I behave badly; but you can't judge people by what they do. You can't go through life measuring right and wrong with a foot-rule. That's what you're always doing, Mary; that's what you're doing now."

She saw herself in the Suffrage Office, delivering judgment, meting out right and wrong, and there seemed to her to be some justice in the charge, although it did not affect her main position.

"I'm not angry with you," she said slowly. "I will go on seeing you, as I said I would."

It was true that she had promised that much already, and it was difficult for him to say what more it was that he wanted—some intimacy, some help against the ghost of Katharine, perhaps, something that he knew he had no right to ask; and yet, as he sank into his chair and looked once more at the dying fire it seemed to him that he had been defeated, not so much by Mary as by life itself. He felt himself thrown back to the beginning of life again, where everything has yet to be won; but in extreme youth one has an ignorant hope. He was no longer certain that he would triumph.

20

Happily for Mary Datchet she returned to the office to find that by some obscure Parliamentary maneuver the vote had once more slipped beyond the attainment of women. Mrs. Seal was in a condition bordering upon frenzy. The duplicity of Ministers, the treachery of mankind, the insult to womanhood, the setback to civilization, the ruin of her life's work, the feelings of her father's daughter—all these topics were discussed in turn, and the office was littered with newspaper cuttings branded with the blue, if ambiguous, marks of her displeasure. She confessed herself at fault in her estimate of human nature.

"The simple elementary acts of justice," she said, waving her hand towards the window, and indicating the foot-passengers and omnibuses then passing down the far side of Russell Square, "are as far beyond them as they ever were. We can only look upon ourselves, Mary, as pioneers in a wilderness. We can only go on patiently putting the truth before them. It isn't *them*," she continued, taking heart from her sight of the traffic, "it's their leaders. It's those gentlemen sitting in Parliament and drawing four hundred a year of the people's money. If we had to put our case to the people, we should soon have justice done to us. I have always believed in the people, and I do so still. But—" She shook her head and implied that she would give them one more chance, and if they didn't take advantage of that she couldn't answer for the consequences.

Mr. Clacton's attitude was more philosophical and better supported by statistics. He came into the room after Mrs. Seal's outburst and pointed out, with historical illustrations, that such reverses had happened in every political campaign of any importance. If anything, his spirits were improved by the disaster. The enemy, he said, had taken the offensive; and it was now up to the Society to outwit the enemy. He gave Mary to understand that he had taken the measure of their cunning, and had already bent his mind to the task which, so far as she could make out, depended solely upon him. It depended, so she came to think, when invited into his room for a private conference, upon a systematic revision of the card-index, upon the issue of certain new lemon-colored leaflets, in which the facts were marshaled once more in a very striking way, and upon a large scale map of England dotted with little pins tufted with differently colored plumes of hair according to their geographical position. Each district, under the new system, had its flag, its bottle of ink, its sheaf of documents tabulated and filed for reference in a drawer, so that by looking under M or S, as the case might be, you had all the facts with respect to the Suffrage organizations of that county at your fingers' ends. This would require a great deal of work, of course.

"We must try to consider ourselves rather in the light of a telephone exchange—for the exchange of ideas, Miss Datchet," he said; and taking pleasure in his image, he continued it. "We should consider ourselves the center of an enormous system of wires, connecting us up with every district of the country. We must have our fingers upon the pulse of the community; we want to know what people all over England are thinking; we want to put them in the way of thinking rightly." The system, of course, was only roughly sketched so far—jotted down, in fact, during the Christmas holidays.

"When you ought to have been taking a rest, Mr. Clacton," said Mary dutifully, but her tone was flat and tired.

"We learn to do without holidays, Miss Datchet," said Mr. Clacton, with a spark of satisfaction in his eye.

He wished particularly to have her opinion of the lemon-colored leaflet. According to his plan, it was to be distributed in immense quantities immediately, in order to stimulate and generate, "to generate and stimulate," he repeated, "right thoughts in the country before the meeting of Parliament."

"We have to take the enemy by surprise," he said. "They don't let the grass grow under their feet. Have you seen Bingham's address to his constituents? That's a hint of the sort of thing we've got to meet, Miss Datchet."

He handed her a great bundle of newspaper cuttings, and, begging her to give him her views upon the yellow leaflet before lunch-time, he turned with alacrity to his different sheets of paper and his different bottles of ink.

Mary shut the door, laid the documents upon her table, and sank her head on her hands. Her brain was curiously empty of any thought. She listened, as if, perhaps, by listening she would become merged again in the atmosphere of the office. From the next room came the rapid spasmodic sounds of Mrs. Seal's erratic typewriting; she, doubtless, was already hard at work helping the people of England, as Mr. Clacton put it, to think rightly; "generating and stimulating," those were his words. She was striking a blow against the enemy, no doubt, who didn't let the grass grow beneath their feet. Mr. Clacton's words repeated themselves accurately in her brain. She pushed the papers wearily over to the farther side of the table. It was no use, though; something or other had happened to her brain—a change of focus so that near things were indistinct again. The same thing had happened to her once before, she remembered, after she had met Ralph in the gardens of Lincoln's Inn Fields; she had spent the whole of a committee meeting in thinking about sparrows and colors, until, almost at the end of the meeting, her old convictions had all come back to her. But they had only come back, she thought with scorn at her feebleness, because she wanted to use them to fight against Ralph. They weren't, rightly speaking, convictions at all. She could not see the world divided into separate compartments of good people and bad people, any more than she could believe so implicitly in the rightness of her own thought as to wish to bring the population of the British Isles into agreement with it. She looked at the lemon-colored leaflet, and thought almost enviously of the faith which could find comfort in the issue of such documents; for herself she would be content to remain silent for ever if a share of personal happiness were granted her. She read Mr. Clacton's statement with a curious division of judgment, noting its weak and pompous verbosity on the one hand, and, at the same time, feeling that faith, faith in an illusion, perhaps, but, at any rate, faith in something, was of all gifts the most to be envied. An illusion it was, no doubt. She looked curiously round her at the furniture of the office, at the machinery in which she had taken so much pride, and marveled to think that once the copying-presses, the card-index, the files of documents, had all been shrouded, wrapped in some mist which gave them a unity and a general dignity and purpose independently of their separate significance. The ugly cumbersomeness of the furniture alone impressed her now. Her attitude had become very lax and despondent when the typewriter stopped in the next room. Mary immediately drew up to the table, laid hands on an unopened envelope, and adopted an expression which might hide her state of mind from Mrs. Seal. Some instinct of decency required that she should not allow Mrs. Seal to see her face. Shading her eyes with her fingers, she watched Mrs. Seal pull out one drawer after another in her search for some envelope or leaflet. She was tempted to drop her fingers and exclaim:

"Do sit down, Sally, and tell me how you manage it—how you manage, that is, to bustle about with perfect confidence in the necessity of your own activities, which to me seem as futile as the buzzing of a belated bluebottle." She said nothing of the kind, however, and the presence of industry which she preserved so long as Mrs. Seal was in the room served to set her brain in motion, so that she dispatched her morning's work much as usual. At one o'clock she was surprised to find how efficiently she had dealt with the morning. As she put her hat on she determined to lunch at a shop in the Strand, so as to set that other piece of mechanism, her body, into action. With a brain working and a body working one could keep step with the crowd and never be found out for the hollow machine, lacking the essential thing, that one was conscious of being.

She considered her case as she walked down the Charing Cross Road. She put to herself a series of questions. Would she mind, for example, if the wheels of that motor-omnibus passed over her and crushed her to death? No, not in the least; or an adventure with that disagreeable-looking man hanging about the entrance of the Tube station? No; she could not conceive fear or excitement. Did suffering in any form appall her? No, suffering was neither good nor bad. And this essential thing? In the eyes of every single person she detected a flame; as if a spark in the brain ignited spontaneously at contact with the things they met and drove them on. The young women looking into the milliners' windows had that look in their eyes; and elderly men turning over books in the second-hand bookshops, and eagerly waiting to hear what the price was—the very lowest price—they had it, too. But she cared nothing at all for clothes or for money either. Books she shrank from, for they were connected too closely with Ralph. She kept on her way resolutely through the crowd of people, among whom she was so much of an alien, feeling them cleave and give way before her.

Strange thoughts are bred in passing through crowded streets should the passenger, by chance, have no exact destination in front of him, much as the mind shapes all kinds of forms, solutions, images when listening inattentively to music. From an acute consciousness of herself as an individual, Mary passed to a conception of the scheme of things in which, as a human being, she must have her share. She half held a vision; the vision shaped and dwindled. She wished she had a pencil and a piece of paper to help her to give a form to this conception which composed itself as she walked down the Charing Cross Road. But if she talked to any one, the conception might escape her. Her vision seemed to lay out the lines of her life until death in a way which satisfied her sense of harmony. It only needed a persistent effort of thought, stimulated in this strange way by the crowd and the noise, to climb the crest of existence and see it all laid out once and for ever. Already her suffering as an individual was left behind her. Of this process, which was to her so full of effort, which comprised infinitely swift and full passages of thought, leading from one crest to another, as she shaped her conception of life in this world, only two articulate words escaped her, muttered beneath her breath—"Not happiness—not happiness."

She sat down on a seat opposite the statue of one of London's heroes upon the Embankment, and spoke the words aloud. To her they represented the rare flower or splinter of rock brought down by a climber in proof that he has stood for a moment, at least, upon the highest peak of the mountain. She had been up there and seen the world spread to the horizon. It was now necessary to alter her course to some extent, according to her new resolve. Her post should be in one of those exposed and desolate stations which are shunned naturally by happy people. She arranged the details of the new plan in her mind, not without a grim satisfaction.

"Now," she said to herself, rising from her seat, "I'll think of Ralph."

Where was he to be placed in the new scale of life? Her exalted mood seemed to make it safe to handle the question. But she was dismayed to find how quickly her passions leapt forward the moment she sanctioned this line of thought. Now she was identified with him and rethought his thoughts with complete self-surrender; now, with a sudden cleavage of spirit, she turned upon him and denounced him for his cruelty.

"But I refuse—I refuse to hate any one," she said aloud; chose the moment to cross the road with circumspection, and ten minutes later lunched in the Strand, cutting her meat firmly into small pieces, but giving her fellow-diners no further cause to judge her eccentric. Her soliloquy crystallized itself into little fragmentary phrases emerging suddenly from the turbulence of her thought, particularly when she had to exert herself in any way, either to move, to count money, or to choose a turning. "To know the truth—to accept without bitterness"—those, perhaps, were the most articulate of her utterances, for no one could have made head or tail of the queer gibberish murmured in front of the statue of Francis, Duke of Bedford, save that the name of Ralph occurred frequently in very strange connections, as if, having spoken it, she wished, superstitiously, to cancel it by adding some other word that robbed the sentence with his name in it of any meaning.

Those champions of the cause of women, Mr. Clacton and Mrs. Seal, did not perceive anything strange in Mary's behavior, save that she was almost half an hour later than usual in coming back to the office. Happily, their own affairs kept them busy, and she was free from their inspection. If they had surprised her they would have found her lost, apparently, in admiration of the large hotel across the square, for, after writing a few words, her pen rested upon the paper, and her mind pursued its own journey among the sun-blazoned windows and the drifts of purplish smoke which formed her view. And, indeed, this background was by no means out of keeping with her thoughts. She saw to the remote spaces behind the strife of the foreground, enabled now to gaze there, since she had renounced her own demands, privileged to see the larger view, to share the vast desires and sufferings of the mass of mankind. She had been too lately and too roughly mastered by facts to take an easy pleasure in the relief of renunciation; such satisfaction as she felt came only from the discovery that, having renounced everything that made life happy, easy, splendid, individual, there remained a hard reality, unimpaired by one's personal adventures, remote as the stars, unquenchable as they are.

While Mary Datchet was undergoing this curious transformation from the particular to the universal, Mrs. Seal remembered her duties with regard to the kettle and the gas-fire. She was a little surprised to find that Mary had drawn her chair to the window, and, having lit the gas, she raised herself from a stooping posture and looked at her. The most obvious reason for such an attitude in a secretary was some kind of indisposition. But Mary, rousing herself with an effort, denied that she was indisposed.

"I'm frightfully lazy this afternoon," she added, with a glance at her table. "You must really get another secretary, Sally."

The words were meant to be taken lightly, but something in the tone of them roused a jealous fear which was always dormant in Mrs. Seal's breast. She was terribly afraid that one of these days Mary, the young woman who typified so many rather sentimental and enthusiastic ideas, who had some sort of visionary existence in white with a sheaf of lilies in her hand, would announce, in a jaunty way, that she was about to be married.

"You don't mean that you're going to leave us?" she said.

"I've not made up my mind about anything," said Mary—a remark which could be taken as a generalization.

Mrs. Seal got the teacups out of the cupboard and set them on the table.

"You're not going to be married, are you?" she asked, pronouncing the words with nervous speed.

"Why are you asking such absurd questions this afternoon, Sally?" Mary asked, not very steadily. "Must we all get married?"

Mrs. Seal emitted a most peculiar chuckle. She seemed for one moment to acknowledge the terrible side of life which is concerned with the emotions, the private lives, of the sexes, and then to sheer off from it with all possible speed into the shades of her own shivering virginity. She was made so uncomfortable by the turn the conversation had taken, that she plunged her head into the cupboard, and endeavored to abstract some very obscure piece of china.

"We have our work," she said, withdrawing her head, displaying cheeks more than usually crimson, and placing a jam-pot emphatically upon the table. But, for the moment, she was unable to launch herself upon one of those enthusiastic, but inconsequent, tirades upon liberty, democracy, the rights of the people, and the iniquities of the Government, in which she delighted. Some memory from her own past or from the past of her sex rose to her mind and kept her abashed. She glanced furtively at Mary, who still sat by the window with her arm upon the sill. She noticed how young she was and full of the promise of womanhood. The sight made her so uneasy that she fidgeted the cups upon their saucers.

"Yes—enough work to last a lifetime," said Mary, as if concluding some passage of thought.

Mrs. Seal brightened at once. She lamented her lack of scientific training, and her deficiency in the processes of logic, but she set her mind to work at once to make the prospects of the cause appear as alluring and important as she could. She delivered herself of an harangue in which she asked a great many rhetorical questions and answered them with a little bang of one fist upon another.

"To last a lifetime? My dear child, it will last all our lifetimes. As one falls another steps into the breach. My father, in his generation, a pioneer—I, coming after him, do my little best. What, alas! can one do more? And now it's you young women—we look to you—the future looks to you. Ah, my dear, if I'd a thousand lives, I'd give them all to our cause. The cause of women, d'you say? I say the cause of humanity. And there are some"—she glanced fiercely at the window—"who don't see it! There are some who are satisfied to go on, year after year, refusing to admit the truth. And we who have the vision—the kettle boiling over? No, no, let me see to it—we who know the truth," she continued, gesticulating with the kettle and the teapot. Owing to these encumbrances, perhaps, she lost the thread of her discourse, and concluded, rather wistfully, "It's all so *simple*." She referred to a matter that was a perpetual source of bewilderment to her—the extraordinary incapacity of the human race, in a world where the good is so unmistakably divided from the bad, of distinguishing one from the other, and embodying what ought to be done in a few large, simple Acts of Parliament, which would, in a very short time, completely change the lot of humanity.

"One would have thought," she said, "that men of University training, like Mr. Asquith—one would have thought that an appeal to reason would not be unheard by them. But reason," she reflected, "what is reason without Reality?"

Doing homage to the phrase, she repeated it once more, and caught the ear of Mr. Clacton, as he issued from his room; and he repeated it a third time, giving it, as he was in the habit of doing with Mrs. Seal's phrases, a dryly humorous intonation. He was well pleased with the world, however, and he remarked, in a flattering manner, that he would like to see that phrase in large letters at the head of a leaflet.

"But, Mrs. Seal, we have to aim at a judicious combination of the two," he added in his magisterial way to check the unbalanced enthusiasm of the women. "Reality has to be voiced by reason before it can make itself felt. The weak point of all these movements, Miss Datchet," he continued, taking his place at the table and turning to Mary as usual when about to deliver his more profound cogitations, "is that they are not based upon sufficiently intellectual grounds. A mistake, in my opinion. The British public likes a pellet of reason in its jam of eloquence—a pill of reason in its pudding of sentiment," he said, sharpening the phrase to a satisfactory degree of literary precision.

His eyes rested, with something of the vanity of an author, upon the yellow leaflet which Mary held in her hand. She rose, took her seat at the head of the table, poured out tea for her colleagues, and gave her opinion upon the leaflet. So she had poured out tea, so she had criticized Mr. Clacton's leaflets a hundred times already; but now it seemed to her that she was doing it in a different spirit; she had enlisted in the army, and was a volunteer no longer. She had renounced something and was now—how could she express it?—not quite "in the running" for life. She had always known that Mr. Clacton and Mrs. Seal were not in the running, and across the gulf that separated them she had seen them in the guise of shadow people, flitting in and out of the ranks of the living—eccentrics, undeveloped human beings, from whose substance some essential part had been cut away. All this had never struck her so clearly as it did this afternoon, when she felt that her lot was cast with them for ever. One view of the world plunged in darkness, so a more volatile temperament might have argued after a season of despair, let the world turn again and show another, more splendid, perhaps. No, Mary thought, with unflinching loyalty to what appeared to her to be the true view, having lost what is best, I do not mean to pretend that any other view does instead. Whatever happens, I mean to have no presences in my life. Her very words had a sort of distinctness which is sometimes produced by sharp, bodily pain. To Mrs. Seal's secret jubilation the rule which forbade discussion of shop at tea-time was overlooked. Mary and Mr. Clacton argued with a cogency and a ferocity which made the little woman feel that something very important—she hardly knew what—was taking place. She became much excited; one crucifix became entangled with another, and she dug a considerable hole in the table with the point of her pencil in order to emphasize the most striking heads of the discourse; and how any combination of Cabinet Ministers could resist such discourse she really did not know.

She could hardly bring herself to remember her own private instrument of justice—the typewriter. The telephone-bell rang, and as she hurried off to answer a voice which always seemed a proof of importance by itself, she felt that it was at this exact spot on the surface of the globe that all the subterranean wires of thought and progress came together. When she returned, with a message from the printer, she found that Mary was putting on her hat firmly; there was something imperious and dominating in her attitude altogether.

"Look, Sally," she said, "these letters want copying. These I've not looked at. The question of the new census will have to be gone into carefully. But I'm going home now. Good night, Mr. Clacton; good night, Sally."

"We are very fortunate in our secretary, Mr. Clacton," said Mrs. Seal, pausing with her hand on the papers, as the door shut behind Mary. Mr. Clacton himself had been vaguely impressed by something in Mary's behavior towards him. He envisaged a time even when it would become necessary to tell her that there could not be two masters in one office—but she was certainly able, very able, and in touch with a group of very clever young men. No doubt they had suggested to her some of her new ideas.

He signified his assent to Mrs. Seal's remark, but observed, with a glance at the clock, which showed only half an hour past five:

"If she takes the work seriously, Mrs. Seal—but that's just what some of your clever young ladies don't do." So saying he returned to his room, and Mrs. Seal, after a moment's hesitation, hurried back to her labors.

21

Mary walked to the nearest station and reached home in an incredibly short space of time, just so much, indeed, as was needed for the intelligent understanding of the news of the world as the *Westminster Gazette* reported it. Within a few minutes of opening her door, she was in trim for a hard evening's work. She unlocked a drawer and took out a manuscript, which consisted of a very few pages, entitled, in a forcible hand, "Some Aspects of the Democratic State." The aspects dwindled out in a cries-cross of blotted lines in the very middle of a sentence, and suggested that the author had been interrupted, or convinced of the futility of proceeding, with her pen in the air. . . . Oh, yes, Ralph had come in at that point. She scored that sheet very effectively, and, choosing a fresh one, began at a great rate with a generalization upon the structure of human society, which was a good deal bolder than her custom. Ralph had told her once that she couldn't write English, which accounted for those frequent blots and insertions; but she put all that behind her, and drove ahead with such words as came her way, until she had accomplished half a page of generalization and might legitimately draw breath. Directly her hand stopped her brain stopped too, and she began to listen. A paper-boy shouted down the street; an omnibus ceased and lurched on again with the heave of duty once more shouldered; the dullness of the sounds suggested that a fog had risen since her return, if, indeed, a fog has power to deaden sound, of which fact, she could not be sure at the present moment. It was the sort of fact Ralph Denham knew. At any rate, it was no concern of hers, and she was about to dip a pen when her ear was caught by the sound of a step upon the stone staircase. She followed it past Mr. Chippen's chambers; past Mr. Gibson's; past Mr. Turner's; after which it became her sound. A postman, a washerwoman, a circular, a bill—she presented herself with each of these perfectly natural possibilities; but, to her surprise, her mind rejected each one of them impatiently, even apprehensively. The step became slow, as it was apt to do at the end of the steep climb, and Mary, listening for the regular sound, was filled with an intolerable nervousness. Leaning against the table, she felt the knock of her heart push her body perceptibly backwards and forwards—a state of nerves astonishing and reprehensible in a stable woman. Grotesque fancies took shape. Alone, at the top of the house, an unknown person approaching nearer and nearer—how could she escape? There was no way of escape. She did not even know whether that oblong mark on the ceiling was a trapdoor to the roof or not. And if she got on to the roof—well, there was a drop of sixty feet or so on to the pavement. But she sat perfectly still, and when the knock sounded, she got up directly and opened the door without hesitation. She saw a tall figure outside, with something ominous to her eyes in the look of it.

"What do you want?" she said, not recognizing the face in the fitful light of the staircase.

"Mary? I'm Katharine Hilbery!"

Mary's self-possession returned almost excessively, and her welcome was decidedly cold, as if she must recoup herself for this ridiculous waste of emotion. She moved her green-shaded lamp to another table, and covered "Some Aspects of the Democratic State" with a sheet of blotting-paper.

"Why can't they leave me alone?" she thought bitterly, connecting Katharine and Ralph in a conspiracy to take from her even this hour of solitary study, even this poor little defence against the world. And, as she smoothed down the sheet of blotting-paper over the manuscript, she braced herself to resist Katharine, whose presence struck her, not merely by its force, as usual, but as something in the nature of a menace.

"You're working?" said Katharine, with hesitation, perceiving that she was not welcome.

"Nothing that matters," Mary replied, drawing forward the best of the chairs and poking the fire.

"I didn't know you had to work after you had left the office," said Katharine, in a tone which gave the impression that she was thinking of something else, as was, indeed, the case.

She had been paying calls with her mother, and in between the calls Mrs. Hilbery had rushed into shops and bought pillow-cases and blotting-books on no perceptible method for the furnishing of Katharine's house. Katharine had a sense of impedimenta accumulating on all sides of her. She had left her at length, and had come on to keep an engagement to dine with Rodney at his rooms. But she did not mean to get to him before seven o'clock, and so had plenty of time to walk all the way from Bond Street to the Temple if she wished it. The flow of faces streaming on either side of her had hypnotized her into a mood of profound despondency, to which her expectation of an evening alone with Rodney contributed. They were very good friends again, better friends, they both said, than ever before. So far as she was concerned this was true. There were many more things in him than she had guessed until emotion brought them forth—strength, affection, sympathy. And she thought of them and looked at the faces passing, and thought how much alike they were, and how distant, nobody feeling anything as she felt nothing, and distance, she thought, lay inevitably between the closest, and their intimacy was the worst presence of all. For, "Oh dear," she thought, looking into a tobacconist's window, "I don't care for any of them, and I don't care for William, and people say this is the thing that matters most, and I can't see what they mean by it."

She looked desperately at the smooth-bowled pipes, and wondered—should she walk on by the Strand or by the Embankment? It was not a simple question, for it concerned not different streets so much as different streams of thought. If she went by the Strand she would force herself to think out the problem of the future, or some mathematical problem; if she went by the river she would certainly begin to think about things that didn't exist—the forest, the ocean beach, the leafy solitudes, the magnanimous hero. No, no, no! A thousand times no!—it wouldn't do; there was something repulsive in such thoughts at present; she must take something else; she was out of that mood at present. And then she thought of Mary; the thought gave her confidence, even pleasure of a sad sort, as if the triumph of Ralph and Mary proved that the fault of her failure lay with herself and not with life. An indistinct idea that the sight of Mary might be of help, combined with her natural trust in her, suggested a visit; for, surely, her liking was of a kind that implied liking upon Mary's side also. After a moment's hesitation she decided, although she seldom acted upon impulse, to act upon this one, and turned down a side street and found Mary's door. But her reception was not encouraging; clearly Mary didn't want to see her, had no help to impart, and the half-formed desire to confide in her was quenched immediately. She was slightly amused at her own delusion, looked rather absent-minded, and swung her gloves to and fro, as if doling out the few minutes accurately before she could say good-by.

Those few minutes might very well be spent in asking for information as to the exact position of the Suffrage Bill, or in expounding her own very sensible view of the situation. But there was a tone in her voice, or a shade in her opinions, or a swing of her gloves which served to irritate Mary Datchet, whose manner became increasingly direct, abrupt, and even antagonistic. She became conscious of a wish to make Katharine realize the importance of this work, which she discussed so coolly, as though she, too, had sacrificed what Mary herself had sacrificed. The swinging of the gloves ceased, and Katharine, after ten minutes, began to make movements preliminary to departure. At the sight of this, Mary was aware—she was abnormally aware of things tonight—of another very strong desire; Katharine was not to be allowed to go, to disappear into the free, happy world of irresponsible individuals. She must be made to realize—to feel.

"I don't quite see," she said, as if Katharine had challenged her explicitly, "how, things being as they are, any one can help trying, at least, to do something."

"No. But how *are* things?"

Mary pressed her lips, and smiled ironically; she had Katharine at her mercy; she could, if she liked, discharge upon her head wagon-loads of revolting proof of the state of things ignored by the casual, the amateur, the looker-on, the cynical observer of life at a distance. And yet she hesitated. As usual, when she found herself in talk with Katharine, she began to feel rapid alternations of opinion about her, arrows of sensation striking strangely through the envelope of personality, which shelters us so conveniently from our fellows. What an egoist, how aloof she was! And yet, not in her words, perhaps, but in her voice, in her face, in her attitude, there were signs of a soft brooding spirit, of a sensibility unblunted and profound, playing over her thoughts and deeds, and investing her manner with an habitual gentleness. The arguments and phrases of Mr. Clacton fell flat against such armor.

"You'll be married, and you'll have other things to think of," she said inconsequently, and with an accent of condescension. She was not going to make Katharine understand in a second, as she would, all she herself had learnt at the cost of such pain. No. Katharine was to be happy; Katharine was to be ignorant; Mary was to keep this knowledge of the impersonal life for herself. The thought of her morning's renunciation stung her conscience, and she tried to expand once more into that impersonal condition which was so lofty and so painless. She must check this desire to be an individual again, whose wishes were in conflict with those of other people. She repented of her bitterness.

Katharine now renewed her signs of leave-taking; she had drawn on one of her gloves, and looked about her as if in search of some trivial saying to end with. Wasn't there some picture, or clock, or chest of drawers which might be singled out for notice? something peaceable and friendly to end the uncomfortable interview? The green-shaded lamp burnt in the corner, and illumined books and pens and blotting-paper. The whole aspect of the place started another train of thought and struck her as enviably free; in such a room one could work—one could have a life of one's own.

"I think you're very lucky," she observed. "I envy you, living alone and having your own things"—and engaged in this exalted way, which had no recognition or engagement-ring, she added in her own mind.

Mary's lips parted slightly. She could not conceive in what respects Katharine, who spoke sincerely, could envy her.

"I don't think you've got any reason to envy me," she said.

"Perhaps one always envies other people," Katharine observed vaguely.

"Well, but you've got everything that any one can want."

Katharine remained silent. She gazed into the fire quietly, and without a trace of self-consciousness. The hostility which she had divined in Mary's tone had completely disappeared, and she forgot that she had been upon the point of going.

"Well, I suppose I have," she said at length. "And yet I sometimes think—" She paused; she did not know how to express what she meant.

"It came over me in the Tube the other day," she resumed, with a smile; "what is it that makes these people go one way rather than the other? It's not love; it's not reason; I think it must be some idea. Perhaps, Mary, our affections are the shadow of an idea. Perhaps there isn't any such thing as affection in itself. . . ." She spoke half-mockingly, asking her question, which she scarcely troubled to frame, not of Mary, or of any one in particular.

But the words seemed to Mary Datchet shallow, supercilious, cold-blooded, and cynical all in one. All her natural instincts were roused in revolt against them.

"I'm the opposite way of thinking, you see," she said.

"Yes; I know you are," Katharine replied, looking at her as if now she were about, perhaps, to explain something very important.

Mary could not help feeling the simplicity and good faith that lay behind Katharine's words.

"I think affection is the only reality," she said.

"Yes," said Katharine, almost sadly. She understood that Mary was thinking of Ralph, and she felt it impossible to press her to reveal more of this exalted condition; she could only respect the fact that, in some few cases, life arranged itself thus satisfactorily and pass on. She rose to her feet accordingly. But Mary exclaimed, with unmistakable earnestness, that she must not go; that they met so seldom; that she wanted to talk to her so much. . . . Katharine was surprised at the earnestness with which she spoke. It seemed to her that there could be no indiscretion in mentioning Ralph by name.

Seating herself "for ten minutes," she said: "By the way, Mr. Denham told me he was going to give up the Bar and live in the country. Has he gone? He was beginning to tell me about it, when we were interrupted."

"He thinks of it," said Mary briefly. The color at once came to her face.

"It would be a very good plan," said Katharine in her decided way.

"You think so?"

"Yes, because he would do something worth while; he would write a book. My father always says that he's the most remarkable of the young men who write for him."

Mary bent low over the fire and stirred the coal between the bars with a poker. Katharine's mention of Ralph had roused within her an almost irresistible desire to explain to her the true state of the case between herself and Ralph. She knew, from the tone of her voice, that in speaking of Ralph she had no desire to probe Mary's secrets, or to insinuate any of her own. Moreover, she liked Katharine; she trusted her; she felt a respect for her. The first step of confidence was comparatively simple; but a further confidence had revealed itself, as Katharine spoke, which was not so simple, and yet it impressed itself upon her as a necessity; she must tell Katharine what it was clear that she had no conception of—she must tell Katharine that Ralph was in love with her.

"I don't know what he means to do," she said hurriedly, seeking time against the pressure of her own conviction. "I've not seen him since Christmas."

Katharine reflected that this was odd; perhaps, after all, she had misunderstood the position. She was in the habit of assuming, however, that she was rather unobservant of the finer shades of feeling, and she noted her present failure as another proof that she was a practical, abstract-minded person, better fitted to deal with figures than with the feelings of men and women. Anyhow, William Rodney would say so.

"And now—" she said.

"Oh, please stay!" Mary exclaimed, putting out her hand to stop her. Directly Katharine moved she felt, inarticulately and violently, that she could not bear to let her go. If Katharine went, her only chance of speaking was lost; her only chance of saying something tremendously important was lost. Half a dozen words were sufficient to wake Katharine's attention, and put flight and further silence beyond her power. But although the words came to her lips, her throat closed upon them and drove them back. After all, she considered, why should she speak? Because it is right, her instinct told her; right to expose oneself without reservations to other human beings. She flinched from the thought. It asked too much of one already stripped bare. Something she must keep of her own. But if she did keep something of her own? Immediately she figured an immured life, continuing for an immense period, the same feelings living for ever, neither dwindling nor changing within the ring of a thick stone wall. The imagination of this loneliness frightened her, and yet to speak—to lose her loneliness, for it had already become dear to her, was beyond her power.

Her hand went down to the hem of Katharine's skirt, and, fingering a line of fur, she bent her head as if to examine it.

"I like this fur," she said, "I like your clothes. And you mustn't think that I'm going to marry Ralph," she continued, in the same tone, "because he doesn't care for me at all. He cares for some one else." Her head remained bent, and her hand still rested upon the skirt.

"It's a shabby old dress," said Katharine, and the only sign that Mary's words had reached her was that she spoke with a little jerk.

"You don't mind my telling you that?" said Mary, raising herself.

"No, no," said Katharine; "but you're mistaken, aren't you?" She was, in truth, horribly uncomfortable, dismayed, indeed, disillusioned. She disliked the turn things had taken quite intensely. The indecency of it afflicted her. The suffering implied by the tone appalled her. She looked at Mary furtively, with eyes that were full of apprehension. But if she had hoped to find that these words had been spoken without understanding of their meaning, she was at once disappointed. Mary lay back in her chair, frowning slightly, and looking, Katharine thought, as if she had lived fifteen years or so in the space of a few minutes.

"There are some things, don't you think, that one can't be mistaken about?" Mary said, quietly and almost coldly. "That is what puzzles me about this question of being in love. I've always prided myself upon being reasonable," she added. "I didn't think I could have felt this—I mean if the other person didn't. I was foolish. I let myself pretend." Here she paused. "For, you see, Katharine," she proceeded, rousing herself and speaking with greater energy, "I *am* in love. There's no doubt about that. . . . I'm tremendously in love . . . with Ralph." The little forward shake of her head, which shook a lock of hair, together with her brighter color, gave her an appearance at once proud and defiant.

Katharine thought to herself, "That's how it feels then." She hesitated, with a feeling that it was not for her to speak; and then said, in a low tone, "You've got that."

"Yes," said Mary; "I've got that. One wouldn't *not* be in love. . . . But I didn't mean to talk about that; I only wanted you to know. There's another thing I want to tell you . . ." She paused. "I haven't any authority from Ralph to say it; but I'm sure of this—he's in love with you."

Katharine looked at her again, as if her first glance must have been deluded, for, surely, there must be some outward sign that Mary was talking in an excited, or bewildered, or fantastic manner. No; she still frowned, as if she sought her way through the clauses of a difficult argument, but she still looked more like one who reasons than one who feels.

"That proves that you're mistaken—utterly mistaken," said Katharine, speaking reasonably, too. She had no need to verify the mistake by a glance at her own recollections, when the fact was so clearly stamped upon her mind that if Ralph had any feeling towards her it was one of critical hostility. She did not give the matter another thought, and Mary, now that she had stated the fact, did not seek to prove it, but tried to explain to herself, rather than to Katharine, her motives in making the statement.

She had nerved herself to do what some large and imperious instinct demanded her doing; she had been swept on the breast of a wave beyond her reckoning.

"I've told you," she said, "because I want you to help me. I don't want to be jealous of you. And I am—I'm fearfully jealous. The only way, I thought, was to tell you."

She hesitated, and groped in her endeavor to make her feelings clear to herself.

"If I tell you, then we can talk; and when I'm jealous, I can tell you. And if I'm tempted to do something frightfully mean, I can tell you; you could make me tell you. I find talking so difficult; but loneliness frightens me. I should shut it up in my mind. Yes, that's what I'm afraid of. Going about with something in my mind all my life that never changes. I find it so difficult to change. When I think a thing's wrong I never stop thinking it wrong, and Ralph was quite right, I see, when he said that there's no such thing as right and wrong; no such thing, I mean, as judging people—"

"Ralph Denham said that?" said Katharine, with considerable indignation. In order to have produced such suffering in Mary, it seemed to her that he must have behaved with extreme callousness. It seemed to her that he had discarded the friendship, when it suited his convenience to do so, with some falsely philosophical theory which made his conduct all the worse. She was going on to express herself thus, had not Mary at once interrupted her.

"No, no," she said; "you don't understand. If there's any fault it's mine entirely; after all, if one chooses to run risks—"

Her voice faltered into silence. It was borne in upon her how completely in running her risk she had lost her prize, lost it so entirely that she had no longer the right, in talking of Ralph, to presume that her knowledge of him supplanted all other knowledge. She no longer completely possessed her love, since his share in it was doubtful; and now, to make things yet more bitter, her clear vision of the way to face life was rendered tremulous and uncertain, because another was witness of it. Feeling her desire for the old unshared intimacy too great to be borne without tears, she rose, walked to the farther end of the room, held the curtains apart, and stood there mastered for a moment. The grief itself was not ignoble; the sting of it lay in the fact that she had been led to this act of treachery against herself. Trapped, cheated, robbed, first by Ralph and then by Katharine, she seemed all dissolved in humiliation, and bereft of anything she could call her own. Tears of weakness welled up and rolled down her cheeks. But tears, at least, she could control, and would this instant, and then, turning, she would face Katharine, and retrieve what could be retrieved of the collapse of her courage.

She turned. Katharine had not moved; she was leaning a little forward in her chair and looking into the fire. Something in the attitude reminded Mary of Ralph. So he would sit, leaning forward, looking rather fixedly in front of him, while his mind went far away, exploring, speculating, until he broke off with his, "Well, Mary?"—and the silence, that had been so full of romance to her, gave way to the most delightful talk that she had ever known.

Something unfamiliar in the pose of the silent figure, something still, solemn, significant about it, made her hold her breath. She paused. Her thoughts were without bitterness. She was surprised by her own quiet and confidence. She came back silently, and sat once more by Katharine's side. Mary had no wish to speak. In the silence she seemed to have lost her isolation; she was at once the sufferer and the pitiful spectator of suffering; she was happier than she had ever been; she was more bereft; she was rejected, and she was immensely beloved. Attempt to express these sensations was vain, and, moreover, she could not help believing that, without any words on her side, they were shared. Thus for some time longer they sat silent, side by side, while Mary fingered the fur on the skirt of the old dress.

22

The fact that she would be late in keeping her engagement with William was not the only reason which sent Katharine almost at racing speed along the Strand in the direction of his rooms. Punctuality might have been achieved by taking a cab, had she not wished the open air to fan into flame the glow kindled by Mary's words. For among all the impressions of the evening's talk one was of the nature of a revelation and subdued the rest to insignificance. Thus one looked; thus one spoke; such was love.

"She sat up straight and looked at me, and then she said, 'I'm in love,'" Katharine mused, trying to set the whole scene in motion. It was a scene to dwell on with so much wonder that not a grain of pity occurred to her; it was a flame blazing suddenly in the dark; by its light Katharine perceived far too vividly for her comfort the mediocrity, indeed the entirely fictitious character of her own feelings so far as they pretended to correspond with Mary's feelings. She made up her mind to act instantly upon the knowledge thus gained, and cast her mind in amazement back to the scene upon the heath, when she had yielded, heaven knows why, for reasons which seemed now imperceptible. So in broad daylight one might revisit the place where one has groped and turned and succumbed to utter bewilderment in a fog.

"It's all so simple," she said to herself. "There can't be any doubt. I've only got to speak now. I've only got to speak," she went on saying, in time to her own footsteps, and completely forgot Mary Datchet.

William Rodney, having come back earlier from the office than he expected, sat down to pick out the melodies in "The Magic Flute" upon the piano. Katharine was late, but that was nothing new, and, as she had no particular liking for music, and he felt in the mood for it, perhaps it was as well. This defect in Katharine was the more strange, William reflected, because, as a rule, the women of her family were unusually musical. Her cousin, Cassandra Otway, for example, had a very fine taste in music, and he had charming recollections of her in a light fantastic attitude, playing the flute in the morning-room at Stogdon House. He recalled with pleasure the amusing way in which her nose, long like all the Otway noses, seemed to extend itself into the flute, as if she were some inimitably graceful species of musical mole. The little picture suggested very happily her melodious and whimsical temperament. The enthusiasms of a young girl of distinguished upbringing appealed to William, and suggested a thousand ways in which, with his training and accomplishments, he could be of service to her. She ought to be given the chance of hearing good music, as it is played by those who have inherited the great tradition. Moreover, from one or two remarks let fall in the course of conversation, he thought it possible that she had what Katharine professed to lack, a passionate, if untaught, appreciation of literature. He had lent her his play. Meanwhile, as Katharine was certain to be late, and "The Magic Flute" is nothing without a voice, he felt inclined to spend the time of waiting in writing a letter to Cassandra, exhorting her to read Pope in preference to Dostoevsky, until her feeling for form was more highly developed. He set himself down to compose this piece of advice in a shape which was light and playful, and yet did no injury to a cause which he had near at heart, when he heard Katharine upon the stairs. A moment later it was plain that he had been mistaken, it was not Katharine; but he could not settle himself to his letter. His temper had changed from one of urbane contentment—indeed of delicious expansion—to one of uneasiness and expectation. The dinner was brought in, and had to be set by the fire to keep hot. It was now a quarter of an hour beyond the specified time. He bethought him of a piece of news which had depressed him in the earlier part of the day. Owing to the illness of one of his fellow-clerks, it was likely that he would get no holiday until later in the year, which would mean the postponement of their marriage. But this possibility, after all, was not so disagreeable as the probability which forced itself upon him with every tick of the clock that Katharine had completely forgotten her engagement. Such things had happened less frequently since Christmas, but what if they were going to begin to happen again? What if their marriage should turn out, as she had said, a farce? He acquitted her of any wish to hurt him wantonly, but there was something in her character which made it impossible for her to help hurting people. Was she cold? Was she self-absorbed? He tried to fit her with each of these descriptions, but he had to own that she puzzled him.

"There are so many things that she doesn't understand," he reflected, glancing at the letter to Cassandra which he had begun and laid aside. What prevented him from finishing the letter which he had so much enjoyed beginning? The reason was that Katharine might, at any moment, enter the room. The thought, implying his bondage to her, irritated him acutely. It occurred to him that he would leave the letter lying open for her to see, and he would take the opportunity of telling her that he had sent his play to Cassandra for her to criticize. Possibly, but not by any means certainly, this would annoy her—and as he reached the doubtful comfort of this conclusion, there was a knock on the door and Katharine came in. They kissed each other coldly and she made no apology for being late. Nevertheless, her mere presence moved him strangely; but he was determined that this should not weaken his resolution to make some kind of stand against her; to get at the truth about her. He let her make her own disposition of clothes and busied himself with the plates.

"I've got a piece of news for you, Katharine," he said directly they sat down to table; "I shan't get my holiday in April. We shall have to put off our marriage."

He rapped the words out with a certain degree of briskness. Katharine started a little, as if the announcement disturbed her thoughts.

"That won't make any difference, will it? I mean the lease isn't signed," she replied. "But why? What has happened?"

He told her, in an off-hand way, how one of his fellow-clerks had broken down, and might have to be away for months, six months even, in which case they would have to think over their position. He said it in a way which struck her, at last, as oddly casual. She looked at him. There was no outward sign that he was annoyed with her. Was she well dressed? She thought sufficiently so. Perhaps she was late? She looked for a clock.

"It's a good thing we didn't take the house then," she repeated thoughtfully.

"It'll mean, too, I'm afraid, that I shan't be as free for a considerable time as I have been," he continued. She had time to reflect that she gained something by all this, though it was too soon to determine what. But the light which had been burning with such intensity as she came along was suddenly overclouded, as much by his manner as by his news. She had been prepared to meet opposition, which is simple to encounter compared with—she did not know what it was that she had to encounter. The meal passed in quiet, well-controlled talk about indifferent things. Music was not a subject about which she knew anything, but she liked him to tell her things; and could, she mused, as he talked, fancy the evenings of married life spent thus, over the fire; spent thus, or with a book, perhaps, for then she would have time to read her books, and to grasp firmly with every muscle of her unused mind what she longed to know. The atmosphere was very free. Suddenly William broke off. She looked up apprehensively, brushing aside these thoughts with annoyance.

"Where should I address a letter to Cassandra?" he asked her. It was obvious again that William had some meaning or other tonight, or was in some mood. "We've struck up a friendship," he added.

"She's at home, I think," Katharine replied.

"They keep her too much at home," said William. "Why don't you ask her to stay with you, and let her hear a little good music? I'll just finish what I was saying, if you don't mind, because I'm particularly anxious that she should hear tomorrow."

Katharine sank back in her chair, and Rodney took the paper on his knees, and went on with his sentence. "Style, you know, is what we tend to neglect—"; but he was far more conscious of Katharine's eye upon him than of what he was saying about style. He knew that she was looking at him, but whether with irritation or indifference he could not guess.

In truth, she had fallen sufficiently into his trap to feel uncomfortably roused and disturbed and unable to proceed on the lines laid down for herself. This indifferent, if not hostile, attitude on William's part made it impossible to break off without animosity, largely and completely. Infinitely preferable was Mary's state, she thought, where there was a simple thing to do and one did it. In fact, she could not help supposing that some littleness of nature had a part in all the refinements, reserves, and subtleties of feeling for which her friends and family were so distinguished. For example, although she liked Cassandra well enough, her fantastic method of life struck her as purely frivolous; now it was socialism, now it was silkworms, now it was music—which last she supposed was the cause of William's sudden interest in her. Never before had William wasted the minutes of her presence in writing his letters. With a curious sense of light opening where all, hitherto, had been opaque, it dawned upon her that, after all, possibly, yes, probably, nay, certainly, the devotion which she had almost wearily taken for granted existed in a much slighter degree than she had suspected, or existed no longer. She looked at him attentively as if this discovery of hers must show traces in his face. Never had she seen so much to respect in his appearance, so much that attracted her by its sensitiveness and intelligence, although she saw these qualities as if they were those one responds to, dumbly, in the face of a stranger. The head bent over the paper, thoughtful as usual, had now a composure which seemed somehow to place it at a distance, like a face seen talking to some one else behind glass.

He wrote on, without raising his eyes. She would have spoken, but could not bring herself to ask him for signs of affection which she had no right to claim. The conviction that he was thus strange to her filled her with despondency, and illustrated quite beyond doubt the infinite loneliness of human beings. She had never felt the truth of this so strongly before. She looked away into the fire; it seemed to her that even physically they were now scarcely within speaking distance; and spiritually there was certainly no human being with whom she could claim comradeship; no dream that satisfied her as she was used to be satisfied; nothing remained in whose reality she could believe, save those abstract ideas—figures, laws, stars, facts, which she could hardly hold to for lack of knowledge and a kind of shame.

When Rodney owned to himself the folly of this prolonged silence, and the meanness of such devices, and looked up ready to seek some excuse for a good laugh, or opening for a confession, he was disconcerted by what he saw. Katharine seemed equally oblivious of what was bad or of what was good in him. Her expression suggested concentration upon something entirely remote from her surroundings. The carelessness of her attitude seemed to him rather masculine than feminine. His impulse to break up the constraint was chilled, and once more the exasperating sense of his own impotency returned to him. He could not help contrasting Katharine with his vision of the engaging, whimsical Cassandra; Katharine undemonstrative, inconsiderate, silent, and yet so notable that he could never do without her good opinion.

She veered round upon him a moment later, as if, when her train of thought was ended, she became aware of his presence.

"Have you finished your letter?" she asked. He thought he heard faint amusement in her tone, but not a trace of jealousy.

"No, I'm not going to write any more tonight," he said. "I'm not in the mood for it for some reason. I can't say what I want to say."

"Cassandra won't know if it's well written or badly written," Katharine remarked.

"I'm not so sure about that. I should say she has a good deal of literary feeling."

"Perhaps," said Katharine indifferently. "You've been neglecting my education lately, by the way. I wish you'd read something. Let me choose a book." So speaking, she went across to his bookshelves and began looking in a desultory way among his books. Anything, she thought, was better than bickering or the strange silence which drove home to her the distance between them. As she pulled one book forward and then another she thought ironically of her own certainty not an hour ago; how it had vanished in a moment, how she was merely marking time as best she could, not knowing in the least where they stood, what they felt, or whether William loved her or not. More and more the condition of Mary's mind seemed to her wonderful and enviable—if, indeed, it could be quite as she figured it—if, indeed, simplicity existed for any one of the daughters of women.

"Swift," she said, at last, taking out a volume at haphazard to settle this question at least. "Let us have some Swift."

Rodney took the book, held it in front of him, inserted one finger between the pages, but said nothing. His face wore a queer expression of deliberation, as if he were weighing one thing with another, and would not say anything until his mind were made up.

Katharine, taking her chair beside him, noted his silence and looked at him with sudden apprehension. What she hoped or feared, she could not have said; a most irrational and indefensible desire for some assurance of his affection was, perhaps, uppermost in her mind. Peevishness, complaints, exacting cross-examination she was used to, but this attitude of composed quiet, which seemed to come from the consciousness of power within, puzzled her. She did not know what was going to happen next.

At last William spoke.

"I think it's a little odd, don't you?" he said, in a voice of detached reflection. "Most people, I mean, would be seriously upset if their marriage was put off for six months or so. But we aren't; now how do you account for that?"

She looked at him and observed his judicial attitude as of one holding far aloof from emotion.

"I attribute it," he went on, without waiting for her to answer, "to the fact that neither of us is in the least romantic about the other. That may be partly, no doubt, because we've known each other so long; but I'm inclined to think there's more in it than that. There's something temperamental. I think you're a trifle cold, and I suspect I'm a trifle self-absorbed. If that were so it goes a long way to explaining our odd lack of illusion about each other. I'm not saying that the most satisfactory marriages aren't founded upon this sort of understanding. But certainly it struck me as odd this morning, when Wilson told me, how little upset I felt. By the way, you're sure we haven't committed ourselves to that house?"

"I've kept the letters, and I'll go through them tomorrow; but I'm certain we're on the safe side."

"Thanks. As to the psychological problem," he continued, as if the question interested him in a detached way, "there's no doubt, I think, that either of us is capable of feeling what, for reasons of simplicity, I call romance for a third person—at least, I've little doubt in my own case."

It was, perhaps, the first time in all her knowledge of him that Katharine had known William enter thus deliberately and without sign of emotion upon a statement of his own feelings. He was wont to discourage such intimate discussions by a little laugh or turn of the conversation, as much as to say that men, or men of the world, find such topics a little silly, or in doubtful taste. His obvious wish to explain something puzzled her, interested her, and neutralized the wound to her vanity. For some reason, too, she felt more at ease with him than usual; or her ease was more the ease of equality—she could not stop to think of that at the moment though. His remarks interested her too much for the light that they threw upon certain problems of her own.

"What is this romance?" she mused.

"Ah, that's the question. I've never come across a definition that satisfied me, though there are some very good ones"—he glanced in the direction of his books.

"It's not altogether knowing the other person, perhaps—it's ignorance," she hazarded.

"Some authorities say it's a question of distance—romance in literature, that is——"

"Possibly, in the case of art. But in the case of people it may be——" she hesitated.

"Have you no personal experience of it?" he asked, letting his eyes rest upon her swiftly for a moment.

"I believe it's influenced me enormously," she said, in the tone of one absorbed by the possibilities of some view just presented to them; "but in my life there's so little scope for it," she added. She reviewed her daily task, the perpetual demands upon her for good sense, self-control, and accuracy in a house containing a romantic mother. Ah, but her romance wasn't *that* romance. It was a desire, an echo, a sound; she could drape it in color, see it in form, hear it in music, but not in words; no, never in words. She sighed, teased by desires so incoherent, so incommunicable.

"But isn't it curious," William resumed, "that you should neither feel it for me, nor I for you?"

Katharine agreed that it was curious—very; but even more curious to her was the fact that she was discussing the question with William. It revealed possibilities which opened a prospect of a new relationship altogether. Somehow it seemed to her that he was helping her to understand what she had never understood; and in her gratitude she was conscious of a most sisterly desire to help him, too—sisterly, save for one pang, not quite to be subdued, that for him she was without romance.

"I think you might be very happy with some one you loved in that way," she said.

"You assume that romance survives a closer knowledge of the person one loves?"

He asked the question formally, to protect himself from the sort of personality which he dreaded. The whole situation needed the most careful management lest it should degenerate into some degrading and disturbing exhibition such as the scene, which he could never think of without shame, upon the heath among the dead leaves. And yet each sentence brought him relief. He was coming to understand something or other about his own desires hitherto undefined by him, the source of his difficulty with Katharine. The wish to hurt her, which had urged him to begin, had completely left him, and he felt that it was only Katharine now who could help him to be sure. He must take his time. There were so many things that he could not say without the greatest difficulty—that name, for example, Cassandra. Nor could he move his eyes from a certain spot, a fiery glen surrounded by high mountains, in the heart of the coals. He waited in suspense for Katharine to continue. She had said that he might be very happy with some one he loved in that way.

"I don't see why it shouldn't last with you," she resumed. "I can imagine a certain sort of person——" she paused; she was aware that he was listening with the greatest intentness, and that his formality was merely the cover for an extreme anxiety of some sort. There *was* some person then—some woman—who could it be? Cassandra? Ah, possibly——

"A person," she added, speaking in the most matter-of-fact tone she could command, "like Cassandra Otway, for instance. Cassandra is the most interesting of the Otways—with the exception of Henry. Even so, I like Cassandra better. She has more than mere cleverness. She is a character—a person by herself."

"Those dreadful insects!" burst from William, with a nervous laugh, and a little spasm went through him as Katharine noticed. It *was* Cassandra then. Automatically and dully she replied, "You could insist that she confined herself to—to—something else. . . . But she cares for music; I believe she writes poetry; and there can be no doubt that she has a peculiar charm——"

She ceased, as if defining to herself this peculiar charm. After a moment's silence William jerked out:

"I thought her affectionate?"

"Extremely affectionate. She worships Henry. When you think what a house that is—Uncle Francis always in one mood or another——"

"Dear, dear, dear," William muttered.

"And you have so much in common."

"My dear Katharine!" William exclaimed, flinging himself back in his chair, and uprooting his eyes from the spot in the fire. "I really don't know what we're talking about. . . . I assure you. . . ."

He was covered with an extreme confusion.

He withdrew the finger that was still thrust between the pages of Gulliver, opened the book, and ran his eye down the list of chapters, as though he were about to select the one most suitable for reading aloud. As Katharine watched him, she was seized with preliminary symptoms of his own panic. At the same time she was convinced that, should he find the right page, take out his spectacles, clear his throat, and open his lips, a chance that would never come again in all their lives would be lost to them both.

"We're talking about things that interest us both very much," she said. "Shan't we go on talking, and leave Swift for another time? I don't feel in the mood for Swift, and it's a pity to read any one when that's the case—particularly Swift."

The presence of wise literary speculation, as she calculated, restored William's confidence in his security, and he replaced the book in the bookcase, keeping his back turned to her as he did so, and taking advantage of this circumstance to summon his thoughts together.

But a second of introspection had the alarming result of showing him that his mind, when looked at from within, was no longer familiar ground. He felt, that is to say, what he had never consciously felt before; he was revealed to himself as other than he was wont to think him; he was afloat upon a sea of unknown and tumultuous possibilities. He paced once up and down the room, and then flung himself impetuously into the chair by Katharine's side. He had never felt anything like this before; he put himself entirely into her hands; he cast off all responsibility. He very nearly exclaimed aloud:

"You've stirred up all these odious and violent emotions, and now you must do the best you can with them."

Her near presence, however, had a calming and reassuring effect upon his agitation, and he was conscious only of an implicit trust that, somehow, he was safe with her, that she would see him through, find out what it was that he wanted, and procure it for him.

"I wish to do whatever you tell me to do," he said. "I put myself entirely in your hands, Katharine."

"You must try to tell me what you feel," she said.

"My dear, I feel a thousand things every second. I don't know, I'm sure, what I feel. That afternoon on the heath—it was then—then——" He broke off; he did not tell her what had happened then. "Your ghastly good sense, as usual, has convinced me—for the moment—but what the truth is, Heaven only knows!" he exclaimed.

"Isn't it the truth that you are, or might be, in love with Cassandra?" she said gently.

William bowed his head. After a moment's silence he murmured:

"I believe you're right, Katharine."

She sighed, involuntarily. She had been hoping all this time, with an intensity that increased second by second against the current of her words, that it would not in the end come to this. After a moment of surprising anguish, she summoned her courage to tell him how she wished only that she might help him, and had framed the first words of her speech when a knock, terrific and startling to people in their overwrought condition, sounded upon the door.

"Katharine, I worship you," he urged, half in a whisper.

"Yes," she replied, withdrawing with a little shiver, "but you must open the door."

23

When Ralph Denham entered the room and saw Katharine seated with her back to him, he was conscious of a change in the grade of the atmosphere such as a traveler meets with sometimes upon the roads, particularly after sunset, when, without warning, he runs from clammy chill to a hoard of unspent warmth in which the sweetness of hay and beanfield is cherished, as if the sun still shone although the moon is up. He hesitated; he shuddered; he walked elaborately to the window and laid aside his coat. He balanced his stick most carefully against the folds of the curtain. Thus occupied with his own sensations and preparations, he had little time to observe what either of the other two was feeling. Such symptoms of agitation as he might perceive (and they had left their tokens in brightness of eye and pallor of cheeks) seemed to him well befitting the actors in so great a drama as that of Katharine Hilbery's daily life. Beauty and passion were the breath of her being, he thought.

She scarcely noticed his presence, or only as it forced her to adopt a manner of composure, which she was certainly far from feeling. William, however, was even more agitated than she was, and her first instalment of promised help took the form of some commonplace upon the age of the building or the architect's name, which gave him an excuse to fumble in a drawer for certain designs, which he laid upon the table between the three of them.

Which of the three followed the designs most carefully it would be difficult to tell, but it is certain that not one of the three found for the moment anything to say. Years of training in a drawing-room came at length to Katharine's help, and she said something suitable, at the same moment withdrawing her hand from the table because she perceived that it trembled. William agreed effusively; Denham corroborated him, speaking in rather high-pitched tones; they thrust aside the plans, and drew nearer to the fireplace.

"I'd rather live here than anywhere in the whole of London," said Denham.

("And I've got nowhere to live") Katharine thought, as she agreed aloud.

"You could get rooms here, no doubt, if you wanted to," Rodney replied.

"But I'm just leaving London for good—I've taken that cottage I was telling you about." The announcement seemed to convey very little to either of his hearers.

"Indeed?—that's sad. . . . You must give me your address. But you won't cut yourself off altogether, surely—"

"You'll be moving, too, I suppose," Denham remarked.

William showed such visible signs of floundering that Katharine collected herself and asked:

"Where is the cottage you've taken?"

In answering her, Denham turned and looked at her. As their eyes met, she realized for the first time that she was talking to Ralph Denham, and she remembered, without recalling any details, that she had been speaking of him quite lately, and that she had reason to think ill of him. What Mary had said she could not remember, but she felt that there was a mass of knowledge in her mind which she had not had time to examine—knowledge now lying on the far side of a gulf. But her agitation flashed the queerest lights upon her past. She must get through the matter in hand, and then think it out in quiet. She bent her mind to follow what Ralph was saying. He was telling her that he had taken a cottage in Norfolk, and she was saying that she knew, or did not know, that particular neighborhood. But after a moment's attention her mind flew to Rodney, and she had an unusual, indeed unprecedented, sense that they were in touch and shared each other's thoughts. If only Ralph were not there, she would at once give way to her desire to take William's hand, then to bend his head upon her shoulder, for this was what she wanted to do more than anything at the moment, unless, indeed, she wished more than anything to be alone—yes, that was what she wanted. She was sick to death of these discussions; she shivered at the effort to reveal her feelings. She had forgotten to answer. William was speaking now.

"But what will you find to do in the country?" she asked at random, striking into a conversation which she had only half heard, in such a way as to make both Rodney and Denham look at her with a little surprise. But directly she took up the conversation, it was William's turn to fall silent. He at once forgot to listen to what they were saying, although he interposed nervously at intervals, "Yes, yes, yes." As the minutes passed, Ralph's presence became more and more intolerable to him, since there was so much that he must say to Katharine; the moment he could not talk to her, terrible doubts, unanswerable questions accumulated, which he must lay before Katharine, for she alone could help him now. Unless he could see her alone, it would be impossible for him ever to sleep, or to know what he had said in a moment of madness, which was not altogether mad, or was it mad? He nodded his head, and said, nervously, "Yes, yes," and looked at Katharine, and thought how beautiful she looked; there was no one in the world that he admired more. There was an emotion in her face which lent it an expression he had never seen there. Then, as he was turning over means by which he could speak to her alone, she rose, and he was taken by surprise, for he had counted on the fact that she would outstay Denham. His only chance, then, of saying something to her in private, was to take her downstairs and walk with her to the street. While he hesitated, however, overcome with the difficulty of putting one simple thought into words when all his thoughts were scattered about, and all were too strong for utterance, he was struck silent by something that was still more unexpected. Denham got up from his chair, looked at Katharine, and said:

"I'm going, too. Shall we go together?"

And before William could see any way of detaining him—or would it be better to detain Katharine?—he had taken his hat, stick, and was holding the door open for Katharine to pass out. The most that William could do was to stand at the head of the stairs and say good-night. He could not offer to go with them. He could not insist that she should stay. He watched her descend, rather slowly, owing to the dusk of the staircase, and he had a last sight of Denham's head and of Katharine's head near together, against the panels, when suddenly a pang of acute jealousy overcame him, and had he not remained conscious of the slippers upon his feet, he would have run after them or cried out. As it was he could not move from the spot. At the turn of the staircase Katharine turned to look back, trusting to this last glance to seal their compact of good friendship. Instead of returning her silent greeting, William grinned back at her a cold stare of sarcasm or of rage.

She stopped dead for a moment, and then descended slowly into the court. She looked to the right and to the left, and once up into the sky. She was only conscious of Denham as a block upon her thoughts. She measured the distance that must be traversed before she would be alone. But when they came to the Strand no cabs were to be seen, and Denham broke the silence by saying:

"There seem to be no cabs. Shall we walk on a little?"

"Very well," she agreed, paying no attention to him.

Aware of her preoccupation, or absorbed in his own thoughts, Ralph said nothing further; and in silence they walked some distance along the Strand. Ralph was doing his best to put his thoughts into such order that one came before the rest, and the determination that when he spoke he should speak worthily, made him put off the moment of speaking till he had found the exact words and even the place that best suited him. The Strand was too busy. There was too much risk, also, of finding an empty cab. Without a word of explanation he turned to the left, down one of the side streets leading to the river. On no account must they part until something of the very greatest importance had happened. He knew perfectly well what he wished to say, and had arranged not only the substance, but the order in which he was to say it. Now, however, that he was alone with her, not only did he find the difficulty of speaking almost insurmountable, but he was aware that he was angry with her for thus disturbing him, and casting, as it was so easy for a person of her advantages to do, these phantoms and pitfalls across his path. He was determined that he would question her as severely as he would question himself; and make them both, once and for all, either justify her dominance or renounce it. But the longer they walked thus alone, the more he was disturbed by the sense of her actual presence. Her skirt blew; the feathers in her hat waved; sometimes he saw her a step or two ahead of him, or had to wait for her to catch him up.

The silence was prolonged, and at length drew her attention to him. First she was annoyed that there was no cab to free her from his company; then she recalled vaguely something that Mary had said to make her think ill of him; she could not remember what, but the recollection, combined with his masterful ways—why did he walk so fast down this side street?—made her more and more conscious of a person of marked, though disagreeable, force by her side. She stopped and, looking round her for a cab, sighted one in the distance. He was thus precipitated into speech.

"Should you mind if we walked a little farther?" he asked. "There's something I want to say to you."

"Very well," she replied, guessing that his request had something to do with Mary Datchet.

"It's quieter by the river," he said, and instantly he crossed over. "I want to ask you merely this," he began. But he paused so long that she could see his head against the sky; the slope of his thin cheek and his large, strong nose were clearly marked against it. While he paused, words that were quite different from those he intended to use presented themselves. "I've made you my standard ever since I saw you. I've dreamt about you; I've thought of nothing but you; you represent to me the only reality in the world."

His words, and the queer strained voice in which he spoke them, made it appear as if he addressed some person who was not the woman beside him, but some one far away.

"And now things have come to such a pass that, unless I can speak to you openly, I believe I shall go mad. I think of you as the most beautiful, the truest thing in the world," he continued, filled with a sense of exaltation, and feeling that he had no need now to choose his words with pedantic accuracy, for what he wanted to say was suddenly become plain to him.

"I see you everywhere, in the stars, in the river; to me you're everything that exists; the reality of everything. Life, I tell you, would be impossible without you. And now I want—"

She had heard him so far with a feeling that she had dropped some material word which made sense of the rest. She could hear no more of this unintelligible rambling without checking him. She felt that she was overhearing what was meant for another.

"I don't understand," she said. "You're saying things that you don't mean."

"I mean every word I say," he replied, emphatically. He turned his head towards her. She recovered the words she was searching for while he spoke. "Ralph Denham is in love with you." They came back to her in Mary Datchet's voice. Her anger blazed up in her.

"I saw Mary Datchet this afternoon," she exclaimed.

He made a movement as if he were surprised or taken aback, but answered in a moment:

"She told you that I had asked her to marry me, I suppose?"

"No!" Katharine exclaimed, in surprise.

"I did though. It was the day I saw you at Lincoln," he continued. "I had meant to ask her to marry me, and then I looked out of the window and saw you. After that I didn't want to ask any one to marry me. But I did it; and she knew I was lying, and refused me. I thought then, and still think, that she cares for me. I behaved very badly. I don't defend myself."

"No," said Katharine, "I should hope not. There's no defence that I can think of. If any conduct is wrong, that is." She spoke with an energy that was directed even more against herself than against him. "It seems to me," she continued, with the same energy, "that people are bound to be honest. There's no excuse for such behavior." She could now see plainly before her eyes the expression on Mary Datchet's face.

After a short pause, he said:

"I am not telling you that I am in love with you. I am not in love with you."

"I didn't think that," she replied, conscious of some bewilderment.

"I have not spoken a word to you that I do not mean," he added.

"Tell me then what it is that you mean," she said at length.

As if obeying a common instinct, they both stopped and, bending slightly over the balustrade of the river, looked into the flowing water.

"You say that we've got to be honest," Ralph began. "Very well. I will try to tell you the facts; but I warn you, you'll think me mad. It's a fact, though, that since I first saw you four or five months ago I have made you, in an utterly absurd way, I expect, my ideal. I'm almost ashamed to tell you what lengths I've gone to. It's become the thing that matters most in my life." He checked himself. "Without knowing you, except that you're beautiful, and all that, I've come to believe that we're in some sort of agreement; that we're after something together; that we see something. . . . I've got into the habit of imagining you; I'm always thinking what you'd say or do; I walk along the street talking to you; I dream of you. It's merely a bad habit, a schoolboy habit, day-dreaming; it's a common experience; half one's friends do the same; well, those are the facts."

Simultaneously, they both walked on very slowly.

"If you were to know me you would feel none of this," she said. "We don't know each other—we've always been—interrupted. . . . Were you going to tell me this that day my aunts came?" she asked, recollecting the whole scene.

He bowed his head.

"The day you told me of your engagement," he said.

She thought, with a start, that she was no longer engaged.

"I deny that I should cease to feel this if I knew you," he went on. "I should feel it more reasonably—that's all. I shouldn't talk the kind of nonsense I've talked tonight. . . . But it wasn't nonsense. It was the truth," he said doggedly. "It's the important thing. You can force me to talk as if this feeling for you were an hallucination, but all our feelings are that. The best of them are half illusions. Still," he added, as if arguing to himself, "if it weren't as real a feeling as I'm capable of, I shouldn't be changing my life on your account."

"What do you mean?" she inquired.

"I told you. I'm taking a cottage. I'm giving up my profession."

"On my account?" she asked, in amazement.

"Yes, on your account," he replied. He explained his meaning no further.

"But I don't know you or your circumstances," she said at last, as he remained silent.

"You have no opinion about me one way or the other?"

"Yes, I suppose I have an opinion—" she hesitated.

He controlled his wish to ask her to explain herself, and much to his pleasure she went on, appearing to search her mind.

"I thought that you criticized me—perhaps disliked me. I thought of you as a person who judges—"

"No; I'm a person who feels," he said, in a low voice.

"Tell me, then, what has made you do this?" she asked, after a break.

He told her in an orderly way, betokening careful preparation, all that he had meant to say at first; how he stood with regard to his brothers and sisters; what his mother had said, and his sister Joan had refrained from saying; exactly how many pounds stood in his name at the bank; what prospect his brother had of earning a livelihood in America; how much of their income went on rent, and other details known to him by heart. She listened to all this, so that she could have passed an examination in it by the time Waterloo Bridge was in sight; and yet she was no more listening to it than she was counting the paving-stones at her feet. She was feeling happier than she had felt in her life. If Denham could have seen how visibly books of algebraic symbols, pages all speckled with dots and dashes and twisted bars, came before her eyes as they trod the Embankment, his secret joy in her attention might have been dispersed. She went on, saying, "Yes, I see. . . . But how would that help you? . . . Your brother has passed his examination?" so sensibly, that he had constantly to keep his brain in check; and all the time she was in fancy looking up through a telescope at white shadow-cleft disks which were other worlds, until she felt herself possessed of two bodies, one walking by the river with Denham, the other concentrated to a silver globe aloft in the fine blue space above the scum of vapors that was covering the visible world. She looked at the sky once, and saw that no star was keen enough to pierce the flight of watery clouds now coursing rapidly before the west wind. She looked down hurriedly again. There was no reason, she assured herself, for this feeling of happiness; she was not free; she was not alone; she was still bound to earth by a million fibres; every step took her nearer home. Nevertheless, she exulted as she had never exulted before. The air was fresher, the lights more distinct, the cold stone of the balustrade colder and harder, when by chance or purpose she struck her hand against it. No feeling of annoyance with Denham remained; he certainly did not hinder any flight she might choose to make, whether in the direction of the sky or of her home; but that her condition was due to him, or to anything that he had said, she had no consciousness at all.

They were now within sight of the stream of cabs and omnibuses crossing to and from the Surrey side of the river; the sound of the traffic, the hooting of motor-horns, and the light chime of tram-bells sounded more and more distinctly, and, with the increase of noise, they both became silent. With a common instinct they slackened their pace, as if to lengthen the time of semi-privacy allowed them. To Ralph, the pleasure of these last yards of the walk with Katharine was so great that he could not look beyond the present moment to the time when she should have left him. He had no wish to use the last moments of their companionship in adding fresh words to what he had already said. Since they had stopped talking, she had become to him not so much a real person, as the very woman he dreamt of; but his solitary dreams had never produced any such keenness of sensation as that which he felt in her presence. He himself was also strangely transfigured. He had complete mastery of all his faculties. For the first time he was in possession of his full powers. The vistas which opened before him seemed to have no perceptible end. But the mood had none of the restlessness or feverish desire to add one delight to another which had hitherto marked, and somewhat spoilt, the most rapturous of his imaginings. It was a mood that took such clear-eyed account of the conditions of human life that he was not disturbed in the least by the gliding presence of a taxicab, and without agitation he perceived that Katharine was conscious of it also, and turned her head in that direction. Their halting steps acknowledged the desirability of engaging the cab; and they stopped simultaneously, and signed to it.

"Then you will let me know your decision as soon as you can?" he asked, with his hand on the door.

She hesitated for a moment. She could not immediately recall what the question was that she had to decide.

"I will write," she said vaguely. "No," she added, in a second, bethinking her of the difficulties of writing anything decided upon a question to which she had paid no attention, "I don't see how to manage it."

She stood looking at Denham, considering and hesitating, with her foot upon the step. He guessed her difficulties; he knew in a second that she had heard nothing; he knew everything that she felt.

"There's only one place to discuss things satisfactorily that I know of," he said quickly; "that's Kew."

"Kew?"

"Kew," he repeated, with immense decision. He shut the door and gave her address to the driver. She instantly was conveyed away from him, and her cab joined the knotted stream of vehicles, each marked by a light, and indistinguishable one from the other. He stood watching for a moment, and then, as if swept by some fierce impulse, from the spot where they had stood, he turned, crossed the road at a rapid pace, and disappeared.

He walked on upon the impetus of this last mood of almost supernatural exaltation until he reached a narrow street, at this hour empty of traffic and passengers. Here, whether it was the shops with their shuttered windows, the smooth and silvered curve of the wood pavement, or a natural ebb of feeling, his exaltation slowly oozed and deserted him. He was now conscious of the loss that follows any revelation; he had lost something in speaking to Katharine, for, after all, was the Katharine whom he loved the same as the real Katharine? She had transcended her entirely at moments; her skirt had blown, her feather waved, her voice spoken; yes, but how terrible sometimes the pause between the voice of one's dreams and the voice that comes from the object of one's dreams! He felt a mixture of disgust and pity at the figure cut by human beings when they try to carry out, in practice, what they have the power to conceive. How small both he and Katharine had appeared when they issued from the cloud of thought that enveloped them! He recalled the small, inexpressive, commonplace words in which they had tried to communicate with each other; he repeated them over to himself. By repeating Katharine's words, he came in a few moments to such a sense of her presence that he worshipped her more than ever. But she was engaged to be married, he remembered with a start. The strength of his feeling was revealed to him instantly, and he gave himself up to an irresistible rage and sense of frustration. The image of Rodney came before him with every circumstance of folly and indignity. That little pink-cheeked dancing-master to marry Katharine? that gibbering ass with the face of a monkey on an organ? that posing, vain, fantastical fop? with his tragedies and his comedies, his innumerable spites and prides and pettinesses? Lord! marry Rodney! She must be as great a fool as he was. His bitterness took possession of him, and as he sat in the corner of the underground carriage, he looked as stark an image of unapproachable severity as could be imagined. Directly he reached home he sat down at his table, and began to write Katharine a long, wild, mad letter, begging her for both their sakes to break with Rodney, imploring her not to do what would destroy for ever the one beauty, the one truth, the one hope; not to be a traitor, not to be a deserter, for if she were—and he wound up with a quiet and brief assertion that, whatever she did or left undone, he would believe to be the best, and accept from her with gratitude. He covered sheet after sheet, and heard the early carts starting for London before he went to bed.

24

The first signs of spring, even such as make themselves felt towards the middle of February, not only produce little white and violet flowers in the more sheltered corners of woods and gardens, but bring to birth thoughts and desires comparable to those faintly colored and sweetly scented petals in the minds of men and women. Lives frozen by age, so far as the present is concerned, to a hard surface, which neither reflects nor yields, at this season become soft and fluid, reflecting the shapes and colors of the present, as well as the shapes and colors of the past. In the case of Mrs. Hilbery, these early spring days were chiefly upsetting inasmuch as they caused a general quickening of her emotional powers, which, as far as the past was concerned, had never suffered much diminution. But in the spring her desire for expression invariably increased. She was haunted by the ghosts of phrases. She gave herself up to a sensual delight in the combinations of words. She sought them in the pages of her favorite authors. She made them for herself on scraps of paper, and rolled them on her tongue when there seemed no occasion for such eloquence. She was upheld in these excursions by the certainty that no language could outdo the splendor of her father's memory, and although her efforts did not notably further the end of his biography, she was under the impression of living more in his shade at such times than at others. No one can escape the power of language, let alone those of English birth brought up from childhood, as Mrs. Hilbery had been, to disport themselves now in the Saxon plainness, now in the Latin splendor of the tongue, and stored with memories, as she was, of old poets exuberating in an infinity of vocables. Even Katharine was slightly affected against her better judgment by her mother's enthusiasm. Not that her judgment could altogether acquiesce in the necessity for a study of Shakespeare's sonnets as a preliminary to the fifth chapter of her grandfather's biography. Beginning with a perfectly frivolous jest, Mrs. Hilbery had evolved a theory that Anne Hathaway had a way, among other things, of writing Shakespeare's sonnets; the idea, struck out to enliven a party of professors, who forwarded a number of privately printed manuals within the next few days for her instruction, had submerged her in a flood of Elizabethan literature; she had come half to believe in her joke, which was, she said, at least as good as other people's facts, and all her fancy for the time being centered upon Stratford-on-Avon. She had a plan, she told Katharine, when, rather later than usual, Katharine came into the room the morning after her walk by the river, for visiting Shakespeare's tomb. Any fact about the poet had become, for the moment, of far greater interest to her than the immediate present, and the certainty that there was existing in England a spot of ground where Shakespeare had undoubtedly stood, where his very bones lay directly beneath one's feet, was so absorbing to her on this particular occasion that she greeted her daughter with the exclamation:

"D'you think he ever passed this house?"

The question, for the moment, seemed to Katharine to have reference to Ralph Denham.

"On his way to Blackfriars, I mean," Mrs. Hilbery continued, "for you know the latest discovery is that he owned a house there."

Katharine still looked about her in perplexity, and Mrs. Hilbery added:

"Which is a proof that he wasn't as poor as they've sometimes said. I should like to think that he had enough, though I don't in the least want him to be rich."

Then, perceiving her daughter's expression of perplexity, Mrs. Hilbery burst out laughing.

"My dear, I'm not talking about *your* William, though that's another reason for liking him. I'm talking, I'm thinking, I'm dreaming of *my* William—William Shakespeare, of course. Isn't it odd," she mused, standing at the window and tapping gently upon the pane, "that for all one can see, that dear old thing in the blue bonnet, crossing the road with her basket on her arm, has never heard that there was such a person? Yet it all goes on: lawyers hurrying to their work, cabmen squabbling for their fares, little boys rolling their hoops, little girls throwing bread to the gulls, as if there weren't a Shakespeare in the world. I should like to stand at that crossing all day long and say: 'People, read Shakespeare!'"

Katharine sat down at her table and opened a long dusty envelope. As Shelley was mentioned in the course of the letter as if he were alive, it had, of course, considerable value. Her immediate task was to decide whether the whole letter should be printed, or only the paragraph which mentioned Shelley's name, and she reached out for a pen and held it in readiness to do justice upon the sheet. Her pen, however, remained in the air. Almost surreptitiously she slipped a clean sheet in front of her, and her hand, descending, began drawing square boxes halved and quartered by straight lines, and then circles which underwent the same process of dissection.

"Katharine! I've hit upon a brilliant idea!" Mrs. Hilbery exclaimed—"to lay out, say, a hundred pounds or so on copies of Shakespeare, and give them to working men. Some of your clever friends who get up meetings might help us, Katharine. And that might lead to a playhouse, where we could all take parts. You'd be Rosalind—but you've a dash of the old nurse in you. Your father's Hamlet, come to years of discretion; and I'm—well, I'm a bit of them all; I'm quite a large bit of the fool, but the fools in Shakespeare say all the clever things. Now who shall William be? A hero? Hotspur? Henry the Fifth? No, William's got a touch of Hamlet in him, too. I can fancy that William talks to himself when he's alone. Ah, Katharine, you must say very beautiful things when you're together!" she added wistfully, with a glance at her daughter, who had told her nothing about the dinner the night before.

"Oh, we talk a lot of nonsense," said Katharine, hiding her slip of paper as her mother stood by her, and spreading the old letter about Shelley in front of her.

"It won't seem to you nonsense in ten years' time," said Mrs. Hilbery. "Believe me, Katharine, you'll look back on these days afterwards; you'll remember all the silly things you've said; and you'll find that your life has been built on them. The best of life is built on what we say when we're in love. It isn't nonsense, Katharine," she urged, "it's the truth, it's the only truth."

Katharine was on the point of interrupting her mother, and then she was on the point of confiding in her. They came strangely close together sometimes. But, while she hesitated and sought for words not too direct, her mother had recourse to Shakespeare, and turned page after page, set upon finding some quotation which said all this about love far, far better than she could. Accordingly, Katharine did nothing but scrub one of her circles an intense black with her pencil, in the midst of which process the telephone-bell rang, and she left the room to answer it.

When she returned, Mrs. Hilbery had found not the passage she wanted, but another of exquisite beauty as she justly observed, looking up for a second to ask Katharine who that was?

"Mary Datchet," Katharine replied briefly.

"Ah—I half wish I'd called you Mary, but it wouldn't have gone with Hilbery, and it wouldn't have gone with Rodney. Now this isn't the passage I wanted. (I never can find what I want.) But it's spring; it's the daffodils; it's the green fields; it's the birds."

She was cut short in her quotation by another imperative telephone-bell. Once more Katharine left the room.

"My dear child, how odious the triumphs of science are!" Mrs. Hilbery exclaimed on her return. "They'll be linking us with the moon next—but who was that?"

"William," Katharine replied yet more briefly.

"I'll forgive William anything, for I'm certain that there aren't any Williams in the moon. I hope he's coming to luncheon?"

"He's coming to tea."

"Well, that's better than nothing, and I promise to leave you alone."

"There's no need for you to do that," said Katharine.

She swept her hand over the faded sheet, and drew herself up squarely to the table as if she refused to waste time any longer. The gesture was not lost upon her mother. It hinted at the existence of something stern and unapproachable in her daughter's character, which struck chill upon her, as the sight of poverty, or drunkenness, or the logic with which Mr. Hilbery sometimes thought good to demolish her certainty of an approaching millennium struck chill upon her. She went back to her own table, and putting on her spectacles with a curious expression of quiet humility, addressed herself for the first time that morning to the task before her. The shock with an unsympathetic world had a sobering effect on her. For once, her industry surpassed her daughter's. Katharine could not reduce the world to that particular perspective in which Harriet Martineau, for instance, was a figure of solid importance, and possessed of a genuine relationship to this figure or to that date. Singularly enough, the sharp call of the telephone-bell still echoed in her ear, and her body and mind were in a state of tension, as if, at any moment, she might hear another summons of greater interest to her than the whole of the nineteenth century. She did not clearly realize what this call was to be; but when the ears have got into the habit of listening, they go on listening involuntarily, and thus Katharine spent the greater part of the morning in listening to a variety of sounds in the back streets of Chelsea. For the first time in her life, probably, she wished that Mrs. Hilbery would not keep so closely to her work. A quotation from Shakespeare would not have come amiss. Now and again she heard a sigh from her mother's table, but that was the only proof she gave of her existence, and Katharine did not think of connecting it with the square aspect of her own position at the table, or, perhaps, she would have thrown her pen down and told her mother the reason of her restlessness. The only writing she managed to accomplish in the course of the morning was one letter, addressed to her cousin, Cassandra Otway—a rambling letter, long, affectionate, playful and commanding all at once. She bade Cassandra put her creatures in the charge of a groom, and come to them for a week or so. They would go and hear some music together. Cassandra's dislike of rational society, she said, was an affectation fast hardening into a prejudice, which would, in the long run, isolate her from all interesting people and pursuits. She was finishing the sheet when the sound she was anticipating all the time actually struck upon her ears. She jumped up hastily, and slammed the door with a sharpness which made Mrs. Hilbery start. Where was Katharine off to? In her preoccupied state she had not heard the bell.

The alcove on the stairs, in which the telephone was placed, was screened for privacy by a curtain of purple velvet. It was a pocket for superfluous possessions, such as exist in most houses which harbor the wreckage of three generations. Prints of great-uncles, famed for their prowess in the East, hung above Chinese teapots, whose sides were riveted by little gold stitches, and the precious teapots, again, stood upon bookcases containing the complete works of William Cowper and Sir Walter Scott. The thread of sound, issuing from the telephone, was always colored by the surroundings which received it, so it seemed to Katharine. Whose voice was now going to combine with them, or to strike a discord?

"Whose voice?" she asked herself, hearing a man inquire, with great determination, for her number. The unfamiliar voice now asked for Miss Hilbery. Out of all the welter of voices which crowd round the far end of the telephone, out of the enormous range of possibilities, whose voice, what possibility, was this? A pause gave her time to ask herself this question. It was solved next moment.

"I've looked out the train. . . . Early on Saturday afternoon would suit me best. . . . I'm Ralph Denham. . . . But I'll write it down. . . ."

With more than the usual sense of being impinged upon the point of a bayonet, Katharine replied:

"I think I could come. I'll look at my engagements. . . . Hold on."

She dropped the machine, and looked fixedly at the print of the great-uncle who had not ceased to gaze, with an air of amiable authority, into a world which, as yet, beheld no symptoms of the Indian Mutiny. And yet, gently swinging against the wall, within the black tube, was a voice which recked nothing of Uncle James, of China teapots, or of red velvet curtains. She watched the oscillation of the tube, and at the same moment became conscious of the individuality of the house in which she stood; she heard the soft domestic sounds of regular existence upon staircases and floors above her head, and movements through the wall in the house next door. She had no very clear vision of Denham himself, when she lifted the telephone to her lips and replied that she thought Saturday would suit her. She hoped that he would not say good-bye at once, although she felt no particular anxiety to attend to what he was saying, and began, even while he spoke, to think of her own upper room, with its books, its papers pressed between the leaves of dictionaries, and the table that could be cleared for work. She replaced the instrument, thoughtfully; her restlessness was assuaged; she finished her letter to Cassandra without difficulty, addressed the envelope, and fixed the stamp with her usual quick decision.

A bunch of anemones caught Mrs. Hilbery's eye when they had finished luncheon. The blue and purple and white of the bowl, standing in a pool of variegated light on a polished Chippendale table in the drawing-room window, made her stop dead with an exclamation of pleasure.

"Who is lying ill in bed, Katharine?" she demanded. "Which of our friends wants cheering up? Who feels that they've been forgotten and passed over, and that nobody wants them? Whose water rates are overdue, and the cook leaving in a temper without waiting for her wages? There was somebody I know——" she concluded, but for the moment the name of this desirable acquaintance escaped her. The best representative of the forlorn company whose day would be brightened by a bunch of anemones was, in Katharine's opinion, the widow of a general living in the Cromwell Road. In default of the actually destitute and starving, whom she would much have preferred, Mrs. Hilbery was forced to acknowledge her claims, for though in comfortable circumstances, she was extremely dull, unattractive, connected in some oblique fashion with literature, and had been touched to the verge of tears, on one occasion, by an afternoon call.

It happened that Mrs. Hilbery had an engagement elsewhere, so that the task of taking the flowers to the Cromwell Road fell upon Katharine. She took her letter to Cassandra with her, meaning to post it in the first pillar-box she came to. When, however, she was fairly out of doors, and constantly invited by pillar-boxes and post-offices to slip her envelope down their scarlet throats, she forbore. She made absurd excuses, as that she did not wish to cross the road, or that she was certain to pass another post-office in a more central position a little farther on. The longer she held the letter in her hand, however, the more persistently certain questions pressed upon her, as if from a collection of voices in the air. These invisible people wished to be informed whether she was engaged to William Rodney, or was the engagement broken off? Was it right, they asked, to invite Cassandra for a visit, and was William Rodney in love with her, or likely to fall in love? Then the questioners paused for a moment, and resumed as if another side of the problem had just come to their notice. What did Ralph Denham mean by what he said to you last night? Do you consider that he is in love with you? Is it right to consent to a solitary walk with him, and what advice are you going to give him about his future? Has William Rodney cause to be jealous of your conduct, and what do you propose to do about Mary Datchet? What are you going to do? What does honor require you to do? they repeated.

"Good Heavens!" Katharine exclaimed, after listening to all these remarks, "I suppose I ought to make up my mind."

But the debate was a formal skirmishing, a pastime to gain breathing-space. Like all people brought up in a tradition, Katharine was able, within ten minutes or so, to reduce any moral difficulty to its traditional shape and solve it by the traditional answers. The book of wisdom lay open, if not upon her mother's knee, upon the knees of many uncles and aunts. She had only to consult them, and they would at once turn to the right page and read out an answer exactly suited to one in her position. The rules which should govern the behavior of an unmarried woman are written in red ink, graved upon marble, if, by some freak of nature, it should fall out that the unmarried woman has not the same writing scored upon her heart. She was ready to believe that some people are fortunate enough to reject, accept, resign, or lay down their lives at the bidding of traditional authority; she could envy them; but in her case the questions became phantoms directly she tried seriously to find an answer, which proved that the traditional answer would be of no use to her individually. Yet it had served so many people, she thought, glancing at the rows of houses on either side of her, where families, whose incomes must be between a thousand and fifteen-hundred a year lived, and kept, perhaps, three servants, and draped their windows with curtains which were always thick and generally dirty, and must, she thought, since you could only see a looking-glass gleaming above a sideboard on which a dish of apples was set, keep the room inside very dark. But she turned her head away, observing that this was not a method of thinking the matter out.

The only truth which she could discover was the truth of what she herself felt—a frail beam when compared with the broad illumination shed by the eyes of all the people who are in agreement to see together; but having rejected the visionary voices, she had no choice but to make this her guide through the dark masses which confronted her. She tried to follow her beam, with an expression upon her face which would have made any passer-by think her reprehensibly and almost ridiculously detached from the surrounding scene. One would have felt alarmed lest this young and striking woman were about to do something eccentric. But her beauty saved her from the worst fate that can befall a pedestrian; people looked at her, but they did not laugh. To seek a true feeling among the chaos of the unfeelings or half-feelings of life, to recognize it when found, and to accept the consequences of the discovery, draws lines upon the smoothest brow, while it quickens the light of the eyes; it is a pursuit which is alternately bewildering, debasing, and exalting, and, as Katharine speedily found, her discoveries gave her equal cause for surprise, shame, and intense anxiety. Much depended, as usual, upon the interpretation of the word love; which word came up again and again, whether she considered Rodney, Denham, Mary Datchet, or herself; and in each case it seemed to stand for something different, and yet for something unmistakable and something not to be passed by. For the more she looked into the confusion of lives which, instead of running parallel, had suddenly intersected each other, the more distinctly she seemed to convince herself that there was no other light on them than was shed by this strange illumination, and no other path save the one upon which it threw its beams. Her blindness in the case of Rodney, her attempt to match his true feeling with her false feeling, was a failure never to be sufficiently condemned; indeed, she could only pay it the tribute of leaving it a black and naked landmark unburied by attempt at oblivion or excuse.

With this to humiliate there was much to exalt. She thought of three different scenes; she thought of Mary sitting upright and saying, "I'm in love—I'm in love"; she thought of Rodney losing his self-consciousness among the dead leaves, and speaking with the abandonment of a child; she thought of Denham leaning upon the stone parapet and talking to the distant sky, so that she thought him mad. Her mind, passing from Mary to Denham, from William to Cassandra, and from Denham to herself—if, as she rather doubted, Denham's state of mind was connected with herself—seemed to be tracing out the lines of some symmetrical pattern, some arrangement of life, which invested, if not herself, at least the others, not only with interest, but with a kind of tragic beauty. She had a fantastic picture of them upholding splendid palaces upon their bent backs. They were the lantern-bearers, whose lights, scattered among the crowd, wove a pattern, dissolving, joining, meeting again in combination. Half forming such conceptions as these in her rapid walk along the dreary streets of South Kensington, she determined that, whatever else might be obscure, she must further the objects of Mary, Denham, William, and Cassandra. The way was not apparent. No course of action seemed to her indubitably right. All she achieved by her thinking was the conviction that, in such a cause, no risk was too great; and that, far from making any rules for herself or others, she would let difficulties accumulate unsolved, situations widen their jaws unsatiated, while she maintained a position of absolute and fearless independence. So she could best serve the people who loved.

Read in the light of this exaltation, there was a new meaning in the words which her mother had penciled upon the card attached to the bunch of anemones. The door of the house in the Cromwell Road opened; gloomy vistas of passage and staircase were revealed; such light as there was seemed to be concentrated upon a silver salver of visiting-cards, whose black borders suggested that the widow's friends had all suffered the same bereavement. The parlor-maid could hardly be expected to fathom the meaning of the grave tone in which the young lady proffered the flowers, with Mrs. Hilbery's love; and the door shut upon the offering.

The sight of a face, the slam of a door, are both rather destructive of exaltation in the abstract; and, as she walked back to Chelsea, Katharine had her doubts whether anything would come of her resolves. If you cannot make sure of people, however, you can hold fairly fast to figures, and in some way or other her thought about such problems as she was wont to consider worked in happily with her mood as to her friends' lives. She reached home rather late for tea.

On the ancient Dutch chest in the hall she perceived one or two hats, coats, and walking-sticks, and the sound of voices reached her as she stood outside the drawing-room door. Her mother gave a little cry as she came in; a cry which conveyed to Katharine the fact that she was late, that the teacups and milk-jugs were in a conspiracy of disobedience, and that she must immediately take her place at the head of the table and pour out tea for the guests. Augustus Pelham, the diarist, liked a calm atmosphere in which to tell his stories; he liked attention; he liked to elicit little facts, little stories, about the past and the great dead, from such distinguished characters as Mrs. Hilbery for the nourishment of his diary, for whose sake he frequented tea-tables and ate yearly an enormous quantity of buttered toast. He, therefore, welcomed Katharine with relief, and she had merely to shake hands with Rodney and to greet the American lady who had come to be shown the relics, before the talk started again on the broad lines of reminiscence and discussion which were familiar to her.

Yet, even with this thick veil between them, she could not help looking at Rodney, as if she could detect what had happened to him since they met. It was in vain. His clothes, even the white slip, the pearl in his tie, seemed to intercept her quick glance, and to proclaim the futility of such inquiries of a discreet, urbane gentleman, who balanced his cup of tea and poised a slice of bread and butter on the edge of the saucer. He would not meet her eye, but that could be accounted for by his activity in serving and helping, and the polite alacrity with which he was answering the questions of the American visitor.

It was certainly a sight to daunt any one coming in with a head full of theories about love. The voices of the invisible questioners were reinforced by the scene round the table, and sounded with a tremendous self-confidence, as if they had behind them the common sense of twenty generations, together with the immediate approval of Mr. Augustus Pelham, Mrs. Vermont Bankes, William Rodney, and, possibly, Mrs. Hilbery herself. Katharine set her teeth, not entirely in the metaphorical sense, for her hand, obeying the impulse towards definite action, laid firmly upon the table beside her an envelope which she had been grasping all this time in complete forgetfulness. The address was uppermost, and a moment later she saw William's eye rest upon it as he rose to fulfil some duty with a plate. His expression instantly changed. He did what he was on the point of doing, and then looked at Katharine with a look which revealed enough of his confusion to show her that he was not entirely represented by his appearance. In a minute or two he proved himself at a loss with Mrs. Vermont Bankes, and Mrs. Hilbery, aware of the silence with her usual quickness, suggested that, perhaps, it was now time that Mrs. Bankes should be shown "our things."

Katharine accordingly rose, and led the way to the little inner room with the pictures and the books. Mrs. Bankes and Rodney followed her.

She turned on the lights, and began directly in her low, pleasant voice: "This table is my grandfather's writing-table. Most of the later poems were written at it. And this is his pen—the last pen he ever used." She took it in her hand and paused for the right number of seconds. "Here," she continued, "is the original manuscript of the 'Ode to Winter.' The early manuscripts are far less corrected than the later ones, as you will see directly. . . . Oh, do take it yourself," she added, as Mrs. Bankes asked, in an awestruck tone of voice, for that privilege, and began a preliminary unbuttoning of her white kid gloves.

"You are wonderfully like your grandfather, Miss Hilbery," the American lady observed, gazing from Katharine to the portrait, "especially about the eyes. Come, now, I expect she writes poetry herself, doesn't she?" she asked in a jocular tone, turning to William. "Quite one's ideal of a poet, is it not, Mr. Rodney? I cannot tell you what a privilege I feel it to be standing just here with the poet's granddaughter. You must know we think a great deal of your grandfather in America, Miss Hilbery. We have societies for reading him aloud. What! His very own slippers!" Laying aside the manuscript, she hastily grasped the old shoes, and remained for a moment dumb in contemplation of them.

While Katharine went on steadily with her duties as show-woman, Rodney examined intently a row of little drawings which he knew by heart already. His disordered state of mind made it necessary for him to take advantage of these little respites, as if he had been out in a high wind and must straighten his dress in the first shelter he reached. His calm was only superficial, as he knew too well; it did not exist much below the surface of tie, waistcoat, and white slip.

On getting out of bed that morning he had fully made up his mind to ignore what had been said the night before; he had been convinced, by the sight of Denham, that his love for Katharine was passionate, and when he addressed her early that morning on the telephone, he had meant his cheerful but authoritative tones to convey to her the fact that, after a night of madness, they were as indissolubly engaged as ever. But when he reached his office his torments began. He found a letter from Cassandra waiting for him. She had read his play, and had taken the very first opportunity to write and tell him what she thought of it. She knew, she wrote, that her praise meant absolutely nothing; but still, she had sat up all night; she thought this, that, and the other; she was full of enthusiasm most elaborately scratched out in places, but enough was written plain to gratify William's vanity exceedingly. She was quite intelligent enough to say the right things, or, even more charmingly, to hint at them. In other ways, too, it was a very charming letter. She told him about her music, and about a Suffrage meeting to which Henry had taken her, and she asserted, half seriously, that she had learnt the Greek alphabet, and found it "fascinating." The word was underlined. Had she laughed when she drew that line? Was she ever serious? Didn't the letter show the most engaging compound of enthusiasm and spirit and whimsicality, all tapering into a flame of girlish freakishness, which flitted, for the rest of the morning, as a will-o'-the-wisp, across Rodney's landscape. He could not resist beginning an answer to her there and then. He found it particularly delightful to shape a style which should express the bowing and curtsying, advancing and retreating, which are characteristic of one of the many million partnerships of men and women. Katharine never trod that particular measure, he could not help reflecting; Katharine—Cassandra; Cassandra—Katharine—they alternated in his consciousness all day long. It was all very well to dress oneself carefully, compose one's face, and start off punctually at half-past four to a tea-party in Cheyne Walk, but Heaven only knew what would come of it all, and when Katharine, after sitting silent with her usual immobility, wantonly drew from her pocket and slapped down on the table beneath his eyes a letter addressed to Cassandra herself, his composure deserted him. What did she mean by her behavior?

He looked up sharply from his row of little pictures. Katharine was disposing of the American lady in far too arbitrary a fashion. Surely the victim herself must see how foolish her enthusiasms appeared in the eyes of the poet's granddaughter. Katharine never made any attempt to spare people's feelings, he reflected; and, being himself very sensitive to all shades of comfort and discomfort, he cut short the auctioneer's catalog, which Katharine was reeling off more and more absent-mindedly, and took Mrs. Vermont Bankes, with a queer sense of fellowship in suffering, under his own protection.

But within a few minutes the American lady had completed her inspection, and inclining her head in a little nod of reverential farewell to the poet and his shoes, she was escorted downstairs by Rodney. Katharine stayed by herself in the little room. The ceremony of ancestor-worship had been more than usually oppressive to her. Moreover, the room was becoming crowded beyond the bounds of order. Only that morning a heavily insured proof-sheet had reached them from a collector in Australia, which recorded a change of the poet's mind about a very famous phrase, and, therefore, had claims to the honor of glazing and framing. But was there room for it? Must it be hung on the staircase, or should some other relic give place to do it honor? Feeling unable to decide the question, Katharine glanced at the portrait of her grandfather, as if to ask his opinion. The artist who had painted it was now out of fashion, and by dint of showing it to visitors, Katharine had almost ceased to see anything but a glow of faintly pleasing pink and brown tints, enclosed within a circular scroll of gilt laurel-leaves. The young man who was her grandfather looked vaguely over her head. The sensual lips were slightly parted, and gave the face an expression of beholding something lovely or miraculous vanishing or just rising upon the rim of the distance. The expression repeated itself curiously upon Katharine's face as she gazed up into his. They were the same age, or very nearly so. She wondered what he was looking for; were there waves beating upon a shore for him, too, she wondered, and heroes riding through the leaf-hung forests? For perhaps the first time in her life she thought of him as a man, young, unhappy, tempestuous, full of desires and faults; for the first time she realized him for herself, and not from her mother's memory. He might have been her brother, she thought. It seemed to her that they were akin, with the mysterious kinship of blood which makes it seem possible to interpret the sights which the eyes of the dead behold so intently, or even to believe that they look with us upon our present joys and sorrows. He would have understood, she thought, suddenly; and instead of laying her withered flowers upon his shrine, she brought him her own perplexities—perhaps a gift of greater value, should the dead be conscious of gifts, than flowers and incense and adoration. Doubts, questionings, and despondencies she felt, as she looked up, would be more welcome to him than homage, and he would hold them but a very small burden if she gave him, also, some share in what she suffered and achieved. The depth of her own pride and love were not more apparent to her than the sense that the dead asked neither flowers nor regrets, but a share in the life which they had given her, the life which they had lived.

Rodney found her a moment later sitting beneath her grandfather's portrait. She laid her hand on the seat next her in a friendly way, and said:

"Come and sit down, William. How glad I was you were here! I felt myself getting ruder and ruder."

"You are not good at hiding your feelings," he returned dryly.

"Oh, don't scold me—I've had a horrid afternoon." She told him how she had taken the flowers to Mrs. McCormick, and how South Kensington impressed her as the preserve of officers' widows. She described how the door had opened, and what gloomy avenues of busts and palm-trees and umbrellas had been revealed to her. She spoke lightly, and succeeded in putting him at his ease. Indeed, he rapidly became too much at his ease to persist in a condition of cheerful neutrality. He felt his composure slipping from him. Katharine made it seem so natural to ask her to help him, or advise him, to say straight out what he had in his mind. The letter from Cassandra was heavy in his pocket. There was also the letter to Cassandra lying on the table in the next room. The atmosphere seemed charged with Cassandra. But, unless Katharine began the subject of her own accord, he could not even hint—he must ignore the whole affair; it was the part of a gentleman to preserve a bearing that was, as far as he could make it, the bearing of an undoubting lover. At intervals he sighed deeply. He talked rather more quickly than usual about the possibility that some of the operas of Mozart would be played in the summer. He had received a notice, he said, and at once produced a pocket-book stuffed with papers, and began shuffling them in search. He held a thick envelope between his finger and thumb, as if the notice from the opera company had become in some way inseparably attached to it.

"A letter from Cassandra?" said Katharine, in the easiest voice in the world, looking over his shoulder. "I've just written to ask her to come here, only I forgot to post it."

He handed her the envelope in silence. She took it, extracted the sheets, and read the letter through.

The reading seemed to Rodney to take an intolerably long time.

"Yes," she observed at length, "a very charming letter."

Rodney's face was half turned away, as if in bashfulness. Her view of his profile almost moved her to laughter. She glanced through the pages once more.

"I see no harm," William blurted out, "in helping her—with Greek, for example—if she really cares for that sort of thing."

"There's no reason why she shouldn't care," said Katharine, consulting the pages once more. "In fact—ah, here it is—'The Greek alphabet is absolutely *fascinating.*' Obviously she does care."

"Well, Greek may be rather a large order. I was thinking chiefly of English. Her criticisms of my play, though they're too generous, evidently immature—she can't be more than twenty-two, I suppose?—they certainly show the sort of thing one wants: real feeling for poetry, understanding, not formed, of course, but it's at the root of everything after all. There'd be no harm in lending her books?"

"No. Certainly not."

"But if it—hum—led to a correspondence? I mean, Katharine, I take it, without going into matters which seem to me a little morbid, I mean," he floundered, "you, from your point of view, feel that there's nothing disagreeable to you in the notion? If so, you've only to speak, and I never think of it again."

She was surprised by the violence of her desire that he never should think of it again. For an instant it seemed to her impossible to surrender an intimacy, which might not be the intimacy of love, but was certainly the intimacy of true friendship, to any woman in the world. Cassandra would never understand him—she was not good enough for him. The letter seemed to her a letter of flattery—a letter addressed to his weakness, which it made her angry to think was known to another. For he was not weak; he had the rare strength of doing what he promised—she had only to speak, and he would never think of Cassandra again.

She paused. Rodney guessed the reason. He was amazed.

"She loves me," he thought. The woman he admired more than any one in the world, loved him, as he had given up hope that she would ever love him. And now that for the first time he was sure of her love, he resented it. He felt it as a fetter, an encumbrance, something which made them both, but him in particular, ridiculous. He was in her power completely, but his eyes were open and he was no longer her slave or her dupe. He would be her master in future. The instant prolonged itself as Katharine realized the strength of her desire to speak the words that should keep William for ever, and the baseness of the temptation which assailed her to make the movement, or speak the word, which he had often begged her for, which she was now near enough to feeling. She held the letter in her hand. She sat silent.

At this moment there was a stir in the other room; the voice of Mrs. Hilbery was heard talking of proof-sheets rescued by miraculous providence from butcher's ledgers in Australia; the curtain separating one room from the other was drawn apart, and Mrs. Hilbery and Augustus Pelham stood in the doorway. Mrs. Hilbery stopped short. She looked at her daughter, and at the man her daughter was to marry, with her peculiar smile that always seemed to tremble on the brink of satire.

"The best of all my treasures, Mr. Pelham!" she exclaimed. "Don't move, Katharine. Sit still, William. Mr. Pelham will come another day."

Mr. Pelham looked, smiled, bowed, and, as his hostess had moved on, followed her without a word. The curtain was drawn again either by him or by Mrs. Hilbery.

But her mother had settled the question somehow. Katharine doubted no longer.

"As I told you last night," she said, "I think it's your duty, if there's a chance that you care for Cassandra, to discover what your feeling is for her now. It's your duty to her, as well as to me. But we must tell my mother. We can't go on pretending."

"That is entirely in your hands, of course," said Rodney, with an immediate return to the manner of a formal man of honor.

"Very well," said Katharine.

Directly he left her she would go to her mother, and explain that the engagement was at an end—or it might be better that they should go together?

"But, Katharine," Rodney began, nervously attempting to stuff Cassandra's sheets back into their envelope; "if Cassandra—should Cassandra—you've asked Cassandra to stay with you."

"Yes; but I've not posted the letter."

He crossed his knees in a discomfited silence. By all his codes it was impossible to ask a woman with whom he had just broken off his engagement to help him to become acquainted with another woman with a view to his falling in love with her. If it was announced that their engagement was over, a long and complete separation would inevitably follow; in those circumstances, letters and gifts were returned; after years of distance the severed couple met, perhaps at an evening party, and touched hands uncomfortably with an indifferent word or two. He would be cast off completely; he would have to trust to his own resources. He could never mention Cassandra to Katharine again; for months, and doubtless years, he would never see Katharine again; anything might happen to her in his absence.

Katharine was almost as well aware of his perplexities as he was. She knew in what direction complete generosity pointed the way; but pride—for to remain engaged to Rodney and to cover his experiments hurt what was nobler in her than mere vanity—fought for its life.

"I'm to give up my freedom for an indefinite time," she thought, "in order that William may see Cassandra here at his ease. He's not the courage to manage it without my help—he's too much of a coward to tell me openly what he wants. He hates the notion of a public breach. He wants to keep us both."

When she reached this point, Rodney pocketed the letter and elaborately looked at his watch. Although the action meant that he resigned Cassandra, for he knew his own incompetence and distrusted himself entirely, and lost Katharine, for whom his feeling was profound though unsatisfactory, still it appeared to him that there was nothing else left for him to do. He was forced to go, leaving Katharine free, as he had said, to tell her mother that the engagement was at an end. But to do what plain duty required of an honorable man, cost an effort which only a day or two ago would have been inconceivable to him. That a relationship such as he had glanced at with desire could be possible between him and Katharine, he would have been the first, two days ago, to deny with indignation. But now his life had changed; his attitude had changed; his feelings were different; new aims and possibilities had been shown him, and they had an almost irresistible fascination and force. The training of a life of thirty-five years had not left him defenceless; he was still master of his dignity; he rose, with a mind made up to an irrevocable farewell.

"I leave you, then," he said, standing up and holding out his hand with an effort that left him pale, but lent him dignity, "to tell your mother that our engagement is ended by your desire."

She took his hand and held it.

"You don't trust me?" she said.

"I do, absolutely," he replied.

"No. You don't trust me to help you. . . . I could help you?"

"I'm hopeless without your help!" he exclaimed passionately, but withdrew his hand and turned his back. When he faced her, she thought that she saw him for the first time without disguise.

"It's useless to pretend that I don't understand what you're offering, Katharine. I admit what you say. Speaking to you perfectly frankly, I believe at this moment that I do love your cousin; there is a chance that, with your help, I might—but no," he broke off, "it's impossible, it's wrong—I'm infinitely to blame for having allowed this situation to arise."

"Sit beside me. Let's consider sensibly——"

"Your sense has been our undoing——" he groaned.

"I accept the responsibility."

"Ah, but can I allow that?" he exclaimed. "It would mean—for we must face it, Katharine—that we let our engagement stand for the time nominally; in fact, of course, your freedom would be absolute."

"And yours too."

"Yes, we should both be free. Let us say that I saw Cassandra once, twice, perhaps, under these conditions; and then if, as I think certain, the whole thing proves a dream, we tell your mother instantly. Why not tell her now, indeed, under pledge of secrecy?"

"Why not? It would be over London in ten minutes, besides, she would never even remotely understand."

"Your father, then? This secrecy is detestable—it's dishonorable."

"My father would understand even less than my mother."

"Ah, who could be expected to understand?" Rodney groaned; "but it's from your point of view that we must look at it. It's not only asking too much, it's putting you into a position—a position in which I could not endure to see my own sister."

"We're not brothers and sisters," she said impatiently, "and if we can't decide, who can? I'm not talking nonsense," she proceeded. "I've done my best to think this out from every point of view, and I've come to the conclusion that there are risks which have to be taken—though I don't deny that they hurt horribly."

"Katharine, you mind? You'll mind too much."

"No I shan't," she said stoutly. "I shall mind a good deal, but I'm prepared for that; I shall get through it, because you will help me. You'll both help me. In fact, we'll help each other. That's a Christian doctrine, isn't it?"

"It sounds more like Paganism to me," Rodney groaned, as he reviewed the situation into which her Christian doctrine was plunging them.

And yet he could not deny that a divine relief possessed him, and that the future, instead of wearing a lead-colored mask, now blossomed with a thousand varied gaieties and excitements. He was actually to see Cassandra within a week or perhaps less, and he was more anxious to know the date of her arrival than he could own even to himself. It seemed base to be so anxious to pluck this fruit of Katharine's unexampled generosity and of his own contemptible baseness. And yet, though he used these words automatically, they had now no meaning. He was not debased in his own eyes by what he had done, and as for praising Katharine, were they not partners, conspirators, people bent upon the same quest together, so that to praise the pursuit of a common end as an act of generosity was meaningless. He took her hand and pressed it, not in thanks so much as in an ecstasy of comradeship.

"We will help each other," he said, repeating her words, seeking her eyes in an enthusiasm of friendship.

Her eyes were grave but dark with sadness as they rested on him. "He's already gone," she thought, "far away—he thinks of me no more." And the fancy came to her that, as they sat side by side, hand in hand, she could hear the earth pouring from above to make a barrier between them, so that, as they sat, they were separated second by second by an impenetrable wall. The process, which affected her as that of being sealed away and for ever from all companionship with the person she cared for most, came to an end at last, and by common consent they unclasped their fingers, Rodney touching hers with his lips, as the curtain parted, and Mrs. Hilbery peered through the opening with her benevolent and sarcastic expression to ask whether Katharine could remember was it Tuesday or Wednesday, and did she dine in Westminster?

"Dearest William," she said, pausing, as if she could not resist the pleasure of encroaching for a second upon this wonderful world of love and confidence and romance. "Dearest children," she added, disappearing with an impulsive gesture, as if she forced herself to draw the curtain upon a scene which she refused all temptation to interrupt.

25

At a quarter-past three in the afternoon of the following Saturday Ralph Denham sat on the bank of the lake in Kew Gardens, dividing the dial-plate of his watch into sections with his forefinger. The just and inexorable nature of time itself was reflected in his face. He might have been composing a hymn to the unhasting and unresting march of that divinity. He seemed to greet the lapse of minute after minute with stern acquiescence in the inevitable order. His expression was so severe, so serene, so immobile, that it seemed obvious that for him at least there was a grandeur in the departing hour which no petty irritation on his part was to mar, although the wasting time wasted also high private hopes of his own.

His face was no bad index to what went on within him. He was in a condition of mind rather too exalted for the trivialities of daily life. He could not accept the fact that a lady was fifteen minutes late in keeping her appointment without seeing in that accident the frustration of his entire life. Looking at his watch, he seemed to look deep into the springs of human existence, and by the light of what he saw there altered his course towards the north and the midnight. . . . Yes, one's voyage must be made absolutely without companions through ice and black water—towards what goal? Here he laid his finger upon the half-hour, and decided that when the minute-hand reached that point he would go, at the same time answering the question put by another of the many voices of consciousness with the reply that there was undoubtedly a goal, but that it would need the most relentless energy to keep anywhere in its direction. Still, still, one goes on, the ticking seconds seemed to assure him, with dignity, with open eyes, with determination not to accept the second-rate, not to be tempted by the unworthy, not to yield, not to compromise. Twenty-five minutes past three were now marked upon the face of the watch. The world, he assured himself, since Katharine Hilbery was now half an hour behind her time, offers no happiness, no rest from struggle, no certainty. In a scheme of things utterly bad from the start the only unpardonable folly is that of hope. Raising his eyes for a moment from the face of his watch, he rested them upon the opposite bank, reflectively and not without a certain wistfulness, as if the sternness of their gaze were still capable of mitigation. Soon a look of the deepest satisfaction filled them, though, for a moment, he did not move. He watched a lady who came rapidly, and yet with a trace of hesitation, down the broad grass-walk towards him. She did not see him. Distance lent her figure an indescribable height, and romance seemed to surround her from the floating of a purple veil which the light air filled and curved from her shoulders.

"Here she comes, like a ship in full sail," he said to himself, half remembering some line from a play or poem where the heroine bore down thus with feathers flying and airs saluting her. The greenery and the high presences of the trees surrounded her as if they stood forth at her coming. He rose, and she saw him; her little exclamation proved that she was glad to find him, and then that she blamed herself for being late.

"Why did you never tell me? I didn't know there was this," she remarked, alluding to the lake, the broad green space, the vista of trees, with the ruffled gold of the Thames in the distance and the Ducal castle standing in its meadows. She paid the rigid tail of the Ducal lion the tribute of incredulous laughter.

"You've never been to Kew?" Denham remarked.

But it appeared that she had come once as a small child, when the geography of the place was entirely different, and the fauna included certainly flamingoes and, possibly, camels. They strolled on, refashioning these legendary gardens. She was, as he felt, glad merely to stroll and loiter and let her fancy touch upon anything her eyes encountered—a bush, a park-keeper, a decorated goose—as if the relaxation soothed her. The warmth of the afternoon, the first of spring, tempted them to sit upon a seat in a glade of beech-trees, with forest drives striking green paths this way and that around them. She sighed deeply.

"It's so peaceful," she said, as if in explanation of her sigh. Not a single person was in sight, and the stir of the wind in the branches, that sound so seldom heard by Londoners, seemed to her as if wafted from fathomless oceans of sweet air in the distance.

While she breathed and looked, Denham was engaged in uncovering with the point of his stick a group of green spikes half smothered by the dead leaves. He did this with the peculiar touch of the botanist. In naming the little green plant to her he used the Latin name, thus disguising some flower familiar even to Chelsea, and making her exclaim, half in amusement, at his knowledge. Her own ignorance was vast, she confessed. What did one call that tree opposite, for instance, supposing one condescended to call it by its English name? Beech or elm or sycamore? It chanced, by the testimony of a dead leaf, to be oak; and a little attention to a diagram which Denham proceeded to draw upon an envelope soon put Katharine in possession of some of the fundamental distinctions between our British trees. She then asked him to inform her about flowers. To her they were variously shaped and colored petals, poised, at different seasons of the year, upon very similar green stalks; but to him they were, in the first instance, bulbs or seeds, and later, living things endowed with sex, and pores, and susceptibilities which adapted themselves by all manner of ingenious devices to live and beget life, and could be fashioned squat or tapering, flame-colored or pale, pure or spotted, by processes which might reveal the secrets of human existence. Denham spoke with increasing ardor of a hobby which had long been his in secret. No discourse could have worn a more welcome sound in Katharine's ears. For weeks she had heard nothing that made such pleasant music in her mind. It wakened echoes in all those remote fastnesses of her being where loneliness had brooded so long undisturbed.

She wished he would go on for ever talking of plants, and showing her how science felt not quite blindly for the law that ruled their endless variations. A law that might be inscrutable but was certainly omnipotent appealed to her at the moment, because she could find nothing like it in possession of human lives. Circumstances had long forced her, as they force most women in the flower of youth, to consider, painfully and minutely, all that part of life which is conspicuously without order; she had had to consider moods and wishes, degrees of liking or disliking, and their effect upon the destiny of people dear to her; she had been forced to deny herself any contemplation of that other part of life where thought constructs a destiny which is independent of human beings. As Denham spoke, she followed his words and considered their bearing with an easy vigor which spoke of a capacity long hoarded and unspent. The very trees and the green merging into the blue distance became symbols of the vast external world which recks so little of the happiness, of the marriages or deaths of individuals. In order to give her examples of what he was saying, Denham led the way, first to the Rock Garden, and then to the Orchid House.

For him there was safety in the direction which the talk had taken. His emphasis might come from feelings more personal than those science roused in him, but it was disguised, and naturally he found it easy to expound and explain. Nevertheless, when he saw Katharine among the orchids, her beauty strangely emphasized by the fantastic plants, which seemed to peer and gape at her from striped hoods and fleshy throats, his ardor for botany waned, and a more complex feeling replaced it. She fell silent. The orchids seemed to suggest absorbing reflections. In defiance of the rules she stretched her ungloved hand and touched one. The sight of the rubies upon her finger affected him so disagreeably that he started and turned away. But next moment he controlled himself; he looked at her taking in one strange shape after another with the contemplative, considering gaze of a person who sees not exactly what is before him, but gropes in regions that lie beyond it. The far-away look entirely lacked self-consciousness. Denham doubted whether she remembered his presence. He could recall himself, of course, by a word or a movement—but why? She was happier thus. She needed nothing that he could give her. And for him, too, perhaps, it was best to keep aloof, only to know that she existed, to preserve what he already had—perfect, remote, and unbroken. Further, her still look, standing among the orchids in that hot atmosphere, strangely illustrated some scene that he had imagined in his room at home. The sight, mingling with his recollection, kept him silent when the door was shut and they were walking on again.

But though she did not speak, Katharine had an uneasy sense that silence on her part was selfishness. It was selfish of her to continue, as she wished to do, a discussion of subjects not remotely connected with any human beings. She roused herself to consider their exact position upon the turbulent map of the emotions. Oh yes—it was a question whether Ralph Denham should live in the country and write a book; it was getting late; they must waste no more time; Cassandra arrived tonight for dinner; she flinched and roused herself, and discovered that she ought to be holding something in her hands. But they were empty. She held them out with an exclamation.

"I've left my bag somewhere—where?" The gardens had no points of the compass, so far as she was concerned. She had been walking for the most part on grass—that was all she knew. Even the road to the Orchid House had now split itself into three. But there was no bag in the Orchid House. It must, therefore, have been left upon the seat. They retraced their steps in the preoccupied manner of people who have to think about something that is lost. What did this bag look like? What did it contain?

"A purse—a ticket—some letters, papers," Katharine counted, becoming more agitated as she recalled the list. Denham went on quickly in advance of her, and she heard him shout that he had found it before she reached the seat. In order to make sure that all was safe she spread the contents on her knee. It was a queer collection, Denham thought, gazing with the deepest interest. Loose gold coins were tangled in a narrow strip of lace; there were letters which somehow suggested the extreme of intimacy; there were two or three keys, and lists of commissions against which crosses were set at intervals. But she did not seem satisfied until she had made sure of a certain paper so folded that Denham could not judge what it contained. In her relief and gratitude she began at once to say that she had been thinking over what Denham had told her of his plans.

He cut her short. "Don't let's discuss that dreary business."

"But I thought—"

"It's a dreary business. I ought never to have bothered you—"

"Have you decided, then?"

He made an impatient sound. "It's not a thing that matters."

She could only say rather flatly, "Oh!"

"I mean it matters to me, but it matters to no one else. Anyhow," he continued, more amiably, "I see no reason why you should be bothered with other people's nuisances."

She supposed that she had let him see too clearly her weariness of this side of life.

"I'm afraid I've been absent-minded," she began, remembering how often William had brought this charge against her.

"You have a good deal to make you absent-minded," he replied.

"Yes," she replied, flushing. "No," she contradicted herself. "Nothing particular, I mean. But I was thinking about plants. I was enjoying myself. In fact, I've seldom enjoyed an afternoon more. But I want to hear what you've settled, if you don't mind telling me."

"Oh, it's all settled," he replied. "I'm going to this infernal cottage to write a worthless book."

"How I envy you," she replied, with the utmost sincerity.

"Well, cottages are to be had for fifteen shillings a week."

"Cottages are to be had—yes," she replied. "The question is—" She checked herself. "Two rooms are all I should want," she continued, with a curious sigh; "one for eating, one for sleeping. Oh, but I should like another, a large one at the top, and a little garden where one could grow flowers. A path—so—down to a river, or up to a wood, and the sea not very far off, so that one could hear the waves at night. Ships just vanishing on the horizon—" She broke off. "Shall you be near the sea?"

"My notion of perfect happiness," he began, not replying to her question, "is to live as you've said."

"Well, now you can. You will work, I suppose," she continued; "you'll work all the morning and again after tea and perhaps at night. You won't have people always coming about you to interrupt."

"How far can one live alone?" he asked. "Have you tried ever?"

"Once for three weeks," she replied. "My father and mother were in Italy, and something happened so that I couldn't join them. For three weeks I lived entirely by myself, and the only person I spoke to was a stranger in a shop where I lunched—a man with a beard. Then I went back to my room by myself and—well, I did what I liked. It doesn't make me out an amiable character, I'm afraid," she added, "but I can't endure living with other people. An occasional man with a beard is interesting; he's detached; he lets me go my way, and we know we shall never meet again. Therefore, we are perfectly sincere—a thing not possible with one's friends."

"Nonsense," Denham replied abruptly.

"Why 'nonsense'?" she inquired.

"Because you don't mean what you say," he expostulated.

"You're very positive," she said, laughing and looking at him. How arbitrary, hot-tempered, and imperious he was! He had asked her to come to Kew to advise him; he then told her that he had settled the question already; he then proceeded to find fault with her. He was the very opposite of William Rodney, she thought; he was shabby, his clothes were badly made, he was ill versed in the amenities of life; he was tongue-tied and awkward to the verge of obliterating his real character. He was awkwardly silent; he was awkwardly emphatic. And yet she liked him.

"I don't mean what I say," she repeated good-humoredly. "Well—?"

"I doubt whether you make absolute sincerity your standard in life," he answered significantly.

She flushed. He had penetrated at once to the weak spot—her engagement, and had reason for what he said. He was not altogether justified now, at any rate, she was glad to remember; but she could not enlighten him and must bear his insinuations, though from the lips of a man who had behaved as he had behaved their force should not have been sharp. Nevertheless, what he said had its force, she mused; partly because he seemed unconscious of his own lapse in the case of Mary Datchet, and thus baffled her insight; partly because he always spoke with force, for what reason she did not yet feel certain.

"Absolute sincerity is rather difficult, don't you think?" she inquired, with a touch of irony.

"There are people one credits even with that," he replied a little vaguely. He was ashamed of his savage wish to hurt her, and yet it was not for the sake of hurting her, who was beyond his shafts, but in order to mortify his own incredibly reckless impulse of abandonment to the spirit which seemed, at moments, about to rush him to the uttermost ends of the earth. She affected him beyond the scope of his wildest dreams. He seemed to see that beneath the quiet surface of her manner, which was almost pathetically at hand and within reach for all the trivial demands of daily life, there was a spirit which she reserved or repressed for some reason either of loneliness or—could it be possible—of love. Was it given to Rodney to see her unmasked, unrestrained, unconscious of her duties? a creature of uncalculating passion and instinctive freedom? No; he refused to believe it. It was in her loneliness that Katharine was unreserved. "I went back to my room by myself and I did—what I liked." She had said that to him, and in saying it had given him a glimpse of possibilities, even of confidences, as if he might be the one to share her loneliness, the mere hint of which made his heart beat faster and his brain spin. He checked himself as brutally as he could. He saw her redden, and in the irony of her reply he heard her resentment.

He began slipping his smooth, silver watch in his pocket, in the hope that somehow he might help himself back to that calm and fatalistic mood which had been his when he looked at its face upon the bank of the lake, for that mood must, at whatever cost, be the mood of his intercourse with Katharine. He had spoken of gratitude and acquiescence in the letter which he had never sent, and now all the force of his character must make good those vows in her presence.

She, thus challenged, tried meanwhile to define her points. She wished to make Denham understand.

"Don't you see that if you have no relations with people it's easier to be honest with them?" she inquired. "That is what I meant. One needn't cajole them; one's under no obligation to them. Surely you must have found with your own family that it's impossible to discuss what matters to you most because you're all herded together, because you're in a conspiracy, because the position is false—" Her reasoning suspended itself a little inconclusively, for the subject was complex, and she found herself in ignorance whether Denham had a family or not. Denham was agreed with her as to the destructiveness of the family system, but he did not wish to discuss the problem at that moment.

He turned to a problem which was of greater interest to him.

"I'm convinced," he said, "that there are cases in which perfect sincerity is possible—cases where there's no relationship, though the people live together, if you like, where each is free, where there's no obligation upon either side."

"For a time perhaps," she agreed, a little despondently. "But obligations always grow up. There are feelings to be considered. People aren't simple, and though they may mean to be reasonable, they end"—in the condition in which she found herself, she meant, but added lamely—"in a muddle."

"Because," Denham instantly intervened, "they don't make themselves understood at the beginning. I could undertake, at this instant," he continued, with a reasonable intonation which did much credit to his self-control, "to lay down terms for a friendship which should be perfectly sincere and perfectly straightforward."

She was curious to hear them, but, besides feeling that the topic concealed dangers better known to her than to him, she was reminded by his tone of his curious abstract declaration upon the Embankment. Anything that hinted at love for the moment alarmed her; it was as much an infliction to her as the rubbing of a skinless wound.

But he went on, without waiting for her invitation.

"In the first place, such a friendship must be unemotional," he laid it down emphatically. "At least, on both sides it must be understood that if either chooses to fall in love, he or she does so entirely at his own risk. Neither is under any obligation to the other. They must be at liberty to break or to alter at any moment. They must be able to say whatever they wish to say. All this must be understood."

"And they gain something worth having?" she asked.

"It's a risk—of course it's a risk," he replied. The word was one that she had been using frequently in her arguments with herself of late.

"But it's the only way—if you think friendship worth having," he concluded.

"Perhaps under those conditions it might be," she said reflectively.

"Well," he said, "those are the terms of the friendship I wish to offer you." She had known that this was coming, but, none the less, felt a little shock, half of pleasure, half of reluctance, when she heard the formal statement.

"I should like it," she began, "but——"

"Would Rodney mind?"

"Oh no," she replied quickly.

"No, no, it isn't that," she went on, and again came to an end. She had been touched by the unreserved and yet ceremonious way in which he had made what he called his offer of terms, but if he was generous it was the more necessary for her to be cautious. They would find themselves in difficulties, she speculated; but, at this point, which was not very far, after all, upon the road of caution, her foresight deserted her. She sought for some definite catastrophe into which they must inevitably plunge. But she could think of none. It seemed to her that these catastrophes were fictitious; life went on and on—life was different altogether from what people said. And not only was she at an end of her stock of caution, but it seemed suddenly altogether superfluous. Surely if any one could take care of himself, Ralph Denham could; he had told her that he did not love her. And, further, she meditated, walking on beneath the beech-trees and swinging her umbrella, as in her thought she was accustomed to complete freedom, why should she perpetually apply so different a standard to her behavior in practice? Why, she reflected, should there be this perpetual disparity between the thought and the action, between the life of solitude and the life of society, this astonishing precipice on one side of which the soul was active and in broad daylight, on the other side of which it was contemplative and dark as night? Was it not possible to step from one to the other, erect, and without essential change? Was this not the chance he offered her—the rare and wonderful chance of friendship? At any rate, she told Denham, with a sigh in which he heard both impatience and relief, that she agreed; she thought him right; she would accept his terms of friendship.

"Now," she said, "let's go and have tea."

In fact, these principles having been laid down, a great lightness of spirit showed itself in both of them. They were both convinced that something of profound importance had been settled, and could now give their attention to their tea and the Gardens. They wandered in and out of glass-houses, saw lilies swimming in tanks, breathed in the scent of thousands of carnations, and compared their respective tastes in the matter of trees and lakes. While talking exclusively of what they saw, so that any one might have overheard them, they felt that the compact between them was made firmer and deeper by the number of people who passed them and suspected nothing of the kind. The question of Ralph's cottage and future was not mentioned again.

26

Although the old coaches, with their gay panels and the guard's horn, and the humors of the box and the vicissitudes of the road, have long moldered into dust so far as they were matter, and are preserved in the printed pages of our novelists so far as they partook of the spirit, a journey to London by express train can still be a very pleasant and romantic adventure. Cassandra Otway, at the age of twenty-two, could imagine few things more pleasant. Satiated with months of green fields as she was, the first row of artisans' villas on the outskirts of London seemed to have something serious about it, which positively increased the importance of every person in the railway carriage, and even, to her impressionable mind, quickened the speed of the train and gave a note of stern authority to the shriek of the engine-whistle. They were bound for London; they must have precedence of all traffic not similarly destined. A different demeanor was necessary directly one stepped out upon Liverpool Street platform, and became one of those preoccupied and hasty citizens for whose needs innumerable taxi-cabs, motor-omnibuses, and underground railways were in waiting. She did her best to look dignified and preoccupied too, but as the cab carried her away, with a determination which alarmed her a little, she became more and more forgetful of her station as a citizen of London, and turned her head from one window to another, picking up eagerly a building on this side or a street scene on that to feed her intense curiosity. And yet, while the drive lasted no one was real, nothing was ordinary; the crowds, the Government buildings, the tide of men and women washing the base of the great glass windows, were all generalized, and affected her as if she saw them on the stage.

All these feelings were sustained and partly inspired by the fact that her journey took her straight to the center of her most romantic world. A thousand times in the midst of her pastoral landscape her thoughts took this precise road, were admitted to the house in Chelsea, and went directly upstairs to Katharine's room, where, invisible themselves, they had the better chance of feasting upon the privacy of the room's adorable and mysterious mistress. Cassandra adored her cousin; the adoration might have been foolish, but was saved from that excess and lent an engaging charm by the volatile nature of Cassandra's temperament. She had adored a great many things and people in the course of twenty-two years; she had been alternately the pride and the desperation of her teachers. She had worshipped architecture and music, natural history and humanity, literature and art, but always at the height of her enthusiasm, which was accompanied by a brilliant degree of accomplishment, she changed her mind and bought, surreptitiously, another grammar. The terrible results which governesses had predicted from such mental dissipation were certainly apparent now that Cassandra was twenty-two, and had never passed an examination, and daily showed herself less and less capable of passing one. The more serious prediction that she could never possibly earn her living was also verified. But from all these short strands of different accomplishments Cassandra wove for herself an attitude, a cast of mind, which, if useless, was found by some people to have the not despicable virtues of vivacity and freshness. Katharine, for example, thought her a most charming companion. The cousins seemed to assemble between them a great range of qualities which are never found united in one person and seldom in half a dozen people. Where Katharine was simple, Cassandra was complex; where Katharine was solid and direct, Cassandra was vague and evasive. In short, they represented very well the manly and the womanly sides of the feminine nature, and, for foundation, there was the profound unity of common blood between them. If Cassandra adored Katharine she was incapable of adoring any one without refreshing her spirit with frequent draughts of raillery and criticism, and Katharine enjoyed her laughter at least as much as her respect.

Respect was certainly uppermost in Cassandra's mind at the present moment. Katharine's engagement had appealed to her imagination as the first engagement in a circle of contemporaries is apt to appeal to the imaginations of the others; it was solemn, beautiful, and mysterious; it gave both parties the important air of those who have been initiated into some rite which is still concealed from the rest of the group. For Katharine's sake Cassandra thought William a most distinguished and interesting character, and welcomed first his conversation and then his manuscript as the marks of a friendship which it flattered and delighted her to inspire.

Katharine was still out when she arrived at Cheyne Walk. After greeting her uncle and aunt and receiving, as usual, a present of two sovereigns for "cab fares and dissipation" from Uncle Trevor, whose favorite niece she was, she changed her dress and wandered into Katharine's room to await her. What a great looking-glass Katharine had, she thought, and how mature all the arrangements upon the dressing-table were compared to what she was used to at home. Glancing round, she thought that the bills stuck upon a skewer and stood for ornament upon the mantelpiece were astonishingly like Katharine, There wasn't a photograph of William anywhere to be seen. The room, with its combination of luxury and bareness, its silk dressing-gowns and crimson slippers, its shabby carpet and bare walls, had a powerful air of Katharine herself; she stood in the middle of the room and enjoyed the sensation; and then, with a desire to finger what her cousin was in the habit of fingering, Cassandra began to take down the books which stood in a row upon the shelf above the bed. In most houses this shelf is the ledge upon which the last relics of religious belief lodge themselves as if, late at night, in the heart of privacy, people, skeptical by day, find solace in sipping one draught of the old charm for such sorrows or perplexities as may steal from their hiding-places in the dark. But there was no hymn-book here. By their battered covers and enigmatical contents, Cassandra judged them to be old school-books belonging to Uncle Trevor, and piously, though eccentrically, preserved by his daughter. There was no end, she thought, to the unexpectedness of Katharine. She had once had a passion for geometry herself, and, curled upon Katharine's quilt, she became absorbed in trying to remember how far she had forgotten what she once knew. Katharine, coming in a little later, found her deep in this characteristic pursuit.

"My dear," Cassandra exclaimed, shaking the book at her cousin, "my whole life's changed from this moment! I must write the man's name down at once, or I shall forget—"

Whose name, what book, which life was changed Katharine proceeded to ascertain. She began to lay aside her clothes hurriedly, for she was very late.

"May I sit and watch you?" Cassandra asked, shutting up her book. "I got ready on purpose."

"Oh, you're ready, are you?" said Katharine, half turning in the midst of her operations, and looking at Cassandra, who sat, clasping her knees, on the edge of the bed.

"There are people dining here," she said, taking in the effect of Cassandra from a new point of view. After an interval, the distinction, the irregular charm, of the small face with its long tapering nose and its bright oval eyes were very notable. The hair rose up off the forehead rather stiffly, and, given a more careful treatment by hairdressers and dressmakers, the light angular figure might possess a likeness to a French lady of distinction in the eighteenth century.

"Who's coming to dinner?" Cassandra asked, anticipating further possibilities of rapture.

"There's William, and, I believe, Aunt Eleanor and Uncle Aubrey."

"I'm so glad William is coming. Did he tell you that he sent me his manuscript? I think it's wonderful—I think he's almost good enough for you, Katharine."

"You shall sit next to him and tell him what you think of him."

"I shan't dare do that," Cassandra asserted.

"Why? You're not afraid of him, are you?"

"A little—because he's connected with you."

Katharine smiled.

"But then, with your well-known fidelity, considering that you're staying here at least a fortnight, you won't have any illusions left about me by the time you go. I give you a week, Cassandra. I shall see my power fading day by day. Now it's at the climax; but tomorrow it'll have begun to fade. What am I to wear, I wonder? Find me a blue dress, Cassandra, over there in the long wardrobe."

She spoke disconnectedly, handling brush and comb, and pulling out the little drawers in her dressing-table and leaving them open. Cassandra, sitting on the bed behind her, saw the reflection of her cousin's face in the looking-glass. The face in the looking-glass was serious and intent, apparently occupied with other things besides the straightness of the parting which, however, was being driven as straight as a Roman road through the dark hair. Cassandra was impressed again by Katharine's maturity; and, as she enveloped herself in the blue dress which filled almost the whole of the long looking-glass with blue light and made it the frame of a picture, holding not only the slightly moving effigy of the beautiful woman, but shapes and colors of objects reflected from the background, Cassandra thought that no sight had ever been quite so romantic. It was all in keeping with the room and the house, and the city round them; for her ears had not yet ceased to notice the hum of distant wheels.

They went downstairs rather late, in spite of Katharine's extreme speed in getting ready. To Cassandra's ears the buzz of voices inside the drawing-room was like the tuning up of the instruments of the orchestra. It seemed to her that there were numbers of people in the room, and that they were strangers, and that they were beautiful and dressed with the greatest distinction, although they proved to be mostly her relations, and the distinction of their clothing was confined, in the eyes of an impartial observer, to the white waistcoat which Rodney wore. But they all rose simultaneously, which was by itself impressive, and they all exclaimed, and shook hands, and she was introduced to Mr. Peyton, and the door sprang open, and dinner was announced, and they filed off, William Rodney offering her his slightly bent black arm, as she had secretly hoped he would. In short, had the scene been looked at only through her eyes, it must have been described as one of magical brilliancy. The pattern of the soup-plates, the stiff folds of the napkins, which rose by the side of each plate in the shape of arum lilies, the long sticks of bread tied with pink ribbon, the silver dishes and the sea-colored champagne glasses, with the flakes of gold congealed in their stems—all these details, together with a curiously pervasive smell of kid gloves, contributed to her exhilaration, which must be repressed, however, because she was grown up, and the world held no more for her to marvel at.

The world held no more for her to marvel at, it is true; but it held other people; and each other person possessed in Cassandra's mind some fragment of what privately she called "reality." It was a gift that they would impart if you asked them for it, and thus no dinner-party could possibly be dull, and little Mr. Peyton on her right and William Rodney on her left were in equal measure endowed with the quality which seemed to her so unmistakable and so precious that the way people neglected to demand it was a constant source of surprise to her. She scarcely knew, indeed, whether she was talking to Mr. Peyton or to William Rodney. But to one who, by degrees, assumed the shape of an elderly man with a mustache, she described how she had arrived in London that very afternoon, and how she had taken a cab and driven through the streets. Mr. Peyton, an editor of fifty years, bowed his bald head repeatedly, with apparent understanding. At least, he understood that she was very young and pretty, and saw that she was excited, though he could not gather at once from her words or remember from his own experience what there was to be excited about. "Were there any buds on the trees?" he asked. "Which line did she travel by?"

He was cut short in these amiable inquiries by her desire to know whether he was one of those who read, or one of those who look out of the window? Mr. Peyton was by no means sure which he did. He rather thought he did both. He was told that he had made a most dangerous confession. She could deduce his entire history from that one fact. He challenged her to proceed; and she proclaimed him a Liberal Member of Parliament.

William, nominally engaged in a desultory conversation with Aunt Eleanor, heard every word, and taking advantage of the fact that elderly ladies have little continuity of conversation, at least with those whom they esteem for their youth and their sex, he asserted his presence by a very nervous laugh.

Cassandra turned to him directly. She was enchanted to find that, instantly and with such ease, another of these fascinating beings was offering untold wealth for her extraction.

"There's no doubt what *you* do in a railway carriage, William," she said, making use in her pleasure of his first name. "You never *once* look out of the window; you read *all* the time."

"And what facts do you deduce from that?" Mr. Peyton asked.

"Oh, that he's a poet, of course," said Cassandra. "But I must confess that I knew that before, so it isn't fair. I've got your manuscript with me," she went on, disregarding Mr. Peyton in a shameless way. "I've got all sorts of things I want to ask you about it."

William inclined his head and tried to conceal the pleasure that her remark gave him. But the pleasure was not unalloyed. However susceptible to flattery William might be, he would never tolerate it from people who showed a gross or emotional taste in literature, and if Cassandra erred even slightly from what he considered essential in this respect he would express his discomfort by flinging out his hands and wrinkling his forehead; he would find no pleasure in her flattery after that.

"First of all," she proceeded, "I want to know why you chose to write a play?"

"Ah! You mean it's not dramatic?"

"I mean that I don't see what it would gain by being acted. But then does Shakespeare gain? Henry and I are always arguing about Shakespeare. I'm certain he's wrong, but I can't prove it because I've only seen Shakespeare acted once in Lincoln. But I'm quite positive," she insisted, "that Shakespeare wrote for the stage."

"You're perfectly right," Rodney exclaimed. "I was hoping you were on that side. Henry's wrong—entirely wrong. Of course, I've failed, as all the moderns fail. Dear, dear, I wish I'd consulted you before."

From this point they proceeded to go over, as far as memory served them, the different aspects of Rodney's drama. She said nothing that jarred upon him, and untrained daring had the power to stimulate experience to such an extent that Rodney was frequently seen to hold his fork suspended before him, while he debated the first principles of the art. Mrs. Hilbery thought to herself that she had never seen him to such advantage; yes, he was somehow different; he reminded her of some one who was dead, some one who was distinguished—she had forgotten his name.

Cassandra's voice rose high in its excitement.

"You've not read *The Idiot!*" she exclaimed.

"I've read *War and Peace,*" William replied, a little testily.

"*War and Peace!*" she echoed, in a tone of derision.

"I confess I don't understand the Russians."

"Shake hands! Shake hands!" boomed Uncle Aubrey from across the table. "Neither do I. And I hazard the opinion that they don't themselves."

The old gentleman had ruled a large part of the Indian Empire, but he was in the habit of saying that he had rather have written the works of Dickens. The table now took possession of a subject much to its liking. Aunt Eleanor showed premonitory signs of pronouncing an opinion. Although she had blunted her taste upon some form of philanthropy for twenty-five years, she had a fine natural instinct for an upstart or a pretender, and knew to a hairbreadth what literature should be and what it should not be. She was born to the knowledge, and scarcely thought it a matter to be proud of.

"Insanity is not a fit subject for fiction," she announced positively.

"There's the well-known case of Hamlet," Mr. Hilbery interposed, in his leisurely, half-humorous tones.

"Ah, but poetry's different, Trevor," said Aunt Eleanor, as if she had special authority from Shakespeare to say so. "Different altogether. And I've never thought, for my part, that Hamlet was as mad as they make out. What is your opinion, Mr. Peyton?" For, as there was a minister of literature present in the person of the editor of an esteemed review, she deferred to him.

Mr. Peyton leant a little back in his chair, and, putting his head rather on one side, observed that that was a question that he had never been able to answer entirely to his satisfaction. There was much to be said on both sides, but as he considered upon which side he should say it, Mrs. Hilbery broke in upon his judicious meditations.

"Lovely, lovely Ophelia!" she exclaimed. "What a wonderful power it is—poetry! I wake up in the morning all bedraggled; there's a yellow fog outside; little Emily turns on the electric light when she brings me my tea, and says, 'Oh, ma'am, the water's frozen in the cistern, and cook's cut her finger to the bone.' And then I open a little green book, and the birds are singing, the stars shining, the flowers twinkling—" She looked about her as if these presences had suddenly manifested themselves round her dining-room table.

"Has the cook cut her finger badly?" Aunt Eleanor demanded, addressing herself naturally to Katharine.

"Oh, the cook's finger is only my way of putting it," said Mrs. Hilbery. "But if she had cut her arm off, Katharine would have sewn it on again," she remarked, with an affectionate glance at her daughter, who looked, she thought, a little sad. "But what horrid, horrid thoughts," she wound up, laying down her napkin and pushing her chair back. "Come, let us find something more cheerful to talk about upstairs."

Upstairs in the drawing-room Cassandra found fresh sources of pleasure, first in the distinguished and expectant look of the room, and then in the chance of exercising her divining-rod upon a new assortment of human beings. But the low tones of the women, their meditative silences, the beauty which, to her at least, shone even from black satin and the knobs of amber which encircled elderly necks, changed her wish to chatter to a more subdued desire merely to watch and to whisper. She entered with delight into an atmosphere in which private matters were being interchanged freely, almost in monosyllables, by the older women who now accepted her as one of themselves. Her expression became very gentle and sympathetic, as if she, too, were full of solicitude for the world which was somehow being cared for, managed and deprecated by Aunt Maggie and Aunt Eleanor. After a time she perceived that Katharine was outside the community in some way, and, suddenly, she threw aside her wisdom and gentleness and concern and began to laugh.

"What are you laughing at?" Katharine asked.

A joke so foolish and unfilial wasn't worth explaining.

"It was nothing–ridiculous–in the worst of taste, but still, if you half shut your eyes and looked—" Katharine half shut her eyes and looked, but she looked in the wrong direction, and Cassandra laughed more than ever, and was still laughing and doing her best to explain in a whisper that Aunt Eleanor, through half-shut eyes, was like the parrot in the cage at Stogdon House, when the gentlemen came in and Rodney walked straight up to them and wanted to know what they were laughing at.

"I utterly refuse to tell you!" Cassandra replied, standing up straight, clasping her hands in front of her, and facing him. Her mockery was delicious to him. He had not even for a second the fear that she had been laughing at him. She was laughing because life was so adorable, so enchanting.

"Ah, but you're cruel to make me feel the barbarity of my sex," he replied, drawing his feet together and pressing his finger-tips upon an imaginary opera-hat or malacca cane. "We've been discussing all sorts of dull things, and now I shall never know what I want to know more than anything in the world."

"You don't deceive us for a minute!" she cried. "Not for a second. We both know that you've been enjoying yourself immensely. Hasn't he, Katharine?"

"No," she replied, "I think he's speaking the truth. He doesn't care much for politics."

Her words, though spoken simply, produced a curious change in the light, sparkling atmosphere. William at once lost his look of animation and said seriously:

"I detest politics."

"I don't think any man has the right to say that," said Cassandra, almost severely.

"I agree. I mean that I detest politicians," he corrected himself quickly.

"You see, I believe Cassandra is what they call a Feminist," Katharine went on. "Or rather, she was a Feminist six months ago, but it's no good supposing that she is now what she was then. That is one of her greatest charms in my eyes. One never can tell." She smiled at her as an elder sister might smile.

"Katharine, you make one feel so horribly small!" Cassandra exclaimed.

"No, no, that's not what she means," Rodney interposed. "I quite agree that women have an immense advantage over us there. One misses a lot by attempting to know things thoroughly."

"He knows Greek thoroughly," said Katharine. "But then he also knows a good deal about painting, and a certain amount about music. He's very cultivated—perhaps the most cultivated person I know."

"And poetry," Cassandra added.

"Yes, I was forgetting his play," Katharine remarked, and turning her head as though she saw something that needed her attention in a far corner of the room, she left them.

For a moment they stood silent, after what seemed a deliberate introduction to each other, and Cassandra watched her crossing the room.

"Henry," she said next moment, "would say that a stage ought to be no bigger than this drawing-room. He wants there to be singing and dancing as well as acting—only all the opposite of Wagner—you understand?"

They sat down, and Katharine, turning when she reached the window, saw William with his hand raised in gesticulation and his mouth open, as if ready to speak the moment Cassandra ceased.

Katharine's duty, whether it was to pull a curtain or move a chair, was either forgotten or discharged, but she continued to stand by the window without doing anything. The elderly people were all grouped together round the fire. They seemed an independent, middle-aged community busy with its own concerns. They were telling stories very well and listening to them very graciously. But for her there was no obvious employment.

"If anybody says anything, I shall say that I'm looking at the river," she thought, for in her slavery to her family traditions, she was ready to pay for her transgression with some plausible falsehood. She pushed aside the blind and looked at the river. But it was a dark night and the water was barely visible. Cabs were passing, and couples were loitering slowly along the road, keeping as close to the railings as possible, though the trees had as yet no leaves to cast shadow upon their embraces. Katharine, thus withdrawn, felt her loneliness. The evening had been one of pain, offering her, minute after minute, plainer proof that things would fall out as she had foreseen. She had faced tones, gestures, glances; she knew, with her back to them, that William, even now, was plunging deeper and deeper into the delight of unexpected understanding with Cassandra. He had almost told her that he was finding it infinitely better than he could have believed. She looked out of the window, sternly determined to forget private misfortunes, to forget herself, to forget individual lives. With her eyes upon the dark sky, voices reached her from the room in which she was standing. She heard them as if they came from people in another world, a world antecedent to her world, a world that was the prelude, the antechamber to reality; it was as if, lately dead, she heard the living talking. The dream nature of our life had never been more apparent to her, never had life been more certainly an affair of four walls, whose objects existed only within the range of lights and fires, beyond which lay nothing, or nothing more than darkness. She seemed physically to have stepped beyond the region where the light of illusion still makes it desirable to possess, to love, to struggle. And yet her melancholy brought her no serenity. She still heard the voices within the room. She was still tormented by desires. She wished to be beyond their range. She wished inconsistently enough that she could find herself driving rapidly through the streets; she was even anxious to be with some one who, after a moment's groping, took a definite shape and solidified into the person of Mary Datchet. She drew the curtains so that the draperies met in deep folds in the middle of the window.

"Ah, there she is," said Mr. Hilbery, who was standing swaying affably from side to side, with his back to the fire. "Come here, Katharine. I couldn't see where you'd got to—our children," he observed parenthetically, "have their uses—I want you to go to my study, Katharine; go to the third shelf on the right-hand side of the door; take down Trelawny's *Recollections of Shelley*; bring it to me. Then, Peyton, you will have to admit to the assembled company that you have been mistaken."

"Trelawny's *Recollections of Shelley.* The third shelf on the right of the door," Katharine repeated. After all, one does not check children in their play, or rouse sleepers from their dreams. She passed William and Cassandra on her way to the door.

"Stop, Katharine," said William, speaking almost as if he were conscious of her against his will. "Let me go." He rose, after a second's hesitation, and she understood that it cost him an effort. She knelt one knee upon the sofa where Cassandra sat, looking down at her cousin's face, which still moved with the speed of what she had been saying.

"Are you—happy?" she asked.

"Oh, my dear!" Cassandra exclaimed, as if no further words were needed. "Of course, we disagree about every subject under the sun," she exclaimed, "but I think he's the cleverest man I've ever met—and you're the most beautiful woman," she added, looking at Katharine, and as she looked her face lost its animation and became almost melancholy in sympathy with Katharine's melancholy, which seemed to Cassandra the last refinement of her distinction.

"Ah, but it's only ten o'clock," said Katharine darkly.

"As late as that! Well——?" She did not understand.

"At twelve my horses turn into rats and off I go. The illusion fades. But I accept my fate. I make hay while the sun shines." Cassandra looked at her with a puzzled expression.

"Here's Katharine talking about rats, and hay, and all sorts of odd things," she said, as William returned to them. He had been quick. "Can you make her out?"

Katharine perceived from his little frown and hesitation that he did not find that particular problem to his taste at present. She stood upright at once and said in a different tone:

"I really am off, though. I wish you'd explain if they say anything, William. I shan't be late, but I've got to see some one."

"At this time of night?" Cassandra exclaimed.

"Whom have you got to see?" William demanded.

"A friend," she remarked, half turning her head towards him. She knew that he wished her to stay, not, indeed, with them, but in their neighborhood, in case of need.

"Katharine has a great many friends," said William rather lamely, sitting down once more, as Katharine left the room.

She was soon driving quickly, as she had wished to drive, through the lamp-lit streets. She liked both light and speed, and the sense of being out of doors alone, and the knowledge that she would reach Mary in her high, lonely room at the end of the drive. She climbed the stone steps quickly, remarking the queer look of her blue silk skirt and blue shoes upon the stone, dusty with the boots of the day, under the light of an occasional jet of flickering gas.

The door was opened in a second by Mary herself, whose face showed not only surprise at the sight of her visitor, but some degree of embarrassment. She greeted her cordially, and, as there was no time for explanations, Katharine walked straight into the sitting-room, and found herself in the presence of a young man who was lying back in a chair and holding a sheet of paper in his hand, at which he was looking as if he expected to go on immediately with what he was in the middle of saying to Mary Datchet. The apparition of an unknown lady in full evening dress seemed to disturb him. He took his pipe from his mouth, rose stiffly, and sat down again with a jerk.

"Have you been dining out?" Mary asked.

"Are you working?" Katharine inquired simultaneously.

The young man shook his head, as if he disowned his share in the question with some irritation.

"Well, not exactly," Mary replied. "Mr. Basnett had brought some papers to show me. We were going through them, but we'd almost done. . . . Tell us about your party."

Mary had a ruffled appearance, as if she had been running her fingers through her hair in the course of her conversation; she was dressed more or less like a Russian peasant girl. She sat down again in a chair which looked as if it had been her seat for some hours; the saucer which stood upon the arm contained the ashes of many cigarettes. Mr. Basnett, a very young man with a fresh complexion and a high forehead from which the hair was combed straight back, was one of that group of "very able young men" suspected by Mr. Clacton, justly as it turned out, of an influence upon Mary Datchet. He had come down from one of the Universities not long ago, and was now charged with the reformation of society. In connection with the rest of the group of very able young men he had drawn up a scheme for the education of labor, for the amalgamation of the middle class and the working class, and for a joint assault of the two bodies, combined in the Society for the Education of Democracy, upon Capital. The scheme had already reached the stage in which it was permissible to hire an office and engage a secretary, and he had been deputed to expound the scheme to Mary, and make her an offer of the Secretaryship, to which, as a matter of principle, a small salary was attached. Since seven o'clock that evening he had been reading out loud the document in which the faith of the new reformers was expounded, but the reading was so frequently interrupted by discussion, and it was so often necessary to inform Mary "in strictest confidence" of the private characters and evil designs of certain individuals and societies that they were still only halfway through the manuscript. Neither of them realized that the talk had already lasted three hours. In their absorption they had forgotten even to feed the fire, and yet both Mr. Basnett in his exposition, and Mary in her interrogation, carefully preserved a kind of formality calculated to check the desire of the human mind for irrelevant discussion. Her questions frequently began, "Am I to understand–" and his replies invariably represented the views of some one called "we."

By this time Mary was almost persuaded that she, too, was included in the "we," and agreed with Mr. Basnett in believing that "our" views, "our" society, "our" policy, stood for something quite definitely segregated from the main body of society in a circle of superior illumination.

The appearance of Katharine in this atmosphere was extremely incongruous, and had the effect of making Mary remember all sorts of things that she had been glad to forget.

"You've been dining out?" she asked again, looking, with a little smile, at the blue silk and the pearl-sewn shoes.

"No, at home. Are you starting something new?" Katharine hazarded, rather hesitatingly, looking at the papers.

"We are," Mr. Basnett replied. He said no more.

"I'm thinking of leaving our friends in Russell Square," Mary explained.

"I see. And then you will do something else."

"Well, I'm afraid I like working," said Mary.

"Afraid," said Mr. Basnett, conveying the impression that, in his opinion, no sensible person could be afraid of liking to work.

"Yes," said Katharine, as if he had stated this opinion aloud. "I should like to start something—something off one's own bat—that's what I should like."

"Yes, that's the fun," said Mr. Basnett, looking at her for the first time rather keenly, and refilling his pipe.

"But you can't limit work—that's what I mean," said Mary. "I mean there are other sorts of work. No one works harder than a woman with little children."

"Quite so," said Mr. Basnett. "It's precisely the women with babies we want to get hold of." He glanced at his document, rolled it into a cylinder between his fingers, and gazed into the fire. Katharine felt that in this company anything that one said would be judged upon its merits; one had only to say what one thought, rather barely and tersely, with a curious assumption that the number of things that could properly be thought about was strictly limited. And Mr. Basnett was only stiff upon the surface; there was an intelligence in his face which attracted her intelligence.

"When will the public know?" she asked.

"What d'you mean—about us?" Mr. Basnett asked, with a little smile.

"That depends upon many things," said Mary. The conspirators looked pleased, as if Katharine's question, with the belief in their existence which it implied, had a warming effect upon them.

"In starting a society such as we wish to start (we can't say any more at present)," Mr. Basnett began, with a little jerk of his head, "there are two things to remember—the Press and the public. Other societies, which shall be nameless, have gone under because they've appealed only to cranks. If you don't want a mutual admiration society, which dies as soon as you've all discovered each other's faults, you must nobble the Press. You must appeal to the public."

"That's the difficulty," said Mary thoughtfully.

"That's where she comes in," said Mr. Basnett, jerking his head in

Mary's direction. "She's the only one of us who's a capitalist. She can make a whole-time job of it. I'm tied to an office; I can only give my spare time. Are you, by any chance, on the look-out for a job?" he asked Katharine, with a queer mixture of distrust and deference.

"Marriage is her job at present," Mary replied for her.

"Oh, I see," said Mr. Basnett. He made allowances for that; he and his friends had faced the question of sex, along with all others, and assigned it an honorable place in their scheme of life. Katharine felt this beneath the roughness of his manner; and a world entrusted to the guardianship of Mary Datchet and Mr. Basnett seemed to her a good world, although not a romantic or beautiful place or, to put it figuratively, a place where any line of blue mist softly linked tree to tree upon the horizon. For a moment she thought she saw in his face, bent now over the fire, the features of that original man whom we still recall every now and then, although we know only the clerk, barrister, Governmental official, or workingman variety of him. Not that Mr. Basnett, giving his days to commerce and his spare time to social reform, would long carry about him any trace of his possibilities of completeness; but, for the moment, in his youth and ardor, still speculative, still uncramped, one might imagine him the citizen of a nobler state than ours. Katharine turned over her small stock of information, and wondered what their society might be going to attempt. Then she remembered that she was hindering their business, and rose, still thinking of this society, and thus thinking, she said to Mr. Basnett:

"Well, you'll ask me to join when the time comes, I hope."

He nodded, and took his pipe from his mouth, but, being unable to think of anything to say, he put it back again, although he would have been glad if she had stayed.

Against her wish, Mary insisted upon taking her downstairs, and then, as there was no cab to be seen, they stood in the street together, looking about them.

"Go back," Katharine urged her, thinking of Mr. Basnett with his papers in his hand.

"You can't wander about the streets alone in those clothes," said Mary, but the desire to find a cab was not her true reason for standing beside Katharine for a minute or two. Unfortunately for her composure, Mr. Basnett and his papers seemed to her an incidental diversion of life's serious purpose compared with some tremendous fact which manifested itself as she stood alone with Katharine. It may have been their common womanhood.

"Have you seen Ralph?" she asked suddenly, without preface.

"Yes," said Katharine directly, but she did not remember when or where she had seen him. It took her a moment or two to remember why Mary should ask her if she had seen Ralph.

"I believe I'm jealous," said Mary.

"Nonsense, Mary," said Katharine, rather distractedly, taking her arm and beginning to walk up the street in the direction of the main road. "Let me see; we went to Kew, and we agreed to be friends. Yes, that's what happened." Mary was silent, in the hope that Katharine would tell her more. But Katharine said nothing.

"It's not a question of friendship," Mary exclaimed, her anger rising, to her own surprise. "You know it's not. How can it be? I've no right to interfere——" She stopped. "Only I'd rather Ralph wasn't hurt," she concluded.

"I think he seems able to take care of himself," Katharine observed. Without either of them wishing it, a feeling of hostility had risen between them.

"Do you really think it's worth it?" said Mary, after a pause.

"How can one tell?" Katharine asked.

"Have you ever cared for any one?" Mary demanded rashly and foolishly.

"I can't wander about London discussing my feelings–Here's a cab–no, there's some one in it."

"We don't want to quarrel," said Mary.

"Ought I to have told him that I wouldn't be his friend?" Katharine asked. "Shall I tell him that? If so, what reason shall I give him?"

"Of course you can't tell him that," said Mary, controlling herself.

"I believe I shall, though," said Katharine suddenly.

"I lost my temper, Katharine; I shouldn't have said what I did."

"The whole thing's foolish," said Katharine, peremptorily. "That's what I say. It's not worth it." She spoke with unnecessary vehemence, but it was not directed against Mary Datchet. Their animosity had completely disappeared, and upon both of them a cloud of difficulty and darkness rested, obscuring the future, in which they had both to find a way.

"No, no, it's not worth it," Katharine repeated. "Suppose, as you say, it's out of the question–this friendship; he falls in love with me. I don't want that. Still," she added, "I believe you exaggerate; love's not everything; marriage itself is only one of the things——" They had reached the main thoroughfare, and stood looking at the omnibuses and passers-by, who seemed, for the moment, to illustrate what Katharine had said of the diversity of human interests. For both of them it had become one of those moments of extreme detachment, when it seems unnecessary ever again to shoulder the burden of happiness and self-assertive existence. Their neighbors were welcome to their possessions.

"I don't lay down any rules,"' said Mary, recovering herself first, as they turned after a long pause of this description. "All I say is that you should know what you're about–for certain; but," she added, "I expect you do."

At the same time she was profoundly perplexed, not only by what she knew of the arrangements for Katharine's marriage, but by the impression which she had of her, there on her arm, dark and inscrutable.

They walked back again and reached the steps which led up to Mary's flat. Here they stopped and paused for a moment, saying nothing.

"You must go in," said Katharine, rousing herself. "He's waiting all this time to go on with his reading." She glanced up at the lighted window near the top of the house, and they both looked at it and waited for a moment. A flight of semicircular steps ran up to the hall, and Mary slowly mounted the first two or three, and paused, looking down upon Katharine.

"I think you underrate the value of that emotion," she said slowly, and a little awkwardly. She climbed another step and looked down once more upon the figure that was only partly lit up, standing in the street with a colorless face turned upwards. As Mary hesitated, a cab came by and Katharine turned and stopped it, saying as she opened the door:

"Remember, I want to belong to your society—remember," she added, having to raise her voice a little, and shutting the door upon the rest of her words.

Mary mounted the stairs step by step, as if she had to lift her body up an extremely steep ascent. She had had to wrench herself forcibly away from Katharine, and every step vanquished her desire. She held on grimly, encouraging herself as though she were actually making some great physical effort in climbing a height. She was conscious that Mr. Basnett, sitting at the top of the stairs with his documents, offered her solid footing if she were capable of reaching it. The knowledge gave her a faint sense of exaltation.

Mr. Basnett raised his eyes as she opened the door.

"I'll go on where I left off," he said. "Stop me if you want anything explained."

He had been re-reading the document, and making pencil notes in the margin while he waited, and he went on again as if there had been no interruption. Mary sat down among the flat cushions, lit another cigarette, and listened with a frown upon her face.

Katharine leant back in the corner of the cab that carried her to Chelsea, conscious of fatigue, and conscious, too, of the sober and satisfactory nature of such industry as she had just witnessed. The thought of it composed and calmed her. When she reached home she let herself in as quietly as she could, in the hope that the household was already gone to bed. But her excursion had occupied less time than she thought, and she heard sounds of unmistakable liveliness upstairs. A door opened, and she drew herself into a ground-floor room in case the sound meant that Mr. Peyton were taking his leave. From where she stood she could see the stairs, though she was herself invisible. Some one was coming down the stairs, and now she saw that it was William Rodney. He looked a little strange, as if he were walking in his sleep; his lips moved as if he were acting some part to himself. He came down very slowly, step by step, with one hand upon the banisters to guide himself. She thought he looked as if he were in some mood of high exaltation, which it made her uncomfortable to witness any longer unseen. She stepped into the hall. He gave a great start upon seeing her and stopped.

"Katharine!" he exclaimed. "You've been out?" he asked.

"Yes. . . . Are they still up?"

He did not answer, and walked into the ground-floor room through the door which stood open.

"It's been more wonderful than I can tell you," he said, "I'm incredibly happy—"

He was scarcely addressing her, and she said nothing. For a moment they stood at opposite sides of a table saying nothing. Then he asked her quickly, "But tell me, how did it seem to you? What did you think, Katharine? Is there a chance that she likes me? Tell me, Katharine!"

Before she could answer a door opened on the landing above and disturbed them. It disturbed William excessively. He started back, walked rapidly into the hall, and said in a loud and ostentatiously ordinary tone:

"Good night, Katharine. Go to bed now. I shall see you soon. I hope I shall be able to come tomorrow."

Next moment he was gone. She went upstairs and found Cassandra on the landing. She held two or three books in her hand, and she was stooping to look at others in a little bookcase. She said that she could never tell which book she wanted to read in bed, poetry, biography, or metaphysics.

"What do you read in bed, Katharine?" she asked, as they walked upstairs side by side.

"Sometimes one thing–sometimes another," said Katharine vaguely. Cassandra looked at her.

"D'you know, you're extraordinarily queer," she said. "Every one seems to me a little queer. Perhaps it's the effect of London."

"Is William queer, too?" Katharine asked.

"Well, I think he is a little," Cassandra replied. "Queer, but very fascinating. I shall read Milton tonight. It's been one of the happiest nights of my life, Katharine," she added, looking with shy devotion at her cousin's beautiful face.

27

London, in the first days of spring, has buds that open and flowers that suddenly shake their petals—white, purple, or crimson—in competition with the display in the garden beds, although these city flowers are merely so many doors flung wide in Bond Street and the neighborhood, inviting you to look at a picture, or hear a symphony, or merely crowd and crush yourself among all sorts of vocal, excitable, brightly colored human beings. But, all the same, it is no mean rival to the quieter process of vegetable florescence. Whether or not there is a generous motive at the root, a desire to share and impart, or whether the animation is purely that of insensate fervor and friction, the effect, while it lasts, certainly encourages those who are young, and those who are ignorant, to think the world one great bazaar, with banners fluttering and divans heaped with spoils from every quarter of the globe for their delight.

As Cassandra Otway went about London provided with shillings that opened turnstiles, or more often with large white cards that disregarded turnstiles, the city seemed to her the most lavish and hospitable of hosts. After visiting the National Gallery, or Hertford House, or hearing Brahms or Beethoven at the Bechstein Hall, she would come back to find a new person awaiting her, in whose soul were imbedded some grains of the invaluable substance which she still called reality, and still believed that she could find. The Hilberys, as the saying is, "knew every one," and that arrogant claim was certainly upheld by the number of houses which, within a certain area, lit their lamps at night, opened their doors after 3 P.M., and admitted the Hilberys to their dining-rooms, say, once a month. An indefinable freedom and authority of manner, shared by most of the people who lived in these houses, seemed to indicate that whether it was a question of art, music, or government, they were well within the gates, and could smile indulgently at the vast mass of humanity which is forced to wait and struggle, and pay for entrance with common coin at the door. The gates opened instantly to admit Cassandra. She was naturally critical of what went on inside, and inclined to quote what Henry would have said; but she often succeeded in contradicting Henry, in his absence, and invariably paid her partner at dinner, or the kind old lady who remembered her grandmother, the compliment of believing that there was meaning in what they said. For the sake of the light in her eager eyes, much crudity of expression and some untidiness of person were forgiven her. It was generally felt that, given a year or two of experience, introduced to good dressmakers, and preserved from bad influences, she would be an acquisition. Those elderly ladies, who sit on the edge of ballrooms sampling the stuff of humanity between finger and thumb and breathing so evenly that the necklaces, which rise and fall upon their breasts, seem to represent some elemental force, such as the waves upon the ocean of humanity, concluded, a little smilingly, that she would do. They meant that she would in all probability marry some young man whose mother they respected.

William Rodney was fertile in suggestions. He knew of little galleries, and select concerts, and private performances, and somehow made time to meet Katharine and Cassandra, and to give them tea or dinner or supper in his rooms afterwards. Each one of her fourteen days thus promised to bear some bright illumination in its sober text. But Sunday approached. The day is usually dedicated to Nature. The weather was almost kindly enough for an expedition. But Cassandra rejected Hampton Court, Greenwich, Richmond, and Kew in favor of the Zoological Gardens. She had once trifled with the psychology of animals, and still knew something about inherited characteristics. On Sunday afternoon, therefore, Katharine, Cassandra, and William Rodney drove off to the Zoo. As their cab approached the entrance, Katharine bent forward and waved her hand to a young man who was walking rapidly in the same direction.

"There's Ralph Denham!" she exclaimed. "I told him to meet us here," she added. She had even come provided with a ticket for him. William's objection that he would not be admitted was, therefore, silenced directly. But the way in which the two men greeted each other was significant of what was going to happen. As soon as they had admired the little birds in the large cage William and Cassandra lagged behind, and Ralph and Katharine pressed on rather in advance. It was an arrangement in which William took his part, and one that suited his convenience, but he was annoyed all the same. He thought that Katharine should have told him that she had invited Denham to meet them.

"One of Katharine's friends," he said rather sharply. It was clear that he was irritated, and Cassandra felt for his annoyance. They were standing by the pen of some Oriental hog, and she was prodding the brute gently with the point of her umbrella, when a thousand little observations seemed, in some way, to collect in one center. The center was one of intense and curious emotion. Were they happy? She dismissed the question as she asked it, scorning herself for applying such simple measures to the rare and splendid emotions of so unique a couple. Nevertheless, her manner became immediately different, as if, for the first time, she felt consciously womanly, and as if William might conceivably wish later on to confide in her. She forgot all about the psychology of animals, and the recurrence of blue eyes and brown, and became instantly engrossed in her feelings as a woman who could administer consolation, and she hoped that Katharine would keep ahead with Mr. Denham, as a child who plays at being grown-up hopes that her mother won't come in just yet, and spoil the game. Or was it not rather that she had ceased to play at being grown-up, and was conscious, suddenly, that she was alarmingly mature and in earnest?

There was still unbroken silence between Katharine and Ralph Denham, but the occupants of the different cages served instead of speech.

"What have you been doing since we met?" Ralph asked at length.

"Doing?" she pondered. "Walking in and out of other people's houses. I wonder if these animals are happy?" she speculated, stopping before a gray bear, who was philosophically playing with a tassel which once, perhaps, formed part of a lady's parasol.

"I'm afraid Rodney didn't like my coming," Ralph remarked.

"No. But he'll soon get over that," she replied. The detachment expressed by her voice puzzled Ralph, and he would have been glad if she had explained her meaning further. But he was not going to press her for explanations. Each moment was to be, as far as he could make it, complete in itself, owing nothing of its happiness to explanations, borrowing neither bright nor dark tints from the future.

"The bears seem happy," he remarked. "But we must buy them a bag of something. There's the place to buy buns. Let's go and get them." They walked to the counter piled with little paper bags, and each simultaneously produced a shilling and pressed it upon the young lady, who did not know whether to oblige the lady or the gentleman, but decided, from conventional reasons, that it was the part of the gentleman to pay.

"I wish to pay," said Ralph peremptorily, refusing the coin which Katharine tendered. "I have a reason for what I do," he added, seeing her smile at his tone of decision.

"I believe you have a reason for everything," she agreed, breaking the bun into parts and tossing them down the bears' throats, "but I can't believe it's a good one this time. What is your reason?"

He refused to tell her. He could not explain to her that he was offering up consciously all his happiness to her, and wished, absurdly enough, to pour every possession he had upon the blazing pyre, even his silver and gold. He wished to keep this distance between them—the distance which separates the devotee from the image in the shrine.

Circumstances conspired to make this easier than it would have been, had they been seated in a drawing-room, for example, with a tea-tray between them. He saw her against a background of pale grottos and sleek hides; camels slanted their heavy-ridded eyes at her, giraffes fastidiously observed her from their melancholy eminence, and the pink-lined trunks of elephants cautiously abstracted buns from her outstretched hands. Then there were the hothouses. He saw her bending over pythons coiled upon the sand, or considering the brown rock breaking the stagnant water of the alligators' pool, or searching some minute section of tropical forest for the golden eye of a lizard or the indrawn movement of the green frogs' flanks. In particular, he saw her outlined against the deep green waters, in which squadrons of silvery fish wheeled incessantly, or ogled her for a moment, pressing their distorted mouths against the glass, quivering their tails straight out behind them. Again, there was the insect house, where she lifted the blinds of the little cages, and marveled at the purple circles marked upon the rich tussore wings of some lately emerged and semi-conscious butterfly, or at caterpillars immobile like the knobbed twigs of a pale-skinned tree, or at slim green snakes stabbing the glass wall again and again with their flickering cleft tongues. The heat of the air, and the bloom of heavy flowers, which swam in water or rose stiffly from great red jars, together with the display of curious patterns and fantastic shapes, produced an atmosphere in which human beings tended to look pale and to fall silent.

Opening the door of a house which rang with the mocking and profoundly unhappy laughter of monkeys, they discovered William and Cassandra. William appeared to be tempting some small reluctant animal to descend from an upper perch to partake of half an apple. Cassandra was reading out, in her high-pitched tones, an account of this creature's secluded disposition and nocturnal habits. She saw Katharine and exclaimed:

"Here you are! Do prevent William from torturing this unfortunate aye-aye."

"We thought we'd lost you," said William. He looked from one to the other, and seemed to take stock of Denham's unfashionable appearance. He seemed to wish to find some outlet for malevolence, but, failing one, he remained silent. The glance, the slight quiver of the upper lip, were not lost upon Katharine.

"William isn't kind to animals," she remarked. "He doesn't know what they like and what they don't like."

"I take it you're well versed in these matters, Denham," said Rodney, withdrawing his hand with the apple.

"It's mainly a question of knowing how to stroke them," Denham replied.

"Which is the way to the Reptile House?" Cassandra asked him, not from a genuine desire to visit the reptiles, but in obedience to her new-born feminine susceptibility, which urged her to charm and conciliate the other sex. Denham began to give her directions, and Katharine and William moved on together.

"I hope you've had a pleasant afternoon," William remarked.

"I like Ralph Denham," she replied.

"Ça se voit," William returned, with superficial urbanity.

Many retorts were obvious, but wishing, on the whole, for peace, Katharine merely inquired:

"Are you coming back to tea?"

"Cassandra and I thought of having tea at a little shop in Portland Place," he replied. "I don't know whether you and Denham would care to join us."

"I'll ask him," she replied, turning her head to look for him. But he and Cassandra were absorbed in the aye-aye once more.

William and Katharine watched them for a moment, and each looked curiously at the object of the other's preference. But resting his eye upon Cassandra, to whose elegance the dressmakers had now done justice, William said sharply:

"If you come, I hope you won't do your best to make me ridiculous."

"If that's what you're afraid of I certainly shan't come," Katharine replied.

They were professedly looking into the enormous central cage of monkeys, and being thoroughly annoyed by William, she compared him to a wretched misanthropical ape, huddled in a scrap of old shawl at the end of a pole, darting peevish glances of suspicion and distrust at his companions. Her tolerance was deserting her. The events of the past week had worn it thin. She was in one of those moods, perhaps not uncommon with either sex, when the other becomes very clearly distinguished, and of contemptible baseness, so that the necessity of association is degrading, and the tie, which at such moments is always extremely close, drags like a halter round the neck. William's exacting demands and his jealousy had pulled her down into some horrible swamp of her nature where the primeval struggle between man and woman still rages.

"You seem to delight in hurting me," William persisted. "Why did you say that just now about my behavior to animals?" As he spoke he rattled his stick against the bars of the cage, which gave his words an accompaniment peculiarly exasperating to Katharine's nerves.

"Because it's true. You never see what any one feels," she said. "You think of no one but yourself."

"That is not true," said William. By his determined rattling he had now collected the animated attention of some half-dozen apes. Either to propitiate them, or to show his consideration for their feelings, he proceeded to offer them the apple which he held.

The sight, unfortunately, was so comically apt in its illustration of the picture in her mind, the ruse was so transparent, that Katharine was seized with laughter. She laughed uncontrollably. William flushed red. No display of anger could have hurt his feelings more profoundly. It was not only that she was laughing at him; the detachment of the sound was horrible.

"I don't know what you're laughing at," he muttered, and, turning, found that the other couple had rejoined them. As if the matter had been privately agreed upon, the couples separated once more, Katharine and Denham passing out of the house without more than a perfunctory glance round them. Denham obeyed what seemed to be Katharine's wish in thus making haste. Some change had come over her. He connected it with her laughter, and her few words in private with Rodney; he felt that she had become unfriendly to him. She talked, but her remarks were indifferent, and when he spoke her attention seemed to wander. This change of mood was at first extremely disagreeable to him; but soon he found it salutary. The pale drizzling atmosphere of the day affected him, also. The charm, the insidious magic in which he had luxuriated, were suddenly gone; his feeling had become one of friendly respect, and to his great pleasure he found himself thinking spontaneously of the relief of finding himself alone in his room that night. In his surprise at the suddenness of the change, and at the extent of his freedom, he bethought him of a daring plan, by which the ghost of Katharine could be more effectually exorcised than by mere abstinence. He would ask her to come home with him to tea. He would force her through the mill of family life; he would place her in a light unsparing and revealing. His family would find nothing to admire in her, and she, he felt certain, would despise them all, and this, too, would help him. He felt himself becoming more and more merciless towards her. By such courageous measures any one, he thought, could end the absurd passions which were the cause of so much pain and waste. He could foresee a time when his experiences, his discovery, and his triumph were made available for younger brothers who found themselves in the same predicament. He looked at his watch, and remarked that the gardens would soon be closed.

"Anyhow," he added, "I think we've seen enough for one afternoon. Where have the others got to?" He looked over his shoulder, and, seeing no trace of them, remarked at once:

"We'd better be independent of them. The best plan will be for you to come back to tea with me."

"Why shouldn't you come with me?" she asked.

"Because we're next door to Highgate here," he replied promptly.

She assented, having very little notion whether Highgate was next door to Regent's Park or not. She was only glad to put off her return to the family tea-table in Chelsea for an hour or two. They proceeded with dogged determination through the winding roads of Regent's Park, and the Sunday-stricken streets of the neighborhood, in the direction of the Tube station. Ignorant of the way, she resigned herself entirely to him, and found his silence a convenient cover beneath which to continue her anger with Rodney.

When they stepped out of the train into the still grayer gloom of Highgate, she wondered, for the first time, where he was taking her. Had he a family, or did he live alone in rooms? On the whole she was inclined to believe that he was the only son of an aged, and possibly invalid, mother. She sketched lightly, upon the blank vista down which they walked, the little white house and the tremulous old lady rising from behind her tea-table to greet her with faltering words about "my son's friends," and was on the point of asking Ralph to tell her what she might expect, when he jerked open one of the infinite number of identical wooden doors, and led her up a tiled path to a porch in the Alpine style of architecture. As they listened to the shaking of the bell in the basement, she could summon no vision to replace the one so rudely destroyed.

"I must warn you to expect a family party," said Ralph. "They're mostly in on Sundays. We can go to my room afterwards."

"Have you many brothers and sisters?" she asked, without concealing her dismay.

"Six or seven," he replied grimly, as the door opened.

While Ralph took off his coat, she had time to notice the ferns and photographs and draperies, and to hear a hum, or rather a babble, of voices talking each other down, from the sound of them. The rigidity of extreme shyness came over her. She kept as far behind Denham as she could, and walked stiffly after him into a room blazing with unshaded lights, which fell upon a number of people, of different ages, sitting round a large dining-room table untidily strewn with food, and unflinchingly lit up by incandescent gas. Ralph walked straight to the far end of the table.

"Mother, this is Miss Hilbery," he said.

A large elderly lady, bent over an unsatisfactory spirit-lamp, looked up with a little frown, and observed:

"I beg your pardon. I thought you were one of my own girls. Dorothy," she continued on the same breath, to catch the servant before she left the room, "we shall want some more methylated spirits—unless the lamp itself is out of order. If one of you could invent a good spirit-lamp——" she sighed, looking generally down the table, and then began seeking among the china before her for two clean cups for the new-comers.

The unsparing light revealed more ugliness than Katharine had seen in one room for a very long time. It was the ugliness of enormous folds of brown material, looped and festooned, of plush curtains, from which depended balls and fringes, partially concealing bookshelves swollen with black school-texts. Her eye was arrested by crossed scabbards of fretted wood upon the dull green wall, and whereever there was a high flat eminence, some fern waved from a pot of crinkled china, or a bronze horse reared so high that the stump of a tree had to sustain his forequarters. The waters of family life seemed to rise and close over her head, and she munched in silence.

At length Mrs. Denham looked up from her teacups and remarked:

"You see, Miss Hilbery, my children all come in at different hours and want different things. (The tray should go up if you've done, Johnnie.) My boy Charles is in bed with a cold. What else can you expect?—standing in the wet playing football. We did try drawing-room tea, but it didn't do."

A boy of sixteen, who appeared to be Johnnie, grumbled derisively both at the notion of drawing-room tea and at the necessity of carrying a tray up to his brother. But he took himself off, being enjoined by his mother to mind what he was doing, and shut the door after him.

"It's much nicer like this," said Katharine, applying herself with determination to the dissection of her cake; they had given her too large a slice. She knew that Mrs. Denham suspected her of critical comparisons. She knew that she was making poor progress with her cake. Mrs. Denham had looked at her sufficiently often to make it clear to Katharine that she was asking who this young woman was, and why Ralph had brought her to tea with them. There was an obvious reason, which Mrs. Denham had probably reached by this time. Outwardly, she was behaving with rather rusty and laborious civility. She was making conversation about the amenities of Highgate, its development and situation.

"When I first married," she said, "Highgate was quite separate from London, Miss Hilbery, and this house, though you wouldn't believe it, had a view of apple orchards. That was before the Middletons built their house in front of us."

"It must be a great advantage to live at the top of a hill," said Katharine. Mrs. Denham agreed effusively, as if her opinion of Katharine's sense had risen.

"Yes, indeed, we find it very healthy," she said, and she went on, as people who live in the suburbs so often do, to prove that it was healthier, more convenient, and less spoilt than any suburb round London. She spoke with such emphasis that it was quite obvious that she expressed unpopular views, and that her children disagreed with her.

"The ceiling's fallen down in the pantry again," said Hester, a girl of eighteen, abruptly.

"The whole house will be down one of these days," James muttered.

"Nonsense," said Mrs. Denham. "It's only a little bit of plaster—I don't see how any house could be expected to stand the wear and tear you give it." Here some family joke exploded, which Katharine could not follow. Even Mrs. Denham laughed against her will.

"Miss Hilbery's thinking us all so rude," she added reprovingly. Miss Hilbery smiled and shook her head, and was conscious that a great many eyes rested upon her, for a moment, as if they would find pleasure in discussing her when she was gone. Owing, perhaps, to this critical glance, Katharine decided that Ralph Denham's family was commonplace, unshapely, lacking in charm, and fitly expressed by the hideous nature of their furniture and decorations. She glanced along a mantelpiece ranged with bronze chariots, silver vases, and china ornaments that were either facetious or eccentric.

She did not apply her judgment consciously to Ralph, but when she looked at him, a moment later, she rated him lower than at any other time of their acquaintanceship.

He had made no effort to tide over the discomforts of her introduction, and now, engaged in argument with his brother, apparently forgot her presence. She must have counted upon his support more than she realized, for this indifference, emphasized, as it was, by the insignificant commonplace of his surroundings, awoke her, not only to that ugliness, but to her own folly. She thought of one scene after another in a few seconds, with that shudder which is almost a blush. She had believed him when he spoke of friendship. She had believed in a spiritual light burning steadily and steadfastly behind the erratic disorder and incoherence of life. The light was now gone out, suddenly, as if a sponge had blotted it. The litter of the table and the tedious but exacting conversation of Mrs. Denham remained: they struck, indeed, upon a mind bereft of all defences, and, keenly conscious of the degradation which is the result of strife whether victorious or not, she thought gloomily of her loneliness, of life's futility, of the barren prose of reality, of William Rodney, of her mother, and the unfinished book.

Her answers to Mrs. Denham were perfunctory to the verge of rudeness, and to Ralph, who watched her narrowly, she seemed further away than was compatible with her physical closeness. He glanced at her, and ground out further steps in his argument, determined that no folly should remain when this experience was over. Next moment, a silence, sudden and complete, descended upon them all. The silence of all these people round the untidy table was enormous and hideous; something horrible seemed about to burst from it, but they endured it obstinately. A second later the door opened and there was a stir of relief; cries of "Hullo, Joan! There's nothing left for you to eat," broke up the oppressive concentration of so many eyes upon the table-cloth, and set the waters of family life dashing in brisk little waves again. It was obvious that Joan had some mysterious and beneficent power upon her family. She went up to Katharine as if she had heard of her, and was very glad to see her at last. She explained that she had been visiting an uncle who was ill, and that had kept her. No, she hadn't had any tea, but a slice of bread would do. Some one handed up a hot cake, which had been keeping warm in the fender; she sat down by her mother's side, Mrs. Denham's anxieties seemed to relax, and every one began eating and drinking, as if tea had begun over again. Hester voluntarily explained to Katharine that she was reading to pass some examination, because she wanted more than anything in the whole world to go to Newnham.

"Now, just let me hear you decline *amo*—I love," Johnnie demanded.

"No, Johnnie, no Greek at meal-times," said Joan, overhearing him instantly. "She's up at all hours of the night over her books, Miss Hilbery, and I'm sure that's not the way to pass examinations," she went on, smiling at Katharine, with the worried humorous smile of the elder sister whose younger brothers and sisters have become almost like children of her own.

"Joan, you don't really think that *amo* is Greek?" Ralph asked.

"Did I say Greek? Well, never mind. No dead languages at tea-time. My dear boy, don't trouble to make me any toast—"

"Or if you do, surely there's the toasting-fork somewhere?" said Mrs. Denham, still cherishing the belief that the bread-knife could be spoilt. "Do one of you ring and ask for one," she said, without any conviction that she would be obeyed. "But is Ann coming to be with Uncle Joseph?" she continued. "If so, surely they had better send Amy to us—" and in the mysterious delight of learning further details of these arrangements, and suggesting more sensible plans of her own, which, from the aggrieved way in which she spoke, she did not seem to expect any one to adopt, Mrs. Denham completely forgot the presence of a well-dressed visitor, who had to be informed about the amenities of Highgate. As soon as Joan had taken her seat, an argument had sprung up on either side of Katharine, as to whether the Salvation Army has any right to play hymns at street corners on Sunday mornings, thereby making it impossible for James to have his sleep out, and tampering with the rights of individual liberty.

"You see, James likes to lie in bed and sleep like a hog," said Johnnie, explaining himself to Katharine, whereupon James fired up and, making her his goal, also exclaimed:

"Because Sundays are my one chance in the week of having my sleep out. Johnnie messes with stinking chemicals in the pantry—"

They appealed to her, and she forgot her cake and began to laugh and talk and argue with sudden animation. The large family seemed to her so warm and various that she forgot to censure them for their taste in pottery. But the personal question between James and Johnnie merged into some argument already, apparently, debated, so that the parts had been distributed among the family, in which Ralph took the lead; and Katharine found herself opposed to him and the champion of Johnnie's cause, who, it appeared, always lost his head and got excited in argument with Ralph.

"Yes, yes, that's what I mean. She's got it right," he exclaimed, after Katharine had restated his case, and made it more precise. The debate was left almost solely to Katharine and Ralph. They looked into each other's eyes fixedly, like wrestlers trying to see what movement is coming next, and while Ralph spoke, Katharine bit her lower lip, and was always ready with her next point as soon as he had done. They were very well matched, and held the opposite views.

But at the most exciting stage of the argument, for no reason that Katharine could see, all chairs were pushed back, and one after another the Denham family got up and went out of the door, as if a bell had summoned them. She was not used to the clockwork regulations of a large family. She hesitated in what she was saying, and rose. Mrs. Denham and Joan had drawn together and stood by the fireplace, slightly raising their skirts above their ankles, and discussing something which had an air of being very serious and very private. They appeared to have forgotten her presence among them. Ralph stood holding the door open for her.

"Won't you come up to my room?" he said. And Katharine, glancing back at Joan, who smiled at her in a preoccupied way, followed Ralph upstairs. She was thinking of their argument, and when, after the long climb, he opened his door, she began at once.

"The question is, then, at what point is it right for the individual to assert his will against the will of the State."

For some time they continued the argument, and then the intervals between one statement and the next became longer and longer, and they spoke more speculatively and less pugnaciously, and at last fell silent. Katharine went over the argument in her mind, remembering how, now and then, it had been set conspicuously on the right course by some remark offered either by James or by Johnnie.

"Your brothers are very clever," she said. "I suppose you're in the habit of arguing?"

"James and Johnnie will go on like that for hours," Ralph replied. "So will Hester, if you start her upon Elizabethan dramatists."

"And the little girl with the pigtail?"

"Molly? She's only ten. But they're always arguing among themselves."

He was immensely pleased by Katharine's praise of his brothers and sisters. He would have liked to go on telling her about them, but he checked himself.

"I see that it must be difficult to leave them," Katharine continued. His deep pride in his family was more evident to him, at that moment, than ever before, and the idea of living alone in a cottage was ridiculous. All that brotherhood and sisterhood, and a common childhood in a common past mean, all the stability, the unambitious comradeship, and tacit understanding of family life at its best, came to his mind, and he thought of them as a company, of which he was the leader, bound on a difficult, dreary, but glorious voyage. And it was Katharine who had opened his eyes to this, he thought.

A little dry chirp from the corner of the room now roused her attention.

"My tame rook," he explained briefly. "A cat had bitten one of its legs." She looked at the rook, and her eyes went from one object to another.

"You sit here and read?" she said, her eyes resting upon his books. He said that he was in the habit of working there at night.

"The great advantage of Highgate is the view over London. At night the view from my window is splendid." He was extremely anxious that she should appreciate his view, and she rose to see what was to be seen. It was already dark enough for the turbulent haze to be yellow with the light of street lamps, and she tried to determine the quarters of the city beneath her. The sight of her gazing from his window gave him a peculiar satisfaction. When she turned, at length, he was still sitting motionless in his chair.

"It must be late," she said. "I must be going." She settled upon the arm of the chair irresolutely, thinking that she had no wish to go home. William would be there, and he would find some way of making things unpleasant for her, and the memory of their quarrel came back to her. She had noticed Ralph's coldness, too. She looked at him, and from his fixed stare she thought that he must be working out some theory, some argument. He had thought, perhaps, of some fresh point in his position, as to the bounds of personal liberty. She waited, silently, thinking about liberty.

"You've won again," he said at last, without moving.

"I've won?" she repeated, thinking of the argument.

"I wish to God I hadn't asked you here," he burst out.

"What do you mean?"

"When you're here, it's different–I'm happy. You've only to walk to the window–you've only to talk about liberty. When I saw you down there among them all—" He stopped short.

"You thought how ordinary I was."

"I tried to think so. But I thought you more wonderful than ever."

An immense relief, and a reluctance to enjoy that relief, conflicted in her heart.

She slid down into the chair.

"I thought you disliked me," she said.

"God knows I tried," he replied. "I've done my best to see you as you are, without any of this damned romantic nonsense. That was why I asked you here, and it's increased my folly. When you're gone I shall look out of that window and think of you. I shall waste the whole evening thinking of you. I shall waste my whole life, I believe."

He spoke with such vehemence that her relief disappeared; she frowned; and her tone changed to one almost of severity.

"This is what I foretold. We shall gain nothing but unhappiness. Look at me, Ralph." He looked at her. "I assure you that I'm far more ordinary than I appear. Beauty means nothing whatever. In fact, the most beautiful women are generally the most stupid. I'm not that, but I'm a matter-of-fact, prosaic, rather ordinary character; I order the dinner, I pay the bills, I do the accounts, I wind up the clock, and I never look at a book."

"You forget—" he began, but she would not let him speak.

"You come and see me among flowers and pictures, and think me mysterious, romantic, and all the rest of it. Being yourself very inexperienced and very emotional, you go home and invent a story about me, and now you can't separate me from the person you've imagined me to be. You call that, I suppose, being in love; as a matter of fact it's being in delusion. All romantic people are the same," she added. "My mother spends her life in making stories about the people she's fond of. But I won't have you do it about me, if I can help it."

"You can't help it," he said.

"I warn you it's the source of all evil."

"And of all good," he added.

"You'll find out that I'm not what you think me."

"Perhaps. But I shall gain more than I lose."

"If such gain's worth having."

They were silent for a space.

"That may be what we have to face," he said. "There may be nothing else. Nothing but what we imagine."

"The reason of our loneliness," she mused, and they were silent for a time.

"When are you to be married?" he asked abruptly, with a change of tone.

"Not till September, I think. It's been put off."

"You won't be lonely then," he said. "According to what people say, marriage is a very queer business. They say it's different from anything else. It may be true. I've known one or two cases where it seems to be true." He hoped that she would go on with the subject. But she made no reply. He had done his best to master himself, and his voice was sufficiently indifferent, but her silence tormented him. She would never speak to him of Rodney of her own accord, and her reserve left a whole continent of her soul in darkness.

"It may be put off even longer than that," she said, as if by an afterthought. "Some one in the office is ill, and William has to take his place. We may put it off for some time in fact."

"That's rather hard on him, isn't it?" Ralph asked.

"He has his work," she replied. "He has lots of things that interest him. . . . I know I've been to that place," she broke off, pointing to a photograph. "But I can't remember where it is—oh, of course it's Oxford. Now, what about your cottage?"

"I'm not going to take it."

"How you change your mind!" she smiled.

"It's not that," he said impatiently. "It's that I want to be where I can see you."

"Our compact is going to hold in spite of all I've said?" she asked.

"For ever, so far as I'm concerned," he replied.

"You're going to go on dreaming and imagining and making up stories about me as you walk along the street, and pretending that we're riding in a forest, or landing on an island—"

"No. I shall think of you ordering dinner, paying bills, doing the accounts, showing old ladies the relics—"

"That's better," she said. "You can think of me tomorrow morning looking up dates in the 'Dictionary of National Biography.'"

"And forgetting your purse," Ralph added.

At this she smiled, but in another moment her smile faded, either because of his words or of the way in which he spoke them. She was capable of forgetting things. He saw that. But what more did he see? Was he not looking at something she had never shown to anybody? Was it not something so profound that the notion of his seeing it almost shocked her? Her smile faded, and for a moment she seemed upon the point of speaking, but looking at him in silence, with a look that seemed to ask what she could not put into words, she turned and bade him good night.

28

Like a strain of music, the effect of Katharine's presence slowly died from the room in which Ralph sat alone. The music had ceased in the rapture of its melody. He strained to catch the faintest lingering echoes; for a moment the memory lulled him into peace; but soon it failed, and he paced the room so hungry for the sound to come again that he was conscious of no other desire left in life. She had gone without speaking; abruptly a chasm had been cut in his course, down which the tide of his being plunged in disorder; fell upon rocks; flung itself to destruction. The distress had an effect of physical ruin and disaster. He trembled; he was white; he felt exhausted, as if by a great physical effort. He sank at last into a chair standing opposite her empty one, and marked, mechanically, with his eye upon the clock, how she went farther and farther from him, was home now, and now, doubtless, again with Rodney. But it was long before he could realize these facts; the immense desire for her presence churned his senses into foam, into froth, into a haze of emotion that removed all facts from his grasp, and gave him a strange sense of distance, even from the material shapes of wall and window by which he was surrounded. The prospect of the future, now that the strength of his passion was revealed to him, appalled him.

The marriage would take place in September, she had said; that allowed him, then, six full months in which to undergo these terrible extremes of emotion. Six months of torture, and after that the silence of the grave, the isolation of the insane, the exile of the damned; at best, a life from which the chief good was knowingly and for ever excluded. An impartial judge might have assured him that his chief hope of recovery lay in this mystic temper, which identified a living woman with much that no human beings long possess in the eyes of each other; she would pass, and the desire for her vanish, but his belief in what she stood for, detached from her, would remain. This line of thought offered, perhaps, some respite, and possessed of a brain that had its station considerably above the tumult of the senses, he tried to reduce the vague and wandering incoherency of his emotions to order. The sense of self-preservation was strong in him, and Katharine herself had strangely revived it by convincing him that his family deserved and needed all his strength. She was right, and for their sake, if not for his own, this passion, which could bear no fruit, must be cut off, uprooted, shown to be as visionary and baseless as she had maintained. The best way of achieving this was not to run away from her, but to face her, and having steeped himself in her qualities, to convince his reason that they were, as she assured him, not those that he imagined. She was a practical woman, a domestic wife for an inferior poet, endowed with romantic beauty by some freak of unintelligent Nature. No doubt her beauty itself would not stand examination. He had the means of settling this point at least. He possessed a book of photographs from the Greek statues; the head of a goddess, if the lower part were concealed, had often given him the ecstasy of being in Katharine's presence. He took it down from the shelf and found the picture. To this he added a note from her, bidding him meet her at the Zoo. He had a flower which he had picked at Kew to teach her botany. Such were his relics. He placed them before him, and set himself to visualize her so clearly that no deception or delusion was possible. In a second he could see her, with the sun slanting across her dress, coming towards him down the green walk at Kew. He made her sit upon the seat beside him. He heard her voice, so low and yet so decided in its tone; she spoke reasonably of indifferent matters. He could see her faults, and analyze her virtues. His pulse became quieter, and his brain increased in clarity. This time she could not escape him. The illusion of her presence became more and more complete. They seemed to pass in and out of each other's minds, questioning and answering. The utmost fullness of communion seemed to be theirs. Thus united, he felt himself raised to an eminence, exalted, and filled with a power of achievement such as he had never known in singleness. Once more he told over conscientiously her faults, both of face and character; they were clearly known to him; but they merged themselves in the flawless union that was born of their association. They surveyed life to its uttermost limits. How deep it was when looked at from this height! How sublime! How the commonest things moved him almost to tears! Thus, he forgot the inevitable limitations; he forgot her absence, he thought it of no account whether she married him or another; nothing mattered, save that she should exist, and that he should love her. Some words of these reflections were uttered aloud, and it happened that among them were the words, "I love her." It was the first time that he had used the word "love" to describe his feeling; madness, romance, hallucination—he had called it by these names before; but having, apparently by accident, stumbled upon the word "love," he repeated it again and again with a sense of revelation.

"But I'm in love with you!" he exclaimed, with something like dismay. He leant against the window-sill, looking over the city as she had looked. Everything had become miraculously different and completely distinct. His feelings were justified and needed no further explanation. But he must impart them to some one, because his discovery was so important that it concerned other people too. Shutting the book of Greek photographs, and hiding his relics, he ran downstairs, snatched his coat, and passed out of doors.

The lamps were being lit, but the streets were dark enough and empty enough to let him walk his fastest, and to talk aloud as he walked. He had no doubt where he was going. He was going to find Mary Datchet. The desire to share what he felt, with some one who understood it, was so imperious that he did not question it. He was soon in her street. He ran up the stairs leading to her flat two steps at a time, and it never crossed his mind that she might not be at home. As he rang her bell, he seemed to himself to be announcing the presence of something wonderful that was separate from himself, and gave him power and authority over all other people. Mary came to the door after a moment's pause. He was perfectly silent, and in the dusk his face looked completely white. He followed her into her room.

"Do you know each other?" she said, to his extreme surprise, for he had counted on finding her alone. A young man rose, and said that he knew Ralph by sight.

"We were just going through some papers," said Mary. "Mr. Basnett has to help me, because I don't know much about my work yet. It's the new society," she explained. "I'm the secretary. I'm no longer at Russell Square."

The voice in which she gave this information was so constrained as to sound almost harsh.

"What are your aims?" said Ralph. He looked neither at Mary nor at Mr. Basnett. Mr. Basnett thought he had seldom seen a more disagreeable or formidable man than this friend of Mary's, this sarcastic-looking, white-faced Mr. Denham, who seemed to demand, as if by right, an account of their proposals, and to criticize them before he had heard them. Nevertheless, he explained his projects as clearly as he could, and knew that he wished Mr. Denham to think well of them.

"I see," said Ralph, when he had done. "D'you know, Mary," he suddenly remarked, "I believe I'm in for a cold. Have you any quinine?" The look which he cast at her frightened her; it expressed mutely, perhaps without his own consciousness, something deep, wild, and passionate. She left the room at once. Her heart beat fast at the knowledge of Ralph's presence; but it beat with pain, and with an extraordinary fear. She stood listening for a moment to the voices in the next room.

"Of course, I agree with you," she heard Ralph say, in this strange voice, to Mr. Basnett. "But there's more that might be done. Have you seen Judson, for instance? You should make a point of getting him."

Mary returned with the quinine.

"Judson's address?" Mr. Basnett inquired, pulling out his notebook and preparing to write. For twenty minutes, perhaps, he wrote down names, addresses, and other suggestions that Ralph dictated to him. Then, when Ralph fell silent, Mr. Basnett felt that his presence was not desired, and thanking Ralph for his help, with a sense that he was very young and ignorant compared with him, he said good-bye.

"Mary," said Ralph, directly Mr. Basnett had shut the door and they were alone together. "Mary," he repeated. But the old difficulty of speaking to Mary without reserve prevented him from continuing. His desire to proclaim his love for Katharine was still strong in him, but he had felt, directly he saw Mary, that he could not share it with her. The feeling increased as he sat talking to Mr. Basnett. And yet all the time he was thinking of Katharine, and marveling at his love. The tone in which he spoke Mary's name was harsh.

"What is it, Ralph?" she asked, startled by his tone. She looked at him anxiously, and her little frown showed that she was trying painfully to understand him, and was puzzled. He could feel her groping for his meaning, and he was annoyed with her, and thought how he had always found her slow, painstaking, and clumsy. He had behaved badly to her, too, which made his irritation the more acute. Without waiting for him to answer, she rose as if his answer were indifferent to her, and began to put in order some papers that Mr. Basnett had left on the table. She hummed a scrap of a tune under her breath, and moved about the room as if she were occupied in making things tidy, and had no other concern.

"You'll stay and dine?" she said casually, returning to her seat.

"No," Ralph replied. She did not press him further. They sat side by side without speaking, and Mary reached her hand for her work basket, and took out her sewing and threaded a needle.

"That's a clever young man," Ralph observed, referring to Mr. Basnett.

"I'm glad you thought so. It's tremendously interesting work, and considering everything, I think we've done very well. But I'm inclined to agree with you; we ought to try to be more conciliatory. We're absurdly strict. It's difficult to see that there may be sense in what one's opponents say, though they are one's opponents. Horace Basnett is certainly too uncompromising. I mustn't forget to see that he writes that letter to Judson. You're too busy, I suppose, to come on to our committee?" She spoke in the most impersonal manner.

"I may be out of town," Ralph replied, with equal distance of manner.

"Our executive meets every week, of course," she observed. "But some of our members don't come more than once a month. Members of Parliament are the worst; it was a mistake, I think, to ask them."

She went on sewing in silence.

"You've not taken your quinine," she said, looking up and seeing the tabloids upon the mantelpiece.

"I don't want it," said Ralph shortly.

"Well, you know best," she replied tranquilly.

"Mary, I'm a brute!" he exclaimed. "Here I come and waste your time, and do nothing but make myself disagreeable."

"A cold coming on does make one feel wretched," she replied.

"I've not got a cold. That was a lie. There's nothing the matter with me. I'm mad, I suppose. I ought to have had the decency to keep away. But I wanted to see you–I wanted to tell you–I'm in love, Mary." He spoke the word, but, as he spoke it, it seemed robbed of substance.

"In love, are you?" she said quietly. "I'm glad, Ralph."

"I suppose I'm in love. Anyhow, I'm out of my mind. I can't think, I can't work, I don't care a hang for anything in the world. Good Heavens, Mary! I'm in torment! One moment I'm happy; next I'm miserable. I hate her for half an hour; then I'd give my whole life to be with her for ten minutes; all the time I don't know what I feel, or why I feel it; it's insanity, and yet it's perfectly reasonable. Can you make any sense of it? Can you see what's happened? I'm raving, I know; don't listen, Mary; go on with your work."

He rose and began, as usual, to pace up and down the room. He knew that what he had just said bore very little resemblance to what he felt, for Mary's presence acted upon him like a very strong magnet, drawing from him certain expressions which were not those he made use of when he spoke to himself, nor did they represent his deepest feelings. He felt a little contempt for himself at having spoken thus; but somehow he had been forced into speech.

"Do sit down," said Mary suddenly. "You make me so—" She spoke with unusual irritability, and Ralph, noticing it with surprise, sat down at once.

"You haven't told me her name–you'd rather not, I suppose?"

"Her name? Katharine Hilbery."

"But she's engaged—"

"To Rodney. They're to be married in September."

"I see," said Mary. But in truth the calm of his manner, now that he was sitting down once more, wrapt her in the presence of something which she felt to be so strong, so mysterious, so incalculable, that she scarcely dared to attempt to intercept it by any word or question that she was able to frame. She looked at Ralph blankly, with a kind of awe in her face, her lips slightly parted, and her brows raised. He was apparently quite unconscious of her gaze. Then, as if she could look no longer, she leant back in her chair, and half closed her eyes. The distance between them hurt her terribly; one thing after another came into her mind, tempting her to assail Ralph with questions, to force him to confide in her, and to enjoy once more his intimacy. But she rejected every impulse, for she could not speak without doing violence to some reserve which had grown between them, putting them a little far from each other, so that he seemed to her dignified and remote, like a person she no longer knew well.

"Is there anything that I could do for you?" she asked gently, and even with courtesy, at length.

"You could see her–no, that's not what I want; you mustn't bother about me, Mary." He, too, spoke very gently.

"I'm afraid no third person can do anything to help," she added.

"No," he shook his head. "Katharine was saying today how lonely we are." She saw the effort with which he spoke Katharine's name, and believed that he forced himself to make amends now for his concealment in the past. At any rate, she was conscious of no anger against him; but rather of a deep pity for one condemned to suffer as she had suffered. But in the case of Katharine it was different; she was indignant with Katharine.

"There's always work," she said, a little aggressively.

Ralph moved directly.

"Do you want to be working now?" he asked.

"No, no. It's Sunday," she replied. "I was thinking of Katharine. She doesn't understand about work. She's never had to. She doesn't know what work is. I've only found out myself quite lately. But it's the thing that saves one—I'm sure of that."

"There are other things, aren't there?" he hesitated.

"Nothing that one can count upon," she returned. "After all, other people—" she stopped, but forced herself to go on. "Where should I be now if I hadn't got to go to my office every day? Thousands of people would tell you the same thing—thousands of women. I tell you, work is the only thing that saved me, Ralph." He set his mouth, as if her words rained blows on him; he looked as if he had made up his mind to bear anything she might say, in silence. He had deserved it, and there would be relief in having to bear it. But she broke off, and rose as if to fetch something from the next room. Before she reached the door she turned back, and stood facing him, self-possessed, and yet defiant and formidable in her composure.

"It's all turned out splendidly for me," she said. "It will for you, too. I'm sure of that. Because, after all, Katharine is worth it."

"Mary—!" he exclaimed. But her head was turned away, and he could not say what he wished to say. "Mary, you're splendid," he concluded. She faced him as he spoke, and gave him her hand. She had suffered and relinquished, she had seen her future turned from one of infinite promise to one of barrenness, and yet, somehow, over what she scarcely knew, and with what results she could hardly foretell, she had conquered. With Ralph's eyes upon her, smiling straight back at him serenely and proudly, she knew, for the first time, that she had conquered. She let him kiss her hand.

The streets were empty enough on Sunday night, and if the Sabbath, and the domestic amusements proper to the Sabbath, had not kept people indoors, a high strong wind might very probably have done so. Ralph Denham was aware of a tumult in the street much in accordance with his own sensations. The gusts, sweeping along the Strand, seemed at the same time to blow a clear space across the sky in which stars appeared, and for a short time the quicks-peeding silver moon riding through clouds, as if they were waves of water surging round her and over her. They swamped her, but she emerged; they broke over her and covered her again; she issued forth indomitable. In the country fields all the wreckage of winter was being dispersed; the dead leaves, the withered bracken, the dry and discolored grass, but no bud would be broken, nor would the new stalks that showed above the earth take any harm, and perhaps tomorrow a line of blue or yellow would show through a slit in their green. But the whirl of the atmosphere alone was in Denham's mood, and what of star or blossom appeared was only as a light gleaming for a second upon heaped waves fast following each other. He had not been able to speak to Mary, though for a moment he had come near enough to be tantalized by a wonderful possibility of understanding. But the desire to communicate something of the very greatest importance possessed him completely; he still wished to bestow this gift upon some other human being; he sought their company. More by instinct than by conscious choice, he took the direction which led to Rodney's rooms. He knocked loudly upon his door; but no one answered. He rang the bell. It took him some time to accept the fact that Rodney was out. When he could no longer pretend that the sound of the wind in the old building was the sound of some one rising from his chair, he ran downstairs again, as if his goal had been altered and only just revealed to him. He walked in the direction of Chelsea.

But physical fatigue, for he had not dined and had tramped both far and fast, made him sit for a moment upon a seat on the Embankment. One of the regular occupants of those seats, an elderly man who had drunk himself, probably, out of work and lodging, drifted up, begged a match, and sat down beside him. It was a windy night, he said; times were hard; some long story of bad luck and injustice followed, told so often that the man seemed to be talking to himself, or, perhaps, the neglect of his audience had long made any attempt to catch their attention seem scarcely worth while. When he began to speak Ralph had a wild desire to talk to him; to question him; to make him understand. He did, in fact, interrupt him at one point; but it was useless. The ancient story of failure, ill-luck, undeserved disaster, went down the wind, disconnected syllables flying past Ralph's ears with a queer alternation of loudness and faintness as if, at certain moments, the man's memory of his wrongs revived and then flagged, dying down at last into a grumble of resignation, which seemed to represent a final lapse into the accustomed despair. The unhappy voice afflicted Ralph, but it also angered him. And when the elderly man refused to listen and mumbled on, an odd image came to his mind of a lighthouse besieged by the flying bodies of lost birds, who were dashed senseless, by the gale, against the glass. He had a strange sensation that he was both lighthouse and bird; he was steadfast and brilliant; and at the same time he was whirled, with all other things, senseless against the glass. He got up, left his tribute of silver, and pressed on, with the wind against him. The image of the lighthouse and the storm full of birds persisted, taking the place of more definite thoughts, as he walked past the Houses of Parliament and down Grosvenor Road, by the side of the river. In his state of physical fatigue, details merged themselves in the vaster prospect, of which the flying gloom and the intermittent lights of lamp-posts and private houses were the outward token, but he never lost his sense of walking in the direction of Katharine's house. He took it for granted that something would then happen, and, as he walked on, his mind became more and more full of pleasure and expectancy. Within a certain radius of her house the streets came under the influence of her presence. Each house had an individuality known to Ralph, because of the tremendous individuality of the house in which she lived. For some yards before reaching the Hilberys' door he walked in a trance of pleasure, but when he reached it, and pushed the gate of the little garden open, he hesitated. He did not know what to do next. There was no hurry, however, for the outside of the house held pleasure enough to last him some time longer. He crossed the road, and leant against the balustrade of the Embankment, fixing his eyes upon the house.

Lights burnt in the three long windows of the drawing-room. The space of the room behind became, in Ralph's vision, the center of the dark, flying wilderness of the world; the justification for the welter of confusion surrounding it; the steady light which cast its beams, like those of a lighthouse, with searching composure over the trackless waste. In this little sanctuary were gathered together several different people, but their identity was dissolved in a general glory of something that might, perhaps, be called civilization; at any rate, all dryness, all safety, all that stood up above the surge and preserved a consciousness of its own, was centered in the drawing-room of the Hilberys. Its purpose was beneficent; and yet so far above his level as to have something austere about it, a light that cast itself out and yet kept itself aloof. Then he began, in his mind, to distinguish different individuals within, consciously refusing as yet to attack the figure of Katharine. His thoughts lingered over Mrs. Hilbery and Cassandra; and then he turned to Rodney and Mr. Hilbery. Physically, he saw them bathed in that steady flow of yellow light which filled the long oblongs of the windows; in their movements they were beautiful; and in their speech he figured a reserve of meaning, unspoken, but understood. At length, after all this half-conscious selection and arrangement, he allowed himself to approach the figure of Katharine herself; and instantly the scene was flooded with excitement. He did not see her in the body; he seemed curiously to see her as a shape of light, the light itself; he seemed, simplified and exhausted as he was, to be like one of those lost birds fascinated by the lighthouse and held to the glass by the splendor of the blaze.

These thoughts drove him to tramp a beat up and down the pavement before the Hilberys' gate. He did not trouble himself to make any plans for the future. Something of an unknown kind would decide both the coming year and the coming hour. Now and again, in his vigil, he sought the light in the long windows, or glanced at the ray which gilded a few leaves and a few blades of grass in the little garden. For a long time the light burnt without changing. He had just reached the limit of his beat and was turning, when the front door opened, and the aspect of the house was entirely changed. A black figure came down the little pathway and paused at the gate. Denham understood instantly that it was Rodney. Without hesitation, and conscious only of a great friendliness for any one coming from that lighted room, he walked straight up to him and stopped him. In the flurry of the wind Rodney was taken aback, and for the moment tried to press on, muttering something, as if he suspected a demand upon his charity.

"Goodness, Denham, what are you doing here?" he exclaimed, recognizing him.

Ralph mumbled something about being on his way home. They walked on together, though Rodney walked quick enough to make it plain that he had no wish for company.

He was very unhappy. That afternoon Cassandra had repulsed him; he had tried to explain to her the difficulties of the situation, and to suggest the nature of his feelings for her without saying anything definite or anything offensive to her. But he had lost his head; under the goad of Katharine's ridicule he had said too much, and Cassandra, superb in her dignity and severity, had refused to hear another word, and threatened an immediate return to her home. His agitation, after an evening spent between the two women, was extreme. Moreover, he could not help suspecting that Ralph was wandering near the Hilberys' house, at this hour, for reasons connected with Katharine. There was probably some understanding between them—not that anything of the kind mattered to him now. He was convinced that he had never cared for any one save Cassandra, and Katharine's future was no concern of his. Aloud, he said, shortly, that he was very tired and wished to find a cab. But on Sunday night, on the Embankment, cabs were hard to come by, and Rodney found himself constrained to walk some distance, at any rate, in Denham's company. Denham maintained his silence. Rodney's irritation lapsed. He found the silence oddly suggestive of the good masculine qualities which he much respected, and had at this moment great reason to need. After the mystery, difficulty, and uncertainty of dealing with the other sex, intercourse with one's own is apt to have a composing and even ennobling influence, since plain speaking is possible and subterfuges of no avail. Rodney, too, was much in need of a confidant; Katharine, despite her promises of help, had failed him at the critical moment; she had gone off with Denham; she was, perhaps, tormenting Denham as she had tormented him. How grave and stable he seemed, speaking little, and walking firmly, compared with what Rodney knew of his own torments and indecisions! He began to cast about for some way of telling the story of his relations with Katharine and Cassandra that would not lower him in Denham's eyes. It then occurred to him that, perhaps, Katharine herself had confided in Denham; they had something in common; it was likely that they had discussed him that very afternoon. The desire to discover what they had said of him now came uppermost in his mind. He recalled Katharine's laugh; he remembered that she had gone, laughing, to walk with Denham.

"Did you stay long after we'd left?" he asked abruptly.

"No. We went back to my house."

This seemed to confirm Rodney's belief that he had been discussed. He turned over the unpalatable idea for a while, in silence.

"Women are incomprehensible creatures, Denham!" he then exclaimed.

"Um," said Denham, who seemed to himself possessed of complete understanding, not merely of women, but of the entire universe. He could read Rodney, too, like a book. He knew that he was unhappy, and he pitied him, and wished to help him.

"You say something and they–fly into a passion. Or for no reason at all, they laugh. I take it that no amount of education will—" The remainder of the sentence was lost in the high wind, against which they had to struggle; but Denham understood that he referred to Katharine's laughter, and that the memory of it was still hurting him. In comparison with Rodney, Denham felt himself very secure; he saw Rodney as one of the lost birds dashed senseless against the glass; one of the flying bodies of which the air was full. But he and Katharine were alone together, aloft, splendid, and luminous with a twofold radiance. He pitied the unstable creature beside him; he felt a desire to protect him, exposed without the knowledge which made his own way so direct. They were united as the adventurous are united, though one reaches the goal and the other perishes by the way.

"You couldn't laugh at some one you cared for."

This sentence, apparently addressed to no other human being, reached Denham's ears. The wind seemed to muffle it and fly away with it directly. Had Rodney spoken those words?

"You love her." Was that his own voice, which seemed to sound in the air several yards in front of him?

"I've suffered tortures, Denham, tortures!"

"Yes, yes, I know that."

"She's laughed at me."

"Never–to me."

The wind blew a space between the words–blew them so far away that they seemed unspoken.

"How I've loved her!"

This was certainly spoken by the man at Denham's side. The voice had all the marks of Rodney's character, and recalled, with; strange vividness, his personal appearance. Denham could see him against the blank buildings and towers of the horizon. He saw him dignified, exalted, and tragic, as he might have appeared thinking of Katharine alone in his rooms at night.

"I am in love with Katharine myself. That is why I am here tonight."

Ralph spoke distinctly and deliberately, as if Rodney's confession had made this statement necessary.

Rodney exclaimed something inarticulate.

"Ah, I've always known it," he cried, "I've known it from the first. You'll marry her!"

The cry had a note of despair in it. Again the wind intercepted their words. They said no more. At length they drew up beneath a lamp-post, simultaneously.

"My God, Denham, what fools we both are!" Rodney exclaimed. They looked at each other, queerly, in the light of the lamp. Fools! They seemed to confess to each other the extreme depths of their folly. For the moment, under the lamp-post, they seemed to be aware of some common knowledge which did away with the possibility of rivalry, and made them feel more sympathy for each other than for any one else in the world. Giving simultaneously a little nod, as if in confirmation of this understanding, they parted without speaking again.

29

Between twelve and one that Sunday night Katharine lay in bed, not asleep, but in that twilight region where a detached and humorous view of our own lot is possible; or if we must be serious, our seriousness is tempered by the swift oncome of slumber and oblivion. She saw the forms of Ralph, William, Cassandra, and herself, as if they were all equally unsubstantial, and, in putting off reality, had gained a kind of dignity which rested upon each impartially. Thus rid of any uncomfortable warmth of partisanship or load of obligation, she was dropping off to sleep when a light tap sounded upon her door. A moment later Cassandra stood beside her, holding a candle and speaking in the low tones proper to the time of night.

"Are you awake, Katharine?"

"Yes, I'm awake. What is it?"

She roused herself, sat up, and asked what in Heaven's name Cassandra was doing?

"I couldn't sleep, and I thought I'd come and speak to you—only for a moment, though. I'm going home tomorrow."

"Home? Why, what has happened?"

"Something happened today which makes it impossible for me to stay here."

Cassandra spoke formally, almost solemnly; the announcement was clearly prepared and marked a crisis of the utmost gravity. She continued what seemed to be part of a set speech.

"I have decided to tell you the whole truth, Katharine. William allowed himself to behave in a way which made me extremely uncomfortable today."

Katharine seemed to waken completely, and at once to be in control of herself.

"At the Zoo?" she asked.

"No, on the way home. When we had tea."

As if foreseeing that the interview might be long, and the night chilly, Katharine advised Cassandra to wrap herself in a quilt. Cassandra did so with unbroken solemnity.

"There's a train at eleven," she said. "I shall tell Aunt Maggie that I have to go suddenly. . . . I shall make Violet's visit an excuse. But, after thinking it over, I don't see how I can go without telling you the truth."

She was careful to abstain from looking in Katharine's direction. There was a slight pause.

"But I don't see the least reason why you should go," said Katharine eventually. Her voice sounded so astonishingly equable that Cassandra glanced at her. It was impossible to suppose that she was either indignant or surprised; she seemed, on the contrary, sitting up in bed, with her arms clasped round her knees and a little frown on her brow, to be thinking closely upon a matter of indifference to her.

"Because I can't allow any man to behave to me in that way," Cassandra replied, and she added, "particularly when I know that he is engaged to some one else."

"But you like him, don't you?" Katharine inquired.

"That's got nothing to do with it," Cassandra exclaimed indignantly. "I consider his conduct, under the circumstances, most disgraceful."

This was the last of the sentences of her premeditated speech; and having spoken it she was left unprovided with any more to say in that particular style. When Katharine remarked:

"I should say it had everything to do with it," Cassandra's self-possession deserted her.

"I don't understand you in the least, Katharine. How can you behave as you behave? Ever since I came here I've been amazed by you!"

"You've enjoyed yourself, haven't you?" Katharine asked.

"Yes, I have," Cassandra admitted.

"Anyhow, my behavior hasn't spoiled your visit."

"No," Cassandra allowed once more. She was completely at a loss. In her forecast of the interview she had taken it for granted that Katharine, after an outburst of incredulity, would agree that Cassandra must return home as soon as possible. But Katharine, on the contrary, accepted her statement at once, seemed neither shocked nor surprised, and merely looked rather more thoughtful than usual. From being a mature woman charged with an important mission, Cassandra shrunk to the stature of an inexperienced child.

"Do you think I've been very foolish about it?" she asked.

Katharine made no answer, but still sat deliberating silently, and a certain feeling of alarm took possession of Cassandra. Perhaps her words had struck far deeper than she had thought, into depths beyond her reach, as so much of Katharine was beyond her reach. She thought suddenly that she had been playing with very dangerous tools.

Looking at her at length, Katharine asked slowly, as if she found the question very difficult to ask.

"But do you care for William?"

She marked the agitation and bewilderment of the girl's expression, and how she looked away from her.

"Do you mean, am I in love with him?" Cassandra asked, breathing quickly, and nervously moving her hands.

"Yes, in love with him," Katharine repeated.

"How can I love the man you're engaged to marry?" Cassandra burst out.

"He may be in love with you."

"I don't think you've any right to say such things, Katharine," Cassandra exclaimed. "Why do you say them? Don't you mind in the least how William behaves to other women? If I were engaged, I couldn't bear it!"

"We're not engaged," said Katharine, after a pause.

"Katharine!" Cassandra cried.

"No, we're not engaged," Katharine repeated. "But no one knows it but ourselves."

"But why—I don't understand—you're not engaged!" Cassandra said again. "Oh, that explains it! You're not in love with him! You don't want to marry him!"

"We aren't in love with each other any longer," said Katharine, as if disposing of something for ever and ever.

"How queer, how strange, how unlike other people you are, Katharine," Cassandra said, her whole body and voice seeming to fall and collapse together, and no trace of anger or excitement remaining, but only a dreamy quietude.

"You're not in love with him?"

"But I love him," said Katharine.

Cassandra remained bowed, as if by the weight of the revelation, for some little while longer. Nor did Katharine speak. Her attitude was that of some one who wishes to be concealed as much as possible from observation. She sighed profoundly; she was absolutely silent, and apparently overcome by her thoughts.

"D'you know what time it is?" she said at length, and shook her pillow, as if making ready for sleep.

Cassandra rose obediently, and once more took up her candle. Perhaps the white dressing-gown, and the loosened hair, and something unseeing in the expression of the eyes gave her a likeness to a woman walking in her sleep. Katharine, at least, thought so.

"There's no reason why I should go home, then?" Cassandra said, pausing. "Unless you want me to go, Katharine? What *do* you want me to do?"

For the first time their eyes met.

"You wanted us to fall in love," Cassandra exclaimed, as if she read the certainty there. But as she looked she saw a sight that surprised her. The tears rose slowly in Katharine's eyes and stood there, brimming but contained—the tears of some profound emotion, happiness, grief, renunciation; an emotion so complex in its nature that to express it was impossible, and Cassandra, bending her head and receiving the tears upon her cheek, accepted them in silence as the consecration of her love.

"Please, miss," said the maid, about eleven o'clock on the following morning, "Mrs. Milvain is in the kitchen."

A long wicker basket of flowers and branches had arrived from the country, and Katharine, kneeling upon the floor of the drawing-room, was sorting them while Cassandra watched her from an arm-chair, and absent-mindedly made spasmodic offers of help which were not accepted. The maid's message had a curious effect upon Katharine.

She rose, walked to the window, and, the maid being gone, said emphatically and even tragically:

"You know what that means."

Cassandra had understood nothing.

"Aunt Celia is in the kitchen," Katharine repeated.

"Why in the kitchen?" Cassandra asked, not unnaturally.

"Probably because she's discovered something," Katharine replied. Cassandra's thoughts flew to the subject of her preoccupation.

"About us?" she inquired.

"Heaven knows," Katharine replied. "I shan't let her stay in the kitchen, though. I shall bring her up here."

The sternness with which this was said suggested that to bring Aunt Celia upstairs was, for some reason, a disciplinary measure.

"For goodness' sake, Katharine," Cassandra exclaimed, jumping from her chair and showing signs of agitation, "don't be rash. Don't let her suspect. Remember, nothing's certain—"

Katharine assured her by nodding her head several times, but the manner in which she left the room was not calculated to inspire complete confidence in her diplomacy.

Mrs. Milvain was sitting, or rather perching, upon the edge of a chair in the servants' room. Whether there was any sound reason for her choice of a subterranean chamber, or whether it corresponded with the spirit of her quest, Mrs. Milvain invariably came in by the back door and sat in the servants' room when she was engaged in confidential family transactions. The ostensible reason she gave was that neither Mr. nor Mrs. Hilbery should be disturbed. But, in truth, Mrs. Milvain depended even more than most elderly women of her generation upon the delicious emotions of intimacy, agony, and secrecy, and the additional thrill provided by the basement was one not lightly to be forfeited. She protested almost plaintively when Katharine proposed to go upstairs.

"I've something that I want to say to you in *private*," she said, hesitating reluctantly upon the threshold of her ambush.

"The drawing-room is empty—"

"But we might meet your mother upon the stairs. We might disturb your father," Mrs. Milvain objected, taking the precaution to speak in a whisper already.

But as Katharine's presence was absolutely necessary to the success of the interview, and as Katharine obstinately receded up the kitchen stairs, Mrs. Milvain had no course but to follow her. She glanced furtively about her as she proceeded upstairs, drew her skirts together, and stepped with circumspection past all doors, whether they were open or shut.

"Nobody will overhear us?" she murmured, when the comparative sanctuary of the drawing-room had been reached. "I see that I have interrupted you," she added, glancing at the flowers strewn upon the floor. A moment later she inquired, "Was some one sitting with you?" noticing a handkerchief that Cassandra had dropped in her flight.

"Cassandra was helping me to put the flowers in water," said Katharine, and she spoke so firmly and clearly that Mrs. Milvain glanced nervously at the main door and then at the curtain which divided the little room with the relics from the drawing-room.

"Ah, Cassandra is still with you," she remarked. "And did William send you those lovely flowers?"

Katharine sat down opposite her aunt and said neither yes nor no. She looked past her, and it might have been thought that she was considering very critically the pattern of the curtains. Another advantage of the basement, from Mrs. Milvain's point of view, was that it made it necessary to sit very close together, and the light was dim compared with that which now poured through three windows upon Katharine and the basket of flowers, and gave even the slight angular figure of Mrs. Milvain herself a halo of gold.

"They're from Stogdon House," said Katharine abruptly, with a little jerk of her head.

Mrs. Milvain felt that it would be easier to tell her niece what she wished to say if they were actually in physical contact, for the spiritual distance between them was formidable. Katharine, however, made no overtures, and Mrs. Milvain, who was possessed of rash but heroic courage, plunged without preface:

"People are talking about you, Katharine. That is why I have come this morning. You forgive me for saying what I'd much rather not say? What I say is only for your own sake, my child."

"There's nothing to forgive yet, Aunt Celia," said Katharine, with apparent good humor.

"People are saying that William goes everywhere with you and Cassandra, and that he is always paying her attentions. At the Markhams' dance he sat out five dances with her. At the Zoo they were seen alone together. They left together. They never came back here till seven in the evening. But that is not all. They say his manner is very marked—he is quite different when she is there."

Mrs. Milvain, whose words had run themselves together, and whose voice had raised its tone almost to one of protest, here ceased, and looked intently at Katharine, as if to judge the effect of her communication. A slight rigidity had passed over Katharine's face. Her lips were pressed together; her eyes were contracted, and they were still fixed upon the curtain. These superficial changes covered an extreme inner loathing such as might follow the display of some hideous or indecent spectacle. The indecent spectacle was her own action beheld for the first time from the outside; her aunt's words made her realize how infinitely repulsive the body of life is without its soul.

"Well?" she said at length.

Mrs. Milvain made a gesture as if to bring her closer, but it was not returned.

"We all know how good you are—how unselfish—how you sacrifice yourself to others. But you've been too unselfish, Katharine. You have made Cassandra happy, and she has taken advantage of your goodness."

"I don't understand, Aunt Celia," said Katharine. "What has Cassandra done?"

"Cassandra has behaved in a way that I could not have thought possible," said Mrs. Milvain warmly. "She has been utterly selfish—utterly heartless. I must speak to her before I go."

"I don't understand," Katharine persisted.

Mrs. Milvain looked at her. Was it possible that Katharine really doubted? That there was something that Mrs. Milvain herself did not understand? She braced herself, and pronounced the tremendous words: "Cassandra has stolen William's love."

Still the words seemed to have curiously little effect.

"Do you mean," said Katharine, "that he has fallen in love with her?"

"There are ways of *making* men fall in love with one, Katharine."

Katharine remained silent. The silence alarmed Mrs. Milvain, and she began hurriedly:

"Nothing would have made me say these things but your own good. I have not wished to interfere; I have not wished to give you pain. I am a useless old woman. I have no children of my own. I only want to see you happy, Katharine."

Again she stretched forth her arms, but they remained empty.

"You are not going to say these things to Cassandra," said Katharine suddenly. "You've said them to me; that's enough."

Katharine spoke so low and with such restraint that Mrs. Milvain had to strain to catch her words, and when she heard them she was dazed by them.

"I've made you angry! I knew I should!" she exclaimed. She quivered, and a kind of sob shook her; but even to have made Katharine angry was some relief, and allowed her to feel some of the agreeable sensations of martyrdom.

"Yes," said Katharine, standing up, "I'm so angry that I don't want to say anything more. I think you'd better go, Aunt Celia. We don't understand each other."

At these words Mrs. Milvain looked for a moment terribly apprehensive; she glanced at her niece's face, but read no pity there, whereupon she folded her hands upon a black velvet bag which she carried in an attitude that was almost one of prayer. Whatever divinity she prayed to, if pray she did, at any rate she recovered her dignity in a singular way and faced her niece.

"Married love," she said slowly and with emphasis upon every word, "is the most sacred of all loves. The love of husband and wife is the most holy we know. That is the lesson Mamma's children learnt from her; that is what they can never forget. I have tried to speak as she would have wished her daughter to speak. You are her grandchild."

Katharine seemed to judge this defence upon its merits, and then to convict it of falsity.

"I don't see that there is any excuse for your behavior," she said.

At these words Mrs. Milvain rose and stood for a moment beside her niece. She had never met with such treatment before, and she did not know with what weapons to break down the terrible wall of resistance offered her by one who, by virtue of youth and beauty and sex, should have been all tears and supplications. But Mrs. Milvain herself was obstinate; upon a matter of this kind she could not admit that she was either beaten or mistaken. She beheld herself the champion of married love in its purity and supremacy; what her niece stood for she was quite unable to say, but she was filled with the gravest suspicions. The old woman and the young woman stood side by side in unbroken silence. Mrs. Milvain could not make up her mind to withdraw while her principles trembled in the balance and her curiosity remained unappeased. She ransacked her mind for some question that should force Katharine to enlighten her, but the supply was limited, the choice difficult, and while she hesitated the door opened and William Rodney came in. He carried in his hand an enormous and splendid bunch of white and purple flowers, and, either not seeing Mrs. Milvain, or disregarding her, he advanced straight to Katharine, and presented the flowers with the words:

"These are for you, Katharine."

Katharine took them with a glance that Mrs. Milvain did not fail to intercept. But with all her experience, she did not know what to make of it. She watched anxiously for further illumination. William greeted her without obvious sign of guilt, and, explaining that he had a holiday, both he and Katharine seemed to take it for granted that his holiday should be celebrated with flowers and spent in Cheyne Walk. A pause followed; that, too, was natural; and Mrs. Milvain began to feel that she laid herself open to a charge of selfishness if she stayed. The mere presence of a young man had altered her disposition curiously, and filled her with a desire for a scene which should end in an emotional forgiveness. She would have given much to clasp both nephew and niece in her arms. But she could not flatter herself that any hope of the customary exaltation remained.

"I must go," she said, and she was conscious of an extreme flatness of spirit.

Neither of them said anything to stop her. William politely escorted her downstairs, and somehow, amongst her protests and embarrassments, Mrs. Milvain forgot to say good-bye to Katharine. She departed, murmuring words about masses of flowers and a drawing-room always beautiful even in the depths of winter.

William came back to Katharine; he found her standing where he had left her.

"I've come to be forgiven," he said. "Our quarrel was perfectly hateful to me. I've not slept all night. You're not angry with me, are you, Katharine?"

She could not bring herself to answer him until she had rid her mind of the impression that her aunt had made on her. It seemed to her that the very flowers were contaminated, and Cassandra's pocket-handkerchief, for Mrs. Milvain had used them for evidence in her investigations.

"She's been spying upon us," she said, "following us about London, overhearing what people are saying—"

"Mrs. Milvain?" Rodney exclaimed. "What has she told you?"

His air of open confidence entirely vanished.

"Oh, people are saying that you're in love with Cassandra, and that you don't care for me."

"They have seen us?" he asked.

"Everything we've done for a fortnight has been seen."

"I told you that would happen!" he exclaimed.

He walked to the window in evident perturbation. Katharine was too indignant to attend to him. She was swept away by the force of her own anger. Clasping Rodney's flowers, she stood upright and motionless.

Rodney turned away from the window.

"It's all been a mistake," he said. "I blame myself for it. I should have known better. I let you persuade me in a moment of madness. I beg you to forget my insanity, Katharine."

"She wished even to persecute Cassandra!" Katharine burst out, not listening to him. "She threatened to speak to her. She's capable of it—she's capable of anything!"

"Mrs. Milvain is not tactful, I know, but you exaggerate, Katharine. People are talking about us. She was right to tell us. It only confirms my own feeling—the position is monstrous."

At length Katharine realized some part of what he meant.

"You don't mean that this influences you, William?" she asked in amazement.

"It does," he said, flushing. "It's intensely disagreeable to me. I can't endure that people should gossip about us. And then there's your cousin—Cassandra—" He paused in embarrassment.

"I came here this morning, Katharine," he resumed, with a change of voice, "to ask you to forget my folly, my bad temper, my inconceivable behavior. I came, Katharine, to ask whether we can't return to the position we were in before this—this season of lunacy. Will you take me back, Katharine, once more and for ever?"

No doubt her beauty, intensified by emotion and enhanced by the flowers of bright color and strange shape which she carried wrought upon Rodney, and had its share in bestowing upon her the old romance. But a less noble passion worked in him, too; he was inflamed by jealousy. His tentative offer of affection had been rudely and, as he thought, completely repulsed by Cassandra on the preceding day. Denham's confession was in his mind. And ultimately, Katharine's dominion over him was of the sort that the fevers of the night cannot exorcise.

"I was as much to blame as you were yesterday," she said gently, disregarding his question. "I confess, William, the sight of you and Cassandra together made me jealous, and I couldn't control myself. I laughed at you, I know."

"You jealous!" William exclaimed. "I assure you, Katharine, you've not the slightest reason to be jealous. Cassandra dislikes me, so far as she feels about me at all. I was foolish enough to try to explain the nature of our relationship. I couldn't resist telling her what I supposed myself to feel for her. She refused to listen, very rightly. But she left me in no doubt of her scorn."

Katharine hesitated. She was confused, agitated, physically tired, and had already to reckon with the violent feeling of dislike aroused by her aunt which still vibrated through all the rest of her feelings. She sank into a chair and dropped her flowers upon her lap.

"She charmed me," Rodney continued. "I thought I loved her. But that's a thing of the past. It's all over, Katharine. It was a dream—an hallucination. We were both equally to blame, but no harm's done if you believe how truly I care for you. Say you believe me!"

He stood over her, as if in readiness to seize the first sign of her assent. Precisely at that moment, owing, perhaps, to her vicissitudes of feeling, all sense of love left her, as in a moment a mist lifts from the earth. And when the mist departed a skeleton world and blankness alone remained—a terrible prospect for the eyes of the living to behold. He saw the look of terror in her face, and without understanding its origin, took her hand in his. With the sense of companionship returned a desire, like that of a child for shelter, to accept what he had to offer her—and at that moment it seemed that he offered her the only thing that could make it tolerable to live. She let him press his lips to her cheek, and leant her head upon his arm. It was the moment of his triumph. It was the only moment in which she belonged to him and was dependent upon his protection.

"Yes, yes, yes," he murmured, "you accept me, Katharine. You love me."

For a moment she remained silent. He then heard her murmur:

"Cassandra loves you more than I do."

"Cassandra?" he whispered.

"She loves you," Katharine repeated. She raised herself and repeated the sentence yet a third time. "She loves you."

William slowly raised himself. He believed instinctively what Katharine said, but what it meant to him he was unable to understand. Could Cassandra love him? Could she have told Katharine that she loved him? The desire to know the truth of this was urgent, unknown though the consequences might be. The thrill of excitement associated with the thought of Cassandra once more took possession of him. No longer was it the excitement of anticipation and ignorance; it was the excitement of something greater than a possibility, for now he knew her and had measure of the sympathy between them. But who could give him certainty? Could Katharine, Katharine who had lately lain in his arms, Katharine herself the most admired of women? He looked at her, with doubt, and with anxiety, but said nothing.

"Yes, yes," she said, interpreting his wish for assurance, "it's true. I know what she feels for you."

"She loves me?"

Katharine nodded.

"Ah, but who knows what I feel? How can I be sure of my feeling myself? Ten minutes ago I asked you to marry me. I still wish it–I don't know what I wish—"

He clenched his hands and turned away. He suddenly faced her and demanded: "Tell me what you feel for Denham."

"For Ralph Denham?" she asked. "Yes!" she exclaimed, as if she had found the answer to some momentarily perplexing question. "You're jealous of me, William; but you're not in love with me. I'm jealous of you. Therefore, for both our sakes, I say, speak to Cassandra at once."

He tried to compose himself. He walked up and down the room; he paused at the window and surveyed the flowers strewn upon the floor. Meanwhile his desire to have Katharine's assurance confirmed became so insistent that he could no longer deny the overmastering strength of his feeling for Cassandra.

"You're right," he exclaimed, coming to a standstill and rapping his knuckles sharply upon a small table carrying one slender vase. "I love Cassandra."

As he said this, the curtains hanging at the door of the little room parted, and Cassandra herself stepped forth.

"I have overheard every word!" she exclaimed.

A pause succeeded this announcement. Rodney made a step forward and said:

"Then you know what I wish to ask you. Give me your answer—"

She put her hands before her face; she turned away and seemed to shrink from both of them.

"What Katharine said," she murmured. "But," she added, raising her head with a look of fear from the kiss with which he greeted her admission, "how frightfully difficult it all is! Our feelings, I mean—yours and mine and Katharine's. Katharine, tell me, are we doing right?"

"Right—of course we're doing right," William answered her, "if, after what you've heard, you can marry a man of such incomprehensible confusion, such deplorable——"

"Don't, William," Katharine interposed; "Cassandra has heard us; she can judge what we are; she knows better than we could tell her."

But, still holding William's hand, questions and desires welled up in Cassandra's heart. Had she done wrong in listening? Why did Aunt Celia blame her? Did Katharine think her right? Above all, did William really love her, for ever and ever, better than any one?

"I must be first with him, Katharine!" she exclaimed. "I can't share him even with you."

"I shall never ask that," said Katharine. She moved a little away from where they sat and began half-consciously sorting her flowers.

"But you've shared with me," Cassandra said. "Why can't I share with you? Why am I so mean? I know why it is," she added. "We understand each other, William and I. You've never understood each other. You're too different."

"I've never admired anybody more," William interposed.

"It's not that"—Cassandra tried to enlighten him—"it's understanding."

"Have I never understood you, Katharine? Have I been very selfish?"

"Yes," Cassandra interposed. "You've asked her for sympathy, and she's not sympathetic; you've wanted her to be practical, and she's not practical. You've been selfish; you've been exacting—and so has Katharine—but it wasn't anybody's fault."

Katharine had listened to this attempt at analysis with keen attention. Cassandra's words seemed to rub the old blurred image of life and freshen it so marvelously that it looked new again. She turned to William.

"It's quite true," she said. "It was nobody's fault."

"There are many things that he'll always come to you for," Cassandra continued, still reading from her invisible book. "I accept that, Katharine. I shall never dispute it. I want to be generous as you've been generous. But being in love makes it more difficult for me."

They were silent. At length William broke the silence.

"One thing I beg of you both, he said, and the old nervousness of manner returned as he glanced at Katharine. "We will never discuss these matters again. It's not that I'm timid and conventional, as you think,

Katharine. It's that it spoils things to discuss them; it unsettles people's minds; and now we're all so happy—"

Cassandra ratified this conclusion so far as she was concerned, and William, after receiving the exquisite pleasure of her glance, with its absolute affection and trust, looked anxiously at Katharine.

"Yes, I'm happy," she assured him. "And I agree. We will never talk about it again."

"Oh, Katharine, Katharine!" Cassandra cried, holding out her arms while the tears ran down her cheeks.

30

The day was so different from other days to three people in the house that the common routine of household life—the maid waiting at table, Mrs. Hilbery writing a letter, the clock striking, and the door opening, and all the other signs of long-established civilization appeared suddenly to have no meaning save as they lulled Mr. and Mrs. Hilbery into the belief that nothing unusual had taken place. It chanced that Mrs. Hilbery was depressed without visible cause, unless a certain crudeness verging upon coarseness in the temper of her favorite Elizabethans could be held responsible for the mood. At any rate, she had shut up "The Duchess of Malfi" with a sigh, and wished to know, so she told Rodney at dinner, whether there wasn't some young writer with a touch of the great spirit—somebody who made you believe that life was *beautiful?* She got little help from Rodney, and after singing her plaintive requiem for the death of poetry by herself, she charmed herself into good spirits again by remembering the existence of Mozart. She begged Cassandra to play to her, and when they went upstairs Cassandra opened the piano directly, and did her best to create an atmosphere of unmixed beauty. At the sound of the first notes Katharine and Rodney both felt an enormous sense of relief at the license which the music gave them to loosen their hold upon the mechanism of behavior. They lapsed into the depths of thought. Mrs. Hilbery was soon spirited away into a perfectly congenial mood, that was half reverie and half slumber, half delicious melancholy and half pure bliss. Mr. Hilbery alone attended. He was extremely musical, and made Cassandra aware that he listened to every note. She played her best, and won his approval. Leaning slightly forward in his chair, and turning his little green stone, he weighed the intention of her phrases approvingly, but stopped her suddenly to complain of a noise behind him. The window was unhasped. He signed to Rodney, who crossed the room immediately to put the matter right. He stayed a moment longer by the window than was, perhaps, necessary, and having done what was needed, drew his chair a little closer than before to Katharine's side. The music went on. Under cover of some exquisite run of melody, he leant towards her and whispered something. She glanced at her father and mother, and a moment later left the room, almost unobserved, with Rodney.

"What is it?" she asked, as soon as the door was shut.

Rodney made no answer, but led her downstairs into the dining-room on the ground floor. Even when he had shut the door he said nothing, but went straight to the window and parted the curtains. He beckoned to Katharine.

"There he is again," he said. "Look, there—under the lamp-post."

Katharine looked. She had no idea what Rodney was talking about. A vague feeling of alarm and mystery possessed her. She saw a man standing on the opposite side of the road facing the house beneath a lamp-post. As they looked the figure turned, walked a few steps, and came back again to his old position. It seemed to her that he was looking fixedly at her, and was conscious of her gaze on him. She knew, in a flash, who the man was who was watching them. She drew the curtain abruptly.

"Denham," said Rodney. "He was there last night too." He spoke sternly. His whole manner had become full of authority. Katharine felt almost as if he accused her of some crime. She was pale and uncomfortably agitated, as much by the strangeness of Rodney's behavior as by the sight of Ralph Denham.

"If he chooses to come—" she said defiantly.

"You can't let him wait out there. I shall tell him to come in." Rodney spoke with such decision that when he raised his arm Katharine expected him to draw the curtain instantly. She caught his hand with a little exclamation.

"Wait!" she cried. "I don't allow you."

"You can't wait," he replied. "You've gone too far." His hand remained upon the curtain. "Why don't you admit, Katharine," he broke out, looking at her with an expression of contempt as well as of anger, "that you love him? Are you going to treat him as you treated me?"

She looked at him, wondering, in spite of all her perplexity, at the spirit that possessed him.

"I forbid you to draw the curtain," she said.

He reflected, and then took his hand away.

"I've no right to interfere," he concluded. "I'll leave you. Or, if you like, we'll go back to the drawing-room."

"No. I can't go back," she said, shaking her head. She bent her head in thought.

"You love him, Katharine," Rodney said suddenly. His tone had lost something of its sternness, and might have been used to urge a child to confess its fault. She raised her eyes and fixed them upon him.

"I love him?" she repeated. He nodded. She searched his face, as if for further confirmation of his words, and, as he remained silent and expectant, turned away once more and continued her thoughts. He observed her closely, but without stirring, as if he gave her time to make up her mind to fulfil her obvious duty. The strains of Mozart reached them from the room above.

"Now," she said suddenly, with a sort of desperation, rising from her chair and seeming to command Rodney to fulfil his part. He drew the curtain instantly, and she made no attempt to stop him. Their eyes at once sought the same spot beneath the lamp-post.

"He's not there!" she exclaimed.

No one was there. William threw the window up and looked out. The wind rushed into the room, together with the sound of distant wheels, footsteps hurrying along the pavement, and the cries of sirens hooting down the river.

"Denham!" William cried.

"Ralph!" said Katharine, but she spoke scarcely louder than she might have spoken to some one in the same room. With their eyes fixed upon the opposite side of the road, they did not notice a figure close to the railing which divided the garden from the street. But Denham had crossed the road and was standing there. They were startled by his voice close at hand.

"Rodney!"

"There you are! Come in, Denham." Rodney went to the front door and opened it. "Here he is," he said, bringing Ralph with him into the dining-room where Katharine stood, with her back to the open window. Their eyes met for a second. Denham looked half dazed by the strong light, and, buttoned in his overcoat, with his hair ruffled across his forehead by the wind, he seemed like somebody rescued from an open boat out at sea. William promptly shut the window and drew the curtains. He acted with a cheerful decision as if he were master of the situation, and knew exactly what he meant to do.

"You're the first to hear the news, Denham," he said. "Katharine isn't going to marry me, after all."

"Where shall I put—" Ralph began vaguely, holding out his hat and glancing about him; he balanced it carefully against a silver bowl that stood upon the sideboard. He then sat himself down rather heavily at the head of the oval dinner-table. Rodney stood on one side of him and

Katharine on the other. He appeared to be presiding over some meeting from which most of the members were absent. Meanwhile, he waited, and his eyes rested upon the glow of the beautifully polished mahogany table.

"William is engaged to Cassandra," said Katharine briefly.

At that Denham looked up quickly at Rodney. Rodney's expression changed. He lost his self-possession. He smiled a little nervously, and then his attention seemed to be caught by a fragment of melody from the floor above. He seemed for a moment to forget the presence of the others. He glanced towards the door.

"I congratulate you," said Denham.

"Yes, yes. We're all mad–quite out of our minds, Denham," he said. "It's partly Katharine's doing–partly mine." He looked oddly round the room as if he wished to make sure that the scene in which he played a part had some real existence. "Quite mad," he repeated. "Even Katharine–" His gaze rested upon her finally, as if she, too, had changed from his old view of her. He smiled at her as if to encourage her. "Katharine shall explain," he said, and giving a little nod to Denham, he left the room.

Katharine sat down at once, and leant her chin upon her hands. So long as Rodney was in the room the proceedings of the evening had seemed to be in his charge, and had been marked by a certain unreality. Now that she was alone with Ralph she felt at once that a constraint had been taken from them both. She felt that they were alone at the bottom of the house, which rose, story upon story, upon the top of them.

"Why were you waiting out there?" she asked.

"For the chance of seeing you," he replied.

"You would have waited all night if it hadn't been for William. It's windy too. You must have been cold. What could you see? Nothing but our windows."

"It was worth it. I heard you call me."

"I called you?" She had called unconsciously.

"They were engaged this morning," she told him, after a pause.

"You're glad?" he asked.

She bent her head. "Yes, yes," she sighed. "But you don't know how good he is–what he's done for me–" Ralph made a sound of understanding. "You waited there last night too?" she asked.

"Yes. I can wait," Denham replied.

The words seemed to fill the room with an emotion which Katharine connected with the sound of distant wheels, the footsteps hurrying along the pavement, the cries of sirens hooting down the river, the darkness and the wind. She saw the upright figure standing beneath the lamp-post.

"Waiting in the dark," she said, glancing at the window, as if he saw what she was seeing. "Ah, but it's different–" She broke off. "I'm not the person you think me. Until you realize that it's impossible—"

Placing her elbows on the table, she slid her ruby ring up and down her finger abstractedly. She frowned at the rows of leather-bound books opposite her. Ralph looked keenly at her. Very pale, but sternly concentrated upon her meaning, beautiful but so little aware of herself as to seem remote from him also, there was something distant and abstract about her which exalted him and chilled him at the same time.

"No, you're right," he said. "I don't know you. I've never known you."

"Yet perhaps you know me better than any one else," she mused.

Some detached instinct made her aware that she was gazing at a book which belonged by rights to some other part of the house. She walked over to the shelf, took it down, and returned to her seat, placing the book on the table between them. Ralph opened it and looked at the portrait of a man with a voluminous white shirt-collar, which formed the frontispiece.

"I say I do know you, Katharine," he affirmed, shutting the book. "It's only for moments that I go mad."

"Do you call two whole nights a moment?"

"I swear to you that now, at this instant, I see you precisely as you are. No one has ever known you as I know you. . . . Could you have taken down that book just now if I hadn't known you?"

"That's true," she replied, "but you can't think how I'm divided–how I'm at my ease with you, and how I'm bewildered. The unreality–the dark–the waiting outside in the wind–yes, when you look at me, not seeing me, and I don't see you either. . . . But I do see," she went on quickly, changing her position and frowning again, "heaps of things, only not you."

"Tell me what you see," he urged.

But she could not reduce her vision to words, since it was no single shape colored upon the dark, but rather a general excitement, an atmosphere, which, when she tried to visualize it, took form as a wind scouring the flanks of northern hills and flashing light upon cornfields and pools.

"Impossible," she sighed, laughing at the ridiculous notion of putting any part of this into words.

"Try, Katharine," Ralph urged her.

"But I can't–I'm talking a sort of nonsense–the sort of nonsense one talks to oneself." She was dismayed by the expression of longing and despair upon his face. "I was thinking about a mountain in the North of England," she attempted. "It's too silly–I won't go on."

"We were there together?" he pressed her.

"No. I was alone." She seemed to be disappointing the desire of a child. His face fell.

"You're always alone there?"

"I can't explain." She could not explain that she was essentially alone there. "It's not a mountain in the North of England. It's an imagination—a story one tells oneself. You have yours too?"

"You're with me in mine. You're the thing I make up, you see."

"Oh, I see," she sighed. "That's why it's so impossible." She turned upon him almost fiercely. "You must try to stop it," she said.

"I won't," he replied roughly, "because I—" He stopped. He realized that the moment had come to impart that news of the utmost importance which he had tried to impart to Mary Datchet, to Rodney upon the Embankment, to the drunken tramp upon the seat. How should he offer it to Katharine? He looked quickly at her. He saw that she was only half attentive to him; only a section of her was exposed to him. The sight roused in him such desperation that he had much ado to control his impulse to rise and leave the house. Her hand lay loosely curled upon the table. He seized it and grasped it firmly as if to make sure of her existence and of his own. "Because I love you, Katharine," he said.

Some roundness or warmth essential to that statement was absent from his voice, and she had merely to shake her head very slightly for him to drop her hand and turn away in shame at his own impotence. He thought that she had detected his wish to leave her. She had discerned the break in his resolution, the blankness in the heart of his vision. It was true that he had been happier out in the street, thinking of her, than now that he was in the same room with her. He looked at her with a guilty expression on his face. But her look expressed neither disappointment nor reproach. Her pose was easy, and she seemed to give effect to a mood of quiet speculation by the spinning of her ruby ring upon the polished table. Denham forgot his despair in wondering what thoughts now occupied her.

"You don't believe me?" he said. His tone was humble, and made her smile at him.

"As far as I understand you—but what should you advise me to do with this ring?" she asked, holding it out.

"I should advise you to let me keep it for you," he replied, in the same tone of half-humorous gravity.

"After what you've said, I can hardly trust you—unless you'll unsay what you've said?"

"Very well. I'm not in love with you."

"But I think you *are* in love with me. . . . As I am with you," she added casually enough. "At least," she said slipping her ring back to its old position, "what other word describes the state we're in?"

She looked at him gravely and inquiringly, as if in search of help.

"It's when I'm with you that I doubt it, not when I'm alone," he stated.

"So I thought," she replied.

In order to explain to her his state of mind, Ralph recounted his experience with the photograph, the letter, and the flower picked at Kew. She listened very seriously.

"And then you went raving about the streets," she mused. "Well, it's bad enough. But my state is worse than yours, because it hasn't anything to do with facts. It's an hallucination, pure and simple—an intoxication. . . . One can be in love with pure reason?" she hazarded. "Because if you're in love with a vision, I believe that that's what I'm in love with."

This conclusion seemed fantastic and profoundly unsatisfactory to Ralph, but after the astonishing variations of his own sentiments during the past half-hour he could not accuse her of fanciful exaggeration.

"Rodney seems to know his own mind well enough," he said almost bitterly. The music, which had ceased, had now begun again, and the melody of Mozart seemed to express the easy and exquisite love of the two upstairs.

"Cassandra never doubted for a moment. But we—" she glanced at him as if to ascertain his position, "we see each other only now and then——"

"Like lights in a storm——"

"In the midst of a hurricane," she concluded, as the window shook beneath the pressure of the wind. They listened to the sound in silence.

Here the door opened with considerable hesitation, and Mrs. Hilbery's head appeared, at first with an air of caution, but having made sure that she had admitted herself to the dining-room and not to some more unusual region, she came completely inside and seemed in no way taken aback by the sight she saw. She seemed, as usual, bound on some quest of her own which was interrupted pleasantly but strangely by running into one of those queer, unnecessary ceremonies that other people thought fit to indulge in.

"Please don't let me interrupt you, Mr.——" she was at a loss, as usual, for the name, and Katharine thought that she did not recognize him. "I hope you've found something nice to read," she added, pointing to the book upon the table. "Byron—ah, Byron. I've known people who knew Lord Byron," she said.

Katharine, who had risen in some confusion, could not help smiling at the thought that her mother found it perfectly natural and desirable that her daughter should be reading Byron in the dining-room late at night alone with a strange young man. She blessed a disposition that was so convenient, and felt tenderly towards her mother and her mother's eccentricities. But Ralph observed that although Mrs. Hilbery held the book so close to her eyes she was not reading a word.

"My dear mother, why aren't you in bed?" Katharine exclaimed, changing astonishingly in the space of a minute to her usual condition of authoritative good sense. "Why are you wandering about?"

"I'm sure I should like your poetry better than I like Lord Byron's," said Mrs. Hilbery, addressing Ralph Denham.

"Mr. Denham doesn't write poetry; he has written articles for father, for the Review," Katharine said, as if prompting her memory.

"Oh dear! How dull!" Mrs. Hilbery exclaimed, with a sudden laugh that rather puzzled her daughter.

Ralph found that she had turned upon him a gaze that was at once very vague and very penetrating.

"But I'm sure you read poetry at night. I always judge by the expression of the eyes," Mrs. Hilbery continued. ("The windows of the soul," she added parenthetically.) "I don't know much about the law," she went on, "though many of my relations were lawyers. Some of them looked very handsome, too, in their wigs. But I think I do know a little about poetry," she added. "And all the things that aren't written down, but—but—" She waved her hand, as if to indicate the wealth of unwritten poetry all about them. "The night and the stars, the dawn coming up, the barges swimming past, the sun setting. . . . Ah dear," she sighed, "well, the sunset is very lovely too. I sometimes think that poetry isn't so much what we write as what we feel, Mr. Denham."

During this speech of her mother's Katharine had turned away, and Ralph felt that Mrs. Hilbery was talking to him apart, with a desire to ascertain something about him which she veiled purposely by the vagueness of her words. He felt curiously encouraged and heartened by the beam in her eye rather than by her actual words. From the distance of her age and sex she seemed to be waving to him, hailing him as a ship sinking beneath the horizon might wave its flag of greeting to another setting out upon the same voyage. He bent his head, saying nothing, but with a curious certainty that she had read an answer to her inquiry that satisfied her. At any rate, she rambled off into a description of the Law Courts which turned to a denunciation of English justice, which, according to her, imprisoned poor men who couldn't pay their debts. "Tell me, shall we ever do without it all?" she asked, but at this point Katharine gently insisted that her mother should go to bed. Looking back from half-way up the staircase, Katharine seemed to see Denham's eyes watching her steadily and intently with an expression that she had guessed in them when he stood looking at the windows across the road.

31

The tray which brought Katharine's cup of tea the next morning brought, also, a note from her mother, announcing that it was her intention to catch an early train to Stratford-on-Avon that very day.

"Please find out the best way of getting there," the note ran, "and wire to dear Sir John Burdett to expect me, with my love. I've been dreaming all night of you and Shakespeare, dearest Katharine."

This was no momentary impulse. Mrs. Hilbery had been dreaming of Shakespeare any time these six months, toying with the idea of an excursion to what she considered the heart of the civilized world. To stand six feet above Shakespeare's bones, to see the very stones worn by his feet, to reflect that the oldest man's oldest mother had very likely seen Shakespeare's daughter—such thoughts roused an emotion in her, which she expressed at unsuitable moments, and with a passion that would not have been unseemly in a pilgrim to a sacred shrine. The only strange thing was that she wished to go by herself. But, naturally enough, she was well provided with friends who lived in the neighborhood of Shakespeare's tomb, and were delighted to welcome her; and she left later to catch her train in the best of spirits. There was a man selling violets in the street. It was a fine day. She would remember to send Mr. Hilbery the first daffodil she saw. And, as she ran back into the hall to tell Katharine, she felt, she had always felt, that Shakespeare's command to leave his bones undisturbed applied only to odious curiosity-mongers—not to dear Sir John and herself. Leaving her daughter to cogitate the theory of Anne Hathaway's sonnets, and the buried manuscripts here referred to, with the implied menace to the safety of the heart of civilization itself, she briskly shut the door of her taxi-cab, and was whirled off upon the first stage of her pilgrimage.

The house was oddly different without her. Katharine found the maids already in possession of her room, which they meant to clean thoroughly during her absence. To Katharine it seemed as if they had brushed away sixty years or so with the first flick of their damp dusters. It seemed to her that the work she had tried to do in that room was being swept into a very insignificant heap of dust. The china shepherdesses were already shining from a bath of hot water. The writing-table might have belonged to a professional man of methodical habits.

Gathering together a few papers upon which she was at work, Katharine proceeded to her own room with the intention of looking through them, perhaps, in the course of the morning. But she was met on the stairs by

Cassandra, who followed her up, but with such intervals between each step that Katharine began to feel her purpose dwindling before they had reached the door. Cassandra leant over the banisters, and looked down upon the Persian rug that lay on the floor of the hall.

"Doesn't everything look odd this morning?" she inquired. "Are you really going to spend the morning with those dull old letters, because if so—"

The dull old letters, which would have turned the heads of the most sober of collectors, were laid upon a table, and, after a moment's pause, Cassandra, looking grave all of a sudden, asked Katharine where she should find the "History of England" by Lord Macaulay. It was downstairs in Mr. Hilbery's study. The cousins descended together in search of it. They diverged into the drawing-room for the good reason that the door was open. The portrait of Richard Alardyce attracted their attention.

"I wonder what he was like?" It was a question that Katharine had often asked herself lately.

"Oh, a fraud like the rest of them—at least Henry says so," Cassandra replied. "Though I don't believe everything Henry says," she added a little defensively.

Down they went into Mr. Hilbery's study, where they began to look among his books. So desultory was this examination that some fifteen minutes failed to discover the work they were in search of.

"Must you read Macaulay's History, Cassandra?" Katharine asked, with a stretch of her arms.

"I must," Cassandra replied briefly.

"Well, I'm going to leave you to look for it by yourself."

"Oh, no, Katharine. Please stay and help me. You see—you see—I told William I'd read a little every day. And I want to tell him that I've begun when he comes."

"When does William come?" Katharine asked, turning to the shelves again.

"To tea, if that suits you?"

"If it suits me to be out, I suppose you mean."

"Oh, you're horrid. . . . Why shouldn't you—?"

"Yes ?"

"Why shouldn't you be happy too?"

"I am quite happy," Katharine replied.

"I mean as I am. Katharine," she said impulsively, "do let's be married on the same day."

"To the same man?"

"Oh, no, no. But why shouldn't you marry—some one else?"

"Here's your Macaulay," said Katharine, turning round with the book in her hand. "I should say you'd better begin to read at once if you mean to be educated by tea-time."

"Damn Lord Macaulay!" cried Cassandra, slapping the book upon the table. "Would you rather not talk?"

"We've talked enough already," Katharine replied evasively.

"I know I shan't be able to settle to Macaulay," said Cassandra, looking ruefully at the dull red cover of the prescribed volume, which, however, possessed a talismanic property, since William admired it. He had advised a little serious reading for the morning hours.

"Have *you* read Macaulay?" she asked.

"No. William never tried to educate me." As she spoke she saw the light fade from Cassandra's face, as if she had implied some other, more mysterious, relationship. She was stung with compunction. She marveled at her own rashness in having influenced the life of another, as she had influenced Cassandra's life.

"We weren't serious," she said quickly.

"But I'm fearfully serious," said Cassandra, with a little shudder, and her look showed that she spoke the truth. She turned and glanced at Katharine as she had never glanced at her before. There was fear in her glance, which darted on her and then dropped guiltily. Oh, Katharine had everything—beauty, mind, character. She could never compete with Katharine; she could never be safe so long as Katharine brooded over her, dominating her, disposing of her. She called her cold, unseeing, unscrupulous, but the only sign she gave outwardly was a curious one—she reached out her hand and grasped the volume of history. At that moment the bell of the telephone rang and Katharine went to answer it. Cassandra, released from observation, dropped her book and clenched her hands. She suffered more fiery torture in those few minutes than she had suffered in the whole of her life; she learnt more of her capacities for feeling. But when Katharine reappeared she was calm, and had gained a look of dignity that was new to her.

"Was that him?" she asked.

"It was Ralph Denham," Katharine replied.

"I meant Ralph Denham."

"Why did you mean Ralph Denham? What has William told you about Ralph Denham?" The accusation that Katharine was calm, callous, and indifferent was not possible in face of her present air of animation. She gave Cassandra no time to frame an answer. "Now, when are you and William going to be married?" she asked.

Cassandra made no reply for some moments. It was, indeed, a very difficult question to answer. In conversation the night before, William had indicated to Cassandra that, in his belief, Katharine was becoming engaged to Ralph Denham in the dining-room. Cassandra, in the rosy light of her own circumstances, had been disposed to think that the matter must be settled already. But a letter which she had received that morning from William, while ardent in its expression of affection, had conveyed to her obliquely that he would prefer the announcement of their engagement to coincide with that of Katharine's. This document Cassandra now produced, and read aloud, with considerable excisions and much hesitation.

". . . a thousand pities–ahem–I fear we shall cause a great deal of natural annoyance. If, on the other hand, what I have reason to think will happen, should happen–within reasonable time, and the present position is not in any way offensive to you, delay would, in my opinion, serve all our interests better than a premature explanation, which is bound to cause more surprise than is desirable—"

"Very like William," Katharine exclaimed, having gathered the drift of these remarks with a speed that, by itself, disconcerted Cassandra.

"I quite understand his feelings," Cassandra replied. "I quite agree with them. I think it would be much better, if you intend to marry Mr. Denham, that we should wait as William says."

"But, then, if I don't marry him for months–or, perhaps, not at all?"

Cassandra was silent. The prospect appalled her. Katharine had been telephoning to Ralph Denham; she looked queer, too; she must be, or about to become, engaged to him. But if Cassandra could have overheard the conversation upon the telephone, she would not have felt so certain that it tended in that direction. It was to this effect:

"I'm Ralph Denham speaking. I'm in my right senses now."

"How long did you wait outside the house?"

"I went home and wrote you a letter. I tore it up."

"I shall tear up everything too."

"I shall come."

"Yes. Come today."

"I must explain to you—"

"Yes. We must explain—"

A long pause followed. Ralph began a sentence, which he canceled with the word, "Nothing." Suddenly, together, at the same moment, they said good-bye. And yet, if the telephone had been miraculously connected with some higher atmosphere pungent with the scent of thyme and the savor of salt, Katharine could hardly have breathed in a keener sense of exhilaration. She ran downstairs on the crest of it. She was amazed to find herself already committed by William and Cassandra to marry the owner of the halting voice she had just heard on the telephone. The tendency of her spirit seemed to be in an altogether different direction; and of a different nature. She had only to look at Cassandra to see what the love that results in an engagement and marriage means. She considered for a moment, and then said: "If you don't want to tell people yourselves, I'll do it for you. I know William has feelings about these matters that make it very difficult for him to do anything."

"Because he's fearfully sensitive about other people's feelings," said Cassandra. "The idea that he could upset Aunt Maggie or Uncle Trevor would make him ill for weeks."

This interpretation of what she was used to call William's conventionality was new to Katharine. And yet she felt it now to be the true one.

"Yes, you're right," she said.

"And then he worships beauty. He wants life to be beautiful in every part of it. Have you ever noticed how exquisitely he finishes everything? Look at the address on that envelope. Every letter is perfect."

Whether this applied also to the sentiments expressed in the letter, Katharine was not so sure; but when William's solicitude was spent upon Cassandra it not only failed to irritate her, as it had done when she was the object of it, but appeared, as Cassandra said, the fruit of his love of beauty.

"Yes," she said, "he loves beauty."

"I hope we shall have a great many children," said Cassandra. "He loves children."

This remark made Katharine realize the depths of their intimacy better than any other words could have done; she was jealous for one moment; but the next she was humiliated. She had known William for years, and she had never once guessed that he loved children. She looked at the queer glow of exaltation in Cassandra's eyes, through which she was beholding the true spirit of a human being, and wished that she would go on talking about William for ever. Cassandra was not unwilling to gratify her. She talked on. The morning slipped away. Katharine scarcely changed her position on the edge of her father's writing-table, and Cassandra never opened the "History of England."

And yet it must be confessed that there were vast lapses in the attention which Katharine bestowed upon her cousin. The atmosphere was wonderfully congenial for thoughts of her own. She lost herself sometimes in such deep reverie that Cassandra, pausing, could look at her for moments unperceived. What could Katharine be thinking about, unless it were Ralph Denham? She was satisfied, by certain random replies, that Katharine had wandered a little from the subject of William's perfections. But Katharine made no sign. She always ended these pauses by saying something so natural that Cassandra was deluded into giving fresh examples of her absorbing theme. Then they lunched, and the only sign that Katharine gave of abstraction was to forget to help the pudding. She looked so like her mother, as she sat there oblivious of the tapioca, that Cassandra was startled into exclaiming:

"How like Aunt Maggie you look!"

"Nonsense," said Katharine, with more irritation than the remark seemed to call for.

In truth, now that her mother was away, Katharine did feel less sensible than usual, but as she argued it to herself, there was much less need for sense. Secretly, she was a little shaken by the evidence which the morning had supplied of her immense capacity for—what could one call it?—rambling over an infinite variety of thoughts that were too foolish to be named. She was, for example, walking down a road in Northumberland in the August sunset; at the inn she left her companion, who was Ralph Denham, and was transported, not so much by her own feet as by some invisible means, to the top of a high hill. Here the scents, the sounds among the dry heather-roots, the grass-blades pressed upon the palm of her hand, were all so perceptible that she could experience each one separately. After this her mind made excursions into the dark of the air, or settled upon the surface of the sea, which could be discovered over there, or with equal unreason it returned to its couch of bracken beneath the stars of midnight, and visited the snow valleys of the moon. These fancies would have been in no way strange, since the walls of every mind are decorated with some such tracery, but she found herself suddenly pursuing such thoughts with an extreme ardor, which became a desire to change her actual condition for something matching the conditions of her dream. Then she started; then she awoke to the fact that Cassandra was looking at her in amazement.

Cassandra would have liked to feel certain that, when Katharine made no reply at all or one wide of the mark, she was making up her mind to get married at once, but it was difficult, if this were so, to account for some remarks that Katharine let fall about the future. She recurred several times to the summer, as if she meant to spend that season in solitary wandering. She seemed to have a plan in her mind which required Bradshaws and the names of inns.

Cassandra was driven finally, by her own unrest, to put on her clothes and wander out along the streets of Chelsea, on the pretence that she must buy something. But, in her ignorance of the way, she became panic-stricken at the thought of being late, and no sooner had she found the shop she wanted, than she fled back again in order to be at home when William came. He came, indeed, five minutes after she had sat down by the tea-table, and she had the happiness of receiving him alone. His greeting put her doubts of his affection at rest, but the first question he asked was:

"Has Katharine spoken to you?"

"Yes. But she says she's not engaged. She doesn't seem to think she's ever going to be engaged."

William frowned, and looked annoyed.

"They telephoned this morning, and she behaves very oddly. She forgets to help the pudding," Cassandra added by way of cheering him.

"My dear child, after what I saw and heard last night, it's not a question of guessing or suspecting. Either she's engaged to him—or—"

He left his sentence unfinished, for at this point Katharine herself appeared. With his recollections of the scene the night before, he was too self-conscious even to look at her, and it was not until she told him of her mother's visit to Stratford-on-Avon that he raised his eyes. It was clear that he was greatly relieved. He looked round him now, as if he felt at his ease, and Cassandra exclaimed:

"Don't you think everything looks quite different?"

"You've moved the sofa?" he asked.

"No. Nothing's been touched," said Katharine. "Everything's exactly the same." But as she said this, with a decision which seemed to make it imply that more than the sofa was unchanged, she held out a cup into which she had forgotten to pour any tea. Being told of her forgetfulness, she frowned with annoyance, and said that Cassandra was demoralizing her. The glance she cast upon them, and the resolute way in which she plunged them into speech, made William and Cassandra feel like children who had been caught prying. They followed her obediently, making conversation. Any one coming in might have judged them acquaintances met, perhaps, for the third time. If that were so, one must have concluded that the hostess suddenly bethought her of an engagement pressing for fulfilment. First Katharine looked at her watch, and then she asked William to tell her the right time. When told that it was ten minutes to five she rose at once, and said:

"Then I'm afraid I must go."

She left the room, holding her unfinished bread and butter in her hand. William glanced at Cassandra.

"Well, she *is* queer!" Cassandra exclaimed.

William looked perturbed. He knew more of Katharine than Cassandra did, but even he could not tell—In a second Katharine was back again dressed in outdoor things, still holding her bread and butter in her bare hand.

"If I'm late, don't wait for me," she said. "I shall have dined," and so saying, she left them.

"But she can't—" William exclaimed, as the door shut, "not without any gloves and bread and butter in her hand!" They ran to the window, and saw her walking rapidly along the street towards the City. Then she vanished.

"She must have gone to meet Mr. Denham," Cassandra exclaimed.

"Goodness knows!" William interjected.

The incident impressed them both as having something queer and ominous about it out of all proportion to its surface strangeness.

"It's the sort of way Aunt Maggie behaves," said Cassandra, as if in explanation.

William shook his head, and paced up and down the room looking extremely perturbed.

"This is what I've been foretelling," he burst out. "Once set the ordinary conventions aside—Thank Heaven Mrs. Hilbery is away. But there's Mr. Hilbery. How are we to explain it to him? I shall have to leave you."

"But Uncle Trevor won't be back for hours, William!" Cassandra implored.

"You never can tell. He may be on his way already. Or suppose Mrs. Milvain—your Aunt Celia—or Mrs. Cosham, or any other of your aunts or uncles should be shown in and find us alone together. You know what they're saying about us already."

Cassandra was equally stricken by the sight of William's agitation, and appalled by the prospect of his desertion.

"We might hide," she exclaimed wildly, glancing at the curtain which separated the room with the relics.

"I refuse entirely to get under the table," said William sarcastically.

She saw that he was losing his temper with the difficulties of the situation. Her instinct told her that an appeal to his affection, at this moment, would be extremely ill-judged. She controlled herself, sat down, poured out a fresh cup of tea, and sipped it quietly. This natural action, arguing complete self-mastery, and showing her in one of those feminine attitudes which William found adorable, did more than any argument to compose his agitation. It appealed to his chivalry. He accepted a cup. Next she asked for a slice of cake. By the time the cake was eaten and the tea drunk the personal question had lapsed, and they were discussing poetry. Insensibly they turned from the question of dramatic poetry in general, to the particular example which reposed in William's pocket, and when the maid came in to clear away the tea-things, William had asked permission to read a short passage aloud, "unless it bored her?"

Cassandra bent her head in silence, but she showed a little of what she felt in her eyes, and thus fortified, William felt confident that it would take more than Mrs. Milvain herself to rout him from his position. He read aloud.

Meanwhile Katharine walked rapidly along the street. If called upon to explain her impulsive action in leaving the tea-table, she could have traced it to no better cause than that William had glanced at Cassandra; Cassandra at William. Yet, because they had glanced, her position was impossible. If one forgot to pour out a cup of tea they rushed to the conclusion that she was engaged to Ralph Denham. She knew that in half an hour or so the door would open, and Ralph Denham would appear. She could not sit there and contemplate seeing him with William's and Cassandra's eyes upon them, judging their exact degree of intimacy, so that they might fix the wedding-day. She promptly decided that she would meet Ralph out of doors; she still had time to reach Lincoln's Inn Fields before he left his office. She hailed a cab, and bade it take her to a shop for selling maps which she remembered in Great Queen Street, since she hardly liked to be set down at his door. Arrived at the shop, she bought a large scale map of Norfolk, and thus provided, hurried into Lincoln's Inn Fields, and assured herself of the position of Messrs. Hoper and Grateley's office. The great gas chandeliers were alight in the office windows. She conceived that he sat at an enormous table laden with papers beneath one of them in the front room with the three tall windows. Having settled his position there, she began walking to and fro upon the pavement. Nobody of his build appeared. She scrutinized each male figure as it approached and passed her. Each male figure had, nevertheless, a look of him, due, perhaps, to the professional dress, the quick step, the keen glance which they cast upon her as they hastened home after the day's work. The square itself, with its immense houses all so fully occupied and stern of aspect, its atmosphere of industry and power, as if even the sparrows and the children were earning their daily bread, as if the sky itself, with its gray and scarlet clouds, reflected the serious intention of the city beneath it, spoke of him. Here was the fit place for their meeting, she thought; here was the fit place for her to walk thinking of him. She could not help comparing it with the domestic streets of Chelsea. With this comparison in her mind, she extended her range a little, and turned into the main road. The great torrent of vans and carts was sweeping down Kingsway; pedestrians were streaming in two currents along the pavements. She stood fascinated at the corner. The deep roar filled her ears; the changing tumult had the inexpressible fascination of varied life pouring ceaselessly with a purpose which, as she looked, seemed to her, somehow, the normal purpose for which life was framed; its complete indifference to the individuals, whom it swallowed up and rolled onwards, filled her with at least a temporary exaltation. The blend of daylight and of lamplight made her an invisible spectator, just as it gave the people who passed her a semi-transparent quality, and left the faces pale ivory ovals in which the eyes alone were dark. They tended the enormous rush of the current—the great flow, the deep stream, the unquenchable tide. She stood unobserved and absorbed, glorying openly in the rapture that had run subterraneously all day. Suddenly she was clutched, unwilling, from the outside, by the recollection of her purpose in coming there. She had come to find Ralph Denham. She hastily turned back into Lincoln's Inn Fields, and looked for her landmark—the light in the three tall windows. She sought in vain. The faces of the houses had now merged in the general darkness, and she had difficulty in determining which she sought. Ralph's three windows gave back on their ghostly glass panels only a reflection of the gray and greenish sky. She rang the bell, peremptorily, under the painted name of the firm. After some delay she was answered by a caretaker, whose pail and brush of themselves told her that the working day was over and the workers gone. Nobody, save perhaps Mr. Grateley himself, was left, she assured Katharine; every one else had been gone these ten minutes.

The news woke Katharine completely. Anxiety gained upon her. She hastened back into Kingsway, looking at people who had miraculously regained their solidity. She ran as far as the Tube station, overhauling clerk after clerk, solicitor after solicitor. Not one of them even faintly resembled Ralph Denham. More and more plainly did she see him; and more and more did he seem to her unlike any one else. At the door of the station she paused, and tried to collect her thoughts. He had gone to her house. By taking a cab she could be there probably in advance of him. But she pictured herself opening the drawing-room door, and William and Cassandra looking up, and Ralph's entrance a moment later, and the glances—the insinuations. No; she could not face it. She would write him a letter and take it at once to his house. She bought paper and pencil at the bookstall, and entered an A.B.C. shop, where, by ordering a cup of coffee, she secured an empty table, and began at vice to write:

"I came to meet you and I have missed you. I could not face William and Cassandra. They want us—" here she paused. "They insist that we are engaged," she substituted, "and we couldn't talk at all, or explain anything. I want—" Her wants were so vast, now that she was in communication with Ralph, that the pencil was utterly inadequate to conduct them on to the paper; it seemed as if the whole torrent of Kingsway had to run down her pencil. She gazed intently at a notice hanging on the gold-encrusted wall opposite. ". . . to say all kinds of things," she added, writing each word with the painstaking of a child. But, when she raised her eyes again to meditate the next sentence, she was aware of a waitress, whose expression intimated that it was closing time, and, looking round, Katharine saw herself almost the last person left in the shop. She took up her letter, paid her bill, and found herself once more in the street. She would now take a cab to Highgate. But at that moment it flashed upon her that she could not remember the address. This check seemed to let fall a barrier across a very powerful current of desire. She ransacked her memory in desperation, hunting for the name, first by remembering the look of the house, and then by trying, in memory, to retrace the words she had written once, at least, upon an envelope. The more she pressed the farther the words receded. Was the house an Orchard Something, on the street a Hill? She gave it up. Never, since she was a child, had she felt anything like this blankness and desolation. There rushed in upon her, as if she were waking from some dream, all the consequences of her inexplicable indolence. She figured Ralph's face as he turned from her door without a word of explanation, receiving his dismissal as a blow from herself, a callous intimation that she did not wish to see him. She followed his departure from her door; but it was far more easy to see him marching far and fast in any direction for any length of time than to conceive that he would turn back to Highgate. Perhaps he would try once more to see her in Cheyne Walk? It was proof of the clearness with which she saw him, that she started forward as this possibility occurred to her, and almost raised her hand to beckon to a cab. No; he was too proud to come again; he rejected the desire and walked on and on, on and on—If only she could read the names of those visionary streets down which he passed! But her imagination betrayed her at this point, or mocked her with a sense of their strangeness, darkness, and distance. Indeed, instead of helping herself to any decision, she only filled her mind with the vast extent of London and the impossibility of finding any single figure that wandered off this way and that way, turned to the right and to the left, chose that dingy little back street where the children were playing in the road, and so—She roused herself impatiently. She walked rapidly along Holborn. Soon she turned and walked as rapidly in the other direction. This indecision was not merely odious, but had something that alarmed her about it, as she had been alarmed slightly once or twice already that day; she felt unable to cope with the strength of her own desires. To a person controlled by habit, there was humiliation as well as alarm in this sudden release of what appeared to be a very powerful as well as an unreasonable force. An aching in the muscles of her right hand now showed her that she was crushing her gloves and the map of Norfolk in a grip sufficient to crack a more solid object. She relaxed her grasp; she looked anxiously at the faces of the passers-by to see whether their eyes rested on her for a moment longer than was natural, or with any curiosity. But having smoothed out her gloves, and done what she could to look as usual, she forgot spectators, and was once more given up to her desperate desire to find Ralph Denham. It was a desire now—wild, irrational, unexplained, resembling something felt in childhood. Once more she blamed herself bitterly for her carelessness. But finding herself opposite the Tube station, she pulled herself up and took counsel swiftly, as of old. It flashed upon her that she would go at once to Mary Datchet, and ask her to give her Ralph's address. The decision was a relief, not only in giving her a goal, but in providing her with a rational excuse for her own actions. It gave her a goal certainly, but the fact of having a goal led her to dwell exclusively upon her obsession; so that when she rang the bell of Mary's flat, she did not for a moment consider how this demand would strike Mary. To her extreme annoyance Mary was not at home; a charwoman opened the door. All Katharine could do was to accept the invitation to wait. She waited for, perhaps, fifteen minutes, and spent them in pacing from one end of the room to the other without intermission. When she heard Mary's key in the door she paused in front of the fireplace, and Mary found her standing upright, looking at once expectant and determined, like a person who has come on an errand of such importance that it must be broached without preface.

Mary exclaimed in surprise.

"Yes, yes," Katharine said, brushing these remarks aside, as if they were in the way.

"Have you had tea?"

"Oh yes," she said, thinking that she had had tea hundreds of years ago, somewhere or other.

Mary paused, took off her gloves, and, finding matches, proceeded to light the fire.

Katharine checked her with an impatient movement, and said:

"Don't light the fire for me. . . . I want to know Ralph Denham's address."

She was holding a pencil and preparing to write on the envelope. She waited with an imperious expression.

"The Apple Orchard, Mount Ararat Road, Highgate," Mary said, speaking slowly and rather strangely.

"Oh, I remember now!" Katharine exclaimed, with irritation at her own stupidity. "I suppose it wouldn't take twenty minutes to drive there?" She gathered up her purse and gloves and seemed about to go.

"But you won't find him," said Mary, pausing with a match in her hand. Katharine, who had already turned towards the door, stopped and looked at her.

"Why? Where is he?" she asked.

"He won't have left his office."

"But he has left the office," she replied. "The only question is will he have reached home yet? He went to see me at Chelsea; I tried to meet him and missed him. He will have found no message to explain. So I must find him—as soon as possible."

Mary took in the situation at her leisure.

"But why not telephone?" she said.

Katharine immediately dropped all that she was holding; her strained expression relaxed, and exclaiming, "Of course! Why didn't I think of that!" she seized the telephone receiver and gave her number. Mary looked at her steadily, and then left the room. At length Katharine heard, through all the superimposed weight of London, the mysterious sound of feet in her own house mounting to the little room, where she could almost see the pictures and the books; she listened with extreme intentness to the preparatory vibrations, and then established her identity.

"Has Mr. Denham called?"

"Yes, miss."

"Did he ask for me?"

"Yes. We said you were out, miss."

"Did he leave any message?"

"No. He went away. About twenty minutes ago, miss."

Katharine hung up the receiver. She walked the length of the room in such acute disappointment that she did not at first perceive Mary's absence. Then she called in a harsh and peremptory tone:

"Mary."

Mary was taking off her outdoor things in the bedroom. She heard Katharine call her. "Yes," she said, "I shan't be a moment." But the moment prolonged itself, as if for some reason Mary found satisfaction in making herself not only tidy, but seemly and ornamented. A stage in her life had been accomplished in the last months which left its traces for ever upon her bearing. Youth, and the bloom of youth, had receded, leaving the purpose of her face to show itself in the hollower cheeks, the firmer lips, the eyes no longer spontaneously observing at random, but narrowed upon an end which was not near at hand. This woman was now a serviceable human being, mistress of her own destiny, and thus, by some combination of ideas, fit to be adorned with the dignity of silver chains and glowing brooches. She came in at her leisure and asked: "Well, did you get an answer?"

"He has left Chelsea already," Katharine replied.

"Still, he won't be home yet," said Mary.

Katharine was once more irresistibly drawn to gaze upon an imaginary map of London, to follow the twists and turns of unnamed streets.

"I'll ring up his home and ask whether he's back." Mary crossed to the telephone and, after a series of brief remarks, announced:

"No. His sister says he hasn't come back yet."

"Ah!" She applied her ear to the telephone once more. "They've had a message. He won't be back to dinner."

"Then what is he going to do?"

Very pale, and with her large eyes fixed not so much upon Mary as upon vistas of unresponding blankness, Katharine addressed herself also not so much to Mary as to the unrelenting spirit which now appeared to mock her from every quarter of her survey.

After waiting a little time Mary remarked indifferently:

"I really don't know." Slackly lying back in her armchair, she watched the little flames beginning to creep among the coals indifferently, as if they, too, were very distant and indifferent.

Katharine looked at her indignantly and rose.

"Possibly he may come here," Mary continued, without altering the abstract tone of her voice. "It would be worth your while to wait if you want to see him tonight." She bent forward and touched the wood, so that the flames slipped in between the interstices of the coal.

Katharine reflected. "I'll wait half an hour," she said.

Mary rose, went to the table, spread out her papers under the green-shaded lamp and, with an action that was becoming a habit, twisted a lock of hair round and round in her fingers. Once she looked unperceived at her visitor, who never moved, who sat so still, with eyes so intent, that you could almost fancy that she was watching something, some face that never looked up at her. Mary found herself unable to go on writing. She turned her eyes away, but only to be aware of the presence of what Katharine looked at. There were ghosts in the room, and one, strangely and sadly, was the ghost of herself. The minutes went by.

"What would be the time now?" said Katharine at last. The half-hour was not quite spent.

"I'm going to get dinner ready," said Mary, rising from her table.

"Then I'll go," said Katharine.

"Why don't you stay? Where are you going?"

Katharine looked round the room, conveying her uncertainty in her glance.

"Perhaps I might find him," she mused.

"But why should it matter? You'll see him another day."

Mary spoke, and intended to speak, cruelly enough.

"I was wrong to come here," Katharine replied.

Their eyes met with antagonism, and neither flinched.

"You had a perfect right to come here," Mary answered.

A loud knocking at the door interrupted them. Mary went to open it, and returning with some note or parcel, Katharine looked away so that Mary might not read her disappointment.

"Of course you had a right to come," Mary repeated, laying the note upon the table.

"No," said Katharine. "Except that when one's desperate one has a sort of right. I am desperate. How do I know what's happening to him now? He may do anything. He may wander about the streets all night. Anything may happen to him."

She spoke with a self-abandonment that Mary had never seen in her.

"You know you exaggerate; you're talking nonsense," she said roughly.

"Mary, I must talk—I must tell you——"

"You needn't tell me anything," Mary interrupted her. "Can't I see for myself?"

"No, no," Katharine exclaimed. "It's not that——"

Her look, passing beyond Mary, beyond the verge of the room and out beyond any words that came her way, wildly and passionately, convinced Mary that she, at any rate, could not follow such a glance to its end. She was baffled; she tried to think herself back again into the height of her love for Ralph. Pressing her fingers upon her eyelids, she murmured:

"You forget that I loved him too. I thought I knew him. I *did* know him."

And yet, what had she known? She could not remember it any more. She pressed her eyeballs until they struck stars and suns into her darkness. She convinced herself that she was stirring among ashes. She desisted. She was astonished at her discovery. She did not love Ralph any more. She looked back dazed into the room, and her eyes rested upon the table with its lamp-lit papers. The steady radiance seemed for a second to have its counterpart within her; she shut her eyes; she opened them and looked at the lamp again; another love burnt in the place of the old one, or so, in a momentary glance of amazement, she guessed before the revelation was over and the old surroundings asserted themselves. She leant in silence against the mantelpiece.

"There are different ways of loving," she murmured, half to herself, at length.

Katharine made no reply and seemed unaware of her words. She seemed absorbed in her own thoughts.

"Perhaps he's waiting in the street again tonight," she exclaimed. "I'll go now. I might find him."

"It's far more likely that he'll come here," said Mary, and Katharine, after considering for a moment, said:

"I'll wait another half-hour."

She sank down into her chair again, and took up the same position which Mary had compared to the position of one watching an unseeing face. She watched, indeed, not a face, but a procession, not of people, but of life itself: the good and bad; the meaning; the past, the present, and the future. All this seemed apparent to her, and she was not ashamed of her extravagance so much as exalted to one of the pinnacles of existence, where it behoved the world to do her homage. No one but she herself knew what it meant to miss Ralph Denham on that particular night; into this inadequate event crowded feelings that the great crises of life might have failed to call forth. She had missed him, and knew the bitterness of all failure; she desired him, and knew the torment of all passion. It did not matter what trivial accidents led to this culmination. Nor did she care how extravagant she appeared, nor how openly she showed her feelings.

When the dinner was ready Mary told her to come, and she came submissively, as if she let Mary direct her movements for her. They ate and drank together almost in silence, and when Mary told her to eat more, she ate more; when she was told to drink wine, she drank it. Nevertheless, beneath this superficial obedience, Mary knew that she was following her own thoughts unhindered. She was not inattentive so much as remote; she looked at once so unseeing and so intent upon some vision of her own that Mary gradually felt more than protective—she became actually alarmed at the prospect of some collision between Katharine and the forces of the outside world. Directly they had done, Katharine announced her intention of going.

"But where are you going to?" Mary asked, desiring vaguely to hinder her.

"Oh, I'm going home—no, to Highgate perhaps."

Mary saw that it would be useless to try to stop her. All she could do was to insist upon coming too, but she met with no opposition; Katharine seemed indifferent to her presence. In a few minutes they were walking along the Strand. They walked so rapidly that Mary was deluded into the belief that Katharine knew where she was going. She herself was not attentive. She was glad of the movement along lamp-lit streets in the open air. She was fingering, painfully and with fear, yet with strange hope, too, the discovery which she had stumbled upon unexpectedly that night. She was free once more at the cost of a gift, the best, perhaps, that she could offer, but she was, thank Heaven, in love no longer. She was tempted to spend the first instalment of her freedom in some dissipation; in the pit of the Coliseum, for example, since they were now passing the door. Why not go in and celebrate her independence of the tyranny of love? Or, perhaps, the top of an omnibus bound for some remote place such as Camberwell, or Sidcup, or the Welsh Harp would suit her better. She noticed these names painted on little boards for the first time for weeks. Or should she return to her room, and spend the night working out the details of a very enlightened and ingenious scheme? Of all possibilities this appealed to her most, and brought to mind the fire, the lamplight, the steady glow which had seemed lit in the place where a more passionate flame had once burnt.

Now Katharine stopped, and Mary woke to the fact that instead of having a goal she had evidently none. She paused at the edge of the crossing, and looked this way and that, and finally made as if in the direction of Haverstock Hill.

"Look here—where are you going?" Mary cried, catching her by the hand. "We must take that cab and go home." She hailed a cab and insisted that Katharine should get in, while she directed the driver to take them to Cheyne Walk.

Katharine submitted. "Very well," she said. "We may as well go there as anywhere else."

A gloom seemed to have fallen on her. She lay back in her corner, silent and apparently exhausted. Mary, in spite of her own preoccupation, was struck by her pallor and her attitude of dejection.

"I'm sure we shall find him," she said more gently than she had yet spoken.

"It may be too late," Katharine replied. Without understanding her, Mary began to pity her for what she was suffering.

"Nonsense," she said, taking her hand and rubbing it. "If we don't find him there we shall find him somewhere else."

"But suppose he's walking about the streets—for hours and hours?"

She leant forward and looked out of the window.

"He may refuse ever to speak to me again," she said in a low voice, almost to herself.

The exaggeration was so immense that Mary did not attempt to cope with it, save by keeping hold of Katharine's wrist. She half expected that Katharine might open the door suddenly and jump out. Perhaps Katharine perceived the purpose with which her hand was held.

"Don't be frightened," she said, with a little laugh. "I'm not going to jump out of the cab. It wouldn't do much good after all."

Upon this, Mary ostentatiously withdrew her hand.

"I ought to have apologized," Katharine continued, with an effort, "for bringing you into all this business; I haven't told you half, either. I'm no longer engaged to William Rodney. He is to marry Cassandra Otway. It's all arranged—all perfectly right. . . . And after he'd waited in the streets for hours and hours, William made me bring him in. He was standing under the lamp-post watching our windows. He was perfectly white when he came into the room. William left us alone, and we sat and talked. It seems ages and ages ago, now. Was it last night? Have I been out long? What's the time?" She sprang forward to catch sight of a clock, as if the exact time had some important bearing on her case.

"Only half-past eight!" she exclaimed. "Then he may be there still." She leant out of the window and told the cabman to drive faster.

"But if he's not there, what shall I do? Where could I find him? The streets are so crowded."

"We shall find him," Mary repeated.

Mary had no doubt but that somehow or other they would find him. But suppose they did find him? She began to think of Ralph with a sort of strangeness, in her effort to understand how he could be capable of satisfying this extraordinary desire. Once more she thought herself back to her old view of him and could, with an effort, recall the haze which surrounded his figure, and the sense of confused, heightened exhilaration which lay all about his neighborhood, so that for months at a time she had never exactly heard his voice or seen his face—or so it now seemed to her. The pain of her loss shot through her. Nothing would ever make up—

not success, or happiness, or oblivion. But this pang was immediately followed by the assurance that now, at any rate, she knew the truth; and Katharine, she thought, stealing a look at her, did not know the truth; yes, Katharine was immensely to be pitied.

The cab, which had been caught in the traffic, was now liberated and sped on down Sloane Street. Mary was conscious of the tension with which Katharine marked its progress, as if her mind were fixed upon a point in front of them, and marked, second by second, their approach to it. She said nothing, and in silence Mary began to fix her mind, in sympathy at first, and later in forgetfulness of her companion, upon a point in front of them. She imagined a point distant as a low star upon the horizon of the dark. There for her too, for them both, was the goal for which they were striving, and the end for the ardors of their spirits was the same: but where it was, or what it was, or why she felt convinced that they were united in search of it, as they drove swiftly down the streets of London side by side, she could not have said.

"At last," Katharine breathed, as the cab drew up at the door. She jumped out and scanned the pavement on either side. Mary, meanwhile, rang the bell. The door opened as Katharine assured herself that no one of the people within view had any likeness to Ralph. On seeing her, the maid said at once:

"Mr. Denham called again, miss. He has been waiting for you for some time."

Katharine vanished from Mary's sight. The door shut between them, and Mary walked slowly and thoughtfully up the street alone.

Katharine turned at once to the dining-room. But with her fingers upon the handle, she held back. Perhaps she realized that this was a moment which would never come again. Perhaps, for a second, it seemed to her that no reality could equal the imagination she had formed. Perhaps she was restrained by some vague fear or anticipation, which made her dread any exchange or interruption. But if these doubts and fears or this supreme bliss restrained her, it was only for a moment. In another second she had turned the handle and, biting her lip to control herself, she opened the door upon Ralph Denham. An extraordinary clearness of sight seemed to possess her on beholding him. So little, so single, so separate from all else he appeared, who had been the cause of these extreme agitations and aspirations. She could have laughed in his face. But, gaining upon this clearness of sight against her will, and to her dislike, was a flood of confusion, of relief, of certainty, of humility, of desire no longer to strive and to discriminate, yielding to which, she let herself sink within his arms and confessed her love.

32

Nobody asked Katharine any questions next day. If cross-examined she might have said that nobody spoke to her. She worked a little, wrote a little, ordered the dinner, and sat, for longer than she knew, with her head on her hand piercing whatever lay before her, whether it was a letter or a dictionary, as if it were a film upon the deep prospects that revealed themselves to her kindling and brooding eyes. She rose once, and going to the bookcase, took out her father's Greek dictionary and spread the sacred pages of symbols and figures before her. She smoothed the sheets with a mixture of affectionate amusement and hope. Would other eyes look on them with her one day? The thought, long intolerable, was now just bearable.

She was quite unaware of the anxiety with which her movements were watched and her expression scanned. Cassandra was careful not to be caught looking at her, and their conversation was so prosaic that were it not for certain jolts and jerks between the sentences, as if the mind were kept with difficulty to the rails, Mrs. Milvain herself could have detected nothing of a suspicious nature in what she overheard.

William, when he came in late that afternoon and found Cassandra alone, had a very serious piece of news to impart. He had just passed Katharine in the street and she had failed to recognize him.

"That doesn't matter with me, of course, but suppose it happened with somebody else? What would they think? They would suspect something merely from her expression. She looked—she looked"—he hesitated—"like some one walking in her sleep."

To Cassandra the significant thing was that Katharine had gone out without telling her, and she interpreted this to mean that she had gone out to meet Ralph Denham. But to her surprise William drew no comfort from this probability.

"Once throw conventions aside," he began, "once do the things that people don't do—" and the fact that you are going to meet a young man is no longer proof of anything, except, indeed, that people will talk.

Cassandra saw, not without a pang of jealousy, that he was extremely solicitous that people should not talk about Katharine, as if his interest in her were still proprietary rather than friendly. As they were both ignorant of Ralph's visit the night before they had not that reason to comfort themselves with the thought that matters were hastening to a crisis. These absences of Katharine's, moreover, left them exposed to interruptions which almost destroyed their pleasure in being alone together. The rainy evening made it impossible to go out; and, indeed, according to William's code, it was considerably more damning to be seen out of doors than surprised within. They were so much at the mercy of bells and doors that they could hardly talk of Macaulay with any conviction, and William preferred to defer the second act of his tragedy until another day.

Under these circumstances Cassandra showed herself at her best. She sympathized with William's anxieties and did her utmost to share them; but still, to be alone together, to be running risks together, to be partners in the wonderful conspiracy, was to her so enthralling that she was always forgetting discretion, breaking out into exclamations and admirations which finally made William believe that, although deplorable and upsetting, the situation was not without its sweetness.

When the door did open, he started, but braved the forthcoming revelation. It was not Mrs. Milvain, however, but Katharine herself who entered, closely followed by Ralph Denham. With a set expression which showed what an effort she was making, Katharine encountered their eyes, and saying, "We're not going to interrupt you," she led Denham behind the curtain which hung in front of the room with the relics. This refuge was none of her willing, but confronted with wet pavements and only some belated museum or Tube station for shelter, she was forced, for Ralph's sake, to face the discomforts of her own house. Under the street lamps she had thought him looking both tired and strained.

Thus separated, the two couples remained occupied for some time with their own affairs. Only the lowest murmurs penetrated from one section of the room to the other. At length the maid came in to bring a message that Mr. Hilbery would not be home for dinner. It was true that there was no need that Katharine should be informed, but William began to inquire Cassandra's opinion in such a way as to show that, with or without reason, he wished very much to speak to her.

From motives of her own Cassandra dissuaded him.

"But don't you think it's a little unsociable?" he hazarded. "Why not do something amusing?–go to the play, for instance? Why not ask Katharine and Ralph, eh?" The coupling of their names in this manner caused Cassandra's heart to leap with pleasure.

"Don't you think they must be—?" she began, but William hastily took her up.

"Oh, I know nothing about that. I only thought we might amuse ourselves, as your uncle's out."

He proceeded on his embassy with a mixture of excitement and embarrassment which caused him to turn aside with his hand on the curtain, and to examine intently for several moments the portrait of a lady, optimistically said by Mrs. Hilbery to be an early work of Sir Joshua Reynolds. Then, with some unnecessary fumbling, he drew aside the curtain, and with his eyes fixed upon the ground, repeated his message and suggested that they should all spend the evening at the play. Katharine accepted the suggestion with such cordiality that it was strange to find her of no clear mind as to the precise spectacle she wished to see. She left the choice entirely to Ralph and William, who, taking counsel fraternally over an evening paper, found themselves in agreement as to the merits of a music-hall. This being arranged, everything else followed easily and enthusiastically. Cassandra had never been to a music-hall. Katharine instructed her in the peculiar delights of an entertainment where Polar bears follow directly upon ladies in full evening dress, and the stage is alternately a garden of mystery, a milliner's band-box, and a fried-fish shop in the Mile End Road. Whatever the exact nature of the program that night, it fulfilled the highest purposes of dramatic art, so far, at least, as four of the audience were concerned.

No doubt the actors and the authors would have been surprised to learn in what shape their efforts reached those particular eyes and ears; but they could not have denied that the effect as a whole was tremendous. The hall resounded with brass and strings, alternately of enormous pomp and majesty, and then of sweetest lamentation. The reds and creams of the background, the lyres and harps and urns and skulls, the protuberances of plaster, the fringes of scarlet plush, the sinking and blazing of innumerable electric lights, could scarcely have been surpassed for decorative effect by any craftsman of the ancient or modern world.

Then there was the audience itself, bare-shouldered, tufted and garlanded in the stalls, decorous but festal in the balconies, and frankly fit for daylight and street life in the galleries. But, however they differed when looked at separately, they shared the same huge, lovable nature in the bulk, which murmured and swayed and quivered all the time the dancing and juggling and love-making went on in front of it, slowly laughed and reluctantly left off laughing, and applauded with a helter-skelter generosity which sometimes became unanimous and overwhelming. Once William saw Katharine leaning forward and clapping her hands with an abandonment that startled him. Her laugh rang out with the laughter of the audience.

For a second he was puzzled, as if this laughter disclosed something that he had never suspected in her. But then Cassandra's face caught his eye, gazing with astonishment at the buffoon, not laughing, too deeply intent and surprised to laugh at what she saw, and for some moments he watched her as if she were a child.

The performance came to an end, the illusion dying out first here and then there, as some rose to put on their coats, others stood upright to salute "God Save the King," the musicians folded their music and encased their instruments, and the lights sank one by one until the house was empty, silent, and full of great shadows. Looking back over her shoulder as she followed Ralph through the swing doors, Cassandra marveled to see how the stage was already entirely without romance. But, she wondered, did they really cover all the seats in brown holland every night?

The success of this entertainment was such that before they separated another expedition had been planned for the next day. The next day was Saturday; therefore both William and Ralph were free to devote the whole afternoon to an expedition to Greenwich, which Cassandra had never seen, and Katharine confused with Dulwich. On this occasion Ralph was their guide. He brought them without accident to Greenwich.

What exigencies of state or fantasies of imagination first gave birth to the cluster of pleasant places by which London is surrounded is matter of indifference now that they have adapted themselves so admirably to the needs of people between the ages of twenty and thirty with Saturday afternoons to spend. Indeed, if ghosts have any interest in the affections of those who succeed them they must reap their richest harvests when the fine weather comes again and the lovers, the sightseers, and the holiday-makers pour themselves out of trains and omnibuses into their old pleasure-grounds. It is true that they go, for the most part, unthanked by name, although upon this occasion William was ready to give such discriminating praise as the dead architects and painters received seldom in the course of the year. They were walking by the river bank, and Katharine and Ralph, lagging a little behind, caught fragments of his lecture. Katharine smiled at the sound of his voice; she listened as if she found it a little unfamiliar, intimately though she knew it; she tested it. The note of assurance and happiness was new. William was very happy. She learnt every hour what sources of his happiness she had neglected. She had never asked him to teach her anything; she had never consented to read Macaulay; she had never expressed her belief that his play was second only to the works of Shakespeare. She followed dreamily in their wake, smiling and delighting in the sound which conveyed, she knew, the rapturous and yet not servile assent of Cassandra.

Then she murmured, "How can Cassandra—" but changed her sentence to the opposite of what she meant to say and ended, "how could she herself have been so blind?" But it was unnecessary to follow out such riddles when the presence of Ralph supplied her with more interesting problems, which somehow became involved with the little boat crossing the river, the majestic and careworn City, and the steamers homecoming with their treasury, or starting in search of it, so that infinite leisure would be necessary for the proper disentanglement of one from the other. He stopped, moreover, and began inquiring of an old boatman as to the tides and the ships. In thus talking he seemed different, and even looked different, she thought, against the river, with the steeples and towers for background. His strangeness, his romance, his power to leave her side and take part in the affairs of men, the possibility that they should together hire a boat and cross the river, the speed and wildness of this enterprise filled her mind and inspired her with such rapture, half of love and half of adventure, that William and Cassandra were startled from their talk, and Cassandra exclaimed, "She looks as if she were offering up a sacrifice! Very beautiful," she added quickly, though she repressed, in deference to William, her own wonder that the sight of Ralph Denham talking to a boatman on the banks of the Thames could move any one to such an attitude of adoration.

That afternoon, what with tea and the curiosities of the Thames tunnel and the unfamiliarity of the streets, passed so quickly that the only method of prolonging it was to plan another expedition for the following day. Hampton Court was decided upon, in preference to Hampstead, for though Cassandra had dreamt as a child of the brigands of Hampstead, she had now transferred her affections completely and for ever to William III. Accordingly, they arrived at Hampton Court about lunch-time on a fine Sunday morning. Such unity marked their expressions of admiration for the red-brick building that they might have come there for no other purpose than to assure each other that this palace was the stateliest palace in the world. They walked up and down the Terrace, four abreast, and fancied themselves the owners of the place, and calculated the amount of good to the world produced indubitably by such a tenancy.

"The only hope for us," said Katharine, "is that William shall die, and Cassandra shall be given rooms as the widow of a distinguished poet."

"Or—" Cassandra began, but checked herself from the liberty of envisaging Katharine as the widow of a distinguished lawyer. Upon this, the third day of junketing, it was tiresome to have to restrain oneself even from such innocent excursions of fancy. She dared not question William; he was inscrutable; he never seemed even to follow the other couple with curiosity when they separated, as they frequently did, to name a plant, or examine a fresco. Cassandra was constantly studying their backs. She noticed how sometimes the impulse to move came from Katharine, and sometimes from Ralph; how, sometimes, they walked slow, as if in profound intercourse, and sometimes fast, as if in passionate. When they came together again nothing could be more unconcerned than their manner.

"We have been wondering whether they ever catch a fish . . ." or, "We must leave time to visit the Maze." Then, to puzzle her further, William and Ralph filled in all interstices of meal-times or railway journeys with perfectly good-tempered arguments; or they discussed politics, or they told stories, or they did sums together upon the backs of old envelopes to prove something. She suspected that Katharine was absent-minded, but it was impossible to tell. There were moments when she felt so young and inexperienced that she almost wished herself back with the silkworms at Stogdon House, and not embarked upon this bewildering intrigue.

These moments, however, were only the necessary shadow or chill which proved the substance of her bliss, and did not damage the radiance which seemed to rest equally upon the whole party. The fresh air of spring, the sky washed of clouds and already shedding warmth from its blue, seemed the reply vouchsafed by nature to the mood of her chosen spirits. These chosen spirits were to be found also among the deer, dumbly basking, and among the fish, set still in mid-stream, for they were mute sharers in a benignant state not needing any exposition by the tongue. No words that Cassandra could come by expressed the stillness, the brightness, the air of expectancy which lay upon the orderly beauty of the grass walks and gravel paths down which they went walking four abreast that Sunday afternoon. Silently the shadows of the trees lay across the broad sunshine; silence wrapt her heart in its folds. The quivering stillness of the butterfly on the half-opened flower, the silent grazing of the deer in the sun, were the sights her eye rested upon and received as the images of her own nature laid open to happiness and trembling in its ecstasy.

But the afternoon wore on, and it became time to leave the gardens. As they drove from Waterloo to Chelsea, Katharine began to have some compunction about her father, which, together with the opening of offices and the need of working in them on Monday, made it difficult to plan another festival for the following day. Mr. Hilbery had taken their absence, so far, with paternal benevolence, but they could not trespass upon it indefinitely. Indeed, had they known it, he was already suffering from their absence, and longing for their return.

He had no dislike of solitude, and Sunday, in particular, was pleasantly adapted for letter-writing, paying calls, or a visit to his club. He was leaving the house on some such suitable expedition towards tea-time when he found himself stopped on his own doorstep by his sister, Mrs. Milvain. She should, on hearing that no one was at home, have withdrawn submissively, but instead she accepted his half-hearted invitation to come in, and he found himself in the melancholy position of being forced to order tea for her and sit in the drawing-room while she drank it. She speedily made it plain that she was only thus exacting because she had come on a matter of business. He was by no means exhilarated at the news.

"Katharine is out this afternoon," he remarked. "Why not come round later and discuss it with her—with us both, eh?"

"My dear Trevor, I have particular reasons for wishing to talk to you alone. . . . Where is Katharine?"

"She's out with her young man, naturally. Cassandra plays the part of chaperone very usefully. A charming young woman that—a great favorite of mine." He turned his stone between his fingers, and conceived different methods of leading Celia away from her obsession, which, he supposed, must have reference to the domestic affairs of Cyril as usual.

"With Cassandra," Mrs. Milvain repeated significantly. "With Cassandra."

"Yes, with Cassandra," Mr. Hilbery agreed urbanely, pleased at the diversion. "I think they said they were going to Hampton Court, and I rather believe they were taking a protege of mine, Ralph Denham, a very clever fellow, too, to amuse Cassandra. I thought the arrangement very suitable." He was prepared to dwell at some length upon this safe topic, and trusted that Katharine would come in before he had done with it.

"Hampton Court always seems to me an ideal spot for engaged couples. There's the Maze, there's a nice place for having tea—I forget what they call it—and then, if the young man knows his business he contrives to take his lady upon the river. Full of possibilities—full. Cake, Celia?" Mr. Hilbery continued. "I respect my dinner too much, but that can't possibly apply to you. You've never observed that feast, so far as I can remember."

Her brother's affability did not deceive Mrs. Milvain; it slightly saddened her; she well knew the cause of it. Blind and infatuated as usual!

"Who is this Mr. Denham?" she asked.

"Ralph Denham?" said Mr. Hilbery, in relief that her mind had taken this turn. "A very interesting young man. I've a great belief in him. He's an authority upon our mediæval institutions, and if he weren't forced to earn his living he would write a book that very much wants writing."

"He is not well off, then?" Mrs. Milvain interposed.

"Hasn't a penny, I'm afraid, and a family more or less dependent on him."

"A mother and sisters?—His father is dead?"

"Yes, his father died some years ago," said Mr. Hilbery, who was prepared to draw upon his imagination, if necessary, to keep Mrs. Milvain supplied with facts about the private history of Ralph Denham since, for some inscrutable reason, the subject took her fancy.

"His father has been dead some time, and this young man had to take his place——"

"A legal family?" Mrs. Milvain inquired. "I fancy I've seen the name somewhere."

Mr. Hilbery shook his head. "I should be inclined to doubt whether they were altogether in that walk of life," he observed. "I fancy that Denham once told me that his father was a corn merchant. Perhaps he said a stockbroker. He came to grief, anyhow, as stockbrokers have a way of doing. I've a great respect for Denham," he added. The remark sounded to his ears unfortunately conclusive, and he was afraid that there was nothing more to be said about Denham. He examined the tips of his fingers carefully. "Cassandra's grown into a very charming young woman," he started afresh. "Charming to look at, and charming to talk to, though her historical knowledge is not altogether profound. Another cup of tea?"

Mrs. Milvain had given her cup a little push, which seemed to indicate some momentary displeasure. But she did not want any more tea.

"It is Cassandra that I have come about," she began. "I am very sorry to say that Cassandra is not at all what you think her, Trevor. She has imposed upon your and Maggie's goodness. She has behaved in a way that would have seemed incredible–in this house of all houses–were it not for other circumstances that are still more incredible."

Mr. Hilbery looked taken aback, and was silent for a second.

"It all sounds very black," he remarked urbanely, continuing his examination of his finger-nails. "But I own I am completely in the dark."

Mrs. Milvain became rigid, and emitted her message in little short sentences of extreme intensity.

"Who has Cassandra gone out with? William Rodney. Who has Katharine gone out with? Ralph Denham. Why are they for ever meeting each other round street corners, and going to music-halls, and taking cabs late at night? Why will Katharine not tell me the truth when I question her? I understand the reason now. Katharine has entangled herself with this unknown lawyer; she has seen fit to condone Cassandra's conduct."

There was another slight pause.

"Ah, well, Katharine will no doubt have some explanation to give me," Mr. Hilbery replied imperturbably. "It's a little too complicated for me to take in all at once, I confess–and, if you won't think me rude, Celia, I think I'll be getting along towards Knightsbridge."

Mrs. Milvain rose at once.

"She has condoned Cassandra's conduct and entangled herself with Ralph Denham," she repeated. She stood very erect with the dauntless air of one testifying to the truth regardless of consequences. She knew from past discussions that the only way to counter her brother's indolence and indifference was to shoot her statements at him in a compressed form once finally upon leaving the room. Having spoken thus, she restrained herself from adding another word, and left the house with the dignity of one inspired by a great ideal.

She had certainly framed her remarks in such a way as to prevent her brother from paying his call in the region of Knightsbridge. He had no fears for Katharine, but there was a suspicion at the back of his mind that Cassandra might have been, innocently and ignorantly, led into some foolish situation in one of their unshepherded dissipations. His wife was an erratic judge of the conventions; he himself was lazy; and with Katharine absorbed, very naturally–Here he recalled, as well as he could, the exact nature of the charge. "She has condoned Cassandra's conduct and entangled herself with Ralph Denham." From which it appeared that

Katharine was *not* absorbed, or which of them was it that had entangled herself with Ralph Denham? From this maze of absurdity Mr. Hilbery saw no way out until Katharine herself came to his help, so that he applied himself, very philosophically on the whole, to a book.

No sooner had he heard the young people come in and go upstairs than he sent a maid to tell Miss Katharine that he wished to speak to her in the study. She was slipping furs loosely onto the floor in the drawing-room in front of the fire. They were all gathered round, reluctant to part. The message from her father surprised Katharine, and the others caught from her look, as she turned to go, a vague sense of apprehension.

Mr. Hilbery was reassured by the sight of her. He congratulated himself, he prided himself, upon possessing a daughter who had a sense of responsibility and an understanding of life profound beyond her years. Moreover, she was looking today unusual; he had come to take her beauty for granted; now he remembered it and was surprised by it. He thought instinctively that he had interrupted some happy hour of hers with Rodney, and apologized.

"I'm sorry to bother you, my dear. I heard you come in, and thought I'd better make myself disagreeable at once—as it seems, unfortunately, that fathers are expected to make themselves disagreeable. Now, your Aunt Celia has been to see me; your Aunt Celia has taken it into her head apparently that you and Cassandra have been—let us say a little foolish. This going about together—these pleasant little parties—there's been some kind of misunderstanding. I told her I saw no harm in it, but I should just like to hear from yourself. Has Cassandra been left a little too much in the company of Mr. Denham?"

Katharine did not reply at once, and Mr. Hilbery tapped the coal encouragingly with the poker. Then she said, without embarrassment or apology:

"I don't see why I should answer Aunt Celia's questions. I've told her already that I won't."

Mr. Hilbery was relieved and secretly amused at the thought of the interview, although he could not license such irreverence outwardly.

"Very good. Then you authorize me to tell her that she's been mistaken, and there was nothing but a little fun in it? You've no doubt, Katharine, in your own mind? Cassandra is in our charge, and I don't intend that people should gossip about her. I suggest that you should be a little more careful in future. Invite me to your next entertainment."

She did not respond, as he had hoped, with any affectionate or humorous reply. She meditated, pondering something or other, and he reflected that even his Katharine did not differ from other women in the capacity to let things be. Or had she something to say?

"Have you a guilty conscience?" he inquired lightly. "Tell me, Katharine," he said more seriously, struck by something in the expression of her eyes.

"I've been meaning to tell you for some time," she said, "I'm not going to marry William."

"You're not going–!" he exclaimed, dropping the poker in his immense surprise. "Why? When? Explain yourself, Katharine."

"Oh, some time ago–a week, perhaps more." Katharine spoke hurriedly and indifferently, as if the matter could no longer concern any one.

"But may I ask–why have I not been told of this–what do you mean by it?"

"We don't wish to be married–that's all."

"This is William's wish as well as yours?"

"Oh, yes. We agree perfectly."

Mr. Hilbery had seldom felt more completely at a loss. He thought that Katharine was treating the matter with curious unconcern; she scarcely seemed aware of the gravity of what she was saying; he did not understand the position at all. But his desire to smooth everything over comfortably came to his relief. No doubt there was some quarrel, some whimsey on the part of William, who, though a good fellow, was a little exacting sometimes–something that a woman could put right. But though he inclined to take the easiest view of his responsibilities, he cared too much for this daughter to let things be.

"I confess I find great difficulty in following you. I should like to hear William's side of the story," he said irritably. "I think he ought to have spoken to me in the first instance."

"I wouldn't let him," said Katharine. "I know it must seem to you very strange," she added. "But I assure you, if you'd wait a little–until mother comes back."

This appeal for delay was much to Mr. Hilbery's liking. But his conscience would not suffer it. People were talking. He could not endure that his daughter's conduct should be in any way considered irregular. He wondered whether, in the circumstances, it would be better to wire to his wife, to send for one of his sisters, to forbid William the house, to pack Cassandra off home–for he was vaguely conscious of responsibilities in her direction, too. His forehead was becoming more and more wrinkled by the multiplicity of his anxieties, which he was sorely tempted to ask Katharine to solve for him, when the door opened and William Rodney appeared. This necessitated a complete change, not only of manner, but of position also.

"Here's William," Katharine exclaimed, in a tone of relief. "I've told father we're not engaged," she said to him. "I've explained that I prevented you from telling him."

William's manner was marked by the utmost formality. He bowed very slightly in the direction of Mr. Hilbery, and stood erect, holding one lapel of his coat, and gazing into the center of the fire. He waited for Mr. Hilbery to speak.

Mr. Hilbery also assumed an appearance of formidable dignity. He had risen to his feet, and now bent the top part of his body slightly forward.

"I should like your account of this affair, Rodney—if Katharine no longer prevents you from speaking."

William waited two seconds at least.

"Our engagement is at an end," he said, with the utmost stiffness.

"Has this been arrived at by your joint desire?"

After a perceptible pause William bent his head, and Katharine said, as if by an afterthought:

"Oh, yes."

Mr. Hilbery swayed to and fro, and moved his lips as if to utter remarks which remained unspoken.

"I can only suggest that you should postpone any decision until the effect of this misunderstanding has had time to wear off. You have now known each other—" he began.

"There's been no misunderstanding," Katharine interposed. "Nothing at all." She moved a few paces across the room, as if she intended to leave them. Her preoccupied naturalness was in strange contrast to her father's pomposity and to William's military rigidity. He had not once raised his eyes. Katharine's glance, on the other hand, ranged past the two gentlemen, along the books, over the tables, towards the door. She was paying the least possible attention, it seemed, to what was happening. Her father looked at her with a sudden clouding and troubling of his expression. Somehow his faith in her stability and sense was queerly shaken. He no longer felt that he could ultimately entrust her with the whole conduct of her own affairs after a superficial show of directing them. He felt, for the first time in many years, responsible for her.

"Look here, we must get to the bottom of this," he said, dropping his formal manner and addressing Rodney as if Katharine were not present. "You've had some difference of opinion, eh? Take my word for it, most people go through this sort of thing when they're engaged. I've seen more trouble come from long engagements than from any other form of human folly. Take my advice and put the whole matter out of your minds—both of you. I prescribe a complete abstinence from emotion. Visit some cheerful seaside resort, Rodney."

He was struck by William's appearance, which seemed to him to indicate profound feeling resolutely held in check. No doubt, he reflected, Katharine had been very trying, unconsciously trying, and had driven him to take up a position which was none of his willing. Mr. Hilbery certainly did not overrate William's sufferings. No minutes in his life had hitherto extorted from him such intensity of anguish. He was now facing the consequences of his insanity. He must confess himself entirely and fundamentally other than Mr. Hilbery thought him. Everything was against him. Even the Sunday evening and the fire and the tranquil library scene were against him. Mr. Hilbery's appeal to him as a man of the world was terribly against him. He was no longer a man of any world that Mr. Hilbery cared to recognize. But some power compelled him, as it had compelled him to come downstairs, to make his stand here and now, alone and unhelped by any one, without prospect of reward. He fumbled with various phrases; and then jerked out:

"I love Cassandra."

Mr. Hilbery's face turned a curious dull purple. He looked at his daughter. He nodded his head, as if to convey his silent command to her to leave the room; but either she did not notice it or preferred not to obey.

"You have the impudence—" Mr. Hilbery began, in a dull, low voice that he himself had never heard before, when there was a scuffling and exclaiming in the hall, and Cassandra, who appeared to be insisting against some dissuasion on the part of another, burst into the room.

"Uncle Trevor," she exclaimed, "I insist upon telling you the truth!" She flung herself between Rodney and her uncle, as if she sought to intercept their blows. As her uncle stood perfectly still, looking very large and imposing, and as nobody spoke, she shrank back a little, and looked first at Katharine and then at Rodney. "You must know the truth," she said, a little lamely.

"You have the impudence to tell me this in Katharine's presence?" Mr. Hilbery continued, speaking with complete disregard of Cassandra's interruption.

"I am aware, quite aware—" Rodney's words, which were broken in sense, spoken after a pause, and with his eyes upon the ground, nevertheless expressed an astonishing amount of resolution. "I am quite aware what you must think of me," he brought out, looking Mr. Hilbery directly in the eyes for the first time.

"I could express my views on the subject more fully if we were alone," Mr. Hilbery returned.

"But you forget me," said Katharine. She moved a little towards Rodney, and her movement seemed to testify mutely to her respect for him, and her alliance with him. "I think William has behaved perfectly rightly, and, after all, it is I who am concerned–I and Cassandra."

Cassandra, too, gave an indescribably slight movement which seemed to draw the three of them into alliance together. Katharine's tone and glance made Mr. Hilbery once more feel completely at a loss, and in addition, painfully and angrily obsolete; but in spite of an awful inner hollowness he was outwardly composed.

"Cassandra and Rodney have a perfect right to settle their own affairs according to their own wishes; but I see no reason why they should do so either in my room or in my house. . . . I wish to be quite clear on this point, however; you are no longer engaged to Rodney."

He paused, and his pause seemed to signify that he was extremely thankful for his daughter's deliverance.

Cassandra turned to Katharine, who drew her breath as if to speak and checked herself; Rodney, too, seemed to await some movement on her part; her father glanced at her as if he half anticipated some further revelation. She remained perfectly silent. In the silence they heard distinctly steps descending the staircase, and Katharine went straight to the door.

"Wait," Mr. Hilbery commanded. "I wish to speak to you—alone," he added.

She paused, holding the door ajar.

"I'll come back," she said, and as she spoke she opened the door and went out. They could hear her immediately speak to some one outside, though the words were inaudible.

Mr. Hilbery was left confronting the guilty couple, who remained standing as if they did not accept their dismissal, and the disappearance of Katharine had brought some change into the situation. So, in his secret heart, Mr. Hilbery felt that it had, for he could not explain his daughter's behavior to his own satisfaction.

"Uncle Trevor," Cassandra exclaimed impulsively, "don't be angry, please. I couldn't help it; I do beg you to forgive me."

Her uncle still refused to acknowledge her identity, and still talked over her head as if she did not exist.

"I suppose you have communicated with the Otways," he said to Rodney grimly.

"Uncle Trevor, we wanted to tell you," Cassandra replied for him. "We waited—" she looked appealingly at Rodney, who shook his head ever so slightly.

"Yes? What were you waiting for?" her uncle asked sharply, looking at her at last.

The words died on her lips. It was apparent that she was straining her ears as if to catch some sound outside the room that would come to her help. He received no answer. He listened, too.

"This is a most unpleasant business for all parties," he concluded, sinking into his chair again, hunching his shoulders and regarding the flames. He seemed to speak to himself, and Rodney and Cassandra looked at him in silence.

"Why don't you sit down?" he said suddenly. He spoke gruffly, but the force of his anger was evidently spent, or some preoccupation had turned his mood to other regions. While Cassandra accepted his invitation, Rodney remained standing.

"I think Cassandra can explain matters better in my absence," he said, and left the room, Mr. Hilbery giving his assent by a slight nod of the head.

Meanwhile, in the dining-room next door, Denham and Katharine were once more seated at the mahogany table. They seemed to be continuing a conversation broken off in the middle, as if each remembered the precise point at which they had been interrupted, and was eager to go on as quickly as possible. Katharine, having interposed a short account of the interview with her father, Denham made no comment, but said:

"Anyhow, there's no reason why we shouldn't see each other."

"Or stay together. It's only marriage that's out of the question," Katharine replied.

"But if I find myself coming to want you more and more?"

"If our lapses come more and more often?"

He sighed impatiently, and said nothing for a moment.

"But at least," he renewed, "we've established the fact that my lapses are still in some odd way connected with you; yours have nothing to do with me. Katharine," he added, his assumption of reason broken up by his agitation, "I assure you that we are in love—what other people call love. Remember that night. We had no doubts whatever then. We were absolutely happy for half an hour. You had no lapse until the day after; I had no lapse until yesterday morning. We've been happy at intervals all day until I—went off my head, and you, quite naturally, were bored."

"Ah," she exclaimed, as if the subject chafed her, "I can't make you understand. It's not boredom—I'm never bored. Reality—reality," she ejaculated, tapping her finger upon the table as if to emphasize and perhaps explain her isolated utterance of this word. "I cease to be real to you. It's the faces in a storm again—the vision in a hurricane. We come together for a moment and we part. It's my fault, too. I'm as bad as you are—worse, perhaps."

They were trying to explain, not for the first time, as their weary gestures and frequent interruptions showed, what in their common language they had christened their "lapses"; a constant source of distress to them, in the past few days, and the immediate reason why Ralph was on his way to leave the house when Katharine, listening anxiously, heard him and prevented him. What was the cause of these lapses? Either because Katharine looked more beautiful, or more strange, because she wore something different, or said something unexpected, Ralph's sense of her romance welled up and overcame him either into silence or into inarticulate expressions, which Katharine, with unintentional but invariable perversity, interrupted or contradicted with some severity or assertion of prosaic fact. Then the vision disappeared, and Ralph expressed vehemently in his turn the conviction that he only loved her shadow and cared nothing for her reality. If the lapse was on her side it took the form of gradual detachment until she became completely absorbed in her own thoughts, which carried her away with such intensity that she sharply resented any recall to her companion's side. It was useless to assert that these trances were always originated by Ralph himself, however little in their later stages they had to do with him. The fact remained that she had no need of him and was very loath to be reminded of him. How, then, could they be in love? The fragmentary nature of their relationship was but too apparent.

Thus they sat depressed to silence at the dining-room table, oblivious of everything, while Rodney paced the drawing-room overhead in such agitation and exaltation of mind as he had never conceived possible, and Cassandra remained alone with her uncle. Ralph, at length, rose and walked gloomily to the window. He pressed close to the pane. Outside were truth and freedom and the immensity only to be apprehended by the mind in loneliness, and never communicated to another. What worse sacrilege was there than to attempt to violate what he perceived by seeking to impart it? Some movement behind him made him reflect that Katharine had the power, if she chose, to be in person what he dreamed of her spirit. He turned sharply to implore her help, when again he was struck cold by her look of distance, her expression of intentness upon some far object. As if conscious of his look upon her she rose and came to him, standing close by his side, and looking with him out into the dusky atmosphere. Their physical closeness was to him a bitter enough comment upon the distance between their minds. Yet distant as she was, her presence by his side transformed the world. He saw himself performing wonderful deeds of courage; saving the drowning, rescuing the forlorn. Impatient with this form of egotism, he could not shake off the conviction that somehow life was wonderful, romantic, a master worth serving so long as she stood there. He had no wish that she should speak; he did not look at her or touch her; she was apparently deep in her own thoughts and oblivious of his presence.

The door opened without their hearing the sound. Mr. Hilbery looked round the room, and for a moment failed to discover the two figures in the window. He started with displeasure when he saw them, and observed them keenly before he appeared able to make up his mind to say anything. He made a movement finally that warned them of his presence; they turned instantly. Without speaking, he beckoned to Katharine to come to him, and, keeping his eyes from the region of the room where Denham stood, he shepherded her in front of him back to the study. When Katharine was inside the room he shut the study door carefully behind him as if to secure himself from something that he disliked.

"Now, Katharine," he said, taking up his stand in front of the fire, "you will, perhaps, have the kindness to explain——" She remained silent. "What inferences do you expect me to draw?" he said sharply. . . . "You tell me that you are not engaged to Rodney; I see you on what appear to be extremely intimate terms with another—with Ralph Denham. What am I to conclude? Are you," he added, as she still said nothing, "engaged to Ralph Denham?"

"No," she replied.

His sense of relief was great; he had been certain that her answer would have confirmed his suspicions, but that anxiety being set at rest, he was the more conscious of annoyance with her for her behavior.

"Then all I can say is that you've very strange ideas of the proper way to behave. . . . People have drawn certain conclusions, nor am I surprised. . . . The more I think of it the more inexplicable I find it," he went on, his anger rising as he spoke. "Why am I left in ignorance of what is going on in my own house? Why am I left to hear of these events for the first time from my sister? Most disagreeable—most upsetting. How I'm to explain to your Uncle Francis—but I wash my hands of it. Cassandra goes tomorrow. I forbid Rodney the house. As for the other young man, the sooner he makes himself scarce the better. After placing the most implicit trust in you, Katharine——" He broke off, disquieted by the ominous silence with which his words were received, and looked at his daughter with the curious doubt as to her state of mind which he had felt before, for the first time, this evening. He perceived once more that she was not attending to what he said, but was listening, and for a moment he, too, listened for sounds outside the room. His certainty that there was some understanding between Denham and Katharine returned, but with a most unpleasant suspicion that there was something illicit about it, as the whole position between the young people seemed to him gravely illicit.

"I'll speak to Denham," he said, on the impulse of his suspicion, moving as if to go.

"I shall come with you," Katharine said instantly, starting forward.

"You will stay here," said her father.

"What are you going to say to him?" she asked.

"I suppose I may say what I like in my own house?" he returned.

"Then I go, too," she replied.

At these words, which seemed to imply a determination to go—to go for ever, Mr. Hilbery returned to his position in front of the fire, and began swaying slightly from side to side without for the moment making any remark.

"I understood you to say that you were not engaged to him," he said at length, fixing his eyes upon his daughter.

"We are not engaged," she said.

"It should be a matter of indifference to you, then, whether he comes here or not—I will not have you listening to other things when I am speaking to you!" he broke off angrily, perceiving a slight movement on her part to one side. "Answer me frankly, what is your relationship with this young man?"

"Nothing that I can explain to a third person," she said obstinately.

"I will have no more of these equivocations," he replied.

"I refuse to explain," she returned, and as she said it the front door banged to. "There!" she exclaimed. "He is gone!" She flashed such a look of fiery indignation at her father that he lost his self-control for a moment.

"For God's sake, Katharine, control yourself!" he cried.

She looked for a moment like a wild animal caged in a civilized dwelling-place. She glanced over the walls covered with books, as if for a second she had forgotten the position of the door. Then she made as if to go, but her father laid his hand upon her shoulder. He compelled her to sit down.

"These emotions have been very upsetting, naturally," he said. His manner had regained all its suavity, and he spoke with a soothing assumption of paternal authority. "You've been placed in a very difficult position, as I understand from Cassandra. Now let us come to terms; we will leave these agitating questions in peace for the present. Meanwhile, let us try to behave like civilized beings. Let us read Sir Walter Scott. What d'you say to 'The Antiquary,' eh? Or 'The Bride of Lammermoor'?"

He made his own choice, and before his daughter could protest or make her escape, she found herself being turned by the agency of Sir Walter Scott into a civilized human being.

Yet Mr. Hilbery had grave doubts, as he read, whether the process was more than skin-deep. Civilization had been very profoundly and unpleasantly overthrown that evening; the extent of the ruin was still undetermined; he had lost his temper, a physical disaster not to be matched for the space of ten years or so; and his own condition urgently required soothing and renovating at the hands of the classics. His house was in a state of revolution; he had a vision of unpleasant encounters on the staircase; his meals would be poisoned for days to come; was literature itself a specific against such disagreeables? A note of hollowness was in his voice as he read.

33

Considering that Mr. Hilbery lived in a house which was accurately numbered in order with its fellows, and that he filled up forms, paid rent, and had seven more years of tenancy to run, he had an excuse for laying down laws for the conduct of those who lived in his house, and this excuse, though profoundly inadequate, he found useful during the interregnum of civilization with which he now found himself faced. In obedience to those laws, Rodney disappeared; Cassandra was dispatched to catch the eleven-thirty on Monday morning; Denham was seen no more; so that only Katharine, the lawful occupant of the upper rooms, remained, and Mr. Hilbery thought himself competent to see that she did nothing further to compromise herself. As he bade her good morning next day he was aware that he knew nothing of what she was thinking, but, as he reflected with some bitterness, even this was an advance upon the ignorance of the previous mornings. He went to his study, wrote, tore up, and wrote again a letter to his wife, asking her to come back on account of domestic difficulties which he specified at first, but in a later draft more discreetly left unspecified. Even if she started the very moment that she got it, he reflected, she would not be home till Tuesday night, and he counted lugubriously the number of hours that he would have to spend in a position of detestable authority alone with his daughter.

What was she doing now, he wondered, as he addressed the envelope to his wife. He could not control the telephone. He could not play the spy. She might be making any arrangements she chose. Yet the thought did not disturb him so much as the strange, unpleasant, illicit atmosphere of the whole scene with the young people the night before. His sense of discomfort was almost physical.

Had he known it, Katharine was far enough withdrawn, both physically and spiritually, from the telephone. She sat in her room with the dictionaries spreading their wide leaves on the table before her, and all the pages which they had concealed for so many years arranged in a pile. She worked with the steady concentration that is produced by the successful effort to think down some unwelcome thought by means of another thought. Having absorbed the unwelcome thought, her mind went on with additional vigor, derived from the victory; on a sheet of paper lines of figures and symbols frequently and firmly written down marked the different stages of its progress. And yet it was broad daylight; there were sounds of knocking and sweeping, which proved that living people were at work on the other side of the door, and the door, which could be thrown open in a second, was her only protection against the world. But she had somehow risen to be mistress in her own kingdom, assuming her sovereignty unconsciously.

Steps approached her unheard. It is true that they were steps that lingered, divagated, and mounted with the deliberation natural to one past sixty whose arms, moreover, are full of leaves and blossoms; but they came on steadily, and soon a tap of laurel boughs against the door arrested Katharine's pencil as it touched the page. She did not move, however, and sat blank-eyed as if waiting for the interruption to cease. Instead, the door opened. At first, she attached no meaning to the moving mass of green which seemed to enter the room independently of any human agency. Then she recognized parts of her mother's face and person behind the yellow flowers and soft velvet of the palm-buds.

"From Shakespeare's tomb!" exclaimed Mrs. Hilbery, dropping the entire mass upon the floor, with a gesture that seemed to indicate an act of dedication. Then she flung her arms wide and embraced her daughter.

"Thank God, Katharine!" she exclaimed. "Thank God!" she repeated.

"You've come back?" said Katharine, very vaguely, standing up to receive the embrace.

Although she recognized her mother's presence, she was very far from taking part in the scene, and yet felt it to be amazingly appropriate that her mother should be there, thanking God emphatically for unknown blessings, and strewing the floor with flowers and leaves from Shakespeare's tomb.

"Nothing else matters in the world!" Mrs. Hilbery continued. "Names aren't everything; it's what we feel that's everything. I didn't want silly, kind, interfering letters. I didn't want your father to tell me. I knew it from the first. I prayed that it might be so."

"You knew it?" Katharine repeated her mother's words softly and vaguely, looking past her. "How did you know it?" She began, like a child, to finger a tassel hanging from her mother's cloak.

"The first evening you told me, Katharine. Oh, and thousands of times—dinner-parties—talking about books—the way he came into the room—your voice when you spoke of him."

Katharine seemed to consider each of these proofs separately. Then she said gravely:

"I'm not going to marry William. And then there's Cassandra——"

"Yes, there's Cassandra," said Mrs. Hilbery. "I own I was a little grudging at first, but, after all, she plays the piano so beautifully. Do tell me, Katharine," she asked impulsively, "where did you go that evening she played Mozart, and you thought I was asleep?"

Katharine recollected with difficulty.

"To Mary Datchet's," she remembered.

"Ah!" said Mrs. Hilbery, with a slight note of disappointment in her voice. "I had my little romance—my little speculation." She looked at her daughter. Katharine faltered beneath that innocent and penetrating gaze; she flushed, turned away, and then looked up with very bright eyes.

"I'm not in love with Ralph Denham," she said.

"Don't marry unless you're in love!" said Mrs. Hilbery very quickly. "But," she added, glancing momentarily at her daughter, "aren't there different ways, Katharine—different—?"

"We want to meet as often as we like, but to be free," Katharine continued.

"To meet here, to meet in his house, to meet in the street." Mrs. Hilbery ran over these phrases as if she were trying chords that did not quite satisfy her ear. It was plain that she had her sources of information, and, indeed, her bag was stuffed with what she called "kind letters" from the pen of her sister-in-law.

"Yes. Or to stay away in the country," Katharine concluded.

Mrs. Hilbery paused, looked unhappy, and sought inspiration from the window.

"What a comfort he was in that shop—how he took me and found the ruins at once—how *safe* I felt with him—"

"Safe? Oh, no, he's fearfully rash—he's always taking risks. He wants to throw up his profession and live in a little cottage and write books, though he hasn't a penny of his own, and there are any number of sisters and brothers dependent on him."

"Ah, he has a mother?" Mrs. Hilbery inquired.

"Yes. Rather a fine-looking old lady, with white hair." Katharine began to describe her visit, and soon Mrs. Hilbery elicited the facts that not only was the house of excruciating ugliness, which Ralph bore without complaint, but that it was evident that every one depended on him, and he had a room at the top of the house, with a wonderful view over London, and a rook.

"A wretched old bird in a corner, with half its feathers out," she said, with a tenderness in her voice that seemed to commiserate the sufferings of humanity while resting assured in the capacity of Ralph Denham to alleviate them, so that Mrs. Hilbery could not help exclaiming:

"But, Katharine, you *are* in love!" at which Katharine flushed, looked startled, as if she had said something that she ought not to have said, and shook her head.

Hastily Mrs. Hilbery asked for further details of this extraordinary house, and interposed a few speculations about the meeting between Keats and Coleridge in a lane, which tided over the discomfort of the moment, and drew Katharine on to further descriptions and indiscretions. In truth, she found an extraordinary pleasure in being thus free to talk to some one who was equally wise and equally benignant, the mother of her earliest childhood, whose silence seemed to answer questions that were never asked. Mrs. Hilbery listened without making any remark for a considerable time. She seemed to draw her conclusions rather by looking at her daughter than by listening to her, and, if cross-examined, she would probably have given a highly inaccurate version of Ralph Denham's life-history except that he was penniless, fatherless, and lived at Highgate—all of which was much in his favor. But by means of these furtive glances she had assured herself that Katharine was in a state which gave her, alternately, the most exquisite pleasure and the most profound alarm.

She could not help ejaculating at last:

"It's all done in five minutes at a Registry Office nowadays, if you think the Church service a little florid—which it is, though there are noble things in it."

"But we don't want to be married," Katharine replied emphatically, and added, "Why, after all, isn't it perfectly possible to live together without being married?"

Again Mrs. Hilbery looked discomposed, and, in her trouble, took up the sheets which were lying upon the table, and began turning them over this way and that, and muttering to herself as she glanced:

"A plus B minus C equals *x y z*. It's so dreadfully ugly, Katharine. That's what I feel—so dreadfully ugly."

Katharine took the sheets from her mother's hand and began shuffling them absent-mindedly together, for her fixed gaze seemed to show that her thoughts were intent upon some other matter.

"Well, I don't know about ugliness," she said at length.

"But he doesn't ask it of you?" Mrs. Hilbery exclaimed. "Not that grave young man with the steady brown eyes?"

"He doesn't ask anything—we neither of us ask anything."

"If I could help you, Katharine, by the memory of what I felt——"

"Yes, tell me what you felt."

Mrs. Hilbery, her eyes growing blank, peered down the enormously long corridor of days at the far end of which the little figures of herself and her husband appeared fantastically attired, clasping hands upon a moonlit beach, with roses swinging in the dusk.

"We were in a little boat going out to a ship at night," she began. "The sun had set and the moon was rising over our heads. There were lovely silver lights upon the waves and three green lights upon the steamer in the middle of the bay. Your father's head looked so grand against the mast. It was life, it was death. The great sea was round us. It was the voyage for ever and ever."

The ancient fairy-tale fell roundly and harmoniously upon Katharine's ears. Yes, there was the enormous space of the sea; there were the three green lights upon the steamer; the cloaked figures climbed up on deck. And so, voyaging over the green and purple waters, past the cliffs and the sandy lagoons and through pools crowded with the masts of ships and the steeples of churches—here they were. The river seemed to have brought them and deposited them here at this precise point. She looked admiringly at her mother, that ancient voyager.

"Who knows," exclaimed Mrs. Hilbery, continuing her reveries, "where we are bound for, or why, or who has sent us, or what we shall find—who knows anything, except that love is our faith—love——" she crooned, and the soft sound beating through the dim words was heard by her daughter as the breaking of waves solemnly in order upon the vast shore that she gazed upon. She would have been content for her mother to repeat that word almost indefinitely—a soothing word when uttered by another, a riveting together of the shattered fragments of the world. But Mrs. Hilbery, instead of repeating the word love, said pleadingly:

"And you won't think those ugly thoughts again, will you, Katharine?" at which words the ship which Katharine had been considering seemed to put into harbor and have done with its seafaring. Yet she was in great need, if not exactly of sympathy, of some form of advice, or, at least, of the opportunity of setting forth her problems before a third person so as to renew them in her own eyes.

"But then," she said, ignoring the difficult problem of ugliness, "you knew you were in love; but we're different. It seems," she continued, frowning a little as she tried to fix the difficult feeling, "as if something came to an end suddenly—gave out—faded—an illusion—as if when we think we're in love we make it up—we imagine what doesn't exist. That's why it's impossible that we should ever marry. Always to be finding the other an illusion, and going off and forgetting about them, never to be certain that you cared, or that he wasn't caring for some one not you at all, the horror of changing from one state to the other, being happy one moment and miserable the next—that's the reason why we can't possibly marry. At the same time," she continued, "we can't live without each other, because——" Mrs. Hilbery waited patiently for the sentence to be completed, but Katharine fell silent and fingered her sheet of figures.

"We have to have faith in our vision," Mrs. Hilbery resumed, glancing at the figures, which distressed her vaguely, and had some connection in her mind with the household accounts, "otherwise, as you say——" She cast a lightning glance into the depths of disillusionment which were, perhaps, not altogether unknown to her.

"Believe me, Katharine, it's the same for every one—for me, too—for your father," she said earnestly, and sighed. They looked together into the abyss and, as the elder of the two, she recovered herself first and asked:

"But where is Ralph? Why isn't he here to see me?"

Katharine's expression changed instantly.

"Because he's not allowed to come here," she replied bitterly.

Mrs. Hilbery brushed this aside.

"Would there be time to send for him before luncheon?" she asked.

Katharine looked at her as if, indeed, she were some magician. Once more she felt that instead of being a grown woman, used to advise and command, she was only a foot or two raised above the long grass and the little flowers and entirely dependent upon the figure of indefinite size whose head went up into the sky, whose hand was in hers, for guidance.

"I'm not happy without him," she said simply.

Mrs. Hilbery nodded her head in a manner which indicated complete understanding, and the immediate conception of certain plans for the future. She swept up her flowers, breathed in their sweetness, and, humming a little song about a miller's daughter, left the room.

The case upon which Ralph Denham was engaged that afternoon was not apparently receiving his full attention, and yet the affairs of the late John Leake of Dublin were sufficiently confused to need all the care that a solicitor could bestow upon them, if the widow Leake and the five Leake children of tender age were to receive any pittance at all. But the appeal to Ralph's humanity had little chance of being heard today; he was no longer a model of concentration. The partition so carefully erected between the different sections of his life had been broken down, with the result that though his eyes were fixed upon the last Will and Testament, he saw through the page a certain drawing-room in Cheyne Walk.

He tried every device that had proved effective in the past for keeping up the partitions of the mind, until he could decently go home; but a little to his alarm he found himself assailed so persistently, as if from outside, by Katharine, that he launched forth desperately into an imaginary interview with her. She obliterated a bookcase full of law reports, and the corners and lines of the room underwent a curious softening of outline like that which sometimes makes a room unfamiliar at the moment of waking from sleep. By degrees, a pulse or stress began to beat at regular intervals in his mind, heaping his thoughts into waves to which words fitted themselves, and without much consciousness of what he was doing, he began to write on a sheet of draft paper what had the appearance of a poem lacking several words in each line. Not many lines had been set down, however, before he threw away his pen as violently as if that were responsible for his misdeeds, and tore the paper into many separate pieces. This was a sign that Katharine had asserted herself and put to him a remark that could not be met poetically. Her remark was entirely destructive of poetry, since it was to the effect that poetry had nothing whatever to do with her; all her friends spent their lives in making up phrases, she said; all his feeling was an illusion, and next moment, as if to taunt him with his impotence, she had sunk into one of those dreamy states which took no account whatever of his existence. Ralph was roused by his passionate attempts to attract her attention to the fact that he was standing in the middle of his little private room in Lincoln's Inn Fields at a considerable distance from Chelsea. The physical distance increased his desperation. He began pacing in circles until the process sickened him, and then took a sheet of paper for the composition of a letter which, he vowed before he began it, should be sent that same evening.

It was a difficult matter to put into words; poetry would have done it better justice, but he must abstain from poetry. In an infinite number of half-obliterated scratches he tried to convey to her the possibility that although human beings are woefully ill-adapted for communication, still, such communion is the best we know; moreover, they make it possible for each to have access to another world independent of personal affairs, a world of law, of philosophy, or more strangely a world such as he had had a glimpse of the other evening when together they seemed to be sharing something, creating something, an ideal—a vision flung out in advance of our actual circumstances. If this golden rim were quenched, if life were no longer circled by an illusion (but was it an illusion after all?), then it would be too dismal an affair to carry to an end; so he wrote with a sudden spurt of conviction which made clear way for a space and left at least one sentence standing whole. Making every allowance for other desires, on the whole this conclusion appeared to him to justify their relationship. But the conclusion was mystical; it plunged him into thought. The difficulty with which even this amount was written, the inadequacy of the words, and the need of writing under them and over them others which, after all, did no better, led him to leave off before he was at ail satisfied with his production, and unable to resist the conviction that such rambling would never be fit for Katharine's eye. He felt himself more cut off from her than ever. In idleness, and because he could do nothing further with words, he began to draw little figures in the blank spaces, heads meant to resemble her head, blots fringed with flames meant to represent—perhaps the entire universe. From this occupation he was roused by the message that a lady wished to speak to him. He had scarcely time to run his hands through his hair in order to look as much like a solicitor as possible, and to cram his papers into his pocket, already overcome with shame that another eye should behold them, when he realized that his preparations were needless. The lady was Mrs. Hilbery.

"I hope you're not disposing of somebody's fortune in a hurry," she remarked, gazing at the documents on his table, "or cutting off an entail at one blow, because I want to ask you to do me a favor. And Anderson won't keep his horse waiting. (Anderson is a perfect tyrant, but he drove my dear father to the Abbey the day they buried him.) I made bold to come to you, Mr. Denham, not exactly in search of legal assistance (though I don't know who I'd rather come to, if I were in trouble), but in order to ask your help in settling some tiresome little domestic affairs that have arisen in my absence. I've been to Stratford-on-Avon (I must tell you all about that one of these days), and there I got a letter from my sister-in-law, a dear kind goose who likes interfering with other people's children because she's got none of her own. (We're dreadfully afraid that she's going to lose the sight of one of her eyes, and I always feel that our physical ailments are so apt to turn into mental ailments. I think Matthew Arnold says something of the same kind about Lord Byron.) But that's neither here nor there."

The effect of these parentheses, whether they were introduced for that purpose or represented a natural instinct on Mrs. Hilbery's part to embellish the bareness of her discourse, gave Ralph time to perceive that she possessed all the facts of their situation and was come, somehow, in the capacity of ambassador.

"I didn't come here to talk about Lord Byron," Mrs. Hilbery continued, with a little laugh, "though I know that both you and Katharine, unlike other young people of your generation, still find him worth reading." She paused. "I'm so glad you've made Katharine read poetry, Mr. Denham!" she exclaimed, "and feel poetry, and look poetry! She can't talk it yet, but she will—oh, she will!"

Ralph, whose hand was grasped and whose tongue almost refused to articulate, somehow contrived to say that there were moments when he felt hopeless, utterly hopeless, though he gave no reason for this statement on his part.

"But you care for her?" Mrs. Hilbery inquired.

"Good God!" he exclaimed, with a vehemence which admitted of no question.

"It's the Church of England service you both object to?" Mrs. Hilbery inquired innocently.

"I don't care a damn what service it is," Ralph replied.

"You would marry her in Westminster Abbey if the worst came to the worst?" Mrs. Hilbery inquired.

"I would marry her in St. Paul's Cathedral," Ralph replied. His doubts upon this point, which were always roused by Katharine's presence, had vanished completely, and his strongest wish in the world was to be with her immediately, since every second he was away from her he imagined her slipping farther and farther from him into one of those states of mind in which he was unrepresented. He wished to dominate her, to possess her.

"Thank God!" exclaimed Mrs. Hilbery. She thanked Him for a variety of blessings: for the conviction with which the young man spoke; and not least for the prospect that on her daughter's wedding-day the noble cadences, the stately periods, the ancient eloquence of the marriage service would resound over the heads of a distinguished congregation gathered together near the very spot where her father lay quiescent with the other poets of England. The tears filled her eyes; but she remembered simultaneously that her carriage was waiting, and with dim eyes she walked to the door. Denham followed her downstairs.

It was a strange drive. For Denham it was without exception the most unpleasant he had ever taken. His only wish was to go as straightly and quickly as possible to Cheyne Walk; but it soon appeared that Mrs. Hilbery either ignored or thought fit to baffle this desire by interposing various errands of her own. She stopped the carriage at post-offices, and coffee-shops, and shops of inscrutable dignity where the aged attendants had to be greeted as old friends; and, catching sight of the dome of St. Paul's above the irregular spires of Ludgate Hill, she pulled the cord impulsively, and gave directions that Anderson should drive them there. But Anderson had reasons of his own for discouraging afternoon worship, and kept his horse's nose obstinately towards the west. After some minutes, Mrs. Hilbery realized the situation, and accepted it good-humoredly, apologizing to Ralph for his disappointment.

"Never mind," she said, "we'll go to St. Paul's another day, and it may turn out, though I can't promise that it *will*, that he'll take us past Westminster Abbey, which would be even better."

Ralph was scarcely aware of what she went on to say. Her mind and body both seemed to have floated into another region of quick-sailing clouds rapidly passing across each other and enveloping everything in a vaporous indistinctness. Meanwhile he remained conscious of his own concentrated desire, his impotence to bring about anything he wished, and his increasing agony of impatience.

Suddenly Mrs. Hilbery pulled the cord with such decision that even Anderson had to listen to the order which she leant out of the window to give him. The carriage pulled up abruptly in the middle of Whitehall before a large building dedicated to one of our Government offices. In a second Mrs. Hilbery was mounting the steps, and Ralph was left in too acute an irritation by this further delay even to speculate what errand took her now to the Board of Education. He was about to jump from the carriage and take a cab, when Mrs. Hilbery reappeared talking genially to a figure who remained hidden behind her.

"There's plenty of room for us all," she was saying. "Plenty of room. We could find space for *four* of you, William," she added, opening the door, and Ralph found that Rodney had now joined their company. The two men glanced at each other. If distress, shame, discomfort in its most acute form were ever visible upon a human face, Ralph could read them all expressed beyond the eloquence of words upon the face of his unfortunate companion. But Mrs. Hilbery was either completely unseeing or determined to appear so. She went on talking; she talked, it seemed to both the young men, to some one outside, up in the air. She talked about Shakespeare, she apostrophized the human race, she proclaimed the virtues of divine poetry, she began to recite verses which broke down in the middle. The great advantage of her discourse was that it was self-supporting. It nourished itself until Cheyne Walk was reached upon half a dozen grunts and murmurs.

"Now," she said, alighting briskly at her door, "here we are!"

There was something airy and ironical in her voice and expression as she turned upon the doorstep and looked at them, which filled both Rodney and Denham with the same misgivings at having trusted their fortunes to such an ambassador; and Rodney actually hesitated upon the threshold and murmured to Denham:

"You go in, Denham. I . . ." He was turning tail, but the door opening and the familiar look of the house asserting its charm, he bolted in on the wake of the others, and the door shut upon his escape. Mrs. Hilbery led the way upstairs. She took them to the drawing-room. The fire burnt as usual, the little tables were laid with china and silver. There was nobody there.

"Ah," she said, "Katharine's not here. She must be upstairs in her room. You have something to say to her, I know, Mr. Denham. You can find your way?" she vaguely indicated the ceiling with a gesture of her hand. She had become suddenly serious and composed, mistress in her own house. The gesture with which she dismissed him had a dignity that Ralph never forgot. She seemed to make him free with a wave of her hand to all that she possessed. He left the room.

The Hilberys' house was tall, possessing many stories and passages with closed doors, all, once he had passed the drawing-room floor, unknown to Ralph. He mounted as high as he could and knocked at the first door he came to.

"May I come in?" he asked.

A voice from within answered "Yes."

He was conscious of a large window, full of light, of a bare table, and of a long looking-glass. Katharine had risen, and was standing with some white papers in her hand, which slowly fluttered to the ground as she saw her visitor. The explanation was a short one. The sounds were inarticulate; no one could have understood the meaning save themselves. As if the forces of the world were all at work to tear them asunder they sat, clasping hands, near enough to be taken even by the malicious eye of Time himself for a united couple, an indivisible unit.

"Don't move, don't go," she begged of him, when he stooped to gather the papers she had let fall. But he took them in his hands and, giving her by a sudden impulse his own unfinished dissertation, with its mystical conclusion, they read each other's compositions in silence.

Katharine read his sheets to an end; Ralph followed her figures as far as his mathematics would let him. They came to the end of their tasks at about the same moment, and sat for a time in silence.

"Those were the papers you left on the seat at Kew," said Ralph at length. "You folded them so quickly that I couldn't see what they were."

She blushed very deeply; but as she did not move or attempt to hide her face she had the appearance of some one disarmed of all defences, or Ralph likened her to a wild bird just settling with wings trembling to fold themselves within reach of his hand. The moment of exposure had been exquisitely painful—the light shed startlingly vivid. She had now to get used to the fact that some one shared her loneliness. The bewilderment was half shame and half the prelude to profound rejoicing. Nor was she unconscious that on the surface the whole thing must appear of the utmost absurdity. She looked to see whether Ralph smiled, but found his gaze fixed on her with such gravity that she turned to the belief that she had committed no sacrilege but enriched herself, perhaps immeasurably, perhaps eternally. She hardly dared steep herself in the infinite bliss. But his glance seemed to ask for some assurance upon another point of vital interest to him. It beseeched her mutely to tell him whether what she had read upon his confused sheet had any meaning or truth to her. She bent her head once more to the papers she held.

"I like your little dot with the flames round it," she said meditatively.

Ralph nearly tore the page from her hand in shame and despair when he saw her actually contemplating the idiotic symbol of his most confused and emotional moments.

He was convinced that it could mean nothing to another, although somehow to him it conveyed not only Katharine herself but all those states of mind which had clustered round her since he first saw her pouring out tea on a Sunday afternoon. It represented by its circumference of smudges surrounding a central blot all that encircling glow which for him surrounded, inexplicably, so many of the objects of life, softening their sharp outline, so that he could see certain streets, books, and situations wearing a halo almost perceptible to the physical eye. Did she smile? Did she put the paper down wearily, condemning it not only for its inadequacy but for its falsity? Was she going to protest once more that he only loved the vision of her? But it did not occur to her that this diagram had anything to do with her. She said simply, and in the same tone of reflection:

"Yes, the world looks something like that to me too."

He received her assurance with profound joy. Quietly and steadily there rose up behind the whole aspect of life that soft edge of fire which gave its red tint to the atmosphere and crowded the scene with shadows so deep and dark that one could fancy pushing farther into their density and still farther, exploring indefinitely. Whether there was any correspondence between the two prospects now opening before them they shared the same sense of the impending future, vast, mysterious, infinitely stored with undeveloped shapes which each would unwrap for the other to behold; but for the present the prospect of the future was enough to fill them with silent adoration. At any rate, their further attempts to communicate articulately were interrupted by a knock on the door, and the entrance of a maid who, with a due sense of mystery, announced that a lady wished to see Miss Hilbery, but refused to allow her name to be given.

When Katharine rose, with a profound sigh, to resume her duties, Ralph went with her, and neither of them formulated any guess, on their way downstairs, as to who this anonymous lady might prove to be. Perhaps the fantastic notion that she was a little black hunchback provided with a steel knife, which she would plunge into Katharine's heart, appeared to Ralph more probable than another, and he pushed first into the dining-room to avert the blow. Then he exclaimed "Cassandra!" with such heartiness at the sight of Cassandra Otway standing by the dining-room table that she put her finger to her lips and begged him to be quiet.

"Nobody must know I'm here," she explained in a sepulchral whisper. "I missed my train. I have been wandering about London all day. I can bear it no longer. Katharine, what am I to do?"

Katharine pushed forward a chair; Ralph hastily found wine and poured it out for her. If not actually fainting, she was very near it.

"William's upstairs," said Ralph, as soon as she appeared to be recovered. "I'll go and ask him to come down to you." His own happiness had given him a confidence that every one else was bound to be happy too. But Cassandra had her uncle's commands and anger too vividly in her mind to dare any such defiance. She became agitated and said that she must leave the house at once. She was not in a condition to go, had they known where to send her. Katharine's common sense, which had been in abeyance for the past week or two, still failed her, and she could only ask, "But where's your luggage?" in the vague belief that to take lodgings depended entirely upon a sufficiency of luggage. Cassandra's reply, "I've lost my luggage," in no way helped her to a conclusion.

"You've lost your luggage," she repeated. Her eyes rested upon Ralph, with an expression which seemed better fitted to accompany a profound thanksgiving for his existence or some vow of eternal devotion than a question about luggage. Cassandra perceived the look, and saw that it was returned; her eyes filled with tears. She faltered in what she was saying. She began bravely again to discuss the question of lodging when Katharine, who seemed to have communicated silently with Ralph, and obtained his permission, took her ruby ring from her finger and giving it to Cassandra, said: "I believe it will fit you without any alteration."

These words would not have been enough to convince Cassandra of what she very much wished to believe had not Ralph taken the bare hand in his and demanded:

"Why don't you tell us you're glad?" Cassandra was so glad that the tears ran down her cheeks. The certainty of Katharine's engagement not only relieved her of a thousand vague fears and self-reproaches, but entirely quenched that spirit of criticism which had lately impaired her belief in Katharine. Her old faith came back to her. She seemed to behold her with that curious intensity which she had lost; as a being who walks just beyond our sphere, so that life in their presence is a heightened process, illuminating not only ourselves but a considerable stretch of the surrounding world. Next moment she contrasted her own lot with theirs and gave back the ring.

"I won't take that unless William gives it me himself," she said. "Keep it for me, Katharine."

"I assure you everything's perfectly all right," said Ralph. "Let me tell William——"

He was about, in spite of Cassandra's protest, to reach the door, when Mrs. Hilbery, either warned by the parlor-maid or conscious with her usual prescience of the need for her intervention, opened the door and smilingly surveyed them.

"My dear Cassandra!" she exclaimed. "How delightful to see you back again! What a coincidence!" she observed, in a general way. "William is upstairs. The kettle boils over. Where's Katharine, I say? I go to look, and I find Cassandra!" She seemed to have proved something to her own satisfaction, although nobody felt certain what thing precisely it was.

"I find Cassandra," she repeated.

"She missed her train," Katharine interposed, seeing that Cassandra was unable to speak.

"Life," began Mrs. Hilbery, drawing inspiration from the portraits on the wall apparently, "consists in missing trains and in finding——" But she pulled herself up and remarked that the kettle must have boiled completely over everything.

To Katharine's agitated mind it appeared that this kettle was an enormous kettle, capable of deluging the house in its incessant showers of steam, the enraged representative of all those household duties which she had neglected. She ran hastily up to the drawing-room, and the rest followed her, for Mrs. Hilbery put her arm round Cassandra and drew her upstairs. They found Rodney observing the kettle with uneasiness but with such absence of mind that Katharine's catastrophe was in a fair way to be fulfilled. In putting the matter straight no greetings were exchanged, but Rodney and Cassandra chose seats as far apart as possible, and sat down with an air of people making a very temporary lodgment. Either Mrs. Hilbery was impervious to their discomfort, or chose to ignore it, or thought it high time that the subject was changed, for she did nothing but talk about Shakespeare's tomb.

"So much earth and so much water and that sublime spirit brooding over it all," she mused, and went on to sing her strange, half-earthly song of dawns and sunsets, of great poets, and the unchanged spirit of noble loving which they had taught, so that nothing changes, and one age is linked with another, and no one dies, and we all meet in spirit, until she appeared oblivious of any one in the room. But suddenly her remarks seemed to contract the enormously wide circle in which they were soaring and to alight, airily and temporarily, upon matters of more immediate moment.

"Katharine and Ralph," she said, as if to try the sound. "William and Cassandra."

"I feel myself in an entirely false position," said William desperately, thrusting himself into this breach in her reflections. "I've no right to be sitting here. Mr. Hilbery told me yesterday to leave the house. I'd no intention of coming back again. I shall now—"

"I feel the same too," Cassandra interrupted. "After what Uncle Trevor said to me last night–"

"I have put you into a most odious position," Rodney went on, rising from his seat, in which movement he was imitated simultaneously by Cassandra. "Until I have your father's consent I have no right to speak to you–let alone in this house, where my conduct"–he looked at Katharine, stammered, and fell silent–"where my conduct has been reprehensible and inexcusable in the extreme," he forced himself to continue. "I have explained everything to your mother. She is so generous as to try and make me believe that I have done no harm–you have convinced her that my behavior, selfish and weak as it was–selfish and weak–" he repeated, like a speaker who has lost his notes.

Two emotions seemed to be struggling in Katharine; one the desire to laugh at the ridiculous spectacle of William making her a formal speech across the tea-table, the other a desire to weep at the sight of something childlike and honest in him which touched her inexpressibly. To every one's surprise she rose, stretched out her hand, and said:

"You've nothing to reproach yourself with–you've been always—" but here her voice died away, and the tears forced themselves into her eyes, and ran down her cheeks, while William, equally moved, seized her hand and pressed it to his lips. No one perceived that the drawing-room door had opened itself sufficiently to admit at least half the person of Mr.

Hilbery, or saw him gaze at the scene round the tea-table with an expression of the utmost disgust and expostulation. He withdrew unseen. He paused outside on the landing trying to recover his self-control and to decide what course he might with most dignity pursue. It was obvious to him that his wife had entirely confused the meaning of his instructions. She had plunged them all into the most odious confusion. He waited a moment, and then, with much preliminary rattling of the handle, opened the door a second time. They had all regained their places; some incident of an absurd nature had now set them laughing and looking under the table, so that his entrance passed momentarily unperceived. Katharine, with flushed cheeks, raised her head and said:

"Well, that's my last attempt at the dramatic."

"It's astonishing what a distance they roll," said Ralph, stooping to turn up the corner of the hearthrug.

"Don't trouble–don't bother. We shall find it—" Mrs. Hilbery began, and then saw her husband and exclaimed: "Oh, Trevor, we're looking for Cassandra's engagement-ring!"

Mr. Hilbery looked instinctively at the carpet. Remarkably enough, the ring had rolled to the very point where he stood. He saw the rubies touching the tip of his boot. Such is the force of habit that he could not refrain from stooping, with an absurd little thrill of pleasure at being the one to find what others were looking for, and, picking the ring up, he presented it, with a bow that was courtly in the extreme, to Cassandra. Whether the making of a bow released automatically feelings of complaisance and urbanity, Mr. Hilbery found his resentment completely washed away during the second in which he bent and straightened himself. Cassandra dared to offer her cheek and received his embrace. He nodded with some degree of stiffness to Rodney and Denham, who had both risen upon seeing him, and now altogether sat down. Mrs. Hilbery seemed to have been waiting for the entrance of her husband, and for this precise moment in order to put to him a question which, from the ardor with which she announced it, had evidently been pressing for utterance for some time past.

"Oh, Trevor, please tell me, what was the date of the first performance of *Hamlet?*"

In order to answer her Mr. Hilbery had to have recourse to the exact scholarship of William Rodney, and before he had given his excellent authorities for believing as he believed, Rodney felt himself admitted once more to the society of the civilized and sanctioned by the authority of no less a person than Shakespeare himself. The power of literature, which had temporarily deserted Mr. Hilbery, now came back to him, pouring over the raw ugliness of human affairs its soothing balm, and providing a form into which such passions as he had felt so painfully the night before could be molded so that they fell roundly from the tongue in shapely phrases, hurting nobody. He was sufficiently sure of his command of language at length to look at Katharine and again at Denham. All this talk about Shakespeare had acted as a soporific, or rather as an incantation upon Katharine. She leaned back in her chair at the head of the tea-table, perfectly silent, looking vaguely past them all, receiving the most generalized ideas of human heads against pictures, against yellow-tinted walls, against curtains of deep crimson velvet. Denham, to whom he turned next, shared her immobility under his gaze. But beneath his restraint and calm it was possible to detect a resolution, a will, set now with unalterable tenacity, which made such turns of speech as Mr. Hilbery had at command appear oddly irrelevant. At any rate, he said nothing. He respected the young man; he was a very able young man; he was likely to get his own way. He could, he thought, looking at his still and very dignified head, understand Katharine's preference, and, as he thought this, he was surprised by a pang of acute jealousy. She might have married Rodney without causing him a twinge. This man she loved. Or what was the state of affairs between them? An extraordinary confusion of emotion was beginning to get the better of him, when Mrs. Hilbery, who had been conscious of a sudden pause in the conversation, and had looked wistfully at her daughter once or twice, remarked:

"Don't stay if you want to go, Katharine. There's the little room over there. Perhaps you and Ralph—"

"We're engaged," said Katharine, waking with a start, and looking straight at her father. He was taken aback by the directness of the statement; he exclaimed as if an unexpected blow had struck him. Had he loved her to see her swept away by this torrent, to have her taken from him by this uncontrollable force, to stand by helpless, ignored? Oh, how he loved her! How he loved her! He nodded very curtly to Denham.

"I gathered something of the kind last night," he said. "I hope you'll deserve her." But he never looked at his daughter, and strode out of the room, leaving in the minds of the women a sense, half of awe, half of amusement, at the extravagant, inconsiderate, uncivilized male, outraged somehow and gone bellowing to his lair with a roar which still sometimes reverberates in the most polished of drawing-rooms. Then Katharine, looking at the shut door, looked down again, to hide her tears.

34

The lamps were lit; their luster reflected itself in the polished wood; good wine was passed round the dinner-table; before the meal was far advanced civilization had triumphed, and Mr. Hilbery presided over a feast which came to wear more and more surely an aspect, cheerful, dignified, promising well for the future. To judge from the expression in Katharine's eyes it promised something—but he checked the approach sentimentality. He poured out wine; he bade Denham help himself.

They went upstairs and he saw Katharine and Denham abstract themselves directly Cassandra had asked whether she might not play him something—some Mozart? some Beethoven? She sat down to the piano; the door closed softly behind them. His eyes rested on the closed door for some seconds unwaveringly, but, by degrees, the look of expectation died out of them, and, with a sigh, he listened to the music.

Katharine and Ralph were agreed with scarcely a word of discussion as to what they wished to do, and in a moment she joined him in the hall dressed for walking. The night was still and moonlit, fit for walking, though any night would have seemed so to them, desiring more than anything movement, freedom from scrutiny, silence, and the open air.

"At last!" she breathed, as the front door shut. She told him how she had waited, fidgeted, thought he was never coming, listened for the sound of doors, half expected to see him again under the lamp-post, looking at the house. They turned and looked at the serene front with its gold-rimmed windows, to him the shrine of so much adoration. In spite of her laugh and the little pressure of mockery on his arm, he would not resign his belief, but with her hand resting there, her voice quickened and mysteriously moving in his ears, he had not time—they had not the same inclination—other objects drew his attention.

How they came to find themselves walking down a street with many lamps, corners radiant with light, and a steady succession of motor-omnibuses plying both ways along it, they could neither of them tell; nor account for the impulse which led them suddenly to select one of these wayfarers and mount to the very front seat. After curving through streets of comparative darkness, so narrow that shadows on the blinds were pressed within a few feet of their faces, they came to one of those great knots of activity where the lights, having drawn close together, thin out again and take their separate ways. They were borne on until they saw the spires of the city churches pale and flat against the sky.

"Are you cold?" he asked, as they stopped by Temple Bar.

"Yes, I am rather," she replied, becoming conscious that the splendid race of lights drawn past her eyes by the superb curving and swerving of the monster on which she sat was at an end. They had followed some such course in their thoughts too; they had been borne on, victors in the forefront of some triumphal car, spectators of a pageant enacted for them, masters of life. But standing on the pavement alone, this exaltation left them; they were glad to be alone together. Ralph stood still for a moment to light his pipe beneath a lamp.

She looked at his face isolated in the little circle of light.

"Oh, that cottage," she said. "We must take it and go there."

"And leave all this?" he inquired.

"As you like," she replied. She thought, looking at the sky above Chancery Lane, how the roof was the same everywhere; how she was now secure of all that this lofty blue and its steadfast lights meant to her; reality, was it, figures, love, truth?

"I've something on my mind," said Ralph abruptly. "I mean I've been thinking of Mary Datchet. We're very near her rooms now. Would you mind if we went there?"

She had turned before she answered him. She had no wish to see any one tonight; it seemed to her that the immense riddle was answered; the problem had been solved; she held in her hands for one brief moment the globe which we spend our lives in trying to shape, round, whole, and entire from the confusion of chaos. To see Mary was to risk the destruction of this globe.

"Did you treat her badly?" she asked rather mechanically, walking on.

"I could defend myself," he said, almost defiantly. "But what's the use, if one feels a thing? I won't be with her a minute," he said. "I'll just tell her—"

"Of course, you must tell her," said Katharine, and now felt anxious for him to do what appeared to be necessary if he, too, were to hold his globe for a moment round, whole, and entire.

"I wish–I wish—" she sighed, for melancholy came over her and obscured at least a section of her clear vision. The globe swam before her as if obscured by tears.

"I regret nothing," said Ralph firmly. She leant towards him almost as if she could thus see what he saw. She thought how obscure he still was to her, save only that more and more constantly he appeared to her a fire burning through its smoke, a source of life.

"Go on," she said. "You regret nothing—"

"Nothing–nothing," he repeated.

"What a fire!" she thought to herself. She thought of him blazing splendidly in the night, yet so obscure that to hold his arm, as she held it, was only to touch the opaque substance surrounding the flame that roared upwards.

"Why nothing?" she asked hurriedly, in order that he might say more and so make more splendid, more red, more darkly intertwined with smoke this flame rushing upwards.

"What are you thinking of, Katharine?" he asked suspiciously, noticing her tone of dreaminess and the inapt words.

"I was thinking of you—yes, I swear it. Always of you, but you take such strange shapes in my mind. You've destroyed my loneliness. Am I to tell you how I see you? No, tell me—tell me from the beginning."

Beginning with spasmodic words, he went on to speak more and more fluently, more and more passionately, feeling her leaning towards him, listening with wonder like a child, with gratitude like a woman. She interrupted him gravely now and then.

"But it was foolish to stand outside and look at the windows. Suppose William hadn't seen you. Would you have gone to bed?"

He capped her reproof with wonderment that a woman of her age could have stood in Kingsway looking at the traffic until she forgot.

"But it was then I first knew I loved you!" she exclaimed.

"Tell me from the beginning," he begged her.

"No, I'm a person who can't tell things," she pleaded. "I shall say something ridiculous—something about flames—fires. No, I can't tell you."

But he persuaded her into a broken statement, beautiful to him, charged with extreme excitement as she spoke of the dark red fire, and the smoke twined round it, making him feel that he had stepped over the threshold into the faintly lit vastness of another mind, stirring with shapes, so large, so dim, unveiling themselves only in flashes, and moving away again into the darkness, engulfed by it. They had walked by this time to the street in which Mary lived, and being engrossed by what they said and partly saw, passed her staircase without looking up. At this time of night there was no traffic and scarcely any foot-passengers, so that they could pace slowly without interruption, arm-in-arm, raising their hands now and then to draw something upon the vast blue curtain of the sky.

They brought themselves by these means, acting on a mood of profound happiness, to a state of clear-sightedness where the lifting of a finger had effect, and one word spoke more than a sentence. They lapsed gently into silence, traveling the dark paths of thought side by side towards something discerned in the distance which gradually possessed them both. They were victors, masters of life, but at the same time absorbed in the flame, giving their life to increase its brightness, to testify to their faith. Thus they had walked, perhaps, twice or three times up and down Mary Datchet's street before the recurrence of a light burning behind a thin, yellow blind caused them to stop without exactly knowing why they did so. It burned itself into their minds.

"That is the light in Mary's room," said Ralph. "She must be at home." He pointed across the street. Katharine's eyes rested there too.

"Is she alone, working at this time of night? What is she working at?" she wondered. "Why should we interrupt her?" she asked passionately. "What have we got to give her? She's happy too," she added. "She has her work." Her voice shook slightly, and the light swam like an ocean of gold behind her tears.

"You don't want me to go to her?" Ralph asked.

"Go, if you like; tell her what you like," she replied.

He crossed the road immediately, and went up the steps into Mary's house. Katharine stood where he left her, looking at the window and expecting soon to see a shadow move across it; but she saw nothing; the blinds conveyed nothing; the light was not moved. It signaled to her across the dark street; it was a sign of triumph shining there for ever, not to be extinguished this side of the grave. She brandished her happiness as if in salute; she dipped it as if in reverence. "How they burn!" she thought, and all the darkness of London seemed set with fires, roaring upwards; but her eyes came back to Mary's window and rested there satisfied. She had waited some time before a figure detached itself from the doorway and came across the road, slowly and reluctantly, to where she stood.

"I didn't go in—I couldn't bring myself," he broke off. He had stood outside Mary's door unable to bring himself to knock; if she had come out she would have found him there, the tears running down his cheeks, unable to speak.

They stood for some moments, looking at the illuminated blinds, an expression to them both of something impersonal and serene in the spirit of the woman within, working out her plans far into the night—her plans for the good of a world that none of them were ever to know. Then their minds jumped on and other little figures came by in procession, headed, in Ralph's view, by the figure of Sally Seal.

"Do you remember Sally Seal?" he asked. Katharine bent her head.

"Your mother and Mary?" he went on. "Rodney and Cassandra? Old Joan up at Highgate?" He stopped in his enumeration, not finding it possible to link them together in any way that should explain the queer combination which he could perceive in them, as he thought of them. They appeared to him to be more than individuals; to be made up of many different things in cohesion; he had a vision of an orderly world.

"It's all so easy—it's all so simple," Katherine quoted, remembering some words of Sally Seal's, and wishing Ralph to understand that she followed the track of his thought. She felt him trying to piece together in a laborious and elementary fashion fragments of belief, unsoldered and separate, lacking the unity of phrases fashioned by the old believers. Together they groped in this difficult region, where the unfinished, the unfulfilled, the unwritten, the unreturned, came together in their ghostly way and wore the semblance of the complete and the satisfactory. The future emerged more splendid than ever from this construction of the present. Books were to be written, and since books must be written in rooms, and rooms must have hangings, and outside the windows there must be land, and an horizon to that land, and trees perhaps, and a hill, they sketched a habitation for themselves upon the outline of great offices in the Strand and continued to make an account of the future upon the omnibus which took them towards Chelsea; and still, for both of them, it swam miraculously in the golden light of a large steady lamp.

As the night was far advanced they had the whole of the seats on the top of the omnibus to choose from, and the roads, save for an occasional couple, wearing even at midnight, an air of sheltering their words from the public, were deserted. No longer did the shadow of a man sing to the shadow of a piano. A few lights in bedroom windows burnt but were extinguished one by one as the omnibus passed them.

They dismounted and walked down to the river. She felt his arm stiffen beneath her hand, and knew by this token that they had entered the enchanted region. She might speak to him, but with that strange tremor in his voice, those eyes blindly adoring, whom did he answer? What woman did he see? And where was she walking, and who was her companion? Moments, fragments, a second of vision, and then the flying waters, the winds dissipating and dissolving; then, too, the recollection from chaos, the return of security, the earth firm, superb and brilliant in the sun. From the heart of his darkness he spoke his thanksgiving; from a region as far, as hidden, she answered him. On a June night the nightingales sing, they answer each other across the plain; they are heard under the window among the trees in the garden. Pausing, they looked down into the river which bore its dark tide of waters, endlessly moving, beneath them. They turned and found themselves opposite the house. Quietly they surveyed the friendly place, burning its lamps either in expectation of them or because Rodney was still there talking to Cassandra. Katharine pushed the door half open and stood upon the threshold. The light lay in soft golden grains upon the deep obscurity of the hushed and sleeping household. For a moment they waited, and then loosed their hands. "Good night," he breathed. "Good night," she murmured back to him.

JACOB'S ROOM

1

"So of course," wrote Betty Flanders, pressing her heels rather deeper in the sand, "there was nothing for it but to leave."

Slowly welling from the point of her gold nib, pale blue ink dissolved the full stop; for there her pen stuck; her eyes fixed, and tears slowly filled them. The entire bay quivered; the lighthouse wobbled; and she had the illusion that the mast of Mr. Connor's little yacht was bending like a wax candle in the sun. She winked quickly. Accidents were awful things. She winked again. The mast was straight; the waves were regular; the lighthouse was upright; but the blot had spread.

". . . nothing for it but to leave," she read.

"Well, if Jacob doesn't want to play" (the shadow of Archer, her eldest son, fell across the notepaper and looked blue on the sand, and she felt chilly—it was the third of September already), "if Jacob doesn't want to play"—what a horrid blot! It must be getting late.

"Where *is* that tiresome little boy?" she said. "I don't see him. Run and find him. Tell him to come at once." ". . . but mercifully," she scribbled, ignoring the full stop, "everything seems satisfactorily arranged, packed though we are like herrings in a barrel, and forced to stand the perambulator which the landlady quite naturally won't allow. . . ."

Such were Betty Flanders's letters to Captain Barfoot—many-paged, tear-stained. Scarborough is seven hundred miles from Cornwall: Captain Barfoot is in Scarborough: Seabrook is dead. Tears made all the dahlias in her garden undulate in red waves and flashed the glass house in her eyes, and spangled the kitchen with bright knives, and made Mrs. Jarvis, the rector's wife, think at church, while the hymn-tune played and Mrs. Flanders bent low over her little boys' heads, that marriage is a fortress and widows stray solitary in the open fields, picking up stones, gleaning a few golden straws, lonely, unprotected, poor creatures. Mrs. Flanders had been a widow for these two years.

"Ja—cob! Ja—cob!" Archer shouted.

"Scarborough," Mrs. Flanders wrote on the envelope, and dashed a bold line beneath; it was her native town; the hub of the universe. But a stamp? She ferreted in her bag; then held it up mouth downwards; then fumbled in her lap, all so vigorously that Charles Steele in the Panama hat suspended his paint-brush.

Like the antennae of some irritable insect it positively trembled. Here was that woman moving—actually going to get up—confound her! He struck the canvas a hasty violet-black dab. For the landscape needed it. It was too pale—greys flowing into lavenders, and one star or a white gull suspended just so—too pale as usual. The critics would say it was too pale, for he was an unknown man exhibiting obscurely, a favourite with his landladies' children, wearing a cross on his watch chain, and much gratified if his landladies liked his pictures—which they often did.

"Ja—cob! Ja—cob!" Archer shouted.

Exasperated by the noise, yet loving children, Steele picked nervously at the dark little coils on his palette.

"I saw your brother—I saw your brother," he said, nodding his head, as Archer lagged past him, trailing his spade, and scowling at the old gentleman in spectacles.

"Over there—by the rock," Steele muttered, with his brush between his teeth, squeezing out raw sienna, and keeping his eyes fixed on Betty Flanders's back.

"Ja—cob! Ja—cob!" shouted Archer, lagging on after a second.

The voice had an extraordinary sadness. Pure from all body, pure from all passion, going out into the world, solitary, unanswered, breaking against rocks—so it sounded.

Steele frowned; but was pleased by the effect of the black—it was just *that* note which brought the rest together. "Ah, one may learn to paint at fifty! There's Titian . . ." and so, having found the right tint, up he looked and saw to his horror a cloud over the bay.

Mrs. Flanders rose, slapped her coat this side and that to get the sand off, and picked up her black parasol.

The rock was one of those tremendously solid brown, or rather black, rocks which emerge from the sand like something primitive. Rough with crinkled limpet shells and sparsely strewn with locks of dry seaweed, a small boy has to stretch his legs far apart, and indeed to feel rather heroic, before he gets to the top.

But there, on the very top, is a hollow full of water, with a sandy bottom; with a blob of jelly stuck to the side, and some mussels. A fish darts across. The fringe of yellow-brown seaweed flutters, and out pushes an opal-shelled crab—

"Oh, a huge crab," Jacob murmured—

and begins his journey on weakly legs on the sandy bottom. Now! Jacob plunged his hand. The crab was cool and very light. But the water was thick with sand, and so, scrambling down, Jacob was about to jump, holding his bucket in front of him, when he saw, stretched entirely rigid, side by side, their faces very red, an enormous man and woman.

An enormous man and woman (it was early-closing day) were stretched motionless, with their heads on pocket-handkerchiefs, side by side, within a few feet of the sea, while two or three gulls gracefully skirted the incoming waves, and settled near their boots.

The large red faces lying on the bandanna handkerchiefs stared up at Jacob. Jacob stared down at them. Holding his bucket very carefully, Jacob then jumped deliberately and trotted away very nonchalantly at first, but faster and faster as the waves came creaming up to him and he had to swerve to avoid them, and the gulls rose in front of him and floated out and settled again a little farther on. A large black woman was sitting on the sand. He ran towards her.

"Nanny! Nanny!" he cried, sobbing the words out on the crest of each gasping breath.

The waves came round her. She was a rock. She was covered with the seaweed which pops when it is pressed. He was lost.

There he stood. His face composed itself. He was about to roar when, lying among the black sticks and straw under the cliff, he saw a whole skull—perhaps a cow's skull, a skull, perhaps, with the teeth in it. Sobbing, but absent-mindedly, he ran farther and farther away until he held the skull in his arms.

"There he is!" cried Mrs. Flanders, coming round the rock and covering the whole space of the beach in a few seconds. "What has he got hold of? Put it down, Jacob! Drop it this moment! Something horrid, I know. Why didn't you stay with us? Naughty little boy! Now put it down. Now come along both of you," and she swept round, holding Archer by one hand and fumbling for Jacob's arm with the other. But he ducked down and picked up the sheep's jaw, which was loose.

Swinging her bag, clutching her parasol, holding Archer's hand, and telling the story of the gunpowder explosion in which poor Mr. Curnow had lost his eye, Mrs. Flanders hurried up the steep lane, aware all the time in the depths of her mind of some buried discomfort.

There on the sand not far from the lovers lay the old sheep's skull without its jaw. Clean, white, wind-swept, sand-rubbed, a more unpolluted piece of bone existed nowhere on the coast of Cornwall. The sea holly would grow through the eye-sockets; it would turn to powder, or some golfer, hitting his ball one fine day, would disperse a little dust—No, but not in lodgings, thought Mrs. Flanders. It's a great experiment coming so far with young children. There's no man to help with the perambulator. And Jacob is such a handful; so obstinate already.

"Throw it away, dear, do," she said, as they got into the road; but

Jacob squirmed away from her; and the wind rising, she took out her bonnet-pin, looked at the sea, and stuck it in afresh. The wind was rising. The waves showed that uneasiness, like something alive, restive, expecting the whip, of waves before a storm. The fishing-boats were leaning to the water's brim. A pale yellow light shot across the purple sea; and shut. The lighthouse was lit. "Come along," said Betty Flanders. The sun blazed in their faces and gilded the great blackberries trembling out from the hedge which Archer tried to strip as they passed.

"Don't lag, boys. You've got nothing to change into," said Betty, pulling them along, and looking with uneasy emotion at the earth displayed so luridly, with sudden sparks of light from greenhouses in gardens, with a sort of yellow and black mutability, against this blazing sunset, this astonishing agitation and vitality of colour, which stirred Betty Flanders and made her think of responsibility and danger. She gripped Archer's hand. On she plodded up the hill.

"What did I ask you to remember?" she said.

"I don't know," said Archer.

"Well, I don't know either," said Betty, humorously and simply, and who shall deny that this blankness of mind, when combined with profusion, mother wit, old wives' tales, haphazard ways, moments of astonishing daring, humour, and sentimentality—who shall deny that in these respects every woman is nicer than any man?

Well, Betty Flanders, to begin with.

She had her hand upon the garden gate.

"The meat!" she exclaimed, striking the latch down.

She had forgotten the meat.

There was Rebecca at the window.

The bareness of Mrs. Pearce's front room was fully displayed at ten o'clock at night when a powerful oil lamp stood on the middle of the table. The harsh light fell on the garden; cut straight across the lawn; lit up a child's bucket and a purple aster and reached the hedge. Mrs. Flanders had left her sewing on the table. There were her large reels of white cotton and her steel spectacles; her needle-case; her brown wool wound round an old postcard. There were the bulrushes and the Strand magazines; and the linoleum sandy from the boys' boots. A daddy-long-legs shot from corner to corner and hit the lamp globe. The wind blew straight dashes of rain across the window, which flashed silver as they passed through the light. A single leaf tapped hurriedly, persistently, upon the glass. There was a hurricane out at sea.

Archer could not sleep.

Mrs. Flanders stooped over him. "Think of the fairies," said Betty

Flanders. "Think of the lovely, lovely birds settling down on their nests. Now shut your eyes and see the old mother bird with a worm in her beak. Now turn and shut your eyes," she murmured, "and shut your eyes."

The lodging-house seemed full of gurgling and rushing; the cistern overflowing; water bubbling and squeaking and running along the pipes and streaming down the windows.

"What's all that water rushing in?" murmured Archer.

"It's only the bath water running away," said Mrs. Flanders.

Something snapped out of doors.

"I say, won't that steamer sink?" said Archer, opening his eyes.

"Of course it won't," said Mrs. Flanders. "The Captain's in bed long ago. Shut your eyes, and think of the fairies, fast asleep, under the flowers."

"I thought he'd never get off—such a hurricane," she whispered to Rebecca, who was bending over a spirit-lamp in the small room next door. The wind rushed outside, but the small flame of the spirit-lamp burnt quietly, shaded from the cot by a book stood on edge.

"Did he take his bottle well?" Mrs. Flanders whispered, and Rebecca nodded and went to the cot and turned down the quilt, and Mrs. Flanders bent over and looked anxiously at the baby, asleep, but frowning. The window shook, and Rebecca stole like a cat and wedged it.

The two women murmured over the spirit-lamp, plotting the eternal conspiracy of hush and clean bottles while the wind raged and gave a sudden wrench at the cheap fastenings.

Both looked round at the cot. Their lips were pursed. Mrs. Flanders crossed over to the cot.

"Asleep?" whispered Rebecca, looking at the cot.

Mrs. Flanders nodded.

"Good-night, Rebecca," Mrs. Flanders murmured, and Rebecca called her ma'm, though they were conspirators plotting the eternal conspiracy of hush and clean bottles.

Mrs. Flanders had left the lamp burning in the front room. There were her spectacles, her sewing; and a letter with the Scarborough postmark. She had not drawn the curtains either.

The light blazed out across the patch of grass; fell on the child's green bucket with the gold line round it, and upon the aster which trembled violently beside it. For the wind was tearing across the coast, hurling itself at the hills, and leaping, in sudden gusts, on top of its own back. How it spread over the town in the hollow! How the lights seemed to wink and quiver in its fury, lights in the harbour, lights in bedroom windows high up! And rolling dark waves before it, it raced over the Atlantic, jerking the stars above the ships this way and that.

There was a click in the front sitting-room. Mr. Pearce had extinguished the lamp. The garden went out. It was but a dark patch. Every inch was rained upon. Every blade of grass was bent by rain. Eyelids would have been fastened down by the rain. Lying on one's back one would have seen nothing but muddle and confusion—clouds turning and turning, and something yellow-tinted and sulphurous in the darkness.

The little boys in the front bedroom had thrown off their blankets and lay under the sheets. It was hot; rather sticky and steamy. Archer lay spread out, with one arm striking across the pillow. He was flushed; and when the heavy curtain blew out a little he turned and half-opened his eyes. The wind actually stirred the cloth on the chest of drawers, and let in a little light, so that the sharp edge of the chest of drawers was visible, running straight up, until a white shape bulged out; and a silver streak showed in the looking-glass.

In the other bed by the door Jacob lay asleep, fast asleep, profoundly unconscious. The sheep's jaw with the big yellow teeth in it lay at his feet. He had kicked it against the iron bed-rail.

Outside the rain poured down more directly and powerfully as the wind fell in the early hours of the morning. The aster was beaten to the earth. The child's bucket was half-full of rainwater; and the opal-shelled crab slowly circled round the bottom, trying with its weakly legs to climb the steep side; trying again and falling back, and trying again and again.

2

"Mrs. Flanders"—"Poor Betty Flanders"—"Dear Betty"—"She's very attractive still"—"Odd she don't marry again!" "There's Captain Barfoot to be sure—calls every Wednesday as regular as clockwork, and never brings his wife."

"But that's Ellen Barfoot's fault," the ladies of Scarborough said. "She don't put herself out for no one."

"A man likes to have a son—that we know."

"Some tumours have to be cut; but the sort my mother had you bear with for years and years, and never even have a cup of tea brought up to you in bed."

(Mrs. Barfoot was an invalid.)

* * *

Elizabeth Flanders, of whom this and much more than this had been said and would be said, was, of course, a widow in her prime. She was half-way between forty and fifty. Years and sorrow between them; the death of Seabrook, her husband; three boys; poverty; a house on the outskirts of Scarborough; her brother, poor Morty's, downfall and possible demise—for where was he? what was he? Shading her eyes, she looked along the road for Captain Barfoot—yes, there he was, punctual as ever; the attentions of the Captain—all ripened Betty Flanders, enlarged her figure, tinged her face with jollity, and flooded her eyes for no reason that any one could see perhaps three times a day.

True, there's no harm in crying for one's husband, and the tombstone, though plain, was a solid piece of work, and on summer's days when the widow brought her boys to stand there one felt kindly towards her. Hats were raised higher than usual; wives tugged their husbands' arms. Seabrook lay six foot beneath, dead these many years; enclosed in three shells; the crevices sealed with lead, so that, had earth and wood been glass, doubtless his very face lay visible beneath, the face of a young man whiskered, shapely, who had gone out duck-shooting and refused to change his boots.

"Merchant of this city," the tombstone said; though why Betty Flanders had chosen so to call him when, as many still remembered, he had only sat behind an office window for three months, and before that had broken horses, ridden to hounds, farmed a few fields, and run a little wild—well, she had to call him something. An example for the boys.

Had he, then, been nothing? An unanswerable question, since even if it weren't the habit of the undertaker to close the eyes, the light so soon goes out of them. At first, part of herself; now one of a company, he had merged in the grass, the sloping hillside, the thousand white stones, some slanting, others upright, the decayed wreaths, the crosses of green tin, the narrow yellow paths, and the lilacs that drooped in April, with a scent like that of an invalid's bedroom, over the churchyard wall. Seabrook was now all that; and when, with her skirt hitched up, feeding the chickens, she heard the bell for service or funeral, that was Seabrook's voice—the voice of the dead.

The rooster had been known to fly on her shoulder and peck her neck, so that now she carried a stick or took one of the children with her when she went to feed the fowls.

"Wouldn't you like my knife, mother?" said Archer.

Sounding at the same moment as the bell, her son's voice mixed life and death inextricably, exhilaratingly.

"What a big knife for a small boy!" she said. She took it to please him. Then the rooster flew out of the hen-house, and, shouting to Archer to shut the door into the kitchen garden, Mrs. Flanders set her meal down, clucked for the hens, went bustling about the orchard, and was seen from over the way by Mrs. Cranch, who, beating her mat against the wall, held it for a moment suspended while she observed to Mrs. Page next door that Mrs. Flanders was in the orchard with the chickens.

Mrs. Page, Mrs. Cranch, and Mrs. Garfit could see Mrs. Flanders in the orchard because the orchard was a piece of Dods Hill enclosed; and Dods Hill dominated the village. No words can exaggerate the importance of Dods Hill. It was the earth; the world against the sky; the horizon of how many glances can best be computed by those who have lived all their lives in the same village, only leaving it once to fight in the Crimea, like old George Garfit, leaning over his garden gate smoking his pipe. The progress of the sun was measured by it; the tint of the day laid against it to be judged.

"Now she's going up the hill with little John," said Mrs. Cranch to Mrs. Garfit, shaking her mat for the last time, and bustling indoors. Opening the orchard gate, Mrs. Flanders walked to the top of Dods Hill, holding John by the hand. Archer and Jacob ran in front or lagged behind; but they were in the Roman fortress when she came there, and shouting out what ships were to be seen in the bay. For there was a magnificent view—moors behind, sea in front, and the whole of Scarborough from one end to the other laid out flat like a puzzle. Mrs. Flanders, who was growing stout, sat down in the fortress and looked about her.

The entire gamut of the view's changes should have been known to her; its winter aspect, spring, summer and autumn; how storms came up from the sea; how the moors shuddered and brightened as the clouds went over; she should have noted the red spot where the villas were building; and the criss-cross of lines where the allotments were cut; and the diamond flash of little glass houses in the sun. Or, if details like these escaped her, she might have let her fancy play upon the gold tint of the sea at sunset, and thought how it lapped in coins of gold upon the shingle. Little pleasure boats shoved out into it; the black arm of the pier hoarded it up. The whole city was pink and gold; domed; mist-wreathed; resonant; strident. Banjoes strummed; the parade smelt of tar which stuck to the heels; goats suddenly cantered their carriages through crowds. It was observed how well the Corporation had laid out the flower-beds. Sometimes a straw hat was blown away. Tulips burnt in the sun. Numbers of sponge-bag trousers were stretched in rows. Purple bonnets fringed soft, pink, querulous faces on pillows in bath chairs. Triangular hoardings were wheeled along by men in white coats. Captain George Boase had caught a monster shark. One side of the triangular hoarding said so in red, blue, and yellow letters; and each line ended with three differently coloured notes of exclamation.

So that was a reason for going down into the Aquarium, where the sallow blinds, the stale smell of spirits of salt, the bamboo chairs, the tables with ash-trays, the revolving fish, the attendant knitting behind six or seven chocolate boxes (often she was quite alone with the fish for hours at a time) remained in the mind as part of the monster shark, he himself being only a flabby yellow receptacle, like an empty Gladstone bag in a tank. No one had ever been cheered by the Aquarium; but the faces of those emerging quickly lost their dim, chilled expression when they perceived that it was only by standing in a queue that one could be admitted to the pier. Once through the turnstiles, every one walked for a yard or two very briskly; some flagged at this stall; others at that. But it was the band that drew them all to it finally; even the fishermen on the lower pier taking up their pitch within its range.

The band played in the Moorish kiosk. Number nine went up on the board. It was a waltz tune. The pale girls, the old widow lady, the three Jews lodging in the same boarding-house, the dandy, the major, the horse-dealer, and the gentleman of independent means, all wore the same blurred, drugged expression, and through the chinks in the planks at their feet they could see the green summer waves, peacefully, amiably, swaying round the iron pillars of the pier.

But there was a time when none of this had any existence (thought the young man leaning against the railings). Fix your eyes upon the lady's skirt; the grey one will do—above the pink silk stockings. It changes; drapes her ankles—the nineties; then it amplifies—the seventies; now it's burnished red and stretched above a crinoline—the sixties; a tiny black foot wearing a white cotton stocking peeps out. Still sitting there? Yes—she's still on the pier. The silk now is sprigged with roses, but somehow one no longer sees so clearly. There's no pier beneath us. The heavy chariot may swing along the turnpike road, but there's no pier for it to stop at, and how grey and turbulent the sea is in the seventeenth century! Let's to the museum. Cannon-balls; arrow-heads; Roman glass and a forceps green with verdigris. The Rev. Jaspar Floyd dug them up at his own expense early in the forties in the Roman camp on Dods Hill—see the little ticket with the faded writing on it.

And now, what's the next thing to see in Scarborough?

Mrs. Flanders sat on the raised circle of the Roman camp, patching Jacob's breeches; only looking up as she sucked the end of her cotton, or when some insect dashed at her, boomed in her ear, and was gone.

John kept trotting up and slapping down in her lap grass or dead leaves which he called "tea," and she arranged them methodically but absent-mindedly, laying the flowery heads of the grasses together, thinking how Archer had been awake again last night; the church clock was ten or thirteen minutes fast; she wished she could buy Garfit's acre.

* * *

"That's an orchid leaf, Johnny. Look at the little brown spots. Come, my dear. We must go home. Ar—cher! Ja—cob!"

"Ar—cher—Ja—cob!" Johnny piped after her, pivoting round on his heel, and strewing the grass and leaves in his hands as if he were sowing seed. Archer and Jacob jumped up from behind the mound where they had been crouching with the intention of springing upon their mother unexpectedly, and they all began to walk slowly home.

"Who is that?" said Mrs. Flanders, shading her eyes.

"That old man in the road?" said Archer, looking below.

"He's not an old man," said Mrs. Flanders. "He's—no, he's not—I thought it was the Captain, but it's Mr. Floyd. Come along, boys."

"Oh, bother Mr. Floyd!" said Jacob, switching off a thistle's head, for he knew already that Mr. Floyd was going to teach them Latin, as indeed he did for three years in his spare time, out of kindness, for there was no other gentleman in the neighbourhood whom Mrs. Flanders could have asked to do such a thing, and the elder boys were getting beyond her, and must be got ready for school, and it was more than most clergymen would have done, coming round after tea, or having them in his own room—as he could fit it in—for the parish was a very large one, and Mr. Floyd, like his father before him, visited cottages miles away on the moors, and, like old Mr. Floyd, was a great scholar, which made it so unlikely—she had never dreamt of such a thing. Ought she to have guessed? But let alone being a scholar he was eight years younger than she was. She knew his mother—old Mrs. Floyd. She had tea there. And it was that very evening when she came back from having tea with old Mrs. Floyd that she found the note in the hall and took it into the kitchen with her when she went to give Rebecca the fish, thinking it must be something about the boys.

"Mr. Floyd brought it himself, did he?—I think the cheese must be in the parcel in the hall—oh, in the hall—" for she was reading. No, it was not about the boys.

"Yes, enough for fish-cakes tomorrow certainly—Perhaps Captain Barfoot—" she had come to the word "love." She went into the garden and read, leaning against the walnut tree to steady herself. Up and down went her breast. Seabrook came so vividly before her. She shook her head and was looking through her tears at the little shifting leaves against the yellow sky when three geese, half-running, half-flying, scuttled across the lawn with Johnny behind them, brandishing a stick.

Mrs. Flanders flushed with anger.

"How many times have I told you?" she cried, and seized him and snatched his stick away from him.

"But they'd escaped!" he cried, struggling to get free.

"You're a very naughty boy. If I've told you once, I've told you a thousand times. I won't *have* you chasing the geese!" she said, and crumpling

Mr. Floyd's letter in her hand, she held Johnny fast and herded the geese back into the orchard.

"How could I think of marriage!" she said to herself bitterly, as she fastened the gate with a piece of wire. She had always disliked red hair in men, she thought, thinking of Mr. Floyd's appearance, that night when the boys had gone to bed. And pushing her work-box away, she drew the blotting-paper towards her, and read Mr. Floyd's letter again, and her breast went up and down when she came to the word "love," but not so fast this time, for she saw Johnny chasing the geese, and knew that it was impossible for her to marry any one—let alone Mr. Floyd, who was so much younger than she was, but what a nice man—and such a scholar too.

"Dear Mr. Floyd," she wrote—"Did I forget about the cheese?" she wondered, laying down her pen. No, she had told Rebecca that the cheese was in the hall. "I am much surprised . . ." she wrote.

But the letter which Mr. Floyd found on the table when he got up early next morning did not begin "I am much surprised," and it was such a motherly, respectful, inconsequent, regretful letter that he kept it for many years; long after his marriage with Miss Wimbush, of Andover; long after he had left the village. For he asked for a parish in Sheffield, which was given him; and, sending for Archer, Jacob, and John to say good-bye, he told them to choose whatever they liked in his study to remember him by. Archer chose a paper-knife, because he did not like to choose anything too good; Jacob chose the works of Byron in one volume; John, who was still too young to make a proper choice, chose Mr. Floyd's kitten, which his brothers thought an absurd choice, but Mr. Floyd upheld him when he said: "It has fur like you." Then Mr. Floyd spoke about the King's Navy (to which Archer was going); and about Rugby (to which Jacob was going); and next day he received a silver salver and went—first to Sheffield, where he met Miss Wimbush, who was on a visit to her uncle, then to Hackney—then to Maresfield House, of which he became the principal, and finally, becoming editor of a well-known series of Ecclesiastical Biographies, he retired to Hampstead with his wife and daughter, and is often to be seen feeding the ducks on Leg of Mutton Pond. As for Mrs. Flanders's letter—when he looked for it the other day he could not find it, and did not like to ask his wife whether she had put it away. Meeting Jacob in Piccadilly lately, he recognized him after three seconds. But Jacob had grown such a fine young man that Mr. Floyd did not like to stop him in the street.

"Dear me," said Mrs. Flanders, when she read in the *Scarborough and Harrogate Courier* that the Rev. Andrew Floyd, etc., etc., had been made Principal of Maresfield House, "that must be our Mr. Floyd."

A slight gloom fell upon the table. Jacob was helping himself to jam;

the postman was talking to Rebecca in the kitchen; there was a bee humming at the yellow flower which nodded at the open window. They were all alive, that is to say, while poor Mr. Floyd was becoming Principal of Maresfield House.

Mrs. Flanders got up and went over to the fender and stroked Topaz on the neck behind the ears.

"Poor Topaz," she said (for Mr. Floyd's kitten was now a very old cat, a little mangy behind the ears, and one of these days would have to be killed).

"Poor old Topaz," said Mrs. Flanders, as he stretched himself out in the sun, and she smiled, thinking how she had had him gelded, and how she did not like red hair in men. Smiling, she went into the kitchen.

Jacob drew rather a dirty pocket-handkerchief across his face. He went upstairs to his room.

The stag-beetle dies slowly (it was John who collected the beetles). Even on the second day its legs were supple. But the butterflies were dead. A whiff of rotten eggs had vanquished the pale clouded yellows which came pelting across the orchard and up Dods Hill and away on to the moor, now lost behind a furze bush, then off again helter-skelter in a broiling sun. A fritillary basked on a white stone in the Roman camp. From the valley came the sound of church bells. They were all eating roast beef in Scarborough; for it was Sunday when Jacob caught the pale clouded yellows in the clover field, eight miles from home.

Rebecca had caught the death's-head moth in the kitchen.

A strong smell of camphor came from the butterfly boxes.

Mixed with the smell of camphor was the unmistakable smell of seaweed. Tawny ribbons hung on the door. The sun beat straight upon them.

The upper wings of the moth which Jacob held were undoubtedly marked with kidney-shaped spots of a fulvous hue. But there was no crescent upon the underwing. The tree had fallen the night he caught it. There had been a volley of pistol-shots suddenly in the depths of the wood. And his mother had taken him for a burglar when he came home late. The only one of her sons who never obeyed her, she said.

Morris called it "an extremely local insect found in damp or marshy places." But Morris is sometimes wrong. Sometimes Jacob, choosing a very fine pen, made a correction in the margin.

The tree had fallen, though it was a windless night, and the lantern, stood upon the ground, had lit up the still green leaves and the dead beech leaves. It was a dry place. A toad was there. And the red underwing had circled round the light and flashed and gone. The red underwing had never come back, though Jacob had waited. It was after twelve when he crossed the lawn and saw his mother in the bright room, playing patience, sitting up.

"How you frightened me!" she had cried. She thought something dreadful had happened. And he woke Rebecca, who had to be up so early.

There he stood pale, come out of the depths of darkness, in the hot room, blinking at the light.

No, it could not be a straw-bordered underwing.

The mowing-machine always wanted oiling. Barnet turned it under Jacob's window, and it creaked—creaked, and rattled across the lawn and creaked again.

Now it was clouding over.

Back came the sun, dazzlingly.

It fell like an eye upon the stirrups, and then suddenly and yet very gently rested upon the bed, upon the alarum clock, and upon the butterfly box stood open. The pale clouded yellows had pelted over the moor; they had zigzagged across the purple clover. The fritillaries flaunted along the hedgerows. The blues settled on little bones lying on the turf with the sun beating on them, and the painted ladies and the peacocks feasted upon bloody entrails dropped by a hawk. Miles away from home, in a hollow among teasles beneath a ruin, he had found the commas. He had seen a white admiral circling higher and higher round an oak tree, but he had never caught it. An old cottage woman living alone, high up, had told him of a purple butterfly which came every summer to her garden. The fox cubs played in the gorse in the early morning, she told him. And if you looked out at dawn you could always see two badgers. Sometimes they knocked each other over like two boys fighting, she said.

"You won't go far this afternoon, Jacob," said his mother, popping her head in at the door, "for the Captain's coming to say good-bye." It was the last day of the Easter holidays.

Wednesday was Captain Barfoot's day. He dressed himself very neatly in blue serge, took his rubber-shod stick—for he was lame and wanted two fingers on the left hand, having served his country—and set out from the house with the flagstaff precisely at four o'clock in the afternoon.

At three Mr. Dickens, the bath-chair man, had called for Mrs. Barfoot.

"Move me," she would say to Mr. Dickens, after sitting on the esplanade for fifteen minutes. And again, "That'll do, thank you, Mr. Dickens." At the first command he would seek the sun; at the second he would stay the chair there in the bright strip.

An old inhabitant himself, he had much in common with Mrs. Barfoot—James Coppard's daughter. The drinking-fountain, where West Street joins Broad Street, is the gift of James Coppard, who was mayor at the time of Queen Victoria's jubilee, and Coppard is painted upon municipal watering-carts and over shop windows, and upon the zinc blinds of solicitors' consulting-room windows. But Ellen Barfoot never visited the Aquarium (though she had known Captain Boase who had caught the shark quite well), and when the men came by with the posters she eyed them superciliously, for she knew that she would never see the Pierrots, or the brothers Zeno, or Daisy Budd and her troupe of performing seals. For Ellen Barfoot in her bath-chair on the esplanade was a prisoner—civilization's prisoner—all the bars of her cage falling across the esplanade on sunny days when the town hall, the drapery stores, the swimming-bath, and the memorial hall striped the ground with shadow.

An old inhabitant himself, Mr. Dickens would stand a little behind her, smoking his pipe. She would ask him questions—who people were—who now kept Mr. Jones's shop—then about the season—and had Mrs. Dickens tried, whatever it might be—the words issuing from her lips like crumbs of dry biscuit.

She closed her eyes. Mr. Dickens took a turn. The feelings of a man had not altogether deserted him, though as you saw him coming towards you, you noticed how one knobbed black boot swung tremulously in front of the other; how there was a shadow between his waistcoat and his trousers; how he leant forward unsteadily, like an old horse who finds himself suddenly out of the shafts drawing no cart. But as Mr. Dickens sucked in the smoke and puffed it out again, the feelings of a man were perceptible in his eyes. He was thinking how Captain Barfoot was now on his way to Mount Pleasant; Captain Barfoot, his master. For at home in the little sitting-room above the mews, with the canary in the window, and the girls at the sewing-machine, and Mrs. Dickens huddled up with the rheumatics—at home where he was made little of, the thought of being in the employ of Captain Barfoot supported him. He liked to think that while he chatted with Mrs. Barfoot on the front, he helped the Captain on his way to Mrs. Flanders. He, a man, was in charge of Mrs. Barfoot, a woman.

Turning, he saw that she was chatting with Mrs. Rogers. Turning again, he saw that Mrs. Rogers had moved on. So he came back to the bath-chair, and Mrs. Barfoot asked him the time, and he took out his great silver watch and told her the time very obligingly, as if he knew a great deal more about the time and everything than she did. But Mrs. Barfoot knew that Captain Barfoot was on his way to Mrs. Flanders.

Indeed he was well on his way there, having left the tram, and seeing Dods Hill to the south-east, green against a blue sky that was suffused with dust colour on the horizon. He was marching up the hill. In spite of his lameness there was something military in his approach. Mrs. Jarvis, as she came out of the Rectory gate, saw him coming, and her Newfoundland dog, Nero, slowly swept his tail from side to side.

"Oh, Captain Barfoot!" Mrs. Jarvis exclaimed.

"Good-day, Mrs. Jarvis," said the Captain.

They walked on together, and when they reached Mrs. Flanders's gate Captain Barfoot took off his tweed cap, and said, bowing very courteously:

"Good-day to you, Mrs. Jarvis."

And Mrs. Jarvis walked on alone.

She was going to walk on the moor. Had she again been pacing her lawn late at night? Had she again tapped on the study window and cried: "Look at the moon, look at the moon, Herbert!"

And Herbert looked at the moon.

Mrs. Jarvis walked on the moor when she was unhappy, going as far as a certain saucer-shaped hollow, though she always meant to go to a more distant ridge; and there she sat down, and took out the little book hidden beneath her cloak and read a few lines of poetry, and looked about her. She was not very unhappy, and, seeing that she was forty-five, never perhaps would be very unhappy, desperately unhappy that is, and leave her husband, and ruin a good man's career, as she sometimes threatened.

Still there is no need to say what risks a clergyman's wife runs when she walks on the moor. Short, dark, with kindling eyes, a pheasant's feather in her hat, Mrs. Jarvis was just the sort of woman to lose her faith upon the moors—to confound her God with the universal that is—but she did not lose her faith, did not leave her husband, never read her poem through, and went on walking the moors, looking at the moon behind the elm trees, and feeling as she sat on the grass high above Scarborough . . . Yes, yes, when the lark soars; when the sheep, moving a step or two onwards, crop the turf, and at the same time set their bells tinkling; when the breeze first blows, then dies down, leaving the cheek kissed; when the ships on the sea below seem to cross each other and pass on as if drawn by an invisible hand; when there are distant concussions in the air and phantom horsemen galloping, ceasing; when the horizon swims blue, green, emotional—then Mrs. Jarvis, heaving a sigh, thinks to herself, "If only some one could give me . . . if I could give some one. . . ." But she does not know what she wants to give, nor who could give it her.

"Mrs. Flanders stepped out only five minutes ago, Captain," said Rebecca. Captain Barfoot sat him down in the arm-chair to wait. Resting his elbows on the arms, putting one hand over the other, sticking his lame leg straight out, and placing the stick with the rubber ferrule beside it, he sat perfectly still. There was something rigid about him. Did he think? Probably the same thoughts again and again. But were they "nice" thoughts, interesting thoughts? He was a man with a temper; tenacious, faithful. Women would have felt, "Here is law. Here is order. Therefore we must cherish this man. He is on the Bridge at night," and, handing him his cup, or whatever it might be, would run on to visions of shipwreck and disaster, in which all the passengers come tumbling from their cabins, and there is the captain, buttoned in his pea-jacket, matched with the storm, vanquished by it but by none other. "Yet I have a soul," Mrs. Jarvis would bethink her, as Captain Barfoot suddenly blew his nose in a great red bandanna handkerchief, "and it's the man's stupidity that's the cause of this, and the storm's my storm as well as his" . . . so Mrs. Jarvis would bethink her when the Captain dropped in to see them and found Herbert out, and spent two or three hours, almost silent, sitting in the arm-chair. But Betty Flanders thought nothing of the kind.

"Oh, Captain," said Mrs. Flanders, bursting into the drawing-room, "I had to run after Barker's man . . . I hope Rebecca . . . I hope Jacob . . ."

She was very much out of breath, yet not at all upset, and as she put down the hearth-brush which she had bought of the oil-man, she said it was hot, flung the window further open, straightened a cover, picked up a book, as if she were very confident, very fond of the Captain, and a great many years younger than he was. Indeed, in her blue apron she did not look more than thirty-five. He was well over fifty.

She moved her hands about the table; the Captain moved his head from side to side, and made little sounds, as Betty went on chattering, completely at his ease—after twenty years.

"Well," he said at length, "I've heard from Mr. Polegate."

He had heard from Mr. Polegate that he could advise nothing better than to send a boy to one of the universities.

"Mr. Floyd was at Cambridge . . . no, at Oxford . . . well, at one or the other," said Mrs. Flanders.

She looked out of the window. Little windows, and the lilac and green of the garden were reflected in her eyes.

"Archer is doing very well," she said. "I have a very nice report from Captain Maxwell."

"I will leave you the letter to show Jacob," said the Captain, putting it clumsily back in its envelope.

"Jacob is after his butterflies as usual," said Mrs. Flanders irritably, but was surprised by a sudden afterthought, "Cricket begins this week, of course."

"Edward Jenkinson has handed in his resignation," said Captain Barfoot.

"Then you will stand for the Council?" Mrs. Flanders exclaimed, looking the Captain full in the face.

"Well, about that," Captain Barfoot began, settling himself rather deeper in his chair.

Jacob Flanders, therefore, went up to Cambridge in October, 1906.

3

"This is not a smoking-carriage," Mrs. Norman protested, nervously but very feebly, as the door swung open and a powerfully built young man jumped in. He seemed not to hear her. The train did not stop before it reached Cambridge, and here she was shut up alone, in a railway carriage, with a young man.

She touched the spring of her dressing-case, and ascertained that the scent-bottle and a novel from Mudie's were both handy (the young man was standing up with his back to her, putting his bag in the rack). She would throw the scent-bottle with her right hand, she decided, and tug the communication cord with her left. She was fifty years of age, and had a son at college. Nevertheless, it is a fact that men are dangerous. She read half a column of her newspaper; then stealthily looked over the edge to decide the question of safety by the infallible test of appearance. . . . She would like to offer him her paper. But do young men read the *Morning Post?* She looked to see what he was reading—the *Daily Telegraph.*

Taking note of socks (loose), of tie (shabby), she once more reached his face. She dwelt upon his mouth. The lips were shut. The eyes bent down, since he was reading. All was firm, yet youthful, indifferent, unconscious—as for knocking one down! No, no, no! She looked out of the window, smiling slightly now, and then came back again, for he didn't notice her. Grave, unconscious . . . now he looked up, past her . . . he seemed so out of place, somehow, alone with an elderly lady . . . then he fixed his eyes—which were blue—on the landscape. He had not realized her presence, she thought. Yet it was none of *her* fault that this was not a smoking-carriage—if that was what he meant.

Nobody sees any one as he is, let alone an elderly lady sitting opposite a strange young man in a railway carriage. They see a whole—they see all sorts of things—they see themselves. . . . Mrs. Norman now read three pages of one of Mr. Norris's novels. Should she say to the young man (and after all he was just the same age as her own boy): "If you want to smoke, don't mind me"? No: he seemed absolutely indifferent to her presence . . . she did not wish to interrupt.

But since, even at her age, she noted his indifference, presumably he was in some way or other—to her at least—nice, handsome, interesting, distinguished, well built, like her own boy? One must do the best one can with her report. Anyhow, this was Jacob Flanders, aged nineteen. It is no use trying to sum people up. One must follow hints, not exactly what is said, nor yet entirely what is done—for instance, when the train drew into the station, Mr. Flanders burst open the door, and put the lady's dressing-case out for her, saying, or rather mumbling: "Let me" very shyly; indeed he was rather clumsy about it.

"Who . . ." said the lady, meeting her son; but as there was a great crowd on the platform and Jacob had already gone, she did not finish her sentence. As this was Cambridge, as she was staying there for the week-end, as she saw nothing but young men all day long, in streets and round tables, this sight of her fellow-traveller was completely lost in her mind, as the crooked pin dropped by a child into the wishing-well twirls in the water and disappears for ever.

They say the sky is the same everywhere. Travellers, the shipwrecked, exiles, and the dying draw comfort from the thought, and no doubt if you are of a mystical tendency, consolation, and even explanation, shower down from the unbroken surface. But above Cambridge—anyhow above the roof of King's College Chapel—there is a difference. Out at sea a great city will cast a brightness into the night. Is it fanciful to suppose the sky, washed into the crevices of King's College Chapel, lighter, thinner, more sparkling than the sky elsewhere? Does Cambridge burn not only into the night, but into the day?

Look, as they pass into service, how airily the gowns blow out, as though nothing dense and corporeal were within. What sculptured faces, what certainty, authority controlled by piety, although great boots march under the gowns. In what orderly procession they advance. Thick wax candles stand upright; young men rise in white gowns; while the subservient eagle bears up for inspection the great white book.

An inclined plane of light comes accurately through each window, purple and yellow even in its most diffused dust, while, where it breaks upon stone, that stone is softly chalked red, yellow, and purple. Neither snow nor greenery, winter nor summer, has power over the old stained glass. As the sides of a lantern protect the flame so that it burns steady even in the wildest night—burns steady and gravely illumines the tree-trunks—so inside the Chapel all was orderly. Gravely sounded the voices; wisely the organ replied, as if buttressing human faith with the assent of the elements. The white-robed figures crossed from side to side; now mounted steps, now descended, all very orderly.

. . . If you stand a lantern under a tree every insect in the forest creeps up to it—a curious assembly, since though they scramble and swing and knock their heads against the glass, they seem to have no purpose—something senseless inspires them. One gets tired of watching them, as they amble round the lantern and blindly tap as if for admittance, one large toad being the most besotted of any and shouldering his way through the rest. Ah, but what's that? A terrifying volley of pistol-shots rings out—

cracks sharply; ripples spread—silence laps smooth over sound. A tree—a tree has fallen, a sort of death in the forest. After that, the wind in the trees sounds melancholy.

But this service in King's College Chapel—why allow women to take part in it? Surely, if the mind wanders (and Jacob looked extraordinarily vacant, his head thrown back, his hymn-book open at the wrong place), if the mind wanders it is because several hat shops and cupboards upon cupboards of coloured dresses are displayed upon rush-bottomed chairs. Though heads and bodies may be devout enough, one has a sense of individuals—some like blue, others brown; some feathers, others pansies and forget-me-nots. No one would think of bringing a dog into church. For though a dog is all very well on a gravel path, and shows no disrespect to flowers, the way he wanders down an aisle, looking, lifting a paw, and approaching a pillar with a purpose that makes the blood run cold with horror (should you be one of a congregation—alone, shyness is out of the question), a dog destroys the service completely. So do these women—though separately devout, distinguished, and vouched for by the theology, mathematics, Latin, and Greek of their husbands. Heaven knows why it is. For one thing, thought Jacob, they're as ugly as sin.

Now there was a scraping and murmuring. He caught Timmy Durrant's eye; looked very sternly at him; and then, very solemnly, winked.

"Waverley," the villa on the road to Girton was called, not that Mr. Plumer admired Scott or would have chosen any name at all, but names are useful when you have to entertain undergraduates, and as they sat waiting for the fourth undergraduate, on Sunday at lunch-time, there was talk of names upon gates.

"How tiresome," Mrs. Plumer interrupted impulsively. "Does anybody know Mr. Flanders?"

Mr. Durrant knew him; and therefore blushed slightly, and said, awkwardly, something about being sure—looking at Mr. Plumer and hitching the right leg of his trouser as he spoke. Mr. Plumer got up and stood in front of the fireplace. Mrs. Plumer laughed like a straightforward friendly fellow. In short, anything more horrible than the scene, the setting, the prospect, even the May garden being afflicted with chill sterility and a cloud choosing that moment to cross the sun, cannot be imagined. There was the garden, of course. Every one at the same moment looked at it. Owing to the cloud, the leaves ruffled grey, and the sparrows—there were two sparrows.

"I think," said Mrs. Plumer, taking advantage of the momentary respite, while the young men stared at the garden, to look at her husband, and he, not accepting full responsibility for the act, nevertheless touched the bell.

There can be no excuse for this outrage upon one hour of human life, save the reflection which occurred to Mr. Plumer as he carved the mutton, that if no don ever gave a luncheon party, if Sunday after Sunday passed, if men went down, became lawyers, doctors, members of Parliament, business men—if no don ever gave a luncheon party—

"Now, does lamb make the mint sauce, or mint sauce make the lamb?" he asked the young man next him, to break a silence which had already lasted five minutes and a half.

"I don't know, sir," said the young man, blushing very vividly.

At this moment in came Mr. Flanders. He had mistaken the time.

Now, though they had finished their meat, Mrs. Plumer took a second helping of cabbage. Jacob determined, of course, that he would eat his meat in the time it took her to finish her cabbage, looking once or twice to measure his speed—only he was infernally hungry. Seeing this, Mrs. Plumer said that she was sure Mr. Flanders would not mind—and the tart was brought in. Nodding in a peculiar way, she directed the maid to give Mr. Flanders a second helping of mutton. She glanced at the mutton. Not much of the leg would be left for luncheon.

It was none of her fault—since how could she control her father begetting her forty years ago in the suburbs of Manchester? and once begotten, how could she do other than grow up cheese-paring, ambitious, with an instinctively accurate notion of the rungs of the ladder and an ant-like assiduity in pushing George Plumer ahead of her to the top of the ladder? What was at the top of the ladder? A sense that all the rungs were beneath one apparently; since by the time that George Plumer became Professor of Physics, or whatever it might be, Mrs. Plumer could only be in a condition to cling tight to her eminence, peer down at the ground, and goad her two plain daughters to climb the rungs of the ladder.

"I was down at the races yesterday," she said, "with my two little girls."

It was none of *their* fault either. In they came to the drawing-room, in white frocks and blue sashes. They handed the cigarettes. Rhoda had inherited her father's cold grey eyes. Cold grey eyes George Plumer had, but in them was an abstract light. He could talk about Persia and the Trade winds, the Reform Bill and the cycle of the harvests. Books were on his shelves by Wells and Shaw; on the table serious six-penny weeklies written by pale men in muddy boots—the weekly creak and screech of brains rinsed in cold water and wrung dry—melancholy papers.

"I don't feel that I know the truth about anything till I've read them both!" said Mrs. Plumer brightly, tapping the table of contents with her bare red hand, upon which the ring looked so incongruous.

"Oh God, oh God, oh God!" exclaimed Jacob, as the four undergraduates left the house. "Oh, my God!"

* * *

"Bloody beastly!" he said, scanning the street for lilac or bicycle—anything to restore his sense of freedom.

"Bloody beastly," he said to Timmy Durrant, summing up his discomfort at the world shown him at lunch-time, a world capable of existing—there was no doubt about that—but so unnecessary, such a thing to believe in—Shaw and Wells and the serious sixpenny weeklies! What were they after, scrubbing and demolishing, these elderly people? Had they never read Homer, Shakespeare, the Elizabethans? He saw it clearly outlined against the feelings he drew from youth and natural inclination. The poor devils had rigged up this meagre object. Yet something of pity was in him. Those wretched little girls——

The extent to which he was disturbed proves that he was already agog. Insolent he was and inexperienced, but sure enough the cities which the elderly of the race have built upon the skyline showed like brick suburbs, barracks, and places of discipline against a red and yellow flame. He was impressionable; but the word is contradicted by the composure with which he hollowed his hand to screen a match. He was a young man of substance.

Anyhow, whether undergraduate or shop boy, man or woman, it must come as a shock about the age of twenty—the world of the elderly—thrown up in such black outline upon what we are; upon the reality; the moors and Byron; the sea and the lighthouse; the sheep's jaw with the yellow teeth in it; upon the obstinate irrepressible conviction which makes youth so intolerably disagreeable—"I am what I am, and intend to be it," for which there will be no form in the world unless Jacob makes one for himself. The Plumers will try to prevent him from making it. Wells and Shaw and the serious sixpenny weeklies will sit on its head. Every time he lunches out on Sunday—at dinner parties and tea parties—there will be this same shock—horror—discomfort—then pleasure, for he draws into him at every step as he walks by the river such steady certainty, such reassurance from all sides, the trees bowing, the grey spires soft in the blue, voices blowing and seeming suspended in the air, the springy air of May, the elastic air with its particles—chestnut bloom, pollen, whatever it is that gives the May air its potency, blurring the trees, gumming the buds, daubing the green. And the river too runs past, not at flood, nor swiftly, but cloying the oar that dips in it and drops white drops from the blade, swimming green and deep over the bowed rushes, as if lavishly caressing them.

Where they moored their boat the trees showered down, so that their topmost leaves trailed in the ripples and the green wedge that lay in the water being made of leaves shifted in leaf-breadths as the real leaves shifted. Now there was a shiver of wind—instantly an edge of sky; and as Durrant ate cherries he dropped the stunted yellow cherries through the green wedge of leaves, their stalks twinkling as they wriggled in and out, and sometimes one half-bitten cherry would go down red into the green. The meadow was on a level with Jacob's eyes as he lay back; gilt with buttercups, but the grass did not run like the thin green water of the graveyard grass about to overflow the tombstones, but stood juicy and thick. Looking up, backwards, he saw the legs of children deep in the grass, and the legs of cows. Munch, munch, he heard; then a short step through the grass; then again munch, munch, munch, as they tore the grass short at the roots. In front of him two white butterflies circled higher and higher round the elm tree.

"Jacob's off," thought Durrant looking up from his novel. He kept reading a few pages and then looking up in a curiously methodical manner, and each time he looked up he took a few cherries out of the bag and ate them abstractedly. Other boats passed them, crossing the backwater from side to side to avoid each other, for many were now moored, and there were now white dresses and a flaw in the column of air between two trees, round which curled a thread of blue—Lady Miller's picnic party. Still more boats kept coming, and Durrant, without getting up, shoved their boat closer to the bank.

"Oh-h-h-h," groaned Jacob, as the boat rocked, and the trees rocked, and the white dresses and the white flannel trousers drew out long and wavering up the bank.

"Oh-h-h-h!" He sat up, and felt as if a piece of elastic had snapped in his face.

"They're friends of my mother's," said Durrant. "So old Bow took no end of trouble about the boat."

And this boat had gone from Falmouth to St. Ives Bay, all round the coast. A larger boat, a ten-ton yacht, about the twentieth of June, properly fitted out, Durrant said . . .

"There's the cash difficulty," said Jacob.

"My people'll see to that," said Durrant (the son of a banker, deceased).

"I intend to preserve my economic independence," said Jacob stiffly. (He was getting excited.)

"My mother said something about going to Harrogate," he said with a little annoyance, feeling the pocket where he kept his letters.

"Was that true about your uncle becoming a Mohammedan?" asked Timmy Durrant.

Jacob had told the story of his Uncle Morty in Durrant's room the night before.

"I expect he's feeding the sharks, if the truth were known," said Jacob. "I say, Durrant, there's none left!" he exclaimed, crumpling the bag which had held the cherries, and throwing it into the river. He saw Lady Miller's picnic party on the island as he threw the bag into the river.

A sort of awkwardness, grumpiness, gloom came into his eyes.

"Shall we move on . . . this beastly crowd . . ." he said.

So up they went, past the island.

The feathery white moon never let the sky grow dark; all night the chestnut blossoms were white in the green; dim was the cow-parsley in the meadows.

The waiters at Trinity must have been shuffling china plates like cards, from the clatter that could be heard in the Great Court. Jacob's rooms, however, were in Neville's Court; at the top; so that reaching his door one went in a little out of breath; but he wasn't there. Dining in Hall, presumably. It will be quite dark in Neville's Court long before midnight, only the pillars opposite will always be white, and the fountains. A curious effect the gate has, like lace upon pale green. Even in the window you hear the plates; a hum of talk, too, from the diners; the Hall lit up, and the swing-doors opening and shutting with a soft thud. Some are late.

Jacob's room had a round table and two low chairs. There were yellow flags in a jar on the mantelpiece; a photograph of his mother; cards from societies with little raised crescents, coats of arms, and initials; notes and pipes; on the table lay paper ruled with a red margin—an essay, no doubt—"Does History consist of the Biographies of Great Men?" There were books enough; very few French books; but then any one who's worth anything reads just what he likes, as the mood takes him, with extravagant enthusiasm. Lives of the Duke of Wellington, for example; Spinoza; the works of Dickens; the *Faerie Queen*; a Greek dictionary with the petals of poppies pressed to silk between the pages; all the Elizabethans. His slippers were incredibly shabby, like boats burnt to the water's rim. Then there were photographs from the Greeks, and a mezzotint from Sir Joshua—all very English. The works of Jane Austen, too, in deference, perhaps, to some one else's standard. Carlyle was a prize. There were books upon the Italian painters of the Renaissance, a *Manual of the Diseases of the Horse,* and all the usual text-books. Listless is the air in an empty room, just swelling the curtain; the flowers in the jar shift. One fibre in the wicker arm-chair creaks, though no one sits there.

Coming down the steps a little sideways [Jacob sat on the window-seat talking to Durrant; he smoked, and Durrant looked at the map], the old man, with his hands locked behind him, his gown floating black, lurched, unsteadily, near the wall; then, upstairs he went into his room. Then another, who raised his hand and praised the columns, the gate, the sky;

another, tripping and smug. Each went up a staircase; three lights were lit in the dark windows.

If any light burns above Cambridge, it must be from three such rooms; Greek burns here; science there; philosophy on the ground floor. Poor old Huxtable can't walk straight—Sopwith, too, has praised the sky any night these twenty years; and Cowan still chuckles at the same stories. It is not simple, or pure, or wholly splendid, the lamp of learning, since if you see them there under its light (whether Rossetti's on the wall, or Van Gogh reproduced, whether there are lilacs in the bowl or rusty pipes), how priestly they look! How like a suburb where you go to see a view and eat a special cake! "We are the sole purveyors of this cake." Back you go to London; for the treat is over.

Old Professor Huxtable, performing with the method of a clock his change of dress, let himself down into his chair; filled his pipe; chose his paper; crossed his feet; and extracted his glasses. The whole flesh of his face then fell into folds as if props were removed. Yet strip a whole seat of an underground railway carriage of its heads and old Huxtable's head will hold them all. Now, as his eye goes down the print, what a procession tramps through the corridors of his brain, orderly, quick-stepping, and reinforced, as the march goes on, by fresh runnels, till the whole hall, dome, whatever one calls it, is populous with ideas. Such a muster takes place in no other brain. Yet sometimes there he'll sit for hours together, gripping the arm of the chair, like a man holding fast because stranded, and then, just because his corn twinges, or it may be the gout, what execrations, and, dear me, to hear him talk of money, taking out his leather purse and grudging even the smallest silver coin, secretive and suspicious as an old peasant woman with all her lies. Strange paralysis and constriction—marvellous illumination. Serene over it all rides the great full brow, and sometimes asleep or in the quiet spaces of the night you might fancy that on a pillow of stone he lay triumphant.

Sopwith, meanwhile, advancing with a curious trip from the fire-place, cut the chocolate cake into segments. Until midnight or later there would be undergraduates in his room, sometimes as many as twelve, sometimes three or four; but nobody got up when they went or when they came; Sopwith went on talking. Talking, talking, talking—as if everything could be talked—the soul itself slipped through the lips in thin silver disks which dissolve in young men's minds like silver, like moonlight. Oh, far away they'd remember it, and deep in dulness gaze back on it, and come to refresh themselves again.

"Well, I never. That's old Chucky. My dear boy, how's the world treating you?" And in came poor little Chucky, the unsuccessful provincial, Stenhouse his real name, but of course Sopwith brought back by using the other everything, everything, "all I could never be"—yes, though next day, buying his newspaper and catching the early train, it all seemed to him childish, absurd; the chocolate cake, the young men; Sopwith summing things up; no, not all; he would send his son there. He would save every penny to send his son there. Sopwith went on talking; twining stiff fibres of awkward speech—things young men blurted out—plaiting them round his own smooth garland, making the bright side show, the vivid greens, the sharp thorns, manliness. He loved it. Indeed to Sopwith a man could say anything, until perhaps he'd grown old, or gone under, gone deep, when the silver disks would tinkle hollow, and the inscription read a little too simple, and the old stamp look too pure, and the impress always the same—a Greek boy's head. But he would respect still. A woman, divining the priest, would, involuntarily, despise.

Cowan, Erasmus Cowan, sipped his port alone, or with one rosy little man, whose memory held precisely the same span of time; sipped his port, and told his stories, and without book before him intoned Latin, Virgil and Catullus, as if language were wine upon his lips. Only—sometimes it will come over one—what if the poet strode in? "*This* my image?" he might ask, pointing to the chubby man, whose brain is, after all, Virgil's representative among us, though the body gluttonize, and as for arms, bees, or even the plough, Cowan takes his trips abroad with a French novel in his pocket, a rug about his knees, and is thankful to be home again in his place, in his line, holding up in his snug little mirror the image of Virgil, all rayed round with good stories of the dons of Trinity and red beams of port. But language is wine upon his lips. Nowhere else would Virgil hear the like. And though, as she goes sauntering along the Backs, old Miss Umphelby sings him melodiously enough, accurately too, she is always brought up by this question as she reaches Clare Bridge: "But if I met him, what should I wear?"—and then, taking her way up the avenue towards Newnham, she lets her fancy play upon other details of men's meeting with women which have never got into print. Her lectures, therefore, are not half so well attended as those of Cowan, and the thing she might have said in elucidation of the text for ever left out. In short, face a teacher with the image of the taught and the mirror breaks. But Cowan sipped his port, his exaltation over, no longer the representative of Virgil. No, the builder, assessor, surveyor, rather; ruling lines between names, hanging lists above doors. Such is the fabric through which the light must shine, if shine it can—the light of all these languages, Chinese and Russian, Persian and Arabic, of symbols and figures, of history, of things that are known and things that are about to be known. So that if at night, far out at sea over the tumbling waves, one saw a haze on the waters, a city illuminated, a whiteness even in the sky, such as that now over the Hall of Trinity where they're still dining, or washing up plates, that would be the light burning there—the light of Cambridge.

"Let's go round to Simeon's room," said Jacob, and they rolled up the map, having got the whole thing settled.

All the lights were coming out round the court, and falling on the cobbles, picking out dark patches of grass and single daisies. The young men were now back in their rooms. Heaven knows what they were doing. What was it that could *drop* like that? And leaning down over a foaming window-box, one stopped another hurrying past, and upstairs they went and down they went, until a sort of fulness settled on the court, the hive full of bees, the bees home thick with gold, drowsy, humming, suddenly vocal; the Moonlight Sonata answered by a waltz.

The Moonlight Sonata tinkled away; the waltz crashed. Although young men still went in and out, they walked as if keeping engagements. Now and then there was a thud, as if some heavy piece of furniture had fallen, unexpectedly, of its own accord, not in the general stir of life after dinner. One supposed that young men raised their eyes from their books as the furniture fell. Were they reading? Certainly there was a sense of concentration in the air. Behind the grey walls sat so many young men, some undoubtedly reading, magazines, shilling shockers, no doubt; legs, perhaps, over the arms of chairs; smoking; sprawling over tables, and writing while their heads went round in a circle as the pen moved—simple young men, these, who would—but there is no need to think of them grown old; others eating sweets; here they boxed; and, well, Mr. Hawkins must have been mad suddenly to throw up his window and bawl: "Jo—seph! Jo—seph!" and then he ran as hard as ever he could across the court, while an elderly man, in a green apron, carrying an immense pile of tin covers, hesitated, balanced, and then went on. But this was a diversion. There were young men who read, lying in shallow arm-chairs, holding their books as if they had hold in their hands of something that would see them through; they being all in a torment, coming from midland towns, clergymen's sons. Others read Keats. And those long histories in many volumes—surely some one was now beginning at the beginning in order to understand the Holy Roman Empire, as one must. That was part of the concentration, though it would be dangerous on a hot spring night—dangerous, perhaps, to concentrate too much upon single books, actual chapters, when at any moment the door opened and Jacob appeared; or Richard Bonamy, reading Keats no longer, began making long pink spills from an old newspaper, bending forward, and looking eager and contented no more, but almost fierce. Why? Only perhaps that Keats died young—one wants to write poetry too and to love—oh, the brutes! It's damnably difficult. But, after all, not so difficult if on the next staircase, in the large room, there are two, three, five young men all convinced of this—of brutality, that is, and the clear division between right and wrong. There was a sofa, chairs, a square table, and the window being open, one could see how they sat—legs issuing here, one there crumpled in a corner of the sofa; and, presumably, for you could not see him, somebody stood by the fender, talking. Anyhow, Jacob, who sat astride a chair and ate dates from a long box, burst out laughing. The answer came from the sofa corner; for his pipe was held in the air, then replaced. Jacob wheeled round. He had something to say to *that,* though the sturdy red-haired boy at the table seemed to deny it, wagging his head slowly from side to side; and then, taking out his penknife, he dug the point of it again and again into a knot in the table, as if affirming that the voice from the fender spoke the truth—which Jacob could not deny. Possibly, when he had done arranging the date-stones, he might find something to say to it—indeed his lips opened—only then there broke out a roar of laughter.

The laughter died in the air. The sound of it could scarcely have reached any one standing by the Chapel, which stretched along the opposite side of the court. The laughter died out, and only gestures of arms, movements of bodies, could be seen shaping something in the room. Was it an argument? A bet on the boat races? Was it nothing of the sort? What was shaped by the arms and bodies moving in the twilight room?

A step or two beyond the window there was nothing at all, except the enclosing buildings—chimneys upright, roofs horizontal; too much brick and building for a May night, perhaps. And then before one's eyes would come the bare hills of Turkey—sharp lines, dry earth, coloured flowers, and colour on the shoulders of the women, standing naked-legged in the stream to beat linen on the stones. The stream made loops of water round their ankles. But none of that could show clearly through the swaddlings and blanketings of the Cambridge night. The stroke of the clock even was muffled; as if intoned by somebody reverent from a pulpit; as if generations of learned men heard the last hour go rolling through their ranks and issued it, already smooth and time-worn, with their blessing, for the use of the living.

Was it to receive this gift from the past that the young man came to the window and stood there, looking out across the court? It was Jacob. He stood smoking his pipe while the last stroke of the clock purred softly round him. Perhaps there had been an argument. He looked satisfied; indeed masterly; which expression changed slightly as he stood there, the sound of the clock conveying to him (it may be) a sense of old buildings and time; and himself the inheritor; and then tomorrow; and friends; at the thought of whom, in sheer confidence and pleasure, it seemed, he yawned and stretched himself.

Meanwhile behind him the shape they had made, whether by argument or not, the spiritual shape, hard yet ephemeral, as of glass compared with the dark stone of the Chapel, was dashed to splinters, young men rising from chairs and sofa corners, buzzing and barging about the room, one driving another against the bedroom door, which giving way, in they fell. Then Jacob was left there, in the shallow arm-chair, alone with Masham? Anderson? Simeon? Oh, it was Simeon. The others had all gone.

". . . Julian the Apostate. . . ." Which of them said that and the other words murmured round it? But about midnight there sometimes rises, like a veiled figure suddenly woken, a heavy wind; and this now flapping through Trinity lifted unseen leaves and blurred everything. "Julian the Apostate"—and then the wind. Up go the elm branches, out blow the sails, the old schooners rear and plunge, the grey waves in the hot Indian Ocean tumble sultrily, and then all falls flat again.

So, if the veiled lady stepped through the Courts of Trinity, she now drowsed once more, all her draperies about her, her head against a pillar.

"Somehow it seems to matter."

The low voice was Simeon's.

The voice was even lower that answered him. The sharp tap of a pipe on the mantelpiece cancelled the words. And perhaps Jacob only said "hum," or said nothing at all. True, the words were inaudible. It was the intimacy, a sort of spiritual suppleness, when mind prints upon mind indelibly.

"Well, you seem to have studied the subject," said Jacob, rising and standing over Simeon's chair. He balanced himself; he swayed a little. He appeared extraordinarily happy, as if his pleasure would brim and spill down the sides if Simeon spoke.

Simeon said nothing. Jacob remained standing. But intimacy—the room was full of it, still, deep, like a pool. Without need of movement or speech it rose softly and washed over everything, mollifying, kindling, and coating the mind with the lustre of pearl, so that if you talk of a light, of Cambridge burning, it's not languages only. It's Julian the Apostate.

But Jacob moved. He murmured good-night. He went out into the court. He buttoned his jacket across his chest. He went back to his rooms, and being the only man who walked at that moment back to his rooms, his footsteps rang out, his figure loomed large. Back from the Chapel, back from the Hall, back from the Library, came the sound of his footsteps, as if the old stone echoed with magisterial authority: "The young man—the young man—the young man—back to his rooms."

4

What's the use of trying to read Shakespeare, especially in one of those little thin paper editions whose pages get ruffled, or stuck together with sea-water? Although the plays of Shakespeare had frequently been praised, even quoted, and placed higher than the Greek, never since they started had Jacob managed to read one through. Yet what an opportunity!

For the Scilly Isles had been sighted by Timmy Durrant lying like mountain-tops almost a-wash in precisely the right place. His calculations had worked perfectly, and really the sight of him sitting there, with his hand on the tiller, rosy gilled, with a sprout of beard, looking sternly at the stars, then at a compass, spelling out quite correctly his page of the eternal lesson-book, would have moved a woman. Jacob, of course, was not a woman. The sight of Timmy Durrant was no sight for him, nothing to set against the sky and worship; far from it. They had quarrelled. Why the right way to open a tin of beef, with Shakespeare on board, under conditions of such splendour, should have turned them to sulky schoolboys, none can tell. Tinned beef is cold eating, though; and salt water spoils biscuits; and the waves tumble and lollop much the same hour after hour—tumble and lollop all across the horizon. Now a spray of seaweed floats past—now a log of wood. Ships have been wrecked here. One or two go past, keeping their own side of the road. Timmy knew where they were bound, what their cargoes were, and, by looking through his glass, could tell the name of the line, and even guess what dividends it paid its shareholders. Yet that was no reason for Jacob to turn sulky.

The Scilly Isles had the look of mountain-tops almost a-wash. . . . Unfortunately, Jacob broke the pin of the Primus stove.

The Scilly Isles might well be obliterated by a roller sweeping straight across.

But one must give young men the credit of admitting that, though breakfast eaten under these circumstances is grim, it is sincere enough. No need to make conversation. They got out their pipes.

Timmy wrote up some scientific observations; and—what was the question that broke the silence—the exact time or the day of the month? anyhow, it was spoken without the least awkwardness; in the most matter-of-fact way in the world; and then Jacob began to unbutton his clothes and sat naked, save for his shirt, intending, apparently, to bathe.

The Scilly Isles were turning bluish; and suddenly blue, purple, and green flushed the sea; left it grey; struck a stripe which vanished; but when Jacob had got his shirt over his head the whole floor of the waves was blue and white, rippling and crisp, though now and again a broad purple mark appeared, like a bruise; or there floated an entire emerald tinged with yellow. He plunged. He gulped in water, spat it out, struck with his right arm, struck with his left, was towed by a rope, gasped, splashed, and was hauled on board.

The seat in the boat was positively hot, and the sun warmed his back as he sat naked with a towel in his hand, looking at the Scilly Isles which—confound it! the sail flapped. Shakespeare was knocked overboard. There you could see him floating merrily away, with all his pages ruffling innumerably; and then he went under.

Strangely enough, you could smell violets, or if violets were impossible in July, they must grow something very pungent on the mainland then. The mainland, not so very far off—you could see clefts in the cliffs, white cottages, smoke going up—wore an extraordinary look of calm, of sunny peace, as if wisdom and piety had descended upon the dwellers there. Now a cry sounded, as of a man calling pilchards in a main street. It wore an extraordinary look of piety and peace, as if old men smoked by the door, and girls stood, hands on hips, at the well, and horses stood; as if the end of the world had come, and cabbage fields and stone walls, and coast-guard stations, and, above all, the white sand bays with the waves breaking unseen by any one, rose to heaven in a kind of ecstasy.

But imperceptibly the cottage smoke droops, has the look of a mourning emblem, a flag floating its caress over a grave. The gulls, making their broad flight and then riding at peace, seem to mark the grave.

No doubt if this were Italy, Greece, or even the shores of Spain, sadness would be routed by strangeness and excitement and the nudge of a classical education. But the Cornish hills have stark chimneys standing on them; and, somehow or other, loveliness is infernally sad. Yes, the chimneys and the coast-guard stations and the little bays with the waves breaking unseen by any one make one remember the overpowering sorrow. And what can this sorrow be?

It is brewed by the earth itself. It comes from the houses on the coast. We start transparent, and then the cloud thickens. All history backs our pane of glass. To escape is vain.

But whether this is the right interpretation of Jacob's gloom as he sat naked, in the sun, looking at the Land's End, it is impossible to say; for he never spoke a word. Timmy sometimes wondered (only for a second) whether his people bothered him. . . . No matter. There are things that can't be said. Let's shake it off. Let's dry ourselves, and take up the first thing that comes handy. . . . Timmy Durrant's notebook of scientific observations.

"Now . . ." said Jacob.

It is a tremendous argument.

Some people can follow every step of the way, and even take a little one, six inches long, by themselves at the end; others remain observant of the external signs.

The eyes fix themselves upon the poker; the right hand takes the poker and lifts it; turns it slowly round, and then, very accurately, replaces it. The left hand, which lies on the knee, plays some stately but intermittent piece of march music. A deep breath is taken; but allowed to evaporate unused. The cat marches across the hearth-rug. No one observes her.

"That's about as near as I can get to it," Durrant wound up.

The next minute is quiet as the grave.

"It follows . . ." said Jacob.

Only half a sentence followed; but these half-sentences are like flags set on tops of buildings to the observer of external sights down below. What was the coast of Cornwall, with its violet scents, and mourning emblems, and tranquil piety, but a screen happening to hang straight behind as his mind marched up?

"It follows . . ." said Jacob.

"Yes," said Timmy, after reflection. "That is so."

Now Jacob began plunging about, half to stretch himself, half in a kind of jollity, no doubt, for the strangest sound issued from his lips as he furled the sail, rubbed the plates—gruff, tuneless—a sort of pasan, for having grasped the argument, for being master of the situation, sunburnt, unshaven, capable into the bargain of sailing round the world in a ten-ton yacht, which, very likely, he would do one of these days instead of settling down in a lawyer's office, and wearing spats.

"Our friend Masham," said Timmy Durrant, "would rather not be seen in our company as we are now." His buttons had come off.

"D'you know Masham's aunt?" said Jacob.

"Never knew he had one," said Timmy.

"Masham has millions of aunts," said Jacob.

"Masham is mentioned in Domesday Book," said Timmy.

"So are his aunts," said Jacob.

"His sister," said Timmy, "is a very pretty girl."

"That's what'll happen to you, Timmy," said Jacob.

"It'll happen to you first," said Timmy.

"But this woman I was telling you about—Masham's aunt—"

"Oh, do get on," said Timmy, for Jacob was laughing so much that he could not speak.

"Masham's aunt . . ."

Timmy laughed so much that he could not speak.

"Masham's aunt . . ."

"What is there about Masham that makes one laugh?" said Timmy.

"Hang it all—a man who swallows his tie-pin," said Jacob.

"Lord Chancellor before he's fifty," said Timmy.

"He's a gentleman," said Jacob.

"The Duke of Wellington was a gentleman," said Timmy.

"Keats wasn't."

"Lord Salisbury was."

"And what about God?" said Jacob.

The Scilly Isles now appeared as if directly pointed at by a golden finger issuing from a cloud; and everybody knows how portentous that sight is, and how these broad rays, whether they light upon the Scilly Isles or upon the tombs of crusaders in cathedrals, always shake the very foundations of scepticism and lead to jokes about God.

> Abide with me:
> Fast falls the eventide;
> The shadows deepen;
> Lord, with me abide,

sang Timmy Durrant.

"At my place we used to have a hymn which began

> Great God, what do I see and hear?"

said Jacob.

Gulls rode gently swaying in little companies of two or three quite near the boat; the cormorant, as if following his long strained neck in eternal pursuit, skimmed an inch above the water to the next rock; and the drone of the tide in the caves came across the water, low, monotonous, like the voice of some one talking to himself.

> Rock of Ages, cleft for me,
> Let me hide myself in thee,

sang Jacob.

Like the blunt tooth of some monster, a rock broke the surface; brown; overflown with perpetual waterfalls.

> Rock of Ages,

Jacob sang, lying on his back, looking up into the sky at midday, from which every shred of cloud had been withdrawn, so that it was like something permanently displayed with the cover off.

By six o'clock a breeze blew in off an icefield; and by seven the water was more purple than blue; and by half-past seven there was a patch of rough gold-beater's skin round the Scilly Isles, and Durrant's face, as he sat steering, was of the colour of a red lacquer box polished for generations. By nine all the fire and confusion had gone out of the sky, leaving wedges of apple-green and plates of pale yellow; and by ten the lanterns on the boat were making twisted colours upon the waves, elongated or squat, as the waves stretched or humped themselves. The beam from the lighthouse strode rapidly across the water. Infinite millions of miles away powdered stars twinkled; but the waves slapped the boat, and crashed, with regular and appalling solemnity, against the rocks.

Although it would be possible to knock at the cottage door and ask for a glass of milk, it is only thirst that would compel the intrusion. Yet perhaps Mrs. Pascoe would welcome it. The summer's day may be wearing heavy. Washing in her little scullery, she may hear the cheap clock on the mantelpiece tick, tick, tick . . . tick, tick, tick. She is alone in the house. Her husband is out helping Farmer Hosken; her daughter married and gone to America. Her elder son is married too, but she does not agree with his wife. The Wesleyan minister came along and took the younger boy. She is alone in the house. A steamer, probably bound for Cardiff, now crosses the horizon, while near at hand one bell of a foxglove swings to and fro with a bumble-bee for clapper. These white Cornish cottages are built on the edge of the cliff; the garden grows gorse more readily than cabbages; and for hedge, some primeval man has piled granite boulders. In one of these, to hold, an historian conjectures, the victim's blood, a basin has been hollowed, but in our time it serves more tamely to seat those tourists who wish for an uninterrupted view of the Gurnard's Head. Not that any one objects to a blue print dress and a white apron in a cottage garden.

"Look—she has to draw her water from a well in the garden."

"Very lonely it must be in winter, with the wind sweeping over those hills, and the waves dashing on the rocks."

Even on a summer's day you hear them murmuring.

Having drawn her water, Mrs. Pascoe went in. The tourists regretted that they had brought no glasses, so that they might have read the name of the tramp steamer. Indeed, it was such a fine day that there was no saying what a pair of field-glasses might not have fetched into view. Two fishing luggers, presumably from St. Ives Bay, were now sailing in an opposite direction from the steamer, and the floor of the sea became alternately clear and opaque. As for the bee, having sucked its fill of honey, it visited the teasle and thence made a straight line to Mrs. Pascoe's patch, once more directing the tourists' gaze to the old woman's print dress and white apron, for she had come to the door of the cottage and was standing there.

There she stood, shading her eyes and looking out to sea.

For the millionth time, perhaps, she looked at the sea. A peacock butterfly now spread himself upon the teasle, fresh and newly emerged, as the blue and chocolate down on his wings testified. Mrs. Pascoe went indoors, fetched a cream pan, came out, and stood scouring it. Her face was assuredly not soft, sensual, or lecherous, but hard, wise, wholesome rather, signifying in a room full of sophisticated people the flesh and blood of life. She would tell a lie, though, as soon as the truth. Behind her on the wall hung a large dried skate. Shut up in the parlour she prized mats, china mugs, and photographs, though the mouldy little room was saved from the salt breeze only by the depth of a brick, and between lace curtains you saw the gannet drop like a stone, and on stormy days the gulls came shuddering through the air, and the steamers' lights were now high, now deep. Melancholy were the sounds on a winter's night.

The picture papers were delivered punctually on Sunday, and she pored long over Lady Cynthia's wedding at the Abbey. She, too, would have liked to ride in a carriage with springs. The soft, swift syllables of educated speech often shamed her few rude ones. And then all night to hear the grinding of the Atlantic upon the rocks instead of hansom cabs and footmen whistling for motor cars. . . . So she may have dreamed, scouring her cream pan. But the talkative, nimble-witted people have taken themselves to towns. Like a miser, she has hoarded her feelings within her own breast. Not a penny piece has she changed all these years, and, watching her enviously, it seems as if all within must be pure gold.

The wise old woman, having fixed her eyes upon the sea, once more withdrew. The tourists decided that it was time to move on to the Gurnard's Head.

Three seconds later Mrs. Durrant rapped upon the door.

"Mrs. Pascoe?" she said.

Rather haughtily, she watched the tourists cross the field path. She came of a Highland race, famous for its chieftains.

Mrs. Pascoe appeared.

"I envy you that bush, Mrs. Pascoe," said Mrs. Durrant, pointing the parasol with which she had rapped on the door at the fine clump of St. John's wort that grew beside it. Mrs. Pascoe looked at the bush deprecatingly.

"I expect my son in a day or two," said Mrs. Durrant. "Sailing from Falmouth with a friend in a little boat. . . . Any news of Lizzie yet, Mrs. Pascoe?"

Her long-tailed ponies stood twitching their ears on the road twenty yards away. The boy, Curnow, flicked flies off them occasionally. He saw his mistress go into the cottage; come out again; and pass, talking energetically to judge by the movements of her hands, round the vegetable plot in front of the cottage. Mrs. Pascoe was his aunt. Both women surveyed a bush. Mrs. Durrant stooped and picked a sprig from it. Next she pointed (her movements were peremptory; she held herself very upright) at the potatoes. They had the blight. All potatoes that year had the blight. Mrs. Durrant showed Mrs. Pascoe how bad the blight was on her potatoes. Mrs. Durrant talked energetically; Mrs. Pascoe listened submissively. The boy Curnow knew that Mrs. Durrant was saying that it is perfectly simple; you mix the powder in a gallon of water; "I have done it with my own hands in my own garden," Mrs. Durrant was saying.

"You won't have a potato left—you won't have a potato left," Mrs. Durrant was saying in her emphatic voice as they reached the gate. The boy Curnow became as immobile as stone.

Mrs. Durrant took the reins in her hands and settled herself on the driver's seat.

"Take care of that leg, or I shall send the doctor to you," she called back over her shoulder; touched the ponies; and the carriage started forward. The boy Curnow had only just time to swing himself up by the toe of his boot. The boy Curnow, sitting in the middle of the back seat, looked at his aunt.

Mrs. Pascoe stood at the gate looking after them; stood at the gate till the trap was round the corner; stood at the gate, looking now to the right, now to the left; then went back to her cottage.

Soon the ponies attacked the swelling moor road with striving forelegs. Mrs. Durrant let the reins fall slackly, and leant backwards. Her vivacity had left her. Her hawk nose was thin as a bleached bone through which you almost see the light. Her hands, lying on the reins in her lap, were firm even in repose. The upper lip was cut so short that it raised itself almost in a sneer from the front teeth. Her mind skimmed leagues where Mrs. Pascoe's mind adhered to its solitary patch. Her mind skimmed leagues as the ponies climbed the hill road. Forwards and backwards she cast her mind, as if the roofless cottages, mounds of slag, and cottage gardens overgrown with foxglove and bramble cast shade upon her mind. Arrived at the summit, she stopped the carriage. The pale hills were round her, each scattered with ancient stones; beneath was the sea, variable as a southern sea; she herself sat there looking from hill to sea, upright, aquiline, equally poised between gloom and laughter. Suddenly she flicked the ponies so that the boy Curnow had to swing himself up by the toe of his boot.

The rooks settled; the rooks rose. The trees which they touched so capriciously seemed insufficient to lodge their numbers. The tree-tops sang with the breeze in them; the branches creaked audibly and dropped now and then, though the season was midsummer, husks or twigs. Up went the rooks and down again, rising in lesser numbers each time as the sager birds made ready to settle, for the evening was already spent enough to make the air inside the wood almost dark. The moss was soft; the tree-trunks spectral. Beyond them lay a silvery meadow. The pampas grass raised its feathery spears from mounds of green at the end of the meadow. A breadth of water gleamed. Already the convolvulus moth was spinning over the flowers. Orange and purple, nasturtium and cherry pie, were washed into the twilight, but the tobacco plant and the passion flower, over which the great moth spun, were white as china. The rooks creaked their wings together on the tree-tops, and were settling down for sleep when, far off, a familiar sound shook and trembled—increased—fairly dinned in their ears—scared sleepy wings into the air again—the dinner bell at the house.

After six days of salt wind, rain, and sun, Jacob Flanders had put on a dinner jacket. The discreet black object had made its appearance now and then in the boat among tins, pickles, preserved meats, and as the voyage went on had become more and more irrelevant, hardly to be believed in. And now, the world being stable, lit by candle-light, the dinner jacket alone preserved him. He could not be sufficiently thankful. Even so his neck, wrists, and face were exposed without cover, and his whole person, whether exposed or not, tingled and glowed so as to make even black cloth an imperfect screen. He drew back the great red hand that lay on the table-cloth. Surreptitiously it closed upon slim glasses and curved silver forks. The bones of the cutlets were decorated with pink frills—and yesterday he had gnawn ham from the bone! Opposite him were hazy, semi-transparent shapes of yellow and blue. Behind them, again, was the grey-green garden, and among the pear-shaped leaves of the escallonia fishing-boats seemed caught and suspended. A sailing ship slowly drew past the women's backs. Two or three figures crossed the terrace hastily in the dusk. The door opened and shut. Nothing settled or stayed unbroken. Like oars rowing now this side, now that, were the sentences that came now here, now there, from either side of the table.

"Oh, Clara, Clara!" exclaimed Mrs. Durrant, and Timothy Durrant adding, "Clara, Clara," Jacob named the shape in yellow gauze Timothy's sister, Clara. The girl sat smiling and flushed. With her brother's dark eyes, she was vaguer and softer than he was. When the laugh died down she said: "But, mother, it was true. He said so, didn't he? Miss Eliot agreed with us. . . ."

But Miss Eliot, tall, grey-headed, was making room beside her for the old man who had come in from the terrace. The dinner would never end, Jacob thought, and he did not wish it to end, though the ship had sailed from one corner of the window-frame to the other, and a light marked the end of the pier. He saw Mrs. Durrant gaze at the light. She turned to him.

"Did you take command, or Timothy?" she said. "Forgive me if I call you Jacob. I've heard so much of you." Then her eyes went back to the sea. Her eyes glazed as she looked at the view.

"A little village once," she said, "and now grown. . . ." She rose, taking her napkin with her, and stood by the window.

"Did you quarrel with Timothy?" Clara asked shyly. "I should have."

Mrs. Durrant came back from the window.

"It gets later and later," she said, sitting upright, and looking down the table. "You ought to be ashamed—all of you. Mr. Clutterbuck, you ought to be ashamed." She raised her voice, for Mr. Clutterbuck was deaf.

"We *are* ashamed," said a girl. But the old man with the beard went on eating plum tart. Mrs. Durrant laughed and leant back in her chair, as if indulging him.

"We put it to you, Mrs. Durrant," said a young man with thick spectacles and a fiery moustache. "I say the conditions were fulfilled. She owes me a sovereign."

"Not *before* the fish—*with* it, Mrs. Durrant," said Charlotte Wilding.

"That was the bet; with the fish," said Clara seriously. "Begonias, mother. To eat them with his fish."

"Oh dear," said Mrs. Durrant.

"Charlotte won't pay you," said Timothy.

"How dare you . . ." said Charlotte.

"That privilege will be mine," said the courtly Mr. Wortley, producing a silver case primed with sovereigns and slipping one coin on to the table. Then Mrs. Durrant got up and passed down the room, holding herself very straight, and the girls in yellow and blue and silver gauze followed her, and elderly Miss Eliot in her velvet; and a little rosy woman, hesitating at the door, clean, scrupulous, probably a governess. All passed out at the open door.

"When you are as old as I am, Charlotte," said Mrs. Durrant, drawing the girl's arm within hers as they paced up and down the terrace.

"Why are you so sad?" Charlotte asked impulsively.

"Do I seem to you sad? I hope not," said Mrs. Durrant.

"Well, just now. You're *not* old."

"Old enough to be Timothy's mother." They stopped.

Miss Eliot was looking through Mr. Clutterbuck's telescope at the edge of the terrace. The deaf old man stood beside her, fondling his beard, and reciting the names of the constellations: "Andromeda, Bootes, Sidonia, Cassiopeia. . . ."

"Andromeda," murmured Miss Eliot, shifting the telescope slightly.

Mrs. Durrant and Charlotte looked along the barrel of the instrument pointed at the skies.

"There are *millions* of stars," said Charlotte with conviction. Miss Eliot turned away from the telescope. The young men laughed suddenly in the dining-room.

"Let *me* look," said Charlotte eagerly.

"The stars bore me," said Mrs. Durrant, walking down the terrace with Julia Eliot. "I read a book once about the stars. . . . What are they saying?" She stopped in front of the dining-room window. "Timothy," she noted.

"The silent young man," said Miss Eliot.

"Yes, Jacob Flanders," said Mrs. Durrant.

"Oh, mother! I didn't recognize you!" exclaimed Clara Durrant, coming from the opposite direction with Elsbeth. "How delicious," she breathed, crushing a verbena leaf.

Mrs. Durrant turned and walked away by herself.

"Clara!" she called. Clara went to her.

"How unlike they are!" said Miss Eliot.

Mr. Wortley passed them, smoking a cigar.

"Every day I live I find myself agreeing . . ." he said as he passed them.

"It's so interesting to guess . . ." murmured Julia Eliot.

"When first we came out we could see the flowers in that bed," said Elsbeth.

"We see very little now," said Miss Eliot.

"She must have been so beautiful, and everybody loved her, of course," said Charlotte. "I suppose Mr. Wortley . . ." she paused.

"Edward's death was a tragedy," said Miss Eliot decidedly.

Here Mr. Erskine joined them.

"There's no such thing as silence," he said positively. "I can hear twenty different sounds on a night like this without counting your voices."

"Make a bet of it?" said Charlotte.

"Done," said Mr. Erskine. "One, the sea; two, the wind; three, a dog; four . . ."

The others passed on.

"Poor Timothy," said Elsbeth.

"A very fine night," shouted Miss Eliot into Mr. Clutterbuck's ear.

"Like to look at the stars?" said the old man, turning the telescope towards Elsbeth.

"Doesn't it make you melancholy—looking at the stars?" shouted Miss Eliot.

"Dear me no, dear me no," Mr. Clutterbuck chuckled when he understood her. "Why should it make me melancholy? Not for a moment—dear me no."

"Thank you, Timothy, but I'm coming in," said Miss Eliot. "Elsbeth, here's a shawl."

"I'm coming in," Elsbeth murmured with her eye to the telescope. "Cassiopeia," she murmured. "Where are you all?" she asked, taking her eye away from the telescope. "How dark it is!"

Mrs. Durrant sat in the drawing-room by a lamp winding a ball of wool. Mr. Clutterbuck read the Times. In the distance stood a second lamp, and round it sat the young ladies, flashing scissors over silver-spangled stuff for private theatricals. Mr. Wortley read a book.

"Yes; he is perfectly right," said Mrs. Durrant, drawing herself up and ceasing to wind her wool. And while Mr. Clutterbuck read the rest of Lord Lansdowne's speech she sat upright, without touching her ball.

"Ah, Mr. Flanders," she said, speaking proudly, as if to Lord Lansdowne himself. Then she sighed and began to wind her wool again.

"Sit *there*," she said.

Jacob came out from the dark place by the window where he had hovered. The light poured over him, illuminating every cranny of his skin; but not a muscle of his face moved as he sat looking out into the garden.

"I want to hear about your voyage," said Mrs. Durrant.

"Yes," he said.

"Twenty years ago we did the same thing."

"Yes," he said. She looked at him sharply.

"He is extraordinarily awkward," she thought, noticing how he fingered his socks. "Yet so distinguished-looking."

"In those days . . ." she resumed, and told him how they had sailed . . . "my husband, who knew a good deal about sailing, for he kept a yacht before we married" . . . and then how rashly they had defied the fishermen, "almost paid for it with our lives, but so proud of ourselves!" She flung the hand out that held the ball of wool.

"Shall I hold your wool?" Jacob asked stiffly.

"You do that for your mother," said Mrs. Durrant, looking at him again keenly, as she transferred the skein. "Yes, it goes much better."

He smiled; but said nothing.

Elsbeth Siddons hovered behind them with something silver on her arm.

"We want," she said. . . . "I've come . . ." she paused.

"Poor Jacob," said Mrs. Durrant, quietly, as if she had known him all his life. "They're going to make you act in their play."

"How I love you!" said Elsbeth, kneeling beside Mrs. Durrant's chair.

"Give me the wool," said Mrs. Durrant.

"He's come—he's come!" cried Charlotte Wilding. "I've won my bet!"

"There's another bunch higher up," murmured Clara Durrant, mounting another step of the ladder. Jacob held the ladder as she stretched out to reach the grapes high up on the vine.

"There!" she said, cutting through the stalk. She looked semi-transparent, pale, wonderfully beautiful up there among the vine leaves and the yellow and purple bunches, the lights swimming over her in coloured islands. Geraniums and begonias stood in pots along planks; tomatoes climbed the walls.

"The leaves really want thinning," she considered, and one green one, spread like the palm of a hand, circled down past Jacob's head.

"I have more than I can eat already," he said, looking up.

"It does seem absurd . . ." Clara began, "going back to London. . . ."

"Ridiculous," said Jacob, firmly.

"Then . . ." said Clara, "you must come next year, properly," she said, snipping another vine leaf, rather at random.

"If . . . if . . ."

A child ran past the greenhouse shouting. Clara slowly descended the ladder with her basket of grapes.

"One bunch of white, and two of purple," she said, and she placed two great leaves over them where they lay curled warm in the basket.

"I have enjoyed myself," said Jacob, looking down the greenhouse.

"Yes, it's been delightful," she said vaguely.

"Oh, Miss Durrant," he said, taking the basket of grapes; but she walked past him towards the door of the greenhouse.

"You're too good—too good," she thought, thinking of Jacob, thinking that he must not say that he loved her. No, no, no.

The children were whirling past the door, throwing things high into the air.

"Little demons!" she cried. "What have they got?" she asked Jacob.

"Onions, I think," said Jacob. He looked at them without moving.

"Next August, remember, Jacob," said Mrs. Durrant, shaking hands with him on the terrace where the fuchsia hung, like a scarlet ear-ring, behind her head. Mr. Wortley came out of the window in yellow slippers, trailing the Times and holding out his hand very cordially.

"Good-bye," said Jacob. "Good-bye," he repeated. "Good-bye," he said once more. Charlotte Wilding flung up her bedroom window and cried out: "Good-bye, Mr. Jacob!"

"Mr. Flanders!" cried Mr. Clutterbuck, trying to extricate himself from his beehive chair. "Jacob Flanders!"

"Too late, Joseph," said Mrs. Durrant.

"Not to sit for me," said Miss Eliot, planting her tripod upon the lawn.

5

"I rather think," said Jacob, taking his pipe from his mouth, "it's in Virgil," and pushing back his chair, he went to the window.

The rashest drivers in the world are, certainly, the drivers of post-office vans. Swinging down Lamb's Conduit Street, the scarlet van rounded the corner by the pillar box in such a way as to graze the kerb and make the little girl who was standing on tiptoe to post a letter look up, half frightened, half curious. She paused with her hand in the mouth of the box; then dropped her letter and ran away. It is seldom only that we see a child on tiptoe with pity—more often a dim discomfort, a grain of sand in the shoe which it's scarcely worth while to remove—that's our feeling, and so—Jacob turned to the bookcase.

Long ago great people lived here, and coming back from Court past midnight stood, huddling their satin skirts, under the carved door-posts while the footman roused himself from his mattress on the floor, hurriedly fastened the lower buttons of his waistcoat, and let them in. The bitter eighteenth-century rain rushed down the kennel. Southampton Row, however, is chiefly remarkable nowadays for the fact that you will always find a man there trying to sell a tortoise to a tailor. "Showing off the tweed, sir; what the gentry wants is something singular to catch the eye, sir—and clean in their habits, sir!" So they display their tortoises.

At Mudie's corner in Oxford Street all the red and blue beads had run together on the string. The motor omnibuses were locked. Mr. Spalding going to the city looked at Mr. Charles Budgeon bound for Shepherd's Bush. The proximity of the omnibuses gave the outside passengers an opportunity to stare into each other's faces. Yet few took advantage of it. Each had his own business to think of. Each had his past shut in him like the leaves of a book known to him by heart; and his friends could only read the title, James Spalding, or Charles Budgeon, and the passengers going the opposite way could read nothing at all—save "a man with a red moustache," "a young man in grey smoking a pipe." The October sunlight rested upon all these men and women sitting immobile; and little Johnnie Sturgeon took the chance to swing down the staircase, carrying his large mysterious parcel, and so dodging a zigzag course between the wheels he reached the pavement, started to whistle a tune and was soon out of sight—for ever. The omnibuses jerked on, and every single person felt relief at being a little nearer to his journey's end, though some cajoled themselves past the immediate engagement by promise of indulgence beyond—steak and kidney pudding, drink or a game of dominoes in the smoky corner of a city restaurant. Oh yes, human life is very tolerable on the top of an omnibus in Holborn, when the policeman holds up his arm and the sun beats on your back, and if there is such a thing as a shell secreted by man to fit man himself here we find it, on the banks of the Thames, where the great streets join and St. Paul's Cathedral, like the volute on the top of the snail shell, finishes it off. Jacob, getting off his omnibus, loitered up the steps, consulted his watch, and finally made up his mind to go in. . . . Does it need an effort? Yes. These changes of mood wear us out.

Dim it is, haunted by ghosts of white marble, to whom the organ for ever chaunts. If a boot creaks, it's awful; then the order; the discipline. The verger with his rod has life ironed out beneath him. Sweet and holy are the angelic choristers. And for ever round the marble shoulders, in and out of the folded fingers, go the thin high sounds of voice and organ. For ever requiem—repose. Tired with scrubbing the steps of the Prudential Society's office, which she did year in year out, Mrs. Lidgett took her seat beneath the great Duke's tomb, folded her hands, and half closed her eyes. A magnificent place for an old woman to rest in, by the very side of the great Duke's bones, whose victories mean nothing to her, whose name she knows not, though she never fails to greet the little angels opposite, as she passes out, wishing the like on her own tomb, for the leathern curtain of the heart has flapped wide, and out steal on tiptoe thoughts of rest, sweet melodies. . . . Old Spicer, jute merchant, thought nothing of the kind though. Strangely enough he'd never been in St. Paul's these fifty years, though his office windows looked on the churchyard. "So that's all? Well, a gloomy old place. . . . Where's Nelson's tomb? No time now—come again—a coin to leave in the box. . . . Rain or fine is it? Well, if it would only make up its mind!" Idly the children stray in—the verger dissuades them—and another and another . . . man, woman, man, woman, boy . . . casting their eyes up, pursing their lips, the same shadow brushing the same faces; the leathern curtain of the heart flaps wide.

Nothing could appear more certain from the steps of St. Paul's than that each person is miraculously provided with coat, skirt, and boots; an income; an object. Only Jacob, carrying in his hand Finlay's *Byzantine Empire,* which he had bought in Ludgate Hill, looked a little different; for in his hand he carried a book, which book he would at nine-thirty precisely, by his own fireside, open and study, as no one else of all these multitudes would do. They have no houses. The streets belong to them; the shops; the churches; theirs the innumerable desks; the stretched office lights; the vans are theirs, and the railway slung high above the street. If you look closer you will see that three elderly men at a little distance from each other run spiders along the pavement as if the street were their parlour, and here, against the wall, a woman stares at nothing, boot-laces extended, which she does not ask you to buy. The posters are theirs too; and the news on them. A town destroyed; a race won. A homeless people, circling beneath the sky whose blue or white is held off by a ceiling cloth of steel filings and horse dung shredded to dust.

There, under the green shade, with his head bent over white paper, Mr. Sibley transferred figures to folios, and upon each desk you observe, like provender, a bunch of papers, the day's nutriment, slowly consumed by the industrious pen. Innumerable overcoats of the quality prescribed hung empty all day in the corridors, but as the clock struck six each was exactly filled, and the little figures, split apart into trousers or moulded into a single thickness, jerked rapidly with angular forward motion along the pavement; then dropped into darkness. Beneath the pavement, sunk in the earth, hollow drains lined with yellow light for ever conveyed them this way and that, and large letters upon enamel plates represented in the underworld the parks, squares, and circuses of the upper. "Marble Arch—Shepherd's Bush"—to the majority the Arch and the Bush are eternally white letters upon a blue ground. Only at one point—it may be Acton, Holloway, Kensal Rise, Caledonian Road—does the name mean shops where you buy things, and houses, in one of which, down to the right, where the pollard trees grow out of the paving stones, there is a square curtained window, and a bedroom.

Long past sunset an old blind woman sat on a camp-stool with her back to the stone wall of the Union of London and Smith's Bank, clasping a brown mongrel tight in her arms and singing out loud, not for coppers, no, from the depths of her gay wild heart—her sinful, tanned heart—for the child who fetches her is the fruit of sin, and should have been in bed, curtained, asleep, instead of hearing in the lamplight her mother's wild song, where she sits against the Bank, singing not for coppers, with her dog against her breast.

Home they went. The grey church spires received them; the hoary city, old, sinful, and majestic. One behind another, round or pointed, piercing the sky or massing themselves, like sailing ships, like granite cliffs, spires and offices, wharves and factories crowd the bank; eternally the pilgrims trudge; barges rest in mid stream heavy laden; as some believe, the city loves her prostitutes.

But few, it seems, are admitted to that degree. Of all the carriages that leave the arch of the Opera House, not one turns eastward, and when the little thief is caught in the empty market-place no one in black-and-white or rose-coloured evening dress blocks the way by pausing with a hand upon the carriage door to help or condemn—though Lady Charles, to do her justice, sighs sadly as she ascends her staircase, takes down Thomas a Kempis, and does not sleep till her mind has lost itself tunnelling into the complexity of things. "Why? Why? Why?" she sighs. On the whole it's best to walk back from the Opera House. Fatigue is the safest sleeping draught.

The autumn season was in full swing. Tristan was twitching his rug up under his armpits twice a week; Isolde waved her scarf in miraculous sympathy with the conductor's baton. In all parts of the house were to be found pink faces and glittering breasts. When a Royal hand attached to an invisible body slipped out and withdrew the red and white bouquet reposing on the scarlet ledge, the Queen of England seemed a name worth dying for. Beauty, in its hothouse variety (which is none of the worst), flowered in box after box; and though nothing was said of profound importance, and though it is generally agreed that wit deserted beautiful lips about the time that Walpole died—at any rate when Victoria in her nightgown descended to meet her ministers, the lips (through an opera glass) remained red, adorable. Bald distinguished men with gold-headed canes strolled down the crimson avenues between the stalls, and only broke from intercourse with the boxes when the lights went down, and the conductor, first bowing to the Queen, next to the bald-headed men, swept round on his feet and raised his wand.

Then two thousand hearts in the semi-darkness remembered, anticipated, travelled dark labyrinths; and Clara Durrant said farewell to Jacob Flanders, and tasted the sweetness of death in effigy; and Mrs. Durrant, sitting behind her in the dark of the box, sighed her sharp sigh; and Mr. Wortley, shifting his position behind the Italian Ambassador's wife, thought that Brangaena was a trifle hoarse; and suspended in the gallery many feet above their heads, Edward Whittaker surreptitiously held a torch to his miniature score; and . . . and . . .

In short, the observer is choked with observations. Only to prevent us from being submerged by chaos, nature and society between them have arranged a system of classification which is simplicity itself; stalls, boxes, amphitheatre, gallery. The moulds are filled nightly. There is no need to distinguish details. But the difficulty remains—one has to choose. For though I have no wish to be Queen of England or only for a moment—I would willingly sit beside her; I would hear the Prime Minister's gossip; the countess whisper, and share her memories of halls and gardens; the massive fronts of the respectable conceal after all their secret code; or why so impermeable? And then, doffing one's own headpiece, how strange to assume for a moment some one's—any one's—to be a man of valour who has ruled the Empire; to refer while Brangaena sings to the fragments of Sophocles, or see in a flash, as the shepherd pipes his tune, bridges and aqueducts. But no—we must choose. Never was there a harsher necessity! or one which entails greater pain, more certain disaster; for wherever I seat myself, I die in exile: Whittaker in his lodging-house; Lady Charles at the Manor.

* * *

A young man with a Wellington nose, who had occupied a seven-and-sixpenny seat, made his way down the stone stairs when the opera ended, as if he were still set a little apart from his fellows by the influence of the music.

At midnight Jacob Flanders heard a rap on his door.

"By Jove!" he exclaimed. "You're the very man I want!" and without more ado they discovered the lines which he had been seeking all day; only they come not in Virgil, but in Lucretius.

"Yes; that should make him sit up," said Bonamy, as Jacob stopped reading. Jacob was excited. It was the first time he had read his essay aloud.

"Damned swine!" he said, rather too extravagantly; but the praise had gone to his head. Professor Bulteel, of Leeds, had issued an edition of Wycherley without stating that he had left out, disembowelled, or indicated only by asterisks, several indecent words and some indecent phrases. An outrage, Jacob said; a breach of faith; sheer prudery; token of a lewd mind and a disgusting nature. Aristophanes and Shakespeare were cited. Modern life was repudiated. Great play was made with the professional title, and Leeds as a seat of learning was laughed to scorn. And the extraordinary thing was that these young men were perfectly right—extraordinary, because, even as Jacob copied his pages, he knew that no one would ever print them; and sure enough back they came from the *Fortnightly*, the *Contemporary*, the *Nineteenth Century*—when Jacob threw them into the black wooden box where he kept his mother's letters, his old flannel trousers, and a note or two with the Cornish postmark. The lid shut upon the truth.

This black wooden box, upon which his name was still legible in white paint, stood between the long windows of the sitting-room. The street ran beneath. No doubt the bedroom was behind. The furniture—three wicker chairs and a gate-legged table—came from Cambridge. These houses (Mrs. Garfit's daughter, Mrs. Whitehorn, was the landlady of this one) were built, say, a hundred and fifty years ago. The rooms are shapely, the ceilings high; over the doorway a rose, or a ram's skull, is carved in the wood. The eighteenth century has its distinction. Even the panels, painted in raspberry-coloured paint, have their distinction. . . .

"Distinction"—Mrs. Durrant said that Jacob Flanders was "distinguished-looking." "Extremely awkward," she said, "but so distinguished-looking." Seeing him for the first time that no doubt is the word for him. Lying back in his chair, taking his pipe from his lips, and saying to Bonamy: "About this opera now" (for they had done with indecency). "This fellow Wagner" . . . distinction was one of the words to use naturally, though, from looking at him, one would have found it difficult to say which seat in the opera house was his, stalls, gallery, or dress circle. A writer? He lacked self-consciousness. A painter? There was something in the shape of his hands (he was descended on his mother's side from a family of the greatest antiquity and deepest obscurity) which indicated taste. Then his mouth—but surely, of all futile occupations this of cataloguing features is the worst. One word is sufficient. But if one cannot find it?

"I like Jacob Flanders," wrote Clara Durrant in her diary. "He is so unworldly. He gives himself no airs, and one can say what one likes to him, though he's frightening because . . ." But Mr. Letts allows little space in his shilling diaries. Clara was not the one to encroach upon Wednesday. Humblest, most candid of women! "No, no, no," she sighed, standing at the greenhouse door, "don't break—don't spoil"—what? Something infinitely wonderful.

But then, this is only a young woman's language, one, too, who loves, or refrains from loving. She wished the moment to continue for ever precisely as it was that July morning. And moments don't. Now, for instance, Jacob was telling a story about some walking tour he'd taken, and the inn was called "The Foaming Pot," which, considering the landlady's name . . . They shouted with laughter. The joke was indecent.

Then Julia Eliot said "the silent young man," and as she dined with Prime Ministers, no doubt she meant: "If he is going to get on in the world, he will have to find his tongue."

Timothy Durrant never made any comment at all.

The housemaid found herself very liberally rewarded.

Mr. Sopwith's opinion was as sentimental as Clara's, though far more skilfully expressed.

Betty Flanders was romantic about Archer and tender about John; she was unreasonably irritated by Jacob's clumsiness in the house.

Captain Barfoot liked him best of the boys; but as for saying why . . .

It seems then that men and women are equally at fault. It seems that a profound, impartial, and absolutely just opinion of our fellow-creatures is utterly unknown. Either we are men, or we are women. Either we are cold, or we are sentimental. Either we are young, or growing old. In any case life is but a procession of shadows, and God knows why it is that we embrace them so eagerly, and see them depart with such anguish, being shadows. And why, if this—and much more than this is true, why are we yet surprised in the window corner by a sudden vision that the young man in the chair is of all things in the world the most real, the most solid, the best known to us—why indeed? For the moment after we know nothing about him.

Such is the manner of our seeing. Such the conditions of our love.

* * *

("I'm twenty-two. It's nearly the end of October. Life is thoroughly pleasant, although unfortunately there are a great number of fools about. One must apply oneself to something or other—God knows what. Everything is really very jolly—except getting up in the morning and wearing a tail coat.")

"I say, Bonamy, what about Beethoven?"

("Bonamy is an amazing fellow. He knows practically everything—not more about English literature than I do—but then he's read all those Frenchmen.")

"I rather suspect you're talking rot, Bonamy. In spite of what you say, poor old Tennyson. . . ."

("The truth is one ought to have been taught French. Now, I suppose, old Barfoot is talking to my mother. That's an odd affair to be sure. But I can't see Bonamy down there. Damn London!") for the market carts were lumbering down the street.

"What about a walk on Saturday?"

("What's happening on Saturday?")

Then, taking out his pocket-book, he assured himself that the night of the Durrants' party came next week.

But though all this may very well be true—so Jacob thought and spoke—so he crossed his legs—filled his pipe—sipped his whisky, and once looked at his pocket-book, rumpling his hair as he did so, there remains over something which can never be conveyed to a second person save by Jacob himself. Moreover, part of this is not Jacob but Richard Bonamy—the room; the market carts; the hour; the very moment of history. Then consider the effect of sex—how between man and woman it hangs wavy, tremulous, so that here's a valley, there's a peak, when in truth, perhaps, all's as flat as my hand. Even the exact words get the wrong accent on them. But something is always impelling one to hum vibrating, like the hawk moth, at the mouth of the cavern of mystery, endowing Jacob Flanders with all sorts of qualities he had not at all—for though, certainly, he sat talking to Bonamy, half of what he said was too dull to repeat; much unintelligible (about unknown people and Parliament); what remains is mostly a matter of guess work. Yet over him we hang vibrating.

"Yes," said Captain Barfoot, knocking out his pipe on Betty Flanders's hob, and buttoning his coat. "It doubles the work, but I don't mind that."

He was now town councillor. They looked at the night, which was the same as the London night, only a good deal more transparent. Church bells down in the town were striking eleven o'clock. The wind was off the sea. And all the bedroom windows were dark—the Pages were asleep; the Garfits were asleep; the Cranches were asleep—whereas in London at this hour they were burning Guy Fawkes on Parliament Hill.

6

The flames had fairly caught.

"There's St. Paul's!" some one cried.

As the wood caught the city of London was lit up for a second; on other sides of the fire there were trees. Of the faces which came out fresh and vivid as though painted in yellow and red, the most prominent was a girl's face. By a trick of the firelight she seemed to have no body. The oval of the face and hair hung beside the fire with a dark vacuum for background. As if dazed by the glare, her green-blue eyes stared at the flames. Every muscle of her face was taut. There was something tragic in her thus staring—her age between twenty and twenty-five.

A hand descending from the chequered darkness thrust on her head the conical white hat of a pierrot. Shaking her head, she still stared. A whiskered face appeared above her. They dropped two legs of a table upon the fire and a scattering of twigs and leaves. All this blazed up and showed faces far back, round, pale, smooth, bearded, some with billycock hats on; all intent; showed too St. Paul's floating on the uneven white mist, and two or three narrow, paper-white, extinguisher-shaped spires.

The flames were struggling through the wood and roaring up when, goodness knows where from, pails flung water in beautiful hollow shapes, as of polished tortoiseshell; flung again and again; until the hiss was like a swarm of bees; and all the faces went out.

"Oh Jacob," said the girl, as they pounded up the hill in the dark, "I'm so frightfully unhappy!"

Shouts of laughter came from the others—high, low; some before, others after.

The hotel dining-room was brightly lit. A stag's head in plaster was at one end of the table; at the other some Roman bust blackened and reddened to represent Guy Fawkes, whose night it was. The diners were linked together by lengths of paper roses, so that when it came to singing "Auld Lang Syne" with their hands crossed a pink and yellow line rose and fell the entire length of the table. There was an enormous tapping of green wine-glasses. A young man stood up, and Florinda, taking one of the purplish globes that lay on the table, flung it straight at his head. It crushed to powder.

"I'm so frightfully unhappy!" she said, turning to Jacob, who sat beside her.

The table ran, as if on invisible legs, to the side of the room, and a barrel organ decorated with a red cloth and two pots of paper flowers reeled out waltz music.

Jacob could not dance. He stood against the wall smoking a pipe.

"We think," said two of the dancers, breaking off from the rest, and bowing profoundly before him, "that you are the most beautiful man we have ever seen."

So they wreathed his head with paper flowers. Then somebody brought out a white and gilt chair and made him sit on it. As they passed, people hung glass grapes on his shoulders, until he looked like the figure-head of a wrecked ship. Then Florinda got upon his knee and hid her face in his waistcoat. With one hand he held her; with the other, his pipe.

"Now let us talk," said Jacob, as he walked down Haverstock Hill between four and five o'clock in the morning of November the sixth arm-in-arm with Timmy Durrant, "about something sensible."

The Greeks—yes, that was what they talked about—how when all's said and done, when one's rinsed one's mouth with every literature in the world, including Chinese and Russian (but these Slavs aren't civilized), it's the flavour of Greek that remains. Durrant quoted Aeschylus—Jacob Sophocles. It is true that no Greek could have understood or professor refrained from pointing out—Never mind; what is Greek for if not to be shouted on Haverstock Hill in the dawn? Moreover, Durrant never listened to Sophocles, nor Jacob to Aeschylus. They were boastful, triumphant; it seemed to both that they had read every book in the world; known every sin, passion, and joy. Civilizations stood round them like flowers ready for picking. Ages lapped at their feet like waves fit for sailing. And surveying all this, looming through the fog, the lamplight, the shades of London, the two young men decided in favour of Greece.

"Probably," said Jacob, "we are the only people in the world who know what the Greeks meant."

They drank coffee at a stall where the urns were burnished and little lamps burnt along the counter.

Taking Jacob for a military gentleman, the stall-keeper told him about his boy at Gibraltar, and Jacob cursed the British army and praised the Duke of Wellington. So on again they went down the hill talking about the Greeks.

A strange thing—when you come to think of it—this love of Greek, flourishing in such obscurity, distorted, discouraged, yet leaping out, all of a sudden, especially on leaving crowded rooms, or after a surfeit of print, or when the moon floats among the waves of the hills, or in hollow, sallow, fruitless London days, like a specific; a clean blade; always a miracle. Jacob knew no more Greek than served him to stumble through a play. Of ancient history he knew nothing. However, as he tramped into London it seemed to him that they were making the flagstones ring on the road to the Acropolis, and that if Socrates saw them coming he would bestir himself and say "my fine fellows," for the whole sentiment of Athens was entirely after his heart; free, venturesome, high-spirited. . . . She had called him Jacob without asking his leave. She had sat upon his knee. Thus did all good women in the days of the Greeks.

At this moment there shook out into the air a wavering, quavering, doleful lamentation which seemed to lack strength to unfold itself, and yet flagged on; at the sound of which doors in back streets burst sullenly open; workmen stumped forth.

Florinda was sick.

Mrs. Durrant, sleepless as usual, scored a mark by the side of certain lines in the *Inferno.*

Clara slept buried in her pillows; on her dressing-table dishevelled roses and a pair of long white gloves.

Still wearing the conical white hat of a pierrot, Florinda was sick.

The bedroom seemed fit for these catastrophes—cheap, mustard-coloured, half attic, half studio, curiously ornamented with silver paper stars, Welshwomen's hats, and rosaries pendent from the gas brackets. As for Florinda's story, her name had been bestowed upon her by a painter who had wished it to signify that the flower of her maidenhood was still unplucked. Be that as it may, she was without a surname, and for parents had only the photograph of a tombstone beneath which, she said, her father lay buried. Sometimes she would dwell upon the size of it, and rumour had it that Florinda's father had died from the growth of his bones which nothing could stop; just as her mother enjoyed the confidence of a Royal master, and now and again Florinda herself was a Princess, but chiefly when drunk. Thus deserted, pretty into the bargain, with tragic eyes and the lips of a child, she talked more about virginity than women mostly do; and had lost it only the night before, or cherished it beyond the heart in her breast, according to the man she talked to. But did she always talk to men? No, she had her confidante: Mother Stuart. Stuart, as the lady would point out, is the name of a Royal house; but what that signified, and what her business way, no one knew; only that Mrs. Stuart got postal orders every Monday morning, kept a parrot, believed in the transmigration of souls, and could read the future in tea leaves. Dirty lodging-house wallpaper she was behind the chastity of Florinda.

Now Florinda wept, and spent the day wandering the streets; stood at Chelsea watching the river swim past; trailed along the shopping streets; opened her bag and powdered her cheeks in omnibuses; read love letters, propping them against the milk pot in the A.B.C. shop; detected glass in the sugar bowl; accused the waitress of wishing to poison her; declared that young men stared at her; and found herself towards evening slowly sauntering down Jacob's street, when it struck her that she liked that man Jacob better than dirty Jews, and sitting at his table (he was copying his essay upon the Ethics of Indecency), drew off her gloves and told him how Mother Stuart had banged her on the head with the tea-cosy.

Jacob took her word for it that she was chaste. She prattled, sitting by the fireside, of famous painters. The tomb of her father was mentioned. Wild and frail and beautiful she looked, and thus the women of the Greeks were, Jacob thought; and this was life; and himself a man and Florinda chaste.

She left with one of Shelley's poems beneath her arm. Mrs. Stuart, she said, often talked of him.

Marvellous are the innocent. To believe that the girl herself transcends all lies (for Jacob was not such a fool as to believe implicitly), to wonder enviously at the unanchored life—his own seeming petted and even cloistered in comparison—to have at hand as sovereign specifics for all disorders of the soul Adonais and the plays of Shakespeare; to figure out a comradeship all spirited on her side, protective on his, yet equal on both, for women, thought Jacob, are just the same as men—innocence such as this is marvellous enough, and perhaps not so foolish after all.

For when Florinda got home that night she first washed her head; then ate chocolate creams; then opened Shelley. True, she was horribly bored. What on earth was it *about?* She had to wager with herself that she would turn the page before she ate another. In fact she slept. But then her day had been a long one, Mother Stuart had thrown the tea-cosy—there are formidable sights in the streets, and though Florinda was ignorant as an owl, and would never learn to read even her love letters correctly, still she had her feelings, liked some men better than others, and was entirely at the beck and call of life. Whether or not she was a virgin seems a matter of no importance whatever. Unless, indeed, it is the only thing of any importance at all.

Jacob was restless when she left him.

All night men and women seethed up and down the well-known beats. Late home-comers could see shadows against the blinds even in the most respectable suburbs. Not a square in snow or fog lacked its amorous couple. All plays turned on the same subject. Bullets went through heads in hotel bedrooms almost nightly on that account. When the body escaped mutilation, seldom did the heart go to the grave unscarred. Little else was talked of in theatres and popular novels. Yet we say it is a matter of no importance at all.

What with Shakespeare and Adonais, Mozart and Bishop Berkeley—choose whom you like—the fact is concealed and the evenings for most of us pass reputably, or with only the sort of tremor that a snake makes sliding through the grass. But then concealment by itself distracts the mind from the print and the sound. If Florinda had had a mind, she might have read with clearer eyes than we can. She and her sort have solved the question by turning it to a trifle of washing the hands nightly before going to bed, the only difficulty being whether you prefer your water hot or cold, which being settled, the mind can go about its business unassailed.

But it did occur to Jacob, half-way through dinner, to wonder whether she had a mind.

They sat at a little table in the restaurant.

Florinda leant the points of her elbows on the table and held her chin in the cup of her hands. Her cloak had slipped behind her. Gold and white with bright beads on her she emerged, her face flowering from her body, innocent, scarcely tinted, the eyes gazing frankly about her, or slowly settling on Jacob and resting there. She talked:

"You know that big black box the Australian left in my room ever so long ago? . . . I do think furs make a woman look old. . . . That's Bechstein come in now. . . . I was wondering what you looked like when you were a little boy, Jacob." She nibbled her roll and looked at him.

"Jacob. You're like one of those statues. . . . I think there are lovely things in the British Museum, don't you? Lots of lovely things . . ." she spoke dreamily. The room was filling; the heat increasing. Talk in a restaurant is dazed sleep-walkers' talk, so many things to look at—so much noise—other people talking. Can one overhear? Oh, but they mustn't overhear *us.*

"That's like Ellen Nagle—that girl . . ." and so on.

"I'm awfully happy since I've known you, Jacob. You're such a *good* man."

The room got fuller and fuller; talk louder; knives more clattering.

"Well, you see what makes her say things like that is . . ."

She stopped. So did every one.

"Tomorrow . . . Sunday . . . a beastly . . . you tell me . . . go then!" Crash! And out she swept.

It was at the table next them that the voice spun higher and higher. Suddenly the woman dashed the plates to the floor. The man was left there. Everybody stared. Then—"Well, poor chap, we mustn't sit staring. What a go! Did you hear what she said? By God, he looks a fool! Didn't come up to the scratch, I suppose. All the mustard on the tablecloth. The waiters laughing."

Jacob observed Florinda. In her face there seemed to him something horribly brainless—as she sat staring.

Out she swept, the black woman with the dancing feather in her hat.

Yet she had to go somewhere. The night is not a tumultuous black ocean in which you sink or sail as a star. As a matter of fact it was a wet November night. The lamps of Soho made large greasy spots of light upon the pavement. The by-streets were dark enough to shelter man or woman leaning against the doorways. One detached herself as Jacob and Florinda approached.

"She's dropped her glove," said Florinda.

Jacob, pressing forward, gave it her.

Effusively she thanked him; retraced her steps; dropped her glove again. But why? For whom? Meanwhile, where had the other woman got to? And the man?

The street lamps do not carry far enough to tell us. The voices, angry, lustful, despairing, passionate, were scarcely more than the voices of caged beasts at night. Only they are not caged, nor beasts. Stop a man; ask him the way; he'll tell it you; but one's afraid to ask him the way. What does one fear?—the human eye. At once the pavement narrows, the chasm deepens. There! They've melted into it—both man and woman. Further on, blatantly advertising its meritorious solidity, a boarding-house exhibits behind uncurtained windows its testimony to the soundness of London. There they sit, plainly illuminated, dressed like ladies and gentlemen, in bamboo chairs. The widows of business men prove laboriously that they are related to judges. The wives of coal merchants instantly retort that their fathers kept coachmen. A servant brings coffee, and the crochet basket has to be moved. And so on again into the dark, passing a girl here for sale, or there an old woman with only matches to offer, passing the crowd from the Tube station, the women with veiled hair, passing at length no one but shut doors, carved door-posts, and a solitary policeman, Jacob, with Florinda on his arm, reached his room and, lighting the lamp, said nothing at all.

"I don't like you when you look like that," said Florinda.

The problem is insoluble. The body is harnessed to a brain. Beauty goes hand in hand with stupidity. There she sat staring at the fire as she had stared at the broken mustard-pot. In spite of defending indecency, Jacob doubted whether he liked it in the raw. He had a violent reversion towards male society, cloistered rooms, and the works of the classics; and was ready to turn with wrath upon whoever it was who had fashioned life thus.

Then Florinda laid her hand upon his knee.

After all, it was none of her fault. But the thought saddened him. It's not catastrophes, murders, deaths, diseases, that age and kill us; it's the way people look and laugh, and run up the steps of omnibuses.

Any excuse, though, serves a stupid woman. He told her his head ached.

But when she looked at him, dumbly, half-guessing, half-understanding, apologizing perhaps, anyhow saying as he had said, "It's none of my fault," straight and beautiful in body, her face like a shell within its cap, then he knew that cloisters and classics are no use whatever. The problem is insoluble.

7

About this time a firm of merchants having dealings with the East put on the market little paper flowers which opened on touching water. As it was the custom also to use finger-bowls at the end of dinner, the new discovery was found of excellent service. In these sheltered lakes the little coloured flowers swam and slid; surmounted smooth slippery waves, and sometimes foundered and lay like pebbles on the glass floor. Their fortunes were watched by eyes intent and lovely. It is surely a great discovery that leads to the union of hearts and foundation of homes. The paper flowers did no less.

It must not be thought, though, that they ousted the flowers of nature. Roses, lilies, carnations in particular, looked over the rims of vases and surveyed the bright lives and swift dooms of their artificial relations. Mr. Stuart Ormond made this very observation; and charming it was thought; and Kitty Craster married him on the strength of it six months later. But real flowers can never be dispensed with. If they could, human life would be a different affair altogether. For flowers fade; chrysanthemums are the worst; perfect over night; yellow and jaded next morning—not fit to be seen. On the whole, though the price is sinful, carnations pay best—it's a question, however, whether it's wise to have them wired. Some shops advise it. Certainly it's the only way to keep them at a dance; but whether it is necessary at dinner parties, unless the rooms are very hot, remains in dispute. Old Mrs. Temple used to recommend an ivy leaf—just one—dropped into the bowl. She said it kept the water pure for days and days. But there is some reason to think that old Mrs. Temple was mistaken.

The little cards, however, with names engraved on them, are a more serious problem than the flowers. More horses' legs have been worn out, more coachmen's lives consumed, more hours of sound afternoon time vainly lavished than served to win us the battle of Waterloo, and pay for it into the bargain. The little demons are the source of as many reprieves, calamities, and anxieties as the battle itself. Sometimes Mrs. Bonham has just gone out; at others she is at home. But, even if the cards should be superseded, which seems unlikely, there are unruly powers blowing life into storms, disordering sedulous mornings, and uprooting the stability of the afternoon—dressmakers, that is to say, and confectioners' shops. Six yards of silk will cover one body; but if you have to devise six hundred shapes for it, and twice as many colours?—in the middle of which there is the urgent question of the pudding with tufts of green cream and battlements of almond paste. It has not arrived.

The flamingo hours fluttered softly through the sky. But regularly they dipped their wings in pitch black; Notting Hill, for instance, or the purlieus of Clerkenwell. No wonder that Italian remained a hidden art, and the piano always played the same sonata. In order to buy one pair of elastic stockings for Mrs. Page, widow, aged sixty-three, in receipt of five shillings out-door relief, and help from her only son employed in Messrs. Mackie's dye-works, suffering in winter with his chest, letters must be written, columns filled up in the same round, simple hand that wrote in Mr. Letts's diary how the weather was fine, the children demons, and Jacob Flanders unworldly. Clara Durrant procured the stockings, played the sonata, filled the vases, fetched the pudding, left the cards, and when the great invention of paper flowers to swim in finger-bowls was discovered, was one of those who most marvelled at their brief lives.

Nor were there wanting poets to celebrate the theme. Edwin Mallett, for example, wrote his verses ending:

And read their doom in Chloe's eyes,

which caused Clara to blush at the first reading, and to laugh at the second, saying that it was just like him to call her Chloe when her name was Clara. Ridiculous young man! But when, between ten and eleven on a rainy morning, Edwin Mallett laid his life at her feet she ran out of the room and hid herself in her bedroom, and Timothy below could not get on with his work all that morning on account of her sobs.

"Which is the result of enjoying yourself," said Mrs. Durrant severely, surveying the dance programme all scored with the same initials, or rather they were different ones this time—R.B. instead of E.M.; Richard Bonamy it was now, the young man with the Wellington nose.

"But I could never marry a man with a nose like that," said Clara.

"Nonsense," said Mrs. Durrant.

"But I am too severe," she thought to herself. For Clara, losing all vivacity, tore up her dance programme and threw it in the fender.

Such were the very serious consequences of the invention of paper flowers to swim in bowls.

"Please," said Julia Eliot, taking up her position by the curtain almost opposite the door, "don't introduce me. I like to look on. The amusing thing," she went on, addressing Mr. Salvin, who, owing to his lameness, was accommodated with a chair, "the amusing thing about a party is to watch the people—coming and going, coming and going."

"Last time we met," said Mr. Salvin, "was at the Farquhars. Poor lady! She has much to put up with."

"Doesn't she look charming?" exclaimed Miss Eliot, as Clara Durrant passed them.

"And which of them . . . ?" asked Mr. Salvin, dropping his voice and speaking in quizzical tones.

"There are so many . . ." Miss Eliot replied. Three young men stood at the doorway looking about for their hostess.

"You don't remember Elizabeth as I do," said Mr. Salvin, "dancing Highland reels at Banchorie. Clara lacks her mother's spirit. Clara is a little pale."

"What different people one sees here!" said Miss Eliot.

"Happily we are not governed by the evening papers," said Mr. Salvin.

"I never read them," said Miss Eliot. "I know nothing about politics," she added.

"The piano is in tune," said Clara, passing them, "but we may have to ask some one to move it for us."

"Are they going to dance?" asked Mr. Salvin.

"Nobody shall disturb you," said Mrs. Durrant peremptorily as she passed.

"Julia Eliot. It *is* Julia Eliot!" said old Lady Hibbert, holding out both her hands. "And Mr. Salvin. What is going to happen to us, Mr. Salvin? With all my experience of English politics—My dear, I was thinking of your father last night—one of my oldest friends, Mr. Salvin. Never tell me that girls often are incapable of love! I had all Shakespeare by heart before I was in my teens, Mr. Salvin!"

"You don't say so," said Mr. Salvin.

"But I do," said Lady Hibbert.

* * *

"Oh, Mr. Salvin, I'm so sorry. . . ."

"I will remove myself if you'll kindly lend me a hand," said Mr. Salvin.

"You shall sit by my mother," said Clara. "Everybody seems to come in here. . . . Mr. Calthorp, let me introduce you to Miss Edwards."

"Are you going away for Christmas?" said Mr. Calthorp.

"If my brother gets his leave," said Miss Edwards.

"What regiment is he in?" said Mr. Calthorp.

"The Twentieth Hussars," said Miss Edwards.

"Perhaps he knows my brother?" said Mr. Calthorp.

"I am afraid I did not catch your name," said Miss Edwards.

"Calthorp," said Mr. Calthorp.

"But what proof was there that the marriage service was actually performed?" said Mr. Crosby.

"There is no reason to doubt that Charles James Fox . . ." Mr. Burley began; but here Mrs. Stretton told him that she knew his sister well; had stayed with her not six weeks ago; and thought the house charming, but bleak in winter.

"Going about as girls do nowadays—" said Mrs. Forster.

Mr. Bowley looked round him, and catching sight of Rose Shaw moved towards her, threw out his hands, and exclaimed: "Well!"

"Nothing!" she replied. "Nothing at all—though I left them alone the entire afternoon on purpose."

"Dear me, dear me," said Mr. Bowley. "I will ask Jimmy to breakfast."

"But who could resist her?" cried Rose Shaw. "Dearest Clara—I know we mustn't try to stop you . . ."

"You and Mr. Bowley are talking dreadful gossip, I know," said Clara.

"Life is wicked—life is detestable!" cried Rose Shaw.

"There's not much to be said for this sort of thing, is there?" said Timothy Durrant to Jacob.

"Women like it."

"Like what?" said Charlotte Wilding, coming up to them.

"Where have you come from?" said Timothy. "Dining somewhere, I suppose."

"I don't see why not," said Charlotte.

"People must go downstairs," said Clara, passing. "Take Charlotte, Timothy. How d'you do, Mr. Flanders."

"How d'you do, Mr. Flanders," said Julia Eliot, holding out her hand. "What's been happening to you?"

Who is Silvia? what is she?
That all our swains commend her?

sang Elsbeth Siddons.

Every one stood where they were, or sat down if a chair was empty.

"Ah," sighed Clara, who stood beside Jacob, half-way through.

Then to Silvia let us sing,
That Silvia is excelling;
She excels each mortal thing
Upon the dull earth dwelling.
To her let us garlands bring,

sang Elsbeth Siddons.

"Ah!" Clara exclaimed out loud, and clapped her gloved hands; and Jacob clapped his bare ones; and then she moved forward and directed people to come in from the doorway.

"You are living in London?" asked Miss Julia Eliot.

"Yes," said Jacob.

"In rooms?"

"Yes."

"There is Mr. Clutterbuck. You always see Mr. Clutterbuck here. He is not very happy at home, I am afraid. They say that Mrs. Clutterbuck . . ." she dropped her voice. "That's why he stays with the Durrants. Were you there when they acted Mr. Wortley's play? Oh, no, of course not—at the last moment, did you hear—you had to go to join your mother, I remember, at Harrogate—At the last moment, as I was saying, just as everything was ready, the clothes finished and everything—Now Elsbeth is going to sing again. Clara is playing her accompaniment or turning over for Mr. Carter, I think. No, Mr. Carter is playing by himself—This is *Bach*," she whispered, as Mr. Carter played the first bars.

"Are you fond of music?" said Mrs. Durrant.

"Yes. I like hearing it," said Jacob. "I know nothing about it."

"Very few people do that," said Mrs. Durrant. "I daresay you were never taught. Why is that, Sir Jasper?—Sir Jasper Bigham—Mr. Flanders. Why is nobody taught anything that they ought to know, Sir Jasper?" She left them standing against the wall.

Neither of the gentlemen said anything for three minutes, though Jacob shifted perhaps five inches to the left, and then as many to the right. Then Jacob grunted, and suddenly crossed the room.

"Will you come and have something to eat?" he said to Clara Durrant.

"Yes, an ice. Quickly. Now," she said.

Downstairs they went.

But half-way down they met Mr. and Mrs. Gresham, Herbert Turner, Sylvia Rashleigh, and a friend, whom they had dared to bring, from America, "knowing that Mrs. Durrant—wishing to show Mr. Pilcher—Mr. Pilcher from New York—This is Miss Durrant."

"Whom I have heard so much of," said Mr. Pilcher, bowing low.

So Clara left him.

8

About half-past nine Jacob left the house, his door slamming, other doors slamming, buying his paper, mounting his omnibus, or, weather permitting, walking his road as other people do. Head bent down, a desk, a telephone, books bound in green leather, electric light. . . . "Fresh coals, sir?" . . . "Your tea, sir." . . . Talk about football, the Hotspurs, the Harlequins; six-thirty Star brought in by the office boy; the rooks of Gray's Inn passing overhead; branches in the fog thin and brittle; and through the roar of traffic now and again a voice shouting: "Verdict—verdict—winner—winner," while letters accumulate in a basket, Jacob signs them, and each evening finds him, as he takes his coat down, with some muscle of the brain new stretched.

Then, sometimes a game of chess; or pictures in Bond Street, or a long way home to take the air with Bonamy on his arm, meditatively marching, head thrown back, the world a spectacle, the early moon above the steeples coming in for praise, the sea-gulls flying high, Nelson on his column surveying the horizon, and the world our ship.

Meanwhile, poor Betty Flanders's letter, having caught the second post, lay on the hall table—poor Betty Flanders writing her son's name, Jacob Alan Flanders, Esq., as mothers do, and the ink pale, profuse, suggesting how mothers down at Scarborough scribble over the fire with their feet on the fender, when tea's cleared away, and can never, never say, whatever it may be—probably this—Don't go with bad women, do be a good boy; wear your thick shirts; and come back, come back, come back to me.

But she said nothing of the kind. "Do you remember old Miss Wargrave, who used to be so kind when you had the whooping-cough?" she wrote; "she's dead at last, poor thing. They would like it if you wrote. Ellen came over and we spent a nice day shopping. Old Mouse gets very stiff, and we have to walk him up the smallest hill. Rebecca, at last, after I don't know how long, went into Mr. Adamson's. Three teeth, he says, must come out. Such mild weather for the time of year, the little buds actually on the pear trees. And Mrs. Jarvis tells me—" Mrs. Flanders liked Mrs. Jarvis, always said of her that she was too good for such a quiet place, and, though she never listened to her discontent and told her at the end of it (looking up, sucking her thread, or taking off her spectacles) that a little peat wrapped round the iris roots keeps them from the frost, and Parrot's great white sale is Tuesday next, "do remember,"—Mrs. Flanders knew precisely how Mrs. Jarvis felt; and how interesting her letters were, about Mrs. Jarvis, could one read them year in, year out—the unpublished works of women, written by the fireside in pale profusion, dried by the flame, for the blotting-paper's worn to holes and the nib cleft and clotted. Then Captain Barfoot. Him she called "the Captain," spoke of frankly, yet never without reserve. The Captain was enquiring for her about Garfit's acre; advised chickens; could promise profit; or had the sciatica; or Mrs. Barfoot had been indoors for weeks; or the Captain says things look bad, politics that is, for as Jacob knew, the Captain would sometimes talk, as the evening waned, about Ireland or India; and then Mrs. Flanders would fall musing about Morty, her brother, lost all these years—had the natives got him, was his ship sunk—would the Admiralty tell her?—the Captain knocking his pipe out, as Jacob knew, rising to go, stiffly stretching to pick up Mrs. Flanders's wool which had rolled beneath the chair. Talk of the chicken farm came back and back, the women, even at fifty, impulsive at heart, sketching on the cloudy future flocks of Leghorns, Cochin Chinas, Orpingtons; like Jacob in the blur of her outline; but powerful as he was; fresh and vigorous, running about the house, scolding Rebecca.

The letter lay upon the hall table; Florinda coming in that night took it up with her, put it on the table as she kissed Jacob, and Jacob seeing the hand, left it there under the lamp, between the biscuit-tin and the tobacco-box. They shut the bedroom door behind them.

The sitting-room neither knew nor cared. The door was shut; and to suppose that wood, when it creaks, transmits anything save that rats are busy and wood dry is childish. These old houses are only brick and wood, soaked in human sweat, grained with human dirt. But if the pale blue envelope lying by the biscuit-box had the feelings of a mother, the heart was torn by the little creak, the sudden stir. Behind the door was the obscene thing, the alarming presence, and terror would come over her as at death, or the birth of a child. Better, perhaps, burst in and face it than sit in the antechamber listening to the little creak, the sudden stir, for her heart was swollen, and pain threaded it. My son, my son—such would be her cry, uttered to hide her vision of him stretched with Florinda, inexcusable, irrational, in a woman with three children living at Scarborough.

And the fault lay with Florinda. Indeed, when the door opened and the couple came out, Mrs. Flanders would have flounced upon her—only it was Jacob who came first, in his dressing-gown, amiable, authoritative, beautifully healthy, like a baby after an airing, with an eye clear as running water. Florinda followed, lazily stretching; yawning a little; arranging her hair at the looking-glass—while Jacob read his mother's letter.

Let us consider letters—how they come at breakfast, and at night, with their yellow stamps and their green stamps, immortalized by the postmark—for to see one's own envelope on another's table is to realize how soon deeds sever and become alien. Then at last the power of the mind to quit the body is manifest, and perhaps we fear or hate or wish annihilated this phantom of ourselves, lying on the table. Still, there are letters that merely say how dinner's at seven; others ordering coal; making appointments. The hand in them is scarcely perceptible, let alone the voice or the scowl. Ah, but when the post knocks and the letter comes always the miracle seems repeated—speech attempted. Venerable are letters, infinitely brave, forlorn, and lost.

Life would split asunder without them. "Come to tea, come to dinner, what's the truth of the story? have you heard the news? life in the capital is gay; the Russian dancers. . . ." These are our stays and props. These lace our days together and make of life a perfect globe. And yet, and yet . . . when we go to dinner, when pressing finger-tips we hope to meet somewhere soon, a doubt insinuates itself; is this the way to spend our days? the rare, the limited, so soon dealt out to us—drinking tea? dining out? And the notes accumulate. And the telephones ring. And everywhere we go wires and tubes surround us to carry the voices that try to penetrate before the last card is dealt and the days are over. "Try to penetrate," for as we lift the cup, shake the hand, express the hope, something whispers, Is this all? Can I never know, share, be certain? Am I doomed all my days to write letters, send voices, which fall upon the tea-table, fade upon the passage, making appointments, while life dwindles, to come and dine? Yet letters are venerable; and the telephone valiant, for the journey is a lonely one, and if bound together by notes and telephones we went in company, perhaps—who knows?—we might talk by the way.

Well, people have tried. Byron wrote letters. So did Cowper. For centuries the writing-desk has contained sheets fit precisely for the communications of friends. Masters of language, poets of long ages, have turned from the sheet that endures to the sheet that perishes, pushing aside the tea-tray, drawing close to the fire (for letters are written when the dark presses round a bright red cave), and addressed themselves to the task of reaching, touching, penetrating the individual heart. Were it possible! But words have been used too often; touched and turned, and left exposed to the dust of the street. The words we seek hang close to the tree. We come at dawn and find them sweet beneath the leaf.

Mrs. Flanders wrote letters; Mrs. Jarvis wrote them; Mrs. Durrant too; Mother Stuart actually scented her pages, thereby adding a flavour which the English language fails to provide; Jacob had written in his day long letters about art, morality, and politics to young men at college. Clara Durrant's letters were those of a child. Florinda—the impediment between Florinda and her pen was something impassable. Fancy a butterfly, gnat, or other winged insect, attached to a twig which, clogged with mud, it rolls across a page. Her spelling was abominable. Her sentiments infantile. And for some reason when she wrote she declared her belief in God. Then there were crosses—tear stains; and the hand itself rambling and redeemed only by the fact—which always did redeem Florinda—by the fact that she cared. Yes, whether it was for chocolate creams, hot baths, the shape of her face in the looking-glass, Florinda could no more pretend a feeling than swallow whisky. Incontinent was her rejection. Great men are truthful, and these little prostitutes, staring in the fire, taking out a powder-puff, decorating lips at an inch of looking-glass, have (so Jacob thought) an inviolable fidelity.

Then he saw her turning up Greek Street upon another man's arm.

The light from the arc lamp drenched him from head to toe. He stood for a minute motionless beneath it. Shadows chequered the street. Other figures, single and together, poured out, wavered across, and obliterated Florinda and the man.

The light drenched Jacob from head to toe. You could see the pattern on his trousers; the old thorns on his stick; his shoe laces; bare hands; and face.

It was as if a stone were ground to dust; as if white sparks flew from a livid whetstone, which was his spine; as if the switchback railway, having swooped to the depths, fell, fell, fell. This was in his face.

Whether we know what was in his mind is another question. Granted ten years' seniority and a difference of sex, fear of him comes first; this is swallowed up by a desire to help—overwhelming sense, reason, and the time of night; anger would follow close on that—with Florinda, with destiny; and then up would bubble an irresponsible optimism. "Surely there's enough light in the street at this moment to drown all our cares in gold!" Ah, what's the use of saying it? Even while you speak and look over your shoulder towards Shaftesbury Avenue, destiny is chipping a dent in him. He has turned to go. As for following him back to his rooms, no—that we won't do.

Yet that, of course, is precisely what one does. He let himself in and shut the door, though it was only striking ten on one of the city clocks.

No one can go to bed at ten. Nobody was thinking of going to bed. It was January and dismal, but Mrs. Wagg stood on her doorstep, as if expecting something to happen. A barrel-organ played like an obscene nightingale beneath wet leaves. Children ran across the road. Here and there one could see brown panelling inside the hall door. . . . The march that the mind keeps beneath the windows of others is queer enough. Now distracted by brown panelling; now by a fern in a pot; here improvising a few phrases to dance with the barrel-organ; again snatching a detached gaiety from a drunken man; then altogether absorbed by words the poor shout across the street at each other (so outright, so lusty)—yet all the while having for centre, for magnet, a young man alone in his room.

"Life is wicked—life is detestable," cried Rose Shaw.

The strange thing about life is that though the nature of it must have been apparent to every one for hundreds of years, no one has left any adequate account of it. The streets of London have their map; but our passions are uncharted. What are you going to meet if you turn this corner?

"Holborn straight ahead of you" says the policeman. Ah, but where are you going if instead of brushing past the old man with the white beard, the silver medal, and the cheap violin, you let him go on with his story, which ends in an invitation to step somewhere, to his room, presumably, off Queen's Square, and there he shows you a collection of birds' eggs and a letter from the Prince of Wales's secretary, and this (skipping the intermediate stages) brings you one winter's day to the Essex coast, where the little boat makes off to the ship, and the ship sails and you behold on the skyline the Azores; and the flamingoes rise; and there you sit on the verge of the marsh drinking rum-punch, an outcast from civilization, for you have committed a crime, are infected with yellow fever as likely as not, and—fill in the sketch as you like. As frequent as street corners in Holborn are these chasms in the continuity of our ways. Yet we keep straight on.

Rose Shaw, talking in rather an emotional manner to Mr. Bowley at Mrs. Durrant's evening party a few nights back, said that life was wicked because a man called Jimmy refused to marry a woman called (if memory serves) Helen Aitken.

Both were beautiful. Both were inanimate. The oval tea-table invariably separated them, and the plate of biscuits was all he ever gave her. He bowed; she inclined her head. They danced. He danced divinely. They sat in the alcove; never a word was said. Her pillow was wet with tears. Kind Mr. Bowley and dear Rose Shaw marvelled and deplored. Bowley had rooms in the Albany. Rose was re-born every evening precisely as the clock struck eight. All four were civilization's triumphs, and if you persist that a command of the English language is part of our inheritance, one can only reply that beauty is almost always dumb. Male beauty in association with female beauty breeds in the onlooker a sense of fear. Often have I seen them—Helen and Jimmy—and likened them to ships adrift, and feared for my own little craft. Or again, have you ever watched fine collie dogs couchant at twenty yards' distance? As she passed him his cup there was that quiver in her flanks. Bowley saw what was up-asked Jimmy to breakfast. Helen must have confided in Rose. For my own part, I find it exceedingly difficult to interpret songs without words. And now Jimmy feeds crows in Flanders and Helen visits hospitals. Oh, life is damnable, life is wicked, as Rose Shaw said.

The lamps of London uphold the dark as upon the points of burning bayonets. The yellow canopy sinks and swells over the great four-poster. Passengers in the mail-coaches running into London in the eighteenth century looked through leafless branches and saw it flaring beneath them. The light burns behind yellow blinds and pink blinds, and above fanlights, and down in basement windows. The street market in Soho is fierce with light. Raw meat, china mugs, and silk stockings blaze in it. Raw voices wrap themselves round the flaring gas-jets. Arms akimbo, they stand on the pavement bawling—Messrs. Kettle and Wilkinson; their wives sit in the shop, furs wrapped round their necks, arms folded, eyes contemptuous. Such faces as one sees. The little man fingering the meat must have squatted before the fire in innumerable lodging-houses, and heard and seen and known so much that it seems to utter itself even volubly from dark eyes, loose lips, as he fingers the meat silently, his face sad as a poet's, and never a song sung. Shawled women carry babies with purple eyelids; boys stand at street corners; girls look across the road—rude illustrations, pictures in a book whose pages we turn over and over as if we should at last find what we look for. Every face, every shop, bedroom window, public-house, and dark square is a picture feverishly turned—in search of what? It is the same with books. What do we seek through millions of pages? Still hopefully turning the pages—oh, here is Jacob's room.

He sat at the table reading the *Globe*. The pinkish sheet was spread flat before him. He propped his face in his hand, so that the skin of his cheek was wrinkled in deep folds. Terribly severe he looked, set, and defiant. (What people go through in half an hour! But nothing could save him. These events are features of our landscape. A foreigner coming to London could scarcely miss seeing St. Paul's.) He judged life. These pinkish and greenish newspapers are thin sheets of gelatine pressed nightly over the brain and heart of the world. They take the impression of the whole.

Jacob cast his eye over it. A strike, a murder, football, bodies found; vociferation from all parts of England simultaneously. How miserable it is that the *Globe* newspaper offers nothing better to Jacob Flanders! When a child begins to read history one marvels, sorrowfully, to hear him spell out in his new voice the ancient words.

The Prime Minister's speech was reported in something over five columns. Feeling in his pocket, Jacob took out a pipe and proceeded to fill it. Five minutes, ten minutes, fifteen minutes passed. Jacob took the paper over to the fire. The Prime Minister proposed a measure for giving Home Rule to Ireland. Jacob knocked out his pipe. He was certainly thinking about Home Rule in Ireland—a very difficult matter. A very cold night.

The snow, which had been falling all night, lay at three o'clock in the afternoon over the fields and the hill. Clumps of withered grass stood out upon the hill-top; the furze bushes were black, and now and then a black shiver crossed the snow as the wind drove flurries of frozen particles before it. The sound was that of a broom sweeping—sweeping.

The stream crept along by the road unseen by any one. Sticks and leaves caught in the frozen grass. The sky was sullen grey and the trees of black iron. Uncompromising was the severity of the country. At four o'clock the snow was again falling. The day had gone out.

A window tinged yellow about two feet across alone combated the white fields and the black trees. . . . At six o'clock a man's figure carrying a lantern crossed the field. . . . A raft of twig stayed upon a stone, suddenly detached itself, and floated towards the culvert. . . . A load of snow slipped and fell from a fir branch. . . . Later there was a mournful cry. . . . A motor car came along the road shoving the dark before it. . . . The dark shut down behind it. . . .

Spaces of complete immobility separated each of these movements. The land seemed to lie dead. . . . Then the old shepherd returned stiffly across the field. Stiffly and painfully the frozen earth was trodden under and gave beneath pressure like a treadmill. The worn voices of clocks repeated the fact of the hour all night long.

Jacob, too, heard them, and raked out the fire. He rose. He stretched himself. He went to bed.

9

The Countess of Rocksbier sat at the head of the table alone with Jacob. Fed upon champagne and spices for at least two centuries (four, if you count the female line), the Countess Lucy looked well fed. A discriminating nose she had for scents, prolonged, as if in quest of them; her underlip protruded a narrow red shelf; her eyes were small, with sandy tufts for eyebrows, and her jowl was heavy. Behind her (the window looked on Grosvenor Square) stood Moll Pratt on the pavement, offering violets for sale; and Mrs. Hilda Thomas, lifting her skirts, preparing to cross the road. One was from Walworth; the other from Putney. Both wore black stockings, but Mrs. Thomas was coiled in furs. The comparison was much in Lady Rocksbier's favour. Moll had more humour, but was violent; stupid too. Hilda Thomas was mealy-mouthed, all her silver frames aslant; egg-cups in the drawing-room; and the windows shrouded. Lady Rocksbier, whatever the deficiencies of her profile, had been a great rider to hounds. She used her knife with authority, tore her chicken bones, asking Jacob's pardon, with her own hands.

"Who is that driving by?" she asked Boxall, the butler.

"Lady Firtlemere's carriage, my lady," which reminded her to send a card to ask after his lordship's health. A rude old lady, Jacob thought. The wine was excellent. She called herself "an old woman"—"so kind to lunch with an old woman"—which flattered him. She talked of Joseph Chamberlain, whom she had known. She said that Jacob must come and meet—one of our celebrities. And the Lady Alice came in with three dogs on a leash, and Jackie, who ran to kiss his grandmother, while Boxall brought in a telegram, and Jacob was given a good cigar.

A few moments before a horse jumps it slows, sidles, gathers itself together, goes up like a monster wave, and pitches down on the further side. Hedges and sky swoop in a semicircle. Then as if your own body ran into the horse's body and it was your own forelegs grown with his that sprang, rushing through the air you go, the ground resilient, bodies a mass of muscles, yet you have command too, upright stillness, eyes accurately judging. Then the curves cease, changing to downright hammer strokes, which jar; and you draw up with a jolt; sitting back a little, sparkling, tingling, glazed with ice over pounding arteries, gasping: "Ah! ho! Hah!" the steam going up from the horses as they jostle together at the cross-roads, where the signpost is, and the woman in the apron stands and stares at the doorway. The man raises himself from the cabbages to stare too.

So Jacob galloped over the fields of Essex, flopped in the mud, lost the hunt, and rode by himself eating sandwiches, looking over the hedges, noticing the colours as if new scraped, cursing his luck.

He had tea at the Inn; and there they all were, slapping, stamping, saying, "After you," clipped, curt, jocose, red as the wattles of turkeys, using free speech until Mrs. Horsefield and her friend Miss Dudding appeared at the doorway with their skirts hitched up, and hair looping down. Then Tom Dudding rapped at the window with his whip. A motor car throbbed in the courtyard. Gentlemen, feeling for matches, moved out, and Jacob went into the bar with Brandy Jones to smoke with the rustics. There was old Jevons with one eye gone, and his clothes the colour of mud, his bag over his back, and his brains laid feet down in earth among the violet roots and the nettle roots; Mary Sanders with her box of wood; and Tom sent for beer, the half-witted son of the sexton—all this within thirty miles of London.

Mrs. Papworth, of Endell Street, Covent Garden, did for Mr. Bonamy in New Square, Lincoln's Inn, and as she washed up the dinner things in the scullery she heard the young gentlemen talking in the room next door. Mr. Sanders was there again; Flanders she meant; and where an inquisitive old woman gets a name wrong, what chance is there that she will faithfully report an argument? As she held the plates under water and then dealt them on the pile beneath the hissing gas, she listened: heard Sanders speaking in a loud rather overbearing tone of voice: "good," he said, and "absolute" and "justice" and "punishment," and "the will of the majority." Then her gentleman piped up; she backed him for argument against Sanders. Yet Sanders was a fine young fellow (here all the scraps went swirling round the sink, scoured after by her purple, almost nailless hands). "Women"—she thought, and wondered what Sanders and her gentleman did in *that* line, one eyelid sinking perceptibly as she mused, for she was the mother of nine—three still-born and one deaf and dumb from birth. Putting the plates in the rack she heard once more Sanders at it again ("He don't give Bonamy a chance," she thought). "Objective something," said Bonamy; and "common ground" and something else—all very long words, she noted. "Book learning does it," she thought to herself, and, as she thrust her arms into her jacket, heard something—might be the little table by the fire—fall; and then stamp, stamp, stamp—as if they were having at each other—round the room, making the plates dance.

"Tomorrow's breakfast, sir," she said, opening the door; and there were Sanders and Bonamy like two bulls of Bashan driving each other up and down, making such a racket, and all them chairs in the way. They never noticed her. She felt motherly towards them. "Your breakfast, sir," she said, as they came near. And Bonamy, all his hair touzled and his tie flying, broke off, and pushed Sanders into the arm-chair, and said Mr. Sanders had smashed the coffee-pot and he was teaching Mr. Sanders—

Sure enough, the coffee-pot lay broken on the hearthrug.

"Any day this week except Thursday," wrote Miss Perry, and this was not the first invitation by any means. Were all Miss Perry's weeks blank with the exception of Thursday, and was her only desire to see her old friend's son? Time is issued to spinster ladies of wealth in long white ribbons. These they wind round and round, round and round, assisted by five female servants, a butler, a fine Mexican parrot, regular meals, Mudie's library, and friends dropping in. A little hurt she was already that Jacob had not called.

"Your mother," she said, "is one of my oldest friends."

Miss Rosseter, who was sitting by the fire, holding the *Spectator* between her cheek and the blaze, refused to have a fire screen, but finally accepted one. The weather was then discussed, for in deference to Parkes, who was opening little tables, graver matters were postponed. Miss Rosseter drew Jacob's attention to the beauty of the cabinet.

"So wonderfully clever in picking things up," she said. Miss Perry had found it in Yorkshire. The North of England was discussed. When Jacob spoke they both listened. Miss Perry was bethinking her of something suitable and manly to say when the door opened and Mr. Benson was announced. Now there were four people sitting in that room. Miss Perry aged 66; Miss Rosseter 42; Mr. Benson 38; and Jacob 25.

"My old friend looks as well as ever," said Mr. Benson, tapping the bars of the parrot's cage; Miss Rosseter simultaneously praised the tea; Jacob handed the wrong plates; and Miss Perry signified her desire to approach more closely. "Your brothers," she began vaguely.

"Archer and John," Jacob supplied her. Then to her pleasure she recovered Rebecca's name; and how one day "when you were all little boys, playing in the drawing-room—"

"But Miss Perry has the kettle-holder," said Miss Rosseter, and indeed Miss Perry was clasping it to her breast. (Had she, then, loved Jacob's father?)

"So clever"—"not so good as usual"—"I thought it most unfair," said Mr. Benson and Miss Rosseter, discussing the Saturday *Westminster.* Did they not compete regularly for prizes? Had not Mr. Benson three times won a guinea, and Miss Rosseter once ten and sixpence? Of course Everard Benson had a weak heart, but still, to win prizes, remember parrots, toady Miss Perry, despise Miss Rosseter, give tea-parties in his rooms (which were in the style of Whistler, with pretty books on tables), all this, so Jacob felt without knowing him, made him a contemptible ass. As for Miss Rosseter, she had nursed cancer, and now painted water-colours.

"Running away so soon?" said Miss Perry vaguely. "At home every afternoon, if you've nothing better to do—except Thursdays."

"I've never known you desert your old ladies once," Miss Rosseter was saying, and Mr. Benson was stooping over the parrot's cage, and Miss Perry was moving towards the bell. . . .

The fire burnt clear between two pillars of greenish marble, and on the mantelpiece there was a green clock guarded by Britannia leaning on her spear. As for pictures—a maiden in a large hat offered roses over the garden gate to a gentleman in eighteenth-century costume. A mastiff lay extended against a battered door. The lower panes of the windows were of ground glass, and the curtains, accurately looped, were of plush and green too.

Laurette and Jacob sat with their toes in the fender side by side, in two large chairs covered in green plush. Laurette's skirts were short, her legs long, thin, and transparently covered. Her fingers stroked her ankles.

"It's not exactly that I don't understand them," she was saying thoughtfully. "I must go and try again."

"What time will you be there?" said Jacob.

She shrugged her shoulders.

"Tomorrow?"

No, not tomorrow.

"This weather makes me long for the country," she said, looking over her shoulder at the back view of tall houses through the window.

"I wish you'd been with me on Saturday," said Jacob.

"I used to ride," she said. She got up gracefully, calmly. Jacob got up. She smiled at him. As she shut the door he put so many shillings on the mantelpiece.

Altogether a most reasonable conversation; a most respectable room; an intelligent girl. Only Madame herself seeing Jacob out had about her that leer, that lewdness, that quake of the surface (visible in the eyes chiefly), which threatens to spill the whole bag of ordure, with difficulty held together, over the pavement. In short, something was wrong.

Not so very long ago the workmen had gilt the final "y" in Lord Macaulay's name, and the names stretched in unbroken file round the dome of the British Museum. At a considerable depth beneath, many hundreds of the living sat at the spokes of a cart-wheel copying from printed books into manuscript books; now and then rising to consult the catalogue; regaining their places stealthily, while from time to time a silent man replenished their compartments.

There was a little catastrophe. Miss Marchmont's pile overbalanced and fell into Jacob's compartment. Such things happened to Miss Marchmont. What was she seeking through millions of pages, in her old plush dress, and her wig of claret-coloured hair, with her gems and her chilblains? Sometimes one thing, sometimes another, to confirm her philosophy that colour is sound—or, perhaps, it has something to do with music. She could never quite say, though it was not for lack of trying. And she could not ask you back to her room, for it was "not very clean, I'm afraid," so she must catch you in the passage, or take a chair in Hyde Park to explain her philosophy. The rhythm of the soul depends on it—("how rude the little boys are!" she would say), and Mr. Asquith's Irish policy, and Shakespeare comes in, "and Queen Alexandra most graciously once acknowledged a copy of my pamphlet," she would say, waving the little boys magnificently away. But she needs funds to publish her book, for "publishers are capitalists—publishers are cowards." And so, digging her elbow into her pile of books it fell over.

Jacob remained quite unmoved.

But Fraser, the atheist, on the other side, detesting plush, more than once accosted with leaflets, shifted irritably. He abhorred vagueness—the Christian religion, for example, and old Dean Parker's pronouncements. Dean Parker wrote books and Fraser utterly destroyed them by force of logic and left his children unbaptized—his wife did it secretly in the washing basin—but Fraser ignored her, and went on supporting blasphemers, distributing leaflets, getting up his facts in the British Museum, always in the same check suit and fiery tie, but pale, spotted, irritable. Indeed, what a work—to destroy religion!

Jacob transcribed a whole passage from Marlowe.

Miss Julia Hedge, the feminist, waited for her books. They did not come. She wetted her pen. She looked about her. Her eye was caught by the final letters in Lord Macaulay's name. And she read them all round the dome—the names of great men which remind us—"Oh damn," said Julia Hedge, "why didn't they leave room for an Eliot or a Bronte?"

Unfortunate Julia! wetting her pen in bitterness, and leaving her shoe laces untied. When her books came she applied herself to her gigantic labours, but perceived through one of the nerves of her exasperated sensibility how composedly, unconcernedly, and with every consideration the male readers applied themselves to theirs. That young man for example. What had he got to do except copy out poetry? And she must study statistics. There are more women than men. Yes; but if you let women work as men work, they'll die off much quicker. They'll become extinct. That was her argument. Death and gall and bitter dust were on her pen-tip; and as the afternoon wore on, red had worked into her cheek-bones and a light was in her eyes.

But what brought Jacob Flanders to read Marlowe in the British Museum?

* * *

Youth, youth—something savage—something pedantic. For example, there is Mr. Masefield, there is Mr. Bennett. Stuff them into the flame of Marlowe and burn them to cinders. Let not a shred remain. Don't palter with the second rate. Detest your own age. Build a better one. And to set that on foot read incredibly dull essays upon Marlowe to your friends. For which purpose one most collate editions in the British Museum. One must do the thing oneself. Useless to trust to the Victorians, who disembowel, or to the living, who are mere publicists. The flesh and blood of the future depends entirely upon six young men. And as Jacob was one of them, no doubt he looked a little regal and pompous as he turned his page, and Julia Hedge disliked him naturally enough.

But then a pudding-faced man pushed a note towards Jacob, and Jacob, leaning back in his chair, began an uneasy murmured conversation, and they went off together (Julia Hedge watched them), and laughed aloud (she thought) directly they were in the hall.

Nobody laughed in the reading-room. There were shirtings, murmurings, apologetic sneezes, and sudden unashamed devastating coughs. The lesson hour was almost over. Ushers were collecting exercises. Lazy children wanted to stretch. Good ones scribbled assiduously—ah, another day over and so little done! And now and then was to be heard from the whole collection of human beings a heavy sigh, after which the humiliating old man would cough shamelessly, and Miss Marchmont hinnied like a horse.

Jacob came back only in time to return his books.

The books were now replaced. A few letters of the alphabet were sprinkled round the dome. Closely stood together in a ring round the dome were Plato, Aristotle, Sophocles, and Shakespeare; the literature of Rome, Greece, China, India, Persia. One leaf of poetry was pressed flat against another leaf, one burnished letter laid smooth against another in a density of meaning, a conglomeration of loveliness.

"One does want one's tea," said Miss Marchmont, reclaiming her shabby umbrella.

Miss Marchmont wanted her tea, but could never resist a last look at the Elgin Marbles. She looked at them sideways, waving her hand and muttering a word or two of salutation which made Jacob and the other man turn round. She smiled at them amiably. It all came into her philosophy—that colour is sound, or perhaps it has something to do with music. And having done her service, she hobbled off to tea. It was closing time. The public collected in the hall to receive their umbrellas.

For the most part the students wait their turn very patiently. To stand and wait while some one examines white discs is soothing. The umbrella will certainly be found. But the fact leads you on all day through Macaulay, Hobbes, Gibbon; through octavos, quartos, folios; sinks deeper and deeper through ivory pages and morocco bindings into this density of thought, this conglomeration of knowledge.

Jacob's walking-stick was like all the others; they had muddled the pigeon-holes perhaps.

There is in the British Museum an enormous mind. Consider that Plato is there cheek by jowl with Aristotle; and Shakespeare with Marlowe. This great mind is hoarded beyond the power of any single mind to possess it. Nevertheless (as they take so long finding one's walking-stick) one can't help thinking how one might come with a notebook, sit at a desk, and read it all through. A learned man is the most venerable of all—a man like Huxtable of Trinity, who writes all his letters in Greek, they say, and could have kept his end up with Bentley. And then there is science, pictures, architecture—an enormous mind.

They pushed the walking-stick across the counter. Jacob stood beneath the porch of the British Museum. It was raining. Great Russell Street was glazed and shining—here yellow, here, outside the chemist's, red and pale blue. People scuttled quickly close to the wall; carriages rattled rather helter-skelter down the streets. Well, but a little rain hurts nobody. Jacob walked off much as if he had been in the country; and late that night there he was sitting at his table with his pipe and his book.

The rain poured down. The British Museum stood in one solid immense mound, very pale, very sleek in the rain, not a quarter of a mile from him. The vast mind was sheeted with stone; and each compartment in the depths of it was safe and dry. The night-watchmen, flashing their lanterns over the backs of Plato and Shakespeare, saw that on the twenty-second of February neither flame, rat, nor burglar was going to violate these treasures—poor, highly respectable men, with wives and families at Kentish Town, do their best for twenty years to protect Plato and Shakespeare, and then are buried at Highgate.

Stone lies solid over the British Museum, as bone lies cool over the visions and heat of the brain. Only here the brain is Plato's brain and Shakespeare's; the brain has made pots and statues, great bulls and little jewels, and crossed the river of death this way and that incessantly, seeking some landing, now wrapping the body well for its long sleep; now laying a penny piece on the eyes; now turning the toes scrupulously to the East. Meanwhile, Plato continues his dialogue; in spite of the rain; in spite of the cab whistles; in spite of the woman in the mews behind Great Ormond Street who has come home drunk and cries all night long, "Let me in! Let me in!"

In the street below Jacob's room voices were raised.

But he read on. For after all Plato continues imperturbably. And Hamlet utters his soliloquy. And there the Elgin Marbles lie, all night long, old Jones's lantern sometimes recalling Ulysses, or a horse's head; or sometimes a flash of gold, or a mummy's sunk yellow cheek. Plato and Shakespeare continue; and Jacob, who was reading the *Phaedrus*, heard people vociferating round the lamp-post, and the woman battering at the door and crying, "Let me in!" as if a coal had dropped from the fire, or a fly, falling from the ceiling, had lain on its back, too weak to turn over.

The *Phaedrus* is very difficult. And so, when at length one reads straight ahead, falling into step, marching on, becoming (so it seems) momentarily part of this rolling, imperturbable energy, which has driven darkness before it since Plato walked the Acropolis, it is impossible to see to the fire.

The dialogue draws to its close. Plato's argument is done. Plato's argument is stowed away in Jacob's mind, and for five minutes Jacob's mind continues alone, onwards, into the darkness. Then, getting up, he parted the curtains, and saw, with astonishing clearness, how the Springetts opposite had gone to bed; how it rained; how the Jews and the foreign woman, at the end of the street, stood by the pillar-box, arguing.

Every time the door opened and fresh people came in, those already in the room shifted slightly; those who were standing looked over their shoulders; those who were sitting stopped in the middle of sentences. What with the light, the wine, the strumming of a guitar, something exciting happened each time the door opened. Who was coming in?

"That's Gibson."

"The painter?"

"But go on with what you were saying."

They were saying something that was far, far too intimate to be said outright. But the noise of the voices served like a clapper in little Mrs. Withers's mind, scaring into the air blocks of small birds, and then they'd settle, and then she'd feel afraid, put one hand to her hair, bind both round her knees, and look up at Oliver Skelton nervously, and say:

"Promise, *promise,* you'll tell no one." . . . so considerate he was, so tender. It was her husband's character that she discussed. He was cold, she said.

Down upon them came the splendid Magdalen, brown, warm, voluminous, scarcely brushing the grass with her sandalled feet. Her hair flew; pins seemed scarcely to attach the flying silks. An actress of course, a line of light perpetually beneath her. It was only "My dear" that she said, but her voice went jodelling between Alpine passes. And down she tumbled on the floor, and sang, since there was nothing to be said, round ah's and oh's. Mangin, the poet, coming up to her, stood looking down at her, drawing at his pipe. The dancing began.

Grey-haired Mrs. Keymer asked Dick Graves to tell her who Mangin was, and said that she had seen too much of this sort of thing in Paris

(Magdalen had got upon his knees; now his pipe was in her mouth) to be shocked. "Who is that?" she said, staying her glasses when they came to Jacob, for indeed he looked quiet, not indifferent, but like some one on a beach, watching.

"Oh, my dear, let me lean on you," gasped Helen Askew, hopping on one foot, for the silver cord round her ankle had worked loose. Mrs. Keymer turned and looked at the picture on the wall.

"Look at Jacob," said Helen (they were binding his eyes for some game).

And Dick Graves, being a little drunk, very faithful, and very simple-minded, told her that he thought Jacob the greatest man he had ever known. And down they sat cross-legged upon cushions and talked about Jacob, and Helen's voice trembled, for they both seemed heroes to her, and the friendship between them so much more beautiful than women's friendships. Anthony Pollett now asked her to dance, and as she danced she looked at them, over her shoulder, standing at the table, drinking together.

The magnificent world—the live, sane, vigorous world. . . . These words refer to the stretch of wood pavement between Hammersmith and Holborn in January between two and three in the morning. That was the ground beneath Jacob's feet. It was healthy and magnificent because one room, above a mews, somewhere near the river, contained fifty excited, talkative, friendly people. And then to stride over the pavement (there was scarcely a cab or policeman in sight) is of itself exhilarating. The long loop of Piccadilly, diamond-stitched, shows to best advantage when it is empty. A young man has nothing to fear. On the contrary, though he may not have said anything brilliant, he feels pretty confident he can hold his own. He was pleased to have met Mangin; he admired the young woman on the floor; he liked them all; he liked that sort of thing. In short, all the drums and trumpets were sounding. The street scavengers were the only people about at the moment. It is scarcely necessary to say how well-disposed Jacob felt towards them; how it pleased him to let himself in with his latch-key at his own door; how he seemed to bring back with him into the empty room ten or eleven people whom he had not known when he set out; how he looked about for something to read, and found it, and never read it, and fell asleep.

Indeed, drums and trumpets is no phrase. Indeed, Piccadilly and Holborn, and the empty sitting-room and the sitting-room with fifty people in it are liable at any moment to blow music into the air. Women perhaps are more excitable than men. It is seldom that any one says anything about it, and to see the hordes crossing Waterloo Bridge to catch the non-stop to Surbiton one might think that reason impelled them. No, no. It is the drums and trumpets. Only, should you turn aside into one of those little bays on Waterloo Bridge to think the matter over, it will probably seem to you all a muddle—all a mystery.

They cross the Bridge incessantly. Sometimes in the midst of carts and omnibuses a lorry will appear with great forest trees chained to it. Then, perhaps, a mason's van with newly lettered tombstones recording how some one loved some one who is buried at Putney. Then the motor car in front jerks forward, and the tombstones pass too quick for you to read more. All the time the stream of people never ceases passing from the Surrey side to the Strand; from the Strand to the Surrey side. It seems as if the poor had gone raiding the town, and now trapesed back to their own quarters, like beetles scurrying to their holes, for that old woman fairly hobbles towards Waterloo, grasping a shiny bag, as if she had been out into the light and now made off with some scraped chicken bones to her hovel underground. On the other hand, though the wind is rough and blowing in their faces, those girls there, striding hand in hand, shouting out a song, seem to feel neither cold nor shame. They are hatless. They triumph.

The wind has blown up the waves. The river races beneath us, and the men standing on the barges have to lean all their weight on the tiller. A black tarpaulin is tied down over a swelling load of gold. Avalanches of coal glitter blackly. As usual, painters are slung on planks across the great riverside hotels, and the hotel windows have already points of light in them. On the other side the city is white as if with age; St. Paul's swells white above the fretted, pointed, or oblong buildings beside it. The cross alone shines rosy-gilt. But what century have we reached? Has this procession from the Surrey side to the Strand gone on for ever? That old man has been crossing the Bridge these six hundred years, with the rabble of little boys at his heels, for he is drunk, or blind with misery, and tied round with old clouts of clothing such as pilgrims might have worn. He shuffles on. No one stands still. It seems as if we marched to the sound of music; perhaps the wind and the river; perhaps these same drums and trumpets—the ecstasy and hubbub of the soul. Why, even the unhappy laugh, and the policeman, far from judging the drunk man, surveys him humorously, and the little boys scamper back again, and the clerk from Somerset House has nothing but tolerance for him, and the man who is reading half a page of Lothair at the bookstall muses charitably, with his eyes off the print, and the girl hesitates at the crossing and turns on him the bright yet vague glance of the young.

Bright yet vague. She is perhaps twenty-two. She is shabby. She crosses the road and looks at the daffodils and the red tulips in the florist's window. She hesitates, and makes off in the direction of Temple Bar. She walks fast, and yet anything distracts her. Now she seems to see, and now to notice nothing.

10

Through the disused graveyard in the parish of St. Pancras, Fanny Elmer strayed between the white tombs which lean against the wall, crossing the grass to read a name, hurrying on when the grave-keeper approached, hurrying into the street, pausing now by a window with blue china, now quickly making up for lost time, abruptly entering a baker's shop, buying rolls, adding cakes, going on again so that any one wishing to follow must fairly trot. She was not drably shabby, though. She wore silk stockings, and silver-buckled shoes, only the red feather in her hat drooped, and the clasp of her bag was weak, for out fell a copy of Madame Tussaud's programme as she walked. She had the ankles of a stag. Her face was hidden. Of course, in this dusk, rapid movements, quick glances, and soaring hopes come naturally enough. She passed right beneath Jacob's window.

The house was flat, dark, and silent. Jacob was at home engaged upon a chess problem, the board being on a stool between his knees. One hand was fingering the hair at the back of his head. He slowly brought it forward and raised the white queen from her square; then put her down again on the same spot. He filled his pipe; ruminated; moved two pawns; advanced the white knight; then ruminated with one finger upon the bishop. Now Fanny Elmer passed beneath the window.

She was on her way to sit to Nick Bramham the painter.

She sat in a flowered Spanish shawl, holding in her hand a yellow novel.

"A little lower, a little looser, so—better, that's right," Bramham mumbled, who was drawing her, and smoking at the same time, and was naturally speechless. His head might have been the work of a sculptor, who had squared the forehead, stretched the mouth, and left marks of his thumbs and streaks from his fingers in the clay. But the eyes had never been shut. They were rather prominent, and rather bloodshot, as if from staring and staring, and when he spoke they looked for a second disturbed, but went on staring. An unshaded electric light hung above her head.

As for the beauty of women, it is like the light on the sea, never constant to a single wave. They all have it; they all lose it. Now she is dull and thick as bacon; now transparent as a hanging glass. The fixed faces are the dull ones. Here comes Lady Venice displayed like a monument for admiration, but carved in alabaster, to be set on the mantelpiece and never dusted. A dapper brunette complete from head to foot serves only as an illustration to lie upon the drawing-room table. The women in the streets have the faces of playing cards; the outlines accurately filled in with pink or yellow, and the line drawn tightly round them. Then, at a top-floor window, leaning out, looking down, you see beauty itself; or in the corner of an omnibus; or squatted in a ditch—beauty glowing, suddenly expressive, withdrawn the moment after. No one can count on it or seize it or have it wrapped in paper. Nothing is to be won from the shops, and Heaven knows it would be better to sit at home than haunt the plate-glass windows in the hope of lifting the shining green, the glowing ruby, out of them alive. Sea glass in a saucer loses its lustre no sooner than silks do. Thus if you talk of a beautiful woman you mean only something flying fast which for a second uses the eyes, lips, or cheeks of Fanny Elmer, for example, to glow through.

She was not beautiful, as she sat stiffly; her underlip too prominent; her nose too large; her eyes too near together. She was a thin girl, with brilliant cheeks and dark hair, sulky just now, or stiff with sitting. When Bramham snapped his stick of charcoal she started. Bramham was out of temper. He squatted before the gas fire warming his hands. Meanwhile she looked at his drawing. He grunted. Fanny threw on a dressing-gown and boiled a kettle.

"By God, it's bad," said Bramham.

Fanny dropped on to the floor, clasped her hands round her knees, and looked at him, her beautiful eyes—yes, beauty, flying through the room, shone there for a second. Fanny's eyes seemed to question, to commiserate, to be, for a second, love itself. But she exaggerated. Bramham noticed nothing. And when the kettle boiled, up she scrambled, more like a colt or a puppy than a loving woman.

Now Jacob walked over to the window and stood with his hands in his pockets. Mr. Springett opposite came out, looked at his shop window, and went in again. The children drifted past, eyeing the pink sticks of sweetstuff. Pickford's van swung down the street. A small boy twirled from a rope. Jacob turned away. Two minutes later he opened the front door, and walked off in the direction of Holborn.

Fanny Elmer took down her cloak from the hook. Nick Bramham unpinned his drawing and rolled it under his arm. They turned out the lights and set off down the street, holding on their way through all the people, motor cars, omnibuses, carts, until they reached Leicester Square, five minutes before Jacob reached it, for his way was slightly longer, and he had been stopped by a block in Holborn waiting to see the King drive by, so that Nick and Fanny were already leaning over the barrier in the promenade at the Empire when Jacob pushed through the swing doors and took his place beside them.

"Hullo, never noticed you," said Nick, five minutes later.

"Bloody rot," said Jacob.

"Miss Elmer," said Nick.

Jacob took his pipe out of his mouth very awkwardly.

Very awkward he was. And when they sat upon a plush sofa and let the smoke go up between them and the stage, and heard far off the high-pitched voices and the jolly orchestra breaking in opportunely he was still awkward, only Fanny thought: "What a beautiful voice!" She thought how little he said yet how firm it was. She thought how young men are dignified and aloof, and how unconscious they are, and how quietly one might sit beside Jacob and look at him. And how childlike he would be, come in tired of an evening, she thought, and how majestic; a little over-bearing perhaps; "But I wouldn't give way," she thought. He got up and leant over the barrier. The smoke hung about him.

And for ever the beauty of young men seems to be set in smoke, however lustily they chase footballs, or drive cricket balls, dance, run, or stride along roads. Possibly they are soon to lose it. Possibly they look into the eyes of faraway heroes, and take their station among us half contemptuously, she thought (vibrating like a fiddle-string, to be played on and snapped). Anyhow, they love silence, and speak beautifully, each word falling like a disc new cut, not a hubble-bubble of small smooth coins such as girls use; and they move decidedly, as if they knew how long to stay and when to go—oh, but Mr. Flanders was only gone to get a programme.

"The dancers come right at the end," he said, coming back to them.

And isn't it pleasant, Fanny went on thinking, how young men bring out lots of silver coins from their trouser pockets, and look at them, instead of having just so many in a purse?

Then there she was herself, whirling across the stage in white flounces, and the music was the dance and fling of her own soul, and the whole machinery, rock and gear of the world was spun smoothly into those swift eddies and falls, she felt, as she stood rigid leaning over the barrier two feet from Jacob Flanders.

Her screwed-up black glove dropped to the floor. When Jacob gave it her, she started angrily. For never was there a more irrational passion. And Jacob was afraid of her for a moment—so violent, so dangerous is it when young women stand rigid; grasp the barrier; fall in love.

It was the middle of February. The roofs of Hampstead Garden Suburb lay in a tremulous haze. It was too hot to walk. A dog barked, barked, barked down in the hollow. The liquid shadows went over the plain.

The body after long illness is languid, passive, receptive of sweetness, but too weak to contain it. The tears well and fall as the dog barks in the hollow, the children skim after hoops, the country darkens and brightens. Beyond a veil it seems. Ah, but draw the veil thicker lest I faint with sweetness, Fanny Elmer sighed, as she sat on a bench in Judges Walk looking at Hampstead Garden Suburb. But the dog went on barking. The motor cars hooted on the road. She heard a far-away rush and humming. Agitation was at her heart. Up she got and walked. The grass was freshly green; the sun hot. All round the pond children were stooping to launch little boats; or were drawn back screaming by their nurses.

At mid-day young women walk out into the air. All the men are busy in the town. They stand by the edge of the blue pond. The fresh wind scatters the children's voices all about. My children, thought Fanny Elmer. The women stand round the pond, beating off great prancing shaggy dogs. Gently the baby is rocked in the perambulator. The eyes of all the nurses, mothers, and wandering women are a little glazed, absorbed. They gently nod instead of answering when the little boys tug at their skirts, begging them to move on.

And Fanny moved, hearing some cry—a workman's whistle perhaps—high in mid-air. Now, among the trees, it was the thrush trilling out into the warm air a flutter of jubilation, but fear seemed to spur him, Fanny thought; as if he too were anxious with such joy at his heart—as if he were watched as he sang, and pressed by tumult to sing. There! Restless, he flew to the next tree. She heard his song more faintly. Beyond it was the humming of the wheels and the wind rushing.

She spent tenpence on lunch.

"Dear, miss, she's left her umbrella," grumbled the mottled woman in the glass box near the door at the Express Dairy Company's shop.

"Perhaps I'll catch her," answered Milly Edwards, the waitress with the pale plaits of hair; and she dashed through the door.

"No good," she said, coming back a moment later with Fanny's cheap umbrella. She put her hand to her plaits.

"Oh, that door!" grumbled the cashier.

Her hands were cased in black mittens, and the finger-tips that drew in the paper slips were swollen as sausages.

"Pie and greens for one. Large coffee and crumpets. Eggs on toast. Two fruit cakes."

Thus the sharp voices of the waitresses snapped. The lunchers heard their orders repeated with approval; saw the next table served with anticipation. Their own eggs on toast were at last delivered. Their eyes strayed no more.

Damp cubes of pastry fell into mouths opened like triangular bags.

Nelly Jenkinson, the typist, crumbled her cake indifferently enough. Every time the door opened she looked up. What did she expect to see?

The coal merchant read the *Telegraph* without stopping, missed the saucer, and, feeling abstractedly, put the cup down on the table-cloth.

"Did you ever hear the like of that for impertinence?" Mrs. Parsons wound up, brushing the crumbs from her furs.

"Hot milk and scone for one. Pot of tea. Roll and butter," cried the waitresses.

The door opened and shut.

Such is the life of the elderly.

It is curious, lying in a boat, to watch the waves. Here are three coming regularly one after another, all much of a size. Then, hurrying after them comes a fourth, very large and menacing; it lifts the boat; on it goes; somehow merges without accomplishing anything; flattens itself out with the rest.

What can be more violent than the fling of boughs in a gale, the tree yielding itself all up the trunk, to the very tip of the branch, streaming and shuddering the way the wind blows, yet never flying in dishevelment away?

The corn squirms and abases itself as if preparing to tug itself free from the roots, and yet is tied down.

Why, from the very windows, even in the dusk, you see a swelling run through the street, an aspiration, as with arms outstretched, eyes desiring, mouths agape. And then we peaceably subside. For if the exaltation lasted we should be blown like foam into the air. The stars would shine through us. We should go down the gale in salt drops—as sometimes happens. For the impetuous spirits will have none of this cradling. Never any swaying or aimlessly lolling for them. Never any making believe, or lying cosily, or genially supposing that one is much like another, fire warm, wine pleasant, extravagance a sin.

"People are so nice, once you know them."

"I couldn't think ill of her. One must remember—" But Nick perhaps, or Fanny Elmer, believing implicitly in the truth of the moment, fling off, sting the cheek, are gone like sharp hail.

"Oh," said Fanny, bursting into the studio three-quarters of an hour late because she had been hanging about the neighbourhood of the Foundling Hospital merely for the chance of seeing Jacob walk down the street, take out his latch-key, and open the door, "I'm afraid I'm late"; upon which Nick said nothing and Fanny grew defiant.

"I'll never come again!" she cried at length.

"Don't, then," Nick replied, and off she ran without so much as goodnight.

* * *

How exquisite it was—that dress in Evelina's shop off Shaftesbury Avenue! It was four o'clock on a fine day early in April, and was Fanny the one to spend four o'clock on a fine day indoors? Other girls in that very street sat over ledgers, or drew long threads wearily between silk and gauze; or, festooned with ribbons in Swan and Edgars, rapidly added up pence and farthings on the back of the bill and twisted the yard and three-quarters in tissue paper and asked "Your pleasure?" of the next comer.

In Evelina's shop off Shaftesbury Avenue the parts of a woman were shown separate. In the left hand was her skirt. Twining round a pole in the middle was a feather boa. Ranged like the heads of malefactors on Temple Bar were hats—emerald and white, lightly wreathed or drooping beneath deep-dyed feathers. And on the carpet were her feet—pointed gold, or patent leather slashed with scarlet.

Feasted upon by the eyes of women, the clothes by four o'clock were flyblown like sugar cakes in a baker's window. Fanny eyed them too.

But coming along Gerrard Street was a tall man in a shabby coat. A shadow fell across Evelina's window—Jacob's shadow, though it was not Jacob. And Fanny turned and walked along Gerrard Street and wished that she had read books. Nick never read books, never talked of Ireland, or the House of Lords; and as for his finger-nails! She would learn Latin and read Virgil. She had been a great reader. She had read Scott; she had read Dumas. At the Slade no one read. But no one knew Fanny at the Slade, or guessed how empty it seemed to her; the passion for ear-rings, for dances, for Tonks and Steer—when it was only the French who could paint, Jacob said. For the moderns were futile; painting the least respectable of the arts; and why read anything but Marlowe and Shakespeare, Jacob said, and Fielding if you must read novels?

"Fielding," said Fanny, when the man in Charing Cross Road asked her what book she wanted.

She bought *Tom Jones.*

At ten o'clock in the morning, in a room which she shared with a school teacher, Fanny Elmer read *Tom Jones*—that mystic book. For this dull stuff (Fanny thought) about people with odd names is what Jacob likes. Good people like it. Dowdy women who don't mind how they cross their legs read *Tom Jones*—a mystic book; for there is something, Fanny thought, about books which if I had been educated I could have liked—much better than ear-rings and flowers, she sighed, thinking of the corridors at the Slade and the fancy-dress dance next week. She had nothing to wear.

They are real, thought Fanny Elmer, setting her feet on the mantelpiece. Some people are. Nick perhaps, only he was so stupid. And women never—except Miss Sargent, but she went off at lunch-time and gave herself airs. There they sat quietly of a night reading, she thought. Not going to music-halls; not looking in at shop windows; not wearing each other's clothes, like Robertson who had worn her shawl, and she had worn his waistcoat, which Jacob could only do very awkwardly; for he liked *Tom Jones.*

There it lay on her lap, in double columns, price three and sixpence; the mystic book in which Henry Fielding ever so many years ago rebuked Fanny Elmer for feasting on scarlet, in perfect prose, Jacob said. For he never read modern novels. He liked *Tom Jones.*

"I do like *Tom Jones,*" said Fanny, at five-thirty that same day early in April when Jacob took out his pipe in the arm-chair opposite.

Alas, women lie! But not Clara Durrant. A flawless mind; a candid nature; a virgin chained to a rock (somewhere off Lowndes Square) eternally pouring out tea for old men in white waistcoats, blue-eyed, looking you straight in the face, playing Bach. Of all women, Jacob honoured her most. But to sit at a table with bread and butter, with dowagers in velvet, and never say more to Clara Durrant than Benson said to the parrot when old Miss Perry poured out tea, was an insufferable outrage upon the liberties and decencies of human nature—or words to that effect. For Jacob said nothing. Only he glared at the fire. Fanny laid down *Tom Jones.*

She stitched or knitted.

"What's that?" asked Jacob.

"For the dance at the Slade."

And she fetched her head-dress; her trousers; her shoes with red tassels. What should she wear?

"I shall be in Paris," said Jacob.

And what is the point of fancy-dress dances? thought Fanny. You meet the same people; you wear the same clothes; Mangin gets drunk; Florinda sits on his knee. She flirts outrageously—with Nick Bramham just now.

"In Paris?" said Fanny.

"On my way to Greece," he replied.

For, he said, there is nothing so detestable as London in May.

He would forget her.

A sparrow flew past the window trailing a straw—a straw from a stack stood by a barn in a farmyard. The old brown spaniel snuffs at the base for a rat. Already the upper branches of the elm trees are blotted with nests. The chestnuts have flirted their fans. And the butterflies are flaunting across the rides in the Forest. Perhaps the Purple Emperor is feasting, as Morris says, upon a mass of putrid carrion at the base of an oak tree.

Fanny thought it all came from *Tom Jones.* He could go alone with a book in his pocket and watch the badgers. He would take a train at eight-thirty and walk all night. He saw fire-flies, and brought back glow-worms in pill-boxes. He would hunt with the New Forest Staghounds. It all came from *Tom Jones;* and he would go to Greece with a book in his pocket and forget her.

She fetched her hand-glass. There was her face. And suppose one wreathed Jacob in a turban? There was his face. She lit the lamp. But as the daylight came through the window only half was lit up by the lamp. And though he looked terrible and magnificent and would chuck the Forest, he said, and come to the Slade, and be a Turkish knight or a Roman emperor (and he let her blacken his lips and clenched his teeth and scowled in the glass), still—there lay *Tom Jones.*

11

"Archer," said Mrs. Flanders with that tenderness which mothers so often display towards their eldest sons, "will be at Gibraltar tomorrow."

The post for which she was waiting (strolling up Dods Hill while the random church bells swung a hymn tune about her head, the clock striking four straight through the circling notes; the glass purpling under a storm-cloud; and the two dozen houses of the village cowering, infinitely humble, in company under a leaf of shadow), the post, with all its variety of messages, envelopes addressed in bold hands, in slanting hands, stamped now with English stamps, again with Colonial stamps, or sometimes hastily dabbed with a yellow bar, the post was about to scatter a myriad messages over the world. Whether we gain or not by this habit of profuse communication it is not for us to say. But that letter-writing is practised mendaciously nowadays, particularly by young men travelling in foreign parts, seems likely enough.

For example, take this scene.

Here was Jacob Flanders gone abroad and staying to break his journey in Paris. (Old Miss Birkbeck, his mother's cousin, had died last June and left him a hundred pounds.)

"You needn't repeat the whole damned thing over again, Cruttendon," said Mallinson, the little bald painter who was sitting at a marble table, splashed with coffee and ringed with wine, talking very fast, and undoubtedly more than a little drunk.

"Well, Flanders, finished writing to your lady?" said Cruttendon, as

Jacob came and took his seat beside them, holding in his hand an envelope addressed to Mrs. Flanders, near Scarborough, England.

"Do you uphold Velasquez?" said Cruttendon.

"By God, he does," said Mallinson.

"He always gets like this," said Cruttendon irritably.

Jacob looked at Mallinson with excessive composure.

"I'll tell you the three greatest things that were ever written in the whole of literature," Cruttendon burst out. "'Hang there like fruit my soul.'" he began. . . .

"Don't listen to a man who don't like Velasquez," said Mallinson.

"Adolphe, don't give Mr. Mallinson any more wine," said Cruttendon.

"Fair play, fair play," said Jacob judicially. "Let a man get drunk if he likes. That's Shakespeare, Cruttendon. I'm with you there. Shakespeare had more guts than all these damned frogs put together. 'Hang there like fruit my soul,'" he began quoting, in a musical rhetorical voice, flourishing his wine-glass. "'The devil damn you black, you cream-faced loon!'" he exclaimed as the wine washed over the rim.

"'Hang there like fruit my soul,'" Cruttendon and Jacob both began again at the same moment, and both burst out laughing.

"Curse these flies," said Mallinson, flicking at his bald head. "What do they take me for?"

"Something sweet-smelling," said Cruttendon.

"Shut up, Cruttendon," said Jacob. "The fellow has no manners," he explained to Mallinson very politely. "Wants to cut people off their drink. Look here. I want grilled bone. What's the French for grilled bone? Grilled bone, Adolphe. Now you juggins, don't you understand?"

"And I'll tell you, Flanders, the second most beautiful thing in the whole of literature," said Cruttendon, bringing his feet down on to the floor, and leaning right across the table, so that his face almost touched Jacob's face.

"'Hey diddle diddle, the cat and the fiddle,'" Mallinson interrupted, strumming his fingers on the table. "The most ex-qui-sitely beautiful thing in the whole of literature. . . . Cruttendon is a very good fellow," he remarked confidentially. "But he's a bit of a fool." And he jerked his head forward.

Well, not a word of this was ever told to Mrs. Flanders; nor what happened when they paid the bill and left the restaurant, and walked along the Boulevard Raspaille.

Then here is another scrap of conversation; the time about eleven in the morning; the scene a studio; and the day Sunday.

"I tell you, Flanders," said Cruttendon, "I'd as soon have one of Mallinson's little pictures as a Chardin. And when I say that . . ." he squeezed the tail of an emaciated tube . . . "Chardin was a great swell. . . . He sells 'em to pay his dinner now. But wait till the dealers get hold of him. A great swell—oh, a very great swell."

"It's an awfully pleasant life," said Jacob, "messing away up here. Still, it's a stupid art, Cruttendon." He wandered off across the room. "There's this man, Pierre Louÿs now." He took up a book.

"Now my good sir, are you going to settle down?" said Cruttendon.

"That's a solid piece of work," said Jacob, standing a canvas on a chair.

"Oh, that I did ages ago," said Cruttendon, looking over his shoulder.

"You're a pretty competent painter in my opinion," said Jacob after a time.

"Now if you'd like to see what I'm after at the present moment," said Cruttendon, putting a canvas before Jacob. "There. That's it. That's more like it. That's . . ." he squirmed his thumb in a circle round a lamp globe painted white.

"A pretty solid piece of work," said Jacob, straddling his legs in front of it. "But what I wish you'd explain . . ."

Miss Jinny Carslake, pale, freckled, morbid, came into the room.

"Oh Jinny, here's a friend. Flanders. An Englishman. Wealthy. Highly connected. Go on, Flanders. . . ."

Jacob said nothing.

"It's *that*—that's not right," said Jinny Carslake.

"No," said Cruttendon decidedly. "Can't be done."

He took the canvas off the chair and stood it on the floor with its back to them.

"Sit down, ladies and gentlemen. Miss Carslake comes from your part of the world, Flanders. From Devonshire. Oh, I thought you said Devonshire. Very well. She's a daughter of the church too. The black sheep of the family. Her mother writes her such letters. I say—have you one about you? It's generally Sundays they come. Sort of church-bell effect, you know."

"Have you met all the painter men?" said Jinny. "Was Mallinson drunk? If you go to his studio he'll give you one of his pictures. I say, Teddy . . ."

"Half a jiff," said Cruttendon. "What's the season of the year?" He looked out of the window.

"We take a day off on Sundays, Flanders."

"Will he . . ." said Jinny, looking at Jacob. "You . . ."

"Yes, he'll come with us," said Cruttendon.

And then, here is Versailles. Jinny stood on the stone rim and leant over the pond, clasped by Cruttendon's arms or she would have fallen in. "There! There!" she cried. "Right up to the top!" Some sluggish, sloping-shouldered fish had floated up from the depths to nip her crumbs. "You look," she said, jumping down. And then the dazzling white water, rough and throttled, shot up into the air. The fountain spread itself. Through it came the sound of military music far away. All the water was puckered with drops. A blue air-ball gently bumped the surface. How all the nurses and children and old men and young crowded to the edge, leant over and waved their sticks! The little girl ran stretching her arms towards her air-ball, but it sank beneath the fountain.

Edward Cruttendon, Jinny Carslake, and Jacob Flanders walked in a row along the yellow gravel path; got on to the grass; so passed under the trees; and came out at the summer-house where Marie Antoinette used to drink chocolate. In went Edward and Jinny, but Jacob waited outside, sitting on the handle of his walking-stick. Out they came again.

"Well?" said Cruttendon, smiling at Jacob.

Jinny waited; Edward waited; and both looked at Jacob.

"Well?" said Jacob, smiling and pressing both hands on his stick.

"Come along," he decided; and started off. The others followed him, smiling.

And then they went to the little café in the by-street where people sit drinking coffee, watching the soldiers, meditatively knocking ashes into trays.

"But he's quite different," said Jinny, folding her hands over the top of her glass. "I don't suppose you know what Ted means when he says a thing like that," she said, looking at Jacob. "But I do. Sometimes I could kill myself. Sometimes he lies in bed all day long—just lies there. . . . I don't want you right on the table"; she waved her hands. Swollen iridescent pigeons were waddling round their feet.

"Look at that woman's hat," said Cruttendon. "How do they come to think of it? . . . No, Flanders, I don't think I could live like you. When one walks down that street opposite the British Museum—what's it called?—that's what I mean. It's all like that. Those fat women—and the man standing in the middle of the road as if he were going to have a fit . . ."

"Everybody feeds them," said Jinny, waving the pigeons away. "They're stupid old things."

"Well, I don't know," said Jacob, smoking his cigarette. "There's St. Paul's."

"I mean going to an office," said Cruttendon.

"Hang it all," Jacob expostulated.

"But you don't count," said Jinny, looking at Cruttendon. "You're mad. I mean, you just think of painting."

"Yes, I know. I can't help it. I say, will King George give way about the peers?"

"He'll jolly well have to," said Jacob.

"There!" said Jinny. "He really knows."

"You see, I would if I could," said Cruttendon, "but I simply can't."

"I *think* I could," said Jinny. "Only, it's all the people one dislikes who do it. At home, I mean. They talk of nothing else. Even people like my mother."

"Now if I came and lived here—" said Jacob. "What's my share, Cruttendon? Oh, very well. Have it your own way. Those silly birds, directly one wants them—they've flown away."

And finally under the arc lamps in the Gare des Invalides, with one of those queer movements which are so slight yet so definite, which may wound or pass unnoticed but generally inflict a good deal of discomfort, Jinny and Cruttendon drew together; Jacob stood apart. They had to separate. Something must be said. Nothing was said. A man wheeled a trolley past Jacob's legs so near that he almost grazed them. When Jacob recovered his balance the other two were turning away, though Jinny looked over her shoulder, and Cruttendon, waving his hand, disappeared like the very great genius that he was.

No—Mrs. Flanders was told none of this, though Jacob felt, it is safe to say, that nothing in the world was of greater importance; and as for Cruttendon and Jinny, he thought them the most remarkable people he had ever met—being of course unable to foresee how it fell out in the course of time that Cruttendon took to painting orchards; had therefore to live in Kent; and must, one would think, see through apple blossom by this time, since his wife, for whose sake he did it, eloped with a novelist; but no; Cruttendon still paints orchards, savagely, in solitude. Then Jinny Carslake, after her affair with Lefanu the American painter, frequented Indian philosophers, and now you find her in pensions in Italy cherishing a little jeweller's box containing ordinary pebbles picked off the road. But if you look at them steadily, she says, multiplicity becomes unity, which is somehow the secret of life, though it does not prevent her from following the macaroni as it goes round the table, and sometimes, on spring nights, she makes the strangest confidences to shy young Englishmen.

Jacob had nothing to hide from his mother. It was only that he could make no sense himself of his extraordinary excitement, and as for writing it down—

"Jacob's letters are so like him," said Mrs. Jarvis, folding the sheet.

"Indeed he seems to be having . . ." said Mrs. Flanders, and paused, for she was cutting out a dress and had to straighten the pattern, ". . . a very gay time."

Mrs. Jarvis thought of Paris. At her back the window was open, for it was a mild night; a calm night; when the moon seemed muffled and the apple trees stood perfectly still.

"I never pity the dead," said Mrs. Jarvis, shifting the cushion at her back, and clasping her hands behind her head. Betty Flanders did not hear, for her scissors made so much noise on the table.

"They are at rest," said Mrs. Jarvis. "And we spend our days doing foolish unnecessary things without knowing why."

Mrs. Jarvis was not liked in the village.

"You never walk at this time of night?" she asked Mrs. Flanders.

"It is certainly wonderfully mild," said Mrs. Flanders.

Yet it was years since she had opened the orchard gate and gone out on Dods Hill after dinner.

"It is perfectly dry," said Mrs. Jarvis, as they shut the orchard door and stepped on to the turf.

"I shan't go far," said Betty Flanders. "Yes, Jacob will leave Paris on Wednesday."

"Jacob was always my friend of the three," said Mrs. Jarvis.

"Now, my dear, I am going no further," said Mrs. Flanders. They had climbed the dark hill and reached the Roman camp.

The rampart rose at their feet—the smooth circle surrounding the camp or the grave. How many needles Betty Flanders had lost there; and her garnet brooch.

"It is much clearer than this sometimes," said Mrs. Jarvis, standing upon the ridge. There were no clouds, and yet there was a haze over the sea, and over the moors. The lights of Scarborough flashed, as if a woman wearing a diamond necklace turned her head this way and that.

"How quiet it is!" said Mrs. Jarvis.

Mrs. Flanders rubbed the turf with her toe, thinking of her garnet brooch.

Mrs. Jarvis found it difficult to think of herself tonight. It was so calm. There was no wind; nothing racing, flying, escaping. Black shadows stood still over the silver moors. The furze bushes stood perfectly still. Neither did Mrs. Jarvis think of God. There was a church behind them, of course. The church clock struck ten. Did the strokes reach the furze bush, or did the thorn tree hear them?

Mrs. Flanders was stooping down to pick up a pebble. Sometimes people do find things, Mrs. Jarvis thought, and yet in this hazy moonlight it was impossible to see anything, except bones, and little pieces of chalk.

"Jacob bought it with his own money, and then I brought Mr. Parker up to see the view, and it must have dropped—" Mrs. Flanders murmured.

Did the bones stir, or the rusty swords? Was Mrs. Flanders's twopenny-halfpenny brooch for ever part of the rich accumulation? and if all the ghosts flocked thick and rubbed shoulders with Mrs. Flanders in the circle, would she not have seemed perfectly in her place, a live English matron, growing stout?

The clock struck the quarter.

The frail waves of sound broke among the stiff gorse and the hawthorn twigs as the church clock divided time into quarters.

Motionless and broad-backed the moors received the statement "It is fifteen minutes past the hour," but made no answer, unless a bramble stirred.

Yet even in this light the legends on the tombstones could be read, brief voices saying, "I am Bertha Ruck," "I am Tom Gage." And they say which day of the year they died, and the New Testament says something for them, very proud, very emphatic, or consoling.

The moors accept all that too.

The moonlight falls like a pale page upon the church wall, and illumines the kneeling family in the niche, and the tablet set up in 1780 to the Squire of the parish who relieved the poor, and believed in God—so the measured voice goes on down the marble scroll, as though it could impose itself upon time and the open air.

Now a fox steals out from behind the gorse bushes.

Often, even at night, the church seems full of people. The pews are worn and greasy, and the cassocks in place, and the hymn-books on the ledges. It is a ship with all its crew aboard. The timbers strain to hold the dead and the living, the ploughmen, the carpenters, the fox-hunting gentlemen and the farmers smelling of mud and brandy. Their tongues join together in syllabling the sharp-cut words, which for ever slice asunder time and the broad-backed moors. Plaint and belief and elegy, despair and triumph, but for the most part good sense and jolly indifference, go trampling out of the windows any time these five hundred years.

Still, as Mrs. Jarvis said, stepping out on to the moors, "How quiet it is!" Quiet at midday, except when the hunt scatters across it; quiet in the afternoon, save for the drifting sheep; at night the moor is perfectly quiet.

A garnet brooch has dropped into its grass. A fox pads stealthily. A leaf turns on its edge. Mrs. Jarvis, who is fifty years of age, reposes in the camp in the hazy moonlight.

". . . and," said Mrs. Flanders, straightening her back, "I never cared for Mr. Parker."

"Neither did I," said Mrs. Jarvis. They began to walk home.

But their voices floated for a little above the camp. The moonlight destroyed nothing. The moor accepted everything. Tom Gage cries aloud so long as his tombstone endures. The Roman skeletons are in safe keeping. Betty Flanders's darning needles are safe too and her garnet brooch. And sometimes at midday, in the sunshine, the moor seems to hoard these little treasures, like a nurse. But at midnight when no one speaks or gallops, and the thorn tree is perfectly still, it would be foolish to vex the moor with questions—what? and why?

The church clock, however, strikes twelve.

12

The water fell off a ledge like lead—like a chain with thick white links. The train ran out into a steep green meadow, and Jacob saw striped tulips growing and heard a bird singing, in Italy.

A motor car full of Italian officers ran along the flat road and kept up with the train, raising dust behind it. There were trees laced together with vines—as Virgil said. Here was a station; and a tremendous leave-taking going on, with women in high yellow boots and odd pale boys in ringed socks. Virgil's bees had gone about the plains of Lombardy. It was the custom of the ancients to train vines between elms. Then at Milan there were sharp-winged hawks, of a bright brown, cutting figures over the roofs.

These Italian carriages get damnably hot with the afternoon sun on them, and the chances are that before the engine has pulled to the top of the gorge the clanking chain will have broken. Up, up, up, it goes, like a train on a scenic railway. Every peak is covered with sharp trees, and amazing white villages are crowded on ledges. There is always a white tower on the very summit, flat red-frilled roofs, and a sheer drop beneath. It is not a country in which one walks after tea. For one thing there is no grass. A whole hillside will be ruled with olive trees. Already in April the earth is clotted into dry dust between them. And there are neither stiles nor footpaths, nor lanes chequered with the shadows of leaves nor eighteenth-century inns with bow-windows, where one eats ham and eggs. Oh no, Italy is all fierceness, bareness, exposure, and black priests shuffling along the roads. It is strange, too, how you never get away from villas.

Still, to be travelling on one's own with a hundred pounds to spend is a fine affair. And if his money gave out, as it probably would, he would go on foot. He could live on bread and wine—the wine in straw bottles—for after doing Greece he was going to knock off Rome. The Roman civilization was a very inferior affair, no doubt. But Bonamy talked a lot of rot, all the same. "You ought to have been in Athens," he would say to Bonamy when he got back. "Standing on the Parthenon," he would say, or "The ruins of the Coliseum suggest some fairly sublime reflections," which he would write out at length in letters. It might turn to an essay upon civilization. A comparison between the ancients and moderns, with some pretty sharp hits at Mr. Asquith—something in the style of Gibbon.

A stout gentleman laboriously hauled himself in, dusty, baggy, slung with gold chains, and Jacob, regretting that he did not come of the Latin race, looked out of the window.

It is a strange reflection that by travelling two days and nights you are in the heart of Italy. Accidental villas among olive trees appear; and menservants watering the cactuses. Black victorias drive in between pompous pillars with plaster shields stuck to them. It is at once momentary and astonishingly intimate—to be displayed before the eyes of a foreigner. And there is a lonely hill-top where no one ever comes, and yet it is seen by me who was lately driving down Piccadilly on an omnibus. And what I should like would be to get out among the fields, sit down and hear the grasshoppers, and take up a handful of earth—Italian earth, as this is Italian dust upon my shoes.

Jacob heard them crying strange names at railway stations through the night. The train stopped and he heard frogs croaking close by, and he wrinkled back the blind cautiously and saw a vast strange marsh all white in the moonlight. The carriage was thick with cigar smoke, which floated round the globe with the green shade on it. The Italian gentleman lay snoring with his boots off and his waistcoat unbuttoned. . . . And all this business of going to Greece seemed to Jacob an intolerable weariness—sitting in hotels by oneself and looking at monuments—he'd have done better to go to Cornwall with Timmy Durrant. . . . "O—h," Jacob protested, as the darkness began breaking in front of him and the light showed through, but the man was reaching across him to get something—the fat Italian man in his dicky, unshaven, crumpled, obese, was opening the door and going off to have a wash.

So Jacob sat up, and saw a lean Italian sportsman with a gun walking down the road in the early morning light, and the whole idea of the Parthenon came upon him in a clap.

"By Jove!" he thought, "we must be nearly there!" and he stuck his head out of the window and got the air full in his face.

It is highly exasperating that twenty-five people of your acquaintance should be able to say straight off something very much to the point about being in Greece, while for yourself there is a stopper upon all emotions whatsoever. For after washing at the hotel at Patras, Jacob had followed the tram lines a mile or so out; and followed them a mile or so back; he had met several droves of turkeys; several strings of donkeys; had got lost in back streets; had read advertisements of corsets and of Maggi's consommé; children had trodden on his toes; the place smelt of bad cheese; and he was glad to find himself suddenly come out opposite his hotel. There was an old copy of the *Daily Mail* lying among coffee-cups; which he read. But what could he do after dinner?

No doubt we should be, on the whole, much worse off than we are without our astonishing gift for illusion. At the age of twelve or so, having given up dolls and broken our steam engines, France, but much more probably Italy, and India almost for a certainty, draws the superfluous imagination. One's aunts have been to Rome; and every one has an uncle who was last heard of—poor man—in Rangoon. He will never come back any more. But it is the governesses who start the Greek myth. Look at that for a head (they say)—nose, you see, straight as a dart, curls, eyebrows—everything appropriate to manly beauty; while his legs and arms have lines on them which indicate a perfect degree of development—the Greeks caring for the body as much as for the face. And the Greeks could paint fruit so that birds pecked at it. First you read Xenophon; then Euripides. One day—that was an occasion, by God—what people have said appears to have sense in it; "the Greek spirit"; the Greek this, that, and the other; though it is absurd, by the way, to say that any Greek comes near Shakespeare. The point is, however, that we have been brought up in an illusion.

Jacob, no doubt, thought something in this fashion, the *Daily Mail* crumpled in his hand; his legs extended; the very picture of boredom.

"But it's the way we're brought up," he went on.

And it all seemed to him very distasteful. Something ought to be done about it. And from being moderately depressed he became like a man about to be executed. Clara Durrant had left him at a party to talk to an American called Pilchard. And he had come all the way to Greece and left her. They wore evening-dresses, and talked nonsense—what damned nonsense—and he put out his hand for the *Globe Trotter*, an international magazine which is supplied free of charge to the proprietors of hotels.

In spite of its ramshackle condition modern Greece is highly advanced in the electric tramway system, so that while Jacob sat in the hotel sitting-room the trams clanked, chimed, rang, rang, rang imperiously to get the donkeys out of the way, and one old woman who refused to budge, beneath the windows. The whole of civilization was being condemned.

The waiter was quite indifferent to that too. Aristotle, a dirty man, carnivorously interested in the body of the only guest now occupying the only arm-chair, came into the room ostentatiously, put something down, put something straight, and saw that Jacob was still there.

"I shall want to be called early tomorrow," said Jacob, over his shoulder. "I am going to Olympia."

This gloom, this surrender to the dark waters which lap us about, is a modern invention. Perhaps, as Cruttendon said, we do not believe enough. Our fathers at any rate had something to demolish. So have we for the matter of that, thought Jacob, crumpling the *Daily Mail* in his hand. He would go into Parliament and make fine speeches—but what use are fine speeches and Parliament, once you surrender an inch to the black waters? Indeed there has never been any explanation of the ebb and flow in our veins—of happiness and unhappiness. That respectability and evening parties where one has to dress, and wretched slums at the back of Gray's Inn—something solid, immovable, and grotesque—is at the back of it, Jacob thought probable. But then there was the British Empire which was beginning to puzzle him; nor was he altogether in favour of giving Home Rule to Ireland. What did the *Daily Mail* say about that?

For he had grown to be a man, and was about to be immersed in things—as indeed the chambermaid, emptying his basin upstairs, fingering keys, studs, pencils, and bottles of tabloids strewn on the dressing-table, was aware.

That he had grown to be a man was a fact that Florinda knew, as she knew everything, by instinct.

And Betty Flanders even now suspected it, as she read his letter, posted at Milan, "Telling me," she complained to Mrs. Jarvis, "really nothing that I want to know"; but she brooded over it.

Fanny Elmer felt it to desperation. For he would take his stick and his hat and would walk to the window, and look perfectly absent-minded and very stern too, she thought.

"I am going," he would say, "to cadge a meal of Bonamy."

"Anyhow, I can drown myself in the Thames," Fanny cried, as she hurried past the Foundling Hospital.

"But the *Daily Mail* isn't to be trusted," Jacob said to himself, looking about for something else to read. And he sighed again, being indeed so profoundly gloomy that gloom must have been lodged in him to cloud him at any moment, which was odd in a man who enjoyed things so, was not much given to analysis, but was horribly romantic, of course, Bonamy thought, in his rooms in Lincoln's Inn.

"He will fall in love," thought Bonamy. "Some Greek woman with a straight nose."

It was to Bonamy that Jacob wrote from Patras—to Bonamy who couldn't love a woman and never read a foolish book.

There are very few good books after all, for we can't count profuse histories, travels in mule carts to discover the sources of the Nile, or the volubility of fiction.

I like books whose virtue is all drawn together in a page or two. I like sentences that don't budge though armies cross them. I like words to be hard—such were Bonamy's views, and they won him the hostility of those whose taste is all for the fresh growths of the morning, who throw up the window, and find the poppies spread in the sun, and can't forbear a shout of jubilation at the astonishing fertility of English literature. That was not Bonamy's way at all. That his taste in literature affected his friendships, and made him silent, secretive, fastidious, and only quite at his ease with one or two young men of his own way of thinking, was the charge against him.

But then Jacob Flanders was not at all of his own way of thinking—far from it, Bonamy sighed, laying the thin sheets of notepaper on the table and falling into thought about Jacob's character, not for the first time.

The trouble was this romantic vein in him. "But mixed with the stupidity which leads him into these absurd predicaments," thought Bonamy, "there is something—something"—he sighed, for he was fonder of Jacob than of any one in the world.

Jacob went to the window and stood with his hands in his pockets. There he saw three Greeks in kilts; the masts of ships; idle or busy people of the lower classes strolling or stepping out briskly, or falling into groups and gesticulating with their hands. Their lack of concern for him was not the cause of his gloom; but some more profound conviction—it was not that he himself happened to be lonely, but that all people are.

Yet next day, as the train slowly rounded a hill on the way to Olympia, the Greek peasant women were out among the vines; the old Greek men were sitting at the stations, sipping sweet wine. And though Jacob remained gloomy he had never suspected how tremendously pleasant it is to be alone; out of England; on one's own; cut off from the whole thing. There are very sharp bare hills on the way to Olympia; and between them blue sea in triangular spaces. A little like the Cornish coast. Well now, to go walking by oneself all day—to get on to that track and follow it up between the bushes—or are they small trees?—to the top of that mountain from which one can see half the nations of antiquity——

"Yes," said Jacob, for his carriage was empty, "let's look at the map."

Blame it or praise it, there is no denying the wild horse in us. To gallop intemperately; fall on the sand tired out; to feel the earth spin; to have—positively—a rush of friendship for stones and grasses, as if humanity were over, and as for men and women, let them go hang—there is no getting over the fact that this desire seizes us pretty often.

* * *

The evening air slightly moved the dirty curtains in the hotel window at Olympia.

"I am full of love for every one," thought Mrs. Wentworth Williams, "—for the poor most of all—for the peasants coming back in the evening with their burdens. And everything is soft and vague and very sad. It is sad, it is sad. But everything has meaning," thought Sandra Wentworth Williams, raising her head a little and looking very beautiful, tragic, and exalted. "One must love everything."

She held in her hand a little book convenient for travelling—stories by Tchekov—as she stood, veiled, in white, in the window of the hotel at Olympia. How beautiful the evening was! and her beauty was its beauty. The tragedy of Greece was the tragedy of all high souls. The inevitable compromise. She seemed to have grasped something. She would write it down. And moving to the table where her husband sat reading she leant her chin in her hands and thought of the peasants, of suffering, of her own beauty, of the inevitable compromise, and of how she would write it down. Nor did Evan Williams say anything brutal, banal, or foolish when he shut his book and put it away to make room for the plates of soup which were now being placed before them. Only his drooping bloodhound eyes and his heavy sallow cheeks expressed his melancholy tolerance, his conviction that though forced to live with circumspection and deliberation he could never possibly achieve any of those objects which, as he knew, are the only ones worth pursuing. His consideration was flawless; his silence unbroken.

"Everything seems to mean so much," said Sandra. But with the sound of her own voice the spell was broken. She forgot the peasants. Only there remained with her a sense of her own beauty, and in front, luckily, there was a looking-glass.

"I am very beautiful," she thought.

She shifted her hat slightly. Her husband saw her looking in the glass; and agreed that beauty is important; it is an inheritance; one cannot ignore it. But it is a barrier; it is in fact rather a bore. So he drank his soup; and kept his eyes fixed upon the window.

"Quails," said Mrs. Wentworth Williams languidly. "And then goat, I suppose; and then . . ."

"Caramel custard presumably," said her husband in the same cadence, with his toothpick out already.

She laid her spoon upon her plate, and her soup was taken away half finished. Never did she do anything without dignity; for hers was the English type which is so Greek, save that villagers have touched their hats to it, the vicarage reveres it; and upper-gardeners and under-gardeners respectfully straighten their backs as she comes down the broad terrace on Sunday morning, dallying at the stone urns with the Prime Minister to pick a rose—which, perhaps, she was trying to forget, as her eye wandered round the dining-room of the inn at Olympia, seeking the window where her book lay, where a few minutes ago she had discovered something—something very profound it had been, about love and sadness and the peasants.

But it was Evan who sighed; not in despair nor indeed in rebellion. But, being the most ambitious of men and temperamentally the most sluggish, he had accomplished nothing; had the political history of England at his finger-ends, and living much in company with Chatham, Pitt, Burke, and Charles James Fox could not help contrasting himself and his age with them and theirs. "Yet there never was a time when great men are more needed," he was in the habit of saying to himself, with a sigh. Here he was picking his teeth in an inn at Olympia. He had done. But Sandra's eyes wandered.

"Those pink melons are sure to be dangerous," he said gloomily. And as he spoke the door opened and in came a young man in a grey check suit.

"Beautiful but dangerous," said Sandra, immediately talking to her husband in the presence of a third person. ("Ah, an English boy on tour," she thought to herself.)

And Evan knew all that too.

Yes, he knew all that; and he admired her. Very pleasant, he thought, to have affairs. But for himself, what with his height (Napoleon was five feet four, he remembered), his bulk, his inability to impose his own personality (and yet great men are needed more than ever now, he sighed), it was useless. He threw away his cigar, went up to Jacob and asked him, with a simple sort of sincerity which Jacob liked, whether he had come straight out from England.

"How very English!" Sandra laughed when the waiter told them next morning that the young gentleman had left at five to climb the mountain. "I am sure he asked you for a bath?" at which the waiter shook his head, and said that he would ask the manager.

"You do not understand," laughed Sandra. "Never mind."

Stretched on the top of the mountain, quite alone, Jacob enjoyed himself immensely. Probably he had never been so happy in the whole of his life.

But at dinner that night Mr. Williams asked him whether he would like to see the paper; then Mrs. Williams asked him (as they strolled on the terrace smoking—and how could he refuse that man's cigar?) whether he'd seen the theatre by moonlight; whether he knew Everard Sherborn; whether he read Greek and whether (Evan rose silently and went in) if he had to sacrifice one it would be the French literature or the Russian?

"And now," wrote Jacob in his letter to Bonamy, "I shall have to read her cursed book"—her Tchekov, he meant, for she had lent it him.

Though the opinion is unpopular it seems likely enough that bare places, fields too thick with stones to be ploughed, tossing sea-meadows half-way between England and America, suit us better than cities.

There is something absolute in us which despises qualification. It is this which is teased and twisted in society. People come together in a room. "So delighted," says somebody, "to meet you," and that is a lie. And then: "I enjoy the spring more than the autumn now. One does, I think, as one gets older." For women are always, always, always talking about what one feels, and if they say "as one gets older," they mean you to reply with something quite off the point.

Jacob sat himself down in the quarry where the Greeks had cut marble for the theatre. It is hot work walking up Greek hills at midday. The wild red cyclamen was out; he had seen the little tortoises hobbling from clump to clump; the air smelt strong and suddenly sweet, and the sun, striking on jagged splinters of marble, was very dazzling to the eyes. Composed, commanding, contemptuous, a little melancholy, and bored with an august kind of boredom, there he sat smoking his pipe.

Bonamy would have said that this was the sort of thing that made him uneasy—when Jacob got into the doldrums, looked like a Margate fisherman out of a job, or a British Admiral. You couldn't make him understand a thing when he was in a mood like that. One had better leave him alone. He was dull. He was apt to be grumpy.

He was up very early, looking at the statues with his Baedeker.

Sandra Wentworth Williams, ranging the world before breakfast in quest of adventure or a point of view, all in white, not so very tall perhaps, but uncommonly upright—Sandra Williams got Jacob's head exactly on a level with the head of the Hermes of Praxiteles. The comparison was all in his favour. But before she could say a single word he had gone out of the Museum and left her.

Still, a lady of fashion travels with more than one dress, and if white suits the morning hour, perhaps sandy yellow with purple spots on it, a black hat, and a volume of Balzac, suit the evening. Thus she was arranged on the terrace when Jacob came in. Very beautiful she looked. With her hands folded she mused, seemed to listen to her husband, seemed to watch the peasants coming down with brushwood on their backs, seemed to notice how the hill changed from blue to black, seemed to discriminate between truth and falsehood, Jacob thought, and crossed his legs suddenly, observing the extreme shabbiness of his trousers.

"But he is very distinguished looking," Sandra decided.

And Evan Williams, lying back in his chair with the paper on his knees, envied them. The best thing he could do would be to publish, with Macmillans, his monograph upon the foreign policy of Chatham. But confound this tumid, queasy feeling—this restlessness, swelling, and heat—it was jealousy! jealousy! jealousy! which he had sworn never to feel again.

"Come with us to Corinth, Flanders," he said with more than his usual energy, stopping by Jacob's chair. He was relieved by Jacob's reply, or rather by the solid, direct, if shy manner in which he said that he would like very much to come with them to Corinth.

"Here is a fellow," thought Evan Williams, "who might do very well in politics."

"I intend to come to Greece every year so long as I live," Jacob wrote to Bonamy. "It is the only chance I can see of protecting oneself from civilization."

"Goodness knows what he means by that," Bonamy sighed. For as he never said a clumsy thing himself, these dark sayings of Jacob's made him feel apprehensive, yet somehow impressed, his own turn being all for the definite, the concrete, and the rational.

Nothing could be much simpler than what Sandra said as she descended the Acro-Corinth, keeping to the little path, while Jacob strode over rougher ground by her side. She had been left motherless at the age of four; and the Park was vast.

"One never seemed able to get out of it," she laughed. Of course there was the library, and dear Mr. Jones, and notions about things. "I used to stray into the kitchen and sit upon the butler's knees," she laughed, sadly though.

Jacob thought that if he had been there he would have saved her; for she had been exposed to great dangers, he felt, and, he thought to himself, "People wouldn't understand a woman talking as she talks."

She made little of the roughness of the hill; and wore breeches, he saw, under her short skirts.

"Women like Fanny Elmer don't," he thought. "What's-her-name Carslake didn't; yet they pretend . . ."

Mrs. Williams said things straight out. He was surprised by his own knowledge of the rules of behaviour; how much more can be said than one thought; how open one can be with a woman; and how little he had known himself before.

Evan joined them on the road; and as they drove along up hill and down hill (for Greece is in a state of effervescence, yet astonishingly clean-cut, a treeless land, where you see the ground between the blades, each hill cut and shaped and outlined as often as not against sparkling deep blue waters, islands white as sand floating on the horizon, occasional groves of palm trees standing in the valleys, which are scattered with black goats, spotted with little olive trees and sometimes have white hollows, rayed and criss-crossed, in their flanks), as they drove up hill and down he scowled in the corner of the carriage, with his paw so tightly closed that the skin was stretched between the knuckles and the little hairs stood upright. Sandra rode opposite, dominant, like a Victory prepared to fling into the air.

"Heartless!" thought Evan (which was untrue).

"Brainless!" he suspected (and that was not true either). "Still . . . !" He envied her.

When bedtime came the difficulty was to write to Bonamy, Jacob found. Yet he had seen Salamis, and Marathon in the distance. Poor old Bonamy! No; there was something queer about it. He could not write to Bonamy.

"I shall go to Athens all the same," he resolved, looking very set, with this hook dragging in his side.

The Williamses had already been to Athens.

Athens is still quite capable of striking a young man as the oddest combination, the most incongruous assortment. Now it is suburban; now immortal. Now cheap continental jewellery is laid upon plush trays. Now the stately woman stands naked, save for a wave of drapery above the knee. No form can he set on his sensations as he strolls, one blazing afternoon, along the Parisian boulevard and skips out of the way of the royal landau which, looking indescribably ramshackle, rattles along the pitted roadway, saluted by citizens of both sexes cheaply dressed in bowler hats and continental costumes; though a shepherd in kilt, cap, and gaiters very nearly drives his herd of goats between the royal wheels; and all the time the Acropolis surges into the air, raises itself above the town, like a large immobile wave with the yellow columns of the Parthenon firmly planted upon it.

The yellow columns of the Parthenon are to be seen at all hours of the day firmly planted upon the Acropolis; though at sunset, when the ships in the Piraeus fire their guns, a bell rings, a man in uniform (the waistcoat unbuttoned) appears; and the women roll up the black stockings which they are knitting in the shadow of the columns, call to the children, and troop off down the hill back to their houses.

There they are again, the pillars, the pediment, the Temple of Victory and the Erechtheum, set on a tawny rock cleft with shadows, directly you unlatch your shutters in the morning and, leaning out, hear the clatter, the clamour, the whip cracking in the street below. There they are.

The extreme definiteness with which they stand, now a brilliant white, again yellow, and in some lights red, imposes ideas of durability, of the emergence through the earth of some spiritual energy elsewhere dissipated in elegant trifles. But this durability exists quite independently of our admiration. Although the beauty is sufficiently humane to weaken us, to stir the deep deposit of mud—memories, abandonments, regrets, sentimental devotions—the Parthenon is separate from all that; and if you consider how it has stood out all night, for centuries, you begin to connect the blaze (at midday the glare is dazzling and the frieze almost invisible) with the idea that perhaps it is beauty alone that is immortal.

Added to this, compared with the blistered stucco, the new love songs rasped out to the strum of guitar and gramophone, and the mobile yet insignificant faces of the street, the Parthenon is really astonishing in its silent composure; which is so vigorous that, far from being decayed, the Parthenon appears, on the contrary, likely to outlast the entire world.

"And the Greeks, like sensible men, never bothered to finish the backs of their statues," said Jacob, shading his eyes and observing that the side of the figure which is turned away from view is left in the rough.

He noted the slight irregularity in the line of the steps which "the artistic sense of the Greeks preferred to mathematical accuracy," he read in his guide-book.

He stood on the exact spot where the great statue of Athena used to stand, and identified the more famous landmarks of the scene beneath.

In short he was accurate and diligent; but profoundly morose. Moreover he was pestered by guides. This was on Monday.

But on Wednesday he wrote a telegram to Bonamy, telling him to come at once. And then he crumpled it in his hand and threw it in the gutter.

"For one thing he wouldn't come," he thought. "And then I daresay this sort of thing wears off." "This sort of thing" being that uneasy, painful feeling, something like selfishness—one wishes almost that the thing would stop—it is getting more and more beyond what is possible—"If it goes on much longer I shan't be able to cope with it—but if some one else were seeing it at the same time—Bonamy is stuffed in his room in Lincoln's Inn—oh, I say, damn it all, I say,"—the sight of Hymettus, Pentelicus, Lycabettus on one side, and the sea on the other, as one stands in the Parthenon at sunset, the sky pink feathered, the plain all colours, the marble tawny in one's eyes, is thus oppressive. Luckily Jacob had little sense of personal association; he seldom thought of Plato or Socrates in the flesh; on the other hand his feeling for architecture was very strong; he preferred statues to pictures; and he was beginning to think a great deal about the problems of civilization, which were solved, of course, so very remarkably by the ancient Greeks, though their solution is no help to us. Then the hook gave a great tug in his side as he lay in bed on Wednesday night; and he turned over with a desperate sort of tumble, remembering Sandra Wentworth Williams with whom he was in love.

Next day he climbed Pentelicus.

The day after he went up to the Acropolis. The hour was early; the place almost deserted; and possibly there was thunder in the air. But the sun struck full upon the Acropolis.

Jacob's intention was to sit down and read, and, finding a drum of marble conveniently placed, from which Marathon could be seen, and yet it was in the shade, while the Erechtheum blazed white in front of him, there he sat. And after reading a page he put his thumb in his book. Why not rule countries in the way they should be ruled? And he read again.

No doubt his position there overlooking Marathon somehow raised his spirits. Or it may have been that a slow capacious brain has these moments of flowering. Or he had, insensibly, while he was abroad, got into the way of thinking about politics.

And then looking up and seeing the sharp outline, his meditations were given an extraordinary edge; Greece was over; the Parthenon in ruins; yet there he was.

(Ladies with green and white umbrellas passed through the courtyard—French ladies on their way to join their husbands in Constantinople.)

Jacob read on again. And laying the book on the ground he began, as if inspired by what he had read, to write a note upon the importance of history—upon democracy—one of those scribbles upon which the work of a lifetime may be based; or again, it falls out of a book twenty years later, and one can't remember a word of it. It is a little painful. It had better be burnt.

Jacob wrote; began to draw a straight nose; when all the French ladies opening and shutting their umbrellas just beneath him exclaimed, looking at the sky, that one did not know what to expect—rain or fine weather?

Jacob got up and strolled across to the Erechtheum. There are still several women standing there holding the roof on their heads. Jacob straightened himself slightly; for stability and balance affect the body first. These statues annulled things so! He stared at them, then turned, and there was Madame Lucien Grave perched on a block of marble with her kodak pointed at his head. Of course she jumped down, in spite of her age, her figure, and her tight boots—having, now that her daughter was married, lapsed with a luxurious abandonment, grand enough in its way, into the fleshy grotesque; she jumped down, but not before Jacob had seen her.

"Damn these women—damn these women!" he thought. And he went to fetch his book which he had left lying on the ground in the Parthenon.

"How they spoil things," he murmured, leaning against one of the pillars, pressing his book tight between his arm and his side. (As for the weather, no doubt the storm would break soon; Athens was under cloud.)

"It is those damned women," said Jacob, without any trace of bitterness, but rather with sadness and disappointment that what might have been should never be.

(This violent disillusionment is generally to be expected in young men in the prime of life, sound of wind and limb, who will soon become fathers of families and directors of banks.)

Then, making sure that the Frenchwomen had gone, and looking cautiously round him, Jacob strolled over to the Erechtheum and looked rather furtively at the goddess on the left-hand side holding the roof on her head. She reminded him of Sandra Wentworth Williams. He looked at her, then looked away. He looked at her, then looked away. He was extraordinarily moved, and with the battered Greek nose in his head, with Sandra in his head, with all sorts of things in his head, off he started to walk right up to the top of Mount Hymettus, alone, in the heat.

That very afternoon Bonamy went expressly to talk about Jacob to tea with Clara Durrant in the square behind Sloane Street where, on hot spring days, there are striped blinds over the front windows, single horses pawing the macadam outside the doors, and elderly gentlemen in yellow waistcoats ringing bells and stepping in very politely when the maid demurely replies that Mrs. Durrant is at home.

Bonamy sat with Clara in the sunny front room with the barrel organ piping sweetly outside; the water-cart going slowly along spraying the pavement; the carriages jingling, and all the silver and chintz, brown and blue rugs and vases filled with green boughs, striped with trembling yellow bars.

The insipidity of what was said needs no illustration—Bonamy kept on gently returning quiet answers and accumulating amazement at an existence squeezed and emasculated within a white satin shoe (Mrs. Durrant meanwhile enunciating strident politics with Sir Somebody in the back room) until the virginity of Clara's soul appeared to him candid; the depths unknown; and he would have brought out Jacob's name had he not begun to feel positively certain that Clara loved him—and could do nothing whatever.

"Nothing whatever!" he exclaimed, as the door shut, and, for a man of his temperament, got a very queer feeling, as he walked through the park, of carriages irresistibly driven; of flower beds uncompromisingly geometrical; of force rushing round geometrical patterns in the most senseless way in the world. "Was Clara," he thought, pausing to watch the boys bathing in the Serpentine, "the silent woman?—would Jacob marry her?"

But in Athens in the sunshine, in Athens, where it is almost impossible to get afternoon tea, and elderly gentlemen who talk politics talk them all the other way round, in Athens sat Sandra Wentworth Williams, veiled, in white, her legs stretched in front of her, one elbow on the arm of the bamboo chair, blue clouds wavering and drifting from her cigarette.

The orange trees which flourish in the Square of the Constitution, the band, the dragging of feet, the sky, the houses, lemon and rose coloured—all this became so significant to Mrs. Wentworth Williams after her second cup of coffee that she began dramatizing the story of the noble and impulsive Englishwoman who had offered a seat in her carriage to the old American lady at Mycenae (Mrs. Duggan)—not altogether a false story, though it said nothing of Evan, standing first on one foot, then on the other, waiting for the women to stop chattering.

"I am putting the life of Father Damien into verse," Mrs. Duggan had said, for she had lost everything—everything in the world, husband and child and everything, but faith remained.

Sandra, floating from the particular to the universal, lay back in a trance.

The flight of time which hurries us so tragically along; the eternal drudge and drone, now bursting into fiery flame like those brief balls of yellow among green leaves (she was looking at orange trees); kisses on lips that are to die; the world turning, turning in mazes of heat and sound—though to be sure there is the quiet evening with its lovely pallor, "For I am sensitive to every side of it," Sandra thought, "and Mrs. Duggan will write to me for ever, and I shall answer her letters." Now the royal band marching by with the national flag stirred wider rings of emotion, and life became something that the courageous mount and ride out to sea on—the hair blown back (so she envisaged it, and the breeze stirred slightly among the orange trees) and she herself was emerging from silver spray—when she saw Jacob. He was standing in the Square with a book under his arm looking vacantly about him. That he was heavily built and might become stout in time was a fact.

But she suspected him of being a mere bumpkin.

"There is that young man," she said, peevishly, throwing away her cigarette, "that Mr. Flanders."

"Where?" said Evan. "I don't see him."

"Oh, walking away—behind the trees now. No, you can't see him. But we are sure to run into him," which, of course, they did.

But how far was he a mere bumpkin? How far was Jacob Flanders at the age of twenty-six a stupid fellow? It is no use trying to sum people up. One must follow hints, not exactly what is said, nor yet entirely what is done. Some, it is true, take ineffaceable impressions of character at once. Others dally, loiter, and get blown this way and that. Kind old ladies assure us that cats are often the best judges of character. A cat will always go to a good man, they say; but then, Mrs. Whitehorn, Jacob's landlady, loathed cats.

There is also the highly respectable opinion that character-mongering is much overdone nowadays. After all, what does it matter—that Fanny Elmer was all sentiment and sensation, and Mrs. Durrant hard as iron? that Clara, owing (so the character-mongers said) largely to her mother's influence, never yet had the chance to do anything off her own bat, and only to very observant eyes displayed deeps of feeling which were positively alarming; and would certainly throw herself away upon some one unworthy of her one of these days unless, so the character-mongers said, she had a spark of her mother's spirit in her—was somehow heroic. But what a term to apply to Clara Durrant! Simple to a degree, others thought her. And that is the very reason, so they said, why she attracts Dick Bonamy—the young man with the Wellington nose. Now *he's* a dark horse if you like. And there these gossips would suddenly pause. Obviously they meant to hint at his peculiar disposition—long rumoured among them.

"But sometimes it is precisely a woman like Clara that men of that temperament need . . ." Miss Julia Eliot would hint.

"Well," Mr. Bowley would reply, "it may be so."

For however long these gossips sit, and however they stuff out their victims' characters till they are swollen and tender as the livers of geese exposed to a hot fire, they never come to a decision.

"That young man, Jacob Flanders," they would say, "so distinguished looking—and yet so awkward." Then they would apply themselves to Jacob and vacillate eternally between the two extremes. He rode to hounds—after a fashion, for he hadn't a penny.

"Did you ever hear who his father was?" asked Julia Eliot.

"His mother, they say, is somehow connected with the Rocksbiers," replied Mr. Bowley.

"He doesn't overwork himself anyhow."

"His friends are very fond of him."

"Dick Bonamy, you mean?"

"No, I didn't mean that. It's evidently the other way with Jacob. He is precisely the young man to fall headlong in love and repent it for the rest of his life."

"Oh, Mr. Bowley," said Mrs. Durrant, sweeping down upon them in her imperious manner, "you remember Mrs. Adams? Well, that is her niece." And Mr. Bowley, getting up, bowed politely and fetched strawberries.

So we are driven back to see what the other side means—the men in clubs and Cabinets—when they say that character-drawing is a frivolous fireside art, a matter of pins and needles, exquisite outlines enclosing vacancy, flourishes, and mere scrawls.

The battleships ray out over the North Sea, keeping their stations accurately apart. At a given signal all the guns are trained on a target which (the master gunner counts the seconds, watch in hand—at the sixth he looks up) flames into splinters. With equal nonchalance a dozen young men in the prime of life descend with composed faces into the depths of the sea; and there impassively (though with perfect mastery of machinery) suffocate uncomplainingly together. Like blocks of tin soldiers the army covers the cornfield, moves up the hillside, stops, reels slightly this way and that, and falls flat, save that, through field glasses, it can be seen that one or two pieces still agitate up and down like fragments of broken match-stick.

These actions, together with the incessant commerce of banks, laboratories, chancellories, and houses of business, are the strokes which oar the world forward, they say. And they are dealt by men as smoothly sculptured as the impassive policeman at Ludgate Circus. But you will observe that far from being padded to rotundity his face is stiff from force of will, and lean from the efforts of keeping it so. When his right arm rises, all the force in his veins flows straight from shoulder to finger-tips; not an ounce is diverted into sudden impulses, sentimental regrets, wire-drawn distinctions. The buses punctually stop.

It is thus that we live, they say, driven by an unseizable force. They say that the novelists never catch it; that it goes hurtling through their nets and leaves them torn to ribbons. This, they say, is what we live by—this unseizable force.

"Where are the men?" said old General Gibbons, looking round the drawing-room, full as usual on Sunday afternoons of well-dressed people. "Where are the guns?"

Mrs. Durrant looked too.

Clara, thinking that her mother wanted her, came in; then went out again.

They were talking about Germany at the Durrants, and Jacob (driven by this unseizable force) walked rapidly down Hermes Street and ran straight into the Williamses.

"Oh!" cried Sandra, with a cordiality which she suddenly felt. And Evan added, "What luck!"

The dinner which they gave him in the hotel which looks on to the Square of the Constitution was excellent. Plated baskets contained fresh rolls. There was real butter. And the meat scarcely needed the disguise of innumerable little red and green vegetables glazed in sauce.

It was strange, though. There were the little tables set out at intervals on the scarlet floor with the Greek King's monogram wrought in yellow. Sandra dined in her hat, veiled as usual. Evan looked this way and that over his shoulder; imperturbable yet supple; and sometimes sighed. It was strange. For they were English people come together in Athens on a May evening. Jacob, helping himself to this and that, answered intelligently, yet with a ring in his voice.

The Williamses were going to Constantinople early next morning, they said.

"Before you are up," said Sandra.

They would leave Jacob alone, then. Turning very slightly, Evan ordered something—a bottle of wine—from which he helped Jacob, with a kind of solicitude, with a kind of paternal solicitude, if that were possible. To be left alone—that was good for a young fellow. Never was there a time when the country had more need of men. He sighed.

"And you have been to the Acropolis?" asked Sandra.

"Yes," said Jacob. And they moved off to the window together, while Evan spoke to the head waiter about calling them early.

"It is astonishing," said Jacob, in a gruff voice.

Sandra opened her eyes very slightly. Possibly her nostrils expanded a little too.

"At half-past six then," said Evan, coming towards them, looking as if he faced something in facing his wife and Jacob standing with their backs to the window.

Sandra smiled at him.

And, as he went to the window and had nothing to say she added, in broken half-sentences:

"Well, but how lovely—wouldn't it be? The Acropolis, Evan—or are you too tired?"

At that Evan looked at them, or, since Jacob was staring ahead of him, at his wife, surlily, sullenly, yet with a kind of distress—not that she would pity him. Nor would the implacable spirit of love, for anything he could do, cease its tortures.

They left him and he sat in the smoking-room, which looks out on to the Square of the Constitution.

"Evan is happier alone," said Sandra. "We have been separated from the newspapers. Well, it is better that people should have what they want. . . . You have seen all these wonderful things since we met. . . . What impression . . . I think that you are changed."

"You want to go to the Acropolis," said Jacob. "Up here then."

"One will remember it all one's life," said Sandra.

"Yes," said Jacob. "I wish you could have come in the day-time."

"This is more wonderful," said Sandra, waving her hand.

Jacob looked vaguely.

"But you should see the Parthenon in the day-time," he said. "You couldn't come tomorrow—it would be too early?"

"You have sat there for hours and hours by yourself?"

"There were some awful women this morning," said Jacob.

"Awful women?" Sandra echoed.

"Frenchwomen."

"But something very wonderful has happened," said Sandra. Ten minutes, fifteen minutes, half an hour—that was all the time before her.

"Yes," he said.

"When one is your age—when one is young. What will you do? You will fall in love—oh yes! But don't be in too great a hurry. I am so much older."

She was brushed off the pavement by parading men.

"Shall we go on?" Jacob asked.

"Let us go on," she insisted.

For she could not stop until she had told him—or heard him say—or was it some action on his part that she required? Far away on the horizon she discerned it and could not rest.

"You'd never get English people to sit out like this," he said.

"Never—no. When you get back to England you won't forget this—or come with us to Constantinople!" she cried suddenly.

"But then . . ."

Sandra sighed.

"You must go to Delphi, of course," she said. "But," she asked herself, "what do I want from him? Perhaps it is something that I have missed. . . ."

"You will get there about six in the evening," she said. "You will see the eagles."

Jacob looked set and even desperate by the light at the street corner and yet composed. He was suffering, perhaps. He was credulous. Yet there was something caustic about him. He had in him the seeds of extreme disillusionment, which would come to him from women in middle life. Perhaps if one strove hard enough to reach the top of the hill it need not come to him—this disillusionment from women in middle life.

"The hotel is awful," she said. "The last visitors had left their basins full of dirty water. There is always that," she laughed.

"The people one meets *are* beastly," Jacob said.

His excitement was clear enough.

"Write and tell me about it," she said. "And tell me what you feel and what you think. Tell me everything."

The night was dark. The Acropolis was a jagged mound.

"I should like to, awfully," he said.

"When we get back to London, we shall meet . . ."

"Yes."

"I suppose they leave the gates open?" he asked.

"We could climb them!" she answered wildly.

Obscuring the moon and altogether darkening the Acropolis the clouds passed from east to west. The clouds solidified; the vapours thickened; the trailing veils stayed and accumulated.

It was dark now over Athens, except for gauzy red streaks where the streets ran; and the front of the Palace was cadaverous from electric light. At sea the piers stood out, marked by separate dots; the waves being invisible, and promontories and islands were dark humps with a few lights.

"I'd love to bring my brother, if I may," Jacob murmured.

"And then when your mother comes to London—" said Sandra.

The mainland of Greece was dark; and somewhere off Euboea a cloud must have touched the waves and spattered them—the dolphins circling deeper and deeper into the sea. Violent was the wind now rushing down the Sea of Marmara between Greece and the plains of Troy.

In Greece and the uplands of Albania and Turkey, the wind scours the sand and the dust, and sows itself thick with dry particles. And then it pelts the smooth domes of the mosques, and makes the cypresses, standing stiff by the turbaned tombstones of Mohammedans, creak and bristle.

Sandra's veils were swirled about her.

"I will give you my copy," said Jacob. "Here. Will you keep it?"

(The book was the poems of Donne.)

Now the agitation of the air uncovered a racing star. Now it was dark. Now one after another lights were extinguished. Now great towns—Paris—Constantinople—London—were black as strewn rocks. Waterways might be distinguished. In England the trees were heavy in leaf. Here perhaps in some southern wood an old man lit dry ferns and the birds were startled. The sheep coughed; one flower bent slightly towards another. The English sky is softer, milkier than the Eastern. Something gentle has passed into it from the grass-rounded hills, something damp. The salt gale blew in at Betty Flanders's bedroom window, and the widow lady, raising herself slightly on her elbow, sighed like one who realizes, but would fain ward off a little longer—oh, a little longer!—the oppression of eternity.

But to return to Jacob and Sandra.

They had vanished. There was the Acropolis; but had they reached it? The columns and the Temple remain; the emotion of the living breaks fresh on them year after year; and of that what remains?

As for reaching the Acropolis who shall say that we ever do it, or that when Jacob woke next morning he found anything hard and durable to keep for ever? Still, he went with them to Constantinople.

Sandra Wentworth Williams certainly woke to find a copy of Donne's poems upon her dressing-table. And the book would be stood on the shelf in the English country house where Sally Duggan's *Life of Father*

Damien in verse would join it one of these days. There were ten or twelve little volumes already. Strolling in at dusk, Sandra would open the books and her eyes would brighten (but not at the print), and subsiding into the arm-chair she would suck back again the soul of the moment; or, for sometimes she was restless, would pull out book after book and swing across the whole space of her life like an acrobat from bar to bar. She had had her moments. Meanwhile, the great clock on the landing ticked and Sandra would hear time accumulating, and ask herself, "What for? What for?"

"What for? What for?" Sandra would say, putting the book back, and strolling to the looking-glass and pressing her hair. And Miss Edwards would be startled at dinner, as she opened her mouth to admit roast mutton, by Sandra's sudden solicitude: "Are you happy, Miss Edwards?"—a thing Cissy Edwards hadn't thought of for years.

"What for? What for?" Jacob never asked himself any such questions, to judge by the way he laced his boots; shaved himself; to judge by the depth of his sleep that night, with the wind fidgeting at the shutters, and half-a-dozen mosquitoes singing in his ears. He was young—a man. And then Sandra was right when she judged him to be credulous as yet. At forty it might be a different matter. Already he had marked the things he liked in Donne, and they were savage enough. However, you might place beside them passages of the purest poetry in Shakespeare.

But the wind was rolling the darkness through the streets of Athens, rolling it, one might suppose, with a sort of trampling energy of mood which forbids too close an analysis of the feelings of any single person, or inspection of features. All faces—Greek, Levantine, Turkish, English—would have looked much the same in that darkness. At length the columns and the Temples whiten, yellow, turn rose; and the Pyramids and St. Peter's arise, and at last sluggish St. Paul's looms up.

The Christians have the right to rouse most cities with their interpretation of the day's meaning. Then, less melodiously, dissenters of different sects issue a cantankerous emendation. The steamers, resounding like gigantic tuning-forks, state the old old fact—how there is a sea coldly, greenly, swaying outside. But nowadays it is the thin voice of duty, piping in a white thread from the top of a funnel, that collects the largest multitudes, and night is nothing but a long-drawn sigh between hammer-strokes, a deep breath—you can hear it from an open window even in the heart of London.

But who, save the nerve-worn and sleepless, or thinkers standing with hands to the eyes on some crag above the multitude, see things thus in skeleton outline, bare of flesh? In Surbiton the skeleton is wrapped in flesh.

"The kettle never boils so well on a sunny morning," says Mrs. Grandage, glancing at the clock on the mantelpiece. Then the grey Persian cat stretches itself on the window-seat, and buffets a moth with soft round paws. And before breakfast is half over (they were late today), a baby is deposited in her lap, and she must guard the sugar basin while Tom Grandage reads the golfing article in the *Times*, sips his coffee, wipes his moustaches, and is off to the office, where he is the greatest authority upon the foreign exchanges and marked for promotion. The skeleton is well wrapped in flesh. Even this dark night when the wind rolls the darkness through Lombard Street and Fetter Lane and Bedford Square it stirs (since it is summer-time and the height of the season), plane trees spangled with electric light, and curtains still preserving the room from the dawn. People still murmur over the last word said on the staircase, or strain, all through their dreams, for the voice of the alarum clock. So when the wind roams through a forest innumerable twigs stir; hives are brushed; insects sway on grass blades; the spider runs rapidly up a crease in the bark; and the whole air is tremulous with breathing; elastic with filaments.

Only here—in Lombard Street and Fetter Lane and Bedford Square—each insect carries a globe of the world in his head, and the webs of the forest are schemes evolved for the smooth conduct of business; and honey is treasure of one sort and another; and the stir in the air is the indescribable agitation of life.

But colour returns; runs up the stalks of the grass; blows out into tulips and crocuses; solidly stripes the tree trunks; and fills the gauze of the air and the grasses and pools.

The Bank of England emerges; and the Monument with its bristling head of golden hair; the dray horses crossing London Bridge show grey and strawberry and iron-coloured. There is a whir of wings as the suburban trains rush into the terminus. And the light mounts over the faces of all the tall blind houses, slides through a chink and paints the lustrous bellying crimson curtains; the green wine-glasses; the coffee-cups; and the chairs standing askew.

Sunlight strikes in upon shaving-glasses; and gleaming brass cans; upon all the jolly trappings of the day; the bright, inquisitive, armoured, resplendent, summer's day, which has long since vanquished chaos; which has dried the melancholy mediaeval mists; drained the swamp and stood glass and stone upon it; and equipped our brains and bodies with such an armoury of weapons that merely to see the flash and thrust of limbs engaged in the conduct of daily life is better than the old pageant of armies drawn out in battle array upon the plain.

13

"The Height of the season," said Bonamy.

The sun had already blistered the paint on the backs of the green chairs in Hyde Park; peeled the bark off the plane trees; and turned the earth to powder and to smooth yellow pebbles. Hyde Park was circled, incessantly, by turning wheels.

"The height of the season," said Bonamy sarcastically.

He was sarcastic because of Clara Durrant; because Jacob had come back from Greece very brown and lean, with his pockets full of Greek notes, which he pulled out when the chair man came for pence; because Jacob was silent.

"He has not said a word to show that he is glad to see me," thought Bonamy bitterly.

The motor cars passed incessantly over the bridge of the Serpentine; the upper classes walked upright, or bent themselves gracefully over the palings; the lower classes lay with their knees cocked up, flat on their backs; the sheep grazed on pointed wooden legs; small children ran down the sloping grass, stretched their arms, and fell.

"Very urbane," Jacob brought out.

"Urbane" on the lips of Jacob had mysteriously all the shapeliness of a character which Bonamy thought daily more sublime, devastating, terrific than ever, though he was still, and perhaps would be for ever, barbaric, obscure.

What superlatives! What adjectives! How acquit Bonamy of sentimentality of the grossest sort; of being tossed like a cork on the waves; of having no steady insight into character; of being unsupported by reason, and of drawing no comfort whatever from the works of the classics?

"The height of civilization," said Jacob.

He was fond of using Latin words.

Magnanimity, virtue–such words when Jacob used them in talk with Bonamy meant that he took control of the situation; that Bonamy would play round him like an affectionate spaniel; and that (as likely as not) they would end by rolling on the floor.

"And Greece?" said Bonamy. "The Parthenon and all that?"

"There's none of this European mysticism," said Jacob.

"It's the atmosphere. I suppose," said Bonamy. "And you went to Constantinople?"

"Yes," said Jacob.

Bonamy paused, moved a pebble; then darted in with the rapidity and certainty of a lizard's tongue.

"You are in love!" he exclaimed.

Jacob blushed.

The sharpest of knives never cut so deep.

As for responding, or taking the least account of it, Jacob stared straight ahead of him, fixed, monolithic—oh, very beautiful!—like a British Admiral, exclaimed Bonamy in a rage, rising from his seat and walking off; waiting for some sound; none came; too proud to look back; walking quicker and quicker until he found himself gazing into motor cars and cursing women. Where was the pretty woman's face? Clara's—Fanny's—Florinda's? Who was the pretty little creature?

Not Clara Durrant.

The Aberdeen terrier must be exercised, and as Mr. Bowley was going that very moment—would like nothing better than a walk—they went together, Clara and kind little Bowley—Bowley who had rooms in the Albany, Bowley who wrote letters to the *Times* in a jocular vein about foreign hotels and the Aurora Borealis—Bowley who liked young people and walked down Piccadilly with his right arm resting on the boss of his back.

"Little demon!" cried Clara, and attached Troy to his chain.

Bowley anticipated—hoped for—a confidence. Devoted to her mother, Clara sometimes felt her a little, well, her mother was so sure of herself that she could not understand other people being—being—"as ludicrous as I am," Clara jerked out (the dog tugging her forwards). And Bowley thought she looked like a huntress and turned over in his mind which it should be—some pale virgin with a slip of the moon in her hair, which was a flight for Bowley.

The colour was in her cheeks. To have spoken outright about her mother—still, it was only to Mr. Bowley, who loved her, as everybody must; but to speak was unnatural to her, yet it was awful to feel, as she had done all day, that she *must* tell some one.

"Wait till we cross the road," she said to the dog, bending down.

Happily she had recovered by that time.

"She thinks so much about England," she said. "She is so anxious——"

Bowley was defrauded as usual. Clara never confided in any one.

"Why don't the young people settle it, eh?" he wanted to ask. "What's all this about England?"—a question poor Clara could not have answered, since, as Mrs. Durrant discussed with Sir Edgar the policy of Sir Edward Grey, Clara only wondered why the cabinet looked dusty, and Jacob had never come. Oh, here was Mrs. Cowley Johnson . . .

And Clara would hand the pretty china teacups, and smile at the compliment—that no one in London made tea so well as she did.

"We get it at Brocklebank's," she said, "in Cursitor Street."

Ought she not to be grateful? Ought she not to be happy? Especially since her mother looked so well and enjoyed so much talking to Sir Edgar about Morocco, Venezuela, or some such place.

"Jacob! Jacob!" thought Clara; and kind Mr. Bowley, who was ever so good with old ladies, looked; stopped; wondered whether Elizabeth wasn't too harsh with her daughter; wondered about Bonamy, Jacob—which young fellow was it?—and jumped up directly Clara said she must exercise Troy.

They had reached the site of the old Exhibition. They looked at the tulips. Stiff and curled, the little rods of waxy smoothness rose from the earth, nourished yet contained, suffused with scarlet and coral pink. Each had its shadow; each grew trimly in the diamond-shaped wedge as the gardener had planned it.

"Barnes never gets them to grow like that," Clara mused; she sighed.

"You are neglecting your friends," said Bowley, as some one, going the other way, lifted his hat. She started; acknowledged Mr. Lionel Parry's bow; wasted on him what had sprung for Jacob.

("Jacob! Jacob!" she thought.)

"But you'll get run over if I let you go," she said to the dog.

"England seems all right," said Mr. Bowley.

The loop of the railing beneath the statue of Achilles was full of parasols and waistcoats; chains and bangles; of ladies and gentlemen, lounging elegantly, lightly observant.

"'This statue was erected by the women of England . . .'" Clara read out with a foolish little laugh. "Oh, Mr. Bowley! Oh!" Gallop—gallop—gallop—a horse galloped past without a rider. The stirrups swung; the pebbles spurted.

"Oh, stop! Stop it, Mr. Bowley!" she cried, white, trembling, gripping his arm, utterly unconscious, the tears coming.

"Tut-tut!" said Mr. Bowley in his dressing-room an hour later. "Tut-tut!"—a comment that was profound enough, though inarticulately expressed, since his valet was handing his shirt studs.

Julia Eliot, too, had seen the horse run away, and had risen from her seat to watch the end of the incident, which, since she came of a sporting family, seemed to her slightly ridiculous. Sure enough the little man came pounding behind with his breeches dusty; looked thoroughly annoyed; and was being helped to mount by a policeman when Julia Eliot, with a sardonic smile, turned towards the Marble Arch on her errand of mercy. It was only to visit a sick old lady who had known her mother and perhaps the Duke of Wellington; for Julia shared the love of her sex for the distressed; liked to visit death-beds; threw slippers at weddings; received confidences by the dozen; knew more pedigrees than a scholar knows dates, and was one of the kindliest, most generous, least continent of women.

Yet five minutes after she had passed the statue of Achilles she had the rapt look of one brushing through crowds on a summer's afternoon, when the trees are rustling, the wheels churning yellow, and the tumult of the present seems like an elegy for past youth and past summers, and there rose in her mind a curious sadness, as if time and eternity showed through skirts and waistcoasts, and she saw people passing tragically to destruction. Yet, Heaven knows, Julia was no fool. A sharper woman at a bargain did not exist. She was always punctual. The watch on her wrist gave her twelve minutes and a half in which to reach Bruton Street. Lady Congreve expected her at five.

The gilt clock at Verrey's was striking five.

Florinda looked at it with a dull expression, like an animal. She looked at the clock; looked at the door; looked at the long glass opposite; disposed her cloak; drew closer to the table, for she was pregnant—no doubt about it, Mother Stuart said, recommending remedies, consulting friends; sunk, caught by the heel, as she tripped so lightly over the surface.

Her tumbler of pinkish sweet stuff was set down by the waiter; and she sucked, through a straw, her eyes on the looking-glass, on the door, now soothed by the sweet taste. When Nick Bramham came in it was plain, even to the young Swiss waiter, that there was a bargain between them. Nick hitched his clothes together clumsily; ran his fingers through his hair; sat down, to an ordeal, nervously. She looked at him; and set off laughing; laughed—laughed—laughed. The young Swiss waiter, standing with crossed legs by the pillar, laughed too.

The door opened; in came the roar of Regent Street, the roar of traffic, impersonal, unpitying; and sunshine grained with dirt. The Swiss waiter must see to the newcomers. Bramham lifted his glass.

"He's like Jacob," said Florinda, looking at the newcomer.

"The way he stares." She stopped laughing.

Jacob, leaning forward, drew a plan of the Parthenon in the dust in Hyde Park, a network of strokes at least, which may have been the Parthenon, or again a mathematical diagram. And why was the pebble so emphatically ground in at the corner? It was not to count his notes that he took out a wad of papers and read a long flowing letter which Sandra had written two days ago at Milton Dower House with his book before her and in her mind the memory of something said or attempted, some moment in the dark on the road to the Acropolis which (such was her creed) mattered for ever.

"He is," she mused, "like that man in Molière."

She meant Alceste. She meant that he was severe. She meant that she could deceive him.

"Or could I not?" she thought, putting the poems of Donne back in the bookcase. "Jacob," she went on, going to the window and looking over the spotted flower-beds across the grass where the piebald cows grazed under beech trees, "Jacob would be shocked."

The perambulator was going through the little gate in the railing. She kissed her hand; directed by the nurse, Jimmy waved his.

"*He's* a small boy," she said, thinking of Jacob.

And yet—Alceste?

"What a nuisance you are!" Jacob grumbled, stretching out first one leg and then the other and feeling in each trouser-pocket for his chair ticket.

"I expect the sheep have eaten it," he said. "Why do you keep sheep?"

"Sorry to disturb you, sir," said the ticket-collector, his hand deep in the enormous pouch of pence.

"Well, I hope they pay you for it," said Jacob. "There you are. No. You can stick to it. Go and get drunk."

He had parted with half-a-crown, tolerantly, compassionately, with considerable contempt for his species.

Even now poor Fanny Elmer was dealing, as she walked along the Strand, in her incompetent way with this very careless, indifferent, sublime manner he had of talking to railway guards or porters; or Mrs. Whitehorn, when she consulted him about her little boy who was beaten by the schoolmaster.

Sustained entirely upon picture post cards for the past two months, Fanny's idea of Jacob was more statuesque, noble, and eyeless than ever. To reinforce her vision she had taken to visiting the British Museum, where, keeping her eyes downcast until she was alongside of the battered Ulysses, she opened them and got a fresh shock of Jacob's presence, enough to last her half a day. But this was wearing thin. And she wrote now—poems, letters that were never posted, saw his face in advertisements on hoardings, and would cross the road to let the barrel-organ turn her musings to rhapsody. But at breakfast (she shared rooms with a teacher), when the butter was smeared about the plate, and the prongs of the forks were clotted with old egg yolk, she revised these visions violently; was, in truth, very cross; was losing her complexion, as Margery Jackson told her, bringing the whole thing down (as she laced her stout boots) to a level of mother-wit, vulgarity, and sentiment, for she had loved too; and been a fool.

"One's godmothers ought to have told one," said Fanny, looking in at the window of Bacon, the mapseller, in the Strand—told one that it is no use making a fuss; this is life, they should have said, as Fanny said it now, looking at the large yellow globe marked with steamship lines.

"This is life. This is life," said Fanny.

"A very hard face," thought Miss Barrett, on the other side of the glass, buying maps of the Syrian desert and waiting impatiently to be served. "Girls look old so soon nowadays."

The equator swam behind tears.

"Piccadilly?" Fanny asked the conductor of the omnibus, and climbed to the top. After all, he would, he must, come back to her.

But Jacob might have been thinking of Rome; of architecture; of jurisprudence; as he sat under the plane tree in Hyde Park.

The omnibus stopped outside Charing Cross; and behind it were clogged omnibuses, vans, motor-cars, for a procession with banners was passing down Whitehall, and elderly people were stiffly descending from between the paws of the slippery lions, where they had been testifying to their faith, singing lustily, raising their eyes from their music to look into the sky, and still their eyes were on the sky as they marched behind the gold letters of their creed.

The traffic stopped, and the sun, no longer sprayed out by the breeze, became almost too hot. But the procession passed; the banners glittered—far away down Whitehall; the traffic was released; lurched on; spun to a smooth continuous uproar; swerving round the curve of Cockspur Street; and sweeping past Government offices and equestrian statues down Whitehall to the prickly spires, the tethered grey fleet of masonry, and the large white clock of Westminster.

Five strokes Big Ben intoned; Nelson received the salute. The wires of the Admiralty shivered with some far-away communication. A voice kept remarking that Prime Ministers and Viceroys spoke in the Reichstag; entered Lahore; said that the Emperor travelled; in Milan they rioted; said there were rumours in Vienna; said that the Ambassador at Constantinople had audience with the Sultan; the fleet was at Gibraltar. The voice continued, imprinting on the faces of the clerks in Whitehall (Timothy Durrant was one of them) something of its own inexorable gravity, as they listened, deciphered, wrote down. Papers accumulated, inscribed with the utterances of Kaisers, the statistics of ricefields, the growling of hundreds of work-people, plotting sedition in back streets, or gathering in the Calcutta bazaars, or mustering their forces in the uplands of Albania, where the hills are sand-coloured, and bones lie unburied.

The voice spoke plainly in the square quiet room with heavy tables, where one elderly man made notes on the margin of typewritten sheets, his silver-topped umbrella leaning against the bookcase.

His head—bald, red-veined, hollow-looking—represented all the heads in the building. His head, with the amiable pale eyes, carried the burden of knowledge across the street; laid it before his colleagues, who came equally burdened; and then the sixteen gentlemen, lifting their pens or turning perhaps rather wearily in their chairs, decreed that the course of history should shape itself this way or that way, being manfully determined, as their faces showed, to impose some coherency upon Rajahs and Kaisers and the muttering in bazaars, the secret gatherings, plainly visible in Whitehall, of kilted peasants in Albanian uplands; to control the course of events.

Pitt and Chatham, Burke and Gladstone looked from side to side with fixed marble eyes and an air of immortal quiescence which perhaps the living may have envied, the air being full of whistling and concussions, as the procession with its banners passed down Whitehall. Moreover, some were troubled with dyspepsia; one had at that very moment cracked the glass of his spectacles; another spoke in Glasgow tomorrow; altogether they looked too red, fat, pale or lean, to be dealing, as the marble heads had dealt, with the course of history.

Timmy Durrant in his little room in the Admiralty, going to consult a Blue book, stopped for a moment by the window and observed the placard tied round the lamp-post.

Miss Thomas, one of the typists, said to her friend that if the Cabinet was going to sit much longer she should miss her boy outside the Gaiety.

Timmy Durrant, returning with his Blue book under his arm, noticed a little knot of people at the street corner; conglomerated as though one of them knew something; and the others, pressing round him, looked up, looked down, looked along the street. What was it that he knew?

Timothy, placing the Blue book before him, studied a paper sent round by the Treasury for information. Mr. Crawley, his fellow-clerk, impaled a letter on a skewer.

Jacob rose from his chair in Hyde Park, tore his ticket to pieces, and walked away.

"Such a sunset," wrote Mrs. Flanders in her letter to Archer at Singapore. "One couldn't make up one's mind to come indoors," she wrote. "It seemed wicked to waste even a moment."

The long windows of Kensington Palace flushed fiery rose as Jacob walked away; a flock of wild duck flew over the Serpentine; and the trees were stood against the sky, blackly, magnificently.

"Jacob," wrote Mrs. Flanders, with the red light on her page, "is hard at work after his delightful journey . . ."

"The Kaiser," the far-away voice remarked in Whitehall, "received me in audience."

* * *

"Now I know that face—" said the Reverend Andrew Floyd, coming out of Carter's shop in Piccadilly, "but who the dickens—?" and he watched Jacob, turned round to look at him, but could not be sure——

"Oh, Jacob Flanders!" he remembered in a flash.

But he was so tall; so unconscious; such a fine young fellow.

"I gave him Byron's works," Andrew Floyd mused, and started forward, as Jacob crossed the road; but hesitated, and let the moment pass, and lost the opportunity.

Another procession, without banners, was blocking Long Acre. Carriages, with dowagers in amethyst and gentlemen spotted with carnations, intercepted cabs and motor-cars turned in the opposite direction, in which jaded men in white waistcoats lolled, on their way home to shrubberies and billiard-rooms in Putney and Wimbledon.

Two barrel-organs played by the kerb, and horses coming out of Aldridge's with white labels on their buttocks straddled across the road and were smartly jerked back.

Mrs. Durrant, sitting with Mr. Wortley in a motor-car, was impatient lest they should miss the overture.

But Mr. Wortley, always urbane, always in time for the overture, buttoned his gloves, and admired Miss Clara.

"A shame to spend such a night in the theatre!" said Mrs. Durrant, seeing all the windows of the coachmakers in Long Acre ablaze.

"Think of your moors!" said Mr. Wortley to Clara.

"Ah! but Clara likes this better," Mrs. Durrant laughed.

"I don't know—really," said Clara, looking at the blazing windows. She started.

She saw Jacob.

"Who?" asked Mrs. Durrant sharply, leaning forward.

But she saw no one.

Under the arch of the Opera House large faces and lean ones, the powdered and the hairy, all alike were red in the sunset; and, quickened by the great hanging lamps with their repressed primrose lights, by the tramp, and the scarlet, and the pompous ceremony, some ladies looked for a moment into steaming bedrooms near by, where women with loose hair leaned out of windows, where girls—where children—(the long mirrors held the ladies suspended) but one must follow; one must not block the way.

Clara's moors were fine enough. The Phoenicians slept under their piled grey rocks; the chimneys of the old mines pointed starkly; early moths blurred the heather-bells; cartwheels could be heard grinding on the road far beneath; and the suck and sighing of the waves sounded gently, persistently, for ever.

Shading her eyes with her hand Mrs. Pascoe stood in her cabbage-garden looking out to sea. Two steamers and a sailing-ship crossed each other; passed each other; and in the bay the gulls kept alighting on a log, rising high, returning again to the log, while some rode in upon the waves and stood on the rim of the water until the moon blanched all to whiteness.

Mrs. Pascoe had gone indoors long ago.

But the red light was on the columns of the Parthenon, and the Greek women who were knitting their stockings and sometimes crying to a child to come and have the insects picked from its head were as jolly as sand-martins in the heat, quarrelling, scolding, suckling their babies, until the ships in the Piraeus fired their guns.

The sound spread itself flat, and then went tunnelling its way with fitful explosions among the channels of the islands.

Darkness drops like a knife over Greece.

"The guns?" said Betty Flanders, half asleep, getting out of bed and going to the window, which was decorated with a fringe of dark leaves.

"Not at this distance," she thought. "It is the sea."

Again, far away, she heard the dull sound, as if nocturnal women were beating great carpets. There was Morty lost, and Seabrook dead; her sons fighting for their country. But were the chickens safe? Was that some one moving downstairs? Rebecca with the toothache? No. The nocturnal women were beating great carpets. Her hens shifted slightly on their perches.

14

"He left everything just as it was," Bonamy marvelled. "Nothing arranged. All his letters strewn about for any one to read. What did he expect? Did he think he would come back?" he mused, standing in the middle of Jacob's room.

The eighteenth century has its distinction. These houses were built, say, a hundred and fifty years ago. The rooms are shapely, the ceilings high; over the doorways a rose or a ram's skull is carved in the wood. Even the panels, painted in raspberry-coloured paint, have their distinction.

Bonamy took up a bill for a hunting-crop.

"That seems to be paid," he said.

There were Sandra's letters.

Mrs. Durrant was taking a party to Greenwich.

Lady Rocksbier hoped for the pleasure. . . .

Listless is the air in an empty room, just swelling the curtain; the flowers in the jar shift. One fibre in the wicker arm-chair creaks, though no one sits there.

Bonamy crossed to the window. Pickford's van swung down the street. The omnibuses were locked together at Mudie's corner. Engines throbbed, and carters, jamming the brakes down, pulled their horses sharp up. A harsh and unhappy voice cried something unintelligible. And then suddenly all the leaves seemed to raise themselves.

"Jacob! Jacob!" cried Bonamy, standing by the window. The leaves sank down again.

"Such confusion everywhere!" exclaimed Betty Flanders, bursting open the bedroom door.

Bonamy turned away from the window.

"What am I to do with these, Mr. Bonamy?"

She held out a pair of Jacob's old shoes.

The text of this book is set in Goudy Old Style,
designed by American printer and typographer
Frederic W. Goudy (1865–1947).
This serif font was chosen for its readability
and beautiful characteristics.

The archival-quality, natural paper is composed of recyclable products
made from wood grown in sustainable forests;
the manufacturing processes conform to the
environmental regulations of the country of origin.
Binder's boards are made from 100% post-consumer waste.

The finished volume demonstrates the convergence of Old World
craftsmanship and modern technology that exemplifies books
manufactured by Edwards Brothers, Inc.
Established in 1893, the family-owned business is a well-respected
leader in book manufacturing, recognized the world
over for quality and attention to detail.
In addition, Ann Arbor Media Group's editorial and design services
provide full-service book publication to business partners.